LOVE ONLY ONCE

———◦◦◦———

TENDER REBEL

———◦◦◦———

GENTLE ROGUE

Johanna Lindsey

LOVE ONLY ONCE

TENDER REBEL

GENTLE ROGUE

Rhapsody®
Garden City, New York

Contents

LOVE ONLY ONCE

For my niece and nephew,
Raegina Kaohukaukuahiwiokaala Howard
and Michael Lani Alii Howard

Chapter One

1817 London

The fingers holding the brandy decanter were long and delicate. Selena Eddington was vain about her hands. She showed them off whenever a chance presented itself, as it did just then. She brought the decanter to Nicholas instead of taking his glass to the brandy. This served another purpose, as well, for she was able to stand in front of him as he reclined on the plush blue sofa, the fire at her back, her figure outlined provocatively through her thin muslin evening dress. Even a hardened rake like Nicholas Eden could still appreciate a lovely body.

A large ruby winked on her left hand as she steadied his glass and poured the brandy. Her wedding ring. She still wore it proudly, though she had been a widow for two years. More rubies circled her throat, but even spectacular rubies did not detract from her décolletage, exceedingly low, which allowed a mere three inches of material before the cinched high waist of the empire gown fell in straight lines to her trim ankles. The gown was a deep, dark magenta, and suited beautifully both the rubies and Selena.

"Are you listening to me, Nicky?"

Nicholas had that irritating pensive look about him that she recognized more and more of late. He was not listening to a word she was saying but was deep in thoughts that surely didn't include her. He hadn't even glanced at her while she poured his brandy.

"Honestly, Nicky, it's not at all flattering the way you go off and

5

leave me when we're in a room alone together." She stood her ground in front of him until he looked up at her.

"What's that, my dear?" Her hazel eyes flashed. She would have stomped her foot if she'd dared let him see her vile temper. How provoking he was, how indifferent, how . . . impossible! If only he weren't such a good catch.

Mindful of her deportment, she said evenly, "The ball, Nicky. I have been going on about it, but you're not paying attention. If you like, I will change the subject, but only if you promise you won't be late coming for me tomorrow night."

"What ball?"

Selena gasped, truly surprised. He was not foxed, and he was not being blasé. The infuriating man really had no idea what she was talking about.

"Don't tease me, Nicky. The Shepford ball. You know how much I have been looking forward to it."

"Ah, yes," he said dryly. "The ball to outdo them all, and this only the beginning of the season."

She pretended not to notice his tone. "You also know how long I have waited for an invitation to one of the Duchess of Shepford's affairs. This ball promises to be her grandest in years. Simply everyone who is anyone will be there."

"So?"

Selena counted slowly to five. "So I will die if I am even the tiniest bit late."

His lips turned up in the familiar mocking smile. "You die much too often, my dear. You shouldn't take the social whirl so seriously."

"I should be like you?"

She would have called that retort back if she'd been able to. Her temper was very close to being unleashed, and that would be disastrous. She knew how he deplored excess of emotion in anyone—though it was all right for him to let loose his temper, which could be quite unpleasant.

Nicholas simply shrugged. "Call me eccentric, my dear, one of the few who doesn't give a bloody damn for the lot of them."

How true that was. He ignored and even insulted whomever he pleased. He made friends with anyone he pleased, too, even known bastards who were snubbed by society. And he never, ever, pandered to anyone. He was every bit as arrogant as people said he was. But he could also be devastatingly charming—when he wanted to be.

Miraculously, Selena kept a tight rein on her temper. "Nevertheless, Nicky, you did promise to escort me to the Shepford ball."

"Did I?" he drawled.

"Yes, you did," she managed evenly. "And you will promise not to be late in coming for me, won't you?"

He shrugged again. "How can I promise such a thing, my dear? I cannot foresee the future. There is no telling what might arise tomorrow to delay me."

She very nearly screamed. There was nothing to delay him except his own perfidious indifference, and they both knew it. It was not to be borne!

Selena made a quick decision and said nonchalantly, "Very well, Nicky. Since this is so important to me and I can't depend on you, I will find myself another escort and simply hope that you will eventually show up at the ball." Two could play his game.

"On such short notice?" he asked.

"You doubt I can?" she challenged.

He smiled, his gaze moving over her appreciatively. "No, indeed. I believe you will have very little trouble replacing me."

Selena turned her back on him before he could see how the remark affected her. Had that been a warning? Oh, how sure of himself he was. It would serve him right if she broke off their affair. No mistress of his had ever done so. He was always the one to end an affair. He was always the one in charge. How would he react if she dropped him? Would it throw him into a rage? Would it force his hand? This merited serious consideration.

Nicholas Eden stretched more comfortably on the sofa and watched Selena pick up her glass of sherry, then lie down on the thick fur rug in front of the fire, her back to him. His lips curled sardonically. How alluring her pose was, but of course she knew that. Selena always knew precisely what she was doing.

They were at her friend Marie's townhouse, having enjoyed an elegant dinner with Marie and her current lover, played whist for an hour or so, and then retired to this cozy drawing room. Marie and her ardent gentleman had retired to a room upstairs, leaving Nicholas and Selena to themselves. How many other nights had been spent like this one? The only constant was that the Countess had a different lover every time. She lived life dangerously whenever her husband the Earl was out of town.

There was another difference tonight, though. The room was just as romantic, a fire burning, a lamp in the corner turned down low, good brandy, servants discreetly retired for the night, Selena as seductive as ever. But tonight Nicholas was bored. It was as simple as that. He had no wish to leave the sofa and join Selena on the rug.

He had known for a while that he was losing interest in Selena. The fact that he didn't especially wish to bed her tonight confirmed his feeling that it was time to end the affair. Theirs had lasted longer than most of his involvements, nearly three months. Perhaps that was why he felt ready to leave her despite the fact that he'd found no one to replace her.

There was no one he felt like pursuing just then. Selena quite outshined all the ladies of his acquaintance, except those odd few who were in love with their husbands and therefore not prone to his charm. Oh, but his hunting field was not limited only to married ladies bored with their husbands, not really. He did not scruple to leave untouched the sweet innocents out for their first or second seasons. If the tender young ladies were prone to succumb, they were not safe from Nicholas. As long as they were eager to be bedded, he would oblige them for however long the affair could escape the notice of their parents. These were quite his shortest dalliances, certainly, but his most challenging, too.

He had enjoyed three virgins in his younger hell-raising days. One, a Duke's daughter, was quickly married off to a second cousin or some such lucky gentleman. The other two had likewise been married off before full-scale scandals blossomed. Which was not to say the gossipmongers hadn't had field days with each affair. But without challenges issued from enraged families, the affairs remained only gossip and speculation. The fact was that the fathers in question were all afraid to face him on the dueling field. He had by that time already won two duels with irate husbands.

He was not proud of deflowering three innocents, or of wounding two men whose only error lay in having promiscuous wives. But he felt no guilt either. If the debutantes were foolish enough to give themselves to him without promise of marriage, well, so it went. And the wives of noblemen had known exactly what they were doing.

It had been said of Nicholas that he didn't particularly care who got hurt while he pursued his pleasures. Perhaps that was true, perhaps not. No one really knew Nicholas well enough to be sure. Even *he* wasn't sure why he did some of the things he did.

He paid for his reputation, in any case. Fathers with titles above his would not consider him for their daughters. Only the very daring and people looking for a rich husband kept Nicholas' name on their social lists.

But he was not looking for a wife. He had long felt he had no right to offer for a young woman of breeding and lineage that his title demanded. In all likelihood he would never marry. No one knew why the Viscount of Montieth was resigned to his bachelor life, so there were still countless hopefuls looking to snag him, to reform him.

Lady Selena Eddington was one of those hopefuls. She took pains not to show it, but he knew when a woman was after his title. Married to a Baron her first time around, she was looking higher now. She was strikingly beautiful, with short black hair surrounding her oval face with delicate curls, in the current fashion. Golden skin enhanced the expressive hazel eyes. Twenty-four, amusing, seductive, she was a lovely woman. It was certainly not her fault that Nicholas' desire for her had cooled.

No woman had ever managed to keep his ardor burning for long. He had expected this affair to fade. They all did. The only thing that surprised him was his willingness to end it before sighting a new conquest. The decision would force him to haunt the social scene for a while, until someone took his interest, and Nicholas hated having to do that.

Perhaps tomorrow's ball would be just the ticket. There would be dozens of new young ladies there, for the season had just opened. Nicholas sighed. At twenty-seven, after seven years of jaded living, he had lost his taste for young innocents.

He wouldn't break with Selena tonight, he decided, for she was already piqued with him, and she would unleash all of the temper he suspected she was capable of. That was to be avoided. He deplored emotional scenes, for his own nature was too passionate by half.

Women could never stand up to his full rage. They were always reduced to tears, and that was just as deplorable. No, he would tell her tomorrow night when he saw her at the ball. She wouldn't dare make a scene in public.

Selena held her crystal glass of sherry up to the fire and marveled that the amber liquid was the exact shade of Nicholas' eyes when he was in an extreme mood. His eyes had been that honey-gold color when he first began to pursue her, but they were also that color when he was either annoyed or pleased about something. When he was feeling nothing special, was calm or indifferent, his eyes were more of a reddish brown, almost the color of newly polished copper. They were always disturbing eyes because even when they were a darker shade, they still glowed with an inner light. The unsettling eyes were offset by his swarthy skin and inordinately long dark eyelashes. His skin tone was dark gold to begin with, and he was bronzed by the sun as well, for he was an avid outdoorsman. He was saved from looking sinister by brown hair streaked with golden highlights. Worn in the currently fashionable windswept style and naturally wavy, his hair had a two-tone appearance in certain lighting.

It was detestable of him to be so handsome that the mere sight of him could start a girl's heart fluttering. She had seen it happen many times. Young girls became giggling ninnies in his presence. Older women offered blatant invitations with their eyes. No wonder he was so hard to handle. Lovely females had no doubt been throwing themselves at him since he'd come of age, or even before. And it was not just his face that was so entrancing. Why couldn't he be short, or even chubby, she asked herself, anything to take away from his devastating effect? But no, he fit the current mode of skintight trousers and cut-away coats as if the style had been created just for him. No having to nip in the coats or pad the shoulders for Nicholas Eden. His body was superb— muscular yet trim, tall yet graceful, the body of an avid athlete.

If only it weren't so. Then Selena's heart wouldn't throb whenever he looked at her with those sherry eyes. She was determined to bring him to the altar, for not only was he the best-looking man she had ever seen, he was also the Fourth Viscount Eden of Montieth, and rich besides. Made to order was what he was, and arrogantly aware of the fact.

What, indeed, could bring him around? Something had to, for it was painfully obvious that he was losing interest in her. What could she do to reignite the flame? Ride naked through Hyde Park? Join one of the whispered-about Black Sabbaths that were said to be excuses for orgies? Behave even more scandalously than he did? She could break into Whites or Brooks—that would really shock him. Under no circumstances were women allowed in those all-male establishments. Or perhaps she could begin to ignore him. Or even . . . by God, yes, throw him over for another man! He would die! He would simply not be able to stand the blow to his vanity. It would arouse his rage and jealousy, and he would rashly demand that she marry him!

Selena became excited thinking about it. It would work. It had to. Anyway, she had no choice but to try. If it didn't work, she would have lost nothing, for she was losing him as it was.

She rolled over to face him and found him stretched out on the sofa with his feet propped up on one end, boots and all, his hands behind his head at the other end. Going to sleep on her! Famous! She could not remember ever being so insulted. Not even her husband of two years had ever gone to sleep in her presence. Yes, desperate measures were definitely called for.

"Nicholas?" She said his name softly and he answered her right away. At least he hadn't been asleep. "Nicholas, I have been giving our relationship a good deal of thought."

"Have you, Selena?"

She flinched at the boredom in his voice.

"Yes," she went on bravely. "And I have come to a conclusion. Due to your lack of . . . shall we say *warmth* . . . I believe I would be better appreciated by someone else."

"No doubt you would be."

She frowned. He was taking this awfully well. "Well, I have had several offers lately to . . . replace you in my affections, and I have decided"—she paused a moment before committing herself to a lie, then closed her eyes and blurted—"I have decided to accept one."

She waited several moments before she opened her eyes. Nicholas had not moved an inch on the sofa and it was another full minute before he finally did. He sat up slowly and his eyes fastened on hers. She held her breath. His expression was inscrutable.

He picked up his empty glass from the table and held it toward her. "Would you, my dear?"

"Yes, of course." She jumped up to do his bidding, not even thinking how autocratic it was of him to expect her to wait on him.

"Who is the lucky man?"

Selena started, spilling brandy on the table. Was his voice just a little sharp, or was that wishful thinking on her part?

"He would like our arrangement to be discreet, so you will understand if I don't divulge his name."

"He's married?"

She brought him his glass, which was precariously full, all the way to the brim, thanks to her nervousness. "No. In fact I have every reason to believe greater things will come of this relationship. As I said, he simply wants to be discreet—for now."

She should not have taken that tack, she quickly realized. She and Nicholas had also been discreet, never making love in her house because of the servants, though he did call for her there, and never using his house on Park Lane. Yet everyone knew she was his mistress. You only had to be seen with Nicholas Eden three times in a row for that assumption to be made.

"Don't ask me to betray him, Nicky," she said with a halfhearted smile. "You will learn who he is soon enough."

"Then, pray tell, why not give me his name now?"

Did he know she was lying? He did. She could tell by his manner. And who the devil *could* replace Nicholas? The men of her acquaintance had all steered clear of her once he became her escort.

"You are being obnoxious, Nicholas." Selena took the attack. "Who he is certainly can't matter to you, for although it hurts me to admit it, I have noticed a lack of ardor in you lately. What else can I think but that you no longer want me?"

Here was the opening for him to deny it all. The moment was lost.

"What is this all about?" his voice was sharp. "That blasted ball? Is that it?"

"Of course not," she replied indignantly.

"Isn't it?" he challenged. "You think to force me into giving you my escort to that affair tomorrow night by telling me this tale. It won't wash, my dear."

His colossal ego was going to be the death of her, it surely was. What conceit! He just couldn't believe that she might prefer someone else to him.

Nicholas' dark brow arched in surprise and Selena realized horribly that she had expressed her thoughts aloud. She was shocked, but then she stiffened her resolve.

"Well, it's true," she said boldly and moved away from him, back to the fireplace.

Selena paced back and forth before the fire, its heat nearly matching the heat of her anger. He didn't deserve to be loved.

"I'm sorry, Nicky," she said after a while, not daring to look at him. "I don't want our affair to end on a bad note. You really have been wonderful—most of the time. Oh, dear," she sighed. "You are the expert at this. Is that how it's done?"

Nicholas very nearly laughed. "Not bad for an amateur, my dear."

"Good," she said on a brighter note and risked a glance at him. She found him grinning at her. Damn, he still wasn't buying her story. "Doubt me, then, Lord Montieth, but time will tell, won't it? Just don't be too surprised when you see me with my new gentleman."

She turned back to the fire again, and the next time she turned toward him, he was gone.

Chapter Two

The Malory mansion on Grosvenor Square was brightly lit, and most of the occupants were in their bedrooms, preparing for the Duke and Duchess of Shepford's ball. The servants were busier than usual, running from one end of the mansion to the other.

Lord Marshall needed more starch in his cravat. Lady Clare wanted a light snack. She had been too nervous to eat all day. Lady Diana needed a posset to calm her. Bless her, her first season and first ball; she had not eaten for two days. Lord Travis needed help finding his new frilly shirt. Lady Amy simply needed cheering up. She was the only one in the family too young to attend the ball, even a masked ball where she wouldn't be recognized anyway. Oh, how awful to be fifteen!

The only person preparing for the ball who wasn't a son or daughter of the house was Lady Regina Ashton, Lord Edward Malory's niece and first cousin to his large brood of children. Of course, Lady Regina had her own maid to fetch for her if she needed anything, but apparently she didn't, for no one had seen either of them for an hour or more.

The house had been humming with activity for hours. Lord and Lady Malory had started their preparations much earlier, having been invited to the formal dinner being given for a select few before the ball. They had left a little more than an hour ago. The two Malory brothers would escort their sisters and cousin, a major responsibility for the young men, one just out of university and the other still attending.

Marshall Malory hadn't been looking forward to escorting the family females until today when, unexpectedly, a lady friend had asked to join his party in the Malory family coach. A stroke of luck, receiving such a request from that particular lady.

He had been head over heels in love with her since he'd first met her, last year, when he'd been home for the holidays. She had not given him any encouragement then. But now he was through with school, twenty-one, a man on his own. Why, he could even set up his own household now if he was of a mind to. He could ask a certain lady to marry him. Oh, how wonderful to have reached his majority!

Lady Clare was also thinking about age. She was twenty, horrid as that was to contemplate. This was her third season and she had yet to win a husband or even an engagement! There had been a few offers, but not from anyone she could have considered seriously. Oh, she was pretty enough, with fair coloring, fair skin, fair everything. That was the problem. She was just . . . pretty. She was nowhere near as striking as her cousin Regina, and she tended to fade away when in the younger girl's company. Worst fate, this was the second season she would have to share with Regina.

Clare fumed. Her cousin should have married already. She'd had dozens of offers. And it wasn't as if she weren't willing. She seemed more than willing, seemed almost more desperate to get settled than Clare was. But one thing or another had brought all the offers to a dead end. Even a tour of Europe this last year had produced no husband. Regina had returned to London last week, still looking.

This year there would also be the competition of Clare's own sister, Diana. Just short of eighteen, she should have been made to wait another year before being brought out. But their parents thought Diana was old enough to have some fun. She was expressly forbidden, however, to think seriously about any young man. She was too young to marry, but she could enjoy herself all she liked.

Next her parents would be letting fifteen-year-old Amy out of the schoolroom when she was sixteen, Clare thought, increasingly annoyed. She could just see it! Next year, if she still hadn't found a husband, she would have both Diana and Amy to contend with. Amy was just as striking as Regina, with that dark coloring only a few of the Malorys possessed. Clare would have to find a husband this season if it killed her.

Little did Clare know it, but those were her beautiful cousin's sentiments as well. Regina Ashton stared at her image in the mirror while her maid, Meg, rolled up her long black hair to hide its length and make it look more fashionable. Regina was not seeing the slightly tilted eyes of a startling cobalt blue, or the slightly pouting full lips, or the slightly too-white skin that set off her dark hair and long soot-black lashes so dramatically. She was seeing men, parades of men, legions of men—French, Swiss, Austrian, Italian, English—and wondering why she still wasn't married. It certainly wasn't for lack of trying.

Reggie, as she was always called, had had so many men to choose from it was actually embarrassing. There'd been at least a dozen she was sure she could be happy with, two dozen she'd thought she was falling in love with, and so many who just wouldn't do for one reason or another. And those whom Reggie had felt would do, her uncles felt would not.

Oh, the disadvantages of having four uncles who loved her dearly! She likewise adored them, all four. Jason, now forty-five, had been head of the family since he was only sixteen, responsible for his three brothers and one sister, Reggie's mother. Jason took his responsibilities seriously—too seriously at times. He was a very serious man.

Edward was his exact opposite, good-humored, jolly, easygoing, indulgent. A year younger than Jason, Edward had married Aunt Charlotte when he was twenty-two, much sooner than Jason married. He had five children, three girls and two boys. Cousin Travis, nineteen, was Reggie's age and in the middle of his family. They had been playmates all their lives, along with Uncle Jason's only son.

Reggie's mother, Melissa, had been far younger than her two older brothers, nearly seven years. But then, two years after her birth, James was born.

James was the wild brother, the one who said to hell with it all and went his own way. He was thirty-five now, and his name was not even supposed to be mentioned anymore. As far as Jason and Edward were concerned, James did not exist. But Reggie still loved him, despite his terrible sins. She missed him sorely and got to see him only secretly. In the past nine years, she'd seen him only six times, the last time more than two years ago.

Anthony, truth to tell, was her favorite uncle. He was also the only one besides Reggie, Amy, and Reggie's mother who had the dark hair and cobalt eyes of Reggie's great-grandmother, whispered to have been a gypsy. No one in the family would confirm that scandalous fact, of course. Perhaps he was her favorite because he was so carefree, like Reggie herself.

Anthony, thirty-four and the baby of the family, was more like a brother than an uncle. He was also, quite amusingly, society's most notorious rake since his brother James had left London. But whereas James could be ruthless, having much of Jason in him, Anthony was gifted with some of Edward's qualities. He was a dashing blade, an outrageous charmer. He didn't give a snort for anyone's opinion of him, but in his own way he did his best to please anyone who mattered to him.

Reggie smiled. For all his mistresses and outlandish friends, for all the scandals that flourished around him, the duels he had fought, the wild wagers he made, Anthony was sometimes the most lovable hypocrite where she was concerned. For one of his rogue friends to even look sideways at her was to receive an invitation into the boxing ring. Even the most lecherous men learned to hide their thoughts when she was visiting her uncle, to settle for harmless banter and nothing more. If Uncle Jason ever learned she had even been in the same room as some of the men she'd met, heads would roll, Tony's in particular. But Jason never knew, and although Edward suspected, he was not as strict as Jason.

All four uncles treated her more like a daughter than a niece because the four had raised her since her parents' death when Reggie was only two. They had literally shared her since she turned six. Edward was living in London by then and so, too, were James and Anthony. The three of them had a big row with Jason because he insisted on keeping her in the country. He gave in and allowed her to live six months of each year with Edward, where she was able to see her two younger uncles often.

When she was eleven, Anthony felt he was old enough to demand equal time with her. He was allowed the summer months, which were strictly for play. He was happy to make the sacrifice of turning his bachelor house into a home each year, and that was easily done, because along with Reggie came her maid, her nurse, and her governess. Anthony and Reggie had twice-weekly dinners with Edward and his family. Still, all that domesticity never gave Anthony a longing to marry. He was still a bachelor. And since her coming out, it was no longer proper for her to spend part of her year with him, so she saw him only irregularly.

Ah, well, she thought, soon she would be married. It was not what she particularly wanted. She would so much rather have enjoyed herself for a few more years. But it was what her uncles wanted. They assumed it was her desire to find a suitable husband and begin a family. Wasn't that what all young girls wanted? They had had a meeting to discuss it, in fact, and no matter how much she declared that she wasn't ready to leave the bosom of her family, their good intentions won out over her protestations until, finally, she gave up.

From then on she'd done her very best to please them because she loved them all so much. She brought forth suitor after suitor, but one uncle or another found fault with each of them. She continued her search through Europe, but by then she was so wretchedly tired of looking at every man she met with a critical eye. She couldn't make friends. She couldn't enjoy herself. Each man had to be carefully dissected and analyzed—was he husband material? Was he the magic one that all of her uncles would approve?

She was beginning to believe there was no such man, and desperately needed a break from this obsessive search. She wanted to see Uncle Tony, the only one who would understand, who would intercede for her with Jason. But Tony had been visiting a friend in the country when she returned to London and hadn't come back until last evening.

Reggie had gone by twice to see him that very day, but he was out both times, so she had left him a note. Surely he had gotten it by now. Then why hadn't he come?

Even as she had that thought she heard a carriage pull up in front of the house. She laughed, a merry, musical sound.

"Finally!"

"What?" Meg wanted to know. "I'm not done yet. I'll have you know it isn't easy gettin' this hair of yours tucked away. I still say you should cut it. Save me and you both time."

"Never mind that, Meg." Reggie jumped up, causing a few pins to drop to the floor. "Uncle Tony's here."

"Here now, where d'you think you're going like that?" Meg's tone was outraged.

But Reggie ignored her and rushed out of her room, hearing Meg's loud "Regina Ashton!" but paying no attention. She ran until she reached the stairs to the main lower hall, and then she became aware of her scanty attire and stopped. She drew back quickly around the corner, determined not to leave until she heard her uncle's voice. But she didn't hear it. She heard a woman's voice instead, and with a hesitant peek around the corner, she was greatly disappointed to see the butler admitting a lady, not Uncle Tony. She recognized the woman as Lady something-or-other, whom Reggie had met in Hyde Park a few days ago. Bother! Where the devil was Tony?

Just then Meg latched onto her arm and dragged her back down the hallway. Meg took liberties, that was a certainty, but no wonder, for she had been with Reggie as long as nurse Tess had, which was forever.

"If I ever saw anything as scandalous as you standin' there in your unmentionables, I'd like to know!" Meg scolded as she pushed Reggie back down on her stool in front of the small vanity. "We taught you better than that."

"I thought it was Uncle Tony."

"That's no excuse."

"I know, but I must see him tonight. You know why, Meg. He's the only one who can help me. He'll write to Uncle Jason and then I'll be able to relax, finally."

"And what do you think he can tell the Marquis that will do you any good?"

Reggie grinned. "What I'm going to suggest is that they find me a husband."

Meg shook her head and sighed. "You won't like the man they choose for you, my girl."

"Perhaps. But I simply don't care anymore," she insisted. "It would be nice to be able to pick my own husband, but I learned quickly enough that my choice doesn't matter if he's a bad choice according to them. I have been on display now for a full year, going to so many parties and routs and balls that I hate them already. I never thought I'd say that. Why, I couldn't wait to dance at my first ball."

"It's understandable, dear," Meg soothed.

"As long as Uncle Tony understands, and is willing to help, that's all I ask. I want nothing more than to retire to the country, to live quietly again—with or without a husband. If I could find the right man this evening, I would marry him tomorrow, *anything* to quit the social whirl. But I know that's not going to happen, so the next best thing is to let my uncles find him. Knowing them, that will take years. They can never agree on anything, you know. And in the meantime, I'll go home to Haverston."

"I don't see what your Uncle Tony can do that you can't do for yourself. You're not afraid of the Marquis. You can wrap that man around your little finger anytime you've a mind to. Haven't you done so often enough? Just tell him how unhappy you are and he'll—"

"I can't do that!" Reggie gasped. "I could never let Uncle Jason think he's made me unhappy. He would never forgive himself!"

"You're too kindhearted for your own good, my girl," Meg grumbled. "So you'll just go on bein' miserable, then?"

"No. See, that's why I want Uncle Tony to write Uncle Jason first. If I did, and he still insisted I stay here, where would that leave me? But if Tony's letter is scoffed at, then I'll know that plan won't work and I'll still have a chance to think of something else."

"Well, I'm sure you'll see Lord Anthony at the ball tonight."

"No. He detests balls. He wouldn't be caught dead attending one, even for me. Oh, bother! I suppose it will just have to wait until morning." Meg frowned then, and looked away. "What's this? What do you know that I don't?" Reggie demanded.

Meg shrugged. "It's . . . only that Lord Anthony's likely to be gone by mornin' and not back for three or four days. You can wait that long, though."

"Who said he was leaving?"

"I overheard Lord Edward telling his wife that the Marquis has sent for him. He's to be called on the carpet again for some trouble he's gotten himself into."

"No!" Then forlornly, "You don't think he's left already, do you?"

"No, indeed." Meg grinned. "That scamp won't be anxious to face his older brother. He'll put off leavin' as long as he can, I'm sure."

"Then I *must* see him tonight. This is perfect. He can convince Uncle Jason in person better than by letter."

"But you can't go to Lord Anthony's house now," Meg protested. "It's nearly time to leave for the ball."

"Then get me into my gown quickly. Tony is only a few blocks away. I can take the coach and be back before my cousins are ready to leave."

The others were in fact ready to leave then and were waiting for her when Reggie rushed down the stairs a few minutes later. This was unsettling, but not daunting. She pulled her oldest cousin aside as she entered the drawing room, giving the others a fleeting smile of greeting.

"Marshall, I really and truly hate to ask this of you, but I simply must borrow the coach for a few minutes before we all leave."

"What?"

She had been whispering, but his loud exclamation turned every eye their way. She sighed. "Honestly, Marshall, you needn't act as if I've asked for the world."

Marshall, aware at once that they were being watched, and appalled by his momentary lack of control, gathered all his dignity about him and said in the most reasonable tone he could muster, "We have been waiting for you for ten minutes already, and now you propose to make us wait even longer?"

Three more gasps of outrage came flying at her, but Reggie didn't spare a glance for her other cousins. "I wouldn't ask if it weren't important, Marshall. It won't take me more than a half hour . . . well, certainly no more than an hour. I need to see Uncle Anthony."

"No, no, no!" This from Diana, who hardly ever raised her voice. "How can you be so thoughtless, Reggie? That's not like you at all. You'll make us late! We should be leaving right now."

"Stuff," Reggie replied. "You don't want to be the first ones there, do you?"

"We don't want to be the last to arrive either," Clare joined in peevishly. "The ball will commence in a half hour and it will take us that long to get there. What is so important that you must see Uncle Anthony now?"

"It's personal. And it can't wait. He's leaving for Haverston first thing in the morning. I won't be able to talk to him unless I go right now."

"Until he gets back," Clare said. "Why can't it wait until then?"

"Because it can't." Looking at her cousins set against her, and Lady what's-her-name looking just as agitated, Reggie gave in. "Oh, very well. I'll settle for a hired chaise or a chair, Marshall, if you'll just send one of the footmen to fetch one for me. I'll join you at the ball as soon as I'm finished."

"Out of the question."

Marshall was annoyed. It was just like his cousin to try and involve him in something foolish so that he, being the oldest, would be the one to get in trouble later. Well, not this time, by God. He was older and wiser, and she couldn't talk circles around him anymore the way she used to.

Marshall said adamantly, "A hired conveyance? At night? It's not safe and you know it, Reggie."

"Travis can come with me."

"But Travis doesn't want to," the escort in question was quick to reply. "And never mind turning those baby blues on me, Reggie. I've no mind to be late for the ball either."

"Please, Travis."

"No."

Reggie looked at all those unsympathetic faces. She wouldn't give in. "Then I shan't go to the ball. I didn't want to go in the first place."

"Oh, no." Marshall shook his head sternly. "I know you too well, dear cousin. No sooner do we leave here than you sneak out of the house and walk over to Uncle Anthony's. Father would kill me."

"I have more sense than that, Marshall," she assured him tartly. "I'll send another message to Tony and wait for him to come here."

"And if he doesn't?" Marshall pointed out. "He's got better things to do than jump at your beck and call. He may not even be at home. No. You're coming with us and that's final."

"I won't."

"You will!"

"She can use my carriage." All eyes turned to their guest. "My driver and the attendant have been with me for years and can be trusted to see her safely on her errand and then to the ball."

Reggie's smile was dazzling. "Famous! You really are a savior, Lady—?"

"Eddington," the lady supplied. "We met earlier in the week."

"Yes, in the park. I do remember. I'm just terrible with names after meeting so many people this last year. I can't thank you enough."

"Don't mention it. I am happy to oblige."

And Selena *was* happy—anything to get them on their way, for heaven's sake. It was bad enough that she'd had to settle for Marshall Malory as escort to *the* ball of the season. But he was the only one of the dozen men she had sent notes to that morning who hadn't put her off with one excuse or another. Malory, younger than she, had been only a last resort. And there she was in the middle of a family squabble, all because of this young chit.

"There now, Marshall," Reggie was saying. "You certainly can't object now."

"No, I suppose not," he said grudgingly. "But just remember you said a half hour, cousin. You had better *be* at the Shepfords' before Father happens to notice that you're not. There will be the devil to pay otherwise, and you know it."

Chapter Three

"But I am serious, Tony!" Reggie exclaimed as she eyed him carefully across his sitting room. "How can you doubt me? This is an emergency, Tony." He was the only one of her uncles who insisted she call him simply by his Christian name.

She had had to wait twenty minutes for him to be roused from sleep, for he had spent the whole day at his club drinking and gambling, then come home and fallen into bed. Another ten minutes had been wasted just trying to get him to believe how serious she was. Her thirty minutes were already up and she'd barely begun. Marshall was going to kill her.

"Come now, puss. You wouldn't be a week in the country before you were missing gay old London. If you need a rest, tell Eddie boy you're sick or something. A few days in your room and you'll thank me for not taking you seriously about this."

"I have had nothing but the gay life for the last year," Reggie went on determinedly. "I traveled from party to party on my tour, not country to country. And it's not only that I'm tired of the constant entertainments, Tony. I could withstand that well enough. I'm not even suggesting I spend the whole season at Haverston, only a few weeks, so I can recuperate. It's this husband hunting that is going to be the death of me. Truly it is."

"No one said you had to marry the first man you met, puss," Anthony said reasonably.

"The first man? There've been hundreds, Tony. I'll have you know they now call me the 'cold fish.'"

"Who does, by God?"

"The name is perfectly appropriate. I have been cold and cutting. I've had to be, because I refuse to give a man hope when there is no hope."

"What the devil are you talking about?" Anthony demanded brusquely.

"I hired Sir John Dodsley long before the last season was over."

"That old reprobate? Hired him for what?"

"To act as, well, an adviser, you might say," she confessed. "That old reprobate, as you call him, knows everyone. He also knows everything there is to know about everyone. After my sixth serious suitor failed to pass muster with you and your brothers, I felt it was useless disappointing myself or any more young men by having to go through it all again. I paid Dodsley to attend every affair I did. He had a list of what you and your brothers might disapprove of in a man, and he shook his head at me for nearly every single man I met. It saved me time and disappointment, but it got me my quaint nickname, too. It's impossible, Tony. I can please Jason, but not you . . . you, but not Edward. Thank heaven Uncle James isn't also here to express his opinion. There isn't a man in existence who would please all of you."

"That's absurd," he protested. "I can think of a dozen off hand who would do very well."

"Would they, Tony?" she asked softly. "Would you really want me to marry any of them?"

He pulled an aggrieved face, then suddenly grinned. "No, I suppose not."

"So you see my predicament then?"

"But don't you want to marry, puss?"

"Of course I do. And I'm sure the man you and your brothers find for me will make me very happy."

"What?" He glared at her. "Oh, no you don't. You're not putting that responsibility on *my* shoulders, Reggie."

"All right then," she agreed. "We'll leave it to Uncle Jason."

"Don't be foolish. He'd have you married to a tyrant just like him."

"Come now, Tony, you know that's not true." She grinned.

"Well, close to it," he grumbled.

"You see, Tony, at least *I* wouldn't have to keep on summing up every man I meet. I want to enjoy myself again, be able to talk to a man without analyzing him, dance without wondering if my partner is husband material. It's gotten so that every man I look at, I ask myself, Shall I marry him? Could I love him? Would he be as good and kind to me as—" She stopped, blushing.

"As?" he prompted.

"Oh, you might as well know," she said with a sigh. "I compare every man to you and my other uncles. I can't help it. I almost wish you all didn't love me so well. You've pampered me outrageously. I want my husband to be a combination of all of you."

"What *have* we done to you?"

He was about to burst into laughter and she lost her temper. "You think it's funny, do you? I don't see *you* facing this problem. And if I don't get a vacation from it, I swear I will try and reach Uncle James and have him take me away."

He sobered instantly. Though he was the closest to James, even he had been furious and unforgiving over what his brother had done.

"Don't say that, Reggie," he warned. "You're not thinking clearly. Calling James into this will make matters worse, not better."

She pressed the point mercilessly. "Then will you tell Uncle Jason I want to come home for a while? That I'm done with looking for a husband and will wait until the three of you can agree on whom I should marry?"

"Blister it, Reggie, Jason isn't going to like this any more than I do. You should be making your own choice, finding someone you love."

"I tried that." There was an awkward silence.

Anthony scowled. "Lord Medhurst was a pompous ass!"

"Did I know that? I thought he was quite the one. Well, so much for my falling in love."

"You could have had Newel if Eddie hadn't been convinced he would make a terrible father." Tony continued to scowl.

"Yes, well, Uncle Edward was undoubtedly right. Again—so much for my falling in love."

"You certainly know how to depress a fellow, puss. We only wanted what was best for you, you know."

"I do know that, and I love you for it. I just know I'll adore whomever the three of you decide will make a perfect husband."

"Will you?" He grinned. "I'm not so sure. If Jason agrees to this, for example, he'll be determined to find a man who's nothing like me."

He was teasing. If there was anyone who would disapprove of someone like him for her, that someone was Tony himself. She laughed. "Well, you know you can always convert my husband, Tony—after I'm safely married."

Chapter Four

Percival Alden shouted in triumph as he reined in his horse at the end of Green Park, Piccadilly side. "That's twenty pounds you owe me, Nick!" he called over his shoulder as the Viscount came charging up behind him riding his bay. Nicholas Eden gave Percy a black scowl.

They began walking their horses around in a circle. The two friends had just come from Boodles, ending a perfectly good game of cards when Percy mentioned his new black stallion. Nicholas was just drunk enough to take up the challenge, and they sent for their horses.

"We could both have broken our bloody necks, you know," Nicholas pronounced quite sensibly, though his vision was blurred almost double. "Remind me not to do this again, will you?"

Percy thought that was terribly funny and began laughing so hard he nearly lost his balance. "As if anyone could stop you from doing what you've a mind to do, especially when you're foxed. But never mind, old chap. You probably won't remember this daring escapade come morning, and if you do, you won't believe your memory. Ah, where the bloody hell was that moon when it was needed?"

Nicholas looked up at the silver orb just coming out from behind a cloud bank. His head was spinning. Damnation! The race should have sobered him a little.

He fastened his wavering gaze on his friend. "How much do you want for that animal, Percy?"

"No wish to sell him. I'll be winning more races with him."

"How much?" Nicholas repeated obdurately.

"I paid two hundred and fifty for him, but—"

"Three hundred."

"He's not for sale."

"Four hundred."

"Oh, come now, Nick," Percy protested.

"Five hundred."

"I'll send him round in the morning."

Nicholas grinned in satisfaction.

"I should have held out for a thousand." Percy grinned back. "But then, I know where I can get his brother for two fifty. And I wouldn't want to take advantage of you."

Nicholas laughed. "You're wasting your talent, Percy. You should get a job in Smithfield Market selling horseflesh."

"And give my dear mother yet another reason to curse the day she bore a son? No, thank you. I'll go on as I am, taking advantage of hard bargainers like yourself to turn a tidy little profit. It's more fun, anyway. And speaking of fun, weren't you supposed to put in an appearance at Shepford's tonight?"

"Bloody hell," Nicholas growled, his good humor disappearing. "Why did you have to remind me?"

"My good deed for the day."

"I wouldn't go near that place if my little bird didn't need her wings clipped," Nicholas confided.

"Ruffled your feathers, did she?"

"Would you credit she thinks to make me jealous?" Nicholas asked, outraged.

"You? Jealous?" Percy guffawed. "I would love to see the day, dearly I would."

"You're welcome to come along and watch my performance. I mean to give a very good one for Lady E. before I call it quits," Nicholas said darkly.

"You're not going to call the poor fellow out, are you?"

"Good God, over a woman? Of course not. But she will think so, while I will in fact give him my blessing of her. She'll be left to blame herself for her folly, for she will have seen the last of me."

"That's a novel way to go about it," Percy mused. "I must remember to try that. Look, why not give me your blessing of her? Fine-looking woman, Lady E. Oh, I say." Percy looked off across the street. "Speaking of . . . isn't that her carriage over there?"

Nicholas followed the direction of his nod to see the bright, outrageously painted pink-and-green curricle he knew so well. "Impossible," he muttered. "She would die rather than be late for that ball, and it's long since started."

"Don't know anyone else who owns such a smart-looking carriage," Percy remarked. "Been meaning to paint my own those colors."

Nicholas threw him a horrified look before glancing back at the street. "Who do we know who lives on this street?" he asked his friend.

"No one I can think of," Percy began. "Wait a minute! I think I know whose house she's stopped in front of. The house belongs to young Malory's kin—oh, what's his name? You know. Not the wild one who hasn't been around for years, but the other one, the one who's so good a marksman that no one will—oh, I have it! Anthony, Lord Anthony. Good God! You don't think she means to make you jealous with *him?* Even you don't dare mess with him, Nick."

Nicholas didn't answer. Slowly, very slowly, he left the park and crossed the street. If that was Selena, then she was right where she knew he would see her, because he passed this way every night on his way home from his club. As it happened, they had come out of the park that night near the end of Piccadilly, and if Percy hadn't spotted the carriage, he might not have either. But now his curiosity was aroused. Was Selena sitting inside the closed carriage, waiting for him to pass, unaware that he had already gone around her? Had she been unable to get an escort to her damned ball, and was again determined to drag him there with her? It was impossible that she could know Anthony Malory. He and his cronies were in a completely different league, rakehells all, thumbing their noses at society. Nicholas might have a tarnished reputation himself, but even he wouldn't be classed with that group of wastrels.

But what if she had somehow met Malory? But she would not dally here tonight of all nights. The Shepford ball meant too much. It was all she had talked about for the last month.

Yet what if she had come here to tryst with Malory? Nicholas stopped by the curb three houses away. Percy caught up with him, looking alarmed. "That wasn't a dare I made back there, you know," Percy said earnestly. "You're not thinking of doing anything foolish, are you?"

"I've just been thinking, Percy." Nicholas was grinning. "If that is Lady E. in there, then she'll be coming out any moment now."

"How do you know that?"

"The ball. She might be late for it, but she isn't going to miss it, not she. However, maybe she *will* miss it after all. Yes, it would do her a world of good to miss it. A woman shouldn't get so involved with something that she ignores the man in her life. That lesson should be made clear to her, don't you think? Yes, quite clear. Very clear. So she won't make the same mistake again."

"Montieth! What the devil are you planning?" Percy demanded in alarm.

Nicholas didn't answer because his attention was drawn by the door opening down the street. His grin widened as Selena Eddington stepped outside. She was securing a short black domino over her eyes, and she had her hands raised to her face, but he would have recognized that black hair anywhere. She was wearing a long fur-edged cape secured at the throat. The cape was thrown back over her shoulders, revealing a lovely rose-colored gown. Nicholas was taken aback. Rose? That wasn't one of her colors. She contemptuously called it the color of innocence, a quality she had long ago lost without regret. He supposed she was out to impress the Duchess of Stepford with her youth.

She turned toward the man standing at her back and Nicholas recognized Anthony Malory. He knew those dark good looks well, saw him often enough at the clubs, though they were not exactly speaking acquaintances. Selena would find him very attractive, Nicholas admitted that. Well, he wished her luck. Malory was even more determined a bachelor than Nicholas. She would never bring that one to the altar. Did she realize that?

He watched in amusement as she embraced Malory, then gave him a quick kiss. He was obviously not taking her to the ball, for he was dressed in only a lounging robe.

"Well, what do you make of that?" Percy said uncomfortably, bringing his horse a bit closer. "It is Lady E., isn't it?"

"Yes, and the carriage is facing this way, Percy, so I'll be going the other way. Do me a favor and hamper it from turning around as long as you can."

"Blister it, what are you going to do?"

"Why, take Lady E. home with me, what else?" Nicholas chuckled. "I'll go around the block and cut through Mayfair to get back to Park Lane with her. Meet me there."

"Damnation take you, Nick!" Percy exclaimed. "Malory's standing right there!"

"Yes, but he's not going to go chasing down the street after me on foot, now is he? And he won't have a weapon handy if he's just tumbled her. He may enjoy this entertainment."

"Don't do it, Nick."

But Nicholas wasn't sober enough to think. He started his mount down the street toward the carriage, picking up just a little speed before he reached it. When he veered off the street and onto the curb, he took everyone by surprise, riding right between the house and the carriage. Slowing for an instant, he grabbed Selena and yanked her across his horse.

Beautifully done, he congratulated himself. He couldn't have done it any better if he'd been sober. Shouting erupted behind him, but he didn't slow down. The woman across his horse started screaming, but he quickly stuffed his white silk handkerchief in her mouth to stifle her, then used his cravat to bind her wrists.

She was squirming so much that he was in danger of losing her, so he twisted her around until she was sitting in front of him, then whisked her cape over her head, bundling her tightly. Just as good as a sack, he thought with satisfaction. He chuckled as they rounded a corner and headed back toward Park Lane. "Sounds like no one's following, my dear. Perhaps your driver, Tovey, recognized me and knows you're in familiar hands." He chuckled again, hearing the muffled sounds she was making inside the cape. "Yes, I know you're miffed with me, Selena. But console yourself that you can give vent to a full temper tantrum when I let you go—in the morning."

She began to struggle again, but in another few moments he was stopping in front of his townhouse on Park Lane. Percival Alden was stationed by the great dark expanse of Hyde Park across the street, and only he saw Nicholas toss the bundle over his shoulder and carry it into the house. His butler tried not to look too startled.

Percy followed him inside and said, "They didn't even try to follow you."

"Ah, that means the driver did recognize me." Nicholas chuckled. "He's probably explained to Malory by now that the lady and I are friends."

"I still can't believe you did this, Nick. She'll never forgive you."

"I know. Now be a good chap and follow me upstairs so you can light a few lamps before I deposit my baggage." He paused just long enough to grin at his butler, who was staring at the feet hanging over his lordship's shoulder. "Tell my man to get my evening clothes out, Tyndale. I want to be out of here in ten minutes. And if anyone comes to call, for any reason, say that I left for the Duke of Shepford's ball an hour ago."

"Very good, my lord."

"You're still going?" Percy asked in amazement as he and the butler followed Nicholas upstairs.

"But of course," Nicholas replied. "I intend to dance the night away."

He stopped in front of a bedroom at the back of the house on the third floor, checking it quickly to make sure there was nothing of value in the room that Selena could destroy in anger. Satisfied, he told Tyndale to fetch the key, then nodded to Percy to light the lamp on the mantel.

"Be a good girl, my dear, and don't make too much fuss." He patted her backside in a familiar manner. "If you start screaming or do anything else foolish, Tyndale will be forced to put a stop to it. I'm sure you won't enjoy spending the next few hours trussed up on the bed."

He motioned for Percy to leave the room before he dropped her on the bed. Then he loosened her wrist bonds and left the room, locking the door with a soft click. He knew she would remove the gag sooner or later, but he wouldn't be around to hear her.

"Come along, Percy. I have extra evening clothes if you would like to join me at the ball."

Percy shook his head in confusion as he followed Nicholas back down to the second floor where his rooms were located. "I might as well, but I don't see why you're going on to the ball now that she won't be there."

"That's the crowning touch." Nicholas chuckled. "What's the point in Lady E.'s missing the ball unless she's told by her dear friends tomorrow that I danced every dance from the time I arrived until I departed."

"That's cruel, Montieth."

"No crueler than her throwing me over for Malory."

"But you don't even care about that," Percy pointed out, exasperated.

"No, I don't. Still, it warrants *some* kind of reaction, doesn't it? After all, the lady would have been devastated if I'd done nothing."

"If she could choose how you would react, Montieth, I don't think she would choose this."

"Oh, well. Better this than my challenging Malory. Don't you think so?"

"Heavens, yes!" Percy was genuinely appalled. "You wouldn't stand a chance against him."

"You think not?" Nicholas murmured. "Well, perhaps not. After all, he *has* had more practice than I. But we'll never know, will we?"

Chapter Five

Reggie wasn't frightened. She had heard enough to know that her kidnapper was a nobleman. He assumed he'd been recognized by the driver of her carriage, so he meant no real harm. No, she wouldn't be hurt.

One other thing made Reggie smile with a deliciously wicked grin. The man had made a dreadful mistake. He thought she was someone else—Selena, he had called her. "It's only me," he had said, as if she should recognize his voice easily.

Selena? What made this man think she was Selena? He had simply picked her up off the sidewalk, so what made him . . . *"The driver recognized me"!* Good God, Lady Eddington! He knew the carriage so he thought she was Lady Eddington.

This was priceless. He would go to the Shepford ball—and *voilà,* there would be Lady Eddington with Reggie's cousins. Oh, how she wished she could see his face. It was just the sort of prank she might have played on someone in her younger years.

And then he would come racing back to his house, full of frantic apologies, begging her forgiveness. He would plead with her not to say anything. She would have to agree, for her reputation was at stake. She would go to the ball and simply say she had stayed longer with Uncle Anthony than she'd planned to. No one would ever know she had been abducted.

Having removed her gag and wrist bands, she stretched out on the bed, perfectly at ease, enjoying the adventure. It wasn't her first, not by any means. She'd had adventures all her life, beginning at age seven, when she'd fallen through the ice on Haverston Pond, and would have drowned if one of the stableboys hadn't heard her calling and pulled her out. The following year the same boy distracted a wild boar that had chased her up a tree. He'd been gored, and while he recovered quickly, happy to tell his friends all about the dramatic rescue, she was restricted from the woods for a year.

No, even her uncles' almost religious devotion to her upbringing hadn't been able to stand in the way of fate, and Reggie had seen more adventure in nineteen years than most men did in all their lives. Looking around her elegant, temporary prison, she smiled. She knew young women dreamed of adventure, yearned to be swept away by handsome strangers on horseback, but she had known the real thing. Twice, as a matter of fact, this evening's escapade being the second.

Two years before, when she was seventeen, she'd been attacked on the road to Bath by three masked highwaymen, and whisked away by the boldest of the three. Thank heaven her daring oldest cousin Derek had been in the coach that day and, taking one of the coach horses, had pursued her abductor furiously, rescuing Reggie from . . . whatever the stranger had had in mind.

And before that, when she was twelve, there had been her high-seas adventure. She was kidnapped for a whole summer, and endured terrifying storms at sea and even an incredible battle.

Well, she was having another adventure, an amusing and fairly safe one this time. And then she sat bolt upright. Uncle Tony! He knew about this! Suddenly it wasn't funny anymore. If he found out who her abductor was, he would come and break the door down. There would be no end of gossip, and then she would be ruined. Anthony Malory wouldn't let it end easily, either. He would challenge the poor fellow and kill him, mistake or not.

Reggie got up and began to walk, barefoot, around the room. Oh, dear, this was becoming a dreadful predicament. She continued pacing, distracting herself by studying the room. It was done in muted greens and browns, and there were a few modern Chippendale pieces. Her cape was draped over an armchair, her slippers on the floor in front of it, her mask tossed on the padded seat. A single window looked out over a garden, dark and full of shadows. She repaired her hair using a mirror framed in the leaves and flowers of the Rocaille style.

She wondered if Tyndale really would tie her up and gag her if she started shouting for help. Better not to find out. She wondered, too, what was taking Nick so long to discover his mistake. The minutes continued to tick by on the Meissen clock on the mantel.

Nicholas watched her waltz by in the arms of some dandy wearing bright green satin that clashed horribly with Selena's plum-colored evening gown. With those colors, they were hardly a pair one could miss, even on that crowded dance floor.

"Bloody hell," Nicholas growled.

Percy, standing beside him, was more articulate. "Oh, good God! You've really gone and done it, haven't you? I knew you shouldn't have started this, and now you've really gone and done it."

"Shut up, Percy."

"Well, that *is* her, isn't it? Then for God's sake who's the bird you've got caged at home? You've stolen Malory's mistress, isn't that it? He'll kill you, Nick," Percy informed him. "He'll bloody well kill you is what he'll do."

Nicholas was ready to kill his excitable friend. "You do go on and on, don't you? The only thing that will come of this is my getting a tongue lashing from a furious woman I've never laid eyes on before. Lord Malory isn't going to call me out over a stupid mistake like this. What harm has been done, after all?"

"The lady's reputation, Nick," Percy began. "If this gets out—"

"How will it get out? Use your head, old boy. If she is Malory's mistress, what reputation has she to lose? What I *would* like to know, is what was she doing with Lady Eddington's carriage?" He sighed, very much the misunderstood, put-upon male. "I suppose I'd better run along home and let her out—whoever she is."

"Need help?" Percy grinned. "I'm rather curious to know who she is actually."

"She isn't likely to be in a receiving mood," Nicholas pointed out. "I'll be lucky if I only get a vase thrown at my head."

"Well, you can manage that on your own, thank you. Tell me all about it tomorrow, all right."

"I thought you'd feel that way," Nicholas said wryly.

Nicholas rode home as fast as he could. He was quite sober by that point and regretting the entire evening deeply. He prayed the mystery lady had a sense of humor.

Tyndale let him in and took his cloak, hat, and gloves. "Any problems?" Nicholas asked, knowing there would be a long list. But there wasn't.

"Not one, my lord."

"No noise?"

"None."

Nicholas took a long, deep breath. She was probably saving all her fury for him.

"Have the carriage brought round, Tyndale," he ordered before starting up the stairs.

The third floor was as quiet as a tomb. The servants had no reason to be in that part of the house after dark. Lucy, the pretty maid he'd been eyeing lately, wouldn't venture upstairs unless sent for, and his valet, Harris, would be sleeping on the second floor, expecting his master much later. At least no one in the house other than Tyndale knew about the lady's presence. That was a break.

Nicholas stood outside Reggie's door for a brief moment, then unlocked the door and opened it quickly. He was braced to receive a bash on the head, but the jolt he got at first sight of her was just as stunning.

She stood framed by the window, gazing at him in a startlingly direct way. There was no shyness in her look and no fear either on that exquisite, delicate, heart-shaped face. The eyes were disturbing, with an exotic slant. Such dark blue eyes in that fair face, so blue and clear, like colored crystal. The lips were soft and full and the nose was straight and slender. A thick fringe of sooty lashes framed those extraordinary eyes, while black brows arched gently above them. Her hair was raven black, too, in tight little ringlets surrounding her face, giving her fair skin a glow like polished ivory.

She was breathtaking. The beauty didn't stop with her face, either. She was petite, yes, but there was nothing childlike about her form. Firm young breasts pressed against the thin muslin of her rose gown. It was not cut as low as some gowns were and stopped short of being provocative, yet somehow it was as tantalizing as anything he'd seen in London. He wanted to pull the rose muslin down a few inches and watch those lovely breasts spring free. He received another jolt then, feeling his manhood rise against his will. Lord, he hadn't lost control like that since his youth!

Desperate to bring everything under control, he cast about for something—anything—to say. "Hello."

His tone implied "What have we here?" and Reggie grinned despite herself. He was gorgeous, simply gorgeous. It wasn't just his face, though that was striking. There was a sexual magnetism about him that was quite unnerving. He was even better looking than Uncle Anthony, whom she'd always considered the most handsome, compelling man in the world.

The comparison was reassuring. He reminded her of Uncle Tony, not only in height and appearance, but in the way his eyes assessed her. His mouth quirked upward in approval. How often she had seen her uncle look at women just that way. Well, he was a rake, she told herself. What other kind of man would abduct his mistress from the doorstep of another man's house? Had he been jealous, thinking his mistress and Uncle Anthony were . . . oh, this was becoming a most amusing situation.

"Hello, yourself," Reggie said impishly. "I was beginning to wonder when you would realize your mistake. You certainly took enough time about it."

"I am just now wondering if I have in fact made a mistake at all. You don't look like a mistake. You look very much like something I did right for a change."

He quietly closed the door and leaned back against it, those beautiful amber eyes boldly moving over her from head to foot. It was not at all safe for a young lady to be alone with a man of his stamp, and Reggie recognized that. Yet for some reason she couldn't fathom, she wasn't afraid of this man. Scandalously, she wondered if it would be such a terrible thing to lose her virtue to him. Oh, it was a reckless mood she was suddenly in!

She eyed the closed door and his large frame blocking that only exit. "Fie on you, sir. I hope you don't mean to compromise me more than you already have."

"I will if you will let me. Will you? Think carefully before you answer," he said with a devastating smile. "My heart is in jeopardy."

She giggled, delighted. "Stuff! Rakes like you don't *have* hearts. Everyone knows that."

Nicholas was enchanted. Could anything he said disconcert her? He doubted it.

"You wound me, love, if you compare my heart to Malory's."

"Never think it, sir," she assured him. "Tony's heart is as fickle as anyone's can be. Any man's heart would be more constant than his. Even yours," she said dryly.

This from the man's mistress? Nicholas couldn't believe his luck. She hadn't even sounded peevish about it. She simply accepted that Malory would never be faithful to her. Was she ripe for a change in lovers?

"Aren't you at all curious as to why I brought you here?" he asked. He was certainly curious. Why wasn't she upset?

"Oh, no," she replied lightly, "I have already figured that out."

"Have you?" He was amused, waiting to hear whatever outlandish explanation she had arrived at.

"You thought I was Lady Eddington," she said, "and you intended she miss the Shepford ball, while you attended and danced every dance. Did you?"

Nicholas shook himself. "What?"

"Dance every dance?"

"Not one."

"Well, you must have seen her there. Oh, I wish I could have seen your expression." She giggled again. "Were you terribly surprised?"

"Uh . . . terribly," he admitted. He was incredulous. How the devil had she put it all together? What had he said when he carried her up here?

"You have me at a disadvantage. I seem to have said a great deal to you earlier."

"Don't you remember?"

"Not clearly," he admitted weakly. "I'm afraid I was good and foxed."

"Well then, I suppose that excuses you, doesn't it? But you didn't really say all that much. It helps to know the people involved, you see."

"You *know* Lady Eddington?"

"Yes. Not well, of course. I only met her this week. But she was kind enough to lend me her carriage tonight."

He came away from the door suddenly then, crossing the room until he stood only inches away from her. She was even lovelier up close. She didn't move away, to his surprise, but looked up at him as if she trusted him fully.

"Who are you?" he asked in a hoarse whisper.

"Regina Ashton."

"Ashton?" He frowned thoughtfully. "Isn't that the family name of the Earl of Penwich?"

"Why, yes, do you know him?"

"No. He owns a piece of land bordering my own that I have been trying to buy for several years, but the pompous . . . he won't return my inquiries. You're not related to him, are you?"

"It is unfortunate, but yes, I am. At least the tie is quite distant."

Nicholas chuckled. "Most ladies would not think it unfortunate to be connected to an Earl."

"Really? Then they haven't met the present Earl of Penwich. I am happy to say I haven't seen the man for many years, but I doubt he has changed much. He is indeed a pompous . . ."

He grinned. "Who *are* your people, then?"

"I am an orphan, sir."

"I'm sorry."

"As am I. But I do have a loving family on my mother's side who saw to my upbringing. And now it is only fair for you to tell me who you are."

"Nicholas Eden."

"Fourth Viscount of Montieth? Oh dear, I *have* heard about you."

"Scandalous lies, I assure you."

"I doubt it." She grinned up at him. "But you needn't fear I'll think badly of you. After all, no one is quite as bad as Tony, or his brother James for that matter, and I love them both very much."

"Both? Tony *and* James Malory?" He was utterly stunned. "Good God, you don't mean you're James Malory's mistress, too!"

Her eyes widened for a moment. She bit her lip hard, but it didn't work. The laughter broke through in spite of her.

"I fail to see any humor," Nicholas began coldly.

"Oh, but there is, I assure you. I was afraid you might think Tony and I . . . oh, this is famous! I must tell Tony . . . no, I better not. He won't think it's funny. You men are so stuffy sometimes," she sighed. "You see, he's my uncle."

"If that is what you prefer to call him."

She laughed again. "You don't believe me, do you?"

"My dear Miss Ashton—"

"Lady Ashton," she corrected him.

"Very well—Lady Ashton. I'll have you know that Jason Malory's son, Derek Malory, is one of my closest friends—"

"I know."

"You do?"

"Yes, your best friend, actually. You went to school with him, though you finished a few years before he did. You took a liking to him when others did not. He loved you for that. I loved you, too, for befriending him, though I was only eleven at the time he told me about it and I had never met you. Where do you think I heard about you, Lord Montieth? Cousin Derek used to go on and on about you when he came home on holiday."

"Why didn't he ever mention you, then?" Nicholas snapped.

"Why would he talk about me?" she asked. "I'm sure you and he had better things to talk about than the children in your families."

Nicholas frowned darkly. "You could be making all of this up."

"Of course I could." She left it like that, without trying to convince him.

Her eyes sparkled with laughter. Damnation, she was beautiful.

"How old are you?" he asked.

"So you're not angry anymore?"

"Was I angry?"

"Oh, my, yes." She smiled. "I can't imagine why. *I* am the one who should have been angry. And I'm nineteen, if you must know, though you shouldn't have asked."

He began to relax again. She was wonderful. He couldn't bear much more. He wanted to hug her, yet he was loath to remind her of the impropriety of their situation.

"Is this your first season, Regina?"

She liked the way he said her name. "You are conceding that I am who I say I am?"

"I suppose I must."

"You don't have to sound so disappointed about it," she retorted.

"I'm devastated, if you must know." His voice became husky and he allowed himself to run a finger along her cheek, gently, so as not to frighten her. "I don't want you to be an innocent. I want you to know exactly what I mean when I tell you I want to make love to you, Regina."

Her heart began to beat faster. "Do you?" she whispered. She shook herself. She must not lose control. "Yes, of course you do," she teased him. "I thought I saw that look in your eyes."

His hand dropped to his side and his eyes narrowed. "How would you know that look?"

"Oh, my, you're angry again," she said innocently.

"Bloody hell!" he snapped. "Can't you be serious?"

"If I become serious, Lord Montieth, then we'll both be in trouble."

Her dark eyes were inscrutable. Good Lord, there was another girl entirely beneath that effervescent surface.

She stepped past him and moved to the center of the room, and when she turned back to look at him, the gamin smile and teasing sparkle were back in place.

"This is my second season, and I have met many men just as improper as you," she assured him.

"I don't believe that."

"That there are men as improper as you?"

"That this is your second season. Are you married?"

"You imply that I should be, because I was brought out last year? Alas, as far as my family is concerned, there is no one good enough for me. A most annoying circumstance, I assure you."

Nicholas laughed. "It is too bad I sailed to the West Indies last year to inspect some property I have there. I would have met you sooner if I'd stayed here."

"Would you have tried for my hand?"

"I would have tried for—some part of you."

For the first time, Reggie blushed. "That was too bold."

"But not as bold as I would like to be."

Oh, he truly was dangerous, Reggie thought. Handsome, charming, wicked. Then why wasn't she frightened of being alone with Nicholas Eden? Common sense told her she should be.

She watched breathlessly as he came toward her, closing the space between them again. She didn't move away, and he smiled. A tiny pulse was beating at the base of her throat and he had an overwhelming desire to run his tongue over it, feel the pulse beating there.

"I wonder, are you as innocent as you claim to be, Regina Ashton?"

She couldn't give in to him, no matter how strongly he worked his magic on her. "Knowing who my family is, you really can't doubt me, Lord Montieth."

"You haven't been scandalized by my bringing you here," he blurted. "Why is that?" He studied her face closely.

"Oh, I suppose I saw the humor in it," she confessed, but then she added, "I was worried for a while, however, when I thought Uncle Tony might find out where you took me and come pounding on your door before you returned to let me go. That would have caused a fine commotion! I don't see how we could have kept a secret like that for long, and you might have ended up having to marry me. Such a shame, because we really wouldn't suit."

"Wouldn't we?" he asked, amused.

"Certainly not!" she said in mock horror. "I would fall madly in love with you, while you would continue to be a disreputable rake and break my heart."

"You are undoubtedly right," he sighed, playing along. "I would make a terrible husband. Nor am I likely to be forced into marriage, by the way."

"Not even if you have ruined my reputation?"

His mouth turned down. "Not even then."

She evidently didn't like his answer, and he was annoyed with himself for being so unnecessarily honest. Anger with himself made his bright amber eyes even brighter, as if an unnatural light glowed behind them. She shivered, wondering what he would be like if he really lost his temper.

"Are you cold?" he asked, seeing her rub the gooseflesh on her arms. Did he dare wrap his arms around her?

She reached for her cape and draped it loosely over her slim shoulders. "I think it's time—"

"I've frightened you," he said gently. "That wasn't my intention."

"I am afraid I know perfectly well what your intentions are, sir," Reggie replied.

She bent down to put her slippers on, and when she straightened, she found herself in his arms. He did it so swiftly that she was being kissed before she could gasp. He tasted of brandy, sweet and intoxicating. Oh, she'd known it would be like this, so heavenly.

Never had she been kissed with such feeling, or such daring. He actually molded her small frame to his, letting her feel for the first time the state of a man's arousal. She was shocked and excited, and her breasts tingled where they pressed against his coat. What was this other, deeper feeling coming from way down inside her?

His lips trailed along her cheek and down to her throat, where he kissed the throbbing pulse, drawing the skin into his mouth, sucking ever so gently.

"You mustn't," Reggie managed to whisper. It didn't sound like her own voice at all.

"Oh, but I must, love, I really must." He scooped her in his arms.

She gasped. There was nothing amusing about what was happening now. His lips brushed her throat again and she groaned.

"Put me down," she said breathlessly. "Derek will hate you."

"I don't care."

"My uncle will kill you."

"It will be worth it."

That did it. "You won't think so when you see his weapon across a dueling field. Now put me *down*, Lord Montieth!"

Nicholas set her down slowly, carefully, causing her body to slide enticingly along his. "You would care, then?"

He was holding her close to him, and the steady heat of his body unsettled her. "Certainly. I wouldn't like to see you die because of a—a harmless escapade."

"Is that what you'd call my making love to you?" he chuckled, delighted.

"I was not referring to that, but to your bringing me here. As it is, I will have the devil's own time talking Tony round to forgetting this matter."

"You mean to protect me, then?" Nicholas said softly.

Reggie pushed away from him, unable to think clearly with her body against his. Her cape had fallen, and he retrieved it gallantly, handing it back to her with a bow.

She sighed. "If Tony doesn't know you are the one who absconded with me, then I shan't mention your name. If he does know, then, well, I suppose I will do my best to save your hide. But I insist you return me to him now, before he does something foolish, such as telling others I am missing."

"At least you give me hope." Nicholas smiled. "I may not make a good husband, but I have been told I make an excellent lover. Will you consider me?"

She was shocked. "I don't want a lover."

"I will have to follow you this season until I change your mind," he warned her.

He was incorrigible, she thought as, at last, he escorted her out of the house, incorrigible and very tempting. Tony had better be successful with Uncle Jason on her behalf, because Nicholas Eden could be a girl's downfall.

Chapter Six

"I'm sorry you missed the ball."

Nicholas stopped his carriage a few doors away from Anthony Malory's townhouse. His eyes caressed Reggie's face.

She grinned. "I'll wager you're even sorrier that Lady Eddington didn't miss it."

"You would lose the wager," he replied with a sigh. "I don't know why I did it anyway. The drink, I suppose. It's certainly doesn't matter one bit now."

"Stuff! You were jealous when you thought she was seeing Tony."

"Wrong again. I have never been jealous in my life, of anyone or anything."

"My, how fortunate for you."

"You don't believe me?"

"I don't see any other reason for your wanting to lock your mistress away for the evening. You didn't even plan to spend the evening with her."

He laughed. "You say that with such a worldly air."

She blushed. "At any rate, you needn't be sorry that I missed the ball. I'm not."

"Because you met me instead?" he ventured. "You give me more and more hope, love."

She sat up stiffly. "I hate to disappoint you, Lord Montieth, but that is not the reason. I would as well have stayed at home tonight."

"As would I have, if you were with me. There's still time, you know. We can return to my house."

She shook her head at him, wanting to laugh. In fact, since meeting him, she had felt a continual ridiculous urge to laugh for the sheer joy of it. She was bubbling over. But she knew she had to leave him now and put this night behind her.

"I must go," she said softly.

"I suppose you must." His fingers closed over her gloved hand, but he made no move to help her down from the carriage. He exerted a pressure on her hand that held her in place. "I want to kiss you again before you go."

"No."

"Just a good-night kiss."

"No."

His free hand cupped her cheek. He hadn't bothered to collect his gloves or hat before they left his house, and his bare fingers were hot against her skin. She couldn't move, and she waited breathlessly for him to steal the kiss she had refused him.

He did, his lips moving in to fasten on hers for a kiss that was nothing like any kiss she'd had before. Warm and masterful, his lips tasted hers until she thought she would explode.

"Come on, before I forget myself," he said roughly. Passion made his voice heavy.

Reggie was dazed as he helped her down from the carriage and led her toward her uncle's townhouse. "You'd better not come with me," she whispered. Lamps burned on each side of the door, and she could just picture the door opening and Tony facing Nicholas Eden with a gun in his hand. "It isn't necessary for you to accompany me."

"My dear, I may be many reprehensible things, but no one has ever said of me that I was not a gentleman, and a gentleman sees a lady to her door."

"Stuff! You're a gentleman only when it pleases you to be one, and now it pleases you to be obstinate."

Nicholas chuckled at her anxiety. "Do you fear for my safety?"

"Yes, I do. Tony is an agreeable fellow most of the time, but there are occasions when he simply has no control over his temper. He mustn't see you until I have been able to tell him that nothing untoward has happened."

Nicholas stopped and turned her around to face him. "If he has such a violent temper, then I will not let you face him alone."

He thought to protect *her* from Tony. She might have laughed, but she suppressed the urge. "You would have to understand how it is between Tony and me to know that I am the last person who needs to fear him. We are very close, you see, so close that he regularly turns his life upside down for me when I stay with him. He always has, even abstaining from most of his usual pursuits for months at a time. *You* should be able to appreciate what that means," she finished dryly.

He led her forward again, grinning. "I concede your point. Nevertheless, there is a reason for everything I do, and I *will* see you to your door."

She started to protest again, but they were already there. She tensed, praying they hadn't been heard, that the door wouldn't open. She turned to face Nicholas, whispering, "What possible reason could you—?"

But he interrupted roguishly, "You see, I now have an excuse to kiss you good night again."

He folded her in his arms, his mouth coming down to sear hers. This was passion, hot, blistering passion that melted her into him. Nothing else mattered. In that moment, she was his.

Nicholas ended the kiss with passion riding him hard. He nearly shoved her away from him, though without releasing her, his fingers biting into her upper arms. He held her there at arm's length, his breathing harsh, his eyes blazing.

"I want you, sweet Regina. Don't make me wait too long before you admit you want me, too."

It took Reggie a moment to realize that he had let her go and begun walking away. She had the wildest urge to run after him but steadied herself. It wasn't easy. Her heart was racing and her legs were wobbly.

Get hold of yourself, goose, she scolded herself. *You've been kissed before.* But oh, never like that!

Reggie waited until she saw Nicholas step into his carriage before she reluctantly turned away, opened the door, and went inside. The entry and hall were brightly lit and, thankfully, empty. The door to Tony's library-study was open and light spilled out of it. She moved toward it slowly, hoping Tony would be there and not out scouring London for her.

He was there, sitting at his desk with his head in his hands, the fingers twined in his thick black hair as if he'd been trying to pull it out. A decanter of brandy and a glass were beside him.

The sight of him looking so woebegone had a steadying effect on Reggie. Guilt helped her pull herself together. While she had been having the sweetest time of her life, the person who meant the most to her in all the world had been worried sick. And she hadn't even rushed back here. She'd taken her time, enjoying every moment spent with Nicholas. How could she have been so selfish?

"Tony?"

He looked up in shock. Then surprise washed over his handsome features, and relief. He hurried to her and gathered her into his arms, squeezing so tightly she thought her ribs would crack.

"Good God, Reggie, I've been half-baked with worry! I haven't been in such bad shape since James took you with him to—well, never mind that now." He set her away from him so he could look her over. "Are you all right? Have you been hurt?"

"I'm fine, Tony, really I am."

She looked fine too. No rents in her gown, no curls out of place. But she had been gone for three bloody hours, and the things he had imagined happening to her . . .

"I'm going to kill him first thing in the morning, as soon as I find out where the bloody hell he lives!"

So that's why there had been no pounding on the doors, Reggie realized.

"It was all perfectly innocent, Tony," she began, "a mistake—"

"I *know* it was a mistake, Reggie. That idiot driver of yours assured me of that. He kept insisting Montieth would bring you back at any moment, that he and Lady Eddington were, ah . . . that they . . . well, I think you know what I mean. Oh, bloody hell!"

"Yes." Reggie grinned at his discomfort. "I do know what you mean." Then she hastened to work him round. "The poor man thought you and his—"

"Don't say it! And that's no excuse anyway!"

"But can't you imagine his expression, Tony, when he saw that he had the wrong lady?" Reggie giggled. "Oh, I wish I could have seen him."

Anthony frowned. "How is it that you didn't see him?"

"I wasn't there. He left me at his house and went to the ball. You see his only intent was to make Lady Eddington miss the ball. You can understand how shocked he was when he saw her there. He didn't know who the devil he had locked up in his house."

"He locked you in his house?"

"But I was perfectly comfortable," she assured him quickly. "And so you see that I wasn't with him all this time—very little time in fact. No harm was done, and he brought me back here safe and sound."

"I can't believe you're defending him. If I had known where he lives, he'd be dead by now. The fool driver didn't know. I sent a man round to the clubs to make inquiries, but because of that blasted ball the clubs were nearly deserted. By the time my man got back to report that he hadn't learned anything, I was bloody well ready to hie myself off to Shepford's to find someone who could give me that scoundrel's address."

"And then Uncle Edward would have been alerted that I wasn't with you, and all hell would have broken loose," she finished for him. "It's a good thing you didn't do that. This way no one knows I haven't been here with you all evening. Which means that all that is left to do is decide whether I should stay here or return to Uncle Edward's house. What do you suggest?"

"Oh, no you don't, my girl." He saw right through her ploy. "You are not going to get me to forget about this."

"If you don't, then I am ruined," she said quite seriously. "Because no one will ever believe that I spent three hours in Lord Montieth's house and came away with my virtue intact. It is intact, by the way."

He glared at her. "Then I won't kill him. But he will be taught a lesson he richly deserves."

"But no harm was done, Tony!" she insisted passionately. "And—and I don't want you to hurt him."

"You don't—by God, you'll tell me why!"

"I like him," she said simply. "He reminds me of you."

Lord Malory turned livid. "I *will* kill him!"

"Stop!" she cried. "You would never have forced yourself on an unwilling maid, and neither did he."

"Did he kiss you?"

"Well—"

"Of course he did. Only a fool wouldn't, and he's no fool. I'll—"

"No, you won't!" she cried again. "You will pretend you never learned his name, and when you see him, you will ignore him. You will do that for me, Tony, because I don't know if I would be able to forgive you if you did anything to hurt Nicholas Eden. I enjoyed myself tonight, more than I have for a very long time." Having said so much, she pleaded with him, "Please, Uncle Tony."

He started to say something, clamped his mouth shut, scowled, sighed heavily, and finally said gently, "He's not for you, puss. You know that, don't you?"

"Yes, I do. If he were a little less disreputable, though, I would set my cap for him."

"Over my dead body!"

She gave him her sweetest smile.

"Somehow I knew you would say that."

Chapter Seven

Reggie sat at her dressing table, staring dreamily at the little bruise on the base of her throat. Nicholas Eden's love mark. She touched the spot. It was fortunate she had not removed her cape when she returned to Tony's house last night. As it was, she would have to wear a scarf until the mark went away.

It was late in the morning, and she had slept much longer than was her habit. Her cousins would have breakfasted already, and if they were still at home, she would have to go through the story she and Tony had come up with last night.

Tony had sent a message to his brother Edward before she returned home, saying simply that Reggie would not be coming to the ball after all. Only that, no reason given. Their story was that Tony hadn't been at home when she got to his house, so she had waited for him for hours. When he did arrive, they had their talk. As it was so late after their conversation, she had simply gone home to bed. The servants at Uncle Edward's would confirm that Tony had brought her back there and she had indeed gone right to bed.

Reggie sighed and rang for Meg, then hastily went through her bureau in search of a scarf. Meg mustn't see her lovebite either.

When she came downstairs a half hour later, it was to find Aunt Charlotte and cousins Clare and Diana receiving. They were in the drawing room with their visitors—the Ladys Braddock, mother and daughter; Mrs. Faraday and her sister Jane; and two ladies Reggie didn't know. They all stared at her as she entered, and Reggie became most uncomfortable over the lies she was about to tell.

"My dear Regina," Mrs. Faraday spoke in a strangely sympathetic tone. "How divine you look—considering."

Reggie felt a tight knot forming in the pit of her stomach. No. It wasn't possible. Only her own guilty conscience made her think they could know about last night's escapade.

Nicholas Eden, Fourth Viscount Eden of Montieth, lay stretched out on his large bed, his arms tucked behind his head, only a thin sheet covering his nakedness. He had lain there after waking for nearly an hour, but made no move to get up and face the day. He had long since missed his usual morning ride through Hyde Park. There was nothing immediate that he needed to see to. Another letter to the Earl of Penwich demanding an answer about the land he wanted, but that could wait. It was bound to be only a source of irritation anyway, since he'd never received an answer from the man.

He needed to contact the manager of his shipping firm in Southampton to cancel the ship he had recently ordered made ready for him. He had planned to put London behind him for a few months, to sail to the West Indies again. But as of last evening, nothing could make him leave London.

Her name was Regina. He said the name aloud, letting it roll deliciously off of his tongue. Regina. Sweet, fair Regina with ebony hair and china-blue eyes. Those eyes. He had only to close his own eyes to see them smiling at him, laughing. Oh, they possessed such life. Regina, fairest of the fair, beauty beyond compare.

Nicholas chuckled at his fancy. Percy would say he had fallen head over heels. Had he? Well, no, of course not. But he couldn't remember ever wanting a woman as much as he did Regina Ashton.

He sighed. Aunt Ellie would tell him to marry the girl and be happy. She was the only one since his father had died who cared a damn about Nicholas. Perhaps his grandmother did, or perhaps she didn't. It was hard to tell about Rebecca, the old tyrant.

And, of course, there was his "mother." She would be the last to wish him well. It was because of her that he couldn't—or wouldn't—marry Regina or any girl of good family. He wouldn't marry, at least not until the woman who was known to the world as his mother was dead. The threat she held over him would die with her.

Nicholas threw his sheet off and sat up, thoughts of the Dowager Countess ruining his pleasant idyll. It was because of her that he very seldom went home to Silverley, his country estate in Hampshire. Yet he loved Silverley, missed it to the point of bitterness. No matter, the only times he would go there were when the Countess was away. She was in residence most of the year, just to keep Nicholas away.

He rang for his man Harris and was informed that the Lords Alden and Malory were waiting for him in the breakfast room. He gave no special thought to it, for those two friends often dropped by without prior notice.

When he joined them a short while later, Derek Malory was seated at the table with a large plate of food, and Percy stood by the sideboard sipping coffee. Derek offered a merry hello before he went back to teasing the young maid. Percy beckoned Nicholas to him with a conspiratorial grin.

"I know who the little bird is that you brought home to your nest last night," Percy whispered, then nodded toward Derek. "*He* doesn't know yet, but of course he will before the day is out."

Nicholas felt as if a mighty fist had been slammed into his midsection. He kept his voice calm when he whispered, "Be so good as to tell me how that information reached you?"

"It's not a secret," Percy chuckled. "In fact, I'll wager it will have made the complete rounds by the end of the day. I heard it on Rotten Row myself. Rode up to a couple of pretties I know and they couldn't wait to tell me the latest *on-dit*."

"How?" This came out explosively, loud enough to gain a look from Derek, who then turned back to the maid.

"Lady E., don't you know. It seems her driver thought she would be most interested in hearing all about your wicked scheme. And wouldn't you know, she was tickled pink to think you were jealous enough to do something so outrageous. She couldn't wait to tell all her dearest friends about it—and even those who are not so dear. Oh, she has had a busy morning of it."

"Damnation take the bitch!"

"Yes, well, if I were you, I would be leaving London for a while."

"And let the girl face this alone?"

"That never bothered you before."

For that remark Percy received the blackest scowl. "Don't bark at me, Nick. She'll fare better than you, no doubt get married off as your other innocents were, and live happily ever after. But there's Derek's uncle to think about, not to mention his father. This girl's got relatives who will demand your hide. You're not going to come off without a scratch for compromising this girl like you did the others."

"Blister it, I didn't touch the girl."

"'Course you didn't, but who'd believe it?" Percy said pointedly. "Your best bet is to be gone before the challenge comes from one of her uncles."

At that moment Tyndale appeared at the door and announced, "Lord Malory's servant begs a word, my lord."

Derek looked up in surprise, seeing the servant standing behind Tyndale. "Oh, I say, Nicky, there must be some mistake. The chap doesn't work for me."

"I didn't think so," Nicholas muttered, and Percy groaned.

Chapter Eight

"No!"

Anthony Malory looked up as his niece ran into the room and stared wide-eyed at the pistol he was cleaning at his desk. He gave her an impatient look before he went back to examining the weapon.

"It's too late for nos, Reggie."

"You've already killed him!" she cried.

He didn't look up, so he didn't see the color wash from her cheeks. "I've sent a man round to his house. I had no trouble learning the address this morning. He should be here soon to discuss the time and place."

"No, no, no!"

When he glanced up, her eyes were shooting sparks at him. "Now, Reggie—" he began, but she advanced on him.

"Is that your answer to everything?" She stabbed a finger at the weapon in his hands. "I thought we had this settled last night?"

"That was before Montieth's escapade became food for the gossip-mongers. Or are you not aware that your name is on everyone's lips this morning?"

Reggie flinched but said evenly, "I do know it. I just left a room full of women who couldn't wait to offer their sympathies."

"And what did you tell them?"

"Well, I couldn't very well deny that it had happened, because Lady Eddington's driver witnessed the whole thing. But I did lie and say that I was brought right back, that Lord Montieth had realized his mistake quickly."

Anthony shook his head. "Which they didn't believe. Did they?"

"Well, no," she admitted reluctantly.

"Because that bloody driver waited a good hour for you to be returned, and everyone knows it. And it doesn't take an hour to do what is being said was done. Your lying about it only suggests that you have something to hide."

"But that's not true!"

"Since when does the truth matter to passionate gossips?"

"Oh, what am I going to do, Tony?" she cried miserably.

"You will do nothing. You will weather it, with the support of your family. *He* will pay the price for besmirching your good name."

"You will not challenge him."

Anthony's eyes narrowed. "If I don't, Jason will, and Jason will get himself killed. He's not the shot I am."

"No one is going to be killed, Tony." She said this as if the matter were entirely up to her. "There has to be another solution. That's why I came. I thought I would be too late to catch you before you left town, though. How did you find out?"

"I was, in fact, leaving town, and my old friend George hailed me to give me warning that the cat was out of the bag. It's bloody damned fortunate that I was late getting started this morning. Otherwise I'd be halfway to Gloucester by now, and old Eddie would have been left to deal with this. I can just imagine the mess he'd make of it."

"At least his answer wouldn't be to grab the nearest pistol," she retorted.

Anthony made a face. "Does he know yet?"

"No. He was closeted in his office all morning. He still is. Aunt Charlotte said she would try and keep it from him as long as possible. I thought maybe you wouldn't mind . . ."

"Coward. Eddie isn't the one you need to worry about, though. It's Jason who is going to fly through the roof."

"Well, at least he won't hear about it for some time."

"Don't count on that, puss. He'll know by the end of the day, tomorrow at the latest. You think he doesn't keep tabs on you when you're in wicked old London?"

"He doesn't!"

"Oh, but he does," Anthony assured her. "He had regular reports on you when you were in Europe, too. Nothing escapes Jason. Even I am not shielded from his all-seeing eye. How do you think he finds out so quickly about all my bloody scrapes?"

Reggie groaned. This was going from bad to worse. Jason could be just as hot-tempered as Tony. Besides that, he was a man of rigid principles. When there was any question of honor, his could not be tampered with.

For him there would be only one solution, and if that didn't work, he would be cleaning his pistols just as Tony was. But that first solution was intolerable. Nicholas Eden would never agree. He would rather face one of her uncles across the dueling field than be forced to marry, she was sure of it.

She worried at her lower lip. "There must be something we can do, Tony, some story we can invent."

"Any one of a dozen, puss, but not one will be believed. The trouble is that Montieth has seduced innocents like you before. That he was alone with you—never mind that it wasn't you he meant to be alone with—implies that he took advantage of the situation. He is such a handsome devil, you couldn't have resisted him. That's what people will think. And say."

Reggie blushed and looked away uncomfortably.

"I don't know why I'm even discussing this with you," Anthony continued curtly. "There is only one thing to be done, and it's up to me to see it done."

Reggie sighed. "You're right, of course. I don't know why I've been resisting the idea so."

He raised a suspicious brow. "No tricks, Reggie."

"No tricks. You will see that he marries me. That is the only thing to be done."

"Bloody hell!" Anthony shot to his feet in full fury. "He's not good enough for you!"

"Nevertheless—"

"No! And no again! And don't think I'm not on to you, Regina Ashton. You think this will solve your other problem, and you won't have to look for a husband anymore."

"Now that you mention it . . . oh, Tony, I really wouldn't mind having him for a husband, really I wouldn't. And he reminds me of you."

"He is too much like me, which is exactly why he's not for you!"

"But he reminds me of Uncle Edward, too. And there's also a touch of Uncle Jason in him. Why, he was quite put out when I suggested that what he had done would ruin me and he would have to marry me."

"You said that?"

"I was in that kind of mood. And he got angry. He acted just as Uncle Jason would have."

"Why, that—"

"No, no, Tony. He's perfect, don't you see? A little like all of you—just what I have been looking for. And besides, it will be a challenge to reform him."

"He'll never change, Reggie," Tony insisted. "He'll never settle down."

"Oh, I don't know." She grinned. "We might make that statement about you, but we don't know for sure about him. And he did like me. That's a start."

"Don't let's put a nice face on it," Anthony said. "He wanted you. But he'll want other women, too, and he'll go after them. He won't be a faithful husband."

"I think I know that," she said quietly.

"And you still want him?"

She didn't want him dead. That was the alternative. "After all," she said quietly, "he should make things right. He has involved me in a scandal, so he should be the one to get me out of it. This is a peaceful solution, and I'm sure Uncle Jason will wholeheartedly agree."

"This is not what I would call Montieth getting his just deserts." Anthony glowered. "He'll be getting you into the bargain, while you will go on suffering."

"He won't see it that way, Tony. In fact, I'm positive he'll refuse."

"Good." Anthony smiled and went back to cleaning his pistol.

"Oh, no," Reggie said. "You must promise me you'll do your best to convince him, Tony."

"All right," he agreed.

He was smiling in a way that made her want to hit him. She knew that smile too well.

"I want Uncle Edward to be with you when you speak to him," she said suspiciously.

"But your Viscount will be here soon, puss," he reminded her.

"Then come with me to see Uncle Edward now. Leave a message for Lord Montieth to return this evening. And Tony," she added slowly, untying her scarf, "I think Uncle Edward should see this, to impress on him the importance of getting Montieth's consent."

Anthony's face darkened. "You said he only kissed you!"

She tied the scarf again, her look quite innocent. "Well, that *was* caused by a kiss, Tony."

"How dare he leave his mark on you?"

Reggie shrugged, carefully avoiding his eyes. "Do you think Uncle Edward will make too much of the mark and assume the worst? I suppose he will feel it's his duty to inform Uncle Jason of it. You don't think they'll want to rush the wedding, do you? I would rather wait a few months, just to be sure my first child is born after a decent interval of time."

"This is blackmail, Reggie."

She opened her dark blue eyes wide. "Is it?"

"Jason should have taken a switch to your backside when you first developed this talent for manipulating people."

"What a terrible thing to say!" Reggie gasped.

He laughed then, shaking his head at her. "You can drop the performance, puss. I'll get your Viscount to marry you, one way or another."

She hugged him, her delight evident. "And there'll be no more talk of killing?"

"None that will matter," he sighed. "Since Eddie is the logical, business-minded one of us, perhaps he can come up with something to bring the man round without resorting to violence."

He disengaged himself and turned to put the gun away. "You said Montieth wouldn't agree, Reggie, and when a man is stubborn, it takes persuasion to change his mind. You can still change *your* mind, you know." He looked at her intently.

"No. The more I think about it, the more I feel this is the right thing to do."

"He might hate you for it, you know. Have you thought about that?"

"He might, yes, but I will take the chance. I wouldn't consider marriage if he hadn't found me attractive. But he did try to seduce me—*try,*

I said. No, he will be my husband, Tony. Tell Uncle Edward and Uncle Jason that I will have no other."

"Very well, then," Tony replied, then added with a sharp look, "But you will keep that blasted scarf on, hear? There is no point in my brothers thinking any worse of their future nephew-in-law than they have to."

Chapter Nine

It was half past ten o'clock in the evening, and Nicholas sat in his carriage outside Edward Malory's house in Grosvenor Square, thirty minutes late for his appointment, but making no move to leave his carriage.

He had given up trying to guess what this was all about. He had understood that morning's summons from Anthony Malory perfectly well, but since that earlier meeting had not come to pass, he no longer knew what to think. He couldn't conceive of Derek's businesslike Uncle Edward demanding a duel, but what else could this be about? Bloody hell!

Reggie watched the dark carriage from an upstairs window, her nervousness having increased to terror. He was not going to like what she had set in motion. No, most assuredly not. He must suspect why he'd been called there. Why else would he hesitate to come inside?

Oh, Uncle Edward had had quite a lot to say about Lord Montieth, emphatic that she know exactly what she was letting herself in for. He had known the Eden family for years, had been very good friends with Nicholas' father, in fact. So Reggie knew it all now, including the stories of the other young women he had embroiled in scandal because they were weak enough to succumb to his charm. He was irresponsible, he was without conscience, he could be cold and arrogant, or ill-tempered. The charm he showed the ladies was not all there was to the man. Yes, she'd heard it all, but to Uncle Tony's disgust, she had not changed her mind.

Reggie was using Amy's room to peek out of the window, thanking her stars that she was alone upstairs. Aunt Charlotte had gathered her whole brood of children, all of them protesting vehemently, and descended on a friend outside London for the night. Reggie had been allowed to stay so that she would not have to wait until the next day to learn her fate. But she was to remain upstairs and not interfere in any way. Uncle Tony had been adamant about that. Even if she heard all hell breaking loose, she was not to venture downstairs.

Nicholas was relieved of his hat and gloves and escorted to the drawing room. The house surprised him by being much larger than it appeared on the outside. He knew that Edward Malory had several children; and the house was certainly big enough to accommodate a large family. The top two floors were probably all bedrooms, he thought, and the downstairs big enough to include even a ballroom.

"They are waiting, my lord," the butler announced as they reached the drawing room door. No expression crossed the servant's face, but his tone was disapproving. Nicholas nearly chuckled. He knew he was late.

All humor disappeared, however, when the butler opened the door, then closed it behind Nicholas. On a cream-colored sofa sat Eleanor Marston, his spinster Aunt Ellie; and beside her, Rebecca Eden, his formidable grandmother. At the moment, she looked ready to call down the wrath of God upon his head.

So. He was to be called on the carpet, was he? Lectured to by his own family as well as Regina's? His one surprise was that they hadn't summoned his "mother," Miriam. How she would have enjoyed this!

"So you finally mustered the courage to come inside, scamp?" the old dame began without preamble.

"Rebecca!" Eleanor admonished.

Nicholas smiled. He knew his grandmother didn't doubt his nerve any more than he did. She simply liked to ruffle his feathers. Aunt Ellie was always quick to come to his defense, bless her. She was, in fact, the only one who dared admonish the old dame. Aunt Ellie had lived with the old woman for twenty years as her companion, and he marveled at her stamina, for his grandmother was a true tyrant, ruling all around her with an iron will.

Long ago, Eleanor had lived with Miriam and Charles Eden at Silverley, in the first few years of his parents' marriage, before Nicholas was born. But the constant bickering between the two sisters had sent Ellie back to her parents. Later, she had gone to visit Charles' mother, Rebecca, out in Cornwall. She'd been there ever since that "visit," coming to visit Silverley often through the years, but only to visit, not to stay.

"How are you, madame?" he asked his grandmother.

"As if *you* care how I am," she retorted. "Do I come to London every year at this time?" she asked him.

"You have made that your habit, yes."

"But have you paid me a visit once since I arrived?"

"I saw you in Cornwall only last month," Nicholas reminded her.

"That is not the point." Then she leaned back and said, "Well, you surely have fallen into it this time, haven't you?"

"So it would seem," he replied dryly, then turned to face the two Malory men.

The older man came forward to greet him cordially. Big and blond and green-eyed, Edward Malory looked nothing like his brother Anthony, and everything like his brother Jason. He was an inch shorter than Nicholas' own six feet, but his build was stockier.

The younger Malory man stood rooted to his place by the fireplace. Dark blue eyes seemed to be envisioning Nicholas' dismemberment. Malory's vivid blue eyes and coal-black hair announced to Nicholas that Regina Ashton was Anthony's blood relation. It was more than that. She actually bore a startling resemblance to Anthony, even to the slight slanting of the eyes. Good God, he wondered, could Regina be his daughter? That would mean he'd sowed his oats a bit young, but it wasn't impossible.

"We haven't met, Nicholas," Edward Malory said and introduced himself. "But I knew your father Charles very well, and I've known Rebecca for some years."

"Edward invests my money for me, and very nicely, too," Rebecca explained. "Didn't know that, did you, scamp?"

Well, that explained how they'd gotten his grandmother here on such short notice. The proximity to family was starting to make him nervous.

Edward continued, "And I believe you know my youngest brother, Anthony?"

"We've crossed each other's paths in the clubs from time to time," Nicholas replied, making no move toward Anthony.

Anthony didn't acknowledge him at all except to fry him with his eyes. He was as tall as Nicholas, and just as broad in the shoulders, too. A hellion since he was sixteen according to Derek. Nicholas wagered there were worse scandals in Anthony's past than this silly flap over Regina. What the hell did Anthony have to look so condemning about?

"That one wants your head on a platter, scamp," his grandmother spoke in the growing silence. Ellie tried to shush her, but she wouldn't be shushed.

"I am already aware of that, madame," Nicholas said, facing Anthony. "Do we name the time, my lord?"

Anthony chuckled wryly. "By God, I really think you'd rather. But much as I would love to accommodate you, I have promised to let them deal with you first."

Nicholas looked around at the others. Sympathy poured from Ellie's brown eyes, and Edward looked resigned. Nicholas' nervousness increased suddenly, and he fixed his gaze on Anthony again.

"My lord," he said stiffly. "I would like to settle with you."

"My niece would have it otherwise."

"She what?"

"She's too kindhearted by half," Anthony sighed. "Doesn't want to see you hurt—more's the pity." He shook his head.

"Nevertheless, I do believe—"

"No, by God!" Rebecca thundered. "I wasn't around to stop those other duels you involved yourself in, but I'll stop this one. I'll have you thrown in jail first, my boy; see if I don't."

Nicholas tried to smile. "The man wants satisfaction, madame. I can offer no other."

"Lord Anthony will settle for something other than a duel because he loves his niece. We may be thankful for that."

"We? I cannot be thankful, madame."

"We can do without your satirical wit, too," she said. "You may be a damned arrogant, irresponsible pup, but you are the last Eden. You will get yourself an heir before you go throwing your life away on a dueling field."

Nicholas flinched. "Nicely put, madame. But what makes you think I don't already have an heir to give you?"

"I know you better than that. Although it often looks as though you're trying to populate the world, you have no bastards. And you know I would never accept one, anyway."

"Is this necessary, Rebecca?" Eleanor asked hastily.

"Yes, it is," the old woman replied, looking pointedly at the two Malory brothers.

"Nicky?" Eleanor beseeched him, and Nicholas sighed.

"Very well, I admit I have no bastards, either male or female. You are quite correct, madame. It is one thing I am most careful about."

"The only thing."

He gave her a slight bow but made no reply. His manner was casual, even bored, but Nicholas was seething inside. He enjoyed verbal battles with his grandmother when they were alone, but not in the company of others. She knew it and was baiting him just to be ornery.

"Oh, do be seated, Nicholas," Rebecca said testily. "I'm tired of craning my neck to look at you."

"Is this going to take long then?" He grinned maddeningly before taking the chair across from her.

"Please don't be difficult, Nicky," Eleanor beseeched again.

He was taken aback. This, from Ellie? She had always been the one he could talk to, the one who understood the bitterness just below his surface. While he was growing up, she'd always been a shoulder to cry on. How many times had he ridden the long road between Hampshire and Cornwall in the thick of night just to see her? After he grew up, she was still closer to him than anybody. She never even scolded him for the way he lived. It was almost as if she knew why he did the things he did.

She didn't, of course. Only Miriam knew the reason he was so reckless, why he forever walked a tightrope, never easing up.

Nicholas looked at his aunt tenderly. At forty-five, she was still good-looking, with light blond hair and soulful brown eyes. Her older sister Miriam had once been the prettier of the two, but bitterness had helped ravage Miriam's beauty. He liked to think Ellie's goodness had kept her so nicely.

This was the woman he had secretly pretended was his mother, all through childhood. Her expression told him many things, and she was as easy to read just then as she'd always been. She was sorry for his predicament. She was praying he wouldn't cause trouble. She was also in agreement with whatever had been decided behind his back. But would she side with his grandmother against him? She had never done that before. Did she really think he had ravished Regina Ashton? Oh, he might have seduced the girl if she'd been willing, yes, but the fact was that he hadn't seduced her. His conscience could overlook his intentions.

"Did they tell you all of it, Aunt Ellie?" he asked her.

"I believe so."

"They told you it was all a mistake?"

"Yes."

"And that I returned the girl unmolested?"

"Yes."

"Then what are you doing here?"

Rebecca frowned. "Leave her alone, scamp. It's not her fault you got yourself into this."

"We know whose fault it is," Anthony's contemptuous voice sounded behind him.

Nicholas had had enough. "What is it to be then?" he demanded, turning around in his chair to look at Anthony.

"You already know what must be done, Nicky," Eleanor said with gentle reproof. "It is unfortunate that any of this happened. No one here believes that you meant to harm the girl, but the fact remains that her reputation *has* been irreparably damaged. She should not be made to suffer the humiliation of vicious gossip because one of your escapades went awry. You do see that, don't you?" She took a long, steadying breath. "You can do no less than accept responsibility for your actions. You must marry her."

Chapter Ten

"I can't stand it, Meg, I really can't!" Reggie cried, agitation overcoming her.

The maid ignored the wail, just as she had ignored all the others. "Are you going to sleep in that scarf?"

Reggie put her hands to her throat. "Yes, of course. Uncle Edward may come to tell me what happened instead of Uncle Tony. I don't want anyone else to see it."

Meg frowned and went back to the sewing in her lap. She had seen the lovebite herself. Reggie couldn't hide anything from her, not for long anyway. She was outraged by the whole affair, and for once she was in complete accord with Anthony Malory instead of siding with the girl who sat cross-legged in the center of her bed, wringing her hands in an agony of suspense.

The Viscount Eden of Montieth should be shot, not given this treasure for a wife. Meg had never heard of anything so grossly unfair. Did you give the petty thief your purse with a thank-you-kindly? How could they give her precious Reggie to the man who was responsible for her shame?

"Will you go downstairs and see if you can hear anything, Meg?"

"No, I will not."

"Then I will."

"You will not either. You'll sit right there. Keep on worryin', if you like. Soon enough you'll be told he said yes."

"But that's the trouble." Reggie pounded her knees for emphasis. "He's going to say no."

Meg shook her head. "You won't convince me that you want him, my girl, so you can stop tryin'."

"But it's true, Meg."

"I know you too well, Reggie. You're just puttin' a good face on it, pretendin' for your uncles' sake, because this seems to be the only solution."

"Stuff." Reggie giggled, her humor breaking through. "You just won't admit that I'm wicked and shameful in wanting a man I only just met."

Meg looked up at her. "Now I see what you're about. You're for this because it will get you a husband quick and you won't have to be lookin' for one anymore. Admit it, my girl."

Reggie grinned. "That's an added bonus, yes."

"A bonus!" Meg snorted. "That's the only reason you want him. It must be."

"You won't say that after you get a look at him, Meg. I think I'm in love."

"If I believed that, I would go down there and kiss his feet. But you've got more sense than to think you're in love after one meeting."

"I suppose so," Reggie sighed, but her eyes twinkled. "It won't take long, though, Meg, really it won't. You wait and see."

"I hope I don't see it. I hope I don't see you married to him. It will be the sorriest day for you and if it happens, mark my words."

"Stuff," Reggie retorted.

"Just remember, I warned you."

"I won't marry her."

"Good." Anthony's smile was full of wicked pleasure. "I was against the idea from the start."

"Be still, Anthony," Edward warned him. "Nothing has been settled."

"I repeat, I won't marry her," Nicholas said evenly, managing just barely to keep calm.

"You will be good enough to tell me why?" Edward's voice was also a study in tranquillity.

Nicholas said the first thing that came to mind. "She deserves better."

"Agreed," Anthony put in smoothly. "Under normal circumstances, you would never be considered."

Edward shot him a silencing look, then addressed Nicholas again. "If you are referring to your reputation, it precedes you. I am the first to admit it is unsavory. Yet such things must be overlooked now."

"I would make the girl miserable," Nicholas said quickly, with a bit more spirit.

"That is pure conjecture. You don't know Regina well enough to know what would make her happy or unhappy."

"You're just hedging, scamp," Rebecca said. "You have no good reason not to marry the girl, and you know it. And it's high time you were married, high time indeed."

"So I can produce your heir?" he replied.

"Now see here, Nicholas," Edward broke in. "Do you deny that you have embroiled my niece in a scandal?"

"Your niece?"

"Who the devil did you think she was, scamp?" Rebecca was exasperated.

Suddenly Anthony was laughing. "Tell me, Montieth, were you hoping she was illegitimate? A poor relation you could claim we were trying to foist off on you?"

"That will be enough," Edward warned again. "Nicholas . . . well, perhaps I shall have to concede that you didn't know who Regina was. Not many people remember Melissa, she died so long ago."

"Melissa?"

"Our only sister. She was much younger than Jason and I, the middle child. She was . . . well, I needn't elaborate on how precious she was to us, being the only girl in the midst of four boys. Regina is her only child."

"She's all they have left of Melissa," Rebecca added. "Do you begin to see how important Regina is to the Malory brothers?"

Nicholas was feeling sick.

"I should tell you, in regard to my brother's remark, that Regina is quite legitimate," Edward went on. "Melissa was happily married to the Earl of Penwich."

"Penwich!" Nicholas nearly choked on the name he had cursed so many times.

"The late Earl, Thomas Ashton," Edward clarified. "Some obscure cousin has the title now. A disagreeable fellow, but he has no involvement with Regina. She has been under our care for the seventeen years since Melissa and Thomas died together in a terrible fire."

Nicholas' mind whirled. Bloody hell. She was in fact Derek's first cousin, the daughter of an Earl, niece to the Marquis of Haverston. He wouldn't be surprised to learn that she was also an heiress. She could easily have landed a husband with a better title than his. Could have. But now that he had linked her name to his, she wasn't quite the prize anymore, not to those families who wouldn't touch a girl with a scandal behind her. Everyone in the room knew it, including himself. Yet there were other men who would want her, regardless, men less rigid than some.

He said as much to Anthony. "*You* don't seem to think she has lost her chance at a good match, so why are you willing to settle for me?"

"Did I say I was, dear boy? No, no. She is the one who wants you, not I."

Nicholas cast about for a reply. "And as a favored niece, she gets want she wants?" he said.

"There is the simple fact," Edward intervened, "that if she married anyone else, the poor fellow would have to live with the scandal you have created being whispered behind his back for the rest of his life. That is a bit much for any man to take, and certainly wouldn't make for a happy marriage."

Nicholas frowned. "But she would tell her husband the truth."

"What does the truth matter when it is the untruth that is believed by everyone?" Edward replied testily.

"Am I to be held hostage to the narrow-mindedness of others, then?"

"What the devil is the matter with you, Nicholas?" Rebecca demanded. "I've met the girl and she is the loveliest little creature I've seen in a long time. You will never get a better match, and you know it. Why are you fighting this?"

"I don't want a wife—*any* wife," Nicholas said harshly.

"What you want became irrelevant," his grandmother retorted, "when you made off with an innocent girl whose family won't overlook it as others have. You're damned lucky they'll let you have her!"

"Be reasonable, Nicky," Eleanor chimed in. "You have to marry sometime. You can't go on forever as you've been doing. And this girl is charming, beautiful. She will make you a wonderful wife."

"Not my wife," he stated flatly. In the silence that followed, his hopes began to rise, but his grandmother dashed them.

"You'll never be the man your father was. Running off to sea for two years, coming back to live the life of a wastrel, delegating your responsibilities to agents and lackeys. By God, I'm ashamed to admit you're my grandson. And I tell you now, you may as well forget you know me if you don't own up and marry this girl." She stood up, her expression stony. "Come, Ellie. I have said all I will say to him."

Rebecca's face remained coldly unrelenting as she left the room, Ellie beside her. But once the door closed behind them, she turned to Eleanor and gave her a huge conspiratorial grin. "What say you, my dear? Do you think that did the trick?"

"That was a bit much about your being ashamed of him. You know you're not. Why, you delight in his wild escapade more than he does. I swear, Rebecca, you should have been a man."

"Don't I know it! But his little escapade is a godsend this time. I didn't think he would put up this much of a fight, though."

"Didn't you?" Eleanor retorted. "You know why he won't marry. You know how he feels. Nicky refuses to force the stigma of his birth on an unsuspecting wife. He feels he cannot offer for a decent girl, yet his position makes it impossible for him to wed beneath his station. He decided simply never to wed. You know that."

Rebecca nodded, impatient, and said, "Which is why this is a godsend. Now he will have to marry, and into a good family, too. Oh, he doesn't like it one bit, but eventually he'll be glad. I tell you this girl won't give a toot if she ever learns the truth."

"Do you really believe that?"

"If I didn't, then she wouldn't be the one for him," Rebecca said stoutly.

They both knew exactly what motivated Nicholas, though he wasn't aware that they knew. To the world, Miriam was his mother, and the day she ended that pretense—as she often threatened to do—was the day he could stop living in dread of the revelation and become the pariah he was trying his best to become beforehand. He wanted to be thought wicked so as to become accustomed to the treatment he could expect if the truth came out.

"Someone ought to tell him that it probably wouldn't matter much if the truth did come out," Rebecca said. "No one would believe it anyhow, not after all these years."

"Why don't you tell him that?" Ellie asked, knowing the answer.

"Not me, my dear. Why don't you?"

"Oh, no." Eleanor shook her head emphatically. "He feels too strongly about it." She sighed. "We've been over this a hundred times, Rebecca. And besides, he's finally going to take a bride and settle down and have his own family."

"So we hope," Rebecca added. "But they haven't got a yes out of him yet."

"Your attitude is most puzzling, Nicholas," Edward was saying inside the drawing room. "If I didn't know for certain that you were a skirt man, I'd begin to wonder."

Nicholas had to smile at that remark, coming from this staid lord. "My inclinations are decidedly female, sir."

"Yet you don't want my niece?"

Anthony spoke up harshly. "Look me in the eye when you answer, Montieth, for I've seen the mark you put on her."

"What's this?" Edward demanded.

"Relax, Eddie. Just something between the Viscount and myself. But what's your answer, Montieth?"

Nicholas flushed darkly in anger. He felt cornered and didn't like it at all. Had he really marked the girl? If so, what the bloody hell was she doing letting her uncle know about it? They said she wanted to marry him. Damnation, had she given Anthony the impression that their encounter was less than innocent? Was that why this youngest uncle was hell-bent on his blood?

"There is nothing wrong with your niece, my lords," Nicholas said tightly, his amber eyes glowing with anger. "But then, you surely know that better than I."

"Yes, it can be said without prejudice that she is desirable in every way. Still, we can't resolve this." Edward sighed here. "Jason isn't going to like this at all. He is her legal guardian, you see."

"Jason is going to tear him apart if there isn't an engagement by the time he gets here," Anthony said flatly. "Give it up, Eddie, and leave him to me. If Jason gets hold of him, there won't be anything left."

Nicholas sat down again and put his head in his hands as they went on arguing between themselves. He liked and respected Derek's father, Jason Malory, had hunted with him at Haverston and spent long evenings with him over good brandy and good talk. He admired the way Jason ran Haverston and dealt with his people. The last thing he wanted was for Jason to be angry with him. But he couldn't marry the girl, and he couldn't tell them why.

Never before had the bitterness of his parentage hurt him quite so much. The truth was that he was a bastard. And any woman who became his wife would suffer the stigma of his bastardy. He would be ostracized if the truth came out. Hadn't he seen it happen to Derek Malory, who was a known bastard? It was why he felt a closeness to Derek that he didn't feel with his other friends.

Edward's voice intruded on his thoughts. "I doubt Regina's financial status would impress you, Nicholas, for your father's wise investments and your own have made you a wealthy young man. Suffice it to say she is very well off. But . . . perhaps this *will* interest you."

Nicholas accepted the sheaf of papers that Edward brought out of his coat. Letters. *His* letters to the Earl of Penwich!

"How the devil do you come by these?" he demanded incredulously.

"They were forwarded to me just recently, as a matter of fact. The Earl is notorious for ignoring things that don't interest him, and that piece of land you want doesn't interest him."

"Why you?"

"Because it belongs to a trust that I manage. It's a nice little piece of land, with nearly a dozen tenants who all pay their rent regularly."

"It's a bloody large estate and you know it, and not nearly put to its full potential," Nicholas retorted.

"I didn't think you had such a fondness for land," Edward remarked shrewdly. "After all, you don't oversee Silverley."

A muscle jerked in Nicholas' jaw. Hell and fire! He stood a better chance against his old enemy Captain Hawke without a weapon than he did against these Malorys.

"Am I to understand I will never get my hands on that land if I don't marry your niece?"

"You might phrase it more delicately, but that's the gist, yes."

"Refuse, Montieth," Anthony tempted in a soft voice. "Meet me in the morning instead. I won't kill you. I'll aim a ways below your heart, so that the next girl you abscond with in the middle of the night will be believed when she says you've left her untouched."

Nicholas had to laugh. Gelding was the threat now? These were his options? He had no doubt that his grandmother could arrange jail, as she threatened. He'd be estranged from her, doubtless, and the truth was, he loved the old witch. Then there was death or grievous wounding if Anthony had his way. Those were the choices.

Or he could marry the loveliest creature he had ever set eyes on. He could probably have the land he wanted. Aunt Ellie was for this marriage. His grandmother and all the Malorys were for it.

Nicholas closed his eyes for a moment, apparently deep in thought. Then he opened them and stood up.

"My lords," he said evenly, "when is the wedding to be?"

Chapter Eleven

"So you've come to escort your fiancée to Vauxhall Gardens? To a concert? Never thought I'd see you attending a bloody concert, and in the daytime, at that!"

Derek Malory was enjoying himself immensely, and the look of pure disgust on Nicholas Eden's face was perfect. They were in the drawing room at Edward's house, in the very room where the infamous meeting had taken place the night before, and Nicholas had just arrived.

"This is apparently the only way I'll get to see her," Nicholas told Derek. "They wouldn't let me near her last night."

"Well, of course not. Wouldn't have been proper. She was told to go to bed."

"You mean she actually takes orders?" Nicholas said in mock astonishment. "I thought everyone followed hers."

"Oh, I say. You really are put out about this. I don't understand why. She's first rate, you know, a real gem. Couldn't do better."

"I would have preferred to pick my own wife, you understand, as opposed to having one forced on me."

Derek grinned. "Heard you put up quite a fuss. Couldn't believe any of this when they told me, especially that you'd given in. Know how you don't like to be told what to do, not one bit."

"Stop rambling, Derek," Nicholas demanded. "What are you doing here, anyway?"

"I'm to come along, don't you know. Cousin Clare and I are coming with you. Orders from Uncle Edward. Didn't think you'd get her alone, did you? Can't have any hanky-panky before the wedding."

Nicholas scowled. "What the hell difference would it make? I'm already supposed to have bedded her."

"No one believes that, Nick, at least no one in the family."

"Except your Uncle Anthony?"

"Don't know what he thinks," Derek said more soberly. "But you'd best watch out for him. They're especially close, you know, he and your intended."

"She's his favorite niece?"

"It's more than that. He was only three years younger than Aunt Melissa, you see, and they were always inseparable. When she died, he was only seventeen. Her daughter kind of took Melissa's place in his affections. All my uncles felt that way, including my father. But Uncle Anthony, being the youngest, was more like a brother to Regina. You wouldn't believe the fights he had with my father once he came of age and moved to London, because the old man wouldn't let him have her part of each year the way Uncle Edward does." Derek chuckled. "The old man finally gave in because she wanted it, too, and there isn't much she wants that he doesn't give her."

Nicholas grunted. Regina was going to be impossibly spoiled. "Why is it I never met her at Haverston?"

"She was always with Uncle Edward or Uncle Anthony when you came. They each had her for four months of the year by the time you started visiting me." Derek laughed. "But you did meet her once, that first time I brought you home. She was the little hoyden who spilled the bowl of pudding in your lap when you teased her."

"But you called the child Reggie!" Nicholas cried.

"We all call Regina Reggie, and she's grown now. Do you remember her?"

He groaned. "How could I forget? She stuck her tongue out at me when I threatened to blister her bottom."

"Yes, well, she didn't like you at all after that. She was at the house once more, I believe, when you came to visit, but she stayed out of your way."

"She told me that, when you told her about me, she loved me," Nicholas said dryly.

"Oh, she did love you then, I'm sure," Derek chuckled. "But that was before she *met* you. She was especially fond of me, you see, and she was pleased with anyone who befriended me."

"Bloody hell. Next you'll tell me she was your playmate."

"Shouldn't surprise you, old chap. After all, I was only six when she came to Haverston. I admit I led her astray, there being only the two of us. Dragged her everywhere with me. 'Course the old man had a bloody fit when he finally realized she was fishing and hunting instead of sewing, out climbing trees and building forts in the woods instead of tending to her music. Did you know he married just to give us a mother? Hoped it would have a steadying influence. Poor choice though. Love the old girl, but sickly, you know. Spent more time at Bath getting the cure than she did at Haverston."

"Are you telling me I'm marrying a tomboy?"

"Heavens no! Remember, she's spent part of every year with Uncle Edward's family for the past thirteen years, and Edward's got three girls near her age. When she was here with them, she was brilliant at her studies, an angel of decorum and all that. Of course, we still had our fun when she was at Haverston. I can't even count all the times we got called on the carpet by the old man. And *she* never got the worst of it, I did. By the time she was fourteen, she had lost her hoydenish ways, though. She was even running the household by then, for our mum was hardly ever there."

"So she was running one household, studying at another, and what, I'd like to know, did she learn at the third?"

Derek chuckled at his vicious tone. "Now don't eat me. Actually, her time with Uncle Anthony was like a holiday. He did his best to see she enjoyed herself. And he prob'ly taught her how to deal with chaps like us." Then he said seriously, "They all love her, Nick. You won't get around that, no matter what."

"Am I then to be burdened with interfering in-laws the rest of my life?" Nicholas asked coldly.

"I doubt it will be so bad. After all, you'll have her to yourself out at Silverley."

The thought was worth relishing, but it would never come to that. Nicholas had given in to their bullying, but he actually had no intention of marrying Regina Ashton. Somehow he had to make her break their engagement. She might have a cousin who was a bastard, but she wouldn't have a husband for one as well.

Derek was luckier than Nicholas, for he had lived his twenty-three years knowing what he was and not letting it bother him. But Nicholas hadn't found out about his birth until the age of ten. And before the revelation, the woman he'd thought was his mother had made his life miserable simply because he did believe her to be his mother. He had never understood why she hated him, treated him worse than a servant, continually belittling him, berating him. She'd never even pretended to like him, not even in his father's presence. It was more than any child should have endured.

One day, when he was ten years old, he'd innocently called her "mother," something he rarely did, and suddenly she screamed at him, *I am not your mother! I am sick of pretending to be. Your mother was a whore trying to take my place—a whore!*

His father had been there, the poor man. Little did his father know that nothing could have made Nicholas happier than to learn that Miriam was not his mother. It was only later that he realized how cruelly the world treated bastards.

His father was forced to tell him the truth that day. Miriam had had many miscarriages in the first four years of her marriage to Charles, and the doctor's warning that it might always be so strained the marriage badly. Charles didn't actually say so, but Nicholas figured out that Miriam acquired an aversion to the marriage bed. Charles found comfort elsewhere.

Miserably, Charles explained that Nicholas' real mother was a lady, a good, kindhearted woman who had loved Charles. He had taken advantage of that love in one night's drunkenness, the only time he and she allowed themselves that freedom. Nicholas was conceived that night. There was never any chance that the woman might keep the child. She was unmarried. But Charles wanted the child, wanted it desperately. Miriam agreed to go away with the woman until the child was born. When she returned, everyone believed the baby boy was hers.

Nicholas understood her bitterness, her resentment of him, though understanding didn't make it easier to live with. He endured Miriam for another twelve years, until his father died. He left England then, at twenty-two, intending never to return. His grandmother never forgave him for those two years of disappearance, but he'd loved sailing the seas on his own ships, living through one adventure after another, even fighting in a few sea battles. He finally came home to England, but he couldn't ever go home to Silverley. He couldn't live with Miriam and her hate and her continual threats to tell the world the truth about his birth.

To date, no one knew except the two of them and his father's lawyers, for Charles had had Nicholas declared his legal heir. And it wasn't that Nicholas couldn't withstand the scorn if the truth came out; he had prepared himself for it. But his father had taken great pains to keep it a secret, to keep the family name pure. He didn't wish to damage his father's reputation.

He couldn't trust Miriam, however. She might speak out eventually. For that reason, he had no right to marry a girl of good family who would become an outcast if Miriam chose to betray him.

No, Regina Ashton was not for him. He would give anything to possess her, he acknowledged. But he would also give anything not to marry her, not to risk putting her through the horror in store for her if his secret was revealed. He had to find some way out of it.

Chapter Twelve

"I'm sorry to have kept you waiting, my lord."

Nicholas whirled around at the sound of her voice. A jolt passed through him. He had forgotten how truly ravishing she was. She stood hesitantly in the doorway, a little afraid. Her cousin Clare was behind her. Tall and blond like most of the Malorys, she was pretty enough, but she faded away next to the exotically beautiful Regina.

Once again he was shocked to feel his body affected by the sight of Regina. Bloody *hell*. He would have to end their engagement quickly or bed her.

She continued to stand there in the doorway, and he said, "Come, I won't bite you, love."

She blushed at the endearment. "You haven't met my cousin Clare," she offered, coming forward slowly.

He acknowledged the introduction, then said to Regina, "Derek has just been refreshing my memory of you. You should have told me we met before."

"I didn't think you would remember," Regina murmured, thoroughly embarrassed.

"Not remember getting pudding dumped in my lap?" he said, eyes wide in mock wonder.

She smiled despite her nervousness. "I won't say I'm sorry for that. You deserved it."

Seeing the twinkle in her cobalt-blue eyes, he asked himself how he was ever going to make her believe he didn't want her when he did want her. She delighted him in every way. Just the sight of her was enough to heat his blood. He had an overwhelming desire to kiss her, to taste the sweetness of her lips again, feel the pulse beating at her throat. Damnation take her, she was too desirable by half.

"Come along then, children," Derek teased. "This is a lovely afternoon for a concert. Egad! I'm really going to a day concert—and as chaperon, to boot." He walked out the door, shaking his head comically.

Nicholas would have stolen a word with Regina, but cousin Clare made that impossible, her critical eye never leaving them for a moment. He sighed, hoping Derek would be able to arrange something for him later.

Regina seemed in uncommonly good spirits during the ride to Vauxhall Gardens, keeping up a steady flow of nonsensical chatter with her cousins. Was it nerves or was she really so happy? He enjoyed watching her. Was she really pleased about the marriage? Why had she told her uncles she wanted him? Why *him?*

Reggie was astonished by Nicholas' friendliness. After being told how many times he had refused to marry her before finally giving in, she'd expected bitterness, even anger. Why was he so warmly accepting? It couldn't be the land, could it? It wasn't at all flattering to know it had taken a piece of land to sway him. Tony bellowed that he'd been bought. But Tony hadn't yet seen the way Nicholas Eden looked at her. *Was* he bought? And why had he fought so hard against the marriage, then given in?

He must want her; the way his eyes smoldered told her he did. Really, it was shameful the way he looked at her, and he did it even in front of her cousins. She'd seen Clare's shocked expression and Derek's amused one. But Nicholas didn't seem to be aware of what he was doing. Or was he doing it intentionally, to embarrass her? Was his amiability being faked? His desire for her wasn't faked, she was sure of that.

They left the carriage and walked along a flowered path, music growing louder as they neared the large area where an orchestra was set up. Nicholas was looking at Derek so intensely that the younger man finally got the message and hurried Clare ahead of them to buy pastries from the vendors circulating through the audience. Reggie laughed as Derek pulled his cousin along against her protests.

The moment he could, Nicholas whisked her off the pathway and behind a large tree. They were not alone. They were shielded from the crowd of people ahead, but not from those still coming up along the path. But it was secluded enough for a few private words.

He had his chance. She was backed up against the tree, his arms braced on each side of her, a captive audience, forced to listen to his every word. She looked up at him expectantly, and he thought, *Hate me, woman. Despise me. Don't marry me.* It was all there in his mind to say, but he lost himself in her eyes.

Without even realizing he was doing it, he bent his head and touched his lips to hers, feeling the petal softness, the sweetness as her lips opened. Fire rushed through him, and he leaned into her, pressing her between him and the tree. Yet even this wasn't close enough. He needed to be closer. . . .

"Lord Montieth, please," she managed, gasping. "We can be seen."

He leaned slightly away, just far enough that he could see her face.

"Don't be so formal, love. You are entitled to call me by my given name, don't you think?"

Did she hear bitterness in his voice? "You don't . . . *why* did you agree to marry me?"

"Why did you want me to?" he snapped.

"It seemed the only solution."

"You could have brazened it out."

"Brazened it—? Why should I have to? I warned you what would happen if we were found out."

"You were joking!" he reminded her harshly.

"Well, yes, because I didn't think we *would* be discovered. Oh, I don't want to argue. What's done is done."

"No it's not," he said tightly. "You can break the engagement."

"Why would I want to do that?"

"Because you don't want to marry me, Regina," he said in a soft, almost threatening voice. "You don't want to." Then he smiled tenderly, his eyes caressing her face. "You want to be my lover instead, for I will love you to distraction."

"For a time, my lord?" she asked curtly.

"Yes."

"And then we'll go our separate ways?"

"Yes."

"That won't do."

"I will have you, you know," he warned her.

"After we are married, yes."

"We won't marry, love. You will come to your senses long before the wedding day. But I will have you anyway. You know we are inevitable, don't you?"

"You seem to think so."

He laughed. How charming she was. His laughter froze when he heard the deep voice behind him.

"I won't say I'm sorry for interrupting, Montieth, because it appears you need interrupting."

Nicholas stiffened. Reggie peaked around Nicholas' shoulder to find her Uncle Tony and a lady holding tightly to his arm. Oh, no! Not her! Nicholas was going to be furious for he would be sure to think Tony had brought Selena Eddington there on purpose.

"*You* in Vauxhall, Tony?" She tried to sound disbelieving. "I don't believe it."

"Spare me your mockery, puss. I've heard raves about this particular orchestra."

She held her breath as Nicholas' gaze fell on his mistress, who was looking confused and angry. Reggie almost felt sorry for the woman, but her sympathy didn't quite surface. After all, Selena had thought nothing of tossing Reggie's name to the scandalmongers.

"We meet again, Lady Eddington," Reggie said with false sweetness. "Now I can thank you for the loan of your carriage the other night."

Anthony cleared his throat loudly and Nicholas laughed unpleasantly. "I, too, must thank you, Selena. Why, I wouldn't have met my future bride if it hadn't been for you."

A myriad of emotions washed over Lady Eddington's face—none of them pleasant. She was calling herself a thousand kinds of a fool. When she'd learned what happened, she was so pleased that Nicholas had meant to kidnap her that she'd told all her friends how romantic her lover was . . . and how unfortunate to have nabbed the wrong female. Her bragging had resulted in disaster for herself.

Anthony said firmly, "You will be coming along now, won't you? Perhaps I should start chaperoning you myself. I must have a talk with that errant nephew of mine. Derek should know better than to leave you two alone. Being engaged is not a license to behave badly. Remember that."

With that he departed, whispering something in Lady Eddington's ear as he ushered her away, more than likely encouraging her not to make a scene. Nicholas' mouth was set in a hard line as he watched them go. "Didn't your uncle trust me to tell her of my engagement myself? I would have, with great pleasure. If it were not for her and her uncontrollable conceited bragging—"

"You wouldn't be marrying me," Reggie finished softly.

The fury went out of him. His expression became maddeningly unreadable. "And you would be my lover instead of my wife. A preferable arrangement."

"Not for me."

"Are you saying you wouldn't succumb, love?"

"No, I'm not sure, not sure at all," she answered truthfully. There was sadness in her admission, and he was instantly remorseful.

"I am sorry, love," he said gently. "I shouldn't be badgering you. I should simply tell you that I don't want to marry you."

She gazed at him unwaveringly. "Am I to be grateful for your honesty?"

"Blister it! Don't take it as an insult. It has nothing to do with you!"

"It has everything to do with me, my lord," Reggie said angrily. "You have linked my name to yours whether you meant to or not. *You* did that, not I. Also, you agreed to marry me. You were coerced into it, yes, but if you had no intention of honoring that agreement, then you should not have been seen in public with me today. Our public appearance binds me more firmly to you. I am afraid I am stuck with you now, whether *I* like it or not. And I am beginning not to like it at all." Without giving him a chance to recover, she turned and walked away.

Nicholas didn't move. He felt ridiculously pleased when she talked of being stuck with him, and then ridiculously hurt when she said she didn't like it. He had no business feeling like this about her. They were not stuck with each other, and he'd damned well better remember that.

Chapter Thirteen

―――᚛᚜―――

"Uncle Jason!"

Reggie threw herself into her uncle's outstretched arms, thrilled to see him. Jason Malory, Third Marquis of Haverston, was a big man, as all her uncles were big men. She liked that.

"I've missed you, my girl. Haverston isn't the same when you're away."

"You say that every time I come home." She smiled at him fondly. "Actually I did want to come home for a while before all this happened. I still do." She looked around the drawing room and saw Uncle Edward and Uncle Tony.

"And leave your bridegroom cooling his heels here in London?"

"Somehow I don't think he would mind," she replied softly.

He led her to the cream-colored sofa where Anthony was sitting. Edward was standing by the fireplace, as was his habit. They had more than likely been having a family discussion before her arrival. It must have been about she-knew-what. Nobody had even told her that Uncle Jason was there.

"I was afraid I wouldn't have time to talk to you before you were due to leave," Jason began. "I'm glad you came down early."

Reggie shrugged. "Well, I kept Nicholas waiting yesterday when he took me to Vauxhall, and I didn't want to do that again."

Jason sat back, looking very solemn. "I can't say as I like having this matter settled before I even got here. My brothers took a lot upon themselves."

"You know we had no choice, Jason," Edward defended himself.

"A few days wouldn't have made any difference," Jason returned.

"Are you saying you will withhold your consent now, after the engagement has been decided on?" Reggie exclaimed.

Anthony chuckled. "I warned you, Jason. She's got her heart set on the young rake, and there's nothing you can do to change that."

"Is that true, Reggie?"

It had been true, yes, but . . . she wasn't so sure now, not after yesterday. She knew Nicholas still wanted her. He had made that plain. And she wanted him. Why pretend otherwise? But marriage?

"I do like him very much, Uncle Jason, but—I'm afraid he doesn't really want to marry me."

There. It was said. Why did it make her feel so desolate?

"I have been told that he refused adamantly before he agreed," Jason said gently. "That was only to be expected. No young man likes to be forced into anything."

Her eyes filled with hope. Could that be the only reason?

"I forget that you do know him," she said, "better than the rest of us."

"Yes, and I've always liked the boy. There is a lot more to him than he allows the world to see."

"Spare us, brother," Anthony said sardonically.

"He'll make her a good husband, Tony, despite what you seem to think."

"Do you really think so, Uncle Jason?" Reggie asked, hope rising.

"I do indeed," he said firmly.

"Then you approve of my marrying him?"

"I'd have preferred to see you married under normal circumstances, but as this unfortunate situation has come upon us, I can't say I'm unhappy that the fellow is Nicholas Eden, no."

Reggie grinned happily, but before she could say any more, her cousins started drifting in. They were all going with her to the Hamiltons' rout, Amy with her and Nicholas, the others with Marshall in his smart new four-seater. Amidst all the merry chatter as Jason was greeted by his nieces and nephews, Nicholas arrived and stood in the doorway unnoticed. Panic washed over him as he viewed this large family. He was supposed to marry into this overwhelming brood? God help him.

It was Reggie who approached him first. He smiled down at her, determined to keep a tight rein on his emotions this time. She was stunning in a cream day gown that complemented her transluscent complexion. The style was unusual, for while most London women delighted in exposing as much of their bosom as possible, she had contrived to cover hers with a gauze insert that rose all the way to her neck, ending in a thick lacy band around her throat. He was amused. Perhaps he *had* marked her there and this was her clever way of concealing it. He wondered.

"Nicholas?" she asked, curious as to what he was thinking.

"So you have decided to have done with formality?" he said softly. "I feared you wouldn't be speaking to me at all today."

"Are we to argue again, then?" She looked crushed.

"Perish the thought, love."

She blushed prettily. Why did he persist in calling her that? It wasn't proper and he knew it wasn't. But that was Nicholas.

The Marquis greeted Nicholas warmly and without mentioning the wild escapade that accounted for the engagement. The ride to the Hamiltons' country house a few miles outside of London went smoothly, too, young Amy filling each lapse in conversation with excited chatter, for she wasn't often allowed to go to late-night parties.

It remained then to see what reactions the engaged couple would receive at the Hamiltons' for Nicholas' engagement to Regina was overtaking the subject of their first improper meeting in the gossip mills. He had found that out the previous evening, at a dinner party.

The Hamilton soirée wasn't a large gathering. There were only a hundred people present in the large country house, so there was plenty of room to move around. Guests sampled the array of food set out on long tables, danced in a salon cleared for that purpose, or chatted in small groups. A few stodgy ones glared at the sight of Nicholas and Regina together, but most engaged in wild speculation concerning their first unorthodox meeting.

It had always been arranged that they marry, was the *on-dit*. He had only been amusing himself with Selena while waiting for Regina to return to London. They had met on the Continent, you know. No, no, my dears, they met at Haverston. He and the Marquis' son have been quite chummy for years, don't you know.

"Have you heard what they're saying, love?" Nicholas asked as he claimed her first waltz. "They have us betrothed since you were in swaddling."

Reggie had heard some of the more outlandish speculations from her cousins. "Never say so," she giggled. "My other beaux will be devastated that they never had a real chance."

"Other beaux?"

"The dozens and dozens who sought my hand." A few glasses of champagne had brought out the imp in her.

"I hope you are exaggerating, Regina."

"I wish I were," she sighed, blissfully unaware of his changing temper. "It has been most tedious, you know, trying to make a choice from so many. I was quite ready to give up . . . and then you came along."

"How fortunate for me." Nicholas was furious. He had no idea that he was jealous. Without another word, he maneuvered them to the side of the room, where he abruptly left her with Marshall and Amy, giving her a curt bow in parting. His back to her, he headed for the card room, where he could get a more potent libation than champagne.

Reggie frowned, utterly bewildered. To tease her about the new gossip, smile at her with great tenderness, warm her with his honey-gold eyes, and then become so angry without reason. What was the matter with him?

Reggie smiled, determined not to let him make her miserable. She was asked to dance again and again, and she renewed acquaintances with the young men who had flocked around her last season. Basil Elliot and George Fowler, two persistent admirers, now dramatically professed their lives at an end because of the Viscount's good fortune. Both young men swore they would love her forever. Reggie was amused and flattered, for George and Basil were both wildly popular. Their attentions made up for Nicholas' rudeness.

It was some two hours before the errant Lord Montieth decided to join Reggie again. She had not seen him in all that time, but he had seen her. Time and again he had stood in the door of the card room and seen her laughing up at a dancing partner, or surrounded by ardent beaux. The sight sent him right back for another drink. He was pleasantly foxed by the time he approached her.

"Will you dance with me, love?"

"Will we *finish* this dance?" she rejoined.

He didn't answer. He didn't wait for her to accept either but clamped his hand onto her waist and moved her out onto the dance floor. It was another waltz, and he held her much too close this time.

"Did I tell you yet this evening that I want you?" he asked her suddenly.

She had been aware that there was something different about him, but it wasn't until he leaned close that she smelled the brandy. She wasn't worried though. No one who could move around a dance floor so gracefully could be foxed.

"I wish you wouldn't say that kind of thing, Nicholas."

" 'Nicholas,' " he repeated. "Sweet of you to call me by my given name, love. After all, most everyone here thinks we are already lovers, so it would seem a bit odd for you to call me Lord Montieth."

"If you don't want me to—"

"Did I say that?" he interrupted. "But something like 'beloved' would be even nicer than just 'Nicholas.' I suppose you must love me if you want to marry me. And I don't want to marry you, but I do want you, love. Never doubt it."

"Nicholas—"

"It's all I can seem to think about," he went on. "I am found guilty, yet I have not been permitted to enjoy my crime. Hardly fair, don't you agree?"

"Nicholas—"

"Beloved," he corrected. Then he changed the subject.

"Let's go see the Hamiltons' lovely gardens." Before she could protest, he led her off the dance floor and out of the house.

The gardens were brilliantly landscaped into rolling lawns dotted with trees, man-made ponds, flower beds, a topiary garden, and even a gazebo, so thickly covered by flowering vines that it resembled a tree.

They did not pause to appreciate these beauties. In a twinkling Reggie found herself inside the gazebo, wrapped in Nicholas' arms, being kissed so thoroughly she was close to fainting.

Moonlight spilled in through the hanging vines, bathing them in soft silver light. Padded benches hugged each short, trellised wall. The floor was wood, smooth and polished. There were large potted plants scattered between the benches, their leaves rustling gently in the warm night air.

Deep down Reggie knew that Nicholas was not going to be satisfied with just kissing her, not this time. It would be up to her to stop him. But a voice inside her demanded to know why she wanted to stop him.

He was going to be her husband, wasn't he? Why should she deny him anything—especially when she didn't *want* to deny him anything? And wasn't it possible that his attitude toward their marriage would change if they . . . ? Well, wasn't it?

How conveniently the mind works to get what it wants. And how predictably the body reacts to pleasant feelings, wanting more and more. Her mind and her body conspired against Reggie, and soon there was no fight left in her. She wrapped her arms around Nicholas in surrender.

He carried her to a bench, sat down, and cradled her in his lap. "You will not be sorry, love," he whispered, and then his warm mouth claimed hers again.

Sorry? How could she be when she was so excited and happy?

He supported her back with one arm while his other hand moved slowly along her neck, then lower, making her gasp as it passed over her breasts. On it went, over her belly, down her thigh. He was feeling her hesitantly, as if he couldn't quite believe she would let him. But as his hand began to trace that same path upward, he became bolder, more possessive.

Through the thin silk of her gown, her skin began to burn. The gown was in the way, a nuisance. He thought so too. The button at her throat came undone first, then the tie that held the gown beneath her breasts. In another moment they were standing and he had it removed completely.

Nicholas gasped at the sight of Regina in silk underclothes that clung, molding her gentle curves. She looked right back at him, unashamed, which fanned the flames licking at him. Her eyes were black in the shadowy light, her young breasts straining at the lacy chemise. She was the most beautiful creature he had ever seen.

The small bruise at the base of her throat drew his gaze and he smiled. "So I did put my mark on you. I suppose I should say I'm sorry."

"You might be sorry if you knew how difficult it has been to conceal. You won't give me any more like it, will you?"

"I can't make any promises," he whispered hoarsely.

Then he looked at her shrewdly and asked, "You aren't frightened, are you, love?"

"No—at least I don't think so."

"Then let me see all of you," he persuaded gently. She let him come to her again, and he began removing the rest of her clothing until she was naked. His eyes explored her slowly, hungrily, and then he pulled her close to him and fastened his mouth on her breasts. His tongue, his teeth, his lips all came into play, making her gasp and cry out again and again. She wrapped her arms around his head, holding him to her. Her head fell back as he began kissing her belly. Good God, she couldn't take much more. . . .

"Shouldn't you . . . Nicholas . . . your clothes, Nicholas," she finally managed.

In seconds he was bare-chested, and Reggie's eyes widened, so amazed was she at what his clothes had concealed. She had known his chest would be broad, but now it seemed so huge. He was darkly tanned all over, the mat of hair on his chest golden brown.

She ran her fingers over his muscular upper arm. Her touch scorched him, making him groan.

"The rest now," she pleaded softly, wanting to see all of him, as he had seen all of her.

She moved away and sat down to watch as he undressed. She didn't feel at all awkward, naked though she was. She feasted her gaze on him, a man in all his glory.

When he was finally naked, she went to him and touched him, first his narrow hip, then his long, thick thigh. He grasped her hand, stopping her.

"Don't, love." His voice was harsh with passion. "I am near to exploding now, yet I must go slowly."

Then she saw what was near to exploding. Unbelievable. Beautiful. Extraordinary.

Slowly she raised her eyes to his. "How am I to learn what pleases you if I can't touch you?"

He cupped her face between his hands. "Later, love. This time it will please me to please you. But I must hurt you first."

"I know," she said softly, shyly. "Aunt Charlotte told me."

"But if you trust me, Regina—if you relax and trust me—I will prepare you. There will be only a little pain, and I promise you will enjoy what comes after."

"I have enjoyed what comes before." She smiled up at him.

"Oh, sweet love, so have I."

He kissed her again, his tongue parting her lips to plunge inside. He was on the very edge of losing control. Her eagerness inflamed him, made him fight for precious time. He caressed her belly, then drifted lower to her parted thighs.

She moaned as he touched the warm essence of her. And then she jerked in surprise when he thrust a finger deep inside her. Her back arched, breasts pressing against his chest. She tore her lips away from his.

"I am . . . prepared, Nicholas, I swear I am."

"Not yet, love," he cautioned.

"Please, Nicholas," she gasped.

That undid him. He glanced down at the narrow bench in frustration. He refused to take her maidenhead on the floor, but—damnation, he should never have brought her to this place, not for her first time.

"Nicholas!" she beseeched him passionately.

He positioned himself and then leaned into her as gently as he could. He heard her gasp as her warmth closed around him. She surged forward until her maidenhead was reached. The pressure stopped her, but in their position, he could not breech her quickly enough to minimize the pain.

There was no help for it. He closed his mouth over hers to receive her cry and then, without warning, he lifted her up and pulled her down hard onto him. He held her like that, impaled.

It took only moments before her nails eased out of his shoulders and she sighed with pleasure again, relaxing against him.

"Nicholas?"

His name had never sounded sweeter. He smiled with relief and answered her without words, clasping her buttocks to lift her, then letting her slide back onto him slowly.

She quickly increased the tempo, clinging to him tightly. A thousand fires were ignited in her, joining into one flame that soon could not be contained. It washed through her, drowning her in sweetest fire.

Nicholas could not remember ever being so sated, or feeling such tenderness after making love. He wanted to hold Regina forever and never let her go.

"Was that . . . normal?" she asked dreamily.

He laughed. "After what we just experienced, you want mere normalcy?"

"No, I suppose not." She lifted her head from his chest, sighing, "I suppose we must go back to the house."

"Oh, bloody hell," he growled. "I suppose we must."

She gazed at him, love and longing lighting her beautiful face. "Nicholas?"

"Yes, love?"

"You don't think they'll guess, do you?" The truth was, she didn't care if they did, but she believed she should ask.

Nicholas grinned at her. "No one would dare suggest we had made love out of doors. It isn't done, love."

Between dressing, teasing, and stealing kisses, it was another twenty minutes before they were on their way walking around the pond toward the house. Nicholas' arm was draped over her shoulder, holding her close, when Amy rushed out at them from behind a wall of shrubbery.

"Oh, Reggie, I'm so glad it's you!" she called breathlessly.

"Have I been missed?" Reggie asked, preparing herself for an ordeal.

"Missed? I don't know. I've been out . . . walking, you see, and I didn't realize so much time—" Amy started to cough, a bad acting job, as the shrubbery behind her began to rustle. "Marshall will be so angry," she said. "Would you mind terribly if I told him I'd been with you?"

Reggie managed to suppress her grin. "Of course not, if you promise not to let the—time—get away from you again. Nicholas?"

"Not at all," he agreed. "I know how easy it is to lose track of time myself."

All three of them managed to keep straight faces as they hurried back to the house.

Chapter Fourteen

The engagement party, given by Edward and Charlotte Malory, was a complete success. The whole family and all of their close friends were there. Even Jason's wife had been persuaded to leave the cures at Bath and be there for the event. Nicholas' grandmother and Aunt Eleanor enjoyed themselves immensely, and Reggie got the impression that they had despaired of Nicholas' ever marrying. His mother, of whom he never spoke, was conspicuously absent.

Nicholas was on his best behavior, and everything went beautifully. The party had taken two weeks to prepare, and all the meticulous attention to detail, all the effort paid off.

Alas, smooth sailing doesn't last. Two months after the party, Regina Malory was at the very bottom of despair. It didn't help that she had reached this level of misery by slow degrees.

It was all for nothing.

She wouldn't have believed it possible, not after he had made love to her. She had been so certain he would be happy to marry her after that night. He had been so wonderful, so incredibly patient and tender with her that night. Certainly he had had too much to drink, but was that enough to make him forget the evening?

Oh, they were still to be married. And he always let her know when he was leaving town. He went to Southampton for weeks at a time, claiming business. He always let her know when he returned to London, but in the last two months, she had seen him no more than five times. And those five times were terrible, every one.

He was never late to call for her each time he escorted her to a party, but he'd brought her home only three times. The other two times she had let her temper get the best of her and left without him. It wasn't that he deserted her to spend the entire evening in the card room or embroiled in political discussions, but he often spent more time with Selena Eddington than with her. When he made an obnoxious fool of himself by following her around, well, that was the outside of enough.

Intentional, all of it. She knew very well he was playing the cad for her benefit. That was what hurt so much. If she for a minute thought he was showing his true colors, well, she would let Tony have at him, just see if she wouldn't. But he was not a cad. He was waging a ruthless campaign to make her cry off. Just as he had been forced into the engagement, so he meant to force her out of it.

The very worst of it was that no matter how much it hurt, she couldn't break with him. She no longer had just herself to think of.

Nicholas removed her short black lace cape and handed it to the footman, along with his own red-lined dark cloak and his top hat. Reggie was wearing a white gown trimmed with thin gold tassels along the hem and short sleeves. The neckline was fashionably low, barely covering her breasts, and she was uncomfortable in the gown because of that and because white was reserved for innocent maids.

She had managed to coax her Uncle Edward into trusting her without a chaperon this once. Not since the engagement party had there been any pleasantness between her and Nicholas.

Whatever she had hoped for, she was already disappointed. They had been alone in his closed carriage on the short ride, and he hadn't tried to get close to her, hadn't said a single word to her.

She stole a glance at him as they walked side by side to the music room, where a young couple, friends of Nicholas', were entertaining the twenty or so dinner guests. Nicholas looked exceptionally fine tonight in a long-tailed dark green coat, embroidered cream waistcoat, and frilled shirt. His cravat was loosely knotted, and he wore long trousers instead of the knee breeches and silk stockings preferred by dandies for evening dress. The material clung to his long legs, revealing the powerful thighs and calves. Just looking at his long, graceful body made her feel embarrassed.

His hair was a riot of short, dark brown waves, with so many golden streaks running through it that it sometimes looked copper, or even blond. She knew it was soft to the touch, knew too that his lips were soft, not the hard, rigid line they had been lately. Oh, why wouldn't he talk to her?

A gleam entered her eyes. She stopped in the hall with a tiny gasp, forcing Nicholas to stop as well. He turned back toward her, and she bent over to adjust her shoe. Clumsily, she lost her balance and swayed toward him. Nicholas caught her under her arms, but she fell onto him anyway, her hands gripping his shoulders to steady herself, her breasts pressing into his chest. He gasped as though hit in the stomach by a powerful blow. Indeed, it was a powerful blow. Heat surged through his body, and the fire entered his eyes, banking them like smoldering coals.

Reggie's dark blue eyes smoldered. "Thank you, Nicholas."

She let go of him and walked on as if nothing had happened while he stood there, eyes closed, teeth clenched, trying to regain some control. How was it that such a tiny incident could snap the tight rein he kept on himself? It was bad enough that the sight of her and her voice and scent took a constant toll, but her touch . . . that was the one weapon that shattered his defenses totally.

"Oh, look, Nicholas. Uncle Tony's here!"

Reggie smiled across the room at Anthony Malory, but her smile was as much for herself as for him. She had heard Nicholas' gasp, felt him tremble, saw the desire in his amber eyes. Deceitful man. He still wanted her. He didn't want her to know it, but now she did know. The knowledge warmed her, made up for a good deal of his abominable treatment.

Nicholas reached Reggie at the entrance to the music room, his eyes falling instantly on the dark head of Anthony Malory, bent toward the lady he was sitting next to. "Bloody hell! What's he doing here?"

Reggie wanted to laugh at his tone, but she managed to keep a straight face. "I wouldn't know. The hostess is your acquaintance, not mine."

His eyes fixed on hers intently. "He doesn't often attend these affairs, invitation or not. He came so that he could keep an eye on you."

"Oh, unfair, Nicholas," she chided. "This is the first time we've come across him."

"You are forgetting Vauxhall."

"Well, that was an accident. I don't believe his intention that day was to keep an eye on me."

"No. We both know what his intention was that day."

"My, but you *are* angry," she murmured, and then she let the subject drop. She knew why her uncle was there. He had heard that Nicholas was being seen with other women, and he was furious. Apparently he had decided his presence might help.

The young couple at the piano ended their duet, and some of the guests began to rise from their chairs to stretch their legs before the next song began. Bright satin coats and matching knee breeches graced the more fashionable men. The married women were distinguished by bold color, because maidens wore pastels or white.

Reggie knew everyone except their hostess, Mrs. Hargreaves. George Fowler was there with his sister and younger brother. She had recently met Lord Percival Alden, Nicholas' good friend. She even knew Tony's current ladylove, who was sitting next to him. And to her profound irritation, Selena Eddington was there, too, her escort an old chum of Tony's.

"Nicholas." Reggie touched his arm gently. "You must introduce me to our hostess before George's sister begins her recital."

She felt him stiffen under her fingers, and she smiled as she walked ahead of him toward Mrs. Hargreaves. My, but she must make a point of touching him more often, she thought.

The evening didn't progress as she wished. At dinner, she found herself placed well away from Nicholas at the long table. He was seated next to their hostess, an attractively voluptuous woman, and he put himself out to be charming, captivating his hostess and all the other women around him.

She talked as graciously as she could to George, but it was hard to bubble when she felt so sad. The rakish Lord Percival, on her right, didn't help at all, continually making comments about Nicholas that drew her eyes to him again and again, forcing her to recognize all the signs she'd witnessed before. Nicholas wasn't just being charming to Mrs. Hargreaves, he wore the look of a man in hot pursuit.

As the evening wore on, Reggie forgot her earlier triumph in discomfiting Nicholas. He did not look at her once during the meal. She found it difficult to summon even the briefest of smiles for her companions, and she thanked heaven that Tony was not nearby. If she'd had to endure his snide comments just then, she would have burst into tears.

It was with profound relief that Reggie at last retired from the room with the other ladies. She had only a few minutes to compose herself, however, before the men sauntered into the drawing room. She held her breath, waiting to see if Nicholas would continue to ignore her. He made his way straight to Mrs. Hargreaves without giving Reggie a glance.

It was the outside of enough. Her pride wouldn't let her stay. And if her uncle said even one word to her about Nicholas, she would explode. She couldn't do that in public.

When she asked George Fowler to take her home, his limpid green eyes widened in delight. Then he said, "But your uncle?"

"I'm rather annoyed with him." She was and she wasn't, but it served as an excuse. "And he has brought a lady with him, anyway. I hate to impose on you, though, George. You have your sister with you."

"My brother can see to her, never fear," he declared, smiling.

Well, she thought crossly, it was nice that *some*body liked her.

Chapter Fifteen

"Why is it, I wonder, that you notice the minute she leaves the room with someone?"

Nicholas swung around to meet the level gaze of Anthony Malory. "Following me, my lord?" he asked.

"No point in staying now that the entertainment is over," Anthony replied agreeably. "And a grand show it was too. Only ten minutes gone, and off you go too. Bad effect that."

Nicholas glared at him. "I'm surprised you didn't follow her to make sure Fowler takes her right home. Isn't that what a good watch-dog would do?"

Anthony chuckled. "Whatever for? She will do what she wants to do, no matter what I say. And I trust her more with Fowler than I do with you"—he paused and cleared his throat—"even if he was one of the chaps after her last season. If he doesn't take her right home, well, you can't very well blame him, can you? You're doing your best to give these young bucks the impression she's still available." He waited a moment. "Aren't you?"

Nicholas' eyes flared. "If you take exception to my behavior, you know what you can do about it."

"Indeed," Anthony said coldly, all humor gone in an instant. "If I didn't think Reggie would make a fuss about it, I'd see you in the ring quickly enough. When she stops defending you, we'll make that appointment—you may depend upon it."

"You're a bloody hypocrite, Malory."

Anthony shrugged. "Yes, I am, when one of my own is involved.

You know, Montieth, Jason may think highly of you, but Jason knows only the more positive aspects of your character. He doesn't know what you're trying to do, but I do."

"Do you?"

They stopped talking as Percy came in. Anthony left the scowling Nicholas, and Percy approached his friend sympathetically. "So you've had another run-in with him, have you?"

"Something like that," Nicholas bit out.

Percy shook his head. Nicholas' problem was that he rarely had any opposition in his life. He was big enough and reckless enough that no one cared to match words with him, let alone fight him. Now he had Lady Ashton's relatives forcing their collective will on him, and the frustration was doing him in.

"You shouldn't take it so hard, Nick. You've just never come up against anyone as formidable as yourself before, and now you've got a whole passel." When Nicholas did not reply, he went on, "It'll be better once you're married."

"Bloody hell!" Nicholas swore. He left Percy and went to fetch his cloak.

Nicholas took a deep breath of the night air as he stepped outside to await his carriage, which was across the street. Then he took another deep breath. It did not calm him.

"Wait up, Nick." Percy came down the stairs. "It might help if you talk to a friend."

"Not tonight, Percy, I'm on the short end of my temper."

"Because of Malory?" Nicholas grunted. "Oh, it's because she left with Georgie, then, is that it?"

"*She* can leave with whomever she bloody well pleases, for all I care!"

"Gad, don't eat me," Percy protested, backing away a little. "Old George is really ... not actually harmless, but ... well, dash it all, she's engaged to you. She—" He saw he was only making matters worse. "I don't believe it. Can the unfeeling Montieth really and truly be jealous for a change?"

"Of course I'm not jealous," Nicholas snapped. "I simply hoped to-night would be the end of it."

Except that he had seen red, dark red, when George Fowler put his hand to Regina's elbow. Fowler was young, he was handsome, and damn Malory for saying he had been after Regina last season!

"What the devil are you talking about, Nick? End of what?"

"This farce of an engagement. You didn't really think I would marry the girl just because I was browbeaten into agreeing to it?"

Percy whistled softly. "So that's what you were doing, sniffing round Mrs. H. I knew she wasn't your type." Nicholas shook his head. "But I thought you were trying to make your lady jealous."

"Furious, enough to jilt me. It's not the first time I've chased after another skirt with her there watching. I even gave my full attention to Selena, as disgusted as I am with her. But Regina has not spoken up about it once."

"Maybe the girl loves you," Percy said simply.

"I don't want her love, I want her hate," Nicholas growled. Now, he told himself, not after he was used to her love, had come to depend on it and returned it. He couldn't bear her hate then.

"Well, you're in a fine pickle. What if she doesn't break off with you? Will you jilt her?"

Nicholas looked skyward. "I gave my word I'd marry her."

"Then you might end up doing just that."

"I know."

"Would it be so bad?"

He was afraid it would be heaven, but he wasn't going to say that to Percy. His carriage pulled up to the curb then and he asked, "Do me a favor, Percy? Go back in there and give my future in-law a message for me. Tell him he had better have a talk with his niece about who she lets take her home." He chuckled. "If he thinks it matters to me, he might redouble his own efforts to get her to jilt me. If nothing else, the message will irritate him. That makes me happy." And he did look better.

"Thanks much, old man. He's liable to take *my* head off, getting a message like that," Percy said.

"Depend upon it." Nicholas smiled. "But you'll do it for me anyway, won't you? That's a good fellow."

Nicholas laughed at the expression on Percy's face, and waved as his carriage moved down the driveway.

It took only a moment for his good humor to flee. Tonight was proof that he couldn't take much more of Regina's presence. Her touch alone had brought him to his knees. Damnation! He had tried staying away from her as much as possible, but while that was more comfortable, it didn't change his predicament. They were still, in fact, engaged.

"End of the road, mate," broke into his reverie.

Mate? From *his* staid driver?

Nicholas glanced out the window and saw, not his house, but trees close at hand. Nothing but dismal black lay beyond. How had he been so preoccupied as not to know he was being taken outside London to the countryside? Or was he in one of London's huge parks? If so, it might as well be the bloody countryside for all the traffic that might pass at night.

What the devil had Malory done, hired a thug to deal with him so Anthony could swear to Regina that he had not touched Nicholas? He could just see her uncle laughing about it with his friends.

Nicholas smiled grimly. This was one way to let off steam. Why hadn't he thought of it himself?

Chapter Sixteen

⌐arlier in the evening, just after Nicholas and Regina arrived at Mrs.
└Hargreaves' in the West End, a short, stocky fellow named Timothy
Pye hailed a passing hack and gave the driver the address of a tavern
near the waterfront.

Timothy did odd jobs, from an honest day's work on the docks to
slitting a man's throat. He admitted to a partiality for easy jobs, and this
one was about as easy as they got. His friend Neddy was working with
him. All they had to do was follow this nabob wherever he went and
every so often report the lord's whereabouts to their employer.

It was Timothy's turn to report, and it didn't take long to reach the
better-class tavern where the bloke was staying. Upstairs, he pounded
on the door. It took only a moment to open.

Two men were in the room. One was a tall, thin fellow with a huge,
bushy red beard. The other was a young man of medium height, a boy
really, pretty in a girlish sort of way, with black hair and darkest blue
eyes. Timothy had seen the younger fellow only once before in the half-
dozen times he had reported to the older man. Their names had never
been given, nor did Timothy care to know who they were. He simply
did as he was paid to do, no questions asked.

"'E's settled in fer the evenin', so it 'pears," Timothy began,
speaking to the red-bearded one. "Some party o'er the West End. Lots
o' fancy hacks linin' the street both sides."

"Alone?"

Timothy grinned here. "Brought the fancy piece wi' 'im in his carriage, same as before. Took her inside. I saw 'em."

"Are you certain it's the same lady, Mr. Pye, the one who left without him last time?"

Timothy nodded. "Can't rightly ferget that'n, sir. She's a bleedin' beauty, she is."

The younger man spoke. "Must be his mistress, don't you think? Me father said he's not the type to waste his time on anyone he's not beddin'."

"Blast it, boy!" Red beard growled. "*My* father. *My,* not *me.* Why is it you never make these slips when your old man is around? It's only my ears that are cursed."

The young man flushed red all the way down his chest, a fact revealed by his loose shirt. His dark blue eyes averted in embarrassment, he moved over to a table where a deck of cards was spread out next to a bottle of wine and two glasses. He sat down there and shuffled the cards, intending to ignore the rest of the report after being humiliated.

"You were saying, Mr. Pye."

"Right, sir." The "sir" came naturally, for the bloke might not look exactly like a gentleman with that bushy red beard, but he talked like one. "I know'd ye want ter be 'earin' 'bout the fancy, 'case she leaves wi'out 'im agin t'night."

"How is the lighting on the street?"

"Fair. But not so bright me and Neddy can't take down the driver nice an' quiet-like."

"Then perhaps tonight is the night." Red beard smiled for the first time. "You know what to do if the opportunity presents itself, Mr. Pye."

"Right, sir. You don't want the fancy involved, I know, sir. If'e comes out alone, we 'ave 'im."

The door closed behind Pye and Conrad Sharpe laughed. It was a deep resounding laugh for such a thin man. "Oh, don't sulk, lad. If all goes well, we may be on our way home tomorrow."

"You didn't have to go correcting me in front of the likes of him, Connie. My father don't correct me in front of others."

"Doesn't," Conrad corrected again. "Your father is a fairly new father and, so being, he takes pains to spare your feelings, Jeremy."

"And you don't?"

"Why should I, brat?"

There was genuine affection in the older man's manners, and young Jeremy grinned at last. "If they get him tonight, will I get to go along?"

"Sorry, lad. It will be a messy business that your father won't want you to see."

"I'm sixteen!" Jeremy protested. "I've lived through a *sea battle*."

"Just barely."

"Regardless—"

"No," Conrad said adamantly. "Even if your father agreed, I wouldn't let you. You don't need to see your father at his worst."

"He's only going to teach him a lesson, Connie."

"Yes, but because you were hurt, the lesson will be harsh. And his pride is involved, too. You didn't hear the slurs and taunts the young lord rubbed into the open wound. You were flat on your back with a near-mortal wound."

"Thanks to him! Which is why—"

"I said no!" Conrad cut him short again.

"Oh, all right," Jeremy grumbled. "But I still don't see why we've gone to all this fuss and bother, having him trailed in Southampton to no luck, then wasting two weeks here in London doing the same thing. It would have been much more fun just to sink one of his ships."

Conrad chuckled. "Your father should hear your idea of fun. But as for that, this lord may have only six ships to his merchant line, but losing one wouldn't tickle his pocket. Your father is determined to even the score on a more personal level."

"And then can we go home?"

"Yes, lad. And you can get back to your proper schooling."

Jeremy made a face and Conrad Sharpe laughed. Then they heard a female giggle coming from the room next door, where Jeremy's father was, and Jeremy's grimace turned to a hot blush, making Conrad laugh all the harder.

Chapter Seventeen

Still baked from the day's heat, the ground was warm beneath his cheek. Or perhaps he had lain in that spot for hours and his own body heat had warmed the ground, he didn't know. These thoughts went through Nicholas' mind when he came to and opened his eyes.

He next called himself a fool, ten kinds of a fool. Gentleman that he was, he had simply stepped out of his carriage, never dreaming he would be attacked even before his foot touched the ground.

He spat dirt out of his mouth. They had apparently left him lying where he'd fallen. Careful movement told him his hands were tied behind his back, and nearly numb besides. Famous. With sharp stabs shooting though his head, he would be lucky if he could get to his knees, let alone his feet. *If* they had left him his carriage, he wouldn't be able to drive it without the use of his hands. Had they left the carriage?

Twisting his head agonizingly to the side, Nicholas saw one of the carriage wheels—and a pair of boots beside it.

"You're still here?" he asked incredulously.

"An' where would I be goin', mate?"

"Back to your den of thieves, I assume," Nicholas answered.

The fellow laughed. What the devil did this mean? Wasn't this just a common robbery, then? He thought of Malory again, but try as he might, he couldn't conceive of the fellow hiring someone to rough him up.

"Have I been unconscious long?" Nicholas asked. His head throbbed.

"A good hour, mate, ter be sure."

"Then would you mind telling me what the bloody hell you're wait-ing for?" Nicholas growled. "Rob me and be about your business!"

Again the fellow laughed. "Did that, mate, right off. Wasn't told I couldn't, so I did. But me business is right 'ere, seein' ye stay put."

Nicholas tried to sit up, but a wave of dizziness toppled him. He cursed, trying again.

"Steady, mate. Don't be tryin' no tricks now, or I'll 'ave ter let yer 'ave another taste o' me cudgel."

Nicholas sat up, his knees bent to support his chest. Deep breath-ing helped. He finally got a look at the slovenly creature. He wasn't impressed. If he could just get to his feet, he would make short work of the fellow even with his hands tied.

"Be a good fellow and help me up, will you?"

"That's funny, mate. Yer twice the size o' me. I weren't born yes-terdy."

So much for that, Nicholas thought. "What have you done with my driver?"

"Dumped 'im in an alley. Ye needn't worry. 'E'll wake up wi' a 'eadache, same as ye 'ave, but he'll be a'right."

"Where are we?"

"I liked ye better when ye were asleep," the footpad answered. "Too many questions."

"You can at least tell me what we are doing here," Nicholas asked impatiently.

"Yer sittin' in the middle o' the road, and I'm makin' sure ye stay there."

"No, what you're doing is making me angry!" Nicholas snapped.

"That worries me, mate," the fellow snickered, "it surely do."

With just a little leverage and effort, he could plow his head right into the ignominious bastard's belly, Nicholas thought. But his planning was interrupted by the sound of another carriage approaching. Since the footpad was not making haste to leave the scene, Nicholas con-cluded uncomfortably that the carriage was expected. What bloody next? "Friends of yours?"

The fellow shook his head. "I told ye, mate, ye ask too many questions."

The outside lamp on the approaching carriage illuminated the area and what Nicholas saw was naggingly familiar. Hyde Park? He rode the paths there every morning and knew them as well as the grounds of Silverley. Would they dare accost him so close to his home?

The carriage stopped twenty feet away, and the driver got down and brought the carriage lantern forward. Behind him two men left the carriage, but Nicholas could see only vague shapes because the light was thrust toward his own face. He tried to stand, but Pye's cudgel pressed down on his shoulder warningly.

"A very pretty picture, eh, Connie?" he heard, and then, "Indeed, yes. All trussed up and awaiting your pleasure."

Their laughter grated on Nicholas' oversensitive nerves. He didn't recognize the voices, but they were cultured accents. What enemies had he made recently among the fashionable set? Good God, dozens! All the past suitors of his bride-to-be.

"A splendid job, my good fellows." A purse was tossed to the cudgel-wielder, and another to the short, stocky carriage driver. "Just light that lamp there for us, and then you may return the hired hack. We'll make use of this carriage since his lordship won't be needing it."

The light moved out of his eyes and Nicholas got his first good look at the two men. Both were tall and bearded, both well dressed, the thinner man in a double-breasted redingote; the other one, with a huge beard, in a several-tiered Garrick coat. He saw dark trousers and well-polished boots. But who were they?

The broader man, slightly shorter than the other, sported an ivory-handled walking stick. That plus his bushy beard gave him a caricaturelike appearance. He was older than his companion, possibly in his early forties. He seemed vaguely familiar, but for the life of him, Nicholas couldn't place either of them.

"Bring that other lamp over here before you go."

Nicholas' own carriage lamp was set on the back of the carriage, casting light on him, but leaving the two gentlemen in shadows. The driver and the thug left in the hired carriage.

"He looks confused, doesn't he, Connie?" the younger man said when the carriage had rumbled away. "You don't think he's going to disappoint me by saying he doesn't remember me?"

"Perhaps you should refresh his memory."

"Perhaps I should jar it."

The boot caught Nicholas on the jaw. He fell back on his bound arms, grunting in pain.

"Come, lad, sit up. That was barely a tap."

Nicholas was hauled roughly to his feet by his bound wrists, wrenching his arms. He swayed for a moment, overcome by a wave of dizziness, but a heavy hand steadied him. Fortunately his jaw was already turning numb. He barely felt a twinge when he parted his lips. "If we are supposed to have met—"

The fist knocked the breath out of him as it slammed into his stomach. He doubled over, gasping for air that eluded him.

The hand that slipped beneath his chin to draw him back up was almost gentle. "Don't disappoint me again, lad." The voice was soft with warning. "Tell me you remember me."

Nicholas flushed with impotent anger as he stared at the man. He was only a few inches shorter than Nicholas. The light brown hair was long and tied back with a ribbon, though shorter, blonder locks fell over his ears. The beard was the same light brown shade as the hair. When he moved his head to the side to study Nicholas, a flash of gold appeared at his ear. An earring? Impossible. The only men who wore earrings were . . . uneasiness began to replace his anger.

"Captain Hawke?"

"Very good, lad! I would hate to think you had forgotten me," Hawke chuckled. "You see what the right prodding can do, Connie? And it was a darkened alley where we last met. I doubt the boy got a good look at me then."

"He saw you well enough on the *Maiden Anne*."

"But do I look the same on board ship? No. He's a clever lad, that's what. It was a matter of deduction, see? I doubt he has another enemy like me."

"I hate to disappoint you," Nicholas said wearily, "but you no longer have a monopoly on hating me."

"No? Splendid! I wouldn't like to think of you having too easy a time of it once I'm gone."

"Then I shall live to see another day?" Nicholas asked.

Connie laughed. "He's as arrogant as you are, Hawke, damned if he isn't. I don't think you frighten him at all. He'll be spitting in your eye next."

"I don't think so," Hawke replied coldly. "I might pluck out his own in that case. How d'you think he'd look wearing a patch like old Billings?"

"With that pretty face?" Connie snorted. "It would only enhance his superb looks. The ladies would love it."

"Well, perhaps I should see to his face, then."

Nicholas did not even see the blow. Fire exploded on his cheek, the impact staggering him. Connie was there to hold him up, however, and then the other cheek received the same powerful blow.

When his head cleared, Nicholas spat blood. His eyes glowed with a murderous light as he met the pirate captain's stare.

"Are you angry enough now to fight me, lad?"

"You need only have asked," Nicholas managed.

"You needed a bit of motivation. I'm here to even the score, not play with you. I demand a good showing, or we'll only have to do this again."

Nicholas snorted, though it hurt to make the effort. "Even the score? You forget who attacked whom on the open sea."

"But that's my trade, don't you know."

"Then how do you dare speak of revenge simply because you were bested?" Nicholas demanded. "Or do I have the honor of being the only man ever to come away with a whole ship after an encounter with the *Maiden Anne?*"

"Not at all," Hawke said honestly. "We have limped into port before. I myself have received wounds in the heat of battle. Though I did not take kindly to having my son injured when you felled my main mast. But even that had to be accepted for having the boy on board. However, as one gentleman to another—"

"A gentleman pirate?" It was dangerous, but Nicholas had to say it.

"Sneer as you will, but you are clever enough to comprehend why we had to meet again."

Nicholas nearly laughed. It was incredible. The pirate had attacked him first, intending to win the cargo Nicholas was carrying. Nicholas had won that sea battle. He supposed he shouldn't have taunted Captain Hawke when he sailed away. That had been hitting below the belt. But, it had happened four years ago, and he'd been young and reckless, heady with victory. Still, those taunts were apparently what had goaded Hawke into evening the score. What gentleman could ignore an insult?

Gentleman! They had met in a darkened alley in Southampton after Nicholas returned to England, three years ago. He had been unable to see his assailant that night, though Hawke took pleasure in introducing himself. That encounter had been interrupted.

Then there'd been a letter, a *letter,* waiting for Nicholas when he returned from the West Indies last year, expressing regret that Hawke had been unable to renew their acquaintance when he was in London. The letter convinced Nicholas that he had made a terrible enemy. Why, oh, why, was he so blessed as to have a scum of the earth thirsty for his blood?

"Cut him loose, Connie."

Nicholas tensed. "Do I fight you both?"

"Come now," Captain Hawke protested. "That would hardly be sporting, would it?"

"Bloody hell," Nicholas growled. "Striking a defenseless man isn't sporting."

"Did I hurt you, lad? You must accept my apologies, but I thought you were made of sterner stuff. And you must understand, I feel justified after all the bother you've cost me waiting for this moment."

"You will understand if I don't agree?"

"Certainly," Hawke replied with a mock bow.

Hawke removed his Garrick. He was dressed for easy movement in a flowing shirt tucked into his trousers. Nicholas was encumbered with cloak, coat, and waistcoat. He saw that he wouldn't be given the opportunity to remove any of these as he watched the pirate flex his fingers impatiently.

Nicholas couldn't stop the groan from escaping as his bonds were finally severed and his arms dropped painfully to his sides. There was no feeling in his fingers for several moments, and then too much feeling as the blood rushed into them. And he had assumed correctly. He was not given a moment's grace to recover before the first staggering blow caught him under the chin. He landed hard.

"Come on, lad," Hawke complained with a weary sigh. "We won't be interrupted this time. Give me a good showing and I'll call it quits."

"And if I don't?"

"Then you may not walk away from here."

Nicholas took the warning. He threw off his cloak while he was on the ground and then propelled himself at the older man, catching him in the midsection and knocking them both to the ground. He followed with a hard right to Hawke's jaw, but the impact so jarred his throbbing hand that he was the one who cried out in pain.

Nicholas gave it his best, but Hawke was relentless, and despite Nicholas' injuries, Hawke was the more furious of the two. He was also heavier and more muscular. His hamlike fists were merciless on Nicholas' already bruised face and body. The fight was a hard one for both, however, and as Nicholas lay bleeding in the dust, he knew the older man was hurting, too. Even so, Hawke could laugh.

"I must hand it to you, Montieth," Captain Hawke panted. "You probably could have beaten me if you'd had a fresh start. I am satisfied now."

Nicholas heard only some of it before he passed into blessed unconsciousness. Conrad Sharpe leaned over and shook him, but he didn't stir.

"He's out, Hawke. You have to take your hat off to the boy, though. For a pampered nabob, he lasted much longer than I would have expected." Conrad chuckled then. "How does your own body feel now about settling scores?"

"Do be quiet, Connie. Hell and fire, the chap's got a nasty right."

"I noticed," Conrad laughed.

Hawke sighed. "You know, under different circumstances I could almost like him. It's a shame I had to come across him when he was such a sharp-tongued young pup."

"Weren't we all at that age?"

"Yes, I suppose we were. And we all must learn from it." Hawke tried to straighten to his full height but groaned and doubled over. "Get me to a bed, Connie. I think I'll need at least a week's rest after this."

"Was it worth it?"

"Yes, by God, it sure as hell was!"

Chapter Eighteen

The last of the officials and the doctor filed out of the room, and Nicholas' valet, Harris, closed the door. Nicholas allowed himself a smile, but the movement turned to a grimace as the cut on his lip stretched.

"If you don't mind, sir, I'll manage that smile for the both of us," Harris offered. And then he actually did, his drooping mustache leveling out as he smiled widely.

"It did end better than I could have hoped, didn't it?" Nicholas said.

"That it did, sir. Instead of coming before the magistrate on a simple matter of assault, he'll face the charge of piracy."

Nicholas wanted to smile again, but thought better of it. Now he knew how Captain Hawke felt about evening scores. Well, Hawke's victory had been very, very short-lived.

"I suppose I shouldn't gloat, but the fellow deserves no better," Nicholas said.

"Indeed not, sir. Why, the doctor said you're lucky your jawbone is still intact. And I never in all my days saw so many bruises and—"

"Oh, that doesn't matter. You don't think *he's* not suffering now, too? It's the principle of the matter. I never would have met the cur if he hadn't attacked my ship to begin with. Yet *he* held a bloody grudge! But I don't think he's laughing about it now, sitting in jail."

"It's fortunate the watch found you when they did, sir."

"Yes. Pure luck, that."

Nicholas had regained consciousness a few moments after Hawke and the red-haired Connie left in Nicholas' carriage. And it was only a few more moments when he heard horses' hooves not too far away. He managed to call out, and the two night watchmen heard him. It took some convincing to get them to leave him and go after his carriage instead. Thirty minutes later they came back for him with the happy news that his carriage was recovered and the injured assailant apprehended—though the other one managed to outrun capture.

Nicholas told the whole story to the good fellows who brought him home, and Hawke's name nagged at one of them. Sure enough, a host of officials descended on Nicholas while the doctor was still working on him. They announced that Hawke was a felon wanted by the Crown.

"It is also fortunate, sir," the valet continued chattily as he straightened the bedcovers over Nicholas, "that Lady Ashton was not with you when you encountered the thugs. I assume the evening went as planned and she left without you again?"

Nicholas did not answer. When he thought of what might have happened . . . no, it did not bear thinking about. She was safe because George Fowler had taken her home.

Hmm. George Fowler indeed. Unreasonable anger, hot and vicious, took hold of him.

"Sir?"

"What?" Nicholas barked, then recovered. "Ah, yes, Harris, the evening went as expected where the lady is concerned."

The middle-aged valet had been with Nicholas for ten years and was privy to his thoughts and feelings the way no one else could be. He knew Nicholas didn't want to marry Regina Ashton, though he didn't know why—nor would he dream of asking. He and Nicholas had discussed the strategy Nicholas was employing to deal with the commitment.

"Lady Ashton had words with you, sir?"

"It didn't go *that* well," Nicholas replied tiredly. The sedative the doctor had given him was starting to take effect. "I am still engaged."

"Well, surely next time . . ."

"Yes."

"But there's not much time before the wedding," Harris added hesitantly. "The doctor wants you to have three weeks' bedrest."

"Bother that," Nicholas retorted. "I will be up and about in three days, no more."

"If you say so, sir."

"I do say so."

"Very good, sir."

Never having suffered such a beating before, Nicholas had no way of knowing he would feel ten times worse the next day. He roundly cursed Captain Hawke and would have liked the pirate hanged.

It took a full week before he could move even slightly without pain. And though he was finally up and moving in another week, the cuts on his face were still raw.

He was in no fit condition to see Regina. But he couldn't afford to lose any more time.

The wedding was only a week away. He had to see her.

He called at the Malory house in Grosvenor Square despite his appearance. He was told Regina was out of the house, shopping for her trousseau. This information increased his panic. He waited for an hour, and when she arrived he very rudely whisked his fiancée away from her cousins the moment she walked in the door.

He led her through the garden and on into the square, saying nothing, his stride long and fast, his expression darkly brooding. Her soft voice breaking into his thoughts brought him to a halt.

"You are recovered?" she asked. A brisk autumn breeze whipped leaves through the air and played havoc with the feathers on Regina's bonnet. Her cheeks were flushed, her eyes sparkled with blue lights. She was too damnably lovely by far, blooming with health and vitality. She was still the most beautiful woman he had ever encountered.

"Recovered?" Nicholas demanded, wondering how on earth she had found out about the attack when he had avoided her these last two weeks just so she wouldn't find out.

"Derek told us of your illness," she explained. "I am sorry you were not well."

Damnation! So he was to receive her sympathy, thanks to Derek's coloring the truth. He would have preferred her anger.

"Actually, I was visiting a favorite tavern of mine on the waterfront and was set upon by ruffians who beat me soundly for my purse. Still, there is a certain excitement in frequenting unsavory places."

She smiled tolerantly. "Tony was sure you would use your illness as an excuse to postpone the wedding. I told him that wasn't your style."

"You know me so well, love?" Nicholas asked sardonically.

"You may be many things, but cowardly isn't one of them."

"You presume—"

"Oh, stuff," she interrupted. "I won't believe it if you try to convince me otherwise, so you needn't try."

Nicholas gritted his teeth and she flashed him an amused grin. Looking at her beauty affected him strongly, as it always did, and his thoughts were quite scattered for the moment.

"I suppose I should ask how you have been getting on?"

"You should, yes," Reggie agreed. "But we both know that what I do with my time doesn't interest you. For instance, you wouldn't be wounded, would you, if you knew I have been so busy I haven't missed you? And you wouldn't care if you knew that other men have escorted me to the affairs my cousins insist I attend?"

"George Fowler?"

"George, Basil, William—"

"Careful, or I will begin to think you are trying to stir my jealousy in retaliation."

"Retaliation? Oh, I see, you judge me by your own behavior. How amusing, Nicholas. Just because you find other women fascinating—"

"Blister it, Regina!" Nicholas finally lost all patience. "Why do you wrap your anger up in polite nonsense? Scream at me!"

"Don't tempt me."

"Aha!" he exclaimed triumphantly. "I was beginning to think you had no spirit."

"Oh, Nicholas." Reggie laughed softly. "Am I supposed to call you a foul, despicable creature, and swear tearfully that I wouldn't marry you if you were the last man and so forth?"

Nicholas glared furiously. "You mock me, madame?"

"What makes you think that?"

She said this with such an innocent expression that he put his hands on her shoulders, ready to shake her. But her magnificent blue eyes widened in surprise as her own hands came up to brace against his chest, and Nicholas flushed red hot.

He stepped back from her, nearly trembling. "The press of time forces me to be blunt, Regina," he said coldly. "I asked you before to end this farce of an engagement. I am asking you again. Nay, I am begging you. I do not want to marry you."

She dropped her gaze, staring fixedly at the high polish of his Hessian boots. "You don't want me . . . in any way then? Not even as a lover?"

His honey-gold eyes flashed at the turmoil the question caused, but he said only, "You would no doubt make a fine mistress."

"But you are not interested?"

"Not any longer."

She turned her back on him, her shoulders drooping, a dejected little figure. Nicholas had to restrain himself with every ounce of will from reaching out and gathering her into his arms. He wanted to take it all back, to show her what a lie it had been. But it was better for her to be disillusioned for a time, and then to forget him. He could not let this lovely woman marry a bastard.

"I really thought I could make you happy, Nicholas." Her words floated to him over her shoulder.

"No woman can, love, not for any length of time."

"I'm sorry then. I really am."

He didn't move. "You *will* jilt me then?"

"No."

"No?" He stiffened, disbelieving. "What the devil do you mean?"

"The word no means—"

"I know what the bloody word means!"

She finally turned around. "You don't have to shout at me, sir."

"Formal again, are we?" he cried, his temper cresting.

"Under the circumstances, yes," she answered curtly. "You have only to absent yourself from London next week. I assure you I am quite strong enough to bear up under the humiliation of being jilted."

"I gave my word!" he exclaimed.

"Ah, yes, the word of a gentleman—who is a gentleman only when it suits him to be one."

"My word is my bond."

"Then you must stick to it, Lord Montieth."

She started to walk away, but he caught her arm, his fingers hard. "Don't do it, Regina," he warned darkly. "You will regret it."

"I already do," was the whispered reply. It took him aback.

"Then *why?*" he asked desperately.

"I—I must," she replied.

He let go of her arm and stepped away, his face a mask of fury. "Damnation take you then! I will be no husband to you, this I swear. If you persist in this farce, then that is what you will have, a mockery of a marriage. I wish you happy."

"You don't mean that, Nicholas!" There were tears in her eyes.

"I give you my word, madame, and a last warning: Do not come to the church."

Chapter Nineteen

"Ah, don't cry any more, sweetheart," Meg pleaded. "Your cousins will be here in a moment to help with the dressin'. You don't want them to see you like this."

"I can't help it," Reggie sobbed miserably. "And aren't brides supposed to cry on their wedding day?"

"But you've been cryin' for a week. It hasn't helped, has it?"

"No." Reggie shook her head.

"And you don't want your eyes to be all puffy, not today of all days."

Reggie shrugged wearily. "I don't care about that. I'll have the veil on."

"But you won't be wearin' a veil tonight."

There was a silence, and then Reggie whispered, "Will there be a wedding night?"

"You can't be thinkin' he won't show up?" Meg gasped, outraged.

"Oh, he'll be there," Reggie sighed. "But I told you what he said."

"Nonsense. Some men are just scared to death of marriage, and your Viscount appears to be one of them."

"But he swore he wouldn't be a husband to me."

"He said that in anger," Meg said patiently. "You can't go holdin' a man to what he says in anger."

"Yet he can hold himself to it, don't you see? Oh, how could I have been so wrong about him, Meg?" Reggie cried. "How could I?" She shook her head. "To think I once compared him to Tony. Nicholas Eden is nothing like my uncle. He hasn't an ounce of feeling—except between his legs," she added bitterly.

"Reggie!"

"Well, it's true," she retorted. "I was just a game to him, another conquest."

Meg stood looking down at her, hands on her hips. "You should have told him about the baby," she said for the hundredth time. "At least he would have understood why you must go through with this."

"He probably wouldn't have believed it. *I* am even beginning to wonder. Look at me! Four months gone and I'm still not showing even a little. And there's been no sickness, no . . . Am I binding myself to this man for nothing? What if I'm not carrying his child?"

"I wish it weren't so, my girl, but you know it is. And I still say you should have told him."

"Fool that I was, I thought his despicable behavior was only a ruse," Reggie said bitterly. She sighed. "You know, Meg, I do still have some pride left."

"Sometimes we must swallow every bit of pride, sweetheart," Meg said gently.

Reggie shook her head. "I'll tell you just what he would have said if I had confessed. He would have told me to stop wasting time on a lost cause and find a father for my child."

"Maybe you should have."

Reggie's eyes flashed. "I would never force one man's child on another! Nicholas Eden has a child on the way, and he can pay the price for it, not someone else."

"You're the one payin', Reggie, with heartache and misery."

"I know," she sighed, the fire gone. "But only because I thought I loved him. Once I see how wrong I was, I will manage."

"It's not too late, you know. You can leave for the Continent before—"

"No!" Reggie said so forcefully the maid jumped. "This is *my* child! I won't hide in shame until it's born and then give it up, just to save myself an unpleasant marriage." Then she elaborated, "I don't have to live with the man, you know, not if it proves too difficult. I don't have to stay with him forever. But my child will bear his father's name. Nicholas Eden will share the responsibility, as he should."

"Then we had best be gettin' to the church on time," Meg sighed.

* * *

Nicholas was already at the church, silently raging and despairing by turns. Family and friends were arriving, proving that this was really happening. His grandmother and aunt were there, but Miriam Eden was conspicuously absent again. It reinforced his conviction that he had done the right thing in warning off his fiancée.

His heart sank when Jason Malory entered the church, the bride a few steps behind him. Exclamations ran through the crowd, for she was truly breathtaking in a silk gown of powder blue and silver, with tiers of white lace trimming. It was strikingly old-fashioned, tight-waisted, long-sleeved, and reaching to the floor. Though the bell of the skirt was not as full as the gowns of the last era had been, the outer skirt was split on both sides and trimmed with lace, revealing wide panels of silver underskirt. There was lace beneath the rounded bodice and at the neck. A circlet of silver and diamond chains held in place a white veil which covered her face to her chin, draping in back nearly to the floor.

She stood in the church door for several long moments, facing Nicholas at the end of the aisle. He couldn't see her face or her eyes, and he waited breathlessly, willing her to turn around and flee.

She didn't. Regina placed her hand on her uncle's arm and began the long walk down the aisle. Cold, calm anger settled inside Nicholas. On the whim of this small child-woman, he was being forced into marriage. Very well, let her have her day of triumph. It would not last long. When she learned she had married a bastard, she would wish she had heeded his warnings. Ironically, Miriam would help. She would take a malicious delight in apprising Regina of all Nicholas' faults. He thought with grim humor that this would be Miriam's first act of kindness toward him. Of course, she wouldn't know it for what it was.

Chapter Twenty

Reggie stared out the coach window, but all she could see was her own reflection. She flushed as her belly growled with hunger but didn't look at Nicholas to see if he had heard. He was across from her in the plush coach, which bore his coat of arms.

The interior lamp had been burning for two hours, but still they hadn't stopped at an inn for dinner. She was hungry, but she was damned if she'd beg.

The wedding guests had been served a huge luncheon at Malory house, but Reggie hadn't been there for it. Nicholas took her home directly from the church, telling her to pack an overnight bag and order the rest of her things sent on to Silverley. The two of them were gone even before their guests arrived.

He had made her ride all afternoon and into the evening, but she didn't feel like complaining, not when he sat there so pensively, never once looking her way. He hadn't spoken a word since leaving London.

He was married and furious about it. Well, she'd expected he would be. But it boded well, didn't it, that he was taking her to his country estate? She didn't expected that. She didn't know what she had expected.

Her stomach growled again and she finally decided to ask, "Will we be stopping soon for dinner?"

"The last inn was in Montieth. Silverley is just up ahead," Nicholas replied brusquely.

It would have been nice if he'd told her that sooner.

"Is Silverley large, Nicholas?"

"About as large as your own estate, which borders mine."

Her eyes widened. "I didn't know that!"

"How could you not?"

"Why are you angry? Why, it's perfect. The estates will now be combined—"

"Which is what I have wanted for years. But surely your uncle told you about that. He used your estate as the inducement to get me to marry you."

Reggie blushed furiously. "I don't believe it."

"That I wanted the land?"

"You know what I mean!" she snapped. "Oh, I knew there was some land involved, and Tony even said it was what swayed you, but— but I didn't believe it. No one told me about this. I didn't know your estate borders the land that came to me through my mother. I haven't lived there since—my parents died, in the fire that destroyed the house. I was only two at the time. I have never returned to Hampshire. Uncle Edward has always seen to what was left of the estate, as well as to the inheritance I got from my father."

"Yes, a tidy sum that, fifty thousand pounds, which he was happy to point out has tripled due to his wise investments, giving you a sizable yearly income."

"Good God, are you angry about that, too?"

"I am not a fortune hunter!"

Her own grievances were riding very close to the edge. "Oh, bother. Who in his right mind could accuse you of that? You're not exactly a pauper."

"It is no secret that I wanted your land, land I assumed belonged to the Earl of Penwich, since the Earl was the last to be in residence there."

"My father was, not the present Earl. But as the land came to him through my mother, it was not entailed to Penwich and it was their wish it come to me."

"I *know* that now! Your Uncle Edward thought it quite amusing to inform me as I left the church that I no longer needed to worry about buying the estate. He couldn't wait to tell me. Wanted to relieve my mind, he said. Bloody hell. Do you know how it looks, madame?"

"Do you realize you are insulting me, sir?"

He had the decency to look surprised. "I didn't mean to imply—"

"Of course you did. That is what you are complaining about, isn't it? That people will say you married me for my inheritance? Well, thank you very much. I was not aware this was the only way I could get a husband."

His brows narrowed and he said coldly, "Shall we *discuss* how you got a husband?"

Her eyes flashed blue sparks, and for a moment she feared she would lose all control. She managed, just barely, to keep silent, and Nicholas refrained from goading her. Both were relieved to find the coach stopping just at that moment.

He stepped outside and extended a hand to help her down. But as soon as she was standing on the ground, he got back into the coach. She stared up at him, her eyes widening in disbelief.

"You wouldn't!" she gasped.

He said bitterly, "You can't be surprised. I am a man of my word, after all."

"You can't just leave me here—not tonight."

"Tonight, tomorrow—what difference?"

"You know what difference!"

"Ah, yes, the wedding night. But we have had ours, haven't we, love?"

She gasped. "If you do this, Nicholas," she said tremulously, "I swear I will never forgive you."

"Then we are well met, aren't we, if we both honor our oaths? You have what you wanted. You bear my name. I give you now my home. Where is it written that I must share it with you?"

"You expect me to stay here while you go on as before, living in London and . . ."

He shook his head. "London is too close for our arrangement. No, I'm leaving England altogether. Would that I had done so before we met!"

"Nicholas, you can't. I am—"

Reggie stopped herself before making the one declaration that might change his mind. Her pride stubbornly reasserted itself. She would not follow the path of thousands of other women, just to keep a man by her side. If he wouldn't stay because he wanted to . . .

"You are—what, love?"

"Your wife," she said smoothly.

"So you are," he agreed, his mouth tightening into a hard line. "But you will recall I didn't ask you to be, and I warned you not to press the marriage. I have always been plainspoken about this, Regina."

He closed the coach door then and tapped on the roof to signal the driver. Reggie stared incredulously as the vehicle moved away.

"Nicholas, come back!" Reggie shouted. "If you leave . . . Nicholas! Oh! I hate you! I hate you!" she cried in frustration, knowing he couldn't hear her anyway.

Stunned, she turned around to face the large gray stone house. It looked like a miniature castle, a gloomy one, in the dark night, with its central tower and corner turrets. This was only a close view, however, so she did not see how it spread out behind and on the sides of the main block in asymmetrical heights and shapes. There even was a large domed conservatory at the back of the house, towering over the servants' wing on the right.

The arched windows on either side of the door were dark. What if there was no one at home? Famous. Abandoned on her wedding night, and to an empty house!

Well, there was nothing for it. Squaring her shoulders, she forced a smile and approached the front door as if there were nothing odd about a bride arriving without her bridegroom. She knocked, first quietly and then loudly.

When the door finally opened, Reggie saw the startled face of a young girl, a maid. She was not at all confident about answering doors. That was Sayers' duty. He took himself so seriously. He would have her hide to know she has usurped his place.

"We weren't expectin' company, my lady, or I'm sure Sayers would've been waitin' round to let you in. But you've such a soft knock . . . gor, listen to me ramblin'. What can I do for you?"

Regina grinned, feeling ever so much better. "You can let me in, to begin with."

The girl opened the door wider. "You've come to call on the Countess, Lady Miriam?"

"I guess I've come to live here—for a while, at least. But I suppose I can start with seeing Lady Miriam."

"Gor! You've come to live here? Are you sure you want to?"

This was said with such patent surprise that Reggie laughed. "Why? Are there dragons and goblins here?"

"There's one I could speak of. Two if you count Mrs. Oates." The girl gasped, then went vivid red. "I didn't mean . . . oh, forgive me, my lady."

"No harm done. What's your name?"

"Hallie, mum."

"Then, Hallie, do you think you could inform Lady Miriam that I have arrived? I am the new Countess of Montieth."

"Gor!" Hallie squealed.

"Precisely. Now, will you show me where I can await Lady Miriam?"

The maid let Reggie in. "I'll just tell Mrs. Oates you're here, and she'll go up and tell the Countess."

The entry hall was marble-floored and narrow, with only a single long refectory table up against a wall. An ornate silver platter was positioned in the center of the table for calling cards, and a lovely tapestry hung behind. A large Venetian mirror dressed the opposite wall with a brace of wall candles on each side, and a pair of double doors directly facing the front door.

Hallie opened the double doors, and a much larger hall was revealed, two stories high, with a magnificent domed ceiling way above. The main staircase was in the center of the right wall. And at the end of the hallway were opened doors that led into an antechamber, and Reggie caught a glimpse of stained-glass windows nearly covering the outside wall. The impression was of an extremely large house.

At the far end of the hall on the left was the library, and this was where Hallie led her. Forty feet long and twenty wide, the library had tall windows along the far wall, giving ample light in the daytime. The other three walls were covered with books, and huge portraits hung high up above the bookcases.

There was a fireplace, and sofas to either side of it. Beautifully crafted chairs, lounges, and tables were spaced near the windows for reading. There was an ancient reading stand in gold lacquer. A carpet in rich browns, blues, and gold covered the floor. A pedestal desk occupied the far end of the room, with chairs around it, and there was a painted leather screen which would turn that far corner into a cozy study set off from the rest of the room.

"It shouldn't be long, mum," Hallie said. "The Countess . . . oh, dear, the Dowager Countess now, isn't she? Just like the old one, his lordship's grandmother. But Lady Miriam will be eager to welcome you, I'm sure," she said politely, not sounding at all convinced. "Can I get you something? There's brandy there on the table, and mulberry wine, too, that the Countess likes."

"No, I'll just make myself comfortable, thank you," Reggie replied with a smile.

"Very good, mum. And can I be the first to say I'm glad you've come? I hope you like it here."

"I do too, Hallie," Reggie sighed. "I do too."

Chapter Twenty-one

Reggie looked at the morning sun that was just barely peeking into the corner of her bedroom. Directly below her south windows was the round dome of the conservatory. Beyond was the servants' court, and beyond that, hidden behind a clump of trees, the stables and carriage house.

She was in the master bedroom in the rear right corner of the central block of the house. That allowed her two walls of windows, all draped in bloodred velvet with gold fringe and tassels. All the colors in the room were dark except for the powder blue wallpaper. Still, when it got later and all the windows let in light, the room would be cheery.

Her other wall of windows looked out over a vast parkland. The view was stunning—trees dotting the lawns, a forest to the left full of orange-and-gold autumn leaves. A small lake to the right was a riot of color, too, with a carpet of late-blooming wildflowers lining its banks and the blue lake sparkling in the sunshine. What a peaceful, tranquil scene, undisturbed at this early hour. It might almost have made Reggie forget her troubles. But not quite.

She rang for a maid, hoping she would *not* get Mrs. Oates, the housekeeper, who was just as Hallie had described her, a dragon. What a crass, pretentious, annoying creature she was. Imagine, insisting on showing Reggie to a guest room, and a small one at that. Reggie had set her straight quickly. Conceding that the rooms meant for the lady of the house were occupied by Miriam Eden, who couldn't be expected to vacate them overnight, she pointed out that the master's rooms were empty and would do very well.

This had appalled the housekeeper. Only a sitting room separated the two large bedrooms, each of which had a door into the sitting room. Lady Miriam had one of the bedrooms.

Reggie won her way after subtly reminding Mrs. Oates that she was the new mistress of the house. Miriam Eden might have continued to run Silverley after her husband's death, but Silverley actually belonged to Nicholas, and Reggie was Nicholas' wife.

Mrs. Oates cautioned her to be quiet when they passed through the sitting room next to Miriam's room. Reggie was told that Miriam wasn't feeling well and had retired early, which was why Reggie hadn't been properly greeted.

Truth to tell, Reggie was relieved. She was exhausted, embarrassed by the absence of her husband of only a few hours, and so full of bitterness that she was unfit to meet anyone.

She settled into Nicholas' room, and found it was utterly devoid of personal items. Somehow, that made everything worse.

The servant who answered Reggie's call was dark-haired and dark-skinned and just the opposite of talkative Hallie. She said hardly a word as she helped Reggie dress and arrange her hair, then showed her to the breakfast room.

This room was at the front of the house and had full benefit of the morning sun. The table was set for one. A slight? On a side wall was a large rosewood china cabinet filled with fine gold-rimmed china with a floral design of pink and white. Between the windows on the back wall was a lovely carved oak and ebony buffet.

Hallie came in, smiling brightly, carrying a large covered platter which she set on the buffet.

"Mornin', mum. Hope you had a pleasant night."

"Indeed I did. Has the Countess come down yet?" Reggie indicated the single setting.

"She's off on her mornin' ride. She never eats this early, mum."

"Neither do I, really. Why don't you show me the rest of the house now instead?"

"But there's all this food," Hallie said in surprise, removing the lid on the platter to reveal eggs, sausage, kippers, ham, jellies, toast and rolls, even two delicious-looking tarts.

"Heavens!" Reggie gasped. "I wasn't supposed to eat all of that, was I?"

Hallie giggled. "Cook was out to make a better impression, seein' as how she only sent up cold dishes for you last night."

"Well, then I'll just take this with me, and one of these," Reggie said, wrapping a fat sausage in a roll and taking one of the tarts. "And now we can have that tour."

"But shouldn't Mrs. Oates—?"

"Yes," Reggie interrupted conspiratorially, "I suppose she should. But I can let her show me around again later. Right now I would like to see just how big Silverley is, and I would like pleasant company along."

Hallie giggled again. "There's none of us likes Mrs. Oates too well, but she does run a tight ship, as she's so fond of sayin'. Come along then, your ladyship. But if Mrs. Oates should come upon us—"

"Not to worry," Reggie assured her. "I'll think of something to explain why you're with me. You won't be blamed."

The house was indeed big. Near the entryway they passed a billiard room with not one but three tables in it. There were more rooms than Reggie could remember, each filled with lovely Chippendale furnishings and Queen Anne pieces. Many of the high ceilings were arched and decorated with lovely gilded plasterwork. Some had large, gorgeously crafted chandeliers.

There was a music room decorated in green and white and, to the right of the drawing room, an antechamber with floor-to-ceiling stained-glass windows bathing the room in colors which were sharply set off against the white marble floor. Plush red benches hugged the walls. Reggie was astonished by the beauty of the place.

At the back of the house, off the large, formal dining room, was the conservatory. Along a walkway that circled the room were chairs and sofas and statues on pedestals. There were potted plants at the sides of wide stone steps leading down to a fountain in the center of the room. Everywhere were trees and autumn flowers. Reggie was sorry she had missed seeing the room in summer when the indoor garden would have been in full bloom.

Upstairs, the whole length of the back of the house was taken up by the master suites. From right to left were the lord's chamber, the sitting room, the lady's chamber, and then a nursery. There were rooms for a nurse and lady's maid.

The tour took just under an hour, and Hallie was able to escape back to the servants' domain in the center of the house right of the main hall before anyone discovered what they had been doing. Reggie settled in the library then to await Lady Miriam.

Her wait was short. The Countess came in straight from her riding excursion, dressed in a deep violet habit and still carrying a riding quirt. She showed only a moment's surprise at finding the room occupied. She then proceeded to ignore Reggie while she removed her hat and gloves.

So that was the way it was to be? Well, it helped explain Nicholas' propensity to rudeness.

Reggie was able to study Miriam Eden while she was being ignored. For a woman likely nearing fifty, she was holding up remarkably well. She was trim and youthful, her posture stiffly erect. Her tightly wound blond hair was fading, but there was no gray in it. Her eyes were a wintry gray. Hard, cold eyes, but perhaps they smiled sometimes? Reggie thought not.

There was a slight physical resemblance to Miriam's sister Eleanor, but the physical similarity was where it began and ended. The younger sister exuded warmth and gentleness, and there was none in the Countess. How could she possibly live with this woman?

"Should I call you Mother?" she asked suddenly, and there was a perceptible start from the Countess. She turned and looked at Reggie squarely. The gray eyes were frigid, the lips pursed. She most likely wasn't used to being addressed before she condescended to speak, Reggie reflected.

In a brittle voice Miriam replied, "Don't. I'm not your mother any more than I'm—"

"Oh, dear," Reggie interrupted, "I gathered there was an estrangement between you and Nicholas when you didn't come to our wedding, but I—"

"I was needed here," Miriam said stiffly.

"—didn't realize you had disowned your son," Reggie finished.

"What are you doing here, and without Nicholas?" Miriam asked.

"Nicholas and I simply don't suit, you see, and so we couldn't possibly live together," Reggie replied.

There was an astonished pause. "Then why marry?"

Reggie shrugged and gave her a dazzling smile. "It seemed a good idea. For me anyway. I was tired of the constant whirl of parties and such. I much prefer the country life."

"Which doesn't explain why Nicholas would marry."

Reggie raised a brow. "Surely you know why. I wasn't present myself when Nicholas agreed to marry me, but your sister and mother-in-law were there."

Miriam frowned. Of course she wouldn't ask the same question again. Nor would she admit that she didn't communicate with Eleanor or Rebecca. She was being left to wonder about the marriage, which was just what Reggie had intended.

"We are rather isolated here," Miriam warned.

Reggie smiled. "That sounds wonderful. My only regret is that I must ask you to select other rooms for yourself."

Miriam drew herself up stiffly. "I am told you have taken over Nicholas' rooms."

"But they won't do for long, you see. I must have the nursery close at hand." She patted her belly lovingly.

The Countess appeared ready to choke. "Nonsense. You can't be expecting. You were married only yesterday, and even if you stopped at some inn after the wedding, you couldn't possibly know—"

"You are forgetting your son's reputation, Lady Miriam. Nicholas is an expert seducer. I was quite helpless against his charm. I am now four months along."

The Countess stared at Reggie's belly, and Reggie said, "Isn't it fortunate I am not showing?"

"I don't see how you can think any of this fortunate in any way," Miriam said with stiff hauteur. "People can count, you know. It's shameful that you don't even blush when you—just shameful."

"I don't blush, madame, because I feel no shame," Reggie replied coldly. "No shame, no guilt. And if my child is born five months after the marriage, well, other babies have been born early. At least I have a husband, even if he won't be around very much. And my child has a name.

Considering your son's reputation, no one will be surprised that Nicholas could not be held off for the four long months of our engagement."

"Well, I never!"

"Haven't you?"

Miriam Eden turned crimson at the innuendo and stalked out of the room. Reggie sighed. Well, she had made her own bed, so to speak. She shouldn't have alienated the sour old bird, but . . . Reggie smiled. That last look of outrage on the Countess' face had been worth whatever unpleasantness she could expect from the woman.

Chapter Twenty-two

"Putting on a little weight, aren't you, puss?" Anthony asked as he kissed Reggie's cheek and then sat down next to her on the lawn. "Must be eating because you're miserable. And no wonder, living with that cold fish."

Reggie put down her sketch pad and smiled fondly at her uncle. "If you mean Miriam, she's not so bad. After our first two rows, we reached an agreement. We simply don't speak to each other."

"I suppose that's one way to get along with someone," Anthony replied in his driest tone.

Reggie laughed delightedly. "Oh, Tony, I've missed you this last month. I really did expect you sooner. Everyone else has been here."

"You wouldn't have cared to see me right after I heard what was going on. It has taken me this long to cool off."

She sighed. "I suppose you wanted to kill him again?"

"Damned right. I tried to find the blackguard but he has disappeared."

"I could have saved you the trouble of looking," she told him levelly. "He told me he was leaving England. I guess he meant it."

Anthony's temper rose. "We had better talk of something else, puss. Your husband is not my favorite subject. What is that you're drawing?"

Reggie handed over her sketch pad. "Just a hound chasing falling leaves. He ran off into the woods a few minutes before you arrived. I've been getting some good poses of the gardeners, though, and the grooms exercising the horses." He turned the pages and admired her work.

"That's Sir Tyrwhitt, a neighbor," she said when he got to her sketch of a middle-aged dandy. "Would you believe he and the Countess—?"

"No!"

"Well, I don't know for certain, mind you, but she's like a different person around him, actually girlish, if you can believe that."

"I can't," he said firmly.

Reggie laughed. "And that's Squire Gibbs and his young wife Faith. I like her a lot. Miriam is furious that she and I have become friends. An invitation to Silverley has always been an honor, you see, and so when I gave Faith an open welcome, the Countess took to her room for two days to express her displeasure."

"Likes to lord it over the lesser gentry, does she?" he asked.

"Oh, she's very serious about it, Tony."

Anthony turned another page. "Good God, who are those characters?"

"Two of the gardeners, I guess. There are so many servants here I haven't met them all yet. I drew these men yesterday down by the lake."

"You must have been particularly gloomy yesterday. You made them look so sinister."

Reggie shrugged. "It wasn't my mood. They *were* sinister-looking. They moved on when they saw me drawing them, so I had to finish the sketch from memory."

"They look like waterfront brawlers," he said, "not gardeners."

"Oh, stuff. All the people here are really nice, once you get to know them."

"Except the cold fish."

"Don't be unkind, Tony. I don't think she's led a very happy life."

"That's no excuse for forcing her unhappiness on others. And speaking of—"

"Don't," she said stonily. "I'm perfectly fine, Tony, really."

"You can't lie to me, puss. Look at you. You wouldn't be putting on weight if you were exercising, and the only time you mope about and ignore your health is when you're unhappy. I know you, remember? You're just like your mother in certain ways. But you don't have to stay here, you know that. You can come home."

"I know I've made a mistake, Tony, but I don't want the world to know it. Do you understand?"

"For his sake?" he asked sharply.

"No," she replied, then added hesitantly, "The weight you keep harping on isn't what you think, Tony. I'm pregnant."

There was a moment's startled silence. Then he said, "You can't know this soon. You've only been married a month."

"I *am* pregnant, Tony. Very, very pregnant."

His cobalt-blue eyes, so like hers, grew wide, then narrowed furiously. "He didn't! I'll kill him!"

"No, you won't," she replied, vetoing his favorite solution. "This is going to be your first great-nephew or -niece. How could you explain to the child that you'd killed his father?"

"He deserves a sound beating at the very least," growled her uncle.

"Perhaps," she agreed. "But not for seducing me before the wedding. I was a willing participant in the making of this child."

"Don't bother defending him, puss. You forget he's just like me and I know *all* the tricks. He seduced you."

"But I knew exactly what I was doing," she insisted. "I . . . it was foolish in the extreme, I know that now, but I thought it would help to change his attitude. He kept trying to get me to break the engagement, you see. He never deceived me into thinking he was willing to marry me."

"He agreed!"

"Yes, but he thought he could make me jilt him before the wedding."

"You should have."

"Should haves don't count, Tony."

"I know, I know, but blister it, Reggie, how could he desert you, knowing—"

"I never told him! You don't think I would try to keep a man *that* way, do you?" She sounded genuinely shocked.

"Oh," Anthony said, brought up short. Then he said somberly, "Honestly, puss, you really are just like your mother. Melissa gave birth to you only a few months after her wedding, too."

Reggie gasped. "Really? But . . . why didn't any of you tell me that?"

Anthony turned red and looked away. "Well, were we to say, 'By the way, dear, you only just made legitimacy.' "

She giggled and leaned over to kiss his cheek. "Well, thank you for telling me. I'm glad to know I'm not the only promiscuous one in the family—besides Uncle Jason, I mean," she teased.

"Promiscuous! At least your father didn't desert Melissa. He adored her. He would have married her sooner if her stiff-necked pride hadn't kept them apart."

"I never heard any of this," she whispered, shocked.

"They had some terrible rows, they did. She broke the engagement three times, swearing each time that she never wanted to see him again."

"But everyone always told me how much they loved each other," Reggie protested.

"They did, puss," he assured her. "But she was as hot-tempered as I am. The slightest little disagreement got out of hand. Thank God you didn't inherit *that* from her."

"Oh, I don't know," Reggie mused. "If he ever does come back, I'm not going to forgive him. He made me love him, and then he wouldn't even give our marriage a chance. I do have some pride, even if I did practically beg him not to leave. My love has turned to . . . well, it infuriates me even to think about him."

"Good for you. Think about coming home, will you? There's no reason you can't be with your family for the birth. We'll keep outsiders well away from you."

"Well, I do have Meg, and I—"

"Think about it," he ordered sternly.

She grinned at him. "Yes, uncle."

Chapter Twenty-three

It was another damp November morning, and Reggie walked down to the lake with her sketch pad. Uncle Tony had spent the night, and she had seen him off early, promising again to think about coming home. She would think about it, or at least think about returning to London, where she would be closer to the family. She could keep up appearances by moving into Nicholas' townhouse. That was an idea. And it would even give her something to do, now that she was restricted as to physical activities. She could redecorate his London house, spend some of his money.

Trouble was, she had come to enjoy the tranquillity of Silverley. At least it was tranquil when Miriam wasn't around. Reggie got along well with the servants, too. Even Mrs. Oates had unbent surprisingly the moment she learned Reggie was expecting a baby. It seemed Mrs. Oates loved babies. Who would have guessed?

Reggie looked at the gray mansion wistfully. She might have been truly happy there. She pictured her children running across the Silverley lawns, sailing little boats on the lake in summer, ice-skating in winter. She even pictured their father giving them their first ponies and showing them their paces. Somehow she knew Nicholas would have a gentle hand with children. She sighed, a deep, long sigh, pulling up the hood of her fur cloak and casting a look at the heavy bank of clouds above her. Meg was right. It was getting too cold to be sketching outdoors.

She tucked her sketchbook under her arm and turned to go back to the house. She would sketch the lake another time. It was then that she saw one of the servants hurrying toward her, coming not from the house but from the woods.

On the other side of those woods lay her own estate. She hadn't gone there yet. The melancholy caused by thinking about that place where her parents had died was too much. She would go there eventually, she told herself. Eventually, yes. And someday she would show it to her child. The estate had belonged to his . . . her grandparents.

As he got closer she recognized the servant as one of the men she had sketched the other day. He was carrying an oversized sack used, she guessed, to gather dead leaves. He looked as strange as she remembered. A vague sense of danger rose in her.

Maybe it was the full, unkempt beard and long shaggy hair. Or maybe it was his bold demeanor. Whatever, she decided not to wait for him to reach her. She would run to the house.

She stopped, calling herself a ninny. She was letting her imagination run wild. Silly of her. He was only a gardener, after all.

Reggie had no sooner finished the thought than the man reached her, took a moment to catch his breath, then smoothly yanked the sack he carried over her head and shoulders. Her first impulse was to scream, but surprise overtook her until the sack was yanked all the way down her body, and her scream was only a tiny muffled sound.

Her assailant wasted no time shouldering his prize and rushing back into the woods. An expensive, well-sprung coach waited there, hidden, with two high-stepping grays straining to be off. A man was in the driver's seat, ready to crack the whip at the first sign of pursuit. The man on the ground glared up at him.

"Ye could at least get your arse down 'ere and open the bleedin' door, 'Onry. She might look like a light bit of fluff, but after that long trek she don't feel light."

Henri, or 'Onry, as his English friends were wont to call him, chuckled at Artie's surliness, a sure sign that he was no longer worried about their mission. "Then no one is giving chase?"

"Not as I saw. Now give us a 'and. Ye know the cap's orders about treatin' 'er real gentle."

They laid Reggie on a thickly padded seat and quickly wrapped a rope around her knees to hold the sack in place. "This will sweeten his temper, yes? Never thought we would catch our fish this soon."

"Give it up, Frenchy. Ye'll never sound like an Englishman, so stop tryin'. And I bet ye thought we'd be freezin out 'ere in these woods for weeks, eh?"

"Well, did you not?"

"Yeah, but I tol' ye it pays to be ready, and see if she didn't come right out to us. A fine piece of luck! If this don't please the cap'n, what will, I ask ye?"

"The little fish catching the bigger one."

"Right ye are. Let's just 'ope that don't take too long either."

"You will ride back here with her to see she does not fall off the seat, or do you wish me—"

"Ye can 'ave the pleasure. I don't trust ye gettin' this lumberin' land ship out o' these woods in one piece. That'll be my job." He chuckled. "I take it ye fancy that arrangement?"

"As you please, Artie." The young Frenchman flashed a grin at the Englishman.

"Just don't get a mind to sample the goods, mate. Cap'n wouldn't like that a'tall," the man said seriously before climbing into the driver's seat again. The coach rocked forward.

Reggie's mind was racing. This had to be a simple kidnapping. A demand for money would be met, and then she would be returned home. Nothing to worry about.

She wished her body would see it that way. She was trembling violently. They were taking her to a captain who didn't want her roughed up. Yes, a kidnapping. And he was a sea captain, she surmised, because there was a large harbor in Southampton. Why, Nicholas' own shipping firm was located there.

She forced herself to recall every word they'd spoken. What was that about the little fish catching the bigger one? She strained all her senses, alert to every sound, every movement.

It wasn't more than half an hour before their pace slowed and she knew they were in Southampton.

"A few more minutes, *chérie,* and we will have you inside and more comfortable," her captor assured her.

"Inside?" Not "on board?" Well, he was French, after all, so maybe that had been a language problem. Oh dear. The tight sack around her cloak was beginning to make her itch and sweat. And to think she'd believed there would be no more adventures once she was grown!

The coach stopped and she was carefully lifted out, the Englishman carrying her this time. There were no sounds of a waterfront, no waves lapping against a ship, no creak of nearby timber at anchor. Where were they? There was no gangplank to maneuver across, either, but steps were mounted. Then a door was opened.

"Hell's bells, Artie, you got her already?"

"Well, this ain't ballast I'm totin', lad. Where do I put 'er?"

"There's a room ready for her upstairs. Why don't you let me carry her?"

"I can box yer ears and not drop 'er, lad. Want to test me?"

There was a deep chuckle. "You're too touchy by half, Artie. Come on, I'll show you where the room is."

"Where's the cap'n?"

"He's not expected back until tonight. I guess that means I get to take care of her, don't it?"

"Will ye listen to this young cockerel, 'Onry?" Artie demanded. "Not on yer life, lado, will we be leavin' ye alone with the likes o' 'er. Yer the only one round 'ere who might think 'e can get away with a little hanky-panky 'cause the cap's yer old man. Don't ye be thinkin' about it while I'm around."

"I said take care of her—not take *care* of her," the boy shot back.

"Is the lad blushin', 'Onry? Is that a real blush I see?"

"Run along, *mon ami,*" Henri said to the boy. "You questioned his strength, and he will not let up on you today."

"Well, at least let me see what she looks like."

"Oh, she's a pretty one, lado." Artie grinned. "In fact, when the cap sets eyes on 'er, 'e's likely to forget what 'e wanted 'er brought 'ere for. Might just keep 'er for 'imself. Might just indeed."

They carried her to her upstairs room, and then she was set down on her feet. She swayed and nearly fell. The rope at her knees was removed, and the sack lifted off. But the little room was so dark, its windows boarded up, that she had trouble seeing for a moment.

A deep breath of air was her first order of business. Then she focused on the three men, her captors and the boy, moving toward the door. The younger one was looking at her over his shoulder, his mouth hanging open.

"Just a minute, *if* you please," she called to the departing men. "I demand to know why I was brought here."

"The cap'n will be tellin' ye that when 'e gets 'ere, m'lady."

"And who is the captain?"

"No need for names," the brawnier of the two answered, offering a placating tone in response to her haughty one.

"Yet I know your name, Artie. And I know your name, Henri. I even—" She stopped before telling them she had sketched both of them. "I wish to know why I am here."

"Ye'll 'ave to wait and talk to the cap'n. Now, there's a lamp there on the table, and ye'll be fed shortly. Just settle down and make yourself comfy-like."

She swung around, furious, her back to them. The door closed and a key was turned in the lock. She let out a sigh. Where had she gotten the nerve to act so hoity-toity? They were sinister-looking characters despite their bantering manner and placating voices. Well, at least she hadn't shown them any fear. They wouldn't see a Malory cringe. That was a huge satisfaction.

She sat down warily on a rickety chair, wondering forlornly if that might just be her last moment of satisfaction for a long while.

Chapter Twenty-four

The food was delicious, even in Reggie's nervous state. She ate her fill of squab pie, rice pudding, and saffron cakes. There was a delicate wine, too. But once the distraction of dining was over, she went back to worrying.

Henri had brought her the food. He had put on a very rakish ruffled silk shirt; black breeches with high, wide-topped boots; and a long, coatlike vest. Good Lord, all he lacked was an earring. He had even shaved everything except his tightly curled mustache. Why?

What *had* she gotten herself into this time? Feminine clothes were laid out on the bed, brand-new from the look of them, silk robe, a more discreet linen nightgown, furry bedroom slippers, and, embarrassingly, underthings. On a vanity were toilet articles, brush, comb, a very expensive perfume, all new.

The young man had come in to start a fire for her early in the afternoon, and Artie stood guard at the door. He smiled timidly at her. She glared back frostily. She ignored the boy entirely.

It was night now, but she refused to make use of the large bed. She would stay awake all night if she had to, but she wouldn't relax until she had met the captain and given him a piece of her mind.

She fed the fire with wood the boy had left her, then drew a chair up to it, tucking her feet beneath her dark blue velvet skirt. The room was warm and she began feeling sleepy.

She almost didn't hear the key turning in the door. The sound made her stiffen, but she didn't turn around. Damned if she would deign to notice either Artie or Henri.

"My son tells me you're a raving beauty," said a deep voice. "Let me see what has him so smitten. Present yourself, Lady Montieth."

She stood and, very slowly, turned to look at him. Her eyes went wide in shock.

"Uncle James!" *"Regan?"* they cried at once.

She recovered first. "Oh, uncle! You can't mean to kidnap me for another three months of fun aboard the *Maiden Anne?* Don't you think I'm a bit old for that now?"

Looking as confused as a man ever did, he held out his arms. "Come here, sweet, and give us a hug. My God, you really have turned into a raving beauty."

She hugged him happily. "Well, it's been three years, Uncle James, and I only saw you for an hour that time. It's unfair, you know, having to sneak around to see my own uncle. Isn't it time you made up with your brothers?"

"I might be willing," he said quietly. "But I doubt they are, Regan."

He had always liked being different, even to having his own special name for her. Her uncle, the pirate, had stolen her from under his brothers' noses when they refused to allow him to see her. He'd taken her for a fabulous adventure aboard his ship, determined to have his rightful time with her. She had been twelve, and those incredible three months still lived vividly in her mind.

Of course, they both paid a price for it. James was already in disgrace for being a pirate. When he returned Reggie, all three brothers had thrashed him soundly for putting her in danger. He was disowned by all of them, even Tony, whom he'd always been so close to. James suffered over the rift, and Reggie suffered for being the cause of it. He never blamed her, but that only made her feel worse.

She pushed away from James and looked him over. He hadn't changed very much in three years. He was still big and blond, as handsome as ever—and as outrageous. Look what he had done by bringing her there.

"I shouldn't even speak to you," she said sternly. "You gave me a terrible fright. You might at least have told your men to inform me it was the notorious Captain Hawke who was having me abducted."

James exploded. "I'll have their bloody hides, depend upon it! Damnation!" He threw open the door and bellowed, "Artie! . . . Henri!"

"Uncle, no," Reggie protested.

James' rages weren't like Tony's. Tony could be talked around. Even Jason, a stubborn bull when he was angry, could be talked to. But James Malory was frightening. Though his anger had never been directed at her, she feared it.

"Uncle James," she said, "the men were really very gentle with me, and they saw diligently to my comfort. I wasn't frightened," she lied.

"A mistake has been made, Regan, and I'll accept no excuses for it."

A black brow rose sharply. "You mean I wasn't supposed to be brought here?"

"Of course not. I would have come to see you before I left England again. I wouldn't have brought you to me—certainly not in this fashion."

The two miscreants appeared in the doorway just then, uneasy under James' cold stare. "You wanted us, Cap'n?"

"Do you know who you have brought me?" James asked softly. It was his unpredictable tone.

Henri divined the trouble first. "The wrong lady?"

"May I present gentlemen"—James extended an arm toward Reggie, exploded—*"my niece!"*

"Merde!"

"Yeah," Artie breathed.

Another man appeared in the doorway. "What the devil are you shouting about, Hawke?"

"Connie!" Reggie cried in delight, and rushed into his arms.

This was the man who had taught her to fence, to climb to the crow's nest, even to sail the ship when her uncle wasn't looking. Conrad Sharpe, James' closest friend in childhood, was now first mate on the *Maiden Anne*. A more roguish, though lovable pirate had never lived.

"Is that you, little squirt?" Conrad bellowed. "Damn me, if it isn't!" He hugged her close.

"It's been years and years!"

"Hasn't it though?" Conrad chuckled. Finally he caught sight of James' scowling face and cleared his throat. "I, ah—I don't think you're supposed to be here, Regan."

"So I gather." She turned back to James. "Well, uncle, here are the scoundrels. Will you have them flogged for this dastardly mistake? If so, I want to watch."

"Regan!"

"You're not going to?" She glanced at her abductors. "Well, gentlemen, you are indeed fortunate my uncle is in such a charitable mood. He's letting you off light. I would have taken the skin from your backs, to be sure."

"All right, Regan, you win," James relented, nodding curtly for Artie and Henri to leave.

"She hasn't changed at all, has she, Hawke?" Conrad chuckled when the door closed behind the two kidnappers.

"Cunning little baggage," James grumbled.

Reggie grinned at them both. "But aren't you glad to see me?"

"Let me think about it."

"Uncle James!"

"Of course, sweet." James gave her his open smile, the one reserved for those he loved. "But you really have stirred up a problem here. I was expecting someone else, and now I suppose the watch will be up at Silverley."

"Do you want to tell me what that is all about?" she asked him.

"Nothing that concerns you, Regan."

"Don't put me off, uncle. I'm not a child anymore, you know."

"So I see." He grinned. "Look at her, Connie. She's the very image of my sister, isn't she?"

"And to think she could have been my daughter," Conrad said wistfully.

"Oh, Connie, you too?" Reggie asked softly.

"Everyone loved your mother, squirt, even me," Conrad admitted gruffly.

"Is that why you took me under your wing?"

"Never think it. You wormed your way into my heart all on your own."

"Then maybe you'll tell me what this is all about?"

"No, squirt." Connie shook his head, grinning at James. "This is all his doing. If you mean to ferret out what you want to know, turn those big blues on him."

"Uncles James?"

"It's . . . some unfinished business I have here. Nothing for you to fret about."

"But isn't the Countess a bit old for you?"

"It's not like that, Regan," James protested. "And what the devil do you mean, old?"

"Well, she's not really ancient-old, I suppose," Reggie corrected herself. "She takes very good care of herself, too. But what business can you have with her?"

"Not her. Her husband."

"He's dead."

"Dead? Dead!" James looked at Connie. "Damnation! He can't be dead!"

Reggie looked at Connie, bewildered. "He had a score to settle, squirt," Connie explained. "Now it looks like fate has intervened."

"When did he die?" James asked harshly. "How?"

Reggie was becoming concerned. "Well, I don't actually know how. It's been quite a few years though."

James' look of fury turned to one of surprise. Then both men began to laugh, confounding Reggie further. "Ah, sweet, you had me going there," James chuckled. "But I don't believe we are thinking about the same man. It's the young Viscount I want."

"Nicholas Eden?" she cried.

"Now you have it. Do you know him?"

"Very well," she said.

"Then perhaps you can tell me where he is. Lord knows no one else can. I've looked everywhere. I swear the lad is hiding from me—and with good reason.

"Good God!" Reggie gasped. "You had me kidnapped as a lure to bring Nicholas to you, didn't you?"

"Not you, sweet," James assured her. "Those idiots thought you were Eden's wife."

Reggie moved closer to Conrad, took a long breath, and then said hesitantly, "Uncle James, your men didn't make a mistake."

"They—"

"—didn't make a mistake," she finished. "I am Nicholas' wife."

The tense silence that followed wracked everyone's nerves. James stiffened. Conrad put a protective arm around Reggie, and together they waited for the explosion. Before it came, the door opened and the young man leaned in. "Henri just told me she's my cousin? Is it true?"

James glowered. "Not now, Jeremy!" The boy flinched.

"No! Don't go, Jeremy." Reggie caught the boy's hand and pulled him into the room. "Uncle James is angry with me, not with you."

"I am not angry with you, Regan." He tightly controlled his voice.

"You were going to yell at me."

"I was not going to yell at you!" he exploded.

"Well, that's a relief," Reggie said.

James opened his mouth, clamped it shut, and sighed with exasperation. His eyes met Conrad's and the message was clearly, *You handle her. I give up.*

Conrad made the introductions. "Jeremy Malory, Lady Regina Mal—ah, Eden, Countess of Montieth."

"Hell's bells!" Jeremy grinned. "So that's why his temper's flown."

"Yes, I don't think he likes . . . well, never mind." She grinned up at the handsome young man whose coloring was exactly the same as hers. "I didn't get a good look at you before. Heavens, you look exactly like your Uncle Tony when he was younger." She turned toward James. "Were you going to keep him a secret forever, uncle?"

"There's no secret," James said gruffly.

"The family doesn't know."

"*I* only found out five years ago. And I haven't exactly been on speaking terms with my brothers since then."

"You could have told *me* when I last saw you."

"There wasn't time to go into it then, Regan. 'By the way, I have a son.' You would have plagued me with your endless questions, and Jason would have sent the servants out to hunt you down and find me."

"I suppose. But how did you find him? It was five years ago?"

"A little less than that actually," he replied. "And we just bumped into each other in a tavern where he was working."

"You should have seen your uncle's face, squirt, when he saw the boy." Conrad smiled, remembering. "He knew the boy looked familiar, yet he didn't quite know why. And Jeremy couldn't take his eyes off him either."

"I recognized him, you see," Jeremy put in. "I'd never actually seen him before, but my mum described him to me so often I would have known him anywhere. I finally got up the nerve to ask him right out if he was James Malory."

"You can imagine the reaction," Conrad said gleefully. "Everyone on the waterfront knew him only as Captain Hawke, and here was this half-pint lad calling him by his real name. And then, to top it, he says he's his son! Hawke wasn't laughing along with me, though. He took in the boy's coloring, asked him some questions, and damned if he wasn't the proud papa overnight."

"So I have a new cousin, one nearly full grown." Reggie grinned. "Oh, this is famous. Welcome to the family, Jeremy."

He was nearly as tall as his father, which was much taller than Reggie. She leaned up on tiptoes to kiss his cheek, and was surprised by the exuberant hug that squeezed her breathless. The boy wouldn't let go.

"That's enough, Jeremy. Jeremy!"

The lad stepped back. "Can cousins marry?" he asked.

Conrad guffawed. James scowled. Reggie blushed. Now she understood the motive behind that hug.

"Another rake in the family, Uncle James?" she said wryly.

"So it would seem," James sighed. "And learning all the tricks too early."

"He only follows your example," Conrad put in smoothly.

"Well, he's off to bed now."

"Hell's bells," Jeremy protested.

"Do it," James ordered sternly. "You can see more of your cousin in the morning if you can mind your manners and remember she's your cousin, not some tavern wench."

After that set-down the boy might have been expected to leave shamefaced. Not Jeremy. He grinned roguishly at Reggie and winked.

"I'll dream of you, sweet Regan, tonight and every night hereafter."

She nearly laughed. The audacity! She gave him a pert look and said, "Don't be obnoxious, cousin. You held me close enough to tell I'm very much married."

Reggie groaned, damning her heedless tongue. Jeremy cast one look at his father and ran for the door. She steeled herself, sure James had taken her meaning quite clearly.

"Is it true?"

"Yes."

"Damnation take him! How did this come about, Regan? How the devil did you come to marry that—that—"

"You sound as bad as Tony," she cut him short. "You each want a piece of Nicholas. So find him, divide him up between you, cut him into pieces, shoot him, kill him. What do I care? He's only my husband and the father of my child."

"Easy, squirt," Conrad said softly. "Your uncle gave up his plans for the lad the moment he learned you were married to him."

"What plans?" she demanded. "What is this all about, Uncle James?"

"It's a long story, sweet, and—"

"Please don't treat me like a child again, Uncle James."

"Very well," he said. "The short of it is I thrashed him soundly for some insults he had dealt me. For this I ended up in jail."

"And nearly hanged," Conrad added.

"No," Reggie gasped, "I can't believe Nicholas—"

"He gave Hawke's name to the authorities, squirt. The *Maiden Anne* might not fly the Jolly Roger anymore, but England never forgets. Hawke was tried for piracy. He managed to escape, no thanks to Montieth."

"You see why the lads were careful not to mention my name in front of you," James said. "I had to arrange my death; otherwise I would have had to leave England immediately. I'm sorry, Regan," he added gently. "I would have preferred you didn't now what kind of mess your husband has been involved in."

"Don't apologize, uncle," Reggie said tightly. "It only amazes me how often I am reminded of how wrong I was about him. I just don't understand how I could have fooled myself into thinking I loved him."

"Don't you?"

"No. And don't look at me that way. I really don't love him."

"Does she protest too much, Hawke?" Conrad grinned.

"Oh, you think so?" Reggie said heatedly. "Well, would *you* love a wife that deserted you the very day she married you? I will never forgive him, never. Even if he didn't want to marry me, even if he felt justified in leaving, he's hateful for not . . . well, he's simply hateful."

The two men exchanged a glance. "Where is he?" asked her uncle.

"He left England. He couldn't even stand to be in the same country with me."

"He has estates elsewhere?"

She shrugged, lost in her own misery once again. "He once mentioned owning property in the West Indies, but I don't know if he went there. What does it matter? He has no intention of coming back. He made that perfectly—"

She stopped as a commotion started downstairs. James nodded to Conrad to see what it was. The moment Conrad opened the door it was clear the scuffle was going on nearer than the floor below. James followed Conrad out, Reggie right behind the men.

A fight was taking place on the stairs, between Henri and—*Tony?* Good Lord, it *was* Tony! Artie already lay sprawled at the bottom of the stairs. Henri was about to join him there.

Reggie pushed her way between James and Conrad. "Tony, stop!"

Anthony saw her and let go of Henri, who slumped down onto the steps.

"So I was right!" Tony glared, seeing his brother. "You didn't learn your lesson the last time you ran off with her, did you, James?"

"May I ask how you found us?" James inquired with profound calm.

"You may not!" Anthony retorted.

"Tony, you don't understand—" she began.

"Reggie!"

She gritted her teeth. Tony was so stubborn. This was an opportunity she couldn't pass up. The brothers were together, and it was a chance for them to mend their rift. But if Tony wanted only to drag her straight out of here, how could she get him to calm down and talk to James?

"Ohhhh!" Reggie gripped James' arm with one hand and her belly with the other, doubling over as if in pain. "I feel . . . ohhhh! Too much . . . excitement. A bed, uncle. Get me to a bed."

James lifted her gently in his arms. He didn't speak, but he did give her a doubtful look when his eye caught hers. Reggie ignored this and groaned again, quite effectively.

Jeremy came running down the hall toward them, tucking an open shirt into his trousers, both donned hastily. "What happened? What's wrong with Regan?" No one answered him as James and Conrad hurried back to the bedroom with Reggie. "Who are you?" Jeremy demanded as Anthony barged past him to follow the others.

Anthony stopped cold. He'd given the boy only a glance, but it was enough. It was like looking into a mirror of the past. "Who the bloody hell are *you?*"

Conrad laughed and came out of the bedroom. "He's not yours, if that's what you're thinking, Sir Anthony. But he's family, all right. James' boy."

Jeremy covered Anthony's gasp of surprise with his own gasp. "Uncle Tony? Hell's bells! I thought I'd never get to meet any of my father's kin, but here's Regan first, and now you, and all in one night." He grabbed Anthony in a bear hug that damned near knocked the breath out of him. Tony gripped the boy's wide shoulders then and returned the hug, surprising Conrad. "Don't go away, youngun," he said gruffly before moving on to the bedroom.

Seeing Reggie stretched out on the bed, James beside her, Tony's fury returned. "Confound you, James! Have you no bloody sense a'tall, dragging her around in her condition?"

"He didn't drag me," Reggie protested.

"Don't lie for me, sweet," James admonished her gently. He rose and faced his younger brother. "You are quite correct, Tony. If I had any sense, I'd have found out who Montieth's new wife was before I had her brought here to flush him out."

Tony looked bewildered, then exasperated. "A mistake?"

"A colossal one."

"That's still no excuse," Tony grumbled.

"Agreed."

"Will you stop agreeing with me!"

James chuckled. "You don't need an excuse to have a go at me, if that's what you're itching to do, brother."

"Don't do it, Uncle Tony," Jeremy said as he entered the room. "I would hate to have a row with you when I've only just met you."

"He's very protective of his old man," Conrad put in. "Thinks his father can't manage on his own anymore after the grueling excercise Montieth put him through."

"I thought I told you to go to bed, Jeremy." But James' scowl was directed at his first mate.

"I thought you said *you* thrashed Nicholas, Uncle James," Reggie said.

"Oh, he did, squirt." Conrad grinned. "He walked away from the encounter—just barely, mind you—whereas your husband, no doubt, did not."

"No doubt?" she echoed. Conrad shrugged. "We left while he was still out."

"You mean," she demanded furiously, "you abandoned him when he was hurt?"

Conrad and James flinched. "He got help quickly enough, Regan, fast enough to land me in jail within the hour."

"What's this?" Anthony cried.

"Oh, the story should delight you, Tony," Reggie said crossly. "It seems you're not the only one who wants my husband's blood."

Anthony frowned. "I thought you were done defending that blackguard?"

"I am," she replied stiffly. "But he's mine to deal with, *not yours*. I don't need my uncles interfering when I am perfectly capable of making Nicholas Eden regret returning to England, if he ever does."

"That sounds ominous enough," Anthony agreed.

"Doesn't it though?" James smiled. "I almost wish he would return to her."

"Famous!" Reggie snapped. "I'm so glad you two have something in common again."

"Don't get your hopes up, puss," Anthony warned her. "I don't associate with pirates who abscond with children."

"Oh, bother, Tony," Reggie said irritably. "That was years ago. Let go of it, do."

"Who are you calling a pirate?" Jeremy demanded belligerently.

"Your father is a pirate," Anthony said reasonably.

"He's not! Not anymore!"

Anthony looked to James for clarification, but James stubbornly refused to explain himself. It was Conrad who said, "The *Maiden Anne* retired soon after Jeremy joined the crew. We couldn't very well raise the lad on board a ship, could we? The only voyages she makes now, aside from a few voyages back here to the homeland, are to take our crops to market. We've become planters in the islands."

"Is it true, James?" a quiet voice spoke behind them in the doorway.

"Uncle Jason!" Reggie cried, seeing her oldest uncle. Jason looked distinctly menacing in a great-tiered Garrick, and his scowl matched his costume.

"Ah, I'm sorry, James," Anthony offered. "Forgot to tell you the elders were close behind me."

"Not close enough," Edward puffed breathlessly as he appeared in the doorway next to Jason. "And you didn't have to rush off ahead of us, Anthony. Nice place you found here, James. What's it costing you?"

"Still the businessman first and last, eh, Edward?" James grinned. Then he said, "Would you mind telling me how the devil you found me? Let alone how you knew I was in England."

"Anthony's doing," Edward replied. "Saw a sketch Reggie drew. Stopped by when he got back to London this morning to let me know how she was getting on, and it came to him then where he had seen one of the fellows in the sketch. One of your crew when you first bought the *Maiden Anne,* he remembered. Jason had just come in from Haverston, and he figured out the rest."

"But how did you know to look here?"

"Easy," Edward answered. "This is the nearest port. I thought just maybe you were brazen enough to bring your ship into harbor here."

"Not that brazen," James replied, stung. "She's waiting off the coast."

"Then that's why we couldn't find her. Of course, Anthony isn't one to give up easily. We spent the rest of the afternoon making inquiries from one end of town to the other. Finally lucked onto a gent who had seen you coming and going from this renter."

"And now what?" James inquired, looking directly at Jason. "Am I to receive a measure from each of you again?"

"Of course not, Uncle James," Reggie answered quickly. "I'm sure they are willing to forget the past if you are. After all, you have given up pirating. You've settled down, and you have a fine son. I know they will want to welcome him into our family."

"A son!"

"Me," Jeremy said proudly, looking at Jason and Edward from across the room.

Reggie continued before her older uncles could recover, "I really don't think I can manage any more excitement today. Why, I could very well lose my baby if—"

"Baby!"

"Why, Tony, didn't you tell them?" Reggie asked in all innocence.

"Very nicely done, puss." Anthony grinned at her. "And I see you have recovered from your earlier upset."

"I just needed to lie down for a few moments."

He shook his head. "Well, I think you can safely leave us alone now to kiss and make up. Run along and find yourself a cup of tea or something. And take my new nephew with you."

"Uncle Jason?" She didn't have to be specific. He nodded. He was wearing his harmless scowl now, so it was all right. "Go on, Reggie. A man can't get a thing said when you're in the room."

Reggie smiled triumphantly and hugged James. "Welcome back to the family, Uncle James."

"Regan, my sweet, don't ever change."

"As if you four would let me change without *your* approval!" She hooked her arm through Jeremy's. "Come along, cousin. Your father will tell them all about you, and you can tell me all about yourself."

"I had best go with them," Conrad said, and did.

As the three left, they heard behind them, "You still have to be different, don't you, James?" This was Jason. "Her name isn't Regan!"

"It isn't Reggie either! And anyway she's outgrown Reggie. Regan is more suitable for a grown woman."

"It sounds to me like you failed to get them to make up," Jeremy said to her.

"Stuff," Reggie giggled. "Tell him, Connie."

"She's right, lad," Conrad said as he escorted the two down the hall. "They wouldn't be happy unless they were arguing about something."

"So just think how happy you've made them, Jeremy," Reggie added sagely. "Now they can disagree over *your* upbringing, too."

Chapter Twenty-five

The stallion left a trail of dust as it galloped over the plantation road. New spring flowers of the European variety joined with tropical blooms along the roadside to create a profusion of wild color. To the right of the road, less than a mile away, the ocean cast huge waves upon a sandy beach. The hot sun glinted off blue waters as far as the eye could see.

Nicholas noticed none of the beauty around him that sultry early April day. He was returning from the island's small harbor and a meeting with Captain Bowdler, who had reported that his ship would be ready to sail with the morning tide. Nicholas was going home to England, home to Regina.

Six months away had not helped to get her out of his mind. He had tried. He had spent months turning a broken-down plantation house into the showcase of the island, months more in getting the land ready for crops and planting. Nearly every moment had been spent in hard work, but his continuing mood was still dangerously maudlin. A hundred times he had decided to go home. As many times he had talked himself out of it. The situation there would not be changed. Miriam and her threats were still hanging over him and Regina.

But in all this time, Nicholas had overlooked the obvious. Regina probably already knew. Miriam could not live six months with the girl and not try to turn her against him. Yes, she must know by now.

That likelihood had been pointed out to him last week when he got thoroughly foxed with Captain Bowdler and poured out his soul to the man. It took someone objective and just as drunk to make him see that he was sitting on the island brooding like a child because he didn't have the woman he wanted. Well, he'd brooded long enough. It was time to go home and see what was what. If his wife detested him, then that would be the end of that.

But if she didn't? Captain Bowdler asked him that, too. What if she scorned public opinion and judged him on his own merits? Well, the truth was, he had treated her abominably and that was all she *had* to judge him by. Too, she had buckled under one scandal, causing her to want to marry him. He would like to believe that she had married him for reasons other than propriety, but it wasn't likely.

So where did that leave him? Nowhere. Until he got home, he couldn't know how much damage had been done.

A barefoot, chocolate-skinned boy ran out of the large white house to take Nicholas' horse. That was the only thing Nicholas hadn't gotten used to here, owning slaves. It was the one thing about the islands he hated.

"Guests you have, sir, in de study," his housekeeper told him. He thanked her and moved off down the wide, open hall, a little annoyed. Who was calling? He had packing to do yet and another meeting with his estate agent. He didn't have time to chitchat.

He stepped into the darkened study, where drawn shades kept out the noon heat. He scanned the occupied chairs surrounding his desk. Rather than believe what he saw, he closed his eyes. This was not to be borne.

"Tell me I've imagined you, Hawke."

"You've imagined me."

Nicholas crossed the room and sat down behind his desk. "Then you won't mind if I ignore you?"

"See what I mean, Jeremy? He'd spit in the devil's eye.

"Is he the best you could do for a third?" Nicholas asked dryly, indicating the young man. "I don't go in for hurting children. Can't you and your red-haired cohort manage without help?"

"You don't seem surprised to see me, Montieth," James said evenly.

"Should I be?"

"Why, yes. You left England before the hanging."

"Ah, the hanging." Nicholas leaned back, smiling. "Did it draw a big crowd?"

"You find it amusing?" Jeremy demanded.

"My dear boy, all I find amusing is my own stupidity. If I had known this fellow was going to make it his life's mission to plague me, I'd never have arranged for the guards to turn their backs so he could get away."

"Bloody liar!" Conrad joined in heatedly. "Those guards were unbribable! I offered them enough to know that."

"Connie, isn't it?"

"It's Mr. Sharpe to you!"

Nicholas chuckled. "You should know money isn't always the answer. It also helps to know the right people."

"Why?" James asked softly.

"Oh, never doubt that my reasons were selfish, old man," Nicholas replied. "Since I wasn't going to be around to attend the hanging myself, I decided to deny the rest of the populace that pleasure, too. If I could have arranged a postponement until my return, you can be sure I'd have done it. So don't feel you have to thank me."

"Let me have him, Hawke." Conrad's fury was overtaking him. "She'll never have to know."

"If you mean my housekeeper, the old girl's probably got her ear to the door right now. But don't let that dissuade you, old man."

Conrad came out of his chair like a shot, but James motioned him to stop. The captain stared thoughtfully at Nicholas for several moments, probing those honey-gold eyes, and then he laughed.

"Damn me if I don't believe half of what you've said, Montieth." He was probing Nicholas' eyes with his own riveting gaze. "But I wonder," he went on slowly, "what your real motive was. Did you figure if you got me out of the mess you'd got me into, I would call it quits? I wouldn't have." Nicholas didn't answer and James laughed again. "Don't tell me a man of your nature has a conscience? A sense of fair play?"

"Not bloody likely," Conrad mumbled.

"Ah, don't forget, Connie, I wasn't to hang for what I did to him, yet he was responsible for my arrest."

"Very amusing," Nicholas said coldly. "Now may we dispense with these pointless speculations? Play your hand, Hawke, or get out. I have things to do."

"As do we. You don't suppose I enjoy hunting you down, do you? It seems that's all I ever do anymore," James sighed. "The last six months have been most tiresome."

"You'll understand if I don't sympathize?"

"How much of his lip are you going to take, Hawke?" Conrad growled. "Are you ready to reconsider now?"

"Connie's right," Jeremy put in. "I can't see what Regan ever saw in him."

"Can't you, lad?" Conrad sneered. "Look at that pretty face."

"Ease off, both of you," James warned. "Regan has more sense than to fall for good looks. She had to have seen more in him than that."

"Well, he's certainly not what I imagined," Jeremy grumbled.

James smiled. "You can't judge him by this visit, Jeremy. He's got his defenses up."

Nicholas felt he'd been pushed far enough. "Hawke, if you have something to say to me, say it. If you want another go at me, get to it. But if you three just want to have an argument over some doxy, you can do that elsewhere."

"You'll take that back, Lord Montieth," Jeremy cried. "She's not a doxy!"

"Who the bloody hell *is* this boy?"

James chuckled. "My son, don't you know. I tried to get him to remain behind on the ship, but he would have none of it. Determined to be here to see how you took our news."

"I doubt you have news that concerns me."

"Your wife is no concern of yours?"

Nicholas stood up slowly, his eyes locked with the captain's. "What about her?"

"She's very lovely, isn't she?"

"How could you—?" With a growl of rage, Nicholas launched himself forward, flew over the desk, and grabbed James by the throat. It took Conrad and Jeremy together to pull him away from the captain. They held Nicholas, each grabbing an arm.

"If you've laid one hand on her, Hawke, I'll kill you!"

James rubbed his sore throat, but there was a twinkle in his dark eyes. He was satisfied. "What did I tell you, Connie? Is this the reaction of man who doesn't care?" he crowed.

"My wife," Nicholas snarled before Conrad could think what to say, "what have you done with her?"

"Oh, this is famous," James chuckled. Conrad and Jeremy clutched Nicholas tighter. "What sweet revenge it would be, lad, to invent a tale to torment you with. I could tell you I had kidnapped your dear wife, which is quite true, as a matter of fact. I had meant to use her to bring you to me. We didn't know you had left the country, you see. And . . . unfortunately, I didn't know who your wife was."

"Don't tell me the fearless Captain Hawke was intimidated by her family?"

This was greeted by such uproarious laughter from the other three that Nicholas was taken aback. He was able to throw off Jeremy's tight hold, then aim a stunning blow to Conrad's midsection. It gained his release for a moment, but only a moment.

"Easy, lad." James put up a hand to stop Nicholas from any more fighting. "I don't want to hurt you." He grinned. "Especially since it took me weeks to recover from the last time."

"Is that supposed to pacify me? It took me just as long to recover, and it prevented me from discouraging Regina . . . well, that is none of your business."

"Depends on how you look at it, lad. I know you tried to get her to jilt you. A shame she didn't," he sighed, "but that's beside the point."

"Get *to* the point!" Nicholas snapped. "What have you done with Regina?"

"My dear boy, Regan would never come to harm through me. You see, she's my beloved niece."

"Regan? I don't give a damn—"

"Don't you?"

There was so much insinuation in his manner that Nicholas stiffened, searching his mind. Suddenly, what he hadn't noticed before came clear as he stared at Hawke. Hawke and the boy bore a distinctive resemblance to each other and to . . .

"James Malory?"

"The same."

"Bloody everlasting hell."

James laughed. "Don't take it too hard. Imagine how I felt, finding out you had married into my family. That put an end to my plans."

"Why?" Nicholas retorted. "As I recall, your family doesn't acknowledge you."

"That was before our reunion. My brothers and I have patched things up, thanks to Regan. She does have a way of getting what she wants."

"Doesn't she," Nicholas murmured, his voice heavy with irony. "What are you doing here then? Came to congratulate me, did you?"

"Hardly, dear boy." James smiled. "I've come to take you home."

Nicholas' eyes shot fire. "Not bloody likely."

James' smile turned sharklike. "You will come with us, one way or another."

Nicholas looked from one to the other of them. He saw that they were serious. "Your escort is not necessary." He decided to try the truth. "My own ship is ready. I am sailing on the morning tide. I had already decided to return to England, you see, so you won't be needed, gentlemen."

"If you say so, dear boy," James replied doubtfully.

"I am telling you the truth."

"Sailing out of this port on your own won't guarantee your reaching England. No, I must insist you come with us."

Nicholas' temper was beginning to simmer again. "Why?"

"My brothers don't like it that you have deserted your wife. They want you back where they can keep an eye on you."

"Of all the absurdities! They can't keep me in England if I wish to leave."

"What you do after you get home is of no concern to me." James shrugged. "I'm just following Jason's orders. He said to fetch you home, and so I will."

As they escorted Nicholas out of the room, Jeremy whispered to his father, "Uncle Jason never said you were supposed to bring him back. He only said you were supposed to tell him about the baby if we found him."

"I haven't done my brother's bidding since I came of age, lad," his father whispered back. "I don't want to start now."

"But if he knew, he might not put up a fuss."

James chuckled. "Did I say I wanted him to enjoy the crossing?"

Chapter Twenty-six

"Nicholas!" Eleanor came quickly to her feet as the three men entered the drawing room of Nicholas' London townhouse.

Reggie stood up more slowly, her eyes narrowing. There were men on either side of her husband. "Uncle James, is this your doing?"

"I just happened to come across him, sweet."

"Well, you can just take him back to wherever you just *happened* to come across him," she said tightly. "He's not welcome here."

"Regina!" Eleanor gasped.

Reggie crossed her arms over her chest, stubbornly refusing to look at Nicholas' aunt. She had become very close to Eleanor in the last months, had even come to love her. But no one, not her relatives or his, was going to make Reggie accept a man who had been forcibly brought back. The humiliation of that was almost as bad as the desertion.

Nicholas studied Regina covertly, pretending he was looking at his aunt. He felt like smashing his fist into something, anything. He also felt like weeping. Look at her! She evidently knew about his parentage, knew and despised him for it. He saw it in the hard set of her lips; the stiff, unyielding line of her posture.

So, Miriam had told her. Well and good. If she hated the thought of being married to a bastard, it was what she deserved for forcing him into the marriage.

Nicholas' being brought home in the hands of her uncle had made him forget that he'd made up his mind to return and had wanted to make amends. He had, in fact, forgotten everything except his fury.

"Not welcome here, madame?" Nicholas said softly. "Am I mistaken, or does this house belong to me?"

Her eyes met his for the first time. Good Lord, she'd forgotten how devastating were those sherry-gold eyes. And he looked wonderful, his skin deeply tanned, his hair brightly sunstreaked. But she couldn't allow him to cast his spell over her.

"You forget, sir, that you refused to share a house with me. To be specific, you *gave* me your home."

"Silverley, not my townhouse. And what the bloody hell have you done to this house?" he demanded, looking around at all the new furniture and floral wallpaper.

Reggie smiled innocently, her voice sweet. "Why, Nicholas, don't you like it? Of course, you weren't here to help me decorate, but I was very frugal with your money. It only cost you four thousand pounds."

James quickly turned around to hide his mirth. Conrad suddenly found the ceiling fascinating. Only Eleanor frowned. The two young people were now glaring at each other.

"Nicholas, is this any way to greet your wife after seven months?"

"What are you doing here, Aunt Ellie?"

"And is that any way to greet me?" His expression did not soften. She sighed. "If you must know, this house is so big I thought Regina could use my company. It wasn't right, your wife living here alone."

"I left her at Silverley!" he thundered.

"Don't you dare shout at Ellie!" Reggie shouted at him. "And *you* go live at Silverley with Miriam. I like it fine right here."

"I think we will both return to Silverley," he said in a cold voice, "now that I have no reason to avoid my *mother* anymore."

"Unacceptable."

"I wasn't asking your permission. A husband doesn't need his wife's permission—for anything," he said harshly.

She gasped at the meaning. "You have relinquished all rights," she said fiercely.

He smiled. "Not relinquished. Just refrained from using . . . until now. After all, your family has gone to *so* much trouble to bring us together again, *I* certainly don't want to disappoint them," he said cruelly.

"Lady Reggie," an older woman servant interrupted from the door-way. "It's time."

"Thank you, Tess." Reggie dismissed the nurse with a nod, then turned to James and Conrad and said, "I know you meant well, but you will understand if I don't thank you for your trouble."

"You did say you could manage very well, Regan," James reminded her.

She smiled for the first time since their arrival. It was her old imp-ish grin, and she gave both men a hug and kiss. "So I did. And so I will. Now if you gentlemen will excuse me, I must see to my son."

James and Conrad burst into great gales of laughter as Reggie left the room. Her husband stood stock-still, rooted to the floor, his mouth open, a look of complete stupefaction on his face.

"What did I tell you, Connie?" James roared. "Is the look on his face worth all the trouble he put us through or is it not?"

Chapter Twenty-seven

Nicholas downed his third brandy in twenty minutes and poured another. James Malory and Conrad Sharpe, his shadows for so long, had just left his house, and he was still stinging from the amusement they had derived at his expense. Even so, he told himself, he had more important matters to simmer over.

He sat in what had so recently been his study, now a small music room. A music room! If that wasn't a piece of malicious spite, he didn't know what was. A man's study was sacred. And she hadn't just changed the study, she'd eliminated it entirely.

Had she expected him never to return? Or had she hoped he would? Damnation take her. His sweet, beautiful wife had turned into a vengeful, hot-tempered woman in the same mold as her two younger uncles. Damnation take them too.

Eleanor paced the room, casting disapproving looks at Nicholas every time he raised the brandy glass to his lips. He was stewing in his resentment.

"What the bloody hell did she do with my papers, my desk, my books?"

Eleanor steeled herself to be calm. "You just learned that you have a son. Is this is all you can ask about?"

"Are you saying you don't know where she put my things?"

Eleanor sighed. "In the attic, Nicky. All of it is in the attic."

"You were here when she turned my house upside down?" he accused.

"I was here, yes."

"And you didn't try to stop her?" he asked incredulously.

"For heaven's sake, Nicky, you took a wife. You couldn't expect to keep a bachelor residence after getting married."

"I didn't ask for a wife," he said bitterly. "And I expected her to remain where I put her, not trespass here. If she wanted to redecorate, why the bloody hell couldn't she satisfy herself with remodeling Silverley?"

"Actually, I believe she liked Silverley the way it was."

"Then why didn't she stay there?" he raged.

"Do you really have to ask?"

"What was the problem?" he sneered. "Wouldn't my dear mother turn over the reins?"

"Regina took her rightful place there, if that is what you mean."

"Then they got along famously? Well, why not?" he laughed derisively. "They have so much in common, both despising me as they do."

"That is unfair, Nicky."

"Don't tell me you're going to defend your sister at this late date?"

"No," Eleanor replied sadly.

"I see. You're taking sides with Regina. Well, you wanted me to marry her. Are you pleased with the way it's turned out?"

Eleanor shook her head. "I swear I just don't know you anymore. Why did you do it, Nicky? She's a wonderful girl. She could have made you so happy."

Sudden pain welled up in his chest, choking him. Happiness with Regina could never be his, no matter how much he wanted it. But Eleanor couldn't understand why because Miriam had never told her the truth. The sisters had been estranged for as long as he could remember. And if Miriam or Regina hadn't told her, he certainly wasn't going to. Sweet Ellie would pity him and he wanted none of that. Better she think him the detestable character everyone else thought him.

He stared down at the glass in his hand and mumbled, "I don't like being forced."

"But the deed was done," Eleanor pointed out. "You did marry her. Couldn't you have given her a chance?"

"No."

"All right. I understand. You were bitter. But now, Nicky, can't you try now?"

"And have her laugh in my face? No thank you."

"She was hurt, that's all. What did you expect when you deserted your bride on her wedding day?"

The hand on the glass tightened. "Is that what she told you? She was hurt?"

Eleanor looked away. "Actually . . ."

"So I thought."

"Don't interrupt, Nicky." She frowned sternly. "I was going to say she won't talk about you to me at all. But give me some credit for understanding the girl after living with her for four months."

"She's wise not to tell you what she thinks of me. She knows you have a soft spot for me."

"You're just not going to unbend, are you?" she cried. He refused to answer and she lost her patience. "What about your *son?* Is he to grow up in a household of strife—as you did? Is that what you want for him?"

Nicholas shot out of the chair and hurled his glass against the wall.

Eleanor was too shocked to speak, and after a moment he explained himself by saying in a hoarse voice, "I am no fool, madame. She may have told everyone the child is mine, but what else can she say? Let her try and tell me the baby is mine!"

"Are you saying you and she . . . that you never . . ."

"Once, Aunt Ellie, only once. And that was four months before I married her!"

Eleanor's expression softened. "She gave birth five months after the wedding, Nicky."

He stopped cold, then stated flatly, "The birth was premature."

"It was not!" Eleanor snapped. "How would you know?"

"Because," he said reasonably, "she would have told me about the baby in order to keep me here if she'd been pregnant when I left. You cannot tell me she wouldn't have known if she'd been four months along. Also, she would have shown some sign of it, which she didn't. She could only have been one or two months pregnant when I left and obviously unaware of her condition.

"Nicholas Eden, until you can stop being so perverse, I shall have nothing to say to you!" With that, Eleanor swept angrily from the room.

Nicholas grabbed the brandy decanter, about to send it the way of the glass. He tilted it to his lips instead. Why not?

Yes, she'd have told him if she'd been pregnant when they married. He recalled the times she let other men take her home. He recalled George Fowler in particular and the red-hot rage he had felt over that. Had it been intuition? Had he known the young bastard wouldn't take her straight home?

Nicholas was so furious he could barely think straight. He had tried not to think about the child from the moment he'd learned of his birth. His son, was he? Just let her try and convince him of that.

Chapter Twenty-eight

Reggie smiled absently as the little fist kneaded her breast. Feeding her son had always been such a lovely, satisfying time for her, but tonight her thoughts were downstairs. She didn't even notice when the small mouth stopped sucking.

"He's off to sleep again, Reggie," Tess whispered.

"Oh, so he is. But not for long, eh?"

Reggie gently lifted the infant to her shoulder and patted his back. His head snuggled there, his mouth sucking air for a moment before it went slack. She smiled up at her old nurse, now her son's nurse.

"Perhaps this time he will stay asleep," Reggie whispered to Tess as she put him back to bed. But the moment she laid him down on his belly, his head popped up jerkily, his feet started to wiggle, and those inquisitive eyes opened.

"It's to be expected." Tess grinned. "He just doesn't need as much sleep now. He's getting older."

"I'll have to start thinking about getting you some help then."

"Bother that," Tess scoffed. "When he's six months old and starting to crawl, then I'll welcome the help."

"If you say so." Reggie laughed. "But you go on and have your dinner now. I'll stay with him until you're through."

"No you won't, my girl. You have company below."

"Yes," Reggie sighed, "my husband. But as I have nothing to say to him, I am not going down. Now go on, Tess. And please have a tray sent up here to me, will you?"

"But—"

"No." Reggie picked up the wide-awake baby again. "This gentleman right here is the only company I want tonight."

Tess gone, Reggie dropped all pretense of ladylike behavior and got down on the floor to play with her son, imitating his sounds and gestures, coaxing him to smile. He wasn't quite up to laughter yet, but that wouldn't be long in coming, for he heard enough laughter around him. His many visitors, from the servants to her uncles, all tried to make him smile with crazy antics that were quite as ridiculous as his mother's.

How she loved this little person. Right before he was born she had fallen into a terrible depression. But after the birth, which had amazed the doctor by being such an easy labor for a first child, Reggie was filled with euphoria. Plainly and simply, her child brightened her life. In fact, in the last two months she had been so busy learning about and enjoying her new motherhood, that she rarely thought of Nicholas, at least not more than a dozen times a day.

"But now he's back, love. What are we going to do?" Reggie sighed.

"You don't expect him to answer that, do you?"

"Oh, Meg, you startled me!"

"D'you want this down there on the floor?" Meg was holding a tray of food. "I caught the maid on the way up here with it."

"Over there on the table, please," Reggie directed. "And now tell me all about your outing with Harris."

Nicholas had left Harris behind, to the valet's endless misery. The poor man had been bereft all these months and especially unhappy after Reggie moved into the townhouse. He was downright hostile, and he and Meg had had a few heated exchanges, defending their territory.

Abruptly, after the baby arrived, all of that changed. Harris warmed to Reggie or, more exactly, to Meg. Meg and Harris astonished themselves by discovering a liking for each other. They had even been going out together lately and got along famously just so long as Meg said nothing derogatory about the Viscount.

Meg put the tray down with a bang. "Never mind about that hardheaded gent I've been passin' time with. I don't think I'll be doin' that anymore. What does he do the moment he hears the Viscount is here? He doesn't give me a by-your-leave, but rushes upstairs to find his lordship! And I could've save him the trouble. Tess informed me another bottle of brandy was just delivered to the music room."

"The music room? Ah, yes," Reggie giggled suddenly. "The music room. I'd forgotten what I did to his study."

"Tess said he and Lady Ellie were shouting in there," Meg informed her.

"Were they? I'm afraid that doesn't interest me."

"Posh," Meg scoffed. "You'd give your eye-teeth to know what they said about you."

"You assume they were arguing about me."

"If not you, what then?"

"What indeed?" Nicholas asked from the open doorway.

Meg turned in a huff, cursing herself for not closing the door. Reggie, lying on the floor, tilted her head back for an upside-down view of her husband. She was flat on her back, her son stretched out on her chest. She sat up slowly.

Nicholas approached her, seeing a small head on her shoulder, one fist jammed firmly into his mouth. Black tufts of hair and vivid blue eyes were unmistakable. A Malory, through and through.

He came around her and offered her his hand. "Do you do this often, love?"

She wasn't fooled by the mellow tone. There was a hard set to his lips, a heated glow in his eyes. Why, he wasn't pleased about his son at all! How could he stand there looking at him and not be delighted? Her mother's pride came rushing to the fore. She held on to his hand and stood up, but the moment she was on her feet, she turned her back to him.

"If you haven't come here to see Thomas, you can leave," she announced frostily.

"Oh, but I have come to see him." Nicholas smiled grimly. "You named him Thomas, after your father?"

Reggie gently put the baby down in his bed and leaned over to kiss him. She turned and faced her husband. "Thomas Ashton Malory Eden."

"Well, that certainly takes care of *your* side of the family, doesn't it?"

His sarcasm made her boil. "If you wanted him named after your side, you should have been around for his birth."

"Why didn't you tell me?"

Her eyes narrowed. In another moment they would be shouting, and this she would not allow in the nursery.

"Meg, stay with Thomas until Tess returns, will you?" Then she said to Nicholas, "My rooms are across the hall. If you care to finish this conversation, you may visit me there."

Reggie didn't wait for him but stalked across the hall and into her sitting room. Nicholas followed, closing the door loudly. She turned around and glared at him. "If you wish to slam doors, kindly do so in another part of the house."

"If I wish to slam doors, which I did not do just now, I will bloody well do so in *any* part of my house. Now answer me! Why didn't you tell me?"

What to answer? She wasn't going to admit that she hadn't wanted to hold him that way. She wasn't at all certain just then that anything could have held him, not when he had failed to show the slightest inkling of pleasure in either her or his son.

At last she simply asked, "Would it have made any difference?"

"How will we ever know, since you didn't tell me?" A sardonic note entered his manner. "Of course, there is the possibility that you didn't know and therefore couldn't tell me."

"Not know that I was four months pregnant?" She smiled. "I did have very few symptoms, it's true. But four months? Any woman would know by then."

He moved closer until he was standing directly in front of her chair. "Usually at four months everyone else knows as well," he said softly. "For the obvious reason of an increased girth. You were lacking that, love."

Reggie's eyes met his and widened at what she read. "You don't think he's yours!" she whispered incredulously. "No wonder you barely looked at him!" She stood up and he moved back to allow her to pass. She spoke to the room at large. "Oh, this is famous. I didn't once consider this."

She could see the humor in it, though, and under other circumstances she'd have laughed. What a perfect revenge for his treatment of her, presenting him with another man's child on his return. But Reggie was in no condition to feel the humorous side of things. There was the shock of seeing him again, and the nastier shock of his ugly conclusion.

He touched her shoulder, swinging her around to face him. "Is this pretended surprise the best performance you can manage, madame? You have had ample time to invent some excuse to explain why your wedding gown clung to your very tiny waist the day I married you. I am most curious to hear your fabrication."

The gypsy slant of her eyes became more pronounced as they narrowed to furious slits, but she kept her voice calm. "Are you? There is the obvious excuse of a tightly laced corset, so shall I say that's what it was? Would you believe that? No? Just as well, since I never lace my corsets tightly."

"Then you admit it?" he snarled.

"Admit what, Nicholas? I tell you that I had a most unusual pregnancy. It was so unusual, in fact, that I began to worry that something was wrong with my baby when I was seven months pregnant and saw a woman only five months pregnant who was twice my size." She took a deep breath. "Uncle Jason assured me that my grandmother was the same way. People hardly knew she was pregnant until the babies were born. He said he and his brothers were all born just as tiny as Thomas was, and look how they turned out. And he was right. Thomas is growing in leaps and bounds, perfectly formed, perfectly normal. He will probably turn out just as large as his father one day." She finished, out of breath, still furious, but a little relieved. She had told him all of it. What he believed or didn't believe was up to him.

"That was a good, original story, love, certainly better than I expected."

Reggie shook her head. He had formed his opinion and wasn't going to let go of it.

"If you don't want to claim Thomas as yours, then don't. I really don't care what you think," she said simply.

Nicholas exploded. "Tell me he is mine! Tell me in plain words."

"He is yours."

"I don't believe it."

"Fine." She nodded her understanding. "Now if you will excuse me, my dinner is getting cold."

He stared in amazement as she passed him and headed for the door. "You won't try to convince me?"

Reggie glanced back at him and hesitated. His bewildered, faintly hopeful look almost made her relent. But she had done all she could. The convincing would have to be up to him. "What for?" she answered. "Thomas doesn't need you. He has me. And he certainly won't lack for male attention, not with four great-uncles to dote on him."

"Not bloody likely!" he bellowed. "I won't have those autocratic bastards raising my—" He clamped his mouth shut, glaring at her furiously. "Go eat your dinner!"

As she returned to the nursery Reggie smiled, her humor greatly restored. Well! That certainly gave her something to think about, didn't it?

Chapter Twenty-nine

Nicholas sat up slowly, frowning at the unfamiliar noise that had wakened him. He shook his head and lay down again, but in no more than a moment he was fully awake. The infant was crying. He was hungry, wasn't he?

He had identified the noise, but he remained wide-awake, wondering how often this business of having one's sleep disturbed occurred. But it didn't matter. Tomorrow he would pack them all back to Silverley. And if he stayed there as well, his rooms were farther away from the nursery there than here.

If he stayed? Why shouldn't he stay? Miriam had kept him from Silverley for years, but Miriam had already done her damage in telling Regina about his birth. That done, the rest of the world finding out didn't matter anymore. Miriam couldn't hurt him now. And he certainly wasn't going to let Regina keep him from Silverley. Silverley was, he reminded himself fiercely, his home. He still had some rights in this world!

The house was quiet now, the infant no doubt being fed by his wet nurse. Had Regina been awakened? He pictured her in the next room, curled up in bed, probably sound asleep. She was probably accustomed to these disturbances and slept right through them.

Having never seen her in bed before, he couldn't get a clear picture of her. Would her hands be clasped under her chin like a child's? Would her dark hair be loose or tucked into a nightcap? How long *was* her hair? He had never seen it other than formally arranged. What did she wear to sleep in? He didn't know anything about her, and she was his wife.

He had every right to walk the few steps to her room, wake her, and make love to her. He wanted to. But he never would. She was no longer the passionate but innocent young woman who gave him her maidenhead on a warm summer night. She would reject him, treat him with contempt and scorn. He wasn't going to let himself in for that.

But . . . she didn't have to know if he tiptoed into her room and looked at her, did she? Nicholas was out of bed and into his robe before the thought was finished. Soon he was in the hall between Regina's sitting room and the nursery. Her door was closed and there was no light beneath it. The nursery door was ajar and soft light spilled out. A woman was softly humming a familiar lullaby.

Nicholas paused with his hand on the closed door, Regina's door. But he felt a strange pull coming from the nursery. The wet nurse wouldn't like being disturbed, yet he suddenly had a powerful urge to enter that room instead of Regina's. He hadn't gotten a good long look at the boy earlier. What better time than now?

Nicholas nudged the nursery door open. The nurse, Tess, was fast asleep in a cot against the wall. A small lamp glowed on a table next to a stuffed armchair. In that chair sat Regina feeding her son.

It brought him up short. Ladies of quality did not suckle their children. It wasn't done. She was in profile to him, her head bent to the child, softly humming. The fashionable short curls of the day framed her face, while the rest of her hair was long and gleaming, spilling over the back of the chair in midnight waves. She wore a long-sleeved sheer white robe, open, revealing a nightgown of the same material, pulled down on one side enough to bare one breast. The infant's mouth was greedily working, and one small hand rested just above the nipple, as if holding the breast in place.

Nicholas was mesmerized. Out of his depth, unfamiliar feelings assailed him, tender feelings, holding him spellbound. Even when she sensed his presence and looked up, he didn't move.

Their eyes met. For a long time, they simply stared at each other. She showed no surprise and no anger. He felt none of the old hostility. They seemed to touch each other without hands, a current passing between them that transcended their differences.

Regina was the first to look away. "I'm sorry if he woke you."

Nicholas shook himself. "No, no, it doesn't matter. I . . . didn't expect you'd be here, though." Then he asked shyly, "Couldn't you locate a wet nurse for him?"

Reggie smiled. "I never looked for one. When Tess told me my mother defied tradition and nursed me herself, I decided to do the same for Thomas. I haven't regretted it for a moment."

"It's rather confining for you, though, isn't it?"

"I have nothing to do, nowhere I want to go that would keep me away from Thomas for any length of time. Naturally I can't make many calls, but that's no hardship for me."

He had nothing to say. But he didn't want to leave. "I've never seen a mother suckling her babe before. Do you mind?" he asked clumsily.

"He's your . . . no, I don't mind," she finished, keeping her eyes on the baby.

He leaned against the door for a moment, studying her. Was the child his? She said he was. And every instinct of his own said he was. Then why was he stubbornly denying the truth? Because leaving a wife who had forced herself on him was one thing. But leaving a pregnant wife was something else again. True, she hadn't told him. But his leaving was still, in view of the pregnancy she'd borne alone, contemptible. Damnation take it. She had put him in this position by keeping silent about her condition. How the devil was he to get out of it?

Reggie turned the boy around to give him her other breast. Nicholas caught his breath as both creamy white globes were revealed to him in the moment before she covered one of them.

He approached her slowly, drawn against his will, and didn't stop until he stood before her chair. She looked up at him, but he didn't trust himself to meet her eyes. It was all he could do to keep from touching her.

He kept his eyes on the child, but that led his gaze to her breast, and to her open throat, and to her soft lips. What would she do if he kissed her? He bent over to find out.

Nicholas heard her gasp just before his mouth took hers. He kept the kiss short and sweet, the lightest touch, ending it before she had a chance to turn away. He straightened, still without meeting her eyes.

"He's a beautiful baby, Regina."

It was several long moments before she replied, "I like to think so."

He smiled hesitantly. "I envy him at this moment."

"Why?"

He looked directly into those dark, clear blue eyes. "You have to ask?"

"You don't want me, Nicholas. You made that quite clear before you left. Have you changed your mind?"

He stiffened. She'd like him to beg, wouldn't she? That would give her a chance to humiliate him. She had sworn she'd never forgive him and she probably wouldn't. He didn't blame her, but he was not going to make things worse. He turned and walked away without a word.

Chapter Thirty

He was serious! He actually meant for them to pack everything that would go to Silverley and leave within the same day. Nicholas made his high-handed announcement at breakfast, having the unmitigated nerve to use the excuse that he could not remain in a house where he had no study. What could she say, she who had given him that excuse in a long-ago moment of pique? Infuriating man!

Well, she wouldn't go without Eleanor. All she needed was to be stuck in the country with two unfriendly people. No, Eleanor must come along. But she didn't tell Nicholas this, she told Eleanor. Ellie refused at first, but Reggie persisted until she gave in.

And so for the rest of the day they were all kept quite busy—except for Nicholas, who simply stood around looking satisfied with the upheaval he had caused. There was no time for Reggie to say any good-byes to her family. Quickly jotted notes had to suffice for that. But even with everyone pitching in to help—everyone except Nicholas—it was nearly evening before the last trunk was loaded onto the extra wagon that had been procured.

Reggie was no longer speaking to the Viscount, but her annoyance with him ran much deeper than today's nonsense. She was in fact disturbed over her encounter with him last night. Whatever Nicholas had been up to, he'd succeeded in making it nearly impossible for her to get back to sleep. It was not that he had kissed her. If she cared to be honest with herself, it was that he had done nothing beyond kissing.

Therein lay her confusion. How could she still want him after everything he had done to her? But want him she did. She had seen him standing there in the doorway, his silk robe open nearly to the waist, his sun-streaked hair all tousled, an intense look in those honey-gold eyes, and she'd been jolted with a desire so strong it frightened her. Seeing him like that was enough to make her forget all the months of cursing him.

Then what was she to do? It wasn't as if she were going to forgive him. She wasn't. She had no business thinking of him amorously.

Eleanor and Tess and the baby rode in the larger coach with Reggie and Nicholas, while Meg, Harris, and Eleanor's maid occupied the smaller coach. With three women near him, Thomas did not lack for soft bosoms to sleep against. He was a silent passenger most of the time, and the women conversed quietly now that they could relax. Nicholas made a point of appearing bored with their chatter. They in turn ignored him, Reggie to the extent that she didn't hesitate to lower her dress and nurse her son when he began to fidget. Let him say something. Just let him.

At this point a change came over Nicholas. He had been amused by his wife's haughty air all day, and even his aunt's frigid looks, for sweet-tempered Eleanor had never been able to stay angry with him for long. He was a little surprised that she was going to Silverley, for she hadn't been there since his father's death six years before. He supposed Eleanor felt Regina needed moral support, and this amused him while hurting him at the same time.

Humor was only part of the maelstrom of his emotions, however. He must be depraved to be stirred by the simple act of Regina's feeding the child, but he was stirred. A commiserating voice whispered in the back of his mind that he was being too hard on himself. He was forgetting that Regina had always had this effect on him.

That realization did not help at all. Regina would shun his advances. And he would make a complete ass of himself by trying to woo his own wife, wouldn't he? If they could share the same bedroom, the proximity might help. After all, she was a passionate woman. But the place they had just left and the one they were going to were both so large that they didn't need to share a room.

There was only one way he could ever share a room with her, and that was through necessity, which wasn't likely . . . or was it? By God, yes! There was one way, and he had almost missed the opportunity, for they were more than halfway to Silverley already. He ran the idea through his mind and concluded it just might work.

Without further analyzing the plan, which would only bring to light possible flaws, Nicholas called out to the driver to stop at the next inn.

"Is something wrong?" Eleanor asked.

"Not at all, Aunt Ellie. I just realized I would prefer a hot meal tonight, rather than the cold fare we can expect at Silverley, arriving at this late hour."

"But it isn't that late yet. Aren't we almost there?" Reggie wanted to know.

"Not quite, love. And I find I am absolutely ravenous. I can't wait."

The inn they came to soon was a place where Nicholas was well known. He knew the proprietor well enough to tell the man exactly what he wanted. Now, he thought, if only luck would stick around for the rest of the night. . . .

Chapter Thirty-one

Reggie giggled as she made her way to the bed. Meg had left after giving her a thorough scolding as she helped her undress. Meg thought she was drunk. Well, of course she wasn't. Eleanor was. That was funny, for Reggie had been obliged to help the older woman up to her room where *her* maid had scolded *her,* too. The cheek of servants these days.

Eleanor had only consumed—what? a half-dozen glasses of that delicious wine the proprietor had been keeping just for them. He had told Nicholas that. Reggie drank just as much, and she was feeling quite wonderful, but she wasn't foxed, no. Her tolerance was just greater than Eleanor's.

She plopped down on the bed, swayed, then righted herself. This wasn't her spacious room at Silverley, but it would do for one night. Halfway through the meal Nicholas had told them to take their time, saying he had been thoughtless in his haste, his excuse being that he wasn't used to traveling with such a large entourage. He'd realized how inconsiderate it would be to arrive at Silverley so late and without notice, for all the servants would have to be roused from their beds to prepare rooms, see to the horses, unload the baggage, and so forth. He had decided they could arrive in the morning, and so he secured rooms for them at the inn.

Dinner was long and enjoyable, Nicholas putting himself out to make amends for the inconvenience he had caused them all. He was quite charming in fact and made his aunt laugh at his humorous anecdotes. Soon Reggie found herself laughing along with them. She hoped

Meg and Tess and the other servants were enjoying themselves as much.

Reggie yawned and reached to extinguish the lamp on the bedside table. Her hand went right past it and she giggled. Before she could manage a second attempt, the door opened and Nicholas stepped into the room.

Reggie was more bemused than anything else when she saw him standing there. He didn't apologize for his error. Was it an error? Why was he in her room?

"Did you want something, Nicholas?"

He smiled. A glance around the room showed him that one of her trunks had been brought up, but nothing of his had been unloaded from the coach. Harris had protested at the arrangements, especially when he was told he would be sleeping in the stable with the footmen to give truth to the story that the inn was too full to accommodate them all comfortably.

Reggie frowned when he began to remove his coat. "What—what are you doing?"

"Getting ready for bed," he said casually.

"But—"

"Didn't I tell you?" He frowned. "I was sure I mentioned it."

She seemed confused. "What didn't you mention?"

"Why, that there are only three rooms to be had here. My aunt and her maid have one. Your maid and the nurse have the other, with a safe bed made up there for Thomas. That left only this room."

He sat down on the opposite side of the bed and removed his boots. Reggie's eyes were wide as she stared at his broad back.

"You intend to sleep here?" This came out in a high-pitched voice. "Here?"

"Where else would I sleep?" He tried to sound wounded.

"But—"

She got no further than that, for he swung around to face her, disturbing her by his closeness.

"Is something wrong?" he asked. "We are married, you know. And I assure you, you can be perfectly safe in the same bed with me."

Did he have to remind her that he didn't desire her any longer?

"You don't snore, do you?" she asked, just to be mean.

"Me? Certainly not."

"Then I don't suppose sharing a room for *one* night will matter *too* much. You will leave some clothes on, though, won't you?"

"I cannot abide constriction."

"Then I will turn the light off now, if you don't mind," she said.

"So I don't shock you with my nakedness? By all means."

Was that amusement in his voice? The cad. She would just have to ignore him.

She caught the lamp with both hands this time—she wasn't going to have him accusing her of being foxed—but then she had a terrible time finding the edge of the turned-down covers so she could scoot her feet under them. When that was finally managed, Nicholas had finished undressing and, with no trouble at all, stretched out under the covers at the same time she did. His weight dipped his side of the bed so much, Reggie had to grip the edge of the covers to keep from rolling into him. She lay, stiff as a board, trying not to touch him with any part of her.

"Good night, wife."

Reggie frowned. "Good night, Nicholas."

Less than a minute later he was snoring. Reggie made a disgusted sound. Didn't snore indeed. How was she supposed to sleep with this racket? She waited no more than another minute before shaking his shoulder.

"Nicholas?"

"Have a heart, love," he mumbled. "Once was enough for tonight."

"Once . . . oh!" she gasped, startled to realize what he meant. He thought she was someone else, and that she wanted him to make love to her—again. The idea!

She fell back on her pillow in a huff. A moment later he began to snore again, but she just gritted her teeth. After a few minutes, Nicholas rolled toward her, and his hand landed alarmingly near her breast. One leg fell across her thigh.

It flashed through her mind that the chest pressing against her arm was naked, that the leg lying on top of her was naked that . . . oh, Lord, if she moved she might wake him. Yet this intimacy was bringing back feelings best forgotten, and she couldn't sleep like this.

Very gently she tried to lift his hand. His reaction was to grip her breast. Her eyes flew wide open. Her breathing quickened. And he slept on, blissfully unaware of what he was doing.

Once again she tried to extricate herself, prying his fingers off her one at a time, slowly. When his hand was released, it moved away of its own accord, but not where she had intended. His hand slid slowly down her belly, across the mound between her legs, and all the way back up, stopping at her other breast. Just then, his knee moved enough to rest on her loins. The fingers caressed her breast.

"Very . . . nice." His warm breath blew against her cheek as he murmured in his sleep.

The moan came from deep within her, surprising her and causing a deep blush. This was insane. He was sleeping! How could he make her feel like this when he was sleeping?

It was the wine. It had to be, for she almost wished she were the man and he the woman, so she could turn him on his back, straddle him, and ease her growing ache.

She had to risk waking him. She had to get him on his own side of the bed. "Nicholas?" she whispered. "Nicholas, you have to—"

"Persistent, aren't you, love?" His hand snaked up and around her neck, drawing her face to his. "Come then, if you insist."

Warm lips touched hers, softly at first, then passionately. The hand at her neck began to caress, softly, making her tingle all over.

"Ah, love," he murmured huskily as his lips trailed over her cheek to nibble an earlobe. "You should insist more often."

Reggie was overwhelmed with erotic delight. What did it matter if he wasn't fully awake and didn't know what he was doing? She curled a hand around his neck, exerting enough pressure to keep him close.

Nicholas wished he could shout in triumph. Accepting his kiss had sealed her fate. His lips moved along her neck with tingling heat. Quickly, expertly, he unlaced her gown and, in one swift movement, whisked it over her head and aside.

Reggie's hand, yanked from his neck in the unrobing, fell back onto his shoulder. His muscles tensed where she touched him. She shivered with her own power. There was no turning back now. He was hers for the night, whether he knew it or not.

Her fingers glided over his back. The skin was soft, warm. She kneaded gently, then harder, then gently again, taking pleasure just in being able to touch him again. It had been so terribly long. And oh, he was making her remember how it was the first time. His lips burned a searing line from her throat to her thighs. Nicholas was becoming intoxicated by the smell and taste of her. Her skin was as firm and as silky smooth as the night he had taken her virginity. Her body had made no change since the baby, except for the fullness of her breasts, and those he was almost afraid to touch, though he yearned to. But they were the territory of her baby now, and he did not want her thinking of the infant just then. He did not want her thinking at all.

Reggie's head moved from side to side, her pulse racing. If Nicholas did not quit the exquisite torture of his exploring fingers, she would soon be begging him.

He must have read her thoughts, for his long body slid over her, the weight so welcome. Her legs raised and wrapped around his hips just as his warm flesh entered her, filled her, thrusting to her depths.

His mouth closed over hers, smothering her cries of pleasure with fevered kisses. She met him thrust for thrust, her arms locked behind his head, fingers gripping his hair.

The climax took them together to shuddering heights, wave after wave washing over them. Pleasure met and savored. Passion spent. The world receded on the same tide, and they slept, wrapped in each other's arms.

Chapter Thirty-two

Nicholas woke at a knock at the door, and became aware of two things simultaneously. He was lying with his limbs entwined with Regina's, and the person who had knocked wasn't going to wait to be invited in.

Finding his wife next to him was a lovely surprise, stirring wonderful memories. He turned toward the door and muttered a curse. Regina's maid stood there, a candle in one hand, Thomas pressed to her shoulder with the other hand. A look of ridiculous surprise spread across her face.

"Isn't it customary to wait until you are bid entry?" Nicholas growled.

But Meg wasn't intimidated. "It's not customary at all, your lordship, not when it's my Lady Reggie's room I am enterin'."

"Well, Lady Reggie is not alone, so if you will turn yourself around, I will make myself presentable."

Meg gasped as he stood up without further notice. She swung around quickly, wax spilling onto the floor. What was he doing in Reggie's bed? The poor girl had been heartbroken when he deserted her, and now here he was back without, she guessed, so much as an apology.

"You may turn around now, and state your business."

Meg bristled. She glanced hesitantly over her shoulder just as he came up behind her, blocking her view of the bed.

Suspiciously, she asked, "Does she know you're here?"

Nicholas laughed. "My dear woman, what *are* you accusing me of?"

Meg drew herself up stiffly, trying to think what she should say.

"Is there some problem that brings you here in the middle of the night?" Nicholas asked before she could speak.

"I've brought Lord Thomas for his late-night feeding," she explained, making him wonder how he could have forgotten so soon that the infant required attention in the middle of the night.

Meg continued as if she had read his thoughts. "It's troublesome, true, but it won't be lastin' much longer, these late feedings. A few nights already he's slept right through. It's the travelin' and the strange room that have him fussin' tonight."

"Very well, you may give him to me."

Meg drew back in amazement. "Beggin' your pardon, your lordship, but wouldn't it be better if you just left the room for a while?"

"No, it would not," Nicholas said firmly. "But you may do so. And no, dear woman, I do not imagine I can satisfy his needs, so you needn't look at me like that. I will give him to his mother and see he is returned to you when he is finished."

He reached for Thomas and Meg was forced to comply, though she warned, "Careful. You must support his neck . . . that's right, just so. He's not a rag doll, you know." At the scowl he shot her, she left.

Nicholas sighed. There was nothing for it, he would have to wake her. Blister it, he didn't want to wake her. She had slept long enough to have lost all the effects of the wine. She would be shocked by his presence. Oh, why couldn't the child suckle without her being awake? Her lovely breasts were already bared, and she was lying on her side. Could the child do it on his own?

He gently lifted the boy and placed him close to Regina. Nothing happened. Nicholas sat back and frowned. Why the devil wouldn't it work? Didn't babies possess some kind of instinct? He turned the little face toward her until the baby's cheek brushed against her nipple. But the little head turned away again, and Thomas began making sounds of frustration.

Exasperated, Nicholas lay down behind Thomas and turned him onto his side, guiding the little mouth to the nipple. Nicholas held the boy in place until at last the nipple was found and Thomas began to suck.

Nicholas smiled, pleased with himself and the baby. With his hand covering the back of the baby's head, holding him firmly to his source of food, Nicholas was able to lie there and watch mother and child at his leisure. Every new father ought to be so lucky, he told himself.

He nearly chuckled aloud at his own cleverness. He was feeling damned proud. This was his son—he would bloody well lay low anyone who said otherwise—and *he* had helped to feed him. Well, he had brought the baby to his food, anyway. It was nearly the same thing. He could understand a little of what Regina must feel each time she fed him. It was a marvelous feeling.

Watching them, he was filled again with the warmth and tenderness he had felt the night before, and a wealth of possessiveness, too. His wife, his child. They belonged to him. Something was going to have to be done to see that they knew it and accepted it.

Nicholas was handling the baby with much more confidence when he walked him down the hall to the room Meg shared with the nurse. He had even managed to turn both mother and child over so that Regina's other breast, quite swollen with milk, could be drained as well. And all without waking her.

Meg opened the door, looking disagreeable. Here, he thought, was a good place to begin gaining acceptance.

"Tell me something, Meg. Is this animosity you have for me personal, or only a reflection of your lady's feelings for me?"

Meg, much older than Nicholas, was bold enough to speak her mind. "Both. You shouldn't have come back. She was doin' just fine without you, and she'll do just fine again once you're gone."

"Gone?" He was truly shocked. "You have me leaving when I've only just returned?"

"Well, won't you?" Meg retorted, working herself into a fine stew. "You didn't want her for your wife. She knows that well enough now."

"And if I don't leave again, Meg? What then?" he asked softly.

Meg held her ground. He was not to be let off easily. "She'll make your life miserable, that's what. No more than you deserve, beggin' your pardon, your lordship. Tess and I didn't raise any insipid miss, I can tell you that. You can't hurt a Malory twice."

Nicholas nodded. He had heard enough. If anyone knew Regina's real feelings, it was Meg, and the maid was outspoken enough to tell him the truth. Was she right? Was there no hope for him and Regina?

Chapter Thirty-three

It was a quarter past eight and Meg bustled around the room, shaking out the violet dress and short-sleeved spencer Reggie would wear. Reggie sat on the edge of the bed, playing with Thomas. She had fed him already and was waiting for Tess to come back for him.

"I'm surprised Thomas slept through the night, aren't you, Meg? I thought the strange surroundings would have him fretting."

"D'you mean to tell me you don't remember my bringing him in here last night?"

Reggie glanced up, bewildered.

"His lordship brought him back to me all comfy and fed," Meg told her. "I'm sure he'd like to take credit for feedin' the baby, but unless they're makin' men differently these days—"

"Nicholas brought him back to you?"

"He did, and I can see you *don't* remember. I told you too much wine—"

"Oh, hush," Reggie cut her short. "Of course I remember. It just took a moment to . . . oh, never mind. Take him back to Tess, will you? I feel a headache coming on."

"Little wonder, with as much—"

"Meg!"

When the door closed, Reggie lay back on the bed. What was wrong with her? She knew Nicholas had spent the night with her. She remembered him coming into the room and falling right asleep. What happened afterward—yes, she couldn't forget any of that. So why couldn't she recall feeding Thomas in the middle of the night?

She began to wonder if she was sure about anything. Maybe she had fallen asleep soon after Nicholas did, and maybe she dreamed the rest of it. Then she remembered she'd been wearing her nightgown when she woke up. Oh. So it was all a dream, then?

The disappointment hit her like a wave.

As they rode in the coach later that morning, Nicholas' mood was black. He kept to his corner, barely deigning to be civil. What a difference from last night at dinner! What had happened to him?

The three women gave a collective sigh when they finally reached Silverley. They were expected. The doors of the great mansion were thrown open, and a troop of servants waited to unload the baggage. It seemed every servant in the house had turned out to welcome their lord home, and even the Countess was standing poised in the doorway.

Belatedly, Reggie realized that some of the fuss had to do with Thomas, the new lord. One by one people tried to get a peek at him as she crossed from the coach to the great double doors.

Miriam gave Thomas a hard look before her frigid eyes took in Reggie and Nicholas. "So," she said matter-of-factly, "you've brought the bastard home."

Eleanor gasped. Giving her sister a furious look she swept into the house. Poor Tess turned scarlet, thankful that feisty Meg wasn't near enough to hear.

Nicholas, standing behind Reggie, went totally rigid, but otherwise no emotion cross his face. He was certain the insult was a reference to himself, not the baby. Miriam would never change. Her soul was so full of bitterness that her venom spilled over sometimes. That was Miriam.

Reggie stood still, her face flushed pink with anger, her eyes fixed on the Countess. The woman seemed pleased that she had successfully disturbed everyone within hearing. Her voice low, Reggie said, "My son is not a bastard, Lady Miriam. If you ever call him that again, I shall be moved to violence."

She went on into the house before Miriam could reply. Tess followed her, leaving Nicholas alone to laugh at Miriam's furious expression.

"You should have been more explicit, mother." He called her that only because he knew how much it infuriated her. "After all, there are so many of us bastards around these days."

Miriam didn't deign to respond to that. "Are you planning to stay this time?" she asked coldly.

Nicholas' smile was mocking. "Yes, I mean to stay. Any objections?"

They both knew she wouldn't object. Silverley was his, and she lived there only through his grace.

After Regina had gone upstairs, Nicholas closed himself away in the library, the room he had always favored at Silverley, his sanctuary. He was thankful to see that nothing had changed. His desk was still in its corner, a well-stocked liquor cabinet next to it. He would go over the books today, see if he could understand Miriam's figures. He would also get foxed.

Nicholas didn't actually get drunk. He couldn't make heads or tails of the books, but that was not surprising. Miriam did it on purpose, he was sure, so that he'd be forced to sit with her for hours while she con-descended to explain what she had done with the estate. Her manner always implied that Silverley would fall to ruin without her.

They both knew that she was the reason he'd stayed away from Sil-verley since his father's death, depending on his agent to keep him informed of conditions. He simply could not stay under the same roof with her for very long. Miriam's threats and barbs made him lose his temper.

She was his father's widow. To the world, she was his mother, so he couldn't very well throw her out. It had always been easier just for him to leave. But now he had his wife and child at Silverley, and Miriam was not going to drive him away anymore.

When he went upstairs to change for dinner, he was in a foul mood. He had not been able to keep from worrying over the problems with Regina, and he was also nagged with guilt for getting her drunk. He had put her nightgown back on so she wouldn't be embarrassed when her maid came in to wake her. But even if she didn't remember their night together, he knew he had tricked her into accepting his ardor.

Three maids were leaving the sitting room that divided the master suites just as Nicholas approached. "Where are you going with all that?" he barked. One was carrying a basket of shoes, and gowns galore were draped over the other two maids' arms.

The servants blanched at his tone, saying nothing. Reggie came up behind them and, after sending them on their way, asked her husband, "What are you snapping at them for?"

"You don't like your rooms?" he asked, wondering why her clothes were being carted out.

"On the contrary, I like them very well. The servants are removing Lady Miriam's belongings, as they did once before. I suppose she moved back in there after I left, thinking I wouldn't return."

That did not appease him. He was too miserable to be appeased. "You wouldn't have returned if I hadn't insisted, would you?"

Reggie shrugged. "I never gave it much thought. I returned to London simply because I wanted to be near my family for Thomas' birth."

"Of course, your dear family," he sneered. "Well, your family is a long way from here, madame, and I thank God for that. You won't be running back to them again."

Reggie stiffened, eyes slanting angrily. "I never *ran* back to them, sir. But if I wanted to do so, I would."

"No, you won't!" Nicholas shouted. "And I'll have you know right now, your bloody uncles are not welcome in this house!"

"You don't mean that," she gasped.

"See if I don't!"

"Oh! Of all the—" She was too enraged to finish the thought. "Oh!"

She swung around and stomped into her bedroom, slamming the door. Nicholas stared at the closed door, his temper past exploding. In two strides he reached it and threw it open.

"Don't you ever walk away from me when I am talking to you!" he bellowed, standing in the doorway.

Reggie swung around, startled, but not at all intimidated by the fury raging through him. She had held back her own fury too long.

"You were not talking!" her voice rose to match his. "You were shouting, and nonsense, too. Do not think you can place such restrictions on me, sir, for I won't have it! I am not your servant!"

"And what, pray tell, are you?"

"Your wife!"

"Exactly! My wife. And if I wish to place restrictions on you, I will bloody well do so!"

"Get out!" she screamed. "Out!"

She shoved the door against him until it closed, with him on the other side. Nicholas scowled, but he didn't try to open the door again. The significance of being banished from her room was too much, symbolizing the rejection he had expected. He looked at the closed door and saw a barrier, solid and unbreakable.

Chapter Thirty-four

"I suppose I ought to mention that I am expecting guests for the week-end."

Miriam's statement drew all eyes to her. They were dining in the formal dining room, Nicholas at one end of the long table, Reggie at the other. Shouting distance described the length separating the lord and lady of the house. This suited Reggie perfectly. She hadn't said a word to her husband for three days.

Miriam and Eleanor were seated facing each other at the center of the table. It was much easier to talk that way, but the two sisters had nothing to say to each other.

Sir Walter Tyrwhitt was next to Miriam. The friendly neighbor had stopped by earlier and she invited him to join them. As usual, Miriam's manner was very different when the debonair gentleman was present. She was almost warm.

Tyrwhitt was in fact a very likable fellow. Middle-aged, a few years younger than Miriam actually, he was a fine-looking man with distinguished silver streaks running along the sides of his dark brown hair. His eyes were green. He was a farmer at heart, and never tired of talking about the land, crops, the weather. It was amusing to see how serious he could become when he spoke of these things, because he treated all other topics with casual indifference.

Nicholas put himself out to be agreeable to their guest, a great relief to all after three days of surliness. He humored Sir Walter with a good deal of talk about spring crops. Or *was* he humoring him? Perhaps he really was interested. Reggie was amazed at how involved he became. Was he, too, a farmer at heart? How little she knew about the man she was married to.

But his amiability did not extend to his wife. Everyone else benefitted. Even Miriam received civil answers. But Reggie he ignored. It hurt. She wasn't still angry over their argument, for she rarely stayed angry long. She was hurt because she could not forget that dream. It had seemed so real. She could not forget how it felt in his arms, how it was when he made love to her. Fool that she was, she had accepted him in her heart. Why was she such a pushover, to forgive so easily?

Miriam's statement about guests made Nicholas frown. "The whole weekend? I take it this is not your usual dinner party?"

"No, actually," Miriam replied. "I hope you don't mind. I'm afraid the invitations went out right before you returned. I wasn't expecting you to come home."

"Nor were you expecting me to stay, I'm sure of that," Nicholas said dryly.

Eleanor intervened before an argument began. "I think it's a fine idea. A bit close to the London season, but that won't start for another week or so. How many guests were you counting on, Miriam?"

"Only about twenty. Not all of them will be staying, however."

"This isn't your usual style, madame," Nicholas commented. "May I ask what the occasion is?"

Miriam turned her head directly toward Nicholas so Walter couldn't see her eyes. "Must there be an occasion?" Her eyes shot daggers at him.

"No. If you have started to enjoy large gatherings, however, I suggest you visit London this year and enjoy them to your heart's content. You may even make use of my townhouse, now that my wife has so thoughtfully refurbished it."

"I would not dream of leaving Silverley unattended," Miriam said stiffly.

"I assure you, madame, I will force myself to stay here and look after the estate. I am capable of doing so, though you like to think otherwise."

Miriam did not take the bait. He was beginning to see that she wouldn't fight as long as Sir Walter was present. What a choice situation. What fun! But Aunt Ellie was frowning at him, and poor Tyrwhitt looked embarrassed. Regina, sweet Regina, looked down at her plate, avoiding his gaze. He sighed.

"Forgive me, mother. I did not mean to imply that I wished to be rid of you, or that you lack confidence in your only son." He grinned as she stiffened. Perhaps there *were* a few small pleasures left to him. "By all means have your party. I'm sure Aunt Ellie and my wife will enjoy helping with the arrangements."

"I have everything in hand already," Miriam said quickly.

"Then that completes the discussion, does it not?"

Nicholas resumed eating, and Reggie shook her head. She had considered her little battles with the Countess beneath her, yet she had always been provoked. Miriam had done nothing to provoke Nicholas tonight. Why did he dedicate himself to being disagreeable?

As soon as the ladies left the men to their brandies, Reggie retired to her rooms. But Thomas was sleeping, and Meg was in the servants' wing with Harris, and it was too early to go to sleep. Still, she refused to go downstairs. Being ignored by her husband in front of others was embarrassing.

Nicholas noticed Regina's absence the moment he entered the drawing room, and approached Eleanor.

"Where is she?" he asked abruptly.

"She mentioned retiring."

"This early? Is she sick?"

"My dear Nicky, where was this interest in your wife when she was with you?"

"Don't chastise, Aunt Ellie. I believe I have been run through the mill quite enough."

"And still you go on in your own stubborn way," Eleanor sighed. "Which is only making you miserable—admit it."

"Nonsense," he said irritably. "And you don't know all of the story, Aunt Ellie."

She sighed, seeing the rigid set of his chin. "Perhaps. But the way you have ignored that poor girl is still deplorable. Why, I don't believe I've heard you say two words to her since we arrived here."

"More than two, I assure you."

"Oh, you can be so exasperating, Nicholas!" Eleanor kept her voice down. "You just won't admit that you were wrong, that you have a wonderful wife and no good reason not to cherish her."

"I do admit that. It is my wife who now regrets her choice of husband. I once told her she would. Bitter thing," he added, "to find yourself proved right about the one thing you wanted to be wrong about."

She watched him walk away, her eyes sad. How she wished she could help. This was something he was going to have to solve on his own.

Much later, Nicholas entered the sitting room which divided the master bedrooms and was startled to find Regina curled up on the sofa, reading. She wore a bright aqua satin dressing gown belted at the waist, clinging enticingly to her small frame. Her midnight hair lay about her slim shoulders in sensual disarray. She lowered the book and looked at him.

Her gaze was direct. It had its usual power to jolt him. Bloody hell. Another night he'd have to spend tossing and turning.

"I thought you'd gone to bed." Frustration made his voice sharp.

Reggie slowly lowered the book to her lap. "I wasn't tired."

"Couldn't you read in your own room?"

She managed to appear unperturbed. "I hadn't realized this room was for your exclusive use."

"It isn't, but if you are going to lie about half-dressed, do it in bed," he snapped. He scowled at her for a moment, then went into his room.

Reggie sat up. So much for being available to him. What ever made her think she might be able to entice him? All she managed to arouse in him was anger. She had better remember that, she told herself.

Chapter Thirty-five

"I just love your house, Nicky," Pamela Ritchie gushed when she found him in the library. "It's—so grand! Your mother was such a dear to show me around."

Nicholas smiled tightly, saying nothing. With anyone else, he'd have been proud to hear his home praised. But he'd learned something about this luscious brunette during their torrid two-week affair of several years past, and that was that she rarely meant anything she said. Oh, she was impressed with Silverley, but she was surely peeved not to be the lady of the manor.

When their affair ended, he heard through the servants' grapevine that she destroyed her bedroom in a fit of temper. He'd seen her occasionally after that. She always had a warm smile for him, but to catch her unawares was to see Pamela fuming.

Women like Pamela and Selena always clashed with his own quick temper eventually. In his wilder days he had known every kind of female temperament, but there was only one he'd been in real danger with, and that was the lovely Caroline Symonds. But fortunately, she was married to the old Duke of Windfield. He had not seen Lady Caroline for three years, and the pain of their separation was long gone.

"We were wondering where you had gone off to, Nicky," Pamela was saying. She perched, uninvited, on the edge of a chair near his desk. "Tea is being served in the drawing room. More people have arrived. Don't know them, some squire or—oh! And your lovely wife finally made an appearance. A charming, sweet girl. Of course, I'd met her before, don't you know, season before last. She was all the rage then. The young bloods were falling all over themselves just for one of her smiles. I was even a little bit envious until it became apparent that something was, well . . . wrong with her, poor thing."

He had known the silly chattering thing was leading up to something, but even so he found himself stiffening. "Am I supposed to guess what you mean by that?"

She laughed, a tittering sound. "I was hoping *you* would tell *me*. Everyone is simply on tenders to know."

"Know?" Nicholas said curtly.

"Why, to know what you found wrong with her."

"I find nothing wrong with my wife, Pamela," he said coldly.

"So you won't fess up? Gallant of you, Nicky, but not very enlightening," she sighed. "You can imagine the stir you've created. It isn't every day one of our most eligible bachelors marries and then leaves his wife practically at the altar. It is rumored that one of Lady Reggie's uncles handed you over to her in chains."

It was not easy for Pamela to be assured that she had scored. Only the tension in his hands showed his anger. She had wanted him to fly into a rage. Pamela harbored more spite for this man than she did for all her other lovers come and gone combined. She had formed serious plans for Nicholas Eden, and he had laid them to ruins. Bloody philandering cur. She was delighted he had ended up with a wife who didn't suit him.

"That particular rumor is an absurdity, Pamela," Nicholas said tightly. "I returned to England in James Malory's company simply because he was kind enough to offer me berth on his ship when he found me stranded in the West Indies. And," he went on quickly before she could say anything, "I hate to disappoint you, but it was business that took me away from my bride. An emergency on an island property that couldn't wait."

"Another man might have taken his bride along, extended honeymoon and all that," she interjected. "Odd you didn't think of it."

"There wasn't time to . . ." he began, but she smiled and rose to leave.

"It will be interesting to watch the two of you, though. Strange that you should be entertaining so soon after your wedding."

"This little gathering was not my idea."

"Yes, your mother sent the invitations, but you were already here, so I assume you wanted a party. Well, they do say the best way to relieve boredom is to have a party. I just hope you weren't thinking of a *personal* party between the two of *us* when you had me included on the guest list. Married men don't attract me, if you know what I mean."

She whirled out of the room before he could reply. Nicholas remained seated, staring at the door. He had been turned down flat, without his even making an offer. The cheek!

A fierce protectiveness rose in him. Something wrong with Reggie, indeed! He left the library with every intention of finding his wife and devoting himself to her fully for as long as a single guest remained in the house. But when he stepped out of the library, glancing toward the entry hall, he saw Selena Eddington alighting from her carriage. Fuming, he went to find Miriam. "What I find amusing is that you kept such close tabs on me all these years," he told her. "Such devotion. Of course it enabled you to know exactly which people I would *not* wish to see."

"Not at all," she replied with a tight little smile. "There are, in fact, many kind souls who feel a mother should be informed of what her son is doing in wicked London . . . and with whom. You can't imagine how many good intentions I had to sit through, appearing grateful, when I didn't care if my so-called son drowned in the Thames." She gave him a look of pure hatred. "Yet, bits of information do sometimes have uses."

Fury flashed in his eyes. He turned and headed for the stairs, Miriam's delighted laughter following him.

"You can't hide all weekend, Lord Montieth," she called scornfully.

Nicholas didn't look back. What the bloody hell did the conniving, spiteful old bitch hope to accomplish by inviting two of his ex-mistresses to his home? And, good God, how many more surprises awaited him?

Chapter Thirty-six

The drawing room was quite crowded, Miriam's twenty people having turned into thirty. The music room was open and sounds of someone tinkering with the harp drifted from it. The dining room was open, the long table set up for a buffet. Guests drifted from room to room.

Selena Eddington had changed little in the year since Reggie had seen her. Dressed in a frilly pink lace creation that made Reggie feel matronly in her dark blue gown, Selena had all the men hanging on her every word. From time to time, she turned toward Reggie with a satisfied smirk.

"Cheer up, my dear. It was bound to happen one day."

Reggie turned to Lady Whately, an acquaintance from years past. She was sitting beside Reggie on the sofa. "What was bound to happen?" Reggie inquired.

"You meeting up with the women from your husband's past, there being so many of them."

"If you mean Lady Selena—"

"Not just her, my dear. There's the Duchess there, and that Ritchie tart, and Mrs. Henslowe, though Anne Henslowe was just a fling, or so I'm told."

Reggie's eyes flew to each woman the old tabby named, widening when they fell on Caroline Symonds, Duchess of Windfield, a stunningly beautiful blond only a few years older than Reggie. The Duchess sat demurely next to a man in his late seventies. He had to be the Duke of Windfield. How utterly miserable the young woman must be with that old husband, thought Reggie.

Pamela Ritchie, Anne Henslowe, Caroline Symonds, and Selena Eddington. Four of Nicholas' past mistresses in the same room with his wife! This was asking too much. Was she supposed to converse with them? Act the gracious hostess?

Nicholas made an appearance just then, and she wished she could glower at him, but that was out of the question. While she watched, Lady Selena took Nicholas' arm and held on tightly.

"That doesn't upset you, does it, my dear?"

Reggie turned to find Lady Whately gone and Anne Henslowe in her place. Was she now to be comforted by one of his mistresses? "Why should it upset me?" Reggie answered stiffly.

Mrs. Henslowe smiled. "It shouldn't. After all, she lost him and you have him. She was upset about it."

"And you?"

"Oh, dear. Someone has been whispering in your ear. I was afraid of that."

Reggie simply could not remain vexed. The woman was genuinely sympathetic, her brown eyes compassionate. She wasn't a bad sort. And her affair with Nicholas had happened long before Reggie met him.

"Don't give it another thought." Reggie smiled.

"*I* won't. I just hope *you* don't. Be assured, my dear, that Nicholas never goes back for second helpings."

Reggie giggled, shocked. "Nicely put."

"And true, to the lamentation of the women in his past. Many have tried to get him back, and all without luck."

"Did you?" Reggie asked bluntly.

"Heavens, no. He wasn't for me and I knew it. I was thankful for my one night with him. It occurred soon after I lost my husband, I was close to losing my sanity as well and Nicholas helped me see that my life wasn't over after all. I'll always be grateful to him for that."

Reggie nodded and Anne Henslowe patted her arm. "Don't let it get to you, my dear. He is yours now, forever."

But he wasn't hers, and he hadn't been hers after that one night nearly a year ago.

She thanked Mrs. Henslowe and looked around for Nicholas. He wasn't there, and he wasn't in the dining room or the music room. That left the conservatory, and she retraced her steps back through the dining room and quietly slipped into the glass-walled sun room. It was warm and dark, the only light coming through the far windows of the dining room. It was just light enough to see as far as the fountain, to see the pink lacy gown and short black curls of Selena Eddington, whose arms were wrapped around Nicholas' neck.

"Are you enjoying your tour of the house, Lady Selena?" Reggie called out, approaching them.

Her voice drew them apart. Selena had the grace to look embarrassed. But Nicholas didn't seem at all contrite. In fact, he turned dark with anger. Seeing his anger, Reggie's outrage turned to throat-tightening pain. Ninny! He hadn't wanted to stop holding Selena.

She turned and left as quickly as she could. Nicholas called after her, but she only hurried her step. The philandering libertine! How could she have been so stupid—so foolish—as to hope?

When she reached the antechamber, Reggie stopped short. No, she would not run and hide as if her heart were breaking. Malorys were made of sterner stuff. They did not make the mistake of falling in love with the same person twice. Love wasn't why she had this tight knot in her throat. No, indeed, she was choking on anger, that was all.

She stepped into the drawing room again, the smile she had worn most of the day right back in place. Calmly, she took a seat and plunged into conversation with Faith and Lady Whately.

Nicholas entered the drawing room the moment after Reggie sat down. He took one look at her tranquil expression and his heart sank. What had he expected? Tears? In order to be jealous, a person had to care. The devil take Selena straight to hell for throwing her arms around him and catching him off guard like that. Had she known Reggie was nearby? He hadn't wanted to escort Selena through the house in the first place, but she had challenged him, hinting that he was afraid to be seen with her, whispering that he was no longer his own man. Like a bloody fool, he dragged her from room to room, giving her the tour. Idiot!

She wanted to see what was behind the closed doors of the conservatory, and once inside, a single flower on a twisting vine caught her eye. Nothing would do but she must have it. After two attempts to reach it herself, she had pleaded sweetly for him to get it. He went for the bloody bloom, and no sooner had he plucked it and turned to hand it to her than she had her arms locked behind his neck. Two seconds had passed, and then Regina spoke. It was unbelievable, the worst piece of luck imaginable.

He looked at Regina again and her eyes met his. In that moment before she turned away, her eyes shot blue flames at him.

Nicholas' hopes soared. He grinned. She didn't care? Then why was she so furious with him? Determined now, he approached the three women on the sofa. "May I join you, ladies? What with all the duties of the host, I haven't had a moment to spare for my lovely wife."

"There isn't room, Nicholas," Reggie said flatly.

And there wasn't, not with the ample posterior of Lady Whately taking up half of the sofa. But he was not deterred by that or by Reggie's stiff tone.

He caught her wrist, tugging her up to stand, then sat down and pulled her down onto his lap.

"Nicholas!" she gasped.

"Don't be embarrassed, love." He grinned, holding her firmly in place.

"Scandalous, Lord Montieth!" Lady Whately was even more embarrassed then Regina. "If you are so eager to be near your wife, you may have my seat."

She left, and then Faith moved away as well, pretending a sudden interest in a painting across the room. Reggie slipped off her husband's lap and sat beside him. She wanted to move away from him entirely, but his arm over her shoulder kept her on the sofa.

"That was—"

"Shush," he whispered. "And smile, love. We are being observed." She smiled up at him tightly but her eyes cursed him anyway. He chuckled. "Is that the best you can do?" Then he said softly, "It was nothing, you know."

She didn't have to ask what he meant. "Of course not," she retorted ironically.

"It really wasn't. She made an attempt to seduce me and she failed. It was no more than that."

"Oh, I believe you, my lord," she said flatly, her voice icy. "I believe you because I have twice been told tonight that your ex-mistresses do not interest you once they fall into the excategory. One of your former ladies assured me that you 'never return for seconds.' So I must believe it even when my eyes tell me differently."

"You're jealous."

"Stuff!"

He grinned devilishly. "Your informant wasn't totally correct, love. Were you the meal, I would return for seconds and thirds and gorge myself to death."

"Oh!" she gasped. "I am in no mood to be quizzed, sir! Good night to you."

She shot to her feet before he could grab her and left the room. He let her go, smiling to himself. He was beginning to think Miriam's gathering was going to be just what was needed to get his wife back. Wouldn't the old bird die to know she had helped him! His grin widened. His mood was becoming positively buoyant.

Chapter Thirty-seven

Warm sunlight spilled into the morning and breakfast rooms, both of which were thrown open to accommodate so many guests. On the long buffet were platters piled high with eggs; kippers; ham and sausage; an assortment of toast, muffins, and rolls; and six kinds of jellies. Hot chocolate was offered, and tea and coffee and clotted cream. Footmen refilled the platters as soon as they emptied.

It was early, and many were still asleep or had availed themselves of the well-stocked stable for a morning ride. Reggie was down because Thomas had awakened at dawn and, after feeding him, she hadn't been able to sleep again. The Whatelys were at breakfast, as well as Pamela Ritchie and the Duke of Windfield. Reggie let their conversation move around her. She wasn't keen to put on a cheerful face again. Brooding thoughts had followed her to bed last night and were still hounding her, Nicholas at the center of those thoughts.

It wasn't as if she hadn't known all along what type of man he was, but, devil take him, couldn't he wait until returning to London before cavorting with another woman? Why was he at Silverley, anyway? She certainly hadn't expected him to be. And that constant scowl of his was so unnerving.

She ought to leave, she knew that. Divorce was out of the question, but she didn't have to live under the same roof with him. She could return to Haverston. Uncle Jason wouldn't mind.

But she had no right to keep Thomas away from his father. And Tess had told her that Nicholas was visiting the nursery at least twice each day, shooing Tess out so he could be alone with his son. He did accept Thomas as his, it was just doubtful he would ever get around to acknowledging that to Reggie.

She sighed deeply. Hadn't she once said it wouldn't matter how her marriage turned out just so long as she didn't have to go on hunting for a husband? How foolishly naive!

"My dear, you have a visitor," Eleanor announced as she came into the room, Lord Dicken Barrett right behind her. "George—? Oh, dear. I don't remember."

"George Fowler," Lord Barrett supplied.

"Oh, yes, Fowler," Eleanor agreed. "Sayers put him in the waiting room, what with the house so full."

Sayers was standing in the doorway, and Reggie frowned to hide her surprise. She stood up. "The waiting room is no place for George. Put him in the library. It should be empty at this hour. And have tea sent in." She dismissed Sayers with a nod, then turned to Eleanor. "You should have slept later, Ellie, if you're still tired."

"I'm fine, dear. We did have a late night of it, but I enjoyed myself." Her eyes met Lord Barrett's briefly. "I'll be wide-awake once I have my tea. Do you know your caller?"

"Yes," Reggie replied. "But I can't imagine what he's doing here."

"Well, you had best see to him. Dicken and I will just have a little something to eat before going on our ride."

Eleanor, riding? Imagine! "I didn't know you enjoyed riding, Ellie."

"Oh, my, yes. But it's so much nicer when you have someone along for company." She leaned closer, adding, "You and Nicholas must try it."

Reggie answered noncommittally and left the room.

George Fowler stood up the moment she entered the library, coming forward to bow over her hand. She had forgotten what a pleasant-looking young man George was, with his mop of sandy brown curls and neatly trimmed mustache, his dark green eyes and well-cut figure. He was a little on the short side—no, not really. She mustn't compare every man to her husband.

"I fear I've come at an inconvenient time," he apologized. "The fellow who took my horse grumbled that there wasn't room for even one more in your stable."

"It's a bit of a squeeze, but I am in no way inconvenienced."

"But you have guests to attend—"

"Not at all," she assured him. "This is my mother-in-law's gathering, planned before we arrived. Mostly her friends—and my husband's—and only a few are up at this hour. Do sit down, George." They seated themselves facing each other. "You're welcome to stay, too, if you like. You probably know most everyone here, and I'm sure we can find you a place for the night, if you don't mind sharing a room."

He grinned happily. "I would accept, if I hadn't already received a summons from my mum. She's on holiday down in Brighton and I thought I would stop by to see you on the way, see how you're getting on."

Reggie smiled at him. He had gone far out of his way in order to see her. "It has been a long time, hasn't it?" She opened the subject happily, remembering how charming he could be.

"A deuced long time," he emphasized.

Hallie brought in tea, and Reggie poured.

"How is your mother, George?"

"As well as can be expected, considering her disposition." He said this with a grimace, as if he expected quite a drubbing when he arrived in Brighton. "The whole family's well. Speaking of family, I saw your Uncle Anthony at the club last week. He seemed in the boughs over something. Nearly came to blows with another fellow just for bumping into him."

Reggie knew what that meant. A week ago would have been the time Anthony learned that Nicholas was back.

"Uncle Tony has his moods, though fortunately he doesn't have them often."

"And do you?" His expression was suddenly serious.

"Have moods, George? Don't we all?"

"You don't mind being buried out here in the country? I would perish within a week."

"I love Silverley. I always did prefer the country."

He seemed disappointed. "I thought perhaps you . . . weren't happy here. One does hear things." He coughed. Was he embarrassed?

"One should close his ears, then," she chided. "I'm happy, George." But she couldn't look him in the eye.

"You're sure?"

"She has told you so, Fowler," Nicholas stated coldly from the doorway. "And since that is obviously what you came to find out, I shall appreciate your leaving."

Reggie jumped to her feet. "Nicholas!"

"That's quite all right, Reggie," George offered, standing.

"That's *Lady Montieth,* old chap," Nicholas said smoothly, eyes bright. "You will remember that, won't you?"

Reggie was incredulous. "You don't have to go, George, really you don't."

"Oh, but he does, I insist." Nicholas then turned and bellowed into the hall. "Sayers! The gentleman is leaving."

Reggie flushed crimson. "I'm sorry, George. There is no excuse for such rudeness."

"Think nothing of it." George bent over her hand, ignoring for a moment the indomitable man in the doorway. "It was a pleasure seeing you again, however briefly."

Reggie waited only two seconds after George slipped out of the room before she emitted a cry of rage, her cobalt eyes shooting sparks at Nicholas. "How dare you? Did *I* throw *your whores* out? Did *I*?" She barely paused for breath. "You are insufferable, sir, utterly!" she raged. "Is this another preposterous rule of yours? First you refuse to allow my family to visit here, and now my friends are not welcome!"

"I would not call an old love a friend," he retorted.

"He was not an old love. And you are a fine one to talk, with four of *your* old loves sleeping in this house last night. Why, you were probably even with one of them—or more than one!"

"If you had shared my bed last night, you would know where I was."

Her mouth dropped open, then angrily snapped shut. Share his bed after she had caught him with another woman? He was annoying her on purpose. Well, he'd succeeded in rousing her fury.

She squared her shoulders. "Your disgraceful behavior has made up my mind for me, sir. I refuse to live another day with such a churlish boor. I am going home."

That brought Nicholas up short. "This *is* your home, Regina."

"It might have been, but you have made it intolerable."

"You're not leaving," he stated flatly.

"You can't stop me."

"I can indeed do just that. See if I don't!"

Silence followed. They glared at each other, and then Regina stalked out.

Nicholas' shoulders drooped. Why the bloody hell had he lost his head like that? He had intended to coax her back to her old self, then woo her into his bed tonight. Everything could have been right by tomorrow. What the everlasting hell was the matter with him? She was right, his behavior was insufferable, and he didn't even begin to understand it himself.

Chapter Thirty-eight

The door crashed open with a resounding bang. Reggie swung around from the vanity seat, brush still raised to her hair.

"What? No trunks packed yet?" he rasped.

Reggie slowly put her brush down. "You're foxed, Nicholas."

"Not quite, love. Just enough to realize I've been pounding my head against a stone wall for no reason."

"You're spouting gibberish."

He shut the door, leaning against it, his amber eyes on her face. "Consider this. The house is mine. The room is mine. The wife is mine. I need no more license than that to take her to bed."

"I—"

"No arguing, love," he broke in.

She warned frostily, "I think you had better leave before—"

"Will you scream, love? Bring the servants and guests running? They don't dare intrude, you know. You will suffer from acute embarrassment tomorrow."

He was smiling at her, the brute. "You will not have your way, Nicholas Eden."

"But I will," he corrected agreeably. "And let's not have any hysterics."

"When I get hysterical," she said through gritted teeth, "you will know it."

"Good of you to be so reasonable, love. Now, why don't you take off that pretty thing you're wearing?"

"Why don't you go—"

"Madame!" he appeared shocked. "If you cannot be civil—"

"Nicholas!" Reggie shouted in frustration. "I am in no mood for nonsense."

"Well, if you're in a hurry, love, I will oblige you."

He started toward her, and she dashed around the large bed, putting it between them. He kept coming, moving around the bed now.

"Don't come any closer." Her voice rose with each word. But he did.

Reggie jumped onto the bed and rolled across it. She looked up to find him grinning. He was enjoying the chase.

"I want you out of here this second!" Her voice cracked with fury.

He stepped up onto the bed, bending to avoid being clobbered by the canopy, and she ran for the door. The crashing sound of Nicholas jumping off the bed made her change direction. Behind the Queen Anne chaise longue was safer.

Nicholas went to the door, locked it, then put the key on the ledge over the door, well out of Reggie's reach.

Reggie looked at the ledge she couldn't possibly reach, then back at Nicholas. She grabbed a book from the table next to her and threw it at him. He nimbly sidestepped it, chuckling at her efforts, and removed his coat.

"If you persist, Nicholas, I swear I will scratch your eyes out!"

"You can try, love." He smiled. He moved toward the chaise and pulled her out from behind it, holding her to him firmly.

"Nicho—"

His lips silenced her. A moment later he dropped her on the bed and pressed her against the mattress with his long body. His mouth devoured hers, leaving her no chance to breathe, let alone rail at him. Her fingers gripping his hair could not move his head, nor could her bucking dislodge him. She bit his lip, and he pulled back, grinning down at her.

"You don't want to do that, love. How can I kiss you properly if you've taken a chunk out of my kisser?" She gave a vicious yank to his hair and he growled, "I should have plied you with wine again. You're much more agreeable when you're foxed."

As he kissed her again, Reggie's eyes widened. Plied her with wine? It hadn't been a dream! He really had made love to her that night at the inn. And he'd planned it! He'd wanted her enough to trick her . . . wanted her enough to give her too much wine . . . wanted her.

Good God, those feelings were sneaking up on her again. How long could she resist?

He looked at her again, his eyes smoldering. "Oh, love," he said huskily, "love me. Love me like you did before," he whispered passionately, and her defenses crumbled. Suddenly she was kissing him back with all the passion she possessed. She wasn't made of stone. She was flesh and blood and her blood was on fire.

Her fingers changed direction, pulling his head toward her. His groans of pleasure were music to her ears. Nicholas wanted her . . . really wanted her. It was her last thought before there was no more time to think.

Chapter Thirty-nine

"Good morning, love." Nicholas' teeth caught at Reggie's lower lip and chewed for a moment. "Did anyone ever tell you what a delightfully rumpled picture you present at sunrise?"

She grinned impishly. "Meg is the only one who sees me at sunrise, and she doesn't say things that go to a girl's head."

Nicholas laughed, pulling her closer. "Your indomitable Meg doesn't like me, you know, and I can't imagine why. I'm such a likable fellow."

"You are an insufferable fellow, and you know it."

"But a *likable* insufferable fellow."

She laughed.

What a marvelous way to be awakened, Reggie thought, snuggling closer to the solid length of her husband. And she wasn't tired, even though she had been loved ardently into the small hours of the night. Not tired. Feeling wonderful. She would have to insist he force himself on her more often.

Thomas' wail was the only thing that could disturb their idyll, and she heard it in a moment.

"I was wondering when he would get around to that."

Reggie grinned at him. "I'd better see to him."

"You will hurry back, won't you?"

"Most definitely, sir."

When Reggie returned to her bedroom twenty minutes later, it was empty. She checked the sitting room, then went to Nicholas' bedroom.

Both rooms were empty. She returned to her own room and waited. He did not appear.

Where had he gone? And why? Would he use her, then treat her with indifference? But she was jumping to conclusions. There had to be a perfectly good explanation for his disappearance.

Reggie rushed Meg with her toilet and then nearly flew out of her room and down the stairs. Voices from the breakfast room drew her in that direction. At the door, she stopped short, suddenly chilled. Nicholas, dressed only in trousers and a short green velvet lounging jacket, stood at the buffet table. His back was to her, as was Selena Eddington's. Selena stood next to him, so close that her shoulder touched his upper arm. His head was bent toward her and Selena was laughing at whatever he was saying.

Red flashed before Reggie's eyes. "Am I intruding—again?"

They whirled around. No one else was in the room, not even a footman, yet Nicholas didn't look at all abashed.

"You didn't have to come down, love." He smiled. "I was just getting a plate of pastries to bring up to you."

"I'm sure you were," she replied frigidly, her eyes locking with Selena's. "Madame, kindly pack your valises and be gone from my house before noon."

Selena's smug expression turned swiftly to outrage. "You can't do that. Lady Miriam invited me."

"Lady Miriam is not mistress here. I am. And we Edens are positively famous for throwing people out of our home." Having gotten that out of her system, Reggie turned and left.

Nicholas caught up with her in the main hall, grabbing her arm. "What the devil was that all about?"

"Let go of me!" she hissed, yanking her arm away. This time he took hold of her shoulder.

"Come in here." He dragged her into the library and closed the door behind them. "Are you mad?"

"I must be, to have believed you had changed!" she said.

"What do you mean?"

"My bed was still warm when you went looking for another conquest! Well, cavort with all the women you want, sir, but do not toy with me again."

"Can you believe I would want another woman after last night?" he replied, truly incredulous. "What you saw was nothing. Selena just happened to be there when I came in for your pastries. I meant to feed you, mind you, so you would have no excuse to leave your room this morning."

"You have a house full of servants to fetch pastries, sir," she pointed out.

"They are being run ragged by all of our guests. I had time to do it because I was waiting for you to return."

"I don't believe you."

He sighed in exasperation. "This is absurd, Regina. You had no call to fly off the handle, and certainly no call to boot Selena out. I told her so."

"You didn't!"

"If you will just consider how ridiculously you are behaving—"

The fire glittering in her eyes gave him pause. "Am I? Yes, I suppose I am. I'm a fool, too, and the stupidest ninny. But you, sir, are a bastard, through and through. You can't bear for your lady friend to leave? Then by all means let her stay. Let her move in for good, in fact, for I won't be here to see it. And if you try to stop me from leaving, I will—shoot you!"

His face darkened to a furious expression, but she was so caught up in releasing the months of fury that she didn't know how dangerously angry he was. When he turned around without making a single reply, she ran in front of him and blocked his exit. "Don't you dare walk out when I'm still fighting with you!"

"What more is there to say, madame?" he said bitterly. "You have finally brought it out in the open. I have no defense, you see."

It bowled her over. No lies, and no excuses.

"You . . . admit you still want her?"

"Want who?" he growled. "I speak of my bastardy, of course. I tried to spare you, if you will recall. I did my best to prevent your marrying a bastard."

"You could have changed," she retorted hotly.

"How do you change the circumstances of your birth?"

"Birth?" She frowned. "What is the matter with you, Nicholas? I'm talking about your behavior. You are a bastard."

There was a charged pause, and then he asked, "Miriam never told you? She never revealed my black secret?"

"What *are* you talking about?" Reggie asked him. "Yes, Miriam told me about your birth. She delighted in telling me. What does that have to do with anything? If you ask me, you should be glad she's not your mother."

It hit him like a thunderbolt. "You mean—you don't care?"

"Care? Don't be absurd," she said. "I have two cousins who are bastards. Does that mean I love them any less? Of course it doesn't. Your birth was no fault of yours." She took a breath, then sailed on. "You, sir, have a mountain of faults without adding that one. I am through being only half a wife. I meant what I said. I will not stay here and watch you renew old alliances. If I see you with that woman once more, I swear I will put to good use the lessons Connie taught me and carve the two of you to pieces!"

He wouldn't—or couldn't—stop laughing. It was enough to make Reggie scream. At that moment, Eleanor entered.

"Is there a war going on in here, my dears, or is this just a family squabble?"

"Family?" Reggie cried. "He doesn't know he's part of a family. He would prefer to be a bachelor. He thinks he *is* a bachelor."

Nicholas sobered. "That's not true."

"You explain it to him, Ellie," Reggie said. "Tell him it's one way or another. He's either a husband or he isn't."

Reggie flounced out of the room, slamming the door behind her. She'd gotten no more than halfway up the stairs when his words came back to her, and she nearly stumbled. *I did my best to prevent your marrying a bastard.*

She stood stock-still, staring into space. Could that be the reason for his horrible behavior? Why hadn't she thought of that when Miriam oh-so-casually dropped the information? Did Nicholas believe she couldn't bear being married to a bastard?

Oh, that fool, that idiot! Reggie sat down on the stairs and her own laughter began spilling out.

Chapter Forty

That evening a cold dinner was served on the back terrace in order to accommodate the croquet matches going on. Reggie brought Thomas down to enjoy the late afternoon sun. With a large blanket spread under him, he delighted in bobbing his head toward sounds that caught his interest. Every guest came by to meet the new Montieth heir.

Only a few of Miriam's guests would be spending another night at Silverley. Most had left that afternoon, including Selena Eddington. Whether Nicholas had spoken to her again or she had thought it prudent to leave, Reggie didn't know.

Pamela Ritchie came over to look at Thomas. An unhappy woman, that. If she weren't careful, those lines of dissatisfaction would become permanent.

Reggie hadn't felt at all distressed when Nicholas and Anne Henslowe played in a croquet match together. They stood side by side waiting their turn and laughing together, but Reggie didn't mind. Her attitude must, she felt, have something to do with all those grins and winks Nicholas had been giving her all afternoon. It was as if they shared a private joke, but they hadn't said a word since coming face to face over lunch. Even so, he had only to look at her to begin chuckling.

He was a happy man. Reggie thought she knew why, and her suspicions made her just as happy as he was.

The sun was beginning to set, and there was a marvelous display of color. Thomas had had enough of the outdoors for one day, and was scooting around on the blanket with extra vigor, a sure sign that he was hungry.

"It's so peaceful out here at this time of day," Eleanor said quietly. "I'm going to miss you and this little fellow."

"You're not thinking of leaving already, are you?" Reggie asked surprised.

"You don't need me here anymore, my dear." They both knew she had stayed only to help Reggie ease into her marriage. "Dicken tells me Rebecca has been nothing short of a harridan since I've been away. Dicken misses me, too. And, truth to tell, this long absence from Cornwall has opened my eyes."

"Why, Eleanor, you and Dicken are . . . ?" Reggie said, delighted.

Eleanor smiled. "He has asked me to marry him many times in the last four years. I think I am finally ready to give it some serious thought."

"Famous! Will you let Nicholas and me do the wedding party, or will Rebecca want to?"

"I'm afraid Rebecca will *insist,*" Eleanor laughed. "She has been pushing Dicken at me for ages." Thomas squawked, demanding attention. "Want me to take him up, my dear?"

"Not unless you can manage to feed him, too." Reggie smiled impishly.

"Do hurry back. Nicky has been keeping such a close eye on you all day, I'm sure he'll go hunting for you if you're gone long."

"Not as long as I know where she is," Nicholas said, approaching from behind them. He scooped Thomas up. "So the rascal's hungry, is he? Good God, he's dripping, too!" He quickly held the boy away from him, and the women laughed. Reggie wrapped a smaller blanket around Thomas' bottom. "That's something babies tend to do, and often. Here, let me have him."

"No, I'll carry him up for you." Nicholas leaned closer, whispering for her ears alone. "Perhaps, after you're finished with him, we might have a little time alone?"

"My, what a pretty picture this makes," Miriam's hard voice intruded. "A father doting on his bastard. You Eden men make wonderful fathers, Nicholas. Too bad you're so terribly lacking as husbands."

Nicholas swung around. "I will not take exception, madame. You are, naturally, upset that your well-wrought plot failed to turn out as expected."

"I don't know what you mean," she replied disdainfully.

"Don't you? Let me thank you now, before I forget. If not for your brilliant guest list, my wife and I might still be estranged. We're not. And we have you to thank for our reconciliation, *mother.*"

Miriam's expression mottled with fury she couldn't contain. "I am sick to death of hearing you call me that. And, Nicholas, you don't know just how brilliant my guest list really is," she laughed. "I have a wonderful surprise for you. You see, your real mother is here! Isn't that marvelous? So why don't you make a fool of yourself by spending the rest of the evening asking every lady here if she's the bitch who whelped you? That would be *such* fun."

Nicholas couldn't move. He was so stunned he couldn't even reach out to stop Miriam from walking away. Reggie's heart twisted when she took Thomas from him, he didn't seem to know she had done so.

"Oh, Nicholas, don't let her upset you," Reggie said gently. "She only said that for spite."

"Did she?" The eyes that met Reggie's were tormented. "Did she? What if she told the truth?"

Desperate for help, Reggie turned toward Eleanor. The older woman was ashen. Reggie understood, but the need had never been greater.

"Tell him," she said quietly, and Ellie gasped.

"Regina!"

"Can't you see? It's time." She grasped Thomas more tightly and waited.

Nicholas looked from Reggie to Eleanor, misery and confusion mixed in his face.

"Oh, Nicky, don't hate me," Eleanor began on a pleading note. "Miriam was being spiteful, but—but she also spoke the truth."

"No!" The word tore out of him. "Not you. You would have told if—"

"I couldn't." Eleanor was crying. "I gave Miriam my word I would never claim you when *she* gave *me* her word she would raise you as her own."

"Is that what you think she did?" he asked painfully. "She was never a mother to me, Ellie, even when I was a child. You were here then. *You know that.*"

"Yes, and I dried your tears and soothed your hurts and died a little every time. Your father didn't want you labeled a bastard, Nicky, and I didn't either. Miriam kept her word that she would never tell, so I had to keep mine."

"She told my wife. And she put me through hell," he hissed at her.

"She judged Regina correctly. She knew the knowledge would go no further and it hasn't."

"She always threatened to let the fact be known."

"Only threats, Nicky."

"But I lived with her threats. They governed my life. Even so, I would have taken the label gladly if I could have had a real mother. Didn't you see that when I poured out my heart to you all those years? *Why didn't you tell me?*"

The bastardy stigma wasn't as important as this war. Both knew it. Eleanor sobbed, "Forgive me," and ran into the house.

Reggie placed her hand on Nicholas' arm. "She was afraid to tell you, afraid you would hate her. Go after her, Nicholas. Listen to her calmly and let her tell you what she told me. It hasn't been easy for her all these years either."

"You knew?" he asked incredulous.

"Since I gave birth to Thomas," she answered gently. "She was with me during labor, and she wanted me to know the real reason why you weren't there. You see, Nicholas, I'm afraid I didn't believe that anyone could be so foolish as to let his having been birthed on the wrong side of the blanket stop him from marrying." She smiled up at him. "I'm sorry, but I never appreciated how much it meant to you."

"It doesn't mean much anymore," he conceded.

"Then don't judge her so harshly, Nicholas, and hear her out without erupting. Please."

He stood there looking at the house and she went on, "Not every woman has the courage to raise an illegitimate child. Look how *you* dealt with it, after all. You decided never to marry because you didn't want a wife to share your burden. Do you think it's not worse for the mother? And remember how young Eleanor was at the time."

"You would have done it, wouldn't you?"

She shrugged. "Yes, but remember we Malorys are already accustomed to having bastards in the family."

He grunted.

"Go on, Nicholas. Talk to her. You'll find she's still the same woman who has always been your best friend. She's been a mother to you all along. Now it's your turn to listen to her sorrow."

His hand cupped her face tenderly. Thomas was squirming in her arms, and Nicholas said, "Go feed my son, madame."

Reggie smiled as he walked away from her, toward the house. Across the lawn, her eyes met Miriam's and she shook her head as Miriam turned away abruptly. Would Miriam ever change?

She rubbed her cheek against Thomas' head and began walking toward the house. "Don't worry, my angel, you will have so much love you will never miss hers. Just wait until you're old enough to hear about your great-uncles. Why, one was a pirate for a while, and . . ."

Chapter Forty-one

Eleanor's bedroom door was closed but Nicholas could hear heartrending sobs from inside. He opened the door soundlessly. She lay across her bed, head buried in her arms, shoulders shaking pathetically. His chest tightened painfully. He closed the door and sat down beside her, gathering her in his arms. "I'm so sorry, Ellie. I wouldn't have made you cry, not for anything, you know that."

She opened golden-brown eyes shimmering with tears. Her eyes were so like his own. Lord, what a fool he was not to have recognized that before.

"You don't hate me, Nicky?"

"Hate you?" he echoed. "You, who have always been my solace, the only person I could count on to love me?" He shook his head. "You can't imagine how many times when I was small I pretended you were my real mother. Why didn't I realize it was true?"

"You weren't supposed to know."

"I should have realized it anyhow, especially when you stopped coming here after Father died. I always wondered why you came here at all. You and Miriam barely spoke to each other. You came because of Father, didn't you?"

"I think you misunderstand, Nicky. Your father and I were together only once. No, I came to Silverley only to be near you. He kept the peace between Miriam and me, making it possible for me to be with you in your home. The reason I didn't come to Silverley after he died was because you were grown. You went to sea for two years, and then you lived in London. You rarely came to Silverley yourself, remember."

"I couldn't stand being with Miriam," he said bitterly. "You saw her all this week. It's never been any different, Ellie."

"You have to understand Miriam, Nicky. She never forgave me for loving Charles, and you were a constant reminder that she'd failed with him."

"Why the bloody hell didn't *you* marry him?"

She smiled hesitantly, a mother's smile for a stubborn child. "Charles was twenty-one when he first came to call on Miriam. She was eighteen, and I, my dear, was only fourteen. I was unnoticeable. He was smitten with her, and I was smitten with him. Fourteen is an impressionable age, you know, and Charles was so very handsome and kind. But they were married the year they met."

"To everyone's misfortune," he said softly, "Everyone's." But she shook her head.

"She loved him, Nicky, those first few years of their marriage. They were very happy. And understand this, Nicky. He never stopped loving her, no matter how difficult she was later on. Miriam was wrong about that. Eden men do make exceptional husbands, for they love only once. But Charles wanted a son, and Miriam had only miscarriages, three of them in as many years. This caused a terrible strain. She was frightened to try for the son he wanted, so she began to resent his attentions. I'm afraid fear turned her against Charles. Her love for him didn't hold up under the strain. But he did love her."

"You lived here then?"

"Yes. You were conceived here." She lowered her eyes, even now guilty over betraying her sister. "I was seventeen years old, and I loved Charles. They had a terrible fight that day because she refused to accept him in her bed. By evening he was drunk, and it just . . . happened, Nicky. I'm not even sure he knew what he was doing, though *I* did. We both regretted it afterward and vowed that Miriam was never to know. I went home to my parents house, and Charles devoted himself to his wife." She sighed. "Eventually Miriam might have gotten over her fear of conceiving. They might have been happy again."

"But I came along?"

"Yes," she admitted. "When I realized I was going to have a baby, I was hysterical. One fall from grace and I was pregnant. I even thought of killing myself. I couldn't tell my parents. I made myself sick with worry. Finally, desperate, I visited Silverley to put my dilemma in Charles' hands. Bless him, he was delighted! I couldn't quite believe that at first, but he was. I had been thinking only of myself, of being ruined, but Charles thought first of you. It made me see how selfish I was in wanting to get rid of you. Forgive me, Nicky, but I did think that was the way out. I was young and terrified, and girls of good families did not have children out of wedlock."

He hugged her to him. "Of course, Ellie. I understand."

"Well," she went on, "Charles wanted you. He was willing to destroy his marriage to have you. He might have done things differently except for Miriam's three miscarriages. He wasn't sure she would ever give him a child. And there I was, three months pregnant."

"So Miriam was told." He knew that much.

"She was shocked, of course. She couldn't believe her own sister would do such a thing. How she hated me from that day on! And she hated Charles, too, never forgiving him. Finally she came to hate you, the only innocent person in the whole mess. She was never the same again, Nicky. Her deepest bitterness was that I'd been able to give Charles the son he wanted. She felt she had failed him, but she blamed him, and me, for interfering before she had a chance to try again. Her bitterness became a monster over the years. Miriam wasn't always the way she is now. I *am* to blame, for I could have stopped Charles the night you were conceived. I could have, but I didn't."

"For God's sake, Ellie, you already said she had stopped loving him by then."

"I know, but she might have gone back to loving him." After a long, thoughtful silence, she resumed. "We were sisters, remember. That did count for something. She even forgot her resentment during those long hours when I was in labor, for it was a difficult labor, and she thought I might die. I was able to get her to swear then that she would never publicly disclaim you. I hoped she would love you, but even then I was afraid she wouldn't. So I made her swear, and she did. But she made me swear that I would never tell you I was your mother. I wanted to tell you so many times, but I'd taken a vow, so I couldn't. And after your father died, Rebecca warned me to leave it alone."

"She knew the whole story?"

Eleanor nodded. "I still don't think I would have told you if Regina hadn't insisted."

"My wife is a gem, isn't she, mother?"

It was the first time he had ever called her that, and Eleanor's face glowed.

"It took you long enough to realize it," she said.

"Oh, I always knew she was wonderful. I've just been ten kinds of a fool about her. How could I blame you for what you did when it was fear of the bastardy stigma that made me almost lose my beautiful Regina? The stigma ruled me as it ruled you."

"You will make it up to her?" she asked him urgently.

"I swear it. And you, love, are moving back to Silverley for good."

"Oh, no Nicky! I mean, well . . . Lord Barrett and I—"

"Bloody hell, you mean I'm losing you to another man when I've only just found you?" he cried, but he was thrilled for her. "Who, may I ask, is Lord Barrett?"

"You know him. He lives near Rebecca, and you've met him there many times. And it's not as if Dicken and I won't visit here often. After all, my first grandchild lives at Silverley."

They looked at each other in complete silence for a long time. He was happy for her. She was happy for him. They had come a long, hard way.

Chapter Forty-two

———❦———

Reggie crossed the sitting room and opened the door to Nicholas' bedroom, quietly slipping inside. To the right was the dressing room, the door leading out into the corridor, and next to it was the master bath, a big square room with walls and floor of blue marble and numerous large mirrors. Huge shelves held all kinds of jars and bottles, towels, shaving apparatus, and other of the lord's necessities. The bath itself was large with cupid spouts for hot and cold water.

Nicholas lay inside, relaxed, eyes closed. Harris was laying out towels and Nicholas' robe and comfortable slippers. It was only nine o'clock, and Miriam's guests were still in the house.

"Good evening, Harris," Reggie greeted him cheerfully. The valet was startled, but he managed to nod and return her greeting. Nicholas gave her a lazy grin.

"Meg has been asking after you, Harris," Reggie continued innocently as though she intruded on a man's toilet all the time and wasn't on a romantic errand at all.

Harris perked up. "Has she, madame?"

"Oh, yes. And you know, it's such a beautiful night. There's a lovely summer moon. What a perfect night for a stroll around the grounds, Meg was saying. Why don't you go find her, Harris? I'm sure his lordship won't mind. Will you, Nicholas?"

"Not at all. Run along, Harris. I won't be needing you again tonight."

"Thank you, sir." Harris made a formal bow before, wholly out of character, he turned and dashed from the room.

Nicholas chuckled. "I don't believe it. Harris and sour Meg?"

"Meg is not sour," she retorted. "And they have been very friendly for some time now."

"Is love blooming there, too? You know about Ellie and Lord Barrett, I assume? You know everything before I do."

"I'm so happy for Ellie."

"You don't think she's too old to be contemplating matrimony?"

"You can't be serious, Nicholas," Reggie giggled.

"I suppose not." He grinned, watching as she trailed her hand through the water. He caught it as it neared him, bringing it to his lips for a kiss. "I have you to thank, you know, for my childhood dreams coming true. She would never have told me if not for you. You know, don't you, Reggie, how awful it is to wonder about your mother all the time? Who was she, what was she like? You lost both of your parents when you were only two."

She smiled gently. "I had four wonderful uncles to tell me everything I wanted to know about them—including faults, of which they spared no detail. But you did have your mother all along, you just never knew it."

"One of the things Ellie told me is that we Eden men only love once. That should delight you."

"Should it?"

"Doesn't it?"

"Oh, I don't know," Reggie said evasively. "I'll let you know after we have our talk. Care to have your back scrubbed?"

She scooped the sponge out of the water without waiting for an answer and moved behind him. She was grinning, but he couldn't see her expression.

"I suppose you would like an apology?" he began uncomfortably.

"That would be nice."

"I do apologize, Regina."

"What for?"

"What do you mean what for?" he growled, turning to look at her.

"If you would be a little more specific, Nicholas."

"I'm sorry I was such a dolt during our engagement."

"No, you weren't very nice at all. But I can forgive you for that. Go on." She began running the sponge along his back, then up around his neck, very slowly.

"Go on?" He sounded bewildered, and Reggie threw the sponge at his head.

"You left me. Or have you forgotten?"

He grabbed hold of the sponge. "Blister it, you know why I did."

Reggie came around to the side of the tub and looked down at him, hands on hips, her eyes glittering. "I beg to differ. I do not know why. It is the only thing I have not been able to figure out."

In a quiet voice, with no fight in him, he said, "I couldn't remain near you without . . ."

She prompted him. "Without?"

"Without making love to you."

There was utter silence. Then she said, "Why couldn't you make love to me?"

"Bloody hell!" he swore. "I was certain you would despise me as soon as you learned of my parentage. I knew I couldn't bear your scorn. I was a bloody fool, I admit it. But I knew Miriam wouldn't keep her mouth shut. I was right about that. I was just wrong about your reaction to my birth."

"Very well. Your explanation will do. You may go on."

He racked his brains. "I told you the truth about Selena. She really did contrive that scene you witnessed in the conservatory."

"I believe you."

This was apparently not what she was waiting to hear. "Oh! Your friend George. I—I suppose I was a bit unreasonable with him, but it wasn't the first time his being with you has rubbed me the wrong way."

"Were you jealous, Nicholas?" Her humor resurfaced.

"I . . . yes, blister it, I was!"

"Duly noted. You may go on," she said, her eyes intent on his face.

"But what else have I done?" he asked, exasperated.

The cobalt eyes sparked. "You are forgetting you had to be returned to me by force."

"No!" His temper exploded. "Now there, you're wrong! I was coming back. My ship was ready to sail. I had decided to tell you everything, explain why I behaved as I did. Your bloody uncle and his thugs arrived the night before I was to sail."

"Oh, dear. I suppose you were too angry over Uncle James' interference to talk to me honestly?"

Nicholas scowled. "I don't like that particular uncle of yours, not at all."

"He'll grow on you."

"I'd rather you grew on me."

"That might be arranged."

"Then you don't mind that I am destined to love only once?" he asked very seriously. But she wasn't ready to declare herself to him, not just then.

"If you could be a little more specific . . ."

"Haven't I told you what you want to hear?"

"You have not," she informed him.

"Then come here."

"Nicholas," she gasped. "I'm not dressed for bathing."

He grabbed her and pulled her into the bath on top of him. "I love you, love you, love you, love you. Is that enough or do you want more?"

"That will do—for tonight." Reggie wrapped her arms around his neck. Their lips met.

After some delightful kissing, he demanded, "Well?"

"Well, what?" she teased. He whacked her bottom. "Oh. Well, I guess I love you, too."

"You *guess?*"

"Well, I must, mustn't I, if I put up with you? No, no!" she shrieked as he began tickling her. "All right. I love you, you impossible man. I set my cap for you, didn't I? And I never gave up hoping you would return my love. Now aren't you glad I'm such a stubborn fellow?"

"Stubborn fellow, but delightful all the same." He kissed her soundly. "You were right, love, you're not dressed for bathing. Shall we remedy that?"

"I thought you'd never ask."

Chapter Forty-three

After bidding farewell to the last guest, Nicholas and Regina stood kissing at the door. "Peace at last," he said with a long sigh.

"Well, not quite," Reggie replied hesitantly, twining a finger in his lapel. "I—I sent a message last night to invite my family out here for the day. Don't be mad, Nicholas. George told me he saw Tony last week and Tony was very upset. I know it was because of us."

"Couldn't you have just written them a letter?" he asked wearily, "and told them you were all right?"

"Letters aren't the same as seeing for themselves how happy I am. They worry about me, Nicholas, and I want them to know everything is finally all right now."

"Then I suppose I will have to bear it for one day." He sighed again.

"You're not angry?"

"I don't dare get angry with you, love." He said this so seriously that she frowned in puzzlement. "You get angry right back."

"Devil!" she retorted.

Nicholas grinned at her. Then, patting her backside, he pushed her gently toward the staircase. "Now run along for a while. You've reminded me that I have some family business of my own to take care of."

He caught Miriam just as she was leaving for her morning ride, delayed until her guests departed. "A word with you, madame, in the library, if you please."

Miriam started to tell him she was too busy, then thought better of it. His manner invited no argument. They walked down the stairs together without a word. "I hope this won't take long," she said curtly as he closed the library door behind them.

"It shouldn't. Do sit down, Miriam."

She frowned. "You have never called me anything but 'mother.' "

Nicholas observed the cold glitter in her brown eyes. It was always there when they were alone. This woman really did hate him. Nothing would change that.

"Imagine," he said, "overnight, two sisters have switched places." Her face went pale, so he said, "I guess you haven't had a chance to talk to Ellie this morning, have you?"

"She told you?"

"Well, you did suggest I ask every lady present if she was my mother." He couldn't resist the barb.

"You didn't!"

"No, Miriam, I didn't. After you opened the wound, my wife healed it. She forced Ellie to confess. I have the whole of it now, finally, and I want to say that I'm sorry for what you've been through, Miriam, now that I understand it all."

"Don't you dare feel sorry for me!" she cried, stunned.

"As you wish," he replied stiffly, no longer uncomfortable over the decision he had come to during the night. "I asked you in here to inform you that, under the circumstance, it is no longer desirable that you live at Silverley. Find yourself a cottage somewhere far from here. I will buy it for you. My father left you a modest income. I will match it. I owe you no more than that."

"Bribery, Nicholas?" she sneered.

"No, Miriam," he said, tired of it all. "If you want to inform the world that it was not you who provided your husband with his heir, by all means do so. My wife knows and doesn't care, and that is all that matters to me."

"You really mean this, don't you?"

"I do."

"You bastard," she said furiously. "You think you have it all, don't you? But wait a few years and your precious wife will hate you—just as I hated your father."

"She's not like you, Miriam." He smiled.

"I always hated it here at Silverley," she said savagely. "I only stayed to keep you away."

"I know that, Miriam," he said quietly.

"I won't stay here a moment longer," she retorted. "And you can be sure it won't be a cottage I'll find, but a mansion!"

She stalked out of the room, and he took a deep breath, grateful to have her gone. It would be worth a fortune to finally have his home back, free of Miriam's bitterness.

A few hours later, a coach rumbled down the driveway with Nicholas' Aunt Miriam in it. The three people on the doorstep breathed a collective sigh as they watched it go. Eleanor went back into the house then, but Nicholas stood there a moment longer, his arms around his wife, holding her close to him, her cheek resting against his chest.

They stayed there too long, for soon two carriages and a coach appeared at the end of the long drive. Nicholas stiffened, then relaxed. What the hell. If Regina loved them, perhaps they weren't all that bad.

"Invaded again," he murmured dryly.

"Don't you dare run away, Nicholas Eden," Reggie scolded.

She held on to him, bubbling with excitement. Jason and Derek and half of Edward's brood alighted from the first carriage. Jason was the first to clasp Nicholas in a hearty embrace.

"Glad to see you came to your senses, my boy. James said you were eager to see your son. Hope your business won't be calling you away too often in the future."

"No, sir, it won't," Nicholas managed to reply cordially, though his hackles rose over what James had told him. Bloody liar.

Derek was next in line, and he got a bear hug. "About time you got around to sending out an invitation, old man."

"Good to see you, Derek."

The cousins were next, and Edward and his wife, all trooping toward the house chattering happily. But then Nicholas caught sight of James and Anthony standing by a carriage glowering at him. He turned to enter the house, muttering about uninvited guests. Reggie heard him and frowned at her younger uncles. "Don't you dare, either of you!" she warned, knowing she didn't need to be explicit. They understood. "I love him and he loves me. And if you two can't make friends with him, I'll—I'll never speak to you again!" She followed her husband into the house, leaving Anthony and James outside.

James looked at his brother and grinned. "I think she means it."

"I know she means it," Anthony replied, clapping James on the back. "Come on then. Let's see what we can do about patching it up with the bounder."

A few minutes later, they cornered Nicholas in the drawing room, dragging him away from the others, one on each side of him. Nicholas sighed in exasperation. Were these Malorys always going to gang up on him? "Yes?"

"Regan wants a truce, lad," James began. "And we're willing if you are."

"Blister it! It's Reggie, not Regan," Anthony snapped at his brother. "When will you ever—"

"What is wrong with Regina?" Nicholas interrupted.

The two men looked at him and began laughing. "Nothing at all, old chap," Anthony conceded. "*You* can call her anything you like. It's this stubborn fellow here who insists on inventing new names all the time."

"And what is 'puss' if not an invention of yours?" James retorted.

"An endearment, that's what."

"And Regan isn't an endearment?"

Nicholas left the brothers to finish the argument on their own. He caught his wife and pulled her down on a sofa beside him.

"You know, love, when I married you, I didn't think I was marrying the Malory brothers, too."

"You're not angry with me for inviting them, are you? I just wanted them to be part of our happiness."

"I know. And I also know you said they were staying only for the day. Your family does take getting used to, especially those two." He nodded toward the corner, and she watched Anthony and James having their heated discussion.

She grinned impishly. "They don't mean half of what they say. And they won't be here that often anyway. Why, Uncle James is sailing next week. He probably won't be back more than once a year from now on."

"And Anthony?"

"Well, Uncle Tony will drop by from time to time to check on me, but you'll get to like him, I promise you will. How can you not when you two have so much in common? Why, the reason I lost my heart to you so quickly was that you reminded me of Tony."

"Bloody hell," he growled.

"Oh, don't sulk," she teased, wrapping her fingers in his. That's not the only reason I love you, you know. Shall I tell you some more reasons?"

"Can we escape for a while?" he asked eagerly.

"I think that can be arranged."

"Then come upstairs with me."

"Nicholas! It's the middle of the afternoon," she hissed, shocked.

"I can't wait any longer, love," he whispered against her ear.

James caught sight of the couple racing out of the room, hand in hand, Reggie holding her other hand against her mouth to stifle her laughter. "Will you look at that?" he cut into Anthony's speech. "Did I tell you he was the man for her?"

"You did not," Anthony retorted hotly. "But of course *I* knew it all along."

TENDER REBEL

*This book is dedicated with love
to all my readers,
with special thanks to those who wanted
Uncle Tony to have his own story.*

Chapter One

England, 1818

"Are ye scared, hinny?"

Roslynn Chadwick turned away from the coach window and the passing scenery she had been staring at for the last hour without actually seeing. Scared? She was alone in the world now with no guardian, no family worth mentioning. She was on her way to an uncertain future and leaving behind all that was familiar to her. Scared? She was terrified.

But Nettie MacDonald wasn't to know that, not if Roslynn could help it. Nettie was too uneasy herself, had been ever since they'd crossed the English border yesterday morning, though she too tried to hide it by turning querulous, as was her way. Nettie had been all chipper and cheer before that, even while crossing the Lowlands, which she disdained. A Highlander all her life, and that was forty-two years' worth, Nettie never thought the day would come when she would be forced to leave her beloved Highlands, let alone cross the border into England. England! But Nettie wouldn't be left behind, no, not dear Nettie.

Roslynn managed a smile for Nettie's benefit, and even a bit of a twinkle in her hazel eyes to reassure her abigail. "Och, and what've I to be scared of, Nettie? Didna we manage to sneak off in the dead of night wi' none the wiser? Geordie'll be searching Aberdeen and Edinburgh for weeks and weeks and never guess we've absconded to London."

"That he will." Nettie spared herself a pleased smile for their success so far, forgetting for the moment her fear and dislike of the English. Her dislike of Geordie Cameron went much deeper. "And I hope that devil chokes on his spleen when he realizes ye've escaped his foul plans, that I do. I didna like Duncan, bless him, making ye promise what ye had tae, but he knew what was best fer ye. And dinna be thinking I'm sae fashed I didna hear ye fergetting yer proper English, lass, that Duncan brought that fine snobbish tutor tae be teaching ye. Ye'll no' be fergetting it, especially now we're here among the devil's kin."

Roslynn grinned when this last was delivered in Nettie's most scolding tone, and couldn't resist teasing a bit more. "When I see an Englishmon will be soon enough for me to be remembering my proper English. You wouldna deny me this wee bit of time left when I dinna have to be thinking about every word I say, would you now?"

"Humph! 'Tis only when ye're that upset that ye ferget anymore, and well I ken it."

Of course Nettie knew it. Nettie knew Roslynn better than herself sometimes. And if Roslynn wasn't in a temper, which was when she most often forgot herself and lapsed into the Scottish brogue she had picked up from Gramp and Nettie, she was still upset, and with reason. But not enough to forget the proper English that had been drummed into her by her tutor. Roslynn sighed.

"I hope the trunks got there, or we'll be in a fine pickle." They had both left with only one change of clothes, to further outwit her cousin Geordie, just in case someone saw them leave and told him.

"That's the least of yer worries, lass. Sure and it saved time bringing that London modiste tae Cameron Hall tae be making ye all those bonny dresses, sae ye dinna have tae be fitted when we get there. Duncan, bless him, thought of everything, even sending the trunks ahead, one by one, sae Geordie wouldna suspect anything if he was watching."

And Nettie had thought it was such a lark, sneaking off in the middle of the night as they had, with their skirts hiked up and wearing old breeches underneath so in the moonlight they might pass for men. Truth be known, Roslynn had thought so too. In fact, that was the only part of this madness she had enjoyed. They had ridden to the nearest town where the prearranged coach and driver were waiting, and had had to wait several hours to be sure they weren't followed before they actually set off on this journey. But all the stealth and bother had been necessary to outwit Geordie Cameron. At least Gramp had made Roslynn believe it was necessary.

And Roslynn could believe it after seeing Geordie's face when Gramp's will was read. After all, Geordie was Duncan Cameron's great-nephew, his youngest brother's grandson, and his only male relative still living. Geordie had every right to assume some of Duncan's great wealth would be left to him, if only a small part. But Duncan had left his entire estate to Roslynn, his only grandchild: Cameron Hall, the mills, the countless other businesses, everything. And Geordie had been hard put not to fly into a rage.

"He shouldna have been sae surprised," Nettie had said after Geordie left the day of the reading. "He knew Duncan hated him, that he blamed him fer yer dear mother's death. Why, 'tis why he was courting ye sae diligently all these years. He knew Duncan'd leave it all tae ye. And 'tis why we've nae time tae lose, now Duncan's gone."

No, there was no time to lose. Roslynn knew it when Geordie once more asked her to marry him after the will was read, and she once more refused. She and Nettie had left that very night, with no time to grieve, no time to regret the promise she had made to her grandfather. But she had done her grieving in the last two months, when they had known Duncan's time was finally up. And it had been a blessing in fact, his death, for he had been wasting away these last seven years and suffering with the pain, and it was only his Scot's stubbornness that had let him linger this long. No, she couldn't be sorry Gramp's suffering was finally over. But oh, how she would miss that dear old man who had been both mother and father to her all these years.

"Ye'll no' grieve fer me, lassie," he'd told her weeks before he died. "I forbid it. Ye've given me too many years, too many wasted years, and I'll no' have ye giving even one day more once I'm gone. Ye'll promise me that too."

One more promise to the old man she loved, the man who had raised her and bullied her and loved her ever since his daughter had returned to him tugging along a six-year-old Roslynn in her wake. What did one more promise matter when she'd already given him the fateful one that had her in such trepidation now? And then there had been no time for grieving anyway, so she had at least fulfilled that promise.

Nettie scowled as she watched Roslynn turn her eyes back to the window and knew she was thinking of Duncan Cameron again. "Gramp" she had disrespectfully called him from the day her mother had first brought her to Cameron Hall to stay, and that just to get his goat. How the little imp had loved nettling the fierce old Scot, and how he had delighted in every bit of teasing and mischief she served him. They would both miss him, but there were too many other things to think of now.

"We're coming tae the inn finally," Nettie observed from her seat facing the front of the coach.

Roslynn leaned forward and turned to the side to see out the window in the same direction, and the setting sun caught her full in the face, touching her hair and making it appear like a sunset itself. Pretty hair, the lass had, red-gold like Janet's, her mother. Nettie's own hair was black as coal, and her eyes were the dull green of a loch shadowed by tall oaks. Roslynn had Janet's eyes too, that greenish-gray color that was saved from being nondescript by the golden flecks that were so brightly noticeable. Come to that, everything about her was a lot like Janet Cameron before she had gone away with her Englishman. In fact, there was nothing at all of Roslynn's father in her, that self same Englishman who had stolen Janet's heart and turned her into a shadow of herself after the tragic accident that killed him. Perhaps it was just as well Janet had died a year afterward, for she had never been the same. And Roslynn, thank God, had her grandfather to lean on then. A seven-year-old child, with both parents gone, was fortunately adaptable, especially with an old Scot to dote on her every whim.

Och, I'm as bad as the lass, tae be thinking about the dead when 'tis the future that's sae in doubt.

"Let's hope the beds are at least softer than last night," Roslynn commented as the coach stopped before the country inn. "That is the *only* thing that has me eager to get to London. I know Frances will have comfortable beds waiting for us."

"Ye mean ye'll no' be glad tae see yer best friend after all these years?"

Roslynn glanced at Nettie with surprise. "Well, of course, there's that. Of course there is. I can't wait to see her again. But the circumstances won't allow a pleasant reunion, will they? I mean, with no time to lose, how much actual visiting will I get to have with Frances? Oh, drat Geordie anyway," she added with a scowl that drew her titian brows closer together. "If it weren't for him—"

"Ye wouldna have made nae promises, and we wouldna be here now, and it does nae good tae be bewailing it, now, does it?" Nettie retorted.

Roslynn grinned. "Who was bewailing what last night when she lay in a hard bed that wasn't fit for bedbugs, let alone a tired body?"

Nettie snorted, refusing to answer that reminder, and shooed Roslynn out of the coach as soon as the driver opened the door and held up his hand for her. Roslynn's chuckle carried back to her abigail as she walked ahead, still thinking about it, and Nettie snorted again, this time to herself.

Ye're no' sae auld that ye canna stand a few nights' discomfort, Nettie, lass, she thought, watching Roslynn's bouncy step that in fact made her feel twice her age at the moment. *The bed can be made of stone and ye'll no' say one word tonight, or ye'll never hear the end of it from the wee lassie.*

But then Nettie grinned, shaking her head. A bit of teasing was just what Roslynn needed to be doing to get her mind off the future. *That bed can be soft as down, but ye better say 'tis full of rocks, lass. 'Tis been too long since ye've heard her laugh and seen the mischief in her eyes. She needs tae tease, that she does.*

As Roslynn approached the inn, she barely noticed the sixteen-year-old lad standing on a stool lighting the lamp above the door, but he unfortunately noticed her. Hearing the husky chuckle that was so different from any sound of humor he'd ever heard before, he glanced over his shoulder, then nearly fell off the stool, he was so boggled by the sight of her. Lit up like a flame, she was, in the reddish glow of the setting sun that streaked across the yard, and getting closer by the second, until he could make out every feature of her heart-shaped face, from the finely molded cheekbones and small tapered nose to the firm little chin and generous, full lips. And then she passed through the door, and his head craned around it to follow her inside, until a sharp *humph* snapped his head back around and he stared at the stern-faced abigail looking up at him, his cheeks flushing hotly.

But Nettie took pity on the lad and didn't dress him down as she usually did anyone caught gawking at her Roslynn. It happened wherever they went, for Lady Roslynn Chadwick had that effect on the male species, and no age seemed to be immune, from small tykes to old men, and everything in breeches in between. And this was the lass to be turned loose on London.

Chapter Two

"And you wondered who his tailor is?" the Honorable William Fairfax snickered aside to his young friend. "Told you his tailor had nothing to do with it, didn't I? You want to turn yourself out in a reasonable facsimile, best take up the gloves. He's been at it for more'n a dozen years, so I hear."

William's young friend, Cully, flinched at the sound of leather connecting with solid flesh again, but squinted his eyes open this time. He had closed them tight a few minutes ago when the first dribble of blood had appeared from an abused nose. He shuddered now, for that same abused nose was gushing blood, and so was the swollen mouth below it, and so was a split brow above it.

"No taste for it, Cully?" William grinned, eyeing his friend's green pallor. "Imagine his partner don't either, not today leastways." He chuckled here, thinking that funny. "Now if Knighton would just climb in the ring with him, we might have something to wager on. He trained him, you know. 'Course, Knighton ain't come out ahead in the last ten years, so I hear, though he does give the lord a better showing. But then Malory's winded now, so that'd even the odds some."

But as they watched along with a few dozen other gentlemen surrounding the boxing ring, Sir Anthony Malory relaxed his stance and turned to glower at the owner of the sporting hall. "Blister it, Knighton, I told you he wasn't ready yet. He hasn't healed from the last time."

John Knighton shrugged, though there was a definite spark of humor in his dark eyes as he gazed back at the disgusted pugilist he considered a friend. "I didn't hear any other takers, my lord, did you?

Maybe if you let someone else win for a change, you'd find more partners to choose from for your exercise."

There were a good many chuckles over that remark. Everyone
there knew it had been a decade since Malory had lost a match or let
anyone get the better of him even in a few rounds of sparring. He was in
superb condition, muscles honed to perfection, but it was his skill in the
ring that made him so remarkable—and unchallenged. The promoters,
Knighton among them, would give their eyeteeth to get him in the ring
for a professional fight. But to a rakehell like Malory, boxing was no
more than a means of exercise to keep him fit and counteract the life of
dissipation he enjoyed. His thrice-weekly visits to Knighton's Hall
were treated in the same vein as his morning rides in the park, simply
for his own pleasure.

Half the gentlemen there were pugilists as well, awaiting their turn
to exercise in the ring. Some, like the Honorable Fairfax, just dropped
by to watch the experts work out, though occasionally there was the
opportunity to do a little gambling if any serious challenges were
issued. A few others who were present were Malory's cronies; they frequently showed up to watch him demolish the sparring partners
Knighton had the misfortune to provide, being wise enough themselves
never to get in the ring with him.

One of them ribbed Anthony now. Nearly of the same height, but
more on the lean side, Lord Amherst was a devil-may-care fellow
whose gray eyes were more often than not crinkled with humor. The
same age, but fair where Anthony was dark, he often shared the same
interests, mainly women, gambling, and women.

"The only way you'll get someone to put his heart into it, Malory,
is if you cuckold some young Corinthian your size and force him to
issue the challenge."

"With my luck, George," Malory shot back, "he'd call for pistols
instead, and what fun is that?"

George Amherst laughed at the dry tone, for if not everyone knew
that Anthony was unbeatable in the ring, they did know he was non-
pareil on the dueling field. He was even known to quite nonchalantly
ask his challengers on what luckless part of their anatomy they would
like to receive their wound of honor, which naturally set the poor fellows trembling in their boots, if they weren't already.

As far as George knew, Anthony had never actually killed anyone in a duel, since nearly all his were fought over women, rake that he was, and he firmly believed there wasn't a woman born worth dying over—well, that was excluding those in his family, of course. Malory was devilish touchy about his family. He might be a bachelor, confirmed positively, but with three older brothers with offspring aplenty, he didn't lack for nieces and nephews to dote on.

"Looking for competition, Tony? You should have sent your man round to find me. You know I'm always happy to oblige you."

George swung around sharply, disbelieving his ears at the sound of a voice he hadn't heard in more than ten years. And then his brows shot up incredulously, for he hadn't been mistaken. Standing in the doorway was James Malory, older certainly, but looking every bit as dangerous as he ever had ten years ago when he had been London's most notorious rakehell. Big, blond, and still handsome too, by God! Incredible!

And then George swung back to see how Anthony was taking this unexpected appearance. The two brothers had been close before, being only a year apart in age and inclined toward the same interests, though James was assuredly the wilder of the two—at least he had been. But then James had disappeared, and for some reason or other that the family never spoke of, the other brothers had disowned him, Anthony included, and wouldn't even mention his name. As close as George was to Anthony all these years since, and he liked to think they were best friends, Anthony had never once confided what it was that James had done to be ousted from the family.

But to George's surprise, Anthony was showing no signs of his formidable temper. In fact, no emotion whatever crossed his handsome countenance for those in the hall to remark on. You had to know him well to recognize that gleam in his cobalt-blue eyes for what it was: pleasure, not fury.

And yet when he spoke, you'd have thought he was addressing his worst enemy. "James, what the bloody hell are you still doing in London? You were to sail this morning!"

James did no more than offer a bored shrug. "Change of plans, thanks to Jeremy's newfound stubbornness. Since he's met the rest of the family, he's become impossible to handle. I swear he's been taking lessons from Regan in manipulation, for he managed somehow or other to talk me into letting him finish his schooling here, though I'm deuced if I know exactly how he did it."

Anthony wanted to laugh at James' expression of bafflement at being outmaneuvered by a seventeen-year-old whelp who looked more Anthony's son than James', and he would have if James hadn't slipped the name Regan into his explanation. The name always rubbed Anthony on the raw, as it did Jason and Edward, their older brothers, and James knew it, which was why he used "Regan" instead of "Reggie," as the rest of the family called Regina Eden. But as far back as Anthony could remember, James had had to be different, going his own way and doing as he bloody well pleased, and to hell with the consequences.

As James had spoken, he had walked forward, casually slipping out of his coat to reveal the sort of loose-sleeved shirt that he preferred when captaining the *Maiden Anne*. Since he gave every appearance of being about to oblige Anthony in the ring, Anthony refrained from taking him to task over his "Regan," which would have started their usual argument and likely jeopardized a little friendly sparring.

"Does this mean you'll be staying as well?" Anthony asked as James handed over his coat to George and accepted the gloves a grinning John Knighton helped him into.

"Only long enough to get the youngun settled and togged up, I think, at least for now. Though Connie has pointed out that the only reason we were willing to set ourselves down in the islands was to give Jeremy a home."

Anthony couldn't help laughing this time. "Two old sea dogs playing mother. God, I wish I could've seen it."

"I wouldn't talk, Tony," James said, unperturbed by the taunting. "You played mother yourself each summer for six years, didn't you?"

"Father," Anthony corrected. "Or more like big brother, which is neither here nor there. I'm surprised you didn't marry like Jason did, just to give Jeremy a mother. 'Course, with Conrad Sharp willing to help you raise the lad, I suppose you didn't think it necessary."

James leaped up into the ring. "That's my best friend you're disparaging."

Anthony bowed slightly. "Point taken. So who gets the dear boy while you and Connie are deciding whether to come home for good?"

James' right connected solidly with Anthony's midsection just before he said, "You do."

While Anthony doubled over, absorbing the punch as well as the answer, the wagers began flying about the room. At last there was someone who looked as if he just might be able to beat the unbeatable Lord Malory. Malory was taller by a few inches, but the other bloke was brawnier, and looked quite capable of wiping the floor with anyone in the room, Malory included. And they were going to be privileged to see it. Only a few there realized these two were brothers.

As soon as Anthony was able to draw breath, he scowled at James for the surprise punch, but as to his revelation, he simply said, "Me? How'd I get so lucky?"

"You're the lad's choice. You're his bloody idol, don't you know— next to me, of course."

"Of course," Anthony replied and took James equally by surprise with an uppercut that staggered James back several paces. As James flexed his jaw, Anthony added, "I'll be glad to have him, as long as you realize I won't curtail my activities as I did for Reggie."

They circled each other now, both getting in another punch before James replied, "Don't expect you to, lad, when I didn't. It's different when you've got a boy underfoot. Hell and fire, he's been wenching since he was fourteen."

Anthony burst into laughter at that, unfortunately letting down his guard to receive a ringing blow to the side of his head. But he was quick enough to counteract with an upper to James' middle that lifted him a good five inches off the floor, amazingly done, since James was a good thirty pounds heavier in solid muscle.

Anthony stood back, allowing his brother a moment to catch his breath. When James glanced up, still bent over, he was grinning.

"Do we really want to take aches and pains to bed tonight, Tony?"

Anthony's teeth flashed in accordance. "Not when something softer can be found, and I assure you, something softer can be found." He came forward to throw an arm around his brother's shoulder.

"Then you'll take the lad until school starts?"

"Love to, but good God, I can see I'll get a fair amount of ribbing from it. Anyone who looks at Jeremy will think he's mine."

"That's why he wants you." James grinned, flashing his own set of pearly whites. "He's got a devilish sense of humor. Now about tonight. I know a couple of wenches—"

"Wenches, indeed. You were a pirate too long, Captain Hawke. Now I know a couple of ladies . . ."

Chapter Three

"But I don't understand, Ros," Lady Frances leaned forward to say. "Why would you want to tie yourself to a man when you don't have to? I mean, if you were already in love, that'd be different. But you're talking about marrying someone you haven't even met yet."

"Frances, if I hadn't promised, do you really think I'd do it?" Roslynn asked.

"Well, I should certainly hope not—but who's to know if you don't keep the promise? I mean, your grandfather's dead and—" Frances broke off at the look on her friend's face. "Forget I said that."

"I will."

"Oh, I just think it's such a shame!" Frances sighed with emphasis.

Lady Frances Grenfell was a striking woman by any standards. On the tiny side, she was not exactly beautiful but was, however, very handsome with her blond hair and dark brown eyes. At one time she had been the most cheerful, effervescent girl Roslynn had ever known, but that was before her disappointing marriage to Henry Grenfell seven years ago. Now she was demure, matronly even, yet she did still have her moments that could remind Roslynn of the happy girl she had once been.

"You're as independent now as anyone could ever ask to be," Frances continued determinedly. "With more money than you know what to do with, and not a soul to tell you what to do. It took me seven years and living with a man I didn't love for five of them to get to where you are now, and still I have a mother who nags if she hears of me doing the slightest thing she doesn't approve of. Even as a widow living alone with my son, I still have someone to answer to. But you, Roslynn, you have no one at all to worry about, and yet you must give yourself over to some man who will delight in putting a harness on your freedom as Lord Henry did to me. And I know you don't want to do it. I know that very well."

"It doesn't matter what I want, Frances. It's what I have to do."

"But why?" Frances cried in exasperation. "That's what I want to know. And don't just say again because you promised your grandfather you would. Tell me why he made you make such a promise. If it was so important to him, he had ample time to have married you off himself."

"Well, as to that," Roslynn replied, "there was no one I wanted to marry. And Gramp wouldn't have forced me on someone I didn't want."

"In all these years? No one at all?"

"Och, I hate the way you say *all these years,* Frances, I really do. Dinna remind me how difficult it's going to be for me."

Frances' brown eyes widened. "Difficult?" She nearly laughed. "Posh! If ever there was going to be anything so easy, it's getting you married. You'll have so many hopefuls, you won't know what to do with them all. And your age, m'dear, won't matter one little jot. Good God, don't you know how incredibly lovely you are? And if that weren't enough, you've got a fortune that would make a banker positively drool."

"I'm twenty-five years old, Frances!" Roslynn said in such a way that she might as well have said one hundred.

Frances grinned. "So am I, and I don't consider that ancient, thank you."

"It's different when you're a widow. You've been married. No one would think anything of you marrying again."

"No, they won't, because I never will."

Roslynn frowned at the interruption. "But the *ton* will take one look at me on the marriage block next to all those young debutantes and laugh their heads off."

Frances smiled. "Honestly, Ros—"

"It's true. Hell's teeth, I'd laugh myself to see a twenty-five-year-old spinster making a fool of herself." Roslynn snorted.

"Now stop it. I tell you—I *swear* to you, your age won't matter."

Roslynn couldn't believe it, much as she wanted to. She hid it well, but she was very close to tears. This was the very reason she was so terrified of putting herself forward in search of a husband. She was going to make a fool of herself, and that was something she couldn't bear.

"They'll think something's terribly wrong with me because I didn't marry before now, Fran. You know they're bound to. It's human nature."

"They'll understand perfectly when they hear you've spent the past six years nursing your grandfather, and they'll commend you for it. Now, not another word about your age. That is the least of your worries. And you have quite managed to avoid answering my question, haven't you?"

Roslynn chuckled at the stern look on her friend's face, a warm, husky sound that was uniquely her own. She and Nettie had arrived at the town house on South Audley Street late last night, so late that there had been no time for the two old friends to talk until this morning. And it was an old friendship, one that had survived twelve years with only one visit in the last ten, and that was when Frances had brought her son, Timmy, to the Highlands for a holiday four years ago.

Roslynn had other women friends in Scotland, but none as close as Frances, and none to whom she felt free to confide all her secrets. They had met when they were thirteen, when Gramp had carted her off to school in England to "ladify" her, since he swore she was turning into a wee hoyden with no sense a-tall of her station—which was certainly true, for all that, but not very fair as far as she was concerned at the time.

Roslynn had lasted two years at school before she was kicked out and carted back to Cameron Hall for "incorrigible behavior." Gramp didn't scold. Fact was he had missed her too much and was glad to have her back. But he enticed one of the fine teachers away from the school to continue Roslynn's education, and there wasn't any mischief terrible enough to make Miss Beechham quit; Gramp was paying her too much.

But during those two years in England, Frances and Roslynn had been inseparable. And if she hadn't had her own coming out when she turned eighteen, she had shared Frances' through their letters. Through Frances, she knew what it was like to fall in love. Through Frances, she also knew what it was like to have a husband you didn't love. And although she never had any children of her own, there wasn't a single thing she didn't know about them, at least about a son, because Frances had shared every phase of Timmy's development with her.

Roslynn had shared everything too in her letters over the years, though her life in the Highlands had been singularly lacking in excitement. But she hadn't wanted to worry Frances these last months with Gramp's fears, so she hadn't told her about Geordie. And how to tell her now? How to make her understand that this was not just an old man's senility to scoff at, but a very real and dangerous situation?

Roslynn decided to start at the beginning. "Frances, do you remember my telling you that my mother drowned in Loch Etive when I was seven?"

"Yes, a year after your father died, wasn't it?" Frances said gently, patting her hand.

Roslynn nodded, trying not to remember how desolate she had been from both deaths. "Gramp always blamed his grandnephew, Geordie, for my mother's death. Geordie was a mean child, you see, always hurting animals and causing accidents that he could laugh over. He was only eleven at the time, but he'd already caused one of our grooms to break a leg, our cook to be severely burned, and one horse to be put down, and no telling what he'd done at his own home that we never heard about. His father was my mother's cousin, and when he came to visit, he always brought Geordie. And the day my mother drowned, they'd been visiting a week already."

"But how could he have caused your mother to drown?"

"There was never any proof, Frances. The boat she took out was assumed to have overturned, and she was too constricted in her heavy clothing, it being winter, to be able to swim to shore."

"What was she doing out on the loch in winter?"

"She had grown up on the loch. It was second nature to her to be in the water. She loved it, swam every day in the summer, and did all her visiting that could be done up and down the shore, both sides of the loch. If she could row herself, she'd have nothing to do with a carriage or a horse, no matter the weather. And she had her own little rowboat that was easy for her to handle. We both did, though I was never allowed to take mine out alone. But anyway, as good a swimmer as she was, she didn't make it out that day."

"There was no one to help?"

"No one saw it happen. She'd planned to cross the loch that day, so likely the boat went down too far in the middle. It was several days later when one of the crofters happened to mention to Gramp that he'd seen Geordie down by where the boats were kept, earlier in the week. If Geordie weren't such a little devil for causing accidents, Gramp would never have thought anything of it. But the fact was, Geordie had taken my mother's death near as bad as I did, which was most surprising since he had never really liked my mother or me."

"So your grandfather thought Geordie had tampered with her boat?"

Roslynn nodded. "Something that would have caused a slow leak. It would have been just the sort of thing Geordie would have laughed over, to have someone get a dousing and lose a good boat. If he did do it, I don't think it was any more than a nasty prank, one gone awry. I don't think he meant to *kill* anyone, just get them wet and mad. He couldn't have known that my mother wouldn't have been rowing near shore. It wasn't often she crossed the loch."

"But still . . ."

"Yes, still." Roslynn sighed. "But Gramp could never prove it, and so what could he do? The boat was never found to show it'd been tampered with. Gramp never trusted Geordie after that, never let him come to the Hall but that he put one of the servants to following him. He *hated* him, Frances, deep down, yet without telling his father what he suspected, he couldn't deny him his home. But he swore Geordie would never get anything out of him, and he was emphatic about that. When Geordie's father died, he left him only a small inheritance. Gramp knew Geordie resented him having so much, while Geordie's side of the family had so little, but that came with Gramp being the oldest son and inheriting the Cameron wealth. And Gramp knew for certain Geordie wanted the money when he asked me to marry him."

"You do yourself a disservice there, Ros. You don't have only money to recommend you."

Roslynn waved that aside. "The fact was that Geordie had never liked me, Frances, even as we got older, and the feeling was more than mutual. He resented me, you see, being Gramp's closest relative. It wasn't until his father died and he learned how little was left him that he did a turnabout and became Mister Charming to me."

"But you turned him down." Frances pointed out the obvious.

"Of course I turned him down. I'm not a stupid looby who can't see through false flattery when it's poured on with such ruthlessness. But he didn't give up. He continued to pretend a great love for me even while I could see the cold hatred in his icy blue eyes."

"Very well, now I have all that, I still don't see why you have to rush onto the marriage block."

"With Gramp gone, I've got no protection. I wouldn't need protection but for Geordie. He's asked me to marry him too many times, you see. He's made it clear in every way he wants the Cameron wealth, and he'll do anything to get it."

"But what can he do?"

Roslynn snorted in disgust. "I thought nothing. But Gramp was wiser."

Frances gasped. "The money wouldn't go to Geordie if anything happened to you, would it?"

"No, Gramp made sure of that. The thing is, Geordie can force me to marry him if he can get his hands on me. There are ways, drugging or beating, or even an unscrupulous parson, and there'd be no signing of the marriage contract that Gramp had drawn up for me. Geordie would have control of everything if he could manage it, and as I said, it would only take his getting his hands on me. Once I'm his wife, he'd have no use for me, would he? In fact, he daren't keep me around to tell all that he'd done."

Frances shivered, despite the warm summer night. "You're not making this up, are you?"

"I wish I was, Frances, I really do. Gramp always hoped Geordie would marry, but he never did. Gramp knew he had just been biding his time, waiting for the day I'd be left alone with no one to protest very loudly if he forced me to marry him. And he's too big for me to fight, even if I am right handy with a dirk and keep one in my boot."

"You don't!"

"Oh, I do. Gramp made sure I knew how to use it too. But what help would a little dirk be if Geordie hired help to abduct me? Now you know why I had to leave Scotland so quickly, why I'm here."

"And why you want a husband."

"Yes, that too. Once I'm married, there's nothing Geordie can do.

Gramp made me promise I'd marry, and quickly. He planned everything, even my escape. Geordie will search Scotland first before he looks for me here, so I have a little time to choose someone, but not much."

"Dash it all, it's not fair, none of it," Frances said with feeling. "How can you fall in love in such a rush?"

Roslynn grinned, remembering Gramp's stern admonishment. "Protect yerself first, lassie, wi' a ring on yer finger. Ye can find love later." And how she had blushed, understanding exactly what he'd meant. But he had also conceded. "Of course, if love falls into yer lap, dinna be pushing it off. Hold fast and dinna let go, fer it could work, and then ye'll have nae need tae be looking fer it later."

Gramp had had other advice too, about whom she should consider. "They say a rake makes a dandy husband, that's if a bonny lass can catch his heart—no' his eye, mind ye—his heart. He's sowed his oats, ye see, more than sowed them, plowed the whole field, sae tae speak. Sae when he settles down, he's ready tae do just that."

"They also say, once a rake, always a rake," Roslynn had been compelled to point out. This bit of advice from Gramp she hadn't been at all thrilled with.

"Who says sae? If that's sae, then the heart hasna been caught. Ye catch the heart, lassie, and ye'll be glad of it, ye will. But I'm no' talking 'bout the young hellions, nae, nae. Ye want tae find a mon wi' enough years on him tae ken he's had his wild days aplenty and doesna need more. But ye dinna want him jaded either. Be careful of that."

"And how do you tell the difference?"

"If he still has feeling. If ye can excite him—och, never mind those blushes, lassie. Ye'll be exciting more young bloods then ye'll ken what tae do wi', and enough rakes as well, sae ye'll have plenty tae choose from."

"But I don't want a rake," she had insisted.

"Ye will," Duncan predicted. "Happens they're the ones the lassies canna resist. Just make sure ye get the ring afore ye allow—"

"Gramp!"

He snorted at her exclamation. "If I dinna tell ye, who will? Ye need tae ken how tae handle such a mon."

"With the back of my hand, that's how."

He chuckled. "Now, hinny, ye're no' being open-minded about this," he cajoled her. "If the mon attracts ye and sets yer heart tae fluttering, are ye going tae ignore him simply because he's a rake?"

"Yes!"

"But I tell ye they make the best husbands!" He had turned to shouting in the face of her stubbornness. "And I want the best mon fer ye, even if ye willna have much time tae find him."

"How in the blue blazes do you know, Gramp? Just tell me that, if you can." She wasn't angry, just flustered. Gramp didn't know she already had knowledge of rakes through Frances, and as far as she was concerned, they were to be avoided like the plague.

"I was one myself, and dinna look sae surprised. I'd had sixteen years of plowing the fields afore I met and married yer grandmother, and I was faithful tae the lass until the day she died."

An exception. One exception. Certainly not enough for Roslynn to change her mind about that particular breed of gentleman. But she didn't tell Duncan that. She let him think he had made his point. Still, this was one part of his advice she wouldn't follow and so made no promises about.

To Frances and her question about love, Roslynn shrugged. "If it doesn't happen right off, then it doesn't. You managed to live through it."

Frances frowned. "I had no choice."

"I'm sorry. I shouldn't have reminded you of that. But as for me, show me a fine-looking fellow who isn't too much of a skirt-chaser and he'll do nicely. If I think I can like him, that should suffice." And then she grinned. "After all, I have my grandfather's permission, suggestion even, to find love later if I don't get it in my marriage."

"He . . . would you?"

Roslynn chuckled at her friend's shocked countenance. "Let me find the husband before I start thinking about the lover. Just cross your fingers for me that they turn out to be one and the same."

Chapter Four

"Well, youngun? What boring bit of nonsense have you to impart? Will it do?" Anthony leaned casually against the doorjamb, watching Jeremy survey his new room with obvious delight.

"Hell's bells, Uncle Tony, I—"

"Stop right there." Anthony put on his most unnerving scowl for the lad's benefit. "You can uncle my brothers to death if you like, but a simple Tony will do here, thank you."

Jeremy smiled widely, not at all intimidated. "It's great, Tony, it really is. The room, the house, you. I can't thank you en—"

"Then don't, please," Anthony cut in quickly. "And before you go on with this bloody hero worship, be apprised I'm going to thoroughly debauch you, dear boy. Serve your father right for entrusting you in my care."

"You promise?"

Anthony had to constrain the short bark of laughter. The lad had taken him seriously. "No, I do not. Good God, d'you think I want Jason down my throat? He's going to go through the roof as it is when he learns James turned you over to me instead of him. No, I'll introduce you to the type of female your father has forgotten exists."

"Like Regan?"

Anthony's scowl was quite real this time. "We'll get on, you and I, as long as I never hear that name. Blister it, you're as bad as your father—"

"Now, I can't let you speak poorly of my father, Uncle Tony," Jeremy interrupted quite seriously.

Anthony stepped forward and tossed the lad's coal-black hair, so like his own. "Understand me, puppy. I love your father. Always have. But I'll run him through the coals anytime I feel the urge to. He was my brother before he was your father, after all, and he doesn't need defending by the likes of you. So keep your hackles down. I never meant anything by it."

Jeremy chuckled, mollified. "Rega—Reggie said you weren't happy unless you were arguing with your brothers."

"Did she? Well, that puss always has been a know-it-all," Anthony replied fondly. "And speaking of the lady, she sent round a note today. Seems she's in town without her viscount for a change and in need of an escort for some ball tonight. How would you like the chore?"

"Me? D'you mean it?" Jeremy asked excitedly.

"I don't see why not. She knows I can't abide such affairs and wouldn't have asked me if someone else were available. But Edward's taken his brood up to Haverston for the week to visit Jason, and Derek's up there too, so that unfortunately leaves you and me the only Malorys in town she can prevail upon—unless, of course, we foist the chore on your father. That's if we could find him in time. He might be laying his pallet here for the week, but he mentioned something about looking up an old friend—"

"Sarah," Jeremy supplied, blue eyes twinkling. "She works in a tavern down—"

"Spare me the details."

"You wouldn't catch him going to a ball anyway, even for his favorite niece. But I'd love to. I even have the clothes for it. And I know how to dance, I really do. Connie taught me."

Anthony nearly choked on that one. "Did he? Who led, you or he?"

Jeremy grinned. "A little of both, but I've had practice with the wenches since, and they haven't complained."

Anthony wasn't about to ask what other forms of practice the lad had been at, for he could well imagine. Too much association with his father's unsavory friends, obviously. Whatever was he going to do with such a charming scamp? But he would have to do something, for Jeremy was sadly lacking in the social graces, thanks to his father. A gentleman pirate—well, retired pirate—and a disreputable rake, yours truly—fine examples to choose from. Perhaps he ought to turn the lad over to his cousins when they returned to London and see if they could teach him the rudiments.

"I'm sure Reggie'll be delighted to dance with you, youngun, but call *her* a wench and she's libel to box your ears. And she knows you well enough now, so she'll be glad to have you for the evening. I understand she's rather fond of you."

"Aye, she took right to me the day we abducted her."

"Must you remind me of that? And it was only after she knew who you were that she took to you, dear boy. Good God, for James to go to so much trouble to even the score with the viscount, then to find Reggie had married him."

"Well, that changed everything."

"Of course it did. But he shouldn't have dragged you along in this quest for vengeance anyway."

"It was a matter of honor."

"Ah, so you know about honor, do you?" Anthony said dryly. "Then there's hope for you, I suppose . . . if we can manage to remove 'wenches' from your vocabulary, that is."

Jeremy blushed slightly. It wasn't his fault he had spent the first years of his life in a tavern until his father discovered his existence and took him in hand. Connie, James' first mate and best friend, was always on him about his speech; now here was another one determined to correct him.

"Perhaps I'm not good enough to escort—"

"There you go taking what I say to heart again." Anthony shook his head at the boy. "Would I have suggested you escort *my* favorite niece if I didn't think you were capable?"

Jeremy was frowning now, but for a different reason. "I can't do it. Hell's bells, what was I even thinking of? Of course I can't. If it was anyone else—no, I just can't."

"What the devil are you mumbling about?"

Jeremy stared at him intently. "I can't take her to no ball if I'm to be her only protection. What if someone like you bothers her?"

"Like *me*?" Anthony wasn't sure whether he wanted to laugh or strangle the whelp.

"You know what I mean, Tony, someone who doesn't take well to a 'no' when he hears it. Not that I wouldn't gullet anyone who dared—"

"But who's to take a seventeen-year-old seriously?" Anthony finished with a scowl. "Damnation, I can't tolerate those bloody affairs! Never could, never will. But you're quite right. I suppose we'll have to compromise. You escort her, and I'll keep an eye on her, too. The Crandal ballroom fronts a garden, I believe, so I ought to manage it without actually making an appearance. That should satisfy even her overprotective husband. Does that suit you, young Galahad?"

"Aye, as long as I know you're there and can step in if she has any real trouble. But hell's bells, Tony, won't you be bored stuck out in the garden all night?"

"Assuredly, but I suppose I can suffer it for one evening. You don't know what the alternative is should I actually show up at one of these affairs, and don't ask. It's the bane of my life, but it's the life I choose, so I've no complaints."

And with that cryptic remark, Anthony left Jeremy to settle into his new quarters.

Chapter Five

"Well, m'dear, do you believe me now?" Frances whispered, coming up behind Roslynn, who stood in a circle of admirers, none of whom had left her alone since she arrived at this ball, the third such affair in as many days.

The question was innocent enough, if anyone had heard, but no one had. Though the eyes of the gentlemen present returned continuously to Roslynn in her teal satin gown, their attention was momentarily engaged by a friendly argument about some race that was supposed to take place tomorrow. *She* had started the argument, which seemed the thing to do since it broke up the previous argument about who was to dance with her next. She was quite tired of dancing, especially with Lord Bradley, who must have the biggest feet this side of the Scottish border.

Fortunately, or unfortunately in Roslynn's case, she didn't need to ask Frances to explain her question. Frances had asked it once too often in the last days, quite thrilled that she had been right about Roslynn's reception by the *ton* and Roslynn had been wrong. She was rubbing it in good, taking Roslynn's success personally, as if it were her own.

"I believe you." Roslynn sighed, hoping this would be the last time she would have to say it. "Honest to God, I do. But however am I to make a choice from so many?"

Frances pulled her back a few steps to admonish her. "You don't *have* to choose any of them. Heavens, you've only just begun the hunt. There are other eligibles you haven't met yet. You're not going to jump into this blindly, now are you?"

"No, no, of course not. I don't intend to marry a *complete* stranger.

Well, he will be one to me in actuality, but I mean to learn everything I can about him first. I believe in knowing my quarry as well as possible to avoid mistakes."

"Quarry indeed." Frances rolled her eyes dramatically. "Is that how you're looking at this?"

Roslynn sighed again. "Oh, I don't know, Frances. It just seems so cold-blooded, no matter how you look at it, especially when no one I've met yet has tickled my interest even a wee bit. I'm going to *buy* myself a husband. There's no nicer way of putting it. And it doesn't look as if I'm going to particularly like the fellow if this is all I have to choose from. But as long as he meets the other criteria—"

"Posh!" Frances admonished sternly. "You're giving up when you've only just begun the search. What's happened to depress you so?"

Roslynn grimaced. "They're all so *young,* Frances. Gilbert Tyrwhitt can't be more than twenty, and Neville Baldwin not much older. The earl is my age, and Lord Bradley is only a few years older, though *he* acts as if he should never have been let out of the schoolroom. Those other two are no better. Damnation, they make me feel so ancient. But Gramp did warn me. He said I should look to an older man, but where are they? And if you tell me they're all married already, I think I'll scream."

Frances laughed. "Ros, you're just rushing it. There are a number of distinguished gentlemen here, widowers, and some confirmed bachelors who I'm sure will reconsider that status once they meet you. But I'll no doubt have to point them out to you, because they're probably intimidated by these young bucks dancing attendance on you and feel the competition's too stiff. After all, you are a smashing success. If you want an older man, you'll have to give the poor fellow some encouragement, let him know that you're interested—well, you know what I mean."

"Hell's teeth, Frances, you don't have to blush. I've no problem with being forward if I have to. I'm even prepared to state my case and do the proposing myself. Now don't raise your eyebrows at me. You know I mean it, and I'll do it if I have to."

"You know very well you'd be too embarrassed to be that bold."

"Under normal circumstances, perhaps. But under these circumstances, I haven't much choice. I've no time to be wasting on a proper courtship, and certainly no time to be sitting around waiting for the right man to come along. So point out the more experienced eligibles, and I'll tell you which ones I want to be introduced to. I've quite had enough of these young bloods."

"So be it," Frances replied and looked casually about the room. "There, by the musicians, that tall one. I can't think of his name off-hand, but I understand he's a widower with two children—no, three, I think it is. He must be forty-one or -two, and is a very likable sort from what I hear. Has a big estate up in Kent where the children are, but he prefers town life. Is he more what you had in mind?"

Roslynn grinned at Frances' inept attempt at sarcasm. "Oh, he's not bad, not bad a-tall. I like that silver at the temples. If I can't have love, I must insist on pleasant-looking, and he is, don't you think? Yes, he'll do for a start. Now who else?"

Frances gave her a disgusted look, for she certainly felt as if *she* were at a market selecting choice goods, even if Roslynn didn't. It was all so unsavory, the logical and businesslike way Ros was approaching this. But then wasn't that really the way it was, only most women had a father or a guardian to handle the particulars, while they concerned themselves merely with the happy fantasies of love evermore, or in the unfortunate cases, love nevermore. Ros didn't have anyone to deal with the realities of marriage for her, so she had to make all the arrangements herself, including the financial settlements.

More in the spirit of the thing now since to fight it was so useless, Frances pointed out another gentleman, and another; after an hour, Roslynn had met them all and had narrowed down a new list of possibles, this one much more acceptable agewise. But the young blades still wouldn't leave her alone and insisted on dance after dance. Although her popularity relieved a good deal of her anxiety, a very great deal of it actually, it was becoming a bit of a nuisance too.

Having lived so long in seclusion with her grandfather and the servants known to her for most of her life, Roslynn had had very little traffic with gentlemen. The males of her acquaintance were used to her, and those she didn't know she very properly didn't take notice of. Unlike Nettie, who took in everything at a glance and was well aware of Roslynn's effect on the male gender, Roslynn was too circumspect when out and about to pay attention to what went on around her. It was not surprising that she had put so little store in her looks, which had never seemed very out-of-the-ordinary to her, and so much store in her age, which seemed inappropriate for her purpose, and had counted solely on her status as an heiress to win her a husband quickly.

She had assumed, given her advanced age in comparison with all the other girls out on their first season, that she would have to settle for the second or third sons with no prospects, or even a gambling rogue, a lord who was down and out and heavily mortgaged. And even if there would be a marriage contract that would leave the control of the bulk of her fortune in her hands, she would be generous. She could afford to be generous. She was so rich it was embarrassing.

But she had had to reevaluate her situation after the first party Frances took her to. She had quickly found that all sorts of gentlemen were interested in her, and the extent of her wealth wasn't even known yet. Of course, her gowns and jewels spoke for themselves, but really, that wealthy earl had already called on her at South Audley Street, and so had the obnoxious Lord Bradley. The older men on her new list were not paupers either, and all had seemed extremely flattered by her interest in them. But would they be willing to marry her? Well, that remained to be seen. Her priority now was to find out more about each of them. She wanted no nasty habits or surprises revealed *after* she was married.

What she was in need of at this point was a confidant and adviser, someone who had known these men for a number of years and could help her whittle down her list. Frances had simply been too sheltered and reclusive since her widowhood to be of any help in a thorough character analysis. She knew no men personally other than her late husband's friends, none of whom she would recommend for consideration. The men she had introduced to Roslynn tonight were mere acquaintances about whom she had only the vaguest knowledge.

A good gossip might help, but that was so unreliable, and old gossip tended to be forgotten in lieu of new, so that wouldn't serve her purpose anyway. If only Roslynn had other friends in London, but Frances was her one and only.

It never occurred to either woman that Roslynn could hire someone to find out anything she wanted to know about her candidates. And even if it had occurred to them, they wouldn't know how to go about finding such a person. But then that would have been too simple, and Roslynn had expected from the beginning that this husband-hunting business would be difficult. She expected to agonize over it, simply because she knew she couldn't afford the time necessary to make a cautious decision.

At least she was making progress tonight, slow but helpful. Sir Artemus Shadwell, her silver-templed widower, had braved her pack of randy bucks, as she was beginning to think of them because of their overzealous pursuit, and stolen her away for a dance. Unfortunately, it wasn't a dance conducive to conversation, and the most she was able to learn from him was that with five children from his first marriage (och, but Frances was way off there!), he wasn't at all interested in starting a new family if he ever married again. How he could avoid it, she'd like to know, but so he said.

That was too bad, because if Roslynn was determined to get anything out of the husband she eventually decided on, it was children. That was the only thing about getting married she was looking forward to. She wanted children, not many, but some, two or three or four, and that was definite. Nor was this something she could wait on either, not at her age. If she was going to have a family, it had to be started immediately. That would have to be understood. There would be no "Maybes" or "We'll sees" about it.

But she needn't write Sir Artemus off her list yet. After all, he wasn't aware that he was one of her "possibles," so he couldn't have considered her question about children serious. And a man's mind could be changed. If she knew anything about men, it was that.

After their dance he took her back to Frances, who was standing by the refreshment table with a young woman Roslynn hadn't met yet. But a waltz began immediately, and Roslynn noticed the persistent Lord Bradley making a beeline toward her. She groaned audibly. It was too much. She was *not* going to get her feet mashed up again by that clumsy fellow.

"What's wrong now, Roslynn?" Frances inquired, hearing her.

"Nothing—och, everything," she answered, exasperated and then quite determined, without the least thought for the stranger who hadn't yet been introduced to her. "I'm not going to dance with that looby Bradley again, Frances. I swear I'm not. I'll faint first, which will embarrass you, so you must excuse me while I go hide this one out."

And with a pleased chuckle for the one decision she had been able to make with ease, she gave both ladies a conspiratorial grin and disappeared into the crowd, leaving them to explain to the persistent Bradley how his quarry could simply vanish.

Quickly making her way to one of several open French doors that led out onto a terrace, Roslynn ducked outside but went no further. Pressed up against the wall beside the door, she spared a quick glance to make sure she wouldn't be observed by anyone taking advantage of the lovely moonlit garden that spread out over a large lawn beyond the flat stone terrace, but thankfully she saw no one. She then twisted and bent over at the waist to peek around the door to make sure her escape was successful. And it was. She was just in time to see Lord Bradley leaving Frances, quite obviously disappointed.

It was shameful, but she couldn't dredge up even the slightest pang of remorse. In fact, she continued to watch Lord Bradley just to make certain he wouldn't think to look outside for her when he couldn't find her on the dance floor. She would have to rush to another hiding place then, and she could see herself crouching ridiculously behind flower beds in the garden, but looking no more ridiculous than she did at the moment, she realized belatedly and spared another nervous glance behind her to make sure the garden was still deserted. It was, as far as she could see. After spying on Lord Bradley for a few moments longer, she finally saw him ask someone else to dance.

Roslynn straightened then with a sigh, silently congratulating herself on saving her feet for the time being. She should have escaped to the garden sooner. The fresh air was welcome, a balm to her muddled thoughts so filled with the complexity her life had become. She could use a few minutes alone, to simply think of nothing, to let it all drain away on the gentle strains of the waltz coming through the open doorways.

Soft gold light spread across the stone terrace in rectangular patches from each doorway and window facing the lawn. A few chairs and tables were scattered about but were too noticeable from inside, so Roslynn wisely avoided them.

She spotted a bench tucked under a tree just on the edge of the terrace where it blended into the lawn, or at least the legs of what looked like a bench. The light reached only that far, what with one low-hanging branch bending toward the house, almost like a shielding curtain. The rest of the area was darkly shadowed because of the thick tree limbs, the moonlight unable to penetrate either. How perfect. She could tuck her feet up on the seat and be almost invisible if someone should come outside. Invisible would be nice for a change.

It was only a few dozen feet away, but still Roslynn ran toward this unexpected haven, hoping in those few seconds she wouldn't be spotted through one of the windows. She actually had a moment's anxiety that she wouldn't reach the safe shadows in time. Their importance was absurd. She was desirous of only a few minutes' respite. She wouldn't crumble if her wish weren't granted. She couldn't stay away long anyway, or Frances would worry.

But none of that seemed to matter next to her anxiety. The silly bench had become essential for a purely emotional need. And then abruptly everything she was feeling froze. She had reached no haven at all. The bench, *her* bench, was already occupied.

She stood there in a pool of light, staring blankly at what had seemed no more than a dark shadow from a dozen feet away but was revealed now to be a man's black-clad leg, just one leg, bent over the backrest of the bench at the corner of it, his foot planted firmly on the seat that *she* had intended to become invisible on. Her eyes traveled upward, discovering the bent knee, seeing finally that he was bracing one hip on the edge of the backrest, half sitting, half standing, no doubt comfortably. She looked higher and saw the forearms casually resting on the bent knee, the hands lax, palms down, fingers long and graceful, details clear only because they were lighter in color next to the black of his trousers. Higher still were wide shoulders relaxed, bent forward, and the contrasting, lighter shade at his neck of a white cravat, loosely tied. She finally looked at his face but could see nothing of his features even at this close distance, just a gray blur defined by dark hair.

He was totally in shadow, where she had meant to be. He was nothing but shades of black and gray to her, but he was there, real, silent. Her feelings melted with a vengeance. She felt violated, angry beyond reason. She knew he could see her clearly in the light from the house, and where that light didn't reach, there was the silvery moonlight. He had probably been able to see her looking utterly ridiculous peeking around the door into the ballroom, like a little child in a game of hide-and-seek. And he said nothing. He hadn't moved. He simply looked at her.

Her skin burned with the shame of it. Her anger soared that he was playing mute, as if he were still invisible to her. He could have put her at ease. A gentleman would have said something to make her believe she had been noticed only now, at this moment, even if it weren't true.

The continued silence tugged on her instinct to flee, but it was too much, not knowing who he was, while he could easily recognize her. To meet new men at some later date, and she surely would, and have to constantly wonder if one of them was this man, the one who would be silently laughing at her. One more worry to add to her others. It just wouldn't do.

She steeled herself to demand who he was, prepared to insist, even prepared to forcefully drag him out into the light if she had to—she was that angry. The words weren't necessary, were actually forgotten. A light appeared in an upstairs room, near enough to the window to cast down a beam of gold that filtered through the upper tree limbs at an angle. It was selective, that beam of light. Where it broke through the leaves above, it touched only certain parts of the man's upper body, his hands, a shoulder clad in black velvet—his face.

Roslynn was simply not prepared. The breath sucked right out of her. For several long moments her mind became such a blank, she couldn't have remembered her own name if asked.

There was a wide mouth gently turned at the corners, a strong, arrogant line of jaw. The nose was chiseled sharply, aquiline, proud. The skin was darkly tanned, swarthy, yet still a sharp contrast to the ebony hair that crowned his head in thick waves. The eyes—God protect the innocent from such eyes—were purest blue, heavy-lidded, with the barest suggestion of a slant. They were exotic, hypnotic, framed by black lashes and slashing brows. They were assessing, probing, boldly sensual—warm, too warm.

It was her weakness from lack of air that jolted Roslynn back to her senses. She breathed in deeply, slowly, and exhaled on a sigh. It simply wasn't fair. Gramp had warned her. She didn't have to be told.

She knew. He was one of them, one of the "not to be considered." He was too ruthlessly handsome not to be.

Her earlier annoyance was forgotten. A new irritation took hold. She had the strangest urge to hit him for being what he was. Why him? Why did the one man who took her breath away have to be the only type of man unacceptable to her?

"You are staring, sir." Where had that come from, when the rest of her thoughts were so chaotic?

"I know," he said simply, his smile deepening.

He refrained from pointing out that she was staring too. He was enjoying himself too much just watching her. Words were unnecessary, an intrusion, even though her husky voice rubbed over his skin like a caress.

Anthony Malory was purely fascinated. He had seen her before she came outside. He had been keeping his eye on Reggie through the nearest window, and then she came into his line of vision. He hadn't seen her face then, just her slim back sheathed in teal satin—and her hair. The glorious red-gold color caught his interest immediately. When she moved out of sight before he had gotten a better look at her, he actually stood up, prepared to brave the masses just this once, the urge to see the face that went with that hair overpowering.

But she came outside. He relaxed back against the bench, patient now. With the light behind her, he still couldn't make out her features clearly, but he would. She wasn't going anywhere until he did.

And then he simply watched her antics in hiding beside the door, and bending over to peek back inside. The shapely derrière she presented to him brought a grin to his lips. *Oh, sweetheart, you can't know the invitation you're offering.*

He almost chuckled aloud, but it was as if she had read his thoughts. She straightened, glancing across the terrace. When she stared in his direction, he thought he was discovered. And then she managed to shock him, coming toward him, *running* toward him, flashing into a patch of bright light, making him doubt his sight with the breathtaking loveliness of her face finally revealed to him, disappearing into the shadows briefly before she reached the patch of light directly in front of the bench. She stopped there, looking now as shocked as he was, only his surprise waned quickly when he realized she hadn't been running to him, hadn't known he was even there. But she did now.

It was amusing, the emotions that flitted over her flawless features. Shock, curiosity, then pink-tinged embarrassment, but no fear. With intense, gold-flecked eyes, she started on his leg and worked her way up. He wondered how much of him she could actually see. Not much probably, standing in the light as she was, but he had no inclination to reveal himself just yet.

On one level he was amazed that she hadn't run off immediately, or fainted, or done some other silly thing that a previously sheltered young debutante was likely to do when presented with a strange man lurking in the shadows. Unconsciously, he sought a reason that she should react differently from all the other innocents he staunchly avoided. When it came to him, it was another shock. She wasn't that young, not too young for him anyway. She wasn't off limits, then.

That knowledge worked on Anthony's system immediately. Where before he had simply appreciated her beauty like a connoisseur, now he registered that he needn't be damned to only look, he could also touch. And then the light came on upstairs, and she was staring at him with a new look, obvious fascination, and he was never so glad in his life that women found him appealing to the senses.

It was suddenly imperative for him to ask, "Who guards you?"

Roslynn was startled to hear his voice again after the long silence; she knew very well she should have walked away after their first brief words had brought no more. Only she had stood fast, unable to take her eyes off him, not caring that she was staring, that he was too.

"Guards me?"

"Yes. Who do you belong to?"

"Oh. No one."

Anthony smiled, amused. "Perhaps I should rephrase my question?"

"No, I understood. So did you. My grandfather recently died, you see. I lived with him. Now I have no one."

"Then have me."

The soft words tripped her heart. Oh, what she wouldn't do to have him. But she was almost certain he didn't mean what she wanted him to mean, but what she should be embarrassed over hearing instead. But she wasn't embarrassed. It was something she would expect a man like him to say. They were never sincere, Frances had told her. And they loved to say shocking things to enhance their image of being dissipated and unprincipled.

Still, she had to ask. She couldn't help herself. "Would you marry me, then?"

"Marry?"

She had managed to discompose him. She almost laughed at his look of horror.

"I don't mince words, sir, though I'm not usually *that* forward. But considering what you said to me, my question was perfectly in order. So I may assume you are not husband material?"

"Good God, no!"

"You needn't be *that* emphatic," she said, disappointment just barely discernible in her tone. "I didn't think you were."

He wasn't so pleased himself now, drawing his own conclusions. "You're not going to dash my hopes this soon, are you, sweetheart? Tell me you're not seeking matrimony along with the masses."

"Oh, but I am, most definitely. It's why I've come to London."

"Don't they all."

"I beg your pardon."

He smiled at her again, and it had the strangest effect on her, sort of like melting into honey. "You're not married yet, are you." He wasn't asking, but clarifying it in her mind as well as his. He leaned forward and caught at her hand, gently tugging her closer. "What name goes with such loveliness?"

What name? What name? Her mind was filled with gloveless fingers lightly gripping her own. Warm, strong. Gooseflesh rushed up her bare arm. Her shins bumped the edge of the bench next to his foot, but she didn't feel it. He had brought her into the shadows.

"You do have one, don't you?" he persisted.

A clean, masculine scent assailed Roslynn's nostrils. "What?"

He chuckled, delighted with her confusion. "My dear girl, a name. We all of us must bear one, good or bad. Mine is Anthony Malory, Tony to my intimates. Now do confess yours."

She closed her eyes. It was the only way she could think. "Ros— Roslynn."

She heard his tongue click. "No wonder you want to marry, Ros Roslynn. You simply want to change your name."

Her eyes snapped open to be dazzled by his smile. He was only teasing. It was nice that he felt free to. The other men she had met recently were too busy trying to make a good impression on her to be at ease in her presence.

She returned his smile. "Roslynn Chadwick, to be precise."

"A name you should keep, sweetheart . . . at least until after we become much better acquainted. And we will, you know. Shall I tell you how?"

She laughed, the husky sound jolting him to his socks. "Ah, you're trying to shock me again, but it won't do. I'm too old to blush, and I've been warned about men like you."

"Like me?"

"A rake."

"Guilty." He gave a mock sigh.

"A master of seduction."

"I should hope so."

She chuckled, and again this was no silly giggle or simper to irritate the senses, but a warm, rich sound that made him want . . . he dared not. This was one woman he didn't want to risk scaring off. She might not be innocent in years, but he didn't know yet whether she was experienced otherwise.

That fateful upstairs light that had started Roslynn on the path to confusion was suddenly put out. Panic was instantaneous. It didn't matter that she had enjoyed his company. It didn't matter that she had felt perfectly at ease with him. They were now enshrouded in darkness, and he was a rake, and she couldn't afford to be seduced.

"I must go."

"Not yet."

"No, I really must."

She tried to pull her hand away, but his grip tightened. His other hand found her cheek, fingertips softly caressing, and something unfurled in her belly. She had to make him understand.

"I—I mun thank you, Mr. Malory." She slipped into the brogue without realizing it, half her mind on his touch, half on her increasing panic. "You've taken my mind off my worries for a spell, but dinna add to them now. It's a husband I'm needing, no' a lover, and you dinna qualify . . . more's the pity."

She got her release, simply because she had managed to surprise him once again.

Anthony watched her passing in and out of the different shades of light before she disappeared inside, and again he had that ridiculous urge to go after her. He didn't. A slow smile started and widened. "More's the pity," she had said with such poignant regret. The little miss didn't know it, but she had sealed her own fate with those words.

Chapter Six

"You've been watching a master at work, Connie."

"Seemed more like a comedy of errors to me," the tall redhead replied. "Opportunity lost is opportunity lost, no matter how you look at it."

Anthony laughed as the two joined him under the tree. "Spying on me, brother?"

James leaned forward to casually rest his forearms on the back of the bench and flashed Anthony a grin. "Truth to tell, I couldn't resist. Was afraid it was going to get embarrassing, though."

"Not bloody likely. I just met her."

"And lost her." Conrad Sharp turned the screw.

Anthony shot the first mate a quelling look as he came around and propped a foot on the opposite end of the bench, but it wasn't effective in the dark.

"Now, Connie, you can't fault him there," James said. "She did throw him quite a turn, appealing to the goodness of his heart and in such a quaint Scottish brogue. And here I thought the lad's halo was perpetually tarnished."

"A lass like that could polish any halo," Conrad replied.

"Yes, she was rather stunning, wasn't she?"

Anthony had heard enough. "And unavailable."

James chuckled. "Staked a claim, have you, lad? Careful, or I might take that as a challenge."

Anthony's blood ran cold. It had been sport in their younger days to compete for the same woman, those days when they had prowled

London together. And every outcome had been a simple matter of which brother had managed to get to the lady first. But the years and overindulgence had tempered Anthony's libido. It was no longer do or die. Or at least it hadn't been, until tonight.

But James, well, he simply didn't know James anymore. Most of their lives they had been close, exceedingly close. It had always been them against the other two brothers, who were a good ten years older. But that was before James had thought it would be a lark to try his hand at pirating on the high seas.

For ten years he had seen James only on rare occasions, the last time ending in a rift that caused all three brothers to disown him—after they had soundly thrashed him for taking Reggie pirating that summer. But now James was reinstated. He had given up pirating. Now he was even likely to return to England for good. And *right* now, Anthony didn't know if he was serious or not about challenging him over Roslynn Chadwick.

At that moment he saw her again, through the window, and noticed that James did too. "Blister it, James, what are you doing here anyway?"

The older brother by one year straightened to his full height, which was a tad shorter than Anthony's. To look at them was not to know they were brothers. James was blond and green-eyed, the marks of a Malory, and stockier in build. It was only Anthony, Regina, Edward's daughter Amy, and now Jeremy who bore the black hair and cobalt-blue eyes of their grandmother, rumored to have had gypsy blood flowing in her veins.

"If you had been a little more informative in that note you left for me, I wouldn't have had to ruin my evening by coming here," James replied. "And now that you've reminded me of it, I've a bone to pick with you, brother. What the devil can you be thinking of, to let that scamp of mine escort Regan anywhere?"

Anthony gritted his teeth over the name Regan. "Is that why you showed up?"

"That was all you saw fit to inform me about. You couldn't scribble a few more words to let me know you would be here as well, could you?"

Anthony spared a glance around the garden. "If you can call my hiding in the shadows being here, well, then, I guess I am."

"Don't be obnoxious, puppy," Conrad joined in. "Until you've had one of your own, you don't know what it's like worrying about what they're up to."

"What could the poor boy possibly get up to with two such diligent fathers hounding him? And besides, much as I would have liked to ignore it, Jeremy was the one who pointed out that he might not be up to scratch in protecting her. That's why I've been dragged along."

"You misunderstand, Tony. It wasn't who was going to protect Regan from the masses that had me worried. It was who was going to protect her from her escort."

Five seconds passed while Anthony wondered how much animosity he would elicit by laughing at this point. "She's his cousin, for God's sake!"

"You think he gives a bloody damn?"

"You're serious, aren't you?" Anthony ventured.

"He's infatuated with her," was all James returned.

"Be that as it may, you are overlooking the 'infatuatee.' She'd have him begging for mercy in less than a minute if he even looked at her wrong. I thought you knew our niece better than that, old boy."

"Aye, I know she can hold her own. But I know my son too, and he isn't easily discouraged."

"Need I remind you this is a seventeen-year-old boy we're talking about?"

"Need I remind you what *you* were like when you were seventeen?" James countered.

Anthony grinned finally. "Point taken. Very well, I'll not only keep an eye on her, I'll keep one on him too."

"That's *if* he can keep his eyes off the Scot," Conrad interjected.

"Then by all means stay," Anthony replied tightly. "There is no reason we can't all three keep this vigil. After all, it's such a pleasant way to spend an evening."

James smiled. "I do believe that's his way of telling us to run along, Connie. Come on, let's leave the poor boy to his pining. You never know. She might even venture forth again and make this chaperoning business more to his liking." Here he chuckled. "It won't be otherwise. He wouldn't brave that den of vultures any more than I would, even for her."

James was wrong on both counts.

Chapter Seven

"Well, what's he doing here? That's what I want to know. Lady Crandal doesn't approve of his sort. She'd never have invited him."

"Sir Anthony doesn't need an invite, m'dear. That one does as he pleases."

"But he's always had the decency to stay away from our parties."

"Decency?" A brief laugh. "There's no decency about it. He simply can't abide these affairs. And it's no wonder. There probably isn't a lady here who wouldn't like to reform that particular rake."

"There's nothing funny about it, Lenore. He shows up, and half the women in the room fall in love with him. I've seen it happen before. That's why a hostess wouldn't dream of inviting him to her party if she wants it to go smoothly. He causes too much of a stir."

"But it does give us something to talk about for months thereafter. Admit it. He does make a delicious subject, doesn't he?"

"That's easy for you to say, Lenore." This from another lady, clearly distressed. "You don't have a daughter out this season. My God, look at my Jane over there. She can't take her eyes off him. I just know she'll never accept Percy now. She can be *so* difficult."

"There's no harm in looking, Alice. You need only tell your girl a few stories about him and she'll be properly horrified and glad he didn't notice her."

"But what's he *doing* here? I still want to know." The question was repeated more sharply.

"Probably keeping an eye on his son," Lenore offered the ladies smugly.

"His *what?*"

"Take a look at the boy dancing with Sarah Lordes. Now, if he isn't the mirror image of Sir Anthony, then they ought to do away with mirrors."

"Good Lord, another Malory bastard! That family really ought to be more circumspect."

"Well, the marquis acknowledged his. I wonder if Sir Anthony will do the same."

"This is priceless! However could they have kept him a secret this long?"

"Must have been hidden away until now. But it appears the Malorys are going to be full of surprises this season. I understand the third brother is back."

"Third brother?" This from a new party. "But there are only three."

"Where have you been, Lidia?" Lenore said cattily. "There are four, and the third is the black sheep."

"But I thought Sir Anthony was that."

"Being the youngest, he's only a close second. Oh, I could tell you stories about the other one. He's been gone for years and years, but no one knows where or why."

"Then it's no wonder I didn't know he existed," Lidia replied stiffly in self-defense.

"Hello again."

Roslynn was annoyed by the untimely interruption, but at least it wasn't one of her young admirers. Fortunately, most of them had retired to the card room for a while, leaving her free to become better acquainted with the gentlemen on her new list. But instead of seeking one out, she had gotten sidetracked by the numerous conversations that erupted when Anthony Malory had stepped into the ballroom.

Roslynn had unobtrusively settled herself behind one group of older ladies and made no bones about eavesdropping. There was no use denying it. She found the subject under discussion infinitely fascinating and listened avidly to every word. But now someone wanted to engage her in conversation, and there was no help for it.

She glanced at Lady Eden, yet still tried to keep one ear tuned in on the older ladies in front of her. "Tired of dancing so soon?"

The younger woman was amused, recognizing inattentiveness when she encountered it. She was further amused when she overheard several remarks nearby and realized the reason for Roslynn's distraction.

"Everyone knows I rarely dance except with my husband, but he wasn't able to join me tonight."

"That's nice."

Regina Eden rolled her eyes, smiled, and hooked her arm through Roslynn's. "Come along, m'dear. It's devilish hot in this spot. Let's move along, shall we?"

Roslynn sighed as she was forcefully dragged away. Lady Eden was certainly pushy for such a young woman. Roslynn had been surprised, in fact, to learn that she was married and had a child already, when she didn't look as though she was very long out of the schoolroom. She was the lady with Frances earlier whom Roslynn hadn't stayed long enough to meet, but Frances had taken care of the introductions upon her return from the garden. At the time she had still been pretty shaken from her encounter with Malory. In fact, she couldn't remember the conversation she had had with Lady Eden then, if she had even had one.

Lady Eden stopped near the refreshment tables. Unfortunately, Roslynn now had a clear view of the subject on everyone's lips. He hadn't really come inside the ballroom. With an air of nonchalance, he stood in the doorway to the garden, one shoulder braced against the frame, arms crossed over his chest, eyes slowly scanning the room—until they lit on her. There they stayed, and he flashed that smile that made her feel like warming honey.

Seeing him in the light, seeing *all* of him in the light, was an experience of the senses. He had a body you couldn't help but admire for its pure symmetry. Wide shoulders, narrow waist, lean hips, and long legs. Yes, he was tall. She hadn't noticed it in the garden. And he fairly reeked of sensuality. She *had* noticed that before.

The cut of his evening clothes was impeccable, though he looked almost sinister in black. But black complemented him. She couldn't imagine him wearing the bright colors of a dandy. That would draw even more attention to him, yet he commanded everyone's attention anyway, just by appearing.

"He *is* devilish handsome, isn't he?"

Roslynn started, realizing she had been caught staring at him. But then it would be unusual if she weren't, for *everyone* was staring at him.

She glanced at Lady Eden and gave a careless shrug. "Do you think so?"

"Oh, most definitely. His brothers are terribly good-looking too, but I've always thought Tony was the handsomest of the lot."

Roslynn wasn't sure if she liked that "Tony" from this beautiful young woman with the midnight hair and vivid blue eyes that glittered with humor. What had he said? "Tony to my intimates."

"I take it you know him well?"

Regina grinned engagingly. "I know the whole family very well."

Roslynn found herself blushing, which was something she so rarely did. She was relieved with that answer but annoyed with herself for how sharp her question had sounded. If the viscountess was well acquainted with the Malorys, then she was the last person Roslynn wanted to be aware of her interest in Sir Anthony. She ought not to be interested at all. She ought to introduce a new topic. She couldn't.

"He's awfully old, isn't he?"

"Well, if you think thirty-five is old—"

"Only thirty-five?"

Regina had to suppress her urge to laugh. The woman was determined to find something wrong with Tony, but heaven knew what that could be. It was obvious he had made another conquest without even trying. Or was he trying? It was really too bad of him to stare like that. If she weren't standing here with Lady Roslynn, the poor woman would be quite undone by what the gossips would make of his interest in her.

Yes, it really was too bad of him, because nothing would come of it. Nothing ever did. And she rather liked Lady Roslynn. She wouldn't like to see her get hurt.

"He's a confirmed bachelor," Regina felt compelled to warn her. "With three older brothers, there's never been any reason for him to marry, you see."

"You don't have to wrap it up prettily. I know he's a rake."

"He prefers 'connoisseur of women.' "

"Then he likes to wrap it up prettily too."

Regina laughed. Oh, she did like this woman. Roslynn might be feigning an indifference toward Tony, but she was refreshingly straight-forward otherwise.

Roslynn stole another glance at Sir Anthony. She felt silly for having called him Mr. Malory, but how was she to have known then that he was a member of the peerage? The eldest brother the Marquis of Haverston, the second an earl, the third the black sheep of the family, and Anthony a close second. Oh, she had heard much about him to-night. Why couldn't she learn as much about her potential "possibles"?

"He doesn't dance?" Roslynn heard herself asking and wondered why she couldn't leave it alone.

"Oh, he does, beautifully, but he doesn't dare ask anyone here. If he did, he'd have to dance with a few dozen other women too, just to throw the vultures off the scent. But Tony wouldn't go through so much bother just to dance with the lady of his choice. That's why he can't tolerate these affairs. They force him to discretion when the word isn't even in his vocabulary."

"Is he really so notorious that just to be seen dancing with him would fairly ruin a girl?"

"I have seen it happen, and it's a shame really, because he's not *that* much of a womanizer. Not that he ever lacks for female companionship. But he's not out to seduce the whole of London either."

"Just his fair share?"

Regina noted the grin and realized Roslynn was amused by Anthony's reputation rather than scandalized. Perhaps she wasn't interested after all. Or perhaps she wisely sensed that it was hopeless.

"Gossips can be cruel, m'dear." Regina leaned closer to whisper. "In fact, I don't dare leave your side. He *is* misbehaving, staring at you like that."

Roslynn avoided the other woman's eyes. "He could be looking at you."

"Of course he isn't. But as long as no one here is quite sure which of us he's ogling, you're safe."

"Ah, there you are, Ros." Frances joined them. "Lord Grahame was just asking for you. He claims you promised him a waltz."

"So I did." Roslynn sighed. It was time to forget Anthony Malory and get back to work. "I just hope the fellow can loosen up and be a little more revealing this time."

Too late, she realized how that must have sounded to Lady Eden, but Regina simply smiled. "It's all right, m'dear. Frances has told me something of your situation. You might be amused to know I had the exact same problem when I was looking for a husband. But unlike yours, my choice had to be approved by my family, which only made it exceedingly difficult because, to them, no one was good enough for me. Thank God my Nicholas compromised me, or I still might be looking for a husband."

It was Frances who appeared shocked. "But I thought you had been promised to him!"

"That was the general assumption after the announcement was made, but the fact was, he had abducted me, thinking I was his current mistress, and that little mistake got out. Oh, he brought me home immediately upon realizing his mistake, but the damage was done. And he came kicking and protesting to the altar, confirmed bachelor that he was. Yet he has settled nicely into marriage. It just goes to show that if someone seems unsuitable in all respects, they might turn out to be the best choice after all. You just never know."

The last was said for Roslynn's benefit, but she forced herself to disregard it. Her chore was hard enough without adding to it the unsuitables. She wasn't going to end up with a bad penny on the off chance that he could be reformed. A gambler she was not.

With that resolve firmly set in her mind, she went off in search of Lord Grahame.

Chapter Eight

If an order had been placed, the weather that morning couldn't have been more perfect. It nearly tripled the amount of riders who were generally found in Hyde Park at such an early hour. Afternoons were the time for promenading, when every conceivable type of carriage could be seen making slow progress along the countrylike lanes. Mornings were reserved for the exercising of stock and body, when one didn't usually encounter one's acquaintances and so was not forced to stop repeatedly for conversation, as would happen in the afternoon.

Anthony Malory was resigned to giving up his customary hard gallop through the park that morning in favor of a brisk trot. Not that Reggie wasn't game, but he doubted her frisky mare could keep up with his powerful stallion, and since she insisted on joining him, he was forced to keep to her pace.

After last night, he had his suspicions as to why she had invited herself along, and he wasn't sure he wanted to discuss the lady. But when Reggie slowed and reigned in, waving James and Jeremy on, he knew there would be no help for it. The little darling could be uncomfortably persevering at times.

"When I asked to ride with you this morning, I rather thought we would be alone," Regina began with just the faintest degree of annoyance in her tone. "Jeremy I could understand wanting to come along with us, but Uncle James? He rarely rises before noon."

Actually, Anthony had pulled brother and nephew out of bed,

browbeating and cajoling them into joining him. That ploy hadn't worked, however, to keep Reggie from her purpose. And blast James. He knew very well the only reason he was along was to keep the conversation impersonal, but there he trotted off, flashing Anthony an amused grin.

Anthony shrugged innocently. "What can I say? James has changed his habits considerably since he became a father. Hasn't that scoundrel you married done the same?"

"Famous! Why is it you always attack Nicholas when your own behavior has been less than exemplary?" And she jumped right into it. "She's half Scot, you know."

He didn't bother to ask who, but said indifferently, "Is she?"

"They're known for terrible tempers."

"All right, puss." He sighed. "What's on your mind that you feel obliged to warn me?"

Her brow wrinkled, blue eyes probing blue eyes of a like shade. "Are you interested in her, Tony?"

"Have I died and don't know it?"

She laughed, unable to help it. "Yes, I suppose that was a silly question. Of course you're interested—you and a few dozen others. I guess my next question should be, are you going to do anything about it?"

"That, my girl, is none of your business."

His tone was gentle but firm, and Regina's frown was back. "I know. But I thought you should learn a little something about her before you make up your mind to pursue her."

"Is this to be a full history?" he asked dryly.

"Don't be difficult, Tony. She's come to London to get married."

"I've already been told that appalling news by the lady herself."

"You mean you've talked to her? When?"

"If you must know, last night in the garden."

She gasped. "You didn't—"

"I didn't."

Regina let out a sigh, but it was only temporary relief. If knowing Lady Roslynn was actively seeking marriage didn't put him off, the poor woman was doomed.

"Perhaps you don't realize how serious she is, Tony. She means to be married by the end of the month. No, you needn't raise your brows. It's not that. In fact, she might as well be sixteen for all the experience she has had of men."

"Now *that* I won't believe."

"There, you see? You don't know anything about her, and yet you're contemplating disrupting her life. The truth is, that life has been extremely sheltered until now. She's been tucked away with her grandfather in the Highlands ever since her parents died, and apparently these past years have been spent nursing him, which is why she hasn't considered marriage until now. Were you aware of that?"

"Our talk was brief, Reggie."

She noted his irritation but pressed on. "Her father was an earl of some consequence. You know Uncle Jason won't like it—"

Anthony interrupted this warning. "Much as I hate to be on big brother's blacklist, I'm not answerable to him, puss."

"There's still more to it, Tony. She's an heiress. Her grandfather was ridiculously wealthy, and he's left it all to Lady Roslynn. That little piece of news isn't common knowledge yet, but you can imagine what will happen if she isn't married before that happens."

"Every scoundrel in London will crawl out from under his rock to pursue her," Anthony answered tightly.

"Exactly. But fortunately, she already has several gentlemen picked out for consideration. As I understand it, it's just a matter now of learning what she can about them before she chooses one. In fact, I'm to ask Nicholas what he knows about them."

"Since you know so much, miss, tell me what the bloody rush is."

Oh, he was definitely interested, enough not to care that his irritation was now plainly showing. It gave Regina pause simply because it was so unique. Never had she seen him stirred up over a woman before. There were just too many for him to choose from for one in particular to mean overmuch to him. She might have to rearrange her own thinking on the matter.

Hesitantly, she offered, "It has something to do with a deathbed promise Lady Roslynn made to her grandfather, the rush, and the reason she's actively looking for a husband. According to her friend Frances Grenfell, she probably wouldn't marry at all if not for that promise. I mean, you don't see a situation like hers very often, a woman so beautiful, so rich, and answerable to no one but herself."

It was indeed a unique situation, but Anthony didn't consider it at the moment, the Grenfell name causing unease. "How close a friend is she to Frances Grenfell?"

He threw Regina off the track with that question. "Why?"

"Lady Frances was one of George's youthful mistakes, though that's not to be repeated, puss."

"No, of course not," she said in one breath, and then in the next, "You mean good old George, your best friend, the one who always teased me so outrageously? *That* George?"

He grinned at her surprise. "One and the same, and you haven't answered my question."

"Well, I don't see that it matters, but they're as close as two friends could be. They met in school and never lost touch with each other."

"Which means bloody confidences and all that," he fairly growled.

Damnation! Anthony could still hear her husky voice confessing, "I've been warned about men like you." He had thought she was teasing, but now he knew where the warnings must have come from and how damning they probably were. She hadn't been teasing at all. She would be on her guard against him no matter what, always remembering what had happened to her friend. He was suddenly of a mind to soundly thrash George Amherst for his youthful indiscretion. Bloody rotten hell!

Seeing his black scowl, Regina was reluctant to say what she knew needed saying, but no one else would dare be so bold with him, so she had to. "You know, Tony, unless you're willing to take the big step yourself, which would shock the whole of London but absolutely delight the family, you really ought to leave the lady alone."

He suddenly laughed. "For God's sake, puss, when did you become my conscience?"

She flushed at that. "Well, it's devilish unfair, you know. I doubt there's a woman alive you couldn't seduce if you set your mind to it."

"You exaggerate my abilities."

"Bother that," she retorted. "I've seen you turn on the charm, Tony, and it's utterly devastating when you do. But I rather like Roslynn Chadwick. Only she has a promise to fulfill that's important to her, and for whatever reason, there's a time limit on it. If you interfere, there's liable to be trouble, not to mention hurt."

Anthony smiled at her fondly. "Your concern is commendable for someone you've just met, Reggie, but a bit premature, don't you think? And besides, she's not some ninnyhammer without a lick of sense. She's independent and answerable to no one but herself. You said so yourself. So don't you think she's old enough, and mature enough, to fend off a rakehell like me if she wants to?"

"That word *want* scares me to death," she groaned, only to hear him laugh again.

"You talked to her for a considerable time last night. Did she happen to mention me?"

Good Lord! That he should ask such a question proved he was most definitely serious, even after everything she had told him.

"If you must know, you were about the only topic we discussed, but that's not unusual, since just about everyone there last night was discussing you. In fact, I'm quite sure she heard an earful from the gossips before I got hold of her."

"Did you paint a pretty picture for me, puss?"

"I tried, but she wasn't buying it. And yet I suppose you'll be delighted to know that however much she feigned indifference, her interest was as plain to recognize as yours is." The smile that remark elicited nearly blinded her. "Oh, dear. I shouldn't have told you that, but since I did, I must also tell you that regardless of her interest, she still went off to better her acquaintance with the gentlemen she is considering for marriage. You might have made an impression, but it hasn't changed her plans in the least."

Regina could see that nothing she said was going to discourage him, and she had said all she could. She might as well have saved her breath. She had never tried to interfere in his love life before, and now she saw how pointless it was to try this once. He was going to do as he pleased, just as he always did. God knew, Uncle Jason had tried for years and years to curb Tony's hedonism without success. What had made her think she would have any better luck?

She realized suddenly how utterly foolish she had been. Here she had been trying to change the very qualities that she had always found most endearing in Anthony. He was a charming rake. That was what he was and what made him her favorite uncle. If he left countless broken hearts behind, it was only because women couldn't help falling in love with him, although he never took any of his affairs seriously. But he did give pleasure and happiness too. That counted for a lot.

"I hope you're not going to be angry with me for putting my nose in where it doesn't belong." She gave him the smile he could never resist.

"It's such a pretty nose."

"But too big at the moment. I'm sorry, Tony, I really am. I just thought—well, never mind. You've managed thus far to get by without anyone's advice. I suppose we should catch up with—"

Regina didn't finish. Her eyes were caught by a magnificent black stallion prancing along at a slow canter to accommodate the pony beside it, but to see who was controlling the powerful beast made her groan inwardly. What horrid luck. Of all the people to encounter at this moment.

She glanced to see if Anthony had noticed Lady Roslynn yet. Of course he had. If the prime horseflesh hadn't caught his eye, the Irish green riding habit and sun-bright hair would have. But his unguarded expression was almost embarrassing to observe.

Good Lord, she had never seen him look at a woman like that before, and she had seen him with dozens of his ladyloves. Last night he had stared, yes, deliberately, a game of seduction played solely with the eyes. This was different. This was a look Nicholas might give Regina, of passion mixed with more tender feelings.

Well, that did it. She felt even more of an idiot now for having tried to warn Anthony off. It was obvious, at least to her, that something special was happening here. And wouldn't it be wonderful if something actually came of it?

Regina's thinking had undergone a complete about-face. She was now wondering how she might help get these two together. Anthony had his own ideas.

"Would you consider staying put, Reggie, while I pay my respects?" Her look said, *Not on your life.* His sigh was long and drawn out. "I didn't think so. Well, come along, then. You owe me one chaperonage, I believe."

Anthony didn't wait for her concurrence but rode straightaway to intercept Roslynn, hoping against hope that Reggie would give him at least a few minutes alone with her first. It wasn't to matter. James, blast him all to hell, chose that moment to return to see what was keeping them and managed to intercept the lady first.

Anthony arrived to hear James saying, "Delighted to see you again, Lady Chadwick."

Roslynn was nervous enough to have trouble controlling Brutus, a circumstance that caused acute embarrassment, since it had never happened before. She had seen Sir Anthony approaching, which was probably why the blond stranger startled her so, seeming to have appeared out of nowhere. It was even worse, and quite irritating, that he should lean forward to steady her horse. The move was so clearly indicative that she couldn't manage Brutus on her own.

Her tone was quite understandably sharp. "Do I know you, sir?"

"No, but I had the opportunity to admire you last evening in the Crandal garden. Unfortunately, you ran away before I could make your acquaintance."

Anthony watched the hot color seep into her cheeks and saw red. "For *that,* dear brother, I think I'll invite you back to Knighton's Hall."

James couldn't have cared less. Roslynn Chadwick by daylight was about the prettiest little lady he had ever encountered. That Anthony had found her first mattered not at all. It made it devilish awkward, but no more than that. Until the lady stated her preference, she was fair game as far as James was concerned.

Roslynn was staring at James, now that she knew who he was. She would never have guessed by his looks that he was Anthony's brother. And after what she had heard about him, she could understand why Anthony was considered the runner-up to being the worst rakehell of the two. They were both breathtakingly handsome, but where Anthony was a charming rogue, she sensed the blond Malory would be much more ruthless in his amorous pursuits—or in any pursuits, for that matter. He fairly reeked of danger. And yet she wasn't frightened. It was Anthony who threatened her peace of mind and rattled her composure.

"So you are the black sheep of the Malory clan?" Roslynn said. "Tell me, what terrible deeds have you done to earn that misnomer?"

"Nothing anyone can prove, I assure you, sweet lady." And then to

Anthony he turned a challenging grin. "Where are your manners, dear boy? Introduce us."

Anthony gritted his teeth. "My brother, James Malory." Without the slightest change in tone, he added, "And that youngun about to run us down is his son, Jeremy."

Jeremy drew up at the last second, exhilarated from the ride and the near disaster. He was just in time to hear Roslynn's comment to James. "Your son? Now why didn't I guess that?" There was such irony in her voice that no one doubted for a moment that she didn't believe a word of it.

Jeremy began laughing hilariously. James was rather amused himself. But Anthony was getting angrier by the second. He had known this would happen, but why did it have to happen for the first time with her? And with the young scamp laughing his head off over the misassumption, there was no point in trying to correct it at present.

Roslynn was surrounded by Malorys now and quite wishing she had not been so cavalier in dismissing Timmy's groom this morning. For a simple ride in the park, she had thought it unnecessary to have a man along for protection. It was something she never did at home. But London was not home.

Anthony seemed to connect with her thoughts. "Have you lost your groom?"

Six-year-old Timmy piped up here. "Ros is my groom and I'm hers. She said all we needed was each other."

"And who might you be?"

"Lord Grenfell," Timmy said importantly.

With George Amherst's blond hair and gray eyes staring up at him, Anthony blundered with a "Know—that is to say, knew your father very well. But the next time Lady Ros thinks to be your groom, you must tell her—"

"I've already concluded that the park is not as safe as I had supposed, Sir Anthony," Roslynn cut in meaningfully. "I assure you I'll not assume the role again."

"Glad to hear it, but in the meantime, I'll escort you home."

James delighted in pointing out, "I hate to remind you, brother, but you already have one charge to look after. I, on the other hand, am available to see the lady home."

"The hell you will!" Anthony shot back.

Regina had held back, enjoying this little encounter without being noticed. But since it was about to get out of hand, she finally nudged her horse forward.

"Before you two come to blows, I think it prudent to point out that Jeremy is also available and will do nicely as an escort for such a short distance. And since I was meaning to call on Lady Frances, I think I'll join them, Tony, so I'll thank you now for indulging me this morning." And to Roslynn, belatedly, "Does that meet with your approval?"

Roslynn sighed in relief, for she hadn't been able to think how to politely refuse either Malory brother after she had already admitted her mistake in riding without an escort. "It does indeed, Lady Eden."

"Please, m'dear, none of that. You'll call me Reggie." She grinned at James before adding, "As most everyone does."

The remark seemed to improve Anthony's humor. He was smiling now as he gazed at Roslynn, and what a smile. She had to force herself not to look at him again even as they exchanged words in departure. She had been wise last night to conclude that it would do her no good to see the man again. This encounter, so innocent yet disconcerting, simply reinforced that conclusion.

Anthony, watching the foursome ride away, was quietly contemplating turning Reggie over his knee next time he saw her. "She's become unbearably bossy since she married Eden."

"Do you think so?" James chuckled. "Perhaps you just never paid any mind to it before, since it was never you she was bossing around."

Rubbed raw by James' humor, Anthony glared at him. "And you—"

James didn't give him a chance to work up a righteous anger. "Now don't be tedious, dear boy. After seeing the way she reacted to you, I can see I haven't much chance of stealing her away." He turned his horse around, then added with a devilish grin just before he put spurs to him, "But bad odds have never stopped me before."

Chapter Nine

"You're being no help a-tall, Frances," Roslynn complained, mimicking, "'Go if you like.' What kind of answer is that, I'd like to be knowing?"

Frances stopped short on the busy walkway fronting the shops on Oxford Street, bringing Nettie plowing into her back for not paying attention. Two packages dropped out of Nettie's hands, one round hatbox rolling toward the curb. Anne, Frances' abigail, made a frantic dash for it before it continued into the street. Frances didn't even notice.

"What's got into you, Ros? If you're having such trouble over a simple decision like this, I shudder to think what agonies you'll go through when it's time to choose your husband. Either you want to go to the Eden party or you don't. Yes or no, either or; how much simpler can it be?"

Roslynn grimaced. Frances was right, of course, at least as far as she knew. But then Roslynn hadn't told her about meeting Anthony Malory at the Crandals' ball. She had intended to, only their conversation on the way home that night had started by her asking if Lady Eden's husband had been a rake before they were married.

"He was indeed."

That answer had been said with such disgust, Roslynn had asked only one more question. "Are they happy together?"

"Actually, I've never seen two people happier or more in love."

This reply had been soft and incredulous, as if Frances couldn't quite believe it was possible. But after that, Roslynn knew her friend would become too upset if she learned that Roslynn had found Anthony

Malory attractive, so she hadn't mentioned him at all. It was too obvious that Frances still abhorred men like him in the extreme.

But regardless of knowing how her friend felt, even being of the same mind, Roslynn had still been full of Anthony that night, so full of him that Nettie had noticed the minute Roslynn walked into her bedroom.

Her very first words had been, "Well, I see ye've met yer mon. What's his name, then?"

Brought out of her cloud, Roslynn had quickly prevaricated that there wasn't one him, but four, and she immediately launched into everything she knew about them so far, which wasn't much but managed to quell Nettie's first assumption quite nicely. Now she was putting too much importance on Lady Eden's invitation, when every other invitation she had received since her introduction to society had been decided on with barely a thought. Definitely out of character.

It was no wonder Frances thought something was wrong with her. But at least she couldn't guess what it was. Nettie, on the other hand, had been watching her like a hawk ever since she had returned from her ride with Timmy yesterday. How she had given herself away she didn't know.

"The decision might be simple for you," she said to Frances rather defensively, "but I have other things to consider."

"Such as?"

"The time involved, for one. Being out of the city for three or four days is just going to delay—"

"Didn't you tell me Regina promised to invite your gentlemen as well?"

"That doesn't mean they'll go, Frances. The season's only just started. She's picked an off time to have a weekend party in the country."

"Silverley's in Hampshire, not days away. And besides, you also mentioned that she promised to speak to her husband and give you all the information he has on your gentlemen as soon as you get there. For that reason alone, I would think you would want to go."

Logic, logic, how to refute it? "Who's to say he knows anything pertinent? It could turn out to be a complete waste of time."

"Then you can turn right around and be back in London the same evening."

"And leave you there?" Roslynn protested. "How would you get back?"

Frances shook her head. "I give up. You obviously don't want to go, so I won't either. We have a half-dozen other invitations for this weekend, so we'll—"

"Now don't be putting words in my mouth. I haven't said no yet."

"Well?"

Roslynn walked on, tossing her next words over her shoulder. "I still need to think on it."

She never should have brought up the party again to begin with, revealing her anxiety about it. She could almost hear the wheels spinning in Nettie's mind. Frances at least didn't have any idea what the trouble was. But Nettie knew her too well. And what could she tell Nettie when she got around to asking, and she would? More of the same excuses, even though Frances had just pointed out she really had none?

Hell's teeth! She was ready to wring her hands over this one. Everything logical said there was nothing to decide. She needed to go to Silverley if for no other reason than to get the information Regina would have for her. Also, she had only to ask herself, what if she didn't go, but all four of her "possibles" did? Then she would be stuck in London accomplishing nothing, and *that* would be a pure waste of time.

On the other hand, and it was a great big other hand, there was a chance Anthony Malory might show up at Silverley for this party, and seeing him again was something Roslynn didn't want to risk, didn't dare risk. He was just too tempting by half. That silly, girlish reaction she had had to him yesterday in the park, in broad daylight, even surrounded by others, proved it without a doubt.

She should have been more specific by asking Lady Eden if the one Malory she didn't want to see again would be there. But she hadn't wanted to give herself away. She had to be oh, so insouciant instead by asking if any Malorys would be there. So she deserved Regina's evasive "I never know when one or more of them will drop by. They know they're always welcome in my home, you see."

That was what she got for being so reticent, for pretending an indifference she was far from feeling. Now it was a matter of delaying her goal by several days or running into that rake again by chance.

There was really only one decision to make, so she might as well stop prevaricating over it. Another encounter with Anthony Malory was to be avoided at all costs. She had to accept the delay.

"Here we are, Ros. Dickens and Smith, my last stop for today," Frances said, then remonstrated, "You know, you're no fun at all to shop with. You could at least come in the shop, even if you don't want to buy anything."

Roslynn couldn't quite manage a smile in her present depression to tease Frances out of her disgruntlement. "I would if you hadn't picked such a hot day to drag me about. Going into the perfumers and the stocking warehouse was enough for me, thank you. I don't know how you could stand the bonnet warehouse and the silk mercers, but then I suppose you're used to it. But you forget we have a colder clime in Scotland. It's just too stuffy in these shops. At least there's a wee breeze out here, even if you can hardly notice it. Go on. I'll wait out here again with Nettie."

It didn't take Nettie but two seconds to start in on her once the door of the drapery shop had closed on Frances and Anne. "Now, lass, ye'll be telling me—"

"Och, Nettie, dinna be onto me now." Roslynn was quick to forestall her. "I'm in no mood to be picked apart, none a-tall."

Nettie was not one to let go easily. "Ye'll no' be denying ye've been acting mighty strange."

"I'm allowed, considering where we are and why and all I've got to be thinking about," Roslynn replied, her tone sharply defensive. "Did you think this business of selecting a husband would be easy work? Hell's teeth! Sometimes I canna think for the worry of it!"

That managed to stir Nettie's sympathy. "Now, hinny, it'll be over afore ye—"

"Shh," Roslynn interrupted with a frown. "There it is again, Nettie. Do you feel it?"

"What?"

"That someone's watching us."

Nettie gave her a doubtful glance, not at all sure whether Roslynn was simply trying to get the subject off herself or if she was serious. But the girl was certainly intent on slowly perusing the street this way and that.

"If someone *is* watching us, it's no' us they be watching, but ye. An admirer, nae doubt."

Roslynn looked back at Nettie impatiently. "I know what it feels like to be looked at like that, and this is not at all the same. I've felt it ever since we stood outside the bonnet warehouse waiting for Frances. I tried to ignore it, but the feeling persists."

"Well, then, it's nae doubt some pickpocket who's marked us, and no' surprising wi' all them jewels ye're wearing. Hold yer purse tightly, lass."

Roslynn sighed. "You're probably right. It'd be too soon for Geordie to have found me, wouldn't it? Still, I'd as soon wait in the carriage than out here in the open. Do you see our driver yet?"

Nettie stretched up on her toes. "Aye, about five shops down, but it appears he's stuck behind a wagon. See him? We can walk, though, and get ye settled inside. Then I'll come back tae tell Lady Frances."

It wasn't that Roslynn was paranoid, but she had never felt such a strange feeling before. It was no doubt her imagination run wild, but just the same, there was no point in her standing outside the drapery shop when the carriage was now in sight. Still, she gave one more glance around her, but there were so many pedestrians on the walkway and vehicles in the street, it was impossible to notice any one person staring at her.

They started down the street but got no farther than twenty feet when an arm snaked around Roslynn's waist from behind, lifting her right off her feet. She didn't think to scream, yet it was almost a relief that her suspicions hadn't been wrong, and she was prepared. No panic, no fear—yet. She simply let the upper half of her body drop over the steely arm that held her, grabbed the edge of her skirt, and plucked the dirk out of her walking boot.

Nettie, meantime, let out a screech to warn the whole of London. She immediately charged the fellow before he moved one foot, swinging her reticule left and right, catching his ear, whipping around his face to flatten his nose. It also caught Roslynn's bonnet as she raised herself, knocking it forward over her eyes so she couldn't see. But her target was felt, cutting off her air as it was. She didn't need to see the beefy arm to take a chunk out of it.

The fellow howled and let go, and Roslynn found herself sitting flat on her backside in the middle of the walkway. She tipped her bonnet back in time to see Nettie still after the man, getting a few more swings at his head and shoulders before he leaped into a dilapidated old carriage and the driver took off, tearing into the horses with a vengeance.

It gave Roslynn the shivers to know that the carriage had been so close, that only a few more steps and she'd have been thrown into it. And everything had happened so fast. There were people standing around her, but all obviously too slow in their reactions to have helped. Only now did one of the grooms from their carriage come running up to offer his assistance—too late.

Nettie turned around, tugging down her spencer, which had come all askew in her attack against the footpad, unable to stop the triumphant smile that was now turning her lips up at the corners. Not even seeing Roslynn sprawled on the ground could lessen her moment of victory—until she saw the dirk still grasped in Roslynn's fist. But still, *she* had made the blackguard run for his life, even if Roslynn had made sure she wasn't carried along with him. They had prevailed, and she was inordinately pleased.

So was Roslynn, come to that, even with her backside smarting. Gramp would have been proud of her for remaining calm and doing what she had to do without hesitation. She had drawn blood for the first time, but even now she didn't feel squeamish about it. What she felt was a good deal safer, knowing she really could take care of herself. Of course, she had been prepared. She might not always have that intuitive warning to put her on guard. And if more than just the one man had tried to grab her, that would be a different story too. She didn't dare get cocky about this success.

Roslynn accepted the groom's help in rising and calmly returned her dirk to her boot before dusting off her skirts. Nettie waved the anxious fellow back and the crowd too, with a few choice words about concern being unwelcome when coming so tardily. Huffily she gathered up the dropped packages, thrust them into the groom's hands, and grabbed Roslynn's arm, fairly dragging her on toward the carriage.

"I should've listened tae yer warning, lass. I will next time."

"Then you think it was Geordie's hirelings?"

Nettie took a moment to consider. "Truth is, it could've been, but I doubt it."

"What else, then?"

"Just look at ye, wearing those sapphires round yer neck like a beacon. They could've thought ye were the wife of some rich lord that'd pay a pretty piece tae be getting ye back."

"I suppose." They were both silent for a moment more, then Roslynn added unexpectedly, "I think I'll go to the Eden party after all. It won't hurt to leave London for a few days, just to be safe. If Geordie is here and watching, he'll think I'm onto him and fleeing again. And until then, I'll keep Frances' servants close to me when I go out."

"Aye, on that I'm in agreement. Ye need tae be more cautious than ye ha' been."

Chapter Ten

It had been a simple matter, escaping London on Brutus' back, two stalwart grooms flanking her. Roslynn didn't bother with a disguise this time. If the town house was being watched, she wanted Geordie to be aware of her leave-taking, to see the hefty satchel of clothes she carried, to think she was fleeing London.

The subterfuge seemed unnecessary, however, when they were several miles away and it appeared no one followed behind them. The brilliant sunrise offered ample light by which to keep watch, but the roads were clogged mainly with farmers bringing their produce to market and with travelers coming to London for the weekend. Only one fancy coach was seen leaving town, and Roslynn left it so far behind it didn't matter whether it had been following her or not.

She had a pleasant breakfast while she waited in the inn where she had arranged to meet Frances, and when Frances showed up with nothing suspicious to report, Roslynn felt safe traveling the rest of the way to Hampshire in the Grenfell coach. Halfway there, she left one worry behind for another, but there was little she could do about this one except hope her concern was unfounded. In her favor was the likelihood that a man like Sir Anthony wouldn't care to leave the excitement of London for a small country gathering, and Lady Eden had confided that this party, planned for months in advance, would be attended mostly by her neighbors, country gentry like herself who generally avoided London during the season.

It was early afternoon when they arrived, quite the first to do so, but then few others were planning on staying over, living as near as they did. Frances opted to nap the rest of the afternoon. Roslynn gave the excuse she would do the same, yet once she was alone in the room allotted to her, she plopped herself down in front of a window facing the front of the house and anxiously watched the drive. Every arriving carriage was noted, every alighting male passenger thoroughly scrutinized. She even kept a close watch on the comings and goings of the servants, making sure no male missed her notice.

When Nettie entered much later to help her mistress prepare for the evening, her patience was tried to the limit by Roslynn's fidgetiness and her constant running toward the window at the least sound of a new arrival. It was taking a good half hour just to complete Roslynn's coiffure.

"And just who is it ye're looking fer, I'd like tae be knowing, that ye canna sit still fer even two minutes?" Nettie finally demanded when Roslynn once again sat down at the dressing table in front of her.

"And who would I be watching for but my gentlemen?" Roslynn replied defensively. "Only Sir Artemus Shadwell has shown up so far."

"If the others are coming, they're coming. Yer watching fer them won't change it."

"I suppose," Roslynn was forced to concede, since her answer had been a lie to begin with.

The truth was, since meeting Anthony Malory, she had given very little thought to her four "possibles." *That* would have to change.

Fortunately for her peace of mind, the last noise she had leaped up to investigate appeared to be the last carriage to arrive. With no other sound from out front, Nettie was able to help her into the sky-blue gown of silk she had chosen for tonight, generously complemented by the Cameron sapphires around her neck and delicate wrists, and Roslynn was able to release some of her tension.

By the time Frances joined her so they could go downstairs together, Roslynn was quite relaxed. *He* wasn't coming, and if there was an annoying twinge of disappointment accompanying that knowledge, Roslynn determinedly ignored it.

Lady Eden met them at the bottom of the wide stairway that rose from the large main hall to divide in the center, one section going to the front of the house where the guest rooms were, the other to the back of the house where the master bedrooms were located. A railinged walkway surrounded this hall on the second floor to reach the many rooms upstairs, leaving the whole area below visible from above, with a mammoth chandelier hanging from the center of the domed ceiling, at the moment glittering down on the white marble floor.

Roslynn was looking forward to a tour of the rest of the house, and Regina didn't disappoint her, insisting her guests could wait. She further put Roslynn at ease with her bright chatter and charming manner as the three of them moved from room to room on the lower floors.

Silverley was an immense country house, almost castlelike with its central main block and corner turrets, but there was nothing medieval inside except perhaps the antique tapestries that graced many of the walls. It was tastefully furnished in different periods, Queen Anne and Chippendale dominating one room, Sheraton another, still another in a combination, including a few quaint French Provincial pieces. Roslynn was left with the impression of a home, not a showpiece, though the latter term could certainly be applied.

The tour ended at the back of the house where the guests were gathered, and simply standing in the small antechamber with its floor-to-ceiling stained-glass windows, they were able to see into the drawing room on the left, which opened into a music room beyond. A large dining room was on the right, and off that was a lovely conservatory, which Roslynn promised herself a closer look at later. But at the moment, what with guests roaming through these connecting rooms, all of which fronted a vast parkland behind the house, Regina was cornered into making introductions before they had even entered the drawing room.

"There is one neighbor of mine I think you'll enjoy meeting," Regina commented to Roslynn when she was finally able to usher her and Frances into the drawing room. "Not everyone hies off to London for the season, you know. I wouldn't have gone myself if I hadn't promised, but I'm glad I did since I got to meet you. And don't worry, we'll have a chance later to discuss what Nicholas had to say about the gentlemen you're interested in."

"I see only Sir Artemus, Ros," Frances said uneasily, remembering how worried Roslynn had been about whether her "possibles" would be here or not.

"That's true," Regina said. "But there is still tomorrow, so I wouldn't discount the other gentlemen yet. I did have acceptances from all four of them. But in the meantime, you really must meet Lord Warton. Nicholas is so jealous of him, you know. In fact, I wonder sometimes what would have happened if I had met Justin Warton first." It was easy to see by her impish grin that she wasn't in the least serious about that last statement.

"Justin's not as old as your other gentlemen, Roslynn," Regina continued. "Only about twenty-eight years old, I believe, but he's *so* nice, I just know you're going to like him. Devoted to his family and abhors London, so you wouldn't have been able to meet him otherwise. He goes to town only once a year to take his mother and sister shopping, and that off season. Now where is he?" With her diminutive height, Regina had to stand on tiptoe to see over a few shoulders, but finally she smiled. "There, by the fireplace. Come along, m'dears."

Roslynn took two steps and stopped abruptly. She had immediately seen the large, handsome man sitting on a cream-and-gold sofa near the fireplace, flanked on one side by a young woman with the same blond looks as he and on the other side by an older woman, obviously Lord Warton's sister and mother, respectively. But she had in the next instant seen the two elegantly attired gentlemen several feet beyond, standing directly in front of the fireplace, the Malory brothers, and it was the dark one she locked eyes with, who made her pause, and groan, and feel the strangest rush of giddiness . . .

It took the greatest effort to tear her eyes away from Anthony Malory and continue to follow her hostess, who hadn't noticed her pause. She would have much preferred to turn around and retreat, rather than close the distance to a mere six feet from the fireplace where the sofa was situated, but there was no help for it. And since there wasn't, she decided it would behoove her to concentrate on the Wartons, Justin Warton in particular, and to keep her back to the Malorys.

It was easy to see why Regina might think Justin would interest her. He was terribly handsome with his blond hair, strong, chiseled features, and the loveliest pair of dark indigo eyes, eyes that were frankly admiring as they lit upon Roslynn. He was also quite the tallest man she had ever met, as she discovered when he rose from the sofa to take her hand and bring it up to his lips. He was large, with wide, wide shoulders, and he was solidly put together, firmly muscled. But with his immense size, if it weren't for his boyish smile and charming manner, he could have been quite intimidating.

As it was, he put Roslynn at ease immediately, and for several minutes she almost forgot who stood behind her—almost. The trouble was, she could actually feel those sensual eyes roaming over her body, could see them in her mind's eye as they had looked at her that night of the Crandal ball. Looked? No—*devoured* her across the space of a room, as they did now from only a few feet away. It was all she could do not to imagine what *he* was imagining as he gazed at her.

The interruption by a new arrival was a welcome distraction. "There you are, love," Nicholas Eden said as he slipped a possessive arm around his wife's tiny waist. "Why is it that whenever I leave the room, this big clod always manages to show up at your side?"

Whether he was jesting or serious was not evident either by his expression or tone, but Justin Warton didn't take offense. He laughed instead, as if he were used to such comments from his host.

"If I was of a mind to steal her away from you, Montieth, you'd know it," Justin replied with a wink for Regina, who was taking these remarks in stride.

"Now don't start, either of you," Regina admonished lightly. "Or you'll have these ladies believing you're serious. They're not, you know, not at all," she confided to her guests. "This, if you haven't guessed, is my husband." And she went on to complete the introductions, for although Frances knew of him, she had never actually met him.

Roslynn had expected someone as beautiful as Regina Eden to have an exceptionally handsome husband, and the Fourth Viscount Eden of Montieth was certainly that. He had gold-streaked brown hair and light brown eyes that glowed like amber each time they rested on his wife, and it was easy to see how he could have been called a rake as recently as a year ago and lived up to the reputation, and just as easy to see that he was now quite domesticated and thoroughly in love with his wife. What was surprising was that he was so young, no more than a few years older than she, Roslynn guessed, and yet his manner was that of an older man; in fact, he reminded her distinctly of Sir Anthony, which brought that rakehell promptly back into her thoughts.

"Come now, puss, how long do you intend to ignore us?" Anthony's deep voice suddenly broke into a lull in the conversation.

"All bloody night, if I have anything to say about it," Nicholas retorted none too pleasantly.

For a heart-stopping moment, Roslynn had thought Anthony was addressing her. But Nicholas' surprising reply, which earned him a sharp jab in the ribs from his wife, disabused her of that giddy notion.

"Oh, bother, must I always play referee?" Regina said to no one in particular, then promptly flounced over to the fireplace and gave each Malory brother a kiss. "As if anyone *could* ignore either of you for very long," she added with a laugh. "But I don't suppose for a minute that it's my attention you're so impatient for. Come along, then, and I'll introduce you." She hooked an arm through each of theirs and dragged them forward. "Lady Frances, I don't believe you've met my uncles, James and Anthony Malory, have you?"

Uncles? *Uncles!* Why was it that that wee bit of information hadn't surfaced sooner? Roslynn wondered angrily. She certainly wouldn't have come here if she had known the Malorys were *that* close to Regina Eden. Their niece. Hell's teeth!

The uneasiness was palatable with four in their group, the Wartons and Frances. Justin in fact made haste to leave with his womenfolk, protectively getting his sister out of the presence of two such notorious rakes. Roslynn could almost wish she had someone to look after her so diligently, someone to whisk her away from this present encounter. But she held her own. Not by look or word did she reveal that she was just as uneasy with the situation. Frances was not so inscrutable, however. Tight-lipped, curt during the introductions, her animosity for these two men couldn't have been more apparent, and she wasted little time in making her own excuses and moving on to the next group of people.

Which left Roslynn in a horrid predicament. To depart as well would have been grossly rude at this point. So she had to stand there, for a while at least, and suffer both Malorys' close scrutiny. And neither of them had any compunctions about openly staring at her.

Neither did James feel it necessary to ignore what had just happened. "I do believe the lass is embarrassed for us, Tony. You needn't be, Lady Roslynn. My brother and I are quite immune to such reactions."

"*You* might be, old man," Anthony remarked with a definite sparkle in his cobalt eyes. "I for one could do with a little sympathy."

Roslynn was left with no doubt as to what kind of sympathy he would like, since he was looking directly at her when he said it. She couldn't help smiling. He couldn't even wait until he found her alone to press his seduction. Now *that* was incorrigible.

Regina must have thought so too. "Now, Tony, you promised you'd behave."

"And so I am," he protested in all innocence. "If I was inclined to do as is my wont, puss, you'd have a scandal on your hands."

Roslynn had the feeling he was quite serious, even though Regina laughed as if he were teasing her. "You're going to scare her off, Tony, if you're not careful."

"Not at all," Roslynn demurred.

"There, you see, sweet?" James put in. "You can feel free to run along and attend to your hostessing. The lady will be quite safe in our hands."

"Oh, I never doubted it for a minute," Regina said, only to add in parting, "Nicholas, don't let either of them out of your sight."

"Splendid." Nicholas scowled.

James chuckled. "A decided lack of trust, that."

"Unfortunately warranted," Nicholas grumbled beneath his breath.

"I do believe he still hasn't forgiven us, Tony," James said.

"Speak for yourself, brother. All I did was point out to him that it would be detrimental to his health if he didn't marry Reggie. You, on the other hand, were responsible for his being confined to bed for several weeks, not to mention your dragging him home from the West Indies when he proved such a reluctant spouse."

"I was never—"

Roslynn interrupted Nicholas' snarl. "Before this gets out of hand, I think I'll just—"

Anthony didn't let her finish. "An excellent idea. While they squabble to their heart's content, you and I shall see what's blooming in the conservatory."

Without giving her a chance to refuse, Anthony took her arm and began escorting her from the room. They moved no more than five feet before she tried to draw away from him. He wasn't letting go.

"Sir Anthony—"

"You're not going to turn coward on me, are you?" His voice sounded near her ear.

Roslynn bristled that he should make it a challenge. "I simply don't want to leave the room with you."

"But you will."

She stopped walking, forcing him to either drag her behind him or stop as well. He stopped, and the tiniest hint of a grin appeared as he bent his head to hers.

"Let me put it this way, sweetheart. Either I kiss you in the conservatory or I kiss you right here, right now. Whichever way, I *am* going to take you in my arms and—"

"The devil you are!" Roslynn got out before she noticed how many people were suddenly watching them. "Very well," she amended in a quiet hiss. "I would like to see the conservatory, but there'll be no kissing, you scoundrel, and I'll have your promise first."

His grin was wide and bold now. "Come along, then."

And he continued to escort her, stopping here and there to have a few words with people he knew, as if they were only strolling through the rooms. Roslynn caught Frances' eye along the way, and her friend's expression was quite disapproving and rightly so. But Roslynn didn't want to press her luck by trying again to extricate herself from this situation. Whether Anthony really would have kissed her in front of everyone was a moot point. She simply couldn't take the chance.

But she should have sealed the bargain. His "Come along, then" was not a promise by any means, which she found out not long after they entered the large conservatory.

"This is really lovely," Roslynn said uneasily as his arm slipped around her waist and he began to guide her along the plant-strewn walkway that circled the room.

"I couldn't agree more," he replied, only he was looking at her.

She kept her eyes averted, gazing intently at the statues along the walk, at the myriad flowers in full bloom, at the fountain that was on a lower level in the center of the room. Foremost in her mind was that hand resting on her hip, burning through the thin material of her high-waisted gown.

"I—I really should take you to task, Sir Anthony." Her voice was thin, shaky, and she had to clear her throat before continuing with more force. "That was devilish unfair of you to leave me no choice back there."

"I know."

"Was it necessary to be so high-handed?"

He stopped, turning her toward him, his eyes moving slowly over her face as he considered her question. In alarm, Roslynn realized that he had maneuvered them to the far side of the room, that thick branches from one of the trees growing below spread out at their level and effectively concealed them from the doorway. In actuality, they were quite alone for the moment, the sound of the party drowned out by the flow of the fountain.

"Yes, it was necessary," he finally answered huskily. "When all I've been able to think about since I first laid eyes on you is this."

To save her soul, Roslynn couldn't find the will to protest as his arm drew her closer. His other hand slid along her neck, the thumb tilting her chin up, and for the breath of a moment her eyes locked with his. Then she felt his lips, warm, beguiling, pressing ever so gently on her own, and her lids closed, accepting the inevitable. She had had to know, and now she did. And for the moment, nothing mattered but the taste of him, the feel of him pressed along her length.

Anthony didn't frighten her with his passion but kept it tightly leashed, even though he felt like an inferno about to explode. He couldn't remember when he had wanted something this much, and he took every care not to overwhelm her with what he was feeling, to fan her desire by slow degrees until she wanted him with equal intensity.

It was the hardest thing he had ever done, restraining himself when his body cried out to take her here and now. And in fact he was not as self-controlled as he supposed. Nearly mindless with wanting, he was unaware of the little things he was doing to her, that his fingers had slid into her hair, dislodging pins from her coiffure, that his knee had slipped between her own, far enough that she was practically straddling his thigh. But fortunately for him, she was as mindless as he was at this point. He just didn't know it.

Actually, that thigh rubbing against her groin was Roslynn's undoing, coupled as it was with his deepening kisses. He had gradually brought his tongue into play, teaching her the exquisite sensations it could invoke, using it to open her mouth, to taste the sweetness within. He eventually enticed her tongue to explore as well, and once it hesitantly passed between his lips, he wouldn't let it go, gently sucking it deeper and deeper into his mouth.

Helpless under his expertise, Roslynn was quite thoroughly seduced, ready and willing to let him do anything he wanted. When Anthony finally became aware of that fact, he groaned in frustration, for he had unwisely chosen his setting, never dreaming that he would be this successful this quickly.

Trailing his lips to her ear, he beseeched her, "Go to your room, sweetheart. I'll follow you there."

She was dazed, hypnotically so, unable to connect one thought with another. "My room?"

He had the urge to shake her. Now was not the time for confusion, for God's sake! He gripped her shoulders instead.

"Look at me, Roslynn," he said urgently. "We can't stay here. Do you understand? There's no privacy here."

She frowned up at him. "What would we be needing privacy for?"

Hell and fire! Was Regina right? Could Roslynn really be that innocent at her age? He found himself torn between chagrin and pleasure at the thought. If it were true, he risked losing what ground he had gained by bringing her back to her senses. And yet a tender cord was struck, heretofore dormant, wishing it were true.

Anthony sighed, dredging up a degree of patience to reach her. "We're going to make love, you and I. That is the natural conclusion to what we've been doing. And since we both want to, the thing to do is find someplace we won't be disturbed. You'll agree your room is the logical place."

Roslynn was shaking her head before he had finished. "Och, mon, what have you done? There was to be no kissing—I told you so."

Her lilting brogue served to stir him even more, and he pulled her tightly back against his chest. "It's too late to prevaricate, sweetheart, after you've surrendered in every way but one. Now be a good girl and do as I say, or I'll take you right here, I swear I will, and the devil take anyone who happens upon us."

If he meant to frighten her into complying, it didn't work. She almost laughed at his effort but didn't think he would appreciate that in this present mood that could make him say such a thing. Common sense told her he wouldn't do anything to cause his niece embarrassment. She should have realized that sooner, before she came in here with him.

"You canna use that bluff on me twice, laddie."

At this moment, Anthony wasn't sure it had been a bluff. But that she was boldly calling it restored his reason, even if it didn't completely cool his ardor. He had made a mess of the situation, and if she wasn't angry, she had every right to be.

His smile came with devastating effect. It was his melting smile. "If now just won't do, then I'll come to your room later tonight."

She pushed away from him, shaking her head. "You'll no' get past the door, I promise you that."

"Leave it unlocked."

"I'll no' do that either."

"Your window, then."

Her hazel eyes flared. "So you'll make me suffocate in my room, locking every window? Why canna you just take no for an answer? Have I no' made it plain enough for you?"

"It's the wrong answer, sweetheart, and until it's the right one, you don't really expect me to give up, do you? I must think of my reputation, you know."

She laughed at this, relieving some of her tension. God, but he was incorrigible, utterly lacking in morals, and oh, so tempting. She had never known a man could have such a powerful sexual allure, so strong that even in her saner moments, knowing full well that he was not the man for her, she could still be drawn to him. But whether he was serious or not in this bold pursuit of her, the only way she was going to survive this present encounter was not to take him seriously at all.

In control again, her eyes chiding him, Roslynn said, "Your reputation is precisely what *I* am thinking of, Sir Anthony."

"Then I must see if I can't chase such thoughts away—again."

"No!"

She gasped as he reached for her, and before she knew it, she was sitting on the railing, her balance precarious at best, and he was grinning at her. She had thought he meant to kiss her again. *This* she didn't find amusing at all. The drop behind her was at least eight or nine feet from the top of the railing where she sat to the ground, her feet were dangling off the floor, and she had nothing to grasp hold of if she should lose her balance—except him.

Scowling, she started to jump down, but Anthony stepped closer, and to Roslynn's horror, he flicked her skirt up to her thighs. Now he moved even closer, forcing her legs to part to accommodate his hips, and he leaned his chest into her, pushing her back, back . . .

"Hold onto me, or you're going to fall over." His voice broke through her panic.

She did, because there was nothing else she could do at the moment. Only he didn't straighten up so she could regain her balance. He kept her dangling half over the railing, his body her only anchor.

"You'll have to do better that that, sweetheart. Wrap your arms around my neck." With one arm he pressed her belly and chest to his. "Now hold tight, because I'm letting go."

"No, dinna—"

"Shh, sweetheart." His breath blew into her ear, sending delicious tremors down her back. "If you won't give in, at least give me this. I need to touch you."

She caught her breath as she felt a hand on each knee, slowly moving up the outside of her thighs, dragging her dress with them. "Stop! You're a bloody . . . let me down!" And then, in a husky whisper, "Anthony."

He shivered at the way she said his name. But before she could say any more, his hands reached her hips, and with a sharp pull he had their loins pressed tightly together.

Roslynn moaned softly, her head falling back, her limbs gone all buttery. He might as well have entered her, the feeling was that evocative. And now his lips burned a moist trail along the neck she had exposed to him, and Roslynn quite understandably forgot her precarious position.

"I don't suppose you'll thank me for intruding, Tony, but Lady Grenfell's searching for your little Scot, and she's bound to look in here at any moment."

With a curse, Anthony glanced at James several feet away, to see him tactfully looking down at the fountain, rather than at them. He lifted Roslynn off the railing, his hands still supporting her hips, and for just a moment more held her like that, savoring the feeling of her in this position, with her legs nearly wrapped around his waist. She was once again in the throes of passion, lips parted, eyes closed, face flushed. He doubted she had even heard James.

"Oh, Christ," he said as he let her slide slowly to her feet, frustrated now beyond measure. "We'll have to continue this another time, sweetheart."

She stepped back, her legs wobbly, and over several long moments he watched her eyes gradually focus, finally widen, and then promptly narrow. Fascinated, Anthony didn't even see her hand coming, but the palm cracked solidly against his cheek.

"There'll no' be another time, mon, for what you're wanting," she said quietly, but with enough force that he couldn't doubt her temper was boiling. "I dinna ken your rules, and you canna be trusted to play fair, so just stay away from me."

She flounced off in the direction they had been taking, continuing around the room. Anthony didn't try to follow her. He sat back on the railing, fingering his cheek, and watched her until she was gone from sight.

"I was wondering when that Scot's temper would surface." He grinned as James came up beside him.

"I'd say you were let off lightly."

Anthony's grin widened. "She didn't even know you were here."

"Bragging, brother?"

"Just feeling inordinately pleased, old man."

"Well, now that you've left her in this raging mood, I don't suppose you'll mind if I try my luck?"

Anthony's humor vanished instantly. "Stay away from her, James."

A blond brow shot up. "Possessive, aren't we? But I believe those words were hers—to you. And after all, dear boy, you haven't won her yet."

Chapter Eleven

Justin Warton proved such delightful company that Roslynn's temper was able to subside completely in less time than she could have hoped for, considering what a foul temper she had when it was fully aroused. And she had been furious, the more so when Frances found her just coming out of the conservatory and promptly whisked her upstairs to repair her coiffure, which she hadn't even realized had fallen into such a telling state of disarray. Horrid man to leave her looking as if she had just been manhandled, which she had been, which forced her to suffer through a stern lecture from Frances, albeit deserved.

She *knew* she had been foolish, *knew* she had taken a terrible risk. She didn't need to be told so with such sterling clarity. But she couldn't take exception to Frances' anger in her behalf, since it was based on love and concern. She could only be more furious with herself, for upsetting Frances and for knowing better in the first place.

After a long harangue about Sir Anthony's sordid reputation, Frances had concluded with, "You simply must never find yourself alone with him again, Ros, especially since you are so obviously attracted to him."

"I never said that, Frances."

"You didn't have to. I saw it the moment Regina brought Sir Anthony forward to be introduced to us. And I saw the way he looked at you too. Kissing you in the conservatory was one thing, but you know it would't have stopped there if you had been in a less conspicuous place."

Roslynn didn't volunteer that it had gone a step beyond kissing, even in that public place, or that she wasn't at all sure that it might not have gone much, much further if Anthony hadn't fortunately come to his senses and released her. *She* certainly hadn't been the one to break away, nor had she even tried, once she was held firmly in his embrace.

"You should have told me you had met him at the Crandal ball." Frances' tone suddenly turned hurtful. "I could have warned you sooner, for it's obvious he's marked you for his next conquest."

"Frances, Frances, you didn't have to warn me. I'd already heard the gossip about him at the ball. I knew what a disreputable rake he is."

"And yet you still let him lead you off."

"I told you, he tricked me!" Roslynn cried in exasperation, then promptly regretted her tone. "I'm sorry, but you must stop worrying. I've told him to stay away from me."

Frances pursed her lips, her finely arched brows drawn tightly together. "Do you think your wishes will make the least bit of difference to him? Men like him don't accept rejection, Ros. For some absurd reason, they only become more intrigued the harder the chase. And *that* one, Sir Anthony, is the worst of the lot, simply because he's the handsomest, the most sought after, and the most confirmed bachelor in the Realm. He'll never marry, Ros. He'll never settle for one woman. And why should he when hundreds scheme and plot to win his favor?"

"Frances, you're forgetting how unique my circumstances are. I'm not just another hopeful debutante on the marriage mart. I've got a goal to accomplish, and I'm not going to let anything upset it. The consequences are too abhorrent to me, not to mention dangerous, if I should fail to quickly secure a marriage."

Frances sighed and gave a little apologetic smile. "You're right, I was forgetting that. But you will be careful, Ros? A man like Malory, with his experience, could have you seduced before you even know it. I suppose we can just be grateful that that brother of his, just as unprincipled, hasn't set his eye on you too."

Roslynn was to remember those words later, but when they returned downstairs and Justin Warton was quick to invite them to share the buffet with him, she was still simmering over her own naiveté with Anthony Malory to give his brother a single thought. And then Justin took her mind off her near catastrophe and she enjoyed herself for a while. He was so charming, his lovely indigo eyes so admiring, that she seriously found herself considering him as a likely candidate to add to her list, despite his young age. At least he was older than she, and he certainly made no attempt to conceal his interest in her, which was gratifying, especially after *she* had had to be so bold as to seek out her other candidates. And still had to, it seemed, since Sir Artemus had yet to approach her tonight, even though she knew he had seen her.

Unfortunately, Lady Warton broke up their threesome soon after they had eaten, complaining of a headache, and Justin was forced to see her home, though he extracted a promise from Roslynn that she would ride with him in the hunt planned for the next morning.

"Well, that was an easy conquest," Frances remarked after Justin had left with his mother.

"Do you think so?" Roslynn grinned. "He is rather nice, isn't he?"

"And so very upstanding. I've heard nothing but good things—"

"Frances, you needn't laud his sterling qualities. If you've noticed, Sir Anthony appears to have left. You can stop worrying."

Frances squeezed her hand. "Very well. I know you've got the sense to distinguish the good from the bad. And as long as Lord Warton has quit for the evening, shouldn't you be furthering your acquaintance with Sir Artemus while you have the opportunity?"

"Indeed." Roslynn sighed. "And I also need to find Lady Eden for the information she promised me. The sooner my list is narrowed down, the better."

But Regina Eden was having a lively conversation with several of her neighbors that Roslynn was loath to interrupt, and she found Sir Artemus embroiled in a game of whist, several such games having started up after dinner.

Roslynn moved near one of the open French doors to wait until she could catch Regina's attention, taking advantage of what little breeze wafted in off the vast parkland. As uncomfortably warm as the drawing room had become, she would have loved to step outside but didn't dare, not after the last time she had thought to escape to a garden had precipitated her first meeting with Sir Anthony. And just because she hadn't seen him since she left him in the conservatory didn't mean he wasn't still on the premises somewhere.

She almost thought to go and drag Frances outside with her just so she could cool off a bit when she was startled by a movement behind her.

"Enjoying yourself, Lady Roslynn?"

She turned around warily, recognizing James Malory's voice and afraid that Anthony would be with him, as before. She relaxed, however, to see he was alone, his golden hair slightly ruffled, obviously having just come in from outside. But her respite lasted only a few seconds, for the way he was pointedly staring at her, waiting for her answer, reminded her that this was the brother she had decided could be dangerous in his dealings, and nothing about him tonight changed that opinion, though she was now inclined to feel that Anthony was the more dangerous, at least to her.

She nodded slightly. "Yes, your niece has made me feel right at home, though I must say I was surprised to learn that she was your niece. She would be the daughter of one of your older brothers, I suppose?"

"Our only sister, Melissa," he corrected. "But she died when Regan was just a baby still, so my brothers and I had the pleasure of raising her."

Roslynn had the distinct impression that four young men really *had* found it a pleasure to raise their only sister's child, which made this particular Malory seem less threatening in her mind until he suggested, "Care for a stroll down to the lake?"

It was unexpected and instantly put her on guard. "No, thank you."

"Then just outside? You look like you could use a breath of fresh air."

"Actually, I'm rather chilled and was just thinking of fetching a shawl."

James chuckled at such a lame excuse. "My dear girl, that fine film of moisture on your brow says otherwise. Come along. You needn't be afraid of me, you know. I'm quite harmless in all respects."

When his hand gripped her elbow to escort her outside, Roslynn felt strangely as if this had happened before, earlier, that she was being rushed along the exact same course, leading to disaster. Only she had no chance to drag James to a halt as she had done with Anthony when he tried to escort her from the room. Just two steps and they were outside, and it was accomplished before she could even think to yank away, nor did he give her a chance to. Instead of walking on, he pulled her to the side of the door and pressed her back against the wall, and his mouth smothered her small cry of alarm.

It was done so swiftly, so cleverly, that Roslynn had had no opportunity to anticipate the trap or get out of it. Nor did she dare make any loud protests now, or she would draw the attention of the occupants inside, only several feet away on the other side of the wall, and she couldn't afford the gossip that that would entail. The most she could do was try to push him away from her, but it was as if she were squeezed in between two walls, his big, solid chest was so unmovable. And then she no longer tried. She could feel the blood pounding in her ears, because of the danger of discovery, she told herself, but actually, she found James Malory's kiss so reminiscent of his brother's that it could have been Anthony kissing her instead. Only it wasn't, and she held onto that thought for dear life.

"You and your brother must take lessons from each other," she hissed the moment he lifted his head.

James laughed despite his disappointment. "Do you think so, little Scot? Now why would you say that?"

She blushed furiously to have as much as admitted that Anthony had also kissed her. Defensively, she snapped, "Was that your idea of being harmless?"

"I lied," he said with a blatant lack of contrition.

"Indeed! Now let me pass, Lord Malory."

He moved back only enough to separate their bodies, not enough to allow her to slip by him. "Don't be angry, sweet. You can't blame a man for trying, though I now concede that Tony has bested me this time. It's devilish unfair that you happened to meet him first."

"What the devil are you blathering about?" But she gasped, afraid she knew. "If you two have placed wagers on me—"

"Never think so, dear girl. It's no more than sibling rivalry, and the simple fact that we share the same tastes, he and I." A finger came up to brush back the damp curls at her temple, and for a moment, Roslynn was mesmerized by intense green eyes. "You are incredibly lovely, you know . . . incredibly. Which makes it bloody difficult to accept defeat." His voice lowered to a husky pitch suddenly. "I could have made your blood sing, sweet lass. Are you quite certain you prefer Tony?"

Roslynn shook herself mentally, fighting off the potent spell he was weaving with little effort, yet with such ruthless success. Good God, these Malorys were devastating at their craft of seduction.

Stiffly, praying he would take her words to heart, she insisted, "I never said I preferred your brother, but that doesn't mean I prefer you to him either. The fact is, Lord Malory, I don't want either of you. Now will you let me pass, or must I throw caution to the winds and call for help?"

He stepped back, bowing slightly, a thoroughly maddening grin turning up his sensual lips. "I can't let you do that, dear lady. Being found out here alone with me would quite ruin you."

"Which you should have considered *before* you dragged me out here!" she retorted and promptly deserted him with all speed.

And as Anthony had done earlier, James watched her flounce away, only he didn't have Anthony's sense of eventual success to buoy his spirits. Quite the contrary. As much as he would have liked to win this particular lady, and no doubt could if he really set his mind to it, her reaction to his kiss was only a muted echo of her reaction to Anthony's. He hadn't left her in a state of bemusement, as his brother so obviously had. Her choice was clear, even if she was not yet aware she had made it. But if it were anyone else but Tony . . .

Damn, but she was a fine piece. His sense of humor returned, laced with irony. She had managed to stir him, and now he was sorely in need of a wench, which meant he would have to take himself off to the nearest village or else annoy Regan by seducing one of her neighbors. So there was nothing for it but to take himself off when he would rather not. Hell and fire, and a bloody pox on love at first sight!

Chapter Twelve

Roslynn rolled over, rubbed the sleep from her eyes, and squinted at the clock on the mantel. Damn. She had really meant to join the hunt this morning. She had even promised Justin she would ride with him and had been looking forward to showing off a bit to impress him with her equestrian talents. But the hunting party would probably be returning soon, if it hadn't already. There had been mention of a picnic planned for midday down by the lake, and it was nearly noon. Double damn.

She sat up, but not before she scowled down at the bed that had offered her no peace last night. Nettie had tried to wake her. She remembered that. But she doubted anything short of fire could have prodded her out of bed early this morning, because it had been dawn before she finally succumbed to sleep. Just one more thing she could lay at Anthony Malory's feet, drat the wretched man.

And there was no excuse for it. She had retired not long after midnight. Having arisen well before dawn yesterday to make the trip to Silverley, and not having napped in the afternoon as Frances had, she had really been exhausted last night. And she had had several hours to get over her chagrin at Anthony's brother for his outlandish conclusions concerning her preferences in men. She had even had her talk with Regina and now knew a good deal more about her "possibles" than she had before, though unfortunately, nothing had been revealed that would really assist her in whittling down her list as she had hoped.

Sir Artemus Shadwell was an avid gambler, but Roslynn had already concluded that observation for herself, and he was rich enough to afford this pastime. Lord Grahame, the distinguished Earl of Dunstanton, was a three-time widower. At least the poor fellow kept trying. Lord David Fleming, the viscount who was also heir to a dukedom, was a confirmed bachelor, his affairs so discreet his name had never been linked with any woman. Commendable. But the Honorable Christopher Savage was still an enigma to her. The Montieths simply weren't acquainted with the fellow.

But her gentlemen, much as they should have, hadn't occupied her thoughts last night as she lay tossing about in her bed. James Malory's effrontery had also been forgotten. It was that black-haired scoundrel with the smoldering blue eyes who had caused her hour after hour of insomnia in reliving those fateful minutes spent with him in the conservatory.

Well, there would be no more of *that,* by God, no more wasted thoughts on blackhearted rascals, and no more procrastinating. She *would* get down to business, and hoped, no, prayed, that the rest of her respected and highly suitable gentlemen would show up today.

Impatient now to quit the room, she rang for Nettie but didn't wait to start her toilette, and was dressed in a lovely peach percale day dress with short, puffed sleeves and heavily flounced at the hem before Nettie even arrived. Rushing Nettie with her coiffure earned her a snort and a brief lecture on the missed opportunities of slugabeds, but even so, the tightly woven chignon and numerous short ringlets that framed her face turned out most becomingly.

But Roslynn spared not a moment to admire the finished package. Snatching up a white satin bonnet adorned with ostrich feathers that matched her shoes, and a lacy parasol, she sped from the room, leaving Nettie to clean up the mess she had made of her wardrobe before Nettie's tardy arrival. And then she was brought up short, for standing at the end of the narrow corridor that led to the guest rooms, leaning casually against the railing that overlooked the central hall, was Anthony Malory.

It was not to be borne, it really wasn't, for he was obviously waiting for her. Hips against the rail, arms crossed over his chest, ankles crossed as well, he had an unimpeded view of her bedroom door, and since he was waiting where he was, there was no way she could have avoided him.

He was casually dressed, almost too casually, minus a cravat and with several buttons open on his embroidered cambric shirt, revealing a darkly tanned V of chest, a few hairs hinting at a thicker patch just below. His coat was dark navy, the shoulders and upper arms filled out tightly. Long, muscular legs were sheathed in soft buckskin, with shiny Hessians molded to his calves. Everything about him proclaimed him an avid outdoorsman, athletic, a bloody Corinthian, which was so contrary to the reputation that would have him a debauched creature of the night, devoted to sensual pleasures and late hours of dissipation. Well, whatever he was, he was dangerously appealing to her senses.

When it appeared that the lady wasn't going to budge another step that would bring her nearer to him, Anthony said, "It's as well you came out now, sweetheart. I was just beginning to fantasize about slipping into your room and finding you still abed—"

"Sir Anthony!"

"Was the door unlocked?" he teased, but at her fulsome glare, finally chuckled. "You needn't bludgeon me with those pretty eyes, my dear. I don't mean a word of it. In fact, you can come ahead without the slightest qualm. Today I fully intend to offer my best behavior, to observe every propriety, and to bury all those wicked instincts that might cause you alarm."

"You promise?"

He grinned. "Must I?"

"Yes."

"Very well. My promise, solemn and most sincere, is yours until you take pity on me and give it back."

The sound of her husky laugh was like music to his ears. "You can have it back, Sir Anthony, when you're too old to want it, and not a day sooner."

She came forward then, stopping just in front of him, her parasol tucked under her arm, her bonnet swinging from the cord held in her hand. She was a vision, by God, with her full lips turned up in a generous smile, her firm little chin that had proved so stubborn, and those lovely gold-flecked eyes sparkling with humor now.

He had been wise to leave Silverley last night, he reflected now, wise indeed. If he had stayed, he would have been drawn to Roslynn again when she needed time to cool her temper. So he had taken himself off to the village to celebrate, for which there was ample cause. She might have slapped him, but by God, he had aroused her, and that was reason enough for his high spirits, and cause for wenching, since she had definitely aroused him as well.

Anthony could have laughed, remembering how his plans had gone awry. The problem was, by the time he had found a willing lass, a comely one too, in the little tavern where he ended up, he no longer needed one or wanted one, other than the one he had left behind at Silverley. So when James unexpectedly showed up at the same tavern not long behind him, he very happily turned the little doxy over to his brother and settled for getting pleasantly drunk while he plotted his next move.

He had decided, quite shrewdly if her present smile was any indication, to change his approach for the time being. And after a lengthy talk with his favorite niece this morning, he had come upon the perfect contrivance. He would offer the lady what she couldn't refuse—help to achieve her goals. Of course, if the advice he gave hindered more than helped, he wouldn't lose any sleep over it. Her goals simply weren't his.

She was waiting, patiently, to hear why he had put himself in her path. Ah, the power of a few words. She was at ease, her guard down, putting full trust in his promise. She had no way of knowing his passions far outweighed his whimsical honor, at least in dealing with those of the female gender.

He came away from the rail, his manner smooth, his voice impersonal. "It would be to your advantage, Lady Roslynn, to come along with me where we might talk privately."

Wariness returned. "I fail to see—"

His smile disarmed her. "My dear, I said talk, nothing more. If you can't bring yourself to trust me, how am I going to help you?"

Nonplussed. "Help me?"

"Of course," he replied. "That is what I had in mind. Now come along."

It was sheer curiosity that prompted Roslynn to hold her tongue and let him lead her downstairs and into the library. She simply couldn't fathom what he thought he was going to help her with. The only difficulties she was having at the moment were her attraction to him and her inability to scratch below the facade that her gentlemen presented to the public. Her gentlemen? No, he couldn't know about them, could he?

Whether he did or didn't, Roslynn found herself aghast to be blushing at the mere possibility. Fortunately, Anthony didn't notice, leading her directly to a sofa, then walking to the end of the long room and stopping before a liquor cart.

"Brandy?" he asked over his shoulder.

"At this hour?"

Her incredulous tone made him smile to himself. "No, of course not. How silly of me."

But he definitely needed one, for the thought flashed through his mind that he had her alone at last and only need lock the doors. But that wasn't what he had brought her here for, and he would have to keep *that* thought uppermost in his mind.

He tossed down the brandy and strolled back to stand before the sofa on which she sat so decorously, legs pressed together, parasol and bonnet in her lap. She was huddled in one corner, leaving him a good five feet of space to occupy himself. He would be a bore to sit next to her when it was perfectly clear she didn't want him to. He did anyway, though he conceded enough to allow a six-inch space to keep her from panicking.

She panicked just the same. "Sir Anthony—"

"D'you think you could start calling me Anthony, or better yet, Tony? After all, if I'm to be your confidant—"

"My *what?*"

He cocked a brow at her. "Too strong a word? Will friend and adviser do? After a long talk with my niece this morning, I realized you're sorely in need of both."

"She told you!" Roslynn's voice gasped accusingly. "Hell's teeth, she had no right!"

"Oh, it was done with the best of intentions, my dear. She wanted to impress on me how serious you are about getting married. Seems to think I have dishonorable intentions toward you. Can't imagine where she got that idea."

She glared at him, but it was impossible to keep her outrage alive after that bit of nonsense. Her laughter broke through, rich and delightful.

"You're a rogue, laddie. Do *you* never take anything seriously?"

"Not if I can help it." He grinned.

"Well, try long enough to tell me why you of all people would want to aid me on my way to matrimony."

"It simply occurred to me that the sooner you're married and bored with it, the sooner I'll have you in my bed," he answered caddishly.

Anything else Roslynn wouldn't have believed. *That* she believed completely.

"A rather long shot you're taking, wouldn't you say?" she bantered. "I could fall passionately in love with my husband, you know."

"Bite your tongue," he said with mock horror. "No one falls passionately in love these days, my dear, except young romantics and doddering old fools. And you're going about this thing much too sensibly for that possibility to occur."

"I'll concede that point for now. So what exactly are you offering to do for me?"

The loaded question brought a twinkle of amusement to his eyes. "Your situation is not unlike Reggie's was when she was looking for a husband. Her pressure came from having got through one season, as well as a tour of the Continent, with no luck whatsoever. Through no fault of her own, of course. She had to attend to finding a man my brothers and I could all agree was suitable for her."

"Yes, I recall her mentioning something like that."

"Did she tell you how she solved her problem?"

"She was compromised."

Roslynn was surprised to see him scowl at that answer. "She had nothing to do with *that*. It was Montieth's cheeky idea of a jest on his current mistress that went awry. And we won't mention that again, if you please. But before then, Reggie had hired an old lord who knew absolutely everyone, and dragged him along with her to every function, as well as on her tour, so with a signal they had worked out together, he could tell her which men she met were worth considering or not."

Roslynn's eyes flared. "I hope you're not suggesting I take you along with *me* everywhere I go, Sir Anthony, because—"

He was quick to forestall her. "Not at all, and unnecessary besides. According to Reggie, you already have several chaps under consideration. As it happens, I know them a damn sight better than Montieth does, since they're all closer to my age than his. Three of them belong to my club; the fourth frequents the same sporting hall I do. I just have one question for you, my dear. Why have you discounted someone closer to your own age?"

Roslynn averted her eyes before murmuring, "An older man is likely to have more patience with my faults than a younger man."

"You have faults? Never say so."

"Everyone has faults!" she snapped.

"A quick temper wouldn't be one of yours, would it?"

Her narrowed gaze brought a laugh, but she went on testily. "An older man will be more settled, having sowed his wild oats already. If I am going to be faithful in this marriage, I must insist upon the same from my husband."

"But you're not going to be faithful, sweetheart," he reminded her.

"If I'm not, then I won't expect him to be. But if I am, I will. Let's leave it at that. The fact is, it was my grandfather who suggested I find a man with a good deal of experience behind him, and truth to tell, the younger men I've met so far haven't impressed me—well, except one, and him I decided to add to my list."

"Who?"

"Justin Warton."

"Warton!" Anthony sat up abruptly, exclaiming, "He's a mama's boy!"

"You needn't be disparaging," she replied curtly.

"My dear girl, if all you want are pristine reports from me on your lucky chaps, then I don't see what help I can be to you. They all present an outward showing that is beyond reproach, which is to be expected of gentlemen of their stature. I had assumed it was the dirt swept under the carpet that you would be interested in."

She felt warm under his censure. "You're right, of course. I'm sorry. Very well, in your opinion, which fellow would make the best husband?"

"You have no particular preference?"

"Not really. I find them all attractive, personable, and quite suitable from what I have been able to learn so far. That has been my difficulty. I don't know which one I should concentrate on to get this matter settled."

Anthony relaxed again, sitting back and casually placing his arm along the back of the sofa, just behind her head. She didn't seem to notice. She was impatiently waiting for him to answer her question, while he was going to carefully avoid doing so.

"It might help if you tell me what attributes you favor," he suggested.

"An easy temperament, a gentle hand, sensitivity, intelligence, patience, as I've said—"

"Delightful." His grin was wickedly maddening. "You'll be bored to tears, my dear, which will have us more intimately acquainted much sooner than I expected." Her pursed lips and scathing gaze elicited a chuckle, not in the least contrite. "You were saying?"

"There is also a marriage contract that must be signed," she said tightly. "It will prohibit my husband from having complete control over me or my holdings."

"Your idea?"

"My grandfather's. He was a stubborn old man with set ways. Since he was leaving his fortune to me, he wanted to make certain it stayed with me and wasn't put in the hands of some stranger he might or might not have approved of. He had the contract drawn up before he died."

"If he was so particular, why didn't he arrange you a marriage?"

Her look was wistful. "We had a special bond, Anthony. I didn't want to leave him while he still lived, and he would never have forced me to."

He smiled at her use of his name, slipping out without thought. It proved she was more comfortable with his company. She had even bent one knee to turn toward him while she spoke, more or less facing him now. It would be so easy to let his arm drop to her shoulders and draw her near . . .

Anthony shook himself mentally. "It's a moot point really. The only one I can think might object to this contract is Savage. Not that he'll be coveting your fortune. He's well enough off, I believe, for wealth not to be a criterion when he weds. But he's not a man who likes to have limitations placed on him. Still, if he wants you, it shouldn't matter."

"Then you recommend him?"

"My dear, I can safely say intelligence is the only criterion of yours that he meets. In fact, none of these chaps will meet every one of the qualities you're looking for. Warton, I suppose, comes closest to the mark, but if you marry him, you'll also be marrying his mother—that is, if she'll even allow him to marry. I've never seen a woman hold the strings so tightly as that formidable lady."

Roslynn was frowning long before he had finished speaking. "Very well, don't recommend one. Just tell me what you know of the others."

"Easy enough. Let's see, shall we start with Fleming? Affectionately known as the bungling viscount, since he must be doing something wrong that no woman will ever be seen with him twice, but perhaps you'll be the exception. He's soft. Some have even called him a coward. Seems he was challenged once by a young man to a duel but wouldn't accept. Never did learn the reason for it. Has he shown a definite interest?"

Actually, he hadn't, but that was not the issue here. "Next?"

Anthony chuckled at her avoidance in answering his query. No need to tell her yet that young Fleming's fancy leaned toward those who wore boots, rather than satin slippers. If she could get the fellow to marry her, which he doubted, she would very quickly be looking outside the marriage bed for a lover.

"The Earl of Dunstanton is a likable enough chap; he just has a way with words that can cut a man to shreds. He seems to be beset with tragedy, however, what with three dead wives in the space of the past five years. It's not common knowledge, but with the death of each wife his estate has doubled."

"You're not suggesting—"

"Not at all," he assured her, taking advantage of her distracted alarm to bring his knee up to where it just touched hers. "It's no more than mere speculation bandied about by envious chaps not so well off."

The seed had been planted, even if it wasn't accurate. Two of the wives had died in childbirth, which truly was a tragedy, occurring one after the other. The third had fallen off a cliff, messy business, but the earl certainly wasn't culpable unless he had it within his power to produce the freak storm that had spooked the lady's horse and led to her fall.

"What about Sir Artemus?"

"Loves to gamble, but don't we all." This said with a wink. "And you'd have a ready-made family if you go with him. He has dozens of little tykes—"

"I was told there were only five children!"

"Five who claim legitimacy. Yes, you'd have your hands full, and very little help from Shadwell, since he tends to forget the fact that he even has children. Are you planning to have some of your own?"

The blush did it, so utterly becoming that Anthony's good intentions flew straight away. His hand slipped to her neck, and without moving, he drew her full against his chest, fingers sliding up into her hair so he could position her mouth to receive his kiss.

It never happened. She pushed him back so quickly and forcefully that he lost his hold due to surprise.

"You promised!"

He sat up, raking a hand through his hair in a manner fraught with impatience and chagrin, yet his voice was a study in tranquillity. "Kindly remember, my dear, that this role of confidant is new to me and will take some getting used to." And then, with a sideways glance that caught the fury of her eyes, "Oh, for God's sake, don't fry me for conditioned instincts. It won't happen again, you may depend on it."

She stood up, faced him, gripping her parasol as if it were a weapon that could hold him off. "If you have nothing more to tell me—"

Oh, sweetheart, if only you knew that it is my will alone that keeps you safe for the time being. "Fact will have to be sifted from rumor. Give me a week or two—"

"One week."

He leaned back again, propping both arms behind him on the sofa, eyeing her languorously. That she was still speaking to him, still willing to depend on his advice, told him enough. She wasn't *that* angry with him.

"Fix your hair, my dear, and I'll escort you down to the lake."

He choked back a laugh at her murmur of exasperation on finding her coiffure once more disturbed by him. With impatient fingers she tightened the effect, then smashed her bonnet down over it. He did laugh then, gaining a murderous stare from her that only amused him the more.

But a few minutes later, as they strolled across the back lawn, she

was treated to the full brunt of his charm, which had her smiling help-
lessly again, quite willing to forgive him his lapse. Only it didn't last,
her improved humor. She hadn't realized how it might look, her having
stayed behind, his having stayed behind, while everyone else rode to
the hunt. But one look at Justin's bemused frown as they approached
the gathering at the lake, and she was brought up short.

"I really don't think it's a good idea for us to be seen together," she
said in an aside to Anthony as she caught sight of several more of her
gentlemen in the party.

"I would agree if we were anywhere but here, my dear," he replied.
"Here I am a relative of the hostess and quite naturally am expected to
socialize."

His total lack of concern suddenly annoyed her, for Lord Grahame
and Lord Fleming, having arrived for today's entertainments, had both
noticed her as well. Whether they thought there was anything untoward
in her tardy arrival on Sir Anthony's arm, she couldn't guess. But neither could she help remembering Regina's friendly warning to the gist
that *any* lady seen to have gained this particular rake's interest was raw
meat for the gossip mills.

At any rate, his escort down to the lake after they both had missed
the hunt couldn't help her cause, not when the men she was in actuality
"courting" would surely wonder about it. Anthony should have known
that. He was much more experienced in these things than she was. And
so her annoyance was directed solely at him, enough to want to burst
his bubble of nonchalance.

"You know, Anthony, even if I do find myself bored with my husband, that doesn't mean you're going to benefit from it."

He seemed to see through her deliberate taunt, at least his grin so
indicated, and his answer sent a tingling thrill of apprehension down
her spine. "On the contrary. You *will* eventually be my mistress, sweetheart. If I weren't absolutely certain of that, I never would have agreed
to help you."

Chapter Thirteen

"**N**o! Dear Lord, let me be dreaming!"

It was in fact a nightmare, to wake up in a room she had not gone to sleep in, to be unable to recall how she came to be there. Roslynn looked around wide-eyed, praying she wasn't really awake, yet knowing she was. Stained and peeling wallpaper. A chipped basin of water with a cockroach scurrying up the pitcher sitting beside it, resting precariously on a three-legged table propped in one corner because the fourth leg was missing. A single narrow bed, coarse woolen blanket covering her to her waist. Bare floor, bare walls, bare window.

How was this possible? She pressed her palms to her temples, trying desperately to remember. Had she been ill? Or had an accident? But all she could recall was last night, if it was last night and not days ago, with the time in between unaccounted for.

She had been unable to sleep, an annoying happenstance, recurring ever since she had met Anthony Malory. She and Frances had returned from the country three days earlier, but she had been unable to forget the time she spent with Anthony there, nor his unexpected about-face in offering to assist her, rather than seduce her.

And yet, despite his promise to end his pursuit of her, at least until after she married, he still hadn't left her alone that day. Oh, he had relinquished her so she could circulate with the other picnickers and work her wiles on her gentlemen, but whenever she noticed him in the crowd, her eyes met his, as if he were constantly watching her. That night, to her chagrin, he danced not once but three times with her, all in the guise of socializing. And he danced with no one else, not even his niece.

She had been furious when she realized what he was doing, but by then the damage had been done. Lord Grahame, the Earl of Dunstanton, had begged off from taking her to the theater after they returned to London, an engagement he had only made that afternoon. He claimed he had suddenly recalled a previous commitment, when it was so obvious he was simply intimidated by Anthony's blatant interest in her.

Yes, she had been unable to sleep last night, full of furious energy, because not one of her gentlemen had called since her return to London, and she didn't deceive herself that they were merely too busy. Anthony's innocent "socializing" had seriously set her back.

So if she remembered all that, how was it possible that she couldn't remember how she came to be here in this horrid little room? Anthony wouldn't . . . no, he wouldn't. And she doubted Frances had gone mad and somehow arranged this. That left only one alternative, unless she was so ill that this was all part of a delirium, and it was too real for that. Geordie had her. Somehow, some way, he had managed to abduct her right out of the house on South Audley Street in Mayfair, and where she was now was anyone's guess. Inconceivable, yet what else was she to believe?

Only there was a part of her that was unwilling to accept that Geordie had won, a part that was too optimistic, hoping there might be some other explanation. So her surprise was genuine when she saw the truth with her own eyes. Her fear was real too, nearly choking her with the tightening of her throat, her palms breaking out in a sweat. Geordie Cameron, in the flesh, walked as nonchalantly as you please into the room, a look on his face that was unmistakable triumph. And after all the things she had imagined would happen if he ever got hold of her, it was no wonder she was so overcome with anxiety that she could do no more than stare at him.

"Och now, it's glad I am tae see Mrs. Pym was right, that ye're awake at last. She's been sae obliging, sitting outside yer door, waiting tae hear ye stir sae she could come and tell me. She knows how impatient I've been, though the coppers in her pocket improved her diligence too. But dinna be thinking she'll be receptive tae yer blathering, lass, fer I've spun her a fine tale, I have, of rescue and returning ye tae the bosom of yer family. She'll no' believe a word ye try tae tell her if it differs from my tale."

After saying all this, he smiled, reminding Roslynn why she had never been able to abide this particular Cameron. His smiles were never genuine, always jeering or mocking, or more often sly, and they brought out the malicious evil in his icy blue eyes, eyes that could have been lovely otherwise.

Roslynn had always thought him tall until she met the Malorys, who were much taller. His carrot-red hair had grown shaggy since last she'd seen him, but then she doubted he'd had much time to attend to his grooming with the merry chase she had led him. He wasn't fat, no, not at all, but there was a beefiness about his body that she knew could overpower her if it came down to her fighting her way out of here. And yet he bore the Cameron good looks, at least when his true self didn't emerge from behind his expression; looks, sadly, that closely resembled Duncan Cameron when he was Geordie's age, so testified the only portrait of her grandfather at Cameron Hall.

"Ye're awful quiet, ye are," Geordie prodded her when she continued to just stare at him. "Have ye nae warm welcome fer yer only cousin?"

The incongruity of that question brought Roslynn back to her senses and dredged forth her anger. That he dared, *dared* do what she had feared he would! Of course, it was why she was here in London, why she was planning to marry when she didn't have to, why she had entered into a bizarre relationship with Anthony, accepting him as her confidant when she knew very well she should avoid him instead. But to be proved right! Her fear was forgotten in light of all the trouble and anxiety this greedy blackguard had put her through.

"Warm welcome?" she snorted. "The only thing I'm wanting to know, *cousin,* is how you managed it!"

He laughed, only too happy to expound on his cleverness and pleased that she hadn't asked why instead. That she knew why she was here saved him the explaining of that, and would save time in convincing her to go along with him. He didn't like being in England or dealing with English hirelings, and the sooner they were set for home, the better.

"It was sae easy, lass, sae very easy," he boasted. "I knew ye'd be trying something once the auld mon was laid tae his grave, only I didna think ye'd be coming here. But I had most of the roads watched, ye see, sae tae England was the only way ye could've traveled wi'out my knowing it."

"Clever you are, to make such a deduction."

His eyes narrowed at her sneer. "Aye, clever, clever enough tae ha' ye where I want ye."

Roslynn flinched, for he was right there. "But how did you find me so quickly, Geordie? London's no' such a small town, is it now?"

"I remembered ye had a friend here. It wasna hard tae find her, and sae tae find ye. But I would've had ye sooner if those bloody idiots I hired hadna been such cowards tae turn tail just because the street crowd was bestirred tae help ye that day on Oxford Street."

So it *had* been Geordie's doing that day she was nearly abducted off the street. But as for the crowd helping, that bit of news elicited a chuckle that Roslynn quickly turned into a cough. She could just imagine the tall tale those two footpads had told Geordie to account for their failure and to avoid his wrath.

"And then ye left town and I thought I'd lost ye," Geordie continued with a frown. "Ye put me tae a good deal of trouble and expense over that, lass, that ye did. I had tae send men oout in every direction tae find yer trail, but ye didna leave one, did ye, no' one that went very far? Only ye came back on yer own." Here he was smiling again, as if to say it was so typically female to make such a blunder. "And then it was only a matter of waiting—and here ye are."

Yes, here she was, and still ignorant of how Geordie had managed it. But his look said he was willing to enlighten her, wanting to in fact, because he was so very pleased with himself in having his plans work out so well, and wanted her to appreciate his cleverness. Oh, she appreciated it all right, like the plague. That had always been Geordie's problem. He was too clever and sly, like a bloody fox. All his life he had thrived on scheming and plotting the little pranks and accidents he was so fond of. Why should this be any different?

Perversely, Roslynn decided to take him down a peg instead of boosting his ego further with her avid curiosity. She yawned in the face of his explanations and said wearily, "So now what, cousin?"

His mouth dropped open. "Are ye no' the least bit interested in how ye came tae wake up here?"

"Does it matter?" she asked in a weary tone. "As you said, I'm here."

She thought he would burst a seam, he puffed up with such chagrin. "Well, I'll be telling ye, seeing as how it was the easiest but most ingenious part of my plans."

"By all means," she replied.

But she gave him another yawn for good measure and delighted in the way his light blue eyes spat daggers at her. He was so easily readable, so petty, and selfish, and hot-tempered. She supposed she ought not to push him anymore. She might have calmed down after her initial shock, but he was still a threat to her. And until she could figure a way out of this, if there was a way, she had best placate him.

"It was the maid, ye see, a clever lass I hired tae get inside the house. It was a simple matter of making certain one of the regular maids didna show up fer work and substituting my lass, claiming she was there tae take the other's place, being as she was sick."

Roslynn's temper sparked at this. "And just what have you done wi' the puir lass that didna show up for work?"

"Dinna fash yerself, cousin." His humor improved again now that he had her full attention. "She wasna harmed, save fer a wee bump on the head, and I've already sent a man tae release her, seeing as how yer absence will be known by now anyway. But as I was saying, wi' my hireling inside the house and in a position tae serve ye, she only needed tae wait until ye ordered something tae eat or drink afore ye retired, sae she could slip a sleeping draught in it."

The milk! The bloody warm milk she had asked for last night, hoping that it might help her sleep, never dreaming she would sleep so soundly she wouldn't even wake up for her own kidnapping!

"Aye, ye can see how it was done now, canna ye?" Geordie chuckled. "As soon as the lass was able, she slipped my men inside the house and hid them and went on home herself, her part over. Then when all the live-in servants had retired and the house was quiet, my men simply carried ye oout and brought ye tae me, and ye didna wake even once."

"So what are yer plans now?" she asked tightly, taunting. "Surely ye've something despicable in mind?"

"I've found me a mon of the cloth who's been persuaded he doesna need tae be hearing yer 'I do's' tae perform a wedding fer us. The gin-soaked sod'll be here as soon as my men can discover what alley he crawled into last night. But it willna be long now, cousin. And dinna think tae be causing a stir while we wait. Mrs. Pym will be keeping an ear open, and she's just outside the door."

As she watched him leave and heard the lock click on the door, she thought about calling him back. If he knew that both Nettie and Frances were aware of her abhorrence for him and that she would never willingly marry him, might he reconsider? But it was his rampant greed that held her tongue. Marrying her would bring him a fortune, and since he had gone this far, it was likely he could go the next step in eliminating anyone who opposed him. As it stood now, his plan could be to simply lock her away somewhere, and none would be the wiser. He could as likely have a "regrettable accident" planned. But it was a certainty that he wouldn't keep her alive if he knew she had friends who would disclaim a marriage between them, and they would be in danger too if she named them.

So where did that leave her? *Married to the blackguard,* was the loathsome answer. Hell's teeth, not while she still had her wits about her. But panic was beginning to take hold. Not long, he had said. How much time did that give her? Even now the drunken reverend could be arriving. And where the bloody hell was she anyway?

Her eyes flew back to the window and she threw off the covers, rushing to the opening. Her heart sank as she saw the two-story drop, with nothing below to break a fall. No wonder Geordie had taken no precautions in boarding up the window. And if she tried to call out it for help, the deceived Mrs. Pym would have the door open in a flash, and Roslynn would no doubt find herself bound and gagged for her efforts.

Briefly, she thought of reasoning with Mrs. Pym, but only briefly. The woman probably thought she was insane or something. Geordie was clever that way, his schemes well thought out, to cover all possibilities. He would leave nothing to chance, not with the fortune he had so long coveted at risk.

Hastily, she surveyed the room again, but only the water pitcher would make a likely weapon, and that only against the first person to come through the door. She had no guarantee that person would be

Geordie, no guarantee either that the pitcher would hurt him enough to render him unconscious, or that he would be alone.

The window, then, was her only chance. It faced a lane of some sort, an alley really, though wide enough for traffic to get through. But there was no traffic. It was utterly deserted, dark and shadowed, as the buildings on each side rose far enough to hold back the daylight. Sticking her head out the window, at each end of the lane she could see streets brightly lit, wagons passing, a child running by, a sailor strolling arm in arm with a garishly dressed woman. A good shout could probably draw someone's attention. Neither end of the lane was *that* far away. But a good shout would draw Mrs. Pym's attention too.

Roslynn ran back to the bed, yanked off the scratchy blanket, and, rushing back, stuck it out the window. She waved it furiously, leaning out the window as well, until finally her arms became exhausted, her breath labored. Nothing. If anyone noticed, it no doubt appeared she was simply airing the blanket, nothing to elicit curiosity.

And then she heard the wagon. Her head swung around to see it slowly entering the lane, and her heart began to race with excitement. It was filled with barrels, possibly using the lane as a shortcut to reach the other street. The lone driver was whistling as he prodded his mule, pausing only to sweet-talk the animal.

Roslynn dropped the blanket, giving up waving it, waving her arms instead. But without her making a sound, the driver simply didn't notice. His hat was wide-brimmed, and since she was above him, she was blocked from his view. The nearer he came, the less chance there was that he would see her at all, and the more she panicked. She hissed, and said *psst,* and waved even more frantically to draw his attention, but to no avail. By the time she thought to throw the water pitcher down at him, he was already too far past her window. Besides, with the noise the wagon was making over the cobbled lane, she doubted he would have heard the crash unless she landed a direct hit, which was unlikely as sore as her arms were already.

Disappointment washed over her and she slumped back against the wall beside the window. This just wouldn't do. Even if the fellow had noticed her, how could she have explained her predicament in a whisper? He wouldn't have been able to understand her. And if she spoke any louder than a whisper, she would give herself away to Mrs. Pym.

Hell's teeth, was there nothing else she could do? She eyed the water pitcher again, but she had little hope she could succeed with it. When Geordie came again, he was likely to have the reverend with him, as well as the men who had fetched him, for witnesses to this unholy ceremony would be needed.

Roslynn was so distraught by picturing herself actually married to Geordie Cameron that she didn't hear the second vehicle passing through the lane until it was almost too late. When she turned at the sound, the hay wagon was nearly beneath her window. This driver, also alone, was cursing the two nags pulling the load of hay, emphasizing his apparent ire by shaking the gin bottle in his hand at them, swilling a long draft, then shaking it with another curse. *He* wouldn't hear her for the noise he himself was making, and he was so close already.

There was nothing for it. She might not have another chance. So without thinking about it, for that would have terrified her and kept her inside, Roslynn climbed up on the window ledge, waited the few seconds until the wagon was directly below, and jumped.

Chapter Fourteen

It was an insane thing to do. That thought passed through Roslynn's mind as she was falling, falling, her feet flying up in front of her eyes, her hands instinctively clutching at air, knowing she was going to die. She cursed Geordie with her last breath, but at least there was some satisfaction that he would think she preferred death to marrying him, though not enough satisfaction to make it worthwhile, for she was the one dying, while that greedy cur would probably produce a marriage certificate and claim her fortune anyway.

She landed with a bone-jarring impact, flat on her back. Breath and wits deserted her, and for a moment she actually passed out. A missing cobblestone was responsible for the wagon's jolt that brought her back to her senses. She groaned, thinking she must surely have a dozen broken bones. But the next jarring of the wagon caused her no discomfort. Incredible. To have done something so stupid, yet come through unscathed. She was surely blessed, but then fools usually were, and she was the greatest of that number today. She could have broken her neck, and well she knew it! But thank God for the cushion of hay. If it had been any other load this wagon was carrying . . .

Miraculously, the drunken driver was unaware he had gained a passenger, but Roslynn supposed her impact with the wagon seemed no different to him in his sottish condition from the wagon hitting a particularly deep rut. Either that, or the man was deaf.

Scattered hay nearly covered her from head to foot, but one glance at the window she had just leaped from, and she swiftly yanked handfuls to complete the camouflage. And not a moment too soon. The wagon rolled out of the shadowed lane into the congested, brightly lit street, and Roslynn finally realized, horribly, that she was wearing nothing more than the thin white cotton nightgown she had gone to sleep in last night, and was barefoot as well.

But she could be thankful for small favors. At least the gown wasn't one of the skimpy negligees that had been made for her trousseau. It covered her from neck to ankle, with flowing long sleeves cuffed at the wrist, and she supposed if she could find something that would make do for a belt, it might pass for a dress at first glance.

Unfortunately, Roslynn had little time to think of that or how she was going to get home without money. The wagon rolled into a stable and stopped, and she just managed to scurry out of it and hide behind an empty stall before the driver came around back to begin unloading the hay. Another man, big and burly, joined him, cursing him in a good-humored way for being late. While they both tackled the hay, Roslynn reconnoitered.

A stable wasn't such a bad place to end her journey thus far. Actually, it was ideal. If she could just rent a horse and get directions to Mayfair, for she still had no idea what part of the city she was in now, she could be home before long and without further incident. The trouble was, the only thing of value on her person was her mother's crucifix, which she wore whenever she wasn't decked out in her more costly jewels, and it was unthinkable to part with it. Still, it didn't look as if she would have much choice in the matter, unless she was closer to Mayfair than she realized. Then she could chance walking, even barefoot.

Roslynn frowned at that idea. It wasn't one of her better ones, and she was forgetting the sort of street traffic she had seen passing by the lane—delivery wagons, drunkards, sailors walking with their doxies, but not one carriage. And this stable wasn't so very far from where she had escaped. Whatever part of town this was, it certainly wasn't elite, and trying to walk through it would likely give her more trouble than she had started with. Which left her again with the desperate need to rent a horse.

Not knowing if Geordie had discovered her absence yet and might already be searching for her in the nearby vicinity made Roslynn a bundle of nerves as she waited for the gin-guzzler to depart with his hay wagon. But she had decided to risk being alone with the other fellow to state her case, for the less people who saw her in her present condition, the better. She could just imagine the scandal should any of this get out. *Lady Chadwick cavorting through the slums in her nightgown.* How the *ton* would eat that up, and down the wayside would go her last chance for a quick, decent marriage.

Still, she had to mentally push herself out of her hiding place once it appeared she was finally alone with the stableman, mortified that anyone, stranger or not, should see her in her bedclothes. And her embarrassment increased a hundredfold when the big fellow actually noticed her and his eyes fairly popped out of his head. Standing with one bare foot unsuccessfully trying to hide the other, her arms crossed over her chest because even though she was completely covered, she still *felt* naked, and her hair streaming about her upper torso, ribboned with straw, she was a sight to behold—a very fetching sight, actually, though she would be the last to think so.

The man must have thought so, however, because he continued to stare, unmoving, unspeaking, his mouth hanging open. He was middle-aged, brown hair feathered with gray, gray stubble on a too-wide jaw. Whether he was proprietor or employee she couldn't tell. It didn't matter, though. He was all she had to help her, and knowing that filled her with a nervousness she wouldn't otherwise have felt.

Roslynn blurted out her predicament with the briefest explanation, but so swiftly, it was doubtful the fellow understood even two words of it. And in fact, it was several long moments before he gave any indication that he had heard her at all. Then he chuckled, hitching up his pants and walking toward her.

"A 'orse, eh? Ye should 'ave said right off, miss. 'Ere I was thinking me good friend Zeke 'ad sent o'er a right fine birthday present. A 'orse?" He chuckled again, shaking his head. "Can't blame a man fer wishful thinking."

Roslynn was blushing furiously before he had finished laughing. "Do you have one to rent?"

"Two I 'ave, both nags, but the good stock goes out early, it does."

"Will you take this, then?" She lifted the cross off her neck and handed it to him. "It'll buy both nags plus several more, but I'll be wanting it back. I'll send someone back with the horse and the proper payment."

He turned the cross over in his hand, then had the audacity to bite on it before nodding his head. "It'll do."

"I don't suppose you'd have a pair of shoes I could borrow too?"

He took one look at her dainty feet and snorted at the request. "Not likely, miss. Me children's all growed an' gone, they are."

Desperately she asked, "A cloak, then, or something to cover myself with?"

"Now, that I can manage. Aye, an' best I do, or ye'd be causing a bleeding riot in the streets, ye would."

Roslynn was too relieved to be annoyed at the sound of his laughter as he went off to fetch her the nag.

Chapter Fifteen

The shadows of twilight grew darker with each passing second. What should have amounted to a thirty-minute ride had turned into a three-hour excursion of wrong turns, delays, and increasing aggravations. But at least Roslynn knew where she was now, and in fact she was grateful for the dark, for in her eagerness to be home she hadn't taken into consideration the ride down South Audley Street, where any number of people might have recognized her. The dark came in handy for concealment, and handier still was the hood of the old moth-eaten cloak the stableman had tossed her.

Hell's teeth, this day couldn't end soon enough for her, but it was far from finished yet. She could no longer stay with Frances, not even for tonight. And she could no longer delay getting married. Geordie's locating her had changed everything. She even expected to find him waiting on the doorstep for her, or secreted in a carriage ready to pounce on her the moment she reached the house.

Luck stayed with her, however, at least in letting her reach home without further mishap. And she even considered it fortunate that Frances wasn't there, for she would have disapproved of what Roslynn meant to do, would have tried to stop her, and Roslynn didn't have the time it would take to convince her she knew what she was doing.

Nettie was another matter. After sending one of the footmen back to the stable with the old horse and the money to retrieve her cross, and briefly assuring the butler and other servants she passed along the way that she was fine, but giving them no explanation, Roslynn rushed upstairs to find Nettie in her room, anxiously pacing the floor and looking more haggard than she had ever seen her. But at first sight of Roslynn, her face filled with surprise and relief.

"Och, hinny, if ye didna give me the worst scare of my life!" And then almost in the same breath, her tune changed. "Where the devil have ye been, I'd like tae be knowing? I thought yer cousin had ye fer sure."

Roslynn nearly smiled at Nettie's ability to jump from one emotion to another with such startling swiftness, but as harried as she was herself, she couldn't even spare a moment for the amusement her abigail stirred, so welcome after such a ghastly day. She hurried straight to her wardrobe, tossing over her shoulder, "He did, Nettie. Now help me dress, quickly, while I tell you about it."

She did, and Nettie interrupted only once with "Ye did what?" when she came to the part about jumping out of the window. After she had finished, the anxiety was back in Nettie's expression.

"Then ye canna stay here nae longer."

"I know," Roslynn replied. "And I'm leaving tonight, we both are, but not together."

"But—"

"Listen now," Roslynn interrupted impatiently. "I've had all afternoon to think what's best to do. Geordie's made his move. Now that his scheme is out in the open, what's to stop him from forcing his way in wherever I am and taking me again, and next time maybe hurting someone in the process? It took me so long to get home, I thought for certain he'd be here waiting. But perhaps he didn't think I could make it this far without money or clothes."

"Then ye think he's still searching fer ye near where ye escaped him?"

"Either that, or he's working on a new plan already. But there's also the likelihood he sent someone here to watch the house. Although I didn't see anyone, that doesn't mean no one's out there, so we've got to confuse them, and pray it's only one man. If we leave together at the same time but in different directions, he'll not know who to follow."

"But where are we going?"

Roslynn finally smiled. "Back to Silverley. He'll have no way to trace us there."

"Ye dinna know that."

"It was Geordie who tried to have me snatched off the street that day. He knew where I was, but apparently no one was watching the house the morning I left so early for the country. When he realized I had gone, he sent men out in all directions, but the trail was lost after we left that inn where we joined up. As long as we avoid public places and aren't followed, we'll be safe."

"But, lass, that accomplishes nothing but tae hide ye fer a time. It doesna get ye married, and ye'll no' really be safe from that blackguard until ye wed."

"I know, which is why I'll be sending for the gentleman of my choice to meet me there and put my proposition to him. If all goes well, I can be married at Silverley too, if Regina doesn't mind."

Nettie's brows shot up. "Then ye've decided which one tae marry?"

"By the time I get there, I'll know which one I want," Roslynn hedged, for that was the only thing still in doubt. "The important thing at the moment is to get there without leaving a trail Geordie can follow. Now, I've already sent one of the servants to fetch us each a rented hack."

"What of Brutus?" Nettie asked, then glanced with wide eyes at Roslynn's full wardrobe. "And all yer clothes? There's nae time tae pack—"

"They must be left here until after I'm wed, Nettie. We can both take a few things now, and I'm sure Regina has a competent seamstress who can supply whatever else we need to see us to the wedding. All I need to do is leave a note for Frances; then we can be off. Where is she, by the way?"

Nettie grunted. "After she fair wore the carpet down tae a frazzle all morning long, one of the maids mentioned she had a brother who knew a certain fellow, who knew how tae go about hiring the kind of men who could find ye quicker than the authorities—"

"Authorities!" Roslynn gasped, horrified that the scandal she had worried about all day was going to break around her head anyway. "Hell's teeth! She didna report me missing, did she?"

Nettie quickly shook her head. "She was near tae doing it, though, that worried she was, but knew once she did, it'd never be kept secret. And if ye'd no' be completely ruined, the talk would still hurt yer efforts tae get a decent husband. That's why she jumped on the maid's suggestion, and even insisted on going herself tae arrange the hiring."

Roslynn frowned. "Still, with so many servants knowing—"

"Och now, ye're no' tae worry as tae that, lass. They're good people Lady Frances has, but tae be safe, I had a wee talk wi' each of them. They're no' likely tae breathe a word outside this house about yer absence."

Roslynn chuckled. "You'll have to tell me sometime what threats you used, but right now we've no more time. Go and pack up several changes of clothes, and I'll do the same, then meet me downstairs. We should leave at exactly the same moment. And, Nettie, head north until you're certain you're not followed; then you can turn toward Hampshire. I'll go south and then backtrack too. But if I don't arrive close behind you, you're not to worry. I'll be going far out of my way first, just to be safe. I don't intend to fall into Geordie's hands again no matter what. He won't be so careless the next time."

Chapter Sixteen

It seemed like an eternity before the front door finally opened to Roslynn's repeated pounding, and pounding she was doing before she finished. She was in such a state of nerves, in fact, expecting to be seized at any moment, that even her own shadow gave her a start when she glanced behind her to make sure the old carriage was still waiting, the driver still keeping an eye on her. Not that he would be much help if Geordie and his hirelings found her.

It was the risk that had her in a such a state. She shouldn't be stopping here. She had promised Nettie she would make all haste out of London, yet she had come directly here instead, not allowing herself time to lose anyone who might have followed her. That was what had her heart hammering to the tune of her fist against the door. Geordie could be sneaking up on her at this very moment, getting closer and closer, while she stood here waiting for the bloody door to open.

When it did open, she shoved her way inside so forcefully, she nearly knocked the butler down. She closed the door herself, leaning back against it, then looked aghast at the fellow, who was looking even more aghast at her.

He collected himself first, straightening his coat with a sharp tug, gathering his dignity about him like a cloak. "Really, miss—"

She jumped in to forestall him, unthinkingly giving him an even worse impression of her. "Och, mon, dinna scold me. I'm sorry to be barging in, but this is an emergency. I must speak wi' Sir Anthony."

"Out of the question," he stated with haughty disdain. "Sir Anthony is not receiving tonight."

"He isna here, then?"

"He is unavailable to callers," the butler stated more bluntly. "I do have my orders, miss. Now if you would be so good—"

"No!" she gasped as he reached for the door handle to show her out. "Did you no' hear me, mon? I *mun* see him!"

Without a pause, he opened the door, forcing her to move away from it. "There are to be no exceptions." But when he reached for her arm to literally shove her outside, Roslynn clobbered him with her reticule. "Now see here!" the man gasped, outraged.

"Och, but you're a dafty, you are," she said calmly enough, but her eyes glared at him furiously. "I'm no' leaving here until I've seen Anthony. I didna take the risk of coming here just to be turned away, you ken? Now tell him—just tell him there's a lady to see him. Do it, mon, or I swear I'll—"

Dobson turned away before she could complete the threat. Stiff-backed, he mounted the stairs, deliberated taking his time. Lady indeed. Never in all his considerable years in Sir Anthony's employ had he seen the like. Ladies didn't accost a man just for doing his duty. The very idea. What *had* Sir Anthony stooped to, to become involved with such a brazen creature?

Out of sight of the foyer where he had left her, Dobson considered waiting a few moments and then simply returning to try again to oust the woman. After all, Sir Anthony had come home in a foul disposition because he was late for a family gathering at his brother Edward's house. Lord James and Master Jeremy had already left for it. Even if Sir Anthony were inclined to see this particular woman, he had no time. He was changing now, and in fact would be down shortly. He would *not* care to be confronted with any further delay in the form of a pushy female of questionable quality. If it were any other appointment, it wouldn't matter so much. But family came first with Sir Anthony. It always had and always would.

And yet . . . Dobson couldn't shake the implied threat from his mind. He had never encountered a caller so insistent on having her way, discounting Sir Anthony's own family, of course. Would she scream, or worse, become violent again? Unthinkable. But perhaps he ought to at least inform Sir Anthony of the problem.

The answer to his knock was curt. Dobson stepped warily into the room. He had only to look at Willis, Sir Anthony's valet, to see there had been no improvement in disposition. The man's expression was harried, as if he had already had a full measure of Sir Anthony's acerbic tongue.

And then Sir Anthony swung around, giving Dobson pause. He rarely saw him in this state of undress. He wore only his trousers and was in the process of towel-drying his thick black hair.

Again the impatient curtness. "What is it, Dobson?"

"A woman, sir. She pushed her way in, demanding to speak with you."

Anthony turned away. "Get rid of her."

"I tried, sir. She refuses to leave."

"Who is she?"

Here Dobson couldn't conceal his disgust. "She wouldn't give her name, but claims to be a lady."

"Is she?"

"I have my doubts, sir."

Anthony tossed the towel aside with obvious annoyance. "Bloody hell, she's probably here for James. I should have known his tavern doxies would start showing up on my doorstep if he stayed for any length of time."

Dobson was reluctant to clarify. "Begging your pardon, sir, but she mentioned your name, not Lord Malory's."

Anthony scowled. "Then use your wits, man. The only women who come here come by invitation. Am I correct?"

"Yes, sir."

"And would I have extended an invitation tonight, with a previous engagement?"

"No, sir."

"Then why are you bothering me with this?"

Dobson could feel the heat rising under his collar. "For permission to force her out the door, sir. She won't leave of her own accord."

"By all means," Anthony replied dryly. "Use one of the footmen if you don't think you can manage on your own, but get rid of her before I come down."

The heat crept up Dobson's cheeks. "Thank you, sir. I will get help, I think. I don't care to confront that Scot's temper again on my own."

"What was that?" Anthony asked so forcefully, Dobson's color washed clean away.

"I—I—"

"Did you say she's Scottish?"

"No, no, she only sounded—"

"Blister it, man, why didn't you say so? Show her up here and hurry, before she decides to leave."

"Before she—" Dobson's mouth dropped open, but a glance about the room prompted a "*Here,* sir?"

"*Now,* Dobson."

Chapter Seventeen

Anthony couldn't believe it. Even when she walked through the door, tossed Dobson a withering look, then turned the same lethal glare on Anthony, he still couldn't believe it.

"That's a very rude mon you have for a butler, Sir Anthony."

He simply grinned at her, standing there with her foot tapping and her arms crossed over her chest. "When I gave you my address, sweetheart, it was so you could send me a message if the need arose, not for you to show up on my doorstep. You do realize the impropriety? This is strictly a bachelor's residence. I even have my brother and nephew staying with me—"

"Well, if they're here, then I'm no' alone wi' you, am I now?"

"I hate to disappoint you, my dear, but they are out for the evening and you are in fact very much alone with me. As you can see, I was preparing to go out myself, which is why Dobson was so reluctant to admit you."

What she saw, when she got a good look at him through the fumes of her anger, was that he looked more as if he were prepared for bed. He wore a short quilted robe of silver-blue satin over trousers, and nothing else. The robe he was just now belting, but not before she had had a glimpse of his bare chest and the sparse mat of black curls there. His hair was damp, hand-combed back from his forehead, with drying tendrils beginning to curl over each temple. He looked more sensual than she had ever seen him, and it was all she could do to tear her eyes away and even remember why she was here.

The trouble was, her eyes lit next on a bed, and it struck her with the force of a blow where he had received her. His *bedroom*. Hell's teeth!

"Did you know it was me—no, you couldna," she answered herself, her eyes flying back to his. "Do you receive all your callers up here?"

Anthony chuckled at this. "Only when I'm in a hurry, my dear."

She frowned, not at all amused, but made a concerted effort to pull herself together. To do that, she had to look away from him again.

"I won't keep you long, Sir Anthony. I haven't the time to waste myself. Something happened—well, that needn't concern you. Suffice it to say, I've run out of time. I need a name from you, and I need it now."

His humor fled. He was afraid he knew exactly what she was talking about, and that certainty produced a tightening in his belly that was most uncomfortable. His being her confidant had been no more than an excuse to get close to her. Not bloody likely would he defeat his own purpose by helping to get her married. He had meant to delay that eventuality indefinitely and seduce her before it ever became a fact. Now here she was demanding a name from him, which he should have if he had actually done what he had told her he would do, which he hadn't. Obviously, her need for a confidant was at an end. If he didn't give her a name, she would make her own choice, good or bad. He had no doubt a-tall.

"What the bloody hell happened?"

She blinked at his harsh tone, coming so unexpectedly. "I told you, that doesn't concern you."

"Then humor me, and while you're at it, you can tell me why you're going about this marriage business in an either-or fashion, and why the rush."

"It's none of your business," she insisted.

"If you want a name, my dear, you'd best make it my business."

"That's—that's—"

"Not very sporting of me, I know."

"Beast!"

His humor returned in the face of her rage. God, she was beautiful when her eyes flashed like that. The golden flecks seemed to blaze, to match the fire of her hair. It dawned on him suddenly that she was really in his house, in his bedroom, where he had imagined her countless times but had been unable to figure a way to get her there himself.

The grin that curled his lips infuriated her even more. *You've come to my lair, sweetheart,* he couldn't help thinking. *I have you now.*

To her, he suggested, "A drink?"

"You'd drive a saint to it," she retorted, but nodded just the same and took a hefty swallow of the brandy he handed her a moment later.

"Well?" he prompted when she did no more than continue to glower resentfully at him.

"It has to do with my grandfather, and his making me promise I'd marry as soon as he passed away."

"I know that," Anthony said calmly. "Now tell me why he wanted such a promise."

"Very well!" she snapped. "I have a distant cousin who means to marry me at any cost."

"So?"

"I didn't say he wants to, but means to, whether *I* want to or not. Do you ken now? If Geordie Cameron gets his hands on me, he'll force me to it."

"I take it you'd rather not have him?"

"Dinna be daft, mon," she said impatiently, beginning to pace a circle around him. "Would I be willing to wed a near stranger for any other reason?"

"No, I don't suppose so."

Roslynn gasped, catching his smile. "You think it's amusing?"

"What I think, sweetheart, is that you've made too much of it. All you need is to have someone persuade this cousin of yours that he'd be healthier if he looked somewhere else for a wife."

"You?"

He shrugged. "Why not? I wouldn't mind doing you such a service."

She nearly hit him. She finished off her brandy instead, grateful for its calming effect.

"Let me tell you something, Anthony Malory. This is my life you're suggesting you gamble with, not yours. You don't know Geordie. You don't know how obsessed he is with getting his hands on my grandfather's fortune through me. He'll do anything to get it, and once he does, what's to stop him from arranging a convenient accident for me, or locking me up somewhere and claiming I've gone daft or something? A little warning from you wouldn't scare him off, even if you could manage to find him to do so. Nothing will. The only way I can protect myself is to marry someone else."

Anthony had taken her glass, refilled it, and handed it back while she laid into him with these facts. She didn't even seem to notice.

"Very well, now I know why you think you must marry quickly. So tell me, what's made it immediate? What brought you to risk your reputation by coming here tonight?"

She flinched at the unnecessary reminder of *that* danger, which had seemed the lesser evil at the time. "Geordie's found me. Last night he managed to have me drugged and taken right out of Frances' house."

"The hell you say!"

She went on as if she hadn't heard his outburst. "I woke up today locked in a strange room down by the waterfront, just waiting for the deceitful parson Geordie had found to arrive. If I hadn't jumped out the window—"

"Good God, woman, you can't be serious!"

She stopped her pacing for a moment to fix him with a look that was frankly contemptuous. "I've no doubt still got some straw in my hair from the hay wagon I landed in. It took me so long to find my way home that there was no time to brush it all out. I would show you, but Nettie's not here to redo my hair if I take it down, and I doubt your Dobson could manage it. And I will *not* leave your house looking as if—as if—"

Anthony threw back his head in laughter when she failed to complete the provocative thought. Roslynn gave him her back and headed straight for the door. He got there at the same moment, his hand sliding past her shoulder to press firmly against the only exit.

"Was it something I said?" he asked in all innocence next to her ear.

Roslynn didn't hesitate to give him the full impact of her elbow, which landed unerringly at such close range. Satisfied with his grunt of discomfort, she slipped around him, putting a more breathable distance between them.

"I believe you've had enough amusement at my expense, Sir Anthony. I only intended to be here a few minutes, and I've wasted all this time on unnecessary explanations. I have a driver waiting and a long trip ahead of me. You said you were in a hurry as well. The name, if you please."

He leaned back against the door, that "long trip" sending off tremors of panic through his body. "You're not leaving London?"

"Of course I am. You don't think I can stay here now that Geordie's found me, do you?"

"Then how do you intend to entice one of your admirers into a marriage proposal if you're not here to help the courtship along?"

"Hell's teeth! As if I have time for a courtship now," she said, exasperated by his never-ending questions. "I'll be doing my own proposing, if you'll—just—give—me—a—name!"

Her furious emphasis on each word warned him to change tactics, and yet he was at a momentary loss. He wouldn't give her a name even if he had one to recommend, but if he told her that, she'd be out of the room in a flash and gone who-knew-where. He wondered if he dared ask her destination. No, she was fed up with his deliberate evasions.

He walked toward her, indicating the thick lounge chair in front of the fireplace. "Sit down, Roslynn."

"Anthony . . ." she began warningly.

"It's not that simple."

Her eyes narrowed suspiciously. "You've had ample time to sift fact from rumor, as you promised to do."

"I asked for a week, if you'll recall."

Her eyes flared in alarm. "Then you haven't—"

"On the contrary," he cut in quickly. "But you're not going to like what I've found out."

She groaned, ignoring the offered chair, and began pacing again. "Tell me."

Anthony's mind raced ahead, scavenging frantically for possible dirt he could pile on her contenders. He began with the only piece that was actually true, hoping inspiration would follow for the rest.

"That duel I told you David Fleming refused to participate in. It not only branded the poor fellow a coward but also—well, actually—"

"Out with it! I suppose it involved some woman? That's hardly surprising."

"The argument wasn't over a woman, my dear, but another man, only it was still a lover's quarrel." He took advantage of her moment of shock to refill her brandy glass once more.

"You mean—"

"I'm afraid so."

"But he seemed so—so, och, never mind. *He* certainly won't do."

"You'll have to scratch Dunstanton too," Anthony said. Since she was leaving London, she couldn't confirm his next words: "He's just announced his betrothal."

"I don't believe it!" she gasped. "Why, just last weekend he asked me to the theater. Of course, he canceled but . . . oh, very well. I wanted the list narrowed down, and so it is. What about Savage?"

Anthony was inspired by the name. "He won't do at all, my dear. Somewhere along his misspent youth he must have taken his name to heart. The man's a sadist."

"Oh, come now—"

"It's true. He enjoys hurting anything weaker than he is—animals, women. His servants are terrified . . ."

"All right! You needn't go into detail. That still leaves Lord Warton, whom even your niece recommended to me, and Sir Artemus."

It was Anthony's turn to pace, for he drew a blank where Warton was concerned. Shadwell's love of gambling could be played up, but there was absolutely nothing to discredit Warton with. In fact, the chap would no doubt make an ideal husband for Roslynn. Fortunately for Anthony, that knowledge so annoyed him, he managed to dredge up the perfect muck to swill on the fellow.

He turned toward Roslynn, imitating a suitably reluctant look. "You might as well forget Warton too. His interest in you was only to throw his mother off the scent."

"What the devil does that mean?"

"He's in love with his sister."

"What?"

"Oh, it's a well-enough-kept secret," Anthony assured her. "Reggie certainly doesn't know, for it's not something Montieth would want to disillusion her with. After all, she's quite friendly with all three Wartons. And he wouldn't have told me if I hadn't mentioned to him your sudden interest in the fellow. But he came upon them in the woods once, quite an embarrassing moment, I would imagine—"

"Enough!" Roslynn finished off her third brandy and handed him the glass. "You've done exactly as I asked, and I thank you. Sir Artemus was the first to appear on my list, so it seems fitting that he should end up being my choice."

"He's destitute, my dear."

"No problem." She smiled. "I have enough money to plump up his purse again."

"I don't think you understand, Roslynn. In the last few years his gambling has become a disease. He's gone from being one of the most wealthy men in England to having nothing. He's had to sell off every estate he owned except the one in Kent, and that's heavily mortgaged."

"How can you know that?"

"My brother Edward has handled the sales."

She was frowning, but insisted stubbornly, "It doesn't matter. In fact, it assures me that he can't possibly refuse the proposal I'll put to him."

"Oh, he'd jump on it, all right. And within a year you'd be just as destitute as he is."

"You're forgetting I will have control of my fortune, Anthony."

"True, but you're overlooking the simple fact that a man can and does gamble on credit, which is utterly impossible to monitor. And his creditors won't hesitate to come to you as his legal wife for payment, nor even to take you to court. And the courts, my dear, will hardly favor your contract when it can be proved you married Shadwell with full knowledge of his penchant for excessive gambling. You would be forced to honor his debts whether you want to or not."

Roslynn paled, eyes wide and incredulous. With so little knowledge of the law herself, she had no reason to doubt Anthony's predictions. She was forced to believe him. And to think she had once assumed a down-and-out gambler would be a perfect choice for her, never dreaming he could actually be the one man to lead her into penury. She might as well give her inheritance to Geordie as settle for a gambler.

"They were all so suitable," she said absently, miserably, before she turned large hazel eyes on Anthony. "Do you ken you've left me no one?"

Her woebegone expression struck right to his heart. He was

responsible, with his half-truths and fabrications. He had interfered with her life with the most selfish of motives. Yet he couldn't bring himself to push her toward another man. He just couldn't do that. And it wasn't only that he wanted her himself. The thought of another man touching her had the strangest, gut-wrenching effect on him.

No, he couldn't regret that he had left her with no one, for his relief was too great on that score. But he couldn't bear her misery either.

In an effort to cheer her, he offered lightly, "Fleming would have you, you know, if only for appearance' sake." If he thought *she* would have *him,* however, he'd simply have to kill the fellow. "For your purposes, he'd be ideal, and then I could be assured of having you all to myself."

If nothing else, he succeeded in sparking her anger again with that observation. "I'd no' take a mon who'd be loath to touch me. If I have to marry, I'm wanting children out of it."

"That can be arranged, my dear, most willingly on my part," he replied softly.

But she was no longer listening to him. "I suppose I could return home and marry a crofter. What difference who I marry now? The thing is to get it done."

He saw his every effort tumbling down the wayside. "Bloody hell! You can't—"

She was still lost in the world of her few remaining options. "It's what I should've done from the start. At least I'll know what I'm getting."

He caught her shoulders, forcing her to hear him. "Confound you, woman, I'm not about to let you throw yourself away on some dirt farmer!" And before Anthony even realized what he was going to say, the words tumbled out. "You'll marry me!"

Chapter Eighteen

When Roslynn's laugher died down to a trickle of chuckles, she realized belatedly that her amusement could be nothing short of a gross insult to Anthony. While she had been blinded by tears of humor, he had moved away from her. She located him now, sitting on the bed, casually leaning back on one elbow.

He didn't *look* insulted. He looked rather bemused, actually. Well, at least her faux pas hadn't aroused his anger, which she wouldn't have blamed him for in the least. But it was so ridiculous. Marry him, indeed. London's most notorious rake? He couldn't possibly have meant it anyway.

But she felt better for having had a good laugh, considering what she was yet facing. With a lingering smile, she took a few steps closer to him, bending her head at an angle to try to gain his attention.

"That's a rare talent you have, Anthony, for lifting the spirits, but then no one could ever accuse you of lacking charm. But it's plain to see you're out of your element when it comes to proposing marriage. I believe the words should come in the form of a request, not a demand. You really must remember that the next time your sense of humor leans toward the absurd."

He said nothing at first, but his eyes rose to meet hers. She grew suddenly uncomfortable under his level stare.

"Quite right, my dear. I'm afraid I lost my head. But then I rarely do things in a conventional manner."

"Well . . ." She drew her ermine-trimmed pelisse closer together. It was a nervous gesture on her part. "I've taken up enough of your time."

He sat up straight, hands pressed to knees. "You're not leaving yet, not without giving me your answer."

"Answer to what?"

"Will you marry me?"

Put to her conventionally, the question sounded no less absurd. "But you were joking!" she said incredulously.

"Afraid not, sweetheart. Though it's as much a surprise to me as it is to you, I'm quite serious."

Roslynn's lips compressed tightly. *This* was not funny at all. "It's out of the question. I wouldn't marry you any more than I would Geordie."

Her previous laughter was understandable. And her reaction to his demand that she marry him was mild compared with his own surprise. But although the words had come of their own volition, once said, Anthony realized the idea of marriage, always so appalling before, suddenly had merit.

Not that he couldn't be talked out of it if she weren't standing there looking so fetching. He had gone thirty-five years without needing a wife and he certainly didn't need one now. So what the bloody hell was he doing insisting he was serious when she had given him an out by doubting him?

The trouble was, he didn't like being backed into a corner, and her threat to marry merely anybody did just that. And he liked even less the idea of her walking out of his life, which she was also threatening to do. For that matter, her leaving this room was the last thing he wanted. She was here. He was bloody well going to take advantage of it.

Her flat refusal to accept him, however, was the seed that tipped the scale. She *would* have him, by God, if he had to compromise her to get her agreement.

"Correct me if I'm wrong, my dear, but you haven't another offer forthcoming, have you? And I recall your saying that it made no difference who you marry as long as you get it done."

She frowned at him. "That's true, but you happen to be the one exception."

"Why?"

"Let's just say you'd make a terrible husband."

"I always thought so," he surprised her by agreeing. "Why else would I have avoided matrimony so long?"

"Well, then, you've made *my* point, haven't you?"

He grinned now. "Just conceding the possibility, sweetheart. But let's also look at the other side of the coin. I could as likely take to marriage right handily. Montieth did, and I'd have been the first to say he was doomed to failure."

"*He* happens to love his wife," she pointed out with annoying emphasis.

"Good God, you're not waiting to hear me say I love you, are you? It's rather soon—"

"Certainly not!" Roslynn cut in stiffly, cheeks flaming.

"But we both know I want you, don't we? And we both know you—"

"Sir Anthony, please!" If it was possible for her face to get any hotter, it did. "There's nothing you could say to me to make me change my mind. You just willna do for me. I swore I'd never marry myself a rake, and you've admitted to me that's what you are. And you canna change what you are, mon."

"I suppose I have Lady Grenfell to thank for your inflexibility?"

Taken aback, she didn't even wonder how he came to that conclusion. "Aye, Frances knows firsthand what happens when you lose your heart to a rake. Hers took to his heels when she needed marrying, forcing her to take what she could, which was an old man she loathed."

The exotic slant to his eyes was much more prominent when he scowled. "I think it's time you heard the full story, Roslynn. Old George simply panicked when faced so unexpectedly with fatherhood. He went off on a two-week spree to resign himself to the loss of his bachelorhood, and by the time he came to his senses, Frances was already married to Grenfell. She never once allowed him to see his son. She refused to see him when Grenfell died. If your friend has been miserable over the whole affair, so has mine been. The truth of the matter is, George would marry her now if she'd have him."

Roslynn moved over to the lounge chair and sat down, dazedly staring at the cold hearth. Why did he have to know George Amherst? Why had he told her that? Frances would probably marry Amherst in a minute if she could bring herself to forgive him for what had doubtless been a most natural reaction on his part, considering what a rakehell he had been at the time. And what about Roslynn herself?

Hell's teeth, there would be nothing she would like better than to marry Anthony Malory . . . *if* he loved her, *if* he would be faithful, *if* she could trust him. None of that was true, however. Nicholas Eden might love Regina, her grandfather might have loved her grandmother, George Amherst possibly had loved Frances and still did, but Anthony had admitted he didn't love her. And unfortunately, it would be too easy for her to love him. If that weren't the case, she would accept his offer. But she wasn't fool enough to leave herself open to the kind of hurt Anthony could and would bring her.

She glanced around to face him, only to see the bed empty now. Startled, she felt her bonnet being tugged on and shot forward to the edge of the chair. She turned to find Anthony casually leaning against the chair, his arms braced on the back.

It took a second for Roslynn to adjust to his nearness and, clearing her throat, she managed to get out, "I'm sorry, but what you've said about Frances and George doesn't change my mind about you."

"Somehow I didn't think it would," he said, shaking his head, and the slow smile appearing added to Roslynn's unease. "You're a stubborn Scot, Lady Chadwick, but that's one of the things I find endearing about you. I give you what you desperately need, and you spite yourself by refusing, and for some ridiculous reason that is pure supposition. I could turn out to be the most exemplary of husbands, you know, but you won't give me the chance to find out one way or the other."

"I told you, I'm not a gambler, Anthony. I'd rather not risk the rest of my life on a 'maybe' when the odds are so stacked against it."

He bent forward to rest his chin on his crossed arms. "You do realize that if I keep you here overnight, you will be quite compromised. I wouldn't even have to touch you, my dear. Circumstances speak for themselves. It's what got Reggie married, when her first meeting with Montieth had been quite innocent."

"You wouldn't!"

"I believe I would."

Roslynn shot to her feet, glaring at him with the chair safely between them. "That's—that's . . . it'd no' work anyway! I'm going home to Scotland. What do I care if my reputation's ruined here? I'd still have my—" She couldn't get the intimate word out, so skirted the thought. "My husband would know the difference, and that's all I care about."

"Is it?" he asked, a devilish gleam appearing in his cobalt eyes. "Then you don't leave me much choice, sweetheart, if I'm to help you despite yourself. So it's to be compromised in truth rather than by pretense?"

"Anthony!"

Her wail brought a grin to his lips. "I rather doubt I could have settled for the pretense anyway. It was good of me to consider it, but I'm too much the rake, as you keep pointing out, not to take advantage of your presence in my bedroom."

She began backing toward the door, more quickly when he came around the chair to follow her. "I'll—I'll settle for the pretense."

He shook his head at her. "My dear girl, if everyone is going to assume you've shared my bed, why deny yourself the pleasure?"

Roslynn had to fight down the thrill of anticipation those words gave her, even though she was sure he was just toying with her. And his teasing manner kept her from being truly alarmed, yet the closer he got, the more she became alarmed in another way.

She knew what could happen if he kissed her. It had happened before. Whether he was serious or not about this supposed seduction, if he touched her it was likely to happen, regardless, and with very little effort on his part.

"I don't want—"

"I know," he said softly as he caught her shoulders and pulled her up against his chest. "But you will, sweetheart. I can promise you that."

He was right, of course. He knew what she wanted, deep down, what she couldn't admit to him or herself. She could fight against it till the sun ceased to shine, but it wouldn't go away. He was the most exciting, compelling man she had ever known, and she had wanted him from the moment she met him. Such intensity of feelings had nothing to do with logic and reasoning. It was the yearning of heart and body, common sense be damned.

Roslynn let go, giving herself up to the senses as he gently enclosed her in his embrace. It felt like coming home, so often had she imagined being held by him again. The warmth of his body, the strength of his arms, the headiness of his passion, she remembered, yet it was all new again, wonderful, and so very welcome.

But his kiss, when it came, was actually so hesitant she barely felt it. And she realized he was giving her this last chance to stop him before he took complete control. He knew very well that he was experienced enough, skillful enough, to overcome any reluctance she might still harbor. He had done it before. That he was holding back warmed her heart more than anything, making her want him even more.

Roslynn said yes simply by slipping her arms around his neck. She was crushed then by the might of his relief, until he recalled himself. But she didn't mind. Breathing was incidental in light of the magic Anthony was now wielding with his mouth. His lips were warm, dry, moving carefully across her own, slowly fanning the heat between them.

He held her like that for a long while, kissing her, letting her feast on the delicious sensations he was evoking. When he leaned back, it was to begin working the buttons on her dress. Her bonnet and cloak had already been discarded without her even realizing he had removed them. Now she watched him begin to slowly undress her, and she couldn't move, didn't want to anyway. His eyes were mesmerizing her, grown dark and heavy-lidded, seeing into her soul. She couldn't look away, even when she felt her dress slithering over her hips to puddle at her feet, or her undergarments following the same path.

He didn't touch her then, except with his eyes as they took a slow journey down her length and back up again. On his lips appeared that sensual smile that had the power to liquefy her limbs, dangerous when her senses were already melted. She swayed, and his hands came out to steady her, grasping her hips, but they didn't stay there. With exquisite slowness, he savored the feel of her bare skin, around her hips, over her narrow waist, stopping finally at her breasts, his thumbs hooked beneath. He didn't touch her in any other way, yet her nipples tightened, her heartbeat accelerated, and a new warmth uncoiled inside her.

And his smile widened. It was positively triumphant, as if he could see inside her and knew exactly what she was feeling. He was a man victorious, rejoicing. And she didn't care. She was smiling herself, but inwardly, because if he had won, so had she, defeating her own common sense to have what she had wanted all along, to make love with this man, to have him initiate her and be her first lover, because with him she knew it would be beautiful.

But as long as she was going to give in to her desires, she wanted to take an active part. She had thought before of undressing him, wondering what he would look like. Her imagination had produced an Adonis. Before her was the man, much more intimidating than a fantasy, yet desire made her bold.

She tugged loose his belt so that his robe fell open, and placing her palms against his skin as he had done against hers, she moved her hands up, touching him as she had longed to do, skin to skin, spreading the robe wide, pushing it back at his shoulders. He let it drop from his arms and reached for her, but she held him at arm's length, wanting to look her fill. Revealed to her was warm skin and muscle, dark, curling hair, a chest that made her fingers tingle. Solid, powerful, he was so much more than she had imagined. She had a strong, compulsive urge to wrap her limbs around him, to get as close as was humanly possible, and there was so much of him to get close to.

"Och, but you're a bonny mon, Anthony."

He had been spellbound, watching Roslynn's fascinated scrutiny of him, but her husky words were the stimulus that nearly sent him over the edge. He yanked her to him, his mouth coming down hard to slash across hers. At the same time he lifted her in his arms and bore her to the bed.

He let her down gently, then leaned back, his eyes smoldering on her face, down her body once more, all of her lying in his bed. How often he had pictured her here, her skin flushed with desire, her eyes heated, beckoning. She was exquisite, more so than he had envisioned, curves perfectly rounded, womanly, and she was here, his, and she wanted him.

He wanted to shout with joy. Instead he cupped her cheeks with exquisite tenderness, fingers moving over her face, into her hair, down her neck. He would never get enough of touching her.

"You can't imagine what you do to me."

"I know what you do to me," she said softly, watching him. "Is it the same?"

The sound he made was half groan, half laugh. "God, I hope so."

And he kissed her, his tongue parting her lips to plunge inside, his chest settling over hers. When she lifted her arms to wrap around him, he caught them, spreading them out wide, twining his fingers with hers to hold them there. She couldn't move, but she could feel, and what she felt was his chest moving across her nipples, back and forth, electrifying the hard little nubs with just the barest sensual touch.

Next he lowered himself to take one sensitive breast into his mouth, gently suckling, or slowly circling his tongue around it. But he wouldn't release her hands, and she felt she would go mad with the need to hold him, caress him.

The moan came from deep in her throat. He paused, grinning up at her.

"You're a devil," she told him, seeing his wicked delight.

"I know." And he licked at her other nipple. "Don't you like it?"

"Don't I like it?" she repeated, as if she had never heard such a ridiculous question. "What I'd like is to be touching you as well. Will you let go?"

"No."

"No?"

"Later you can touch me to your heart's content. Right now I don't think I could bear it."

"Oh." She sighed. "Well, as to that, I canna bear much more either."

He buried his head between her breasts, groaning. "Sweetheart, if you don't hush, you'll have me behaving like an inexperienced boy."

Roslynn chuckled, and the throaty sound was Anthony's undoing. He whipped off his trousers but fortunately recalled himself before literally pouncing on her. There were still her stockings and shoes to remove, and he saw to them in quick order. Desire was riding him hard now, his previous unhurried pace at an end.

It was the dirk falling out of her shoe that returned a measure of control to him. He grinned inwardly, amazed. She was full of surprises, his little Scot. Marriage to her would be not only extremely pleasurable but interesting as well, and he was suddenly looking forward to it, all previous doubts forgotten.

He hefted the dagger in his hand. "Do you actually know how to use this?"

"Aye, and I did when one of Geordie's hirelings tried to snatch me off the street."

Anthony tossed the dirk aside, his smile meant to reassure her. "That's one worry you won't have after tonight, sweetheart."

Roslynn had her doubts about that but kept them to herself. Nothing was settled. He still wasn't the type of man she could enter into a marriage with, no matter how much she wished it were otherwise. He was a lover, and as such she could readily accept him. What did she need with her virginity anyway, since recent events assured her that her marriage, when it came about, would now be no more than a business arrangement?

But tomorrow's decisions were a long way off, and Anthony's hands were gliding up her legs, parting them, and making it impossible for her to think of anything else. He bent to kiss the inside of her thigh as he moved up as well, her hip, dipped his tongue into her belly button. Hot flames curled her toes, made her squirm. She clasped his head, pulling on him, but he still stopped to pay homage to her breasts again, lathing each sensitized peak until she was mindless with wanting. Her back arched, molding her belly to his chest, demanding the contact. It wasn't enough. She didn't know exactly what was needed but understood instinctively there had to be some purpose to the fires ravaging her senses.

She pulled on him frantically now, but he was unmovable, fully in control. Not until he was ready did he slide up a little more, assaulting her neck with lips that were now scorching, moving toward her ear. When his tongue slipped inside, the jolt was so powerful her body bucked, nearly dislodging him, and then settled into a delicious trembling that made her want to curl into him.

Her loins were aching, an inferno of moist heat, and when she felt something touching there for the first time, her body instinctively closed around it, hungering for the pressure in that burning region. And it managed to fill her, a glorious, welcoming fullness that she pushed against, locking her legs around him so she wouldn't lose it, finally feeling she had gained a measure of control. She wouldn't let go, and the pressure built in her, grew, until it seemed to pop, opening a new channel of feeling deep inside her that brought a certain relief of tension, but not enough relief to last.

He was kissing her again, deeply, with a fierce hunger that matched her own, his arms locked on both sides of her like iron bars, his fingers threaded in her hair, holding her, controlling her. And his body was moving against her with a kind of urgency that she responded to, felt also, as the tension grew again, pulsed, and then finally exploded into blissful oblivion.

Moments later Anthony collapsed on her, his own climax draining him so completely that for a while he was too weak to even lift his head. Never had he experienced anything like it, and he was about to tell her so when he realized she was out cold. Whether she had fallen into exhausted slumber or had fainted, he didn't know. He smiled, though, smoothing back the hair from her cheeks, inordinately pleased with himself and her.

He had the consuming urge to wake her, to start all over again, but he tamped it down, recalling the barrier he had felt that marked her a virgin. Reggie had said she was. Roslynn's passionate responses disclaimed it. The truth filled him with an inexplicable pleasure. And although she hadn't even seemed to notice the breach of her maidenhead, the loss demanded recovery. There was the morning. There was the rest of his life.

He shook his head, bemused. When had he become so bloody chivalrous?

Carefully he left the bed, drawing the covers up over her. Her languorous stretch and sigh made him smile. God, she was beautiful, and so alluring she made a man ache with wanting to know every inch of her. He promised himself he would. But for the moment, he donned his robe, gathered up her clothes, and quietly left the room. There was her driver to dismiss, arrangements to be made—the lady wasn't going anywhere.

Chapter Nineteen

Roslynn came awake to the tickling of rose petals against her cheek. She opened her eyes, focused on the pink rose first with confusion knitting her brow, then saw the man behind it, smiling at her.

"Good morning, my dear. And it is, you know. The sun has decided to shine for our wedding."

Roslynn groaned and turned over to bury her head in the pillow, unwilling to face the day and the consequences of her own actions. Hell's teeth, what had she done? Nettie would have gone on to Silverley and would be out of her mind with worry, thinking their ruse had failed, that Geordie had grabbed her again. And her driver! How could she have forgotten leaving the fellow to wait for her? Granted, she had tipped him well, but not well enough to wait all night. He had probably gone off with her bag of clothes, which also contained most of her jewels and important papers, including her marriage contract. Drat those three brandies!

Amidst the mounting consequences running through her mind, Roslynn felt Anthony's hand roving over her backside to the accompaniment of his chuckle. "If you really want to stay in bed—"

"Go away!" she mumbled into the pillow, furious with herself for feeling a thrill at his touch even in the face of her misery, and furious with him for sounding so cheerful.

"I don't see what the problem is," he said reasonably. "I have taken the tedious chore of decision making out of your hands. You are well and truly compromised, sweetheart."

She swung around. "The devil you say. I felt no pain, only—"

He laughed as the blush spread across her cheeks and her mouth snapped shut. "I admit to a certain finesse, but I didn't realize I was *that* skillful. I felt your maidenhead give way, dear girl." He quirked a brow at her, his grin maddening. "Are you saying you didn't?"

"Oh, be quiet and let me think!"

"What's to think about? While you whiled the night away in sated slumber, I obtained a special license that will allow us to marry immediately without hying off to Gretna Green. I never realized until now how beneficial it is to hold the markers on men with influence."

He seemed so bloody proud of himself she wanted to hit him. "I haven't said I'll marry you."

"No, you haven't. But you will." He walked to the door, opened it, allowing the well-remembered butler to step into the room. "Lady Chadwick would like her clothes and some breakfast, Dobson. You are hungry, aren't you, sweetheart? I always find I'm ravenous after a night of—"

The pillow hit him squarely in the face, and he had to choke back his laughter as he caught sight of his butler's incredulous expression. "That will be all, Dobson."

"Yes, yes, of course, sir. Very good, sir."

The poor, embarrassed man couldn't leave the chamber fast enough, but the moment the door had closed, Roslynn lit into Anthony with a fury. "You're a bloody beast, a damnable swine! Why did you have to tell him my name?"

He shrugged, not in the least contrite over his deliberate ploy. "Just a little insurance, sweetheart. Dobson wouldn't dream of spreading tales about the future Lady Malory. On the other hand . . ." He left the thought unfinished, but it wasn't necessary to spell out these new consequences.

"You're forgetting I dinna care if my reputation's ruined here."

"Now that's not exactly true," he replied smoothly, confidently. "You would care. You just don't have your priorities in the right order at the moment."

True, but irrelevant. She tried turning the tables on him. "I'm wondering why a mon like yourself would be wanting to marry so suddenly. Is it my fortune you're interested in?"

"Good God, where did you get that idea?"

He seemed so surprised, she felt rather ashamed for having mentioned it but pointed out, "You're a fourth son."

"So I am. But you're forgetting that I'm already aware of your unusual marriage contract, which, by the by, I'm quite willing to sign. You're also forgetting the fact that we made love last night, Roslynn. You could at this moment be carrying my child."

She glanced away, chewing on her lower lip. They had, and she could be. She had to tamp down the pleasure that thought gave her.

"What do you get out of this marriage, then?" she asked reasonably.

He came back to the bed on the side she was closest to. He pulled a piece of straw out of her hair and examined it, smiling. "You," he said simply.

Her heart seemed to flip over. It was sounding too bloody good, so much so that she couldn't seem to remember what her objections were. This simply wouldn't do.

She let out an exasperated sigh. "I canna think when I just wake up. You didna give me time to think last night either." This is an accusing tone.

"You're the one in the all-fired hurry, sweetheart. I'm only trying to accommodate you."

Must he point out things like that? "I need time to consider."

"How much time?"

"I was going to Silverley. My abigail's already gone there, so I still have to. If you'll give me until this afternoon, I'll have an answer for you. But I must tell you, Anthony, I can't see myself marrying you."

Abruptly, Roslynn found herself lifted up and kissed with a thoroughness that curled her toes. "Can't you?"

She pushed away from him until he let her fall back on the bed. "You only prove that I canna think at all when I'm around you. I'll be leaving now, if you'll just get me my clothes. And what the devil were you doing by taking them away?"

"Just making sure you would still be here when I got back from obtaining the license."

"Did you . . . sleep with me?"

He grinned at her hesitation. "My dear, I made love to you. Sleeping with you is rather beside the point after that, wouldn't you say?"

She decided to say nothing more to that, regretting having brought up the subject at all. He could talk circles around her anyway.

"My clothes, Anthony?"

"Dobson is bringing them. And the portmanteau you left in your carriage is in my dressing room, if you need anything from it."

Roslynn's brows shot up. "You retrieved it? Thank heavens!"

"Good Lord, don't tell me you were careless enough to leave something of value in a hired hack?"

She resented his censure. "I was upset when I came here," she said tartly in her defense. "And more upset after I got here, if you'll recall."

"Quite so," he conceded. "But you had better check to see that nothing is missing."

"It was only the marriage contract I was worried about. It would take too long to have another drawn up."

"Ah." Anthony smiled, humor dancing in his cobalt eyes. "The infamous contract. You may as well leave it with me so I can get the reading of it out of the way."

"And have you conveniently lose it? Not likely."

"My dear girl, you really must try trusting me just a little. It really would make for a more agreeable relationship, don't you think?" When she stubbornly refused to answer, he sighed. "Very well, have it your way." But to give her a taste of her own distrust, he added, "You *will* be at Silverley when I show up, won't you?"

Roslynn had the grace to blush. "Yes. You were kind enough to make the offer. I owe you an answer. But I'll have no arguing over it. You must accept my decision, whatever it is."

With a grin that lacked concurrence, Anthony left the room. The fact was, he trusted her at this point no more than she did him. He would have to have someone follow her to make sure she didn't take off straight for Scotland. He needed someone to keep Warton away from Silverley while she was there too. Couldn't have them meeting again after he had blackened the fellow with such a walloping lie.

As for her coming up with the right answer, that didn't worry him. Her cousin wasn't the only one who could see them married one way or another.

Chapter Twenty

"**I** don't believe it! Tony asked you to marry him? *My* uncle Tony?"

"I know what you mean," Roslynn said, considering Regina's wide-eyed wonder rather amusing. "I find it difficult to believe myself."

"But it's so sudden . . . well, of course he knows your circumstances. It would have to be sudden, wouldn't it, if he was going to get you? Oh, this is famous! Uncle Jason is going to just die! The whole family is. We never thought he'd do it, you know. Oh, it's just wonderful!"

Whether it was wonderful or not was debatable, but Roslynn smiled, not wanting to put a damper on Regina's obvious delight. She had made her decision on the long ride to Silverley, which was fortunate, because she hadn't had a moment's respite since she arrived. First Nettie had laid into her, deservedly, blistering her ears with a thorough scolding for her thoughtlessness. Then Regina had had to hear all about the abduction and the harrowing escape from Geordie firsthand, which Nettie had mentioned as their reason for the unexpected visit.

Now Roslynn had had to admit that Anthony would be here soon for her answer. That Regina hadn't thought to ask what that answer would be was telling. Of course she would be prejudiced. She wouldn't be able to understand how a woman might have doubts about marrying someone of Anthony's good looks and wicked charm, even if he did have a rakehell past.

"Everyone will have to be notified," Regina continued enthusiastically. "I'll do that, if you like. And I'm sure you'll want the wedding just as soon as the banns—"

"No banns, puss." Anthony sauntered into the drawing room without warning. "You can let the family know that congratulations are in order, but I've already sent for the parson, inviting him to dinner, and afterward we'll have a little ceremony. Is that quick enough to suit you, Roslynn?"

Forcing her to reveal her decision in this casual way, the moment he walked in, was not how Roslynn had imagined it. But he was looking directly at her, waiting for her confirmation or denial, and if she didn't know better, she would have sworn he seemed different. Nervous, perhaps? Could her answer really be that important to him?

"Yes, those arrangements will do . . . but we have some things to discuss first."

Anthony let out his breath slowly, a wide grin curling his lips. "By all means. Will you excuse us, puss?"

Regina jumped up and threw her arms around his neck. "Excuse you? I could clobber you! You never even let on."

"And spoil the surprise?"

"Oh, it *is* wonderful, Tony," she agreed happily. "And I can't wait to tell Nicholas, so I'll just run along." She laughed here. "Before you throw me out."

Anthony smiled fondly after her, delaying the moment he must face the music. He supposed he shouldn't have put Roslynn on the spot like that. And her "things to discuss" had sounded too serious by far.

"I hope you're not always going to be so high-handed?"

Roslynn's voice could have cut through lead. Anthony spun about, offering a crooked grin.

"Never think so. I can be putty in the hands of the right woman."

She wasn't amused. If anything, her expression turned more frigid. "Sit down, Anthony. There are some things you'll have to agree to before I'll marry you."

"Is this going to hurt?" When her eyes began to narrow, he sighed. "Very well, give me the worst of it."

"I want a child."

"Only one?"

Hell's teeth, she wanted to throw something at him! Could he ever treat anything seriously?

"Actually, I would like at least three, but one will do for now," she bit out.

"Well, this is cause for sitting down, isn't it?" he said and joined her on the sofa. "Have you a preference for gender too? I mean, if it's girls you want but we only have boys, I'm willing to keep on trying if you are."

His tone might be jesting, but she had the feeling he actually meant it. "You don't mind having children?"

"My dear girl, whatever made you think I would mind? After all, the mode of getting them has always been a favorite practice of mine."

The blush spread clear to her roots. She glanced down at her hands, held tightly in her lap. She could feel his eyes smiling at her, amused by her embarrassment. Well, he hadn't heard all of it yet.

Still avoiding his eyes, she said, "I'm glad you're being so reasonable about it, but I have another condition you must agree to that is rather unorthodox, though related in a way. Your mistress, or mistresses, as the case may be—"

His hand on her chin stopped her, turning her face to his. "This isn't necessary, you know," he said gently. "A gentleman always gives up his mistresses when he marries."

"Not always."

"Be that as it may, in my case—"

"You should have let me finish, Anthony." Her voice was sharp again, her little chin at a stubborn tilt. "I'm not asking you to give up anything. On the contrary. I insist you keep your mistresses."

He sat back, shaking his head. "I've heard of accommodating wives, but don't you think you're overdoing it a touch?"

"I'm serious."

"The devil you are." He scowled, infuriated not only that she really seemed to be serious, but also with the suggestion itself. "If you think for one bloody minute I'll agree to a marriage in name only—"

"No, no, you misunderstand." She was frankly surprised at this show of anger on his part. She had thought he would be delighted with this arrangement. "How can I get a child if our marriage is in name only?"

"How indeed!" he snapped.

"Anthony." She sighed, realizing he must be exhibiting wounded pride. He obviously expected a jealous wife, and that he wasn't getting one was deflating. "I intend to be a wife to you in every way. It's the least I can do, after you've come to my rescue, so to speak. If you'll just listen to me for a moment."

"My breath is bated."

She sighed again. Why was he fighting her on this of all things? It had seemed the ideal solution. In fact, she couldn't marry him otherwise.

She tried again. "I don't see what you're so up in the air about. You don't love me. You said as much. And my feelings aren't involved yet either. But I do like you, and we are—at least I am attracted to you."

"You know bloody well the attraction is mutual!"

She ignored his snarled interruption. "That was one of my prerequisites, that the husband I finally choose at least be pleasing in appearance so that I wouldn't mind too much—"

She broke off at his snort, knowing full well he was thinking of last night and how well she had enjoyed it. No, it wasn't necessary to mention that with him she would find certain marital duties quite pleasurable.

"You are personable," she continued. "And charming. There's no denying that. And I'm sure we can deal well with each other. But because there's no love involved, you're not committed. Neither am I, for that matter, though I'm the one in desperate need of a husband. In your case, however, it would be unrealistic of me to expect you to be completely faithful to your vows, don't you see? And so I'm not asking you to be. What we will have is a business arrangement, a marriage of convenience, if you like. Trust isn't required."

He was staring at her as if she had lost her mind. She supposed that *was* doing it up a bit much, but how else could she put a nice dressing on the simple fact that she didn't trust him and probably never would? Hell's teeth, he was the first to admit he was a rake. And a rake doesn't reform unless his heart is caught—her grandfather's own words, and words she could well believe because they made sense. Anthony had no business getting annoyed with her. *She* should be angry that it was necessary to even make this stipulation.

"Perhaps we should just forget it," she said stiffly.

"A splendid notion finally," he drawled.

Her lips thinned out at his quick agreement to *that*. "I didn't want to marry you to begin with. I told you so."

"What?" He sat bolt upright. "Now wait a minute, Roslynn. I didn't mean not getting married was a splendid notion. I thought you meant—"

"Well, I didna!" she snapped, quite losing her temper at last. "And if you willna agree to keep your mistresses, then we've nothing further to discuss, have we? It isna as if I'm no' asking for an equal share of your body. But I ken what you are, mon, and that your eyes will be wandering again once the novelty wears thin. You canna help it. It's your nature."

"Bloody hell."

She went on as if she hadn't heard his curse. "But I was willing to have you anyway, fool that I am. You would have given me bonny bairns. You would have saved me from Geordie. That was enough. I wasna asking for more."

"Perhaps I am willing to give you more. Or hadn't that thought crossed your mind when you came up with this magnanimous gesture?"

Roslynn stiffened under his derision, but she was in control again. "It comes down to one simple thing, Anthony. I could never trust you where other women are concerned. If I should . . . should come to care for you eventually, a betrayal would be too painful. I would rather know from the start that you won't be faithful to me; then our relationship will progress no further than it is now. We would be friends as well as—"

"Lovers?"

"Yes, well, there you have it. But since you won't agree, that's an end to it, then, isn't it?"

"Did I say I wouldn't agree?" His voice was calm again, but it was a forced calm. His set expression, his rigid posture, said he was still simmering. "Let me see if I have this right, my dear. You want to get a child by me, but at the same time you don't want my full devotion. You will act the wife in every way, but I'm to go on as I have been, seeing as many women as I like."

"Discreetly, Anthony."

"Ah, yes, discreetly. I can see where you might not want it bandied about, especially since you're pushing me out the door before I've even gotten inside it. So if I don't come home two or three nights a week, you'll be happy, I take it?"

She wouldn't deign to answer that. "You agree?"

"Of course." His smile was brittle, lacking warmth, but Roslynn didn't notice. "What man could resist having his piece of cake so thickly frosted?"

Roslynn didn't know if she liked that analogy. She didn't know if she liked his surrender either, now that she had it. He certainly hadn't argued very long. A token resistance, then grudging acceptance. Hah! Wretched man. He was undoubtedly delighted with her terms, and now she had to live with them.

Chapter Twenty-one

The Eden coach was well sprung, comfortable, with conveniences in the way of pillows and blankets, glasses and champagne. Roslynn had no need of the former, her husband's shoulder doing quite nicely in that capacity. She declined the champagne as well, having tipped enough glasses in toasts after the ceremony.

They had really done it, gotten married. Made love one night, married the next. It was so incredible that Roslynn had to wonder if unconsciously she hadn't wanted this to happen all along, if this wasn't why she had gone to Anthony's last night instead of going straight to Silverley as she had intended. But no, it wasn't going to be an ideal marriage. She had seen to that with her own perversity and mustn't forget it. And yet she still had him, didn't she? He was her husband, part-time or not.

She smiled, snuggling up close to him, glad that she was feeling just intoxicated enough not to feel self-conscious about it. Anthony was sipping champagne himself, staring thoughtfully out the window. The silence was companionable, the champagne she had already consumed making her drowsy.

She wasn't sure why they weren't staying the night at Silverley, as she had assumed they would. Anthony had said something about not wanting to worry about the noise, and his own bed, and starting things out right. It had sounded rather ominous at the time, the part about the noise, but she couldn't remember why now. Probably only bride's jitters. After all, she had just signed away her independence, giving herself into the hands of a man she barely knew, and one who was full of surprises, least of which was that he wanted to marry her.

She had every right to be nervous before and after the fact. Hadn't he surprised her twice today, first by arguing about her conditions, and second by signing the marriage contract without having read it first? Nicholas, who was witnessing the signing, had protested. She had herself, for that matter. But even after signing the damn thing, Anthony had still refused to read it. And now he was taking her back to London, the last thing she'd expected for tonight.

Frankly, she would have felt a lot more secure staying with the Edens this first night of her marriage. But she had made enough demands for one day and so hadn't protested when Anthony cut the celebrating short to leave. Granted, they'd had an early dinner, and the wedding ceremony had taken no time at all. It wasn't that late in the evening, though it would probably be midnight before they arrived at Anthony's town house.

She supposed she ought to take advantage of the ride and get some sleep while she could. She smiled again, for her first thoughts on seeing the blankets and pillows piled on the seats hadn't been about sleep. She had been appalled to think they would be having their wedding night in the coach. After all, Nettie had been relegated to a smaller carriage to follow at a slower pace. They were alone, just the two of them, in a coach that was certainly roomy enough to accommodate them for anything they might have in mind. The yellow glow of the coach lamp gave off a soft, romantic light. But no, Anthony had only suggested she nap for the return ride to London. He hadn't even taken advantage of their solitude to kiss her, just pulled her close and settled her against him.

She could blame the champagne for making her think her wedding night was going to start early. She wasn't even sure she was going to have a wedding night. After the fuss Anthony had made over her conditions, even if he did agree to them, she wouldn't be surprised if he just dropped her off and went on to visit one of his many women. And what could she say about it? In his own words, she had pushed him out the door.

Anthony heard his wife's sigh and wondered what she was thinking. Probably devising more ways to keep herself detached from this marriage. It was laughable, it really was, but of course he hadn't thought so earlier. Here he was taking a wife for the first time in his life, and she wanted to be no more than a mistress, and not even a possessive one. Did she feel nothing for him that she could blithely let him go from her arms to those of another woman? If he had wanted to continue to tomcat about town, he could have remained a bachelor.

It was perhaps a half hour later that the pistol shot shattered the quiet of the late hour and the coach came to a jostling halt. Roslynn jerked upright, blinking her eyes awake, in time to hear Anthony's soft curse.

"Have we arrived?" she asked, confused, as she glanced out the window to see nothing but pitch black.

"Not quite, my dear."

"Then—"

"I believe we're about to be robbed."

Her eyes swung to his. "Highwaymen? Then why are you just sitting there, mon? Are you no' going to do something?"

"My dear girl, this is England, and robbery is such a common occurrence that you come to think of it as donations to the needy. No one in his right mind travels these roads at night with anything of real value. We empty our pockets and go on our way, with no real harm done. It will be over in a matter of moments."

She stared at him, aghast. "Just like that? And what if I dinna want to be robbed?"

He sighed. "I assume this is your first time?"

"Of course it is! And I'm amazed that you can sit there calmly doing nothing."

"And what would you suggest I do when I haven't a weapon at my disposal?"

"*I* have one."

He caught her wrist as she reached for her boot and the concealed dirk. "Don't even think about it," he warned.

"But—"

"No!"

She sat back in a huff, glaring at him. "A fine thing when a husband willna protect his wife from brigands."

"Give over. Roslynn," he replied impatiently. "It's only a few pounds and trinkets."

"And a fortune in jewels in my portmanteau."

He gave her a level look, glanced at the bag on the seat opposite them, the same damn bag she had carelessly left in the hired hack last night, and snarled, "Bloody hell! You *would* cart about a fortune, wouldn't you? Very well." A quick examination of the interior inspired no strategy. His eyes came back to settle on Roslynn speculatively. "Toss your cloak back over your shoulders . . . yes." The deep scoop of her décolletage revealed the upper swell of her breasts, but the neckline was rather demure actually, in comparison to some others in this day and age. "Now, lower your dress a little—"

"Anthony!"

"This is no time for offended modesty," he explained wearily as he moved to the seat across from her. "You're to be a distraction."

"Och, well, in that case."

"That's quite low enough, my dear." He frowned at her. "*You* might not care if any number of women view my body in the nude, but I'm not quite so generous when it comes to other men and your charms."

"I was only trying to help," Roslynn retorted, annoyed with the reminder of the bargain she had insisted on.

"Commendable, but we want the chap to ogle you, not bust his breeches."

"Bust his breeches? Whatever are you talking about?"

He finally smiled. "I will be delighted to demonstrate at another time."

Anthony might have said more, but the highwayman made his appearance just then, yanking the door open and thrusting his head inside. Roslynn gave a little start. It was one thing to talk about being robbed even when you were about to be robbed, but quite another thing to meet the robber face-to-face.

The coach was high enough off the ground that only the man's upper torso was framed in the doorway, but it was a huge torso, great-brawny shoulders in a too-tight jacket, dark, scraggly hair on a large head wrapped in a dirty scarf. Fat fingers gripped an old, rusty pistol, also thrust into the coach and pointed directly at Anthony.

Roslynn could do nothing but stare at the pistol, her heart beginning a drumroll. This was not how she had imagined it . . . well, she hadn't really imagined anything. Not knowing any highwaymen personally, how was she to know how very dangerous they could be? But she had goaded Anthony into doing something, so it would be her fault if he got shot. And for what? Some stupid jewels that were replaceable?

She glanced at Anthony, wondering how she could tell him to forget it, when the highwayman spoke up. "Evenin', m'lord," he said congenially enough, his voice muffled behind the scarf. "Good o' ye t' sit tight and await me, it was. 'Ad a bit o' trouble wi' me 'orse after lettin' yer driver know what's what. But I'll be relievin' ye o' yer—cor!"

It was at this point that the chap caught sight of Roslynn in the dim light. It took only a moment more for Anthony to grab hold of his wrist and jerk it forward, which brought the fellow's face slamming into Anthony's fist.

It happened so fast it was over with before Roslynn had time to be alarmed that it was the hand holding the pistol that Anthony had grabbed. The highwayman, unsuspecting lout, was out cold, facedown on the floor. And as calmly as you please, Anthony placed a foot on his back to keep him from sliding out the door while he pried the pistol loose.

"Be a good girl and stay put while I see if he rode alone or has chums lurking about."

Before Roslynn could say a word, Anthony was out the door, the highwayman slid out the other one, and she was left in the empty coach, the words dying on her lips. She had never been so frightened in her life, not even for herself. Anthony in danger was a revelation. She found she couldn't stand the suspense, waiting to hear more shots fired.

Fortunately, it was only a matter of moments before he was back, smiling now. "According to our very shaken driver—it seems this was his first robbery too—the chap was alone."

Roslynn's relief came out in an explosive "What the devil do you mean, scaring me to death like that? You could've been killed!"

Both brows shot up in amazement at her vehemence. "My dear girl, what did you expect me to do when you demanded I *do* something?"

"I didna mean for you to get yourself killed!"

"Glad to hear it," was his dry reply. "But it's done now, so enough."

"Dinna be telling me—"

He yanked her across his lap and smothered her words with a very forceful kiss. A moment later it became soft nibbles, and finally he grinned at her.

"That's better. Now you have something else to think about, and you can be sure we'll continue this later." He set her gently back on the seat beside him and reached for the bottle of champagne. "But right now I could use another drink, and you can go back to sleep."

"As if I could," Roslynn retorted, but the steam had gone out of her anger.

"You'd best try, sweetheart, because I promise you, you won't have much opportunity to sleep later."

She said nothing to that but waited until he sat back with glass in hand and settled herself against him again. Her heart rate had returned to normal, although she could have done without the experience. This was her wedding night, for God's sake. Things like this just didn't happen on one's wedding night.

Peevish now that she had gotten so frightened for nothing, she said, "Next time pay me no mind and don't be so heroic. The jewels weren't *that* important."

"Perhaps, but it would have fallen to me as your husband to replace them, and I would rather not so dent my pocket."

"So you *did* marry me for my money?"

"Why else?"

With such irony in his tone, she glanced at him to see his eyes fixed on the bodice of her gown, which she had yet to raise. She nearly laughed. Why else indeed! The man was a rake through and through, but she had known that, knew too that there was no hope of changing him.

She sighed, briefly wondering if she ought to tell him that if he had married her for her money, he would be pleasantly surprised. Her marriage contract dealt very generously with him. And even though Anthony was obviously well-to-do enough not to have to work for a living, he was still a fourth son and couldn't possibly be rich enough to scorn what she had brought him through the marriage.

She would have to tell him, but not now. The excitement of the attempted robbery had drained her. Within moments, she was fast asleep again.

Chapter Twenty-two

Anthony shook Roslynn awake as they turned off the King's Road onto Grosvenor Place. They were nearing Piccadilly now, where his town house was located across from Green Park. He hoped that James would still be out for the evening and Jeremy would be in bed, because, as late as it was, the last thing he wanted to do was tender explanations. Besides, he had spent the whole of the ride home, less the short interruption by the highwayman, contemplating the delights of his bed. He didn't think he could wait much longer.

Roslynn couldn't have cared less at the moment. She had slept soundly this second time and couldn't seem to rouse herself sufficiently to appreciate that they had finally arrived. She just wanted to continue sleeping. Thoughts of her wedding night, of her new husband, of anything, were far removed. And yet someone continued to shake her.

Anthony was nonplussed when all Roslynn did was sigh an irritated moan and slap his hand away, refusing to open her eyes. Women didn't usually sleep in his presence, so he was unaccustomed to dealing with one who wouldn't wake up. He had suggested a nap to refresh her, not to put her out for the night, for God's sake.

He tried once more. "Come on, my girl, or have you forgotten what day this is?"

"Mmm?"

"Do wedding bells bring anything to mind? Or a husband thinking about you slipping into something sheer and sexy for his delectation?"

She yawned, but did manage to sit up, blinking her eyes several times before rubbing the sleep from them in a very childlike way. "I don't travel with anything like *that*."

He grinned to himself. At least her mind was finally working, even if it was a bit slow in realizing he was only teasing her.

"Not to worry, my dear. I sent for your things this morning."

That certainly woke her up. "You didn't! That was a fool thing to do when you didn't even know yet if I'd marry you or not. Geordie could have been watching and waiting for just that so he could follow and find out where I've gone."

Anthony certainly hoped so. That was just why he'd done it. And with any luck, the man he'd set to follow the "followees" would have an address for him tomorrow. But as to her concern, he chuckled.

"I know it's not every day that you become a bride, sweetheart, but it's a bit disconcerting, not to mention a blow to the ego, that you keep forgetting your changed status. You're married now. The sooner your cousin knows it, the sooner he'll trouble you no more."

The smile began hesitantly but blossomed into a dazzling display of delight. "That's true, isn't it? I'm so used to hiding from Geordie, I suppose it'll take me a while to relax now that I don't have to anymore. It's done. I'm free."

"Not quite free, my dear."

"No, I didn't mean—"

"I know." He chucked her under the chin. "But you are in fact mine now, and I am discovering, very quickly, what a possessive bore I can be."

How utterly absurd was that statement, but Roslynn was certain he was joshing her, as was his habit. If and when he ever treated a subject seriously, she would probably perish from the shock.

On a new thought, she asked, "Anthony, why did you insist on returning to London tonight?"

His eyes twinkled with amusement. "Brides are nervous enough on their wedding night. I thought you might be more at ease in a bed you're already familiar with."

Blushing, she got out in a whisper, "I asked for that, I suppose."

"You did."

"But you mentioned noise?"

"Did I? Think nothing of it. Like as not, we'll be as quiet as church mice."

He was teasing her again. She wasn't sure she liked it tonight. She wasn't sure she would ever get used to it, his allusions to lovemaking. But tonight . . .

She yawned, Anthony grinned, and the coach stopped.

"At last," he said and leaped down without awaiting the coach step. 'Come, my dear, and I will endeavor to carry you over the threshold."

She took his hand and was lifted to the ground. "It isn't necessary—"

"Allow me to play my part," he cut in, at the same moment sweeping her off her feet. "After all, they must have invented this quaint custom for a reason. Perhaps so the bride can't possibly escape?"

"What nonsense." She chuckled, wrapping an arm about his neck. "More likely it was a few brides fainting on the threshold so they had to be carried inside that started it."

"Only a few?" he teased. "I assure you that ignorance of the marriage bed is more widespread than that. Mothers just can't bring themselves to discuss such things these days, you know. A shame, because it makes it devilish hard on the poor grooms, easing fears and nervousness when they'd rather get right to the deflowering."

"Anthony!" she cried, though it was difficult not to smile at his wicked grin. "*Must* you say such things?" But she added, to have the last word, "Besides, some brides don't have mothers to enlighten them."

"Ah, now we're getting personal." He reached the door and pounded on it before giving her a tender look. "But you weren't frightened, were you, sweetheart?"

"You didn't exactly give me time to be frightened," she admitted, warming with another blush.

"And now that you know what it's all about?"

"I believe I feel a faint coming on."

He burst into laughter, but coughed it down as the door opened and a stoic-faced Dobson stared out at them. Roslynn was a trifle disappointed that the fellow could look so blasé, as if he were quite accustomed to finding his employer at the door with a woman in his arms.

But she was mollified a moment later as they passed him and she caught Dobson's unguarded expression. That was more like it, astonishment in the extreme. She hid her smile against Anthony's shoulder.

But watching the butler, she missed seeing James Malory just stepping into the hall, a drink in hand. If he was surprised, he didn't show it. The voice that drew Roslynn's attention to him was bland as well.

"I don't suppose I should be witnessing this."

"I was hoping you wouldn't," Anthony retorted without breaking his stride toward the stairs. "But since you have, you may as well know I married the girl."

"The devil you say!"

"He really did." Roslynn chuckled, delighted with this reaction even more than with Dobson's. "You don't think I'd allow just anyone to carry me over the threshold, do you?"

Anthony stopped short, rather amazed himself that he had managed to discompose this particular brother. "Good God, James, I've waited a lifetime to see you at a loss for words. But you'll understand if I don't wait around for you to recover, won't you?" And he didn't, continuing on his way.

At the top of the stairs, Roslynn whispered, laughter in her voice, "That was naughty of us, don't you think?"

"Not a-tall, dear girl," he promptly disagreed. "If I'm to have you to myself for a while, rendering my brother speechless was not only necessary but priceless. We will be bombarded with the family's good wishes and endless questions soon enough." Inside his room, he leaned back against the door with a sigh. "Alone at last."

Before Roslynn could say anything, he let her legs drop, turning her toward him at the same time. She ended up practically lying on him, a position they both savored for several long moments while he teased her lips with soft nibbles.

The backs of his fingers caressed her cheek, bringing her eyes slowly open. His own were grown dark and heavy-lidded with passion. And his voice was a caress too, his breath warm against her lips.

"Did you ever stop to think that this is the one night of your life when everyone knows you intend to make love? Ah, sweetheart, I love it when you blush for me."

"It's something I've been doing only recently—since I met you."

For some reason, her husky reply savaged Anthony's senses. He set her away from him, his hands trembling, a soft groan in his throat.

"I was a bloody fool to wait this long. I'll give you five minutes to do whatever you have to, but for God's sake, take pity on me, Roslynn, and be in bed when I return."

"Wearing something sheer and sexy?"

"Good God, no!" he exclaimed. "I don't think I could bear it now."

With that he disappeared into his dressing room, leaving Roslynn with a silly smile on her lips and a warmth of anticipation churning in her belly. Had she done that to him, made him lose control like that? Extraordinary. But she wasn't too composed herself. Knowing what was going to happen was a lot different from not knowing. It made it easier. There was an eagerness. But she was still too inexperienced not to be a trifle nervous too.

Her fingers were rather clumsy in stripping off her clothes, though she made quick work of it. Her heart was pumping at an abnormal rate. Her ears were attuned to the door as she waited to hear it open. Climbing into the bed, she was undecided whether to pull the sheet over her completely or to leave it only partially draped. Modesty won out, for now. She wondered if frequency would help, if she might eventually manage a certain detachment. With Anthony, she doubted it. This was more likely to become habit-forming.

He was wearing a long robe of crimson velvet when he finally returned. With acute embarrassment, Roslynn realized that she hadn't even thought to put on a nightgown. Not that it would have stayed on for long, but wasn't it unseemly for a wife to wait naked in bed for her husband? Perhaps not—at least not tonight. And Anthony's appreciative smile as he approached the bed said he certainly approved.

"May I?" He sat down next to her and began removing the pins from her hair.

She touched a red-gold lock that fell onto her shoulder. "I forgot."

"I'm glad."

He was. He loved her hair, loved touching it and running his fingers through it. Setting the pins aside, he massaged her scalp until her eyes closed and a dreamy smile appeared on her lips.

"That's nice," she breathed softly.

"Is it? And what about this?"

His lips pressed to her temple, moving down, stopping at her mouth for a long, deep kiss before continuing down her neck in a path that led to her breasts. Ripples of warmth shot along her nerves, making her toes curl.

"That's *too* nice," she murmured.

Anthony's chuckle was rich with pleasure. "Ah, sweetheart, was it only last night? It seems an eternity has passed between now and then."

She reached out to cup her palm to his cheek and ended by running a finger over his lips. "Only an eternity?"

He said her name impassionedly before he caught her wrist and kissed her palm, his dark eyes never leaving hers. An electricity passed between them, hot and tingling. And his intense stare continued to hold her transfixed as he shrugged out of his robe, yanked the sheet down, and covered her body with his. He commenced then to kiss her so long and passionately that she was in a state of mindless need when he finally entered her, so much so that her climax was immediate and earth-shattering, her cry of fulfillment sending Anthony over the edge as well.

In a cocoon of contentment, Roslynn held his sweat-moistened body, waiting for their breathing to return to normal. She was in no hurry to have him move, and so her hold was rather tight. Not that it could have kept him there, but he was in no hurry to move either. His head rested on her shoulder, his breath fanning her neck, stirring the hair there, tickling her. Gooseflesh rushed down her arms and she gave a little shiver, enough for him to notice.

"I have managed to act the typical groom," he said with a sigh. "Impatient, speedy, and now contrite." He lifted his weight onto his elbows, which gave her a little thrill as his groin pressed more tightly to hers. "I give you leave to castigate me, my dear."

"For what?"

"Well, if you don't know—"

"For what, Anthony?"

"For my lack of control, of course. A man of my age and experience has no excuse, so I must put the blame on you. You quite make me lose my head."

"Is that bad?"

"I'll let you be the judge in a little while, when I make love to you at a more leisurely pace."

Her laugh was deep in her throat. "If I didn't know better, I'd say you were fishing for compliments. You must know your performance wasn't lacking. Quite the contrary. You were wonderful."

He gave her his melting smile, which sent a weakness racing through her limbs. She gasped, her lips parting, tempting him to bend down and brush them lightly with a kiss.

But then he got up, surprising her by tossing the sheet up over her and retrieving his robe where he'd carelessly dropped it on the floor. He sat down again on the edge of the bed, but at a distance, which should have given her warning.

With a mock sigh, he said, "And now for the noise."

Hazel eyes blinked. "The noise?"

"The unleashing of your Scot's temper."

Roslynn grinned at him, thinking he was once again teasing her. "I'm going to lose it, am I?"

"More than likely, since I'm honor-bound to tell you that I lied to you today."

Her amusement fled. "About what?"

"Can't you guess, my dear? I have no intention of keeping a mistress on the side now that I've married. It utterly defeats the purpose, doesn't it?"

"But you agreed!"

His smile was one of sheer male satisfaction. "I can safely say I would have agreed to anything today to make you legally mine, even to putting it in writing, which fortunately you didn't think to request."

Roslynn stared at him incredulously, hot anger banishing the languor of her limbs. She felt tricked, cheated. She was furious.

"You married me falsely!"

"I married you in good faith."

"I offered you an ideal situation, mon!"

"One I didn't ask for or want. And, my dear, if you'll just think about it, you'll see how utterly absurd your request was. You didn't ask me to marry you, I asked you, and I'll have you know I've never done that before. Nor is it something I would have done lightly. I've had mistresses enough to last me a lifetime. What I want now is a wife."

It was ludicrous how calm he was next to her fury, shaming her into lowering her voice. "You say so now, but what of next month, next year? Your eyes will be a-wandering again soon enough."

Anthony grinned at her, knowing that would probably infuriate her all the more. "My eyes have been a-wandering, as you put it, for the last nineteen years. Give them a rest, Roslynn. They settled on you and don't want to move on."

Her own eyes narrowed to a seething glare, just as he had anticipated. "So you think it's a matter to be joking about, do you? Well, let me tell you—"

She didn't get a chance to. He reached over and caught her around the waist, dragging her across the bed and up against his chest. The sheet was lost in the process, but Roslynn was too angry to notice. Anthony wasn't. And the new stirring below his belt demanded he end this bickering soon and get back to the pleasures of the wedding night. The silly girl. All this fuss because he wanted no one but her. She ought to be happy about it instead of raising hell. But he had expected this, and had an answer for her.

"What say we compromise, sweetheart? D'you still insist I keep a mistress?"

"Hell's teeth! Now isna that what I've been saying?" she retorted.

"Very well." His eyes caressed her face, stopped on her lips, and his voice deepened. "Are you prepared to fill the role?"

"Me?"

His grin was back, maddeningly. "Who else? You happen to be the only woman I'm interested in at the moment."

"That's no' what I meant, and you know it!"

"Perhaps, but it's the best I can do."

Roslynn didn't believe this for a moment. "You must have a woman you've been seeing."

"Assuredly. Several, in fact. But none could actually be called my mistress, sweetheart. And if you must know, I haven't seen any of them since I met you. But that's beside the point, isn't it? The point is, I have no desire to take any of them to my bed again, or anyone else for that matter. You are quite stuck with me."

"Anthony, be serious just for once!" she pleaded in exasperation.

"My dear, I've never been more serious in my life. How can I make love to another woman when you're the only woman I want? It can't be done, you know. Desire isn't just called forth at will. Or hadn't you thought of that?"

She was looking at him with confusion and a touch of wonder, only these expressions quickly turned to a frown and a tightening of her lips. "But that doesn't mean you'll no' see someone eventually that you'll be liking."

Anthony sighed wearily. "If that day comes, I swear to you, Roslynn, it won't matter in the least. I'll have only to imagine you, here like this, and be a contented man."

She made a sound that was very nearly a snort. "Very prettily said. I give you that. But you're forgetting you dinna love me."

He tossed her back onto the bed and quickly covered her body with his own. "Then let us examine what I do feel, shall we?" His voice purred, but it was obvious he had lost patience with her. "There's lust, in abundance. It's been bloody hell keeping my hands off you until now. There's possessiveness, which I've only recently discovered. There's jealousy, which I've known about for weeks." His brow rose sharply as her eyes rounded. "Don't tell me I've actually surprised you, my dear."

"You were jealous? Of who?"

"Bloody well everyone, even my blasted brother. And you may as well know, while we're at it, that the gentlemen you were considering for marriage were all immensely suitable, with the exception of Fleming, who really is a queer fellow. It was all lies, Roslynn, because I couldn't stand the thought of any of them having you."

He was holding her down now, because he fully expected her to become violent after this particular confession. But Roslynn was perfectly still, rage at what he'd done overshadowed by utter amazement.

"Then you must . . . care a little?" Her question was whisper-soft, hesitant.

"Bloody hell!" he finally exploded. "Would I have married you if I didn't?"

Not the least bit intimidated, she reminded him, "You married me to help me out of a horrid situation, which I'm grateful for."

Anthony closed his eyes for a moment, pleading for self-control. When he opened them, there was a hard gleam there. But his voice was moderate, if a touch arrogant.

"My dear, if I had only wanted to help you out, as you put it, I could have hurried your bothersome cousin to an early demise with little difficulty. But I wanted you for myself, it's that simple." Here his tone changed, became stern. "And if you tell me once more to enjoy other women when I'll be bloody damned if I will, I'll play the archaic husband for you and thrash you soundly. Have I made myself clear? There will be no other women, not now, not ever!"

He waited for her temper to snap again. He got a smile instead, a very beautiful one that reached her eyes, brightening the golden flecks there.

Anthony didn't know what to make of this sudden change, until she said, "Dinna you mention earlier doing something at a more leisurely pace? I was suppose to judge—"

His laughter cut her off, deep and exultant. "Never change, sweetheart. I wouldn't have you any other way."

And he proceeded to have her his way, with her full and delighted cooperation.

Chapter Twenty-three

"Och, now, what is this? Sitting there grinning at yerself, are ye?"

Roslynn turned the hand-held mirror slightly and caught Nettie's image reflected behind her. Her grin widened, and her eyes, already sparkling, tried for a look of innocence as she swung around on the stool.

"Was I grinning? I can't imagine why."

Nettie snorted, but her lips were twitching at the corners too. "Pleased wi' yerself, ain't ye?"

Roslynn gave up the pretense. "Yes! Oh, Nettie, I never thought I could be this happy!"

"Aye, it's nae wonder. That's a bonny-looking mon ye caught. But did ye have tae be keeping him such a secret?"

"There was no secret. He wasn't really under consideration, Nettie. His asking to marry me was as much a surprise to me as to anyone."

"Well, now, as long as yer happy wi' him, that's all I could be asking, and sae much more than I was expecting, wi' all the haste. It doesna even matter that this house is sae Spartan and the servants boorish snobs."

Roslynn chuckled. "You've met Dobson, I take it?"

"Aye, that lout. What a cold one. But it's nae wonder he's sae snooty, him being in charge of all the servants here. There's nae housekeeper, nae other women servants a-tall, just two maids who come in several times a week tae clean. Even the cook's a mon, and there's another uppity one fer ye."

"I see you have a few complaints, Nettie. But don't take it so to heart. You're forgetting this was a bachelor residence until now. I'm sure Anthony won't object if we make some changes. There's new furnishings to buy." At this she glanced about her new bedroom, envisioning putting her touch to it. "New servants to hire. We'll be busy in the next few weeks, you can be sure."

"Now dinna be going off on a spending spree on my account. And remember ye've a husband now tae be asking afore ye go spending his money. The creatures are particular about such things as that."

"Don't be such a worrier, Nettie. I'm not going to use *his* money when I've so much of my own."

"Ye better talk that over wi' him first, lassie. A mon's funny about wanting tae pay his wife's bills, ye know? Yer trouble is, ye've been doing fer yerself too long, even afore Duncan, bless him, passed on. But yer married now. Ye've got tae make allowances and do things a might differently if ye want tae be keeping the peace atween ye." A knock sounded on the door just then, and Nettie explained. "That'll be yer bath water. Are ye in a hurry tae be joining yer mon fer lunch, or have ye time—"

"There's plenty of time, Nettie. Anthony went out, I believe." Roslynn blushed here. "I was still half asleep when he told me. But he mentioned something about his daily ride and attending to a few things. I don't expect him back before dinner, however, so I can spend the day acquainting myself with the house and servants. And I really must send a note off to Frances to let her know what's happened." After getting so little sleep last night, Roslynn thought those were enough priorities for one day.

An hour later, wearing a cool muslin dress of yellow-and-rose spring flowers on a beige background, Roslynn left Anthony's room, *their* room now, and started down the short hallway. She had seen next to nothing of his home the last time she was here, nor last night either, but that would soon be corrected. She would need Dobson's help, though. Since there were other Malorys in residence, she couldn't just open doors indiscriminately.

She spared a moment's thought for the other two occupants of the house, Anthony's brother and son. She wondered if her husband would now admit that Jeremy Malory was his son. There was no reason for him to still deny it, at least not to her. He was a handsome lad, a boy to be proud of, and the image of his father. Actually, it was ludicrous for Anthony to deny patrimony when anyone merely had to look at Jeremy to know who sired him.

She would need to make friends with the lad, but she could foresee no difficulty there. James Malory was another matter. There was no reason to get too friendly with him, and every reason not to. Should she tell Anthony about James having kissed her once? Or maybe he already knew. He *had* said he had been jealous of his brother.

She smiled, remembering their crazy conversation last night. She didn't know how he had done it, but she had let him convince her he was going to make a wonderful husband. All of her long-standing, preconceived notions about rakes were put to rest. He was going to be faithful. She felt it, believed it now wholeheartedly, and was ecstatic about it. What more could she have asked for than to have Anthony Malory all to herself? His love, she reminded herself. But that would come. It would. It had to.

"Hell's bells, what are *you* doing here?"

Roslynn paused at the top of the stairs. Jeremy Malory, on his way up, stopped dead in his tracks too, his mouth left open in an O of wonder after he had got his question out. The imp in Roslynn decided to be mischievous, since it was obvious he hadn't heard of the marriage yet.

"I spent the night, don't you know."

"Spent the night?" he repeated.

"Yes, and I'm thinking of moving in."

"But—but there's only bachelors here!"

"But there's lots of room, don't you think? And this house could use a woman's touch."

"It could?" he said in bemusement, only to shake his head. "But it wouldn't be proper, would it? I mean, you're a lady—I mean, well, you know what I mean. It just wouldn't be proper."

"No?" Roslynn grinned. "Then I'll have to speak with your father. He's the one insisting I stay."

"*He* did?" Jeremy nearly choked. "Hell's bells, he's gone and done it now! Uncle Tony's going to fly through the roof. He had his eye on you himself. Hell's bells, he'll probably throw us out now."

"Jeremy," she began gently, giving up the game. She hadn't thought he would be this upset. "There's no need to keep up the pretense. I know Anthony is your father. And I'm sorry I teased you like that. The reason I'm staying is because I married your father yesterday. He really should have told you."

His mouth dropped open again, but this time he was quicker to recover. "My father, meaning—Anthony? You married Anthony Malory?"

"You don't have to sound *that* surprised."

"But . . . I don't believe it. Tony getting married? He wouldn't."

"And why not, I'd like to be knowing?"

"He just wouldn't. He's a confirmed bachelor. He's got all the women he could want chasing after him. What would he need a wife—"

"Careful, laddie," Roslynn warned stiffly. "You're getting very close to insulting me."

Color flamed his cheeks. "I—I beg your pardon, Lady Chadwick. Truly, I meant no offense."

"It's Lady Malory now, Jeremy," she said, holding up her hand in front of him and tapping her wedding ring. "It happened last evening at Silverley, with your cousin Regina as witness. So you might as well believe it, laddie. I've no reason to lie about it, and you can ask your father as soon as he comes home."

"My father was there too?"

Roslynn sighed. "How could he not be at his own wedding?"

"No, I meant James. He *is* my father, you know. He really is."

It was Roslynn's turn to be surprised, because Jeremy was too earnest to be lying about it now. "But you look so much like Anthony!"

"I know." He grinned. "But so does Reggie, and so does Amy, Uncle Edward's daughter. And my aunt Melissa, Reggie's mother, did too, though I never met her. She died when Reggie was still a baby. All the rest of the Malorys are blonds. It's just us five who took after my great-grandmother Malory."

"I can see I've a lot to learn about this family, there's so many of you."

"Then he really married you? He really did?"

"Yes, Jeremy, he really did." She grinned, coming down a few steps to lock arms with him. "Come along and I'll tell you all about it. James—your father—was here last night when Anthony carried me over the threshold, you know. Now, if you think *you* were surprised, you should have seen him."

"I'll bet." His chuckle was deep for someone so young, but infectious.

Chapter Twenty-four

When Anthony and James walked inside the tavern and paused to look over the crowded room, the same phenomenon occurred that had happened again and again throughout the afternoon. One by one, the occupants of the room noticed them, nudged their companions, and the room began to quiet, until the silence was as thick as the cloud of smoke floating above the scarred tables.

The riffraff of the wharves didn't take too kindly to the gentry invading their territory, and there was usually always some down-on-his-luck fellow filled with enough resentment of the upper classes to pick a fight with the unsuspecting slummers, as any well-dressed gents were assumed to be. It could be the highlight of an evening, a chance for the lower masses to get a little of their own back from the wealthy who think it their due to exploit them, by wiping the floor with the nabobs' beaten bodies and casting them out in the street half dead, and sometimes, actually dead.

But the sheer size of these two aristocrats gave even the meanest bruisers pause. They didn't have the look of the dandies who thought it a lark to frequent establishments they scorned in the sober light of day. No, these two were obviously of a different quality, the menacing aura about them penetrating even the most sodden brain. Anyone who briefly thought of causing trouble quickly changed his mind at a second look and went on with his drinking and revelry, determined to ignore these particular nabobs.

The silence had lasted perhaps twenty seconds. Anthony didn't even notice it this time. He was tired, frustrated, and just a little bit intoxicated, since they had ordered drinks in each of the nine taverns they had entered while questioning the barkeeps. James did notice, and was berating himself once again for not dressing properly for this excursion. Clothes fitted a man to his elements, and theirs were distinctly out of place in these elements. But how had either of them known this would turn into an all-day excursion?

Anthony was deciding he had had enough for one day when his eyes lit on a thatch of bright red hair. He looked at his brother and rolled his eyes toward the bar. James followed the indicated direction and saw the fellow too. Red hair did not make him Geordie Cameron, but it did raise the odds that he was likely a Scotsman. James sighed, hoping this was the end of their search. Wild-goose chases were not how he preferred to while away his time.

"Why don't we take that table near the bar and see what we can overhear?" James suggested.

"Why don't I just go ask him?" Anthony countered.

"Men of this ilk don't like to be questioned, dear boy. They've usually, every one of them, got something or other to hide. Haven't you surmised that yet?"

Anthony scowled but nodded. James was right. They had had deuced little cooperation from everyone they'd questioned today, but blister it all, he wanted this done with so he could go home. He had a wife waiting for him, and this was not how he had imagined spending the second day of his marriage.

What was supposed to have taken only a few hours' time at the most this morning had turned into a comedy of exasperation. Anthony had been in the process of explaining to James about Geordie Cameron, the reason that he had married in such haste, when his man John had interrupted their breakfast with the fellow's address, having successfully followed Cameron's hirelings yesterday to his lair.

It must have been the look of predatory delight on Anthony's face that prompted James to offer to come along. Not that Anthony was going to really harm the scoundrel. No, just impress him with a sound thrashing, give him the good news that Roslynn was out of his reach, since he wasn't taking any chances that Cameron might miss the notice of her marriage in the papers, and send him off with a warning to trouble her no more. Very simple. He didn't need James' help, but he was glad of his company as the day wore on.

The first in a long list of frustrations was to find Cameron vacated from the flat he had rented. That he hadn't left until last night, when Roslynn had escaped him the day before, was interesting. He was either confident that she wouldn't alert the authorities of her kidnapping or just plain stupid. Whichever, he had smartened up by last night and had changed locations. And since it was too soon for him to have found out about Roslynn's marrying, Anthony doubted the chap had given up to return to Scotland, which was why he had spent the rest of the day making inquiries at every lodging and tavern in the vicinity, albeit fruitlessly.

All he had was Geordie Cameron's description from his landlady, but this fitted the fellow at the bar. Tall, carrot-red hair, light blue eyes, presentable, and oh, yes, very good-looking, according to Mrs. Pym. Anthony couldn't see the eyes yet, and whether the chap was good-looking or not was a matter of opinion, but the rest agreed with him, even to the halfway decent togs he was sporting. The man had a companion, perhaps one of his hirelings, standing there with him, a short chap with a woolen cap pulled so far down over his head, his features were obscured even from a side angle.

They were talking together, at any rate, and James' suggestion to listen in on the conversation was reasonable, despite the fact that Anthony's patience was worn thin. After all the trouble he had been through today, he was no longer just looking forward to thrashing the fellow, but pleasantly contemplating an alternative of a more permanent nature. Missed his lunch, missed his dinner, missed making love to his wife all day. He bloody well hoped she would appreciate his efforts on her behalf.

He followed his brother across the room to a table already occupied by two rough-looking men and felt a small bit of his humor returning as he watched James stop there and stare the fellows into hastily vacating their seats. "Amazing how you do that, old man."

James grinned innocently. "Do what?"

"Put murder and mayhem in those two little green orbs of yours."

"Can I help it if the chaps thought I meant them bodily harm? I didn't, you know. I am the most peaceable fellow this side of—"

"Hell?" Anthony suggested with a wry smile. "It's a good thing Connie's not here, or he'd choke on that fairy tale."

"Put a lid on it, puppy. We need a drink if we're not to look any more inconspicuous than we already do."

Anthony turned around to locate a barmaid and got more than he bargained for. The wench was curvaceous without being plump, amazingly pretty for such a rough establishment, and had set herself down on his lap, wrapping soft arms about his neck in blatant invitation. It was done too quickly for him to discourage her, and he was so surprised by her action that he drew a blank for a moment on how to get rid of her.

James took pity on him, however, vastly amused at Anthony's dilemma. "You've chosen the wrong lap, dear girl." His dry tone brought the barmaid's head around to him, and at her bemused look, James grinned. "You see before you one of the world's most pitiable creatures—a married man—also one very preoccupied this evening. Now, if you'd care to bounce your pretty little backside over to this side of the table, you might get a rise for your trouble."

The maid giggled at James' crudity, words she was used to but not expecting from such an elegant-looking nabob. Yet she gave a last wistful look at Anthony, the one who had first boggled her eyes when the men walked in. He was worth at least another try, though the other one was just as appealing, now she'd had a better look at him.

She ignored Anthony's frown of displeasure, caused by James' words, and wrapped her long blond hair around his neck to pull him closer to her, while below the table, her buttocks wiggled in his lap provocatively. "Sure ye don't want some, luv. I'd be 'appy—"

His wits returning *too* quickly, Anthony lifted her up and set her on her feet, giving her a little shove in James' direction. "Another time, luv," he said not unkindly, but his eyes were narrowed when he met James' amused gaze.

James wasn't in the least perturbed. He caught the girl around the waist, caressed her backside with promise, whispered a few words in her ear, and sent her off with their order for two ales.

"Caught your fancy?" Anthony sneered.

"Whether this is your man or not, dear boy, I'm done for the day. I might as well have some compensation for my trouble, and she'll do nicely."

Anthony finally smiled. "Yes, I suppose she will. But you'll recall whose lap she preferred."

"Your recent victory has apparently gone to your head, lad. I hate to bring you back to earth, but you obviously need to be reminded that all you can do is look from now on—while I on the other hand can still sample to my heart's content."

"You don't see me bemoaning my state, do you?"

"Remember those words when you do. Women are to be savored for the moment. Anything longer is a threat to a man's sanity."

Anthony smiled serenely, even though those used to be his own sentiments as well. James didn't notice. His eyes had drifted to the two at the bar in such intimate conversation, particularly to the shorter fellow, and he frowned, looking at the cutest little backside to ever grace a supposedly male anatomy.

Anthony was distracted as well a moment later when the redhead, no more than six feet away, raised his voice a little. The thick Scottish brogue was unmistakable, reminding him forcefully of why they were here.

"I've heard enough," Anthony said tersely, swiftly rising to his feet.

James grabbed his arm, hissing, "You've heard nothing. Be sensible, Tony. There's no telling how many of these chaps in here might be in his pay. We can bloody well wait a little more to see if he might leave the premises."

"*You* can wait a little more. I have a new wife at home I've kept waiting long enough."

Before he took another step, however, James sensibly called out, "Cameron?" hoping for no response since Anthony was no longer in a reasonable state of mind. Unfortunately, he got ample response, both characters swinging around at once and searching the room, one fearful, the other assuming an aggressive stance. Both pairs of eyes lit on Anthony as he shook off James' hand and closed the distance in two steps, but he had eyes only for the tall Scot.

"Cameron?" he asked in a deceptively quiet tone.

"The name's MacDonell, mon, Ian MacDonell."

"You're lying," Anthony growled, catching the man's lapels in his fists and jerking him forward and up, until their eyes were at a level only inches apart.

Too late, Anthony saw his mistake. The narrowed eyes now blazing at him were light gray, not blue. But at the same moment Anthony realized it, the little man next to them slipped a knife out of his sleeve.

James intervened at this point, since Anthony was too involved with the redhead to take notice of his companion. He neatly knocked the knife aside, only to be attacked for his trouble, fists and feet both flying his way. Hardly any damage ensued. The little bugger had no more strength than a child. But James was not about to just stand there and take this barrage. With no effort at all, he flipped his opponent about and hefted him off his feet. Somehow he wasn't surprised to find a full, soft breast cupped in his hand.

Anthony had glanced their way at the start of the commotion, but now his eyes widened as he took in the delicate chin, smooth lips, and pert little nose. The cap had come down further to completely cover the eyes, but the perfectly molded cheekbones were unmistakably feminine too.

His voice was a trifle loud in his surprise. "Good God, *he's* a woman!"

James grinned. "I know."

"Now you've done it, you miserable curs!" the girl snarled at them both as several men within hearing glanced their way. "Mac, do something!"

MacDonell did. He pulled back his arm and swung at Anthony. The decision was made quickly not to fight, much as Anthony needed that outlet to let off some of his frustration. He caught the fist and slammed it down on the bar.

"There's no need for that, MacDonell," Anthony said. "I made a mistake. I apologize."

MacDonell was disconcerted at how easily he had been outmaneuvered. He wasn't that much smaller than the Englishman, yet he couldn't raise his fist off the bar to save his soul. And he had the feeling that even if he could, it wouldn't do him much good.

Prudently, the Scotsman nodded his acceptance and got his release by doing so. But his companion was still held tight, and it was to James his aggression turned now.

"Ye'll be letting go, mon, if ye ken what's good fer ye. I canna let ye monhandle—"

"Be easy, MacDonell," Anthony interjected in a hushed tone. "He means the lass no harm. Perhaps you'll let us accompany you outside?"

"There's nae need—"

"Look around you, dear fellow," James interrupted the Scot. "There appears to be every need, thanks to my brother's loud blunder."

So saying, he hefted the wench under his arm and started for the door. Her protest died with a tight squeeze about the ribs, and since MacDonell heard no complaint from her, he followed behind. Anthony did as well, after tossing a few coins on the table for the ales that had never arrived. He spared a glance for the room to see that most eyes were still on James and the girl, or rather, just on the girl. He wondered how long she had been in the tavern before her disguise was uncovered. It didn't matter. Dressed as she was in skin-tight breeches, even if her sweater was baggy in the extreme, there probably wasn't a man there who wouldn't have made a try for her if James didn't have her firmly in hand.

Anthony supposed it was too much to hope that they could exit the place without some further incident occurring. He caught up with the others only because the barmaid had appeared out of nowhere, it seemed, and latched possessively onto James' arm, stopping him.

Anthony arrived to hear her demand, " 'Ere now, ye're not leavin', are ye?"

James, instead of brushing her off, gave her a smile to quite dazzle her. "I'll be back later, my dear."

She brightened, not even bothering to glance at the bundle under his arm. "I finish work at two."

"Then two it is."

"Two's one too many, I'm thinking." This from a brawny sailor who had stood up and was now blocking James' path to the door.

Anthony sighed, coming up to stand next to his brother. "I don't suppose you'd care to put her down and take care of this, James."

"Not particularly."

"I didn't think so."

"Stay out of this, mate," the sailor warned Anthony. "He's got no right coming in here and stealing not one but two of our women."

"Two? Is this little ragamuffin yours?" Anthony glanced at the bundle in dispute, who had pulled her wool cap up enough to see by and was peering at them with murder in her eyes. He was almost hesitant to put it to the test. "Are you his, sweetheart?"

She was wise enough to give a negative shake of her head. Fortunately, the sailor was an ugly-looking brute, or she might have given a different answer, she was so angry at the way she was being manhandled. Anthony couldn't blame her. James was holding on a bit tighter than necessary, and the position he had her in was far from dignified.

"I believe that settles it, doesn't it." It was not a question by any means. Anthony was tired of the whole affair, especially when he had no one to blame but himself for being there in the first place. "Now be a good chap and move out of the way."

Surprisingly, the sailor stood firm. "He's not taking her out of here."

"Oh, bloody hell," Anthony said wearily just before flattening his fist on the fellow's jaw.

The sailor landed several feet away from them, out cold. The man he had been sitting with rose from their table with a growl, but not soon enough. A short jab and he fell back in his chair, his hand flying up to stanch the blood now seeping from his nose.

Anthony turned around slowly, one black brow arched questioningly. "Any more comers?"

MacDonell was grinning behind him, realizing now how fortunate he had been not to take on the Englishman. Not another man in the room made a move to accept the challenge, drawing the same conclusion. It had happened too quickly. They recognized a skilled pugilist when they saw one.

"Very nicely done, dear boy," James congratulated him. "Now can we quit this place?"

Anthony bowed low, coming up with a grin. "After you, old man."

Outside, James set the girl on her feet in front of him. She got her first good look at him then in the glow of the tavern lamp above the door, enough to make her hesitate a hairbreadth before she kicked him in the shin and bolted down the street. He swore violently and started after her, but stopped after a few feet, seeing that it was useless. She was already out of sight on the darkened street.

He turned back, swearing again when he saw that MacDonell had disappeared as well. "Now where the bloody hell did the Scot go?"

Anthony was too busy laughing to have heard him. "What's that?"

James smiled tightly. "The Scot. He's gone."

Anthony sobered, turning around. "Well, that's gratitude for you. I wanted to ask him why they both turned when they heard the name Cameron."

"To hell with that," James snapped. "How am I going to find her again when I don't know who she is?"

"Find her?" Anthony was chuckling once more. "Gad, you're a glutton for punishment, brother. What do you want with a wench who insists on damaging your person when you have another one counting the minutes until you return?"

"She intrigued me," James replied simply, then shrugged. "But I suppose you're right. The little barmaid will do just as well." Yet he glanced down the empty street again before they headed toward the waiting carriage.

Chapter Twenty-five

Roslynn stood by the window in the parlor, her cheek pressed to the cool glass, her hands gripping the blue tasseled drapes next to her. She had stood like that for the past thirty minutes, ever since she had left the dining room and an uncomfortable dinner with Jeremy and his cousin Derek, who had come by to take the youngster out for the evening.

At least Derek Malory's arrival had proved a diversion for a while. The marquis' heir was a handsome young man about her own age, with an unruly thatch of blond hair and eyes more hazel than green. He cut quite a dashing figure in his evening togs, and it took Roslynn only half a minute to discover he was fast following in his uncles' footsteps—another rake for a family that had too many already. But there was still a certain boyish quality about Derek Malory that made him seem harmless and quite charming.

He reacted to the news of his uncle's marriage just as Jeremy had, at first with disbelief, then delight. He was also the first to call her Aunt Roslynn, and not in jest, giving her quite a start for a moment. She really was an aunt now, to a whole brood of nephews and nieces. An instant family, thanks to her marriage to Anthony, and a warm and loving one, if Jeremy was to be believed.

But Jeremy and Derek were gone now, and Roslynn had gone back to her brooding, hardly even aware that she had stood in the same spot for the past half hour, gazing out at the passing traffic on Piccadilly.

On the one hand, she was worried sick. Something had happened to Anthony. He was hurt, unable to get word to her. That was the only reason the whole day had gone by and she had heard nothing from him.

On the other hand, what had started as a slight irritation upon being abandoned, so to speak, had grown to a simmering anger as the hours dragged by, especially when Derek arrived and she couldn't explain Anthony's absence. He had simply gone about his business for the day without a by-your-leave, never mind that he had a wife now who might worry about him.

These conflicting feelings hadn't sat well together and had spoiled her appetite for the special dinner that she had held up for more than an hour, hoping Anthony would arrive in time. He hadn't, of course, and her anxiety was growing now, taking precedence over the anger, tying her belly up in knots.

Hell's teeth, where was he? This was only the second day of their marriage. Had he completely forgotten that fact? They should have spent the day together, getting to know each other better.

A carriage finally stopped in front of the house. Roslynn raced out of the room, waving Dobson away when he started for the door. She yanked it open herself before Anthony even reached it, and scanned his tall frame for injuries. There were none. He was all right. She wanted to hug him and clobber him at the same time. She stood there gripping her hands instead, to keep from giving in to either urge.

When Anthony spotted her, looking like a confection in a pale green gown with delicate white lace trim, his face lit up with a dazzling smile. "God, you're a sight for sore eyes, sweetheart. I can't tell you what a bloody rotten day I've had."

Roslynn didn't move so he could enter, but stood her ground in the center of the doorway. "Why dinna you tell me anyway?"

The brogue gave her away. He stepped back to get a better look at her and noted the mulish angle of jaw, the tightly compressed lips.

"Is something amiss, my dear?"

"Do you ken what time it is, mon?"

"Ah, so that's it." He chuckled. "Did you miss me, sweetheart?"

"Miss you?" she gasped. "Ye conceited toad! I dinna care if you go off for days at a time if that's your wont. But it's common courtesy, isna it, to be telling someone when they're no' to expect you home?"

"Yes, I suppose it is," he surprised her by agreeing. "And I'll be sure to remember that the next time I spend the day trying to track down your elusive cousin."

"Geordie? But—why?"

"Why else? To give him the good news. Or hadn't you realized that until he is made aware of your new status, he's still a danger to you?"

Roslynn could feel the blush starting, and it was a furious one. He was late on her behalf, and how did she meet him at the door? Like a shrew.

"I'm sorry, Anthony."

Her contrite, downcast look was irresistible. He pulled her close until her head rested on his shoulder. "Silly girl," he teased her gently. "You've nothing to be sorry about. I rather like having someone worry about me. You *were* worried, weren't you? That's why all the fuss?"

She nodded, having heard him, but she wasn't that attuned to what he was saying. Her nose was twitching, assaulted by an offensive, sweet smell coming from his coat, almost like . . . perfume, cheap perfume at that. She leaned back, frowning, and caught sight of a thin yellow string on his shoulder—no, not a string, a blond hair. She picked it off and pulled, but it kept coming, until at least a twelve-inch length dangled from her fingers. She might have thought it was her own, even though it was so light in color, but it was brittle, not fine.

"I knew it!" she hissed, looking up at him with outraged fury in her eyes.

"Knew what? What's got into you now?"

"This!" She shoved the hair in his face. "It's no' mine, mon, and it certainly isna yours, is it now?"

Anthony scowled, swiping the hair from her fingers. "It's not what you think, Roslynn."

She stood back, crossing her arms over her chest. "Oh? I suppose it was some brazen wench who just happened to plop down on your lap uninvited, rubbing her cheap smell all over you before you could be stopping her?"

Good God, he groaned inwardly, *did she have to hit it right on the nose?* "As a matter of fact—"

"Hell's teeth, you canna even make up your own tales!" she shrieked.

This was so ridiculous, it was laughable, but Anthony didn't dare laugh when her expression at the moment boded murder. Very calmly, he said, "Actually, it was a barmaid. And I wouldn't have been in a position to have found her tumbling into my lap if I wasn't in a tavern, one of many, mind you, looking for your cousin."

"Aye, put the blame on me for your unfaithfulness. That's typical of a mon's arrogance, isna it? But I'll be telling you what I'm to blame for, and that's believing you last night! I'll no' be making *that* mistake again!"

"Roslynn—"

She jumped back when he reached for her, and before he could stop her, she slammed the door in his face. Anthony swore foully, his temper finally unleashed, but with nothing to vent it on now.

He turned around, facing the empty street, gritting his teeth. At least James had gone on in the carriage to White's to kill a few hours before his rendezvous with self-same barmaid. He didn't think he could have borne having his brother be a witness to this absurdity and watching him laugh his head off as he reminded Anthony about marital bliss.

Bloody everlasting hell. Kicked out of his own house! A fine topping for a day that had gone from bad to worse. If the *ton* ever got wind . . .

Anthony's head came up with a jolt. It was *his* bloody house. What the devil did she think she was doing, kicking him out of his own house?

He swung around and started to kick the door, he was so angry. He thought better of that at the last moment and tried the latch first. But finding it unlocked, he threw it open forcefully. The resounding bang was satisfying; however, it did nothing to appease his temper. Nor did the fact that he caught his wife by surprise, halfway up the stairs.

"Get back down here, Lady Malory. We haven't finished this discussion."

He was amazed that she obeyed him immediately, coming stiffly down the stairs. But when she reached him, it was to give him a look of contempt.

"If you'll no' go away, then I will," she said, and she actually walked toward the still-open door.

Anthony caught her wrist and spun her around. "The devil you will! You aren't leaving this house, and neither am I. We're married, remember? Married people live together, last I heard."

"You canna make me stay here!"

"Can't I?"

He could, and it infuriated Roslynn more that she had given him that right.

She jerked her hand away from him, rubbing the wrist that would be bruised come morning. "Very well, but I'll be taking another room for myself, and if you've anything to say about that, you can save it for another time."

She turned back toward the stairs, only to be brought around again with a hand to her shoulder. "I prefer right now, my dear," he said darkly. "You're condemning me out of hand."

"You've brought the evidence home wi' you, mon. It speaks for itself."

His eyes closed in exasperation for a moment. "Even if that were true, which it isn't, you're not allowing me to speak in my own defense. Unfair, by any means."

"Unfair?" she retorted, eyes frying him. "I'm only saving you the trouble, because no matter what you say, I'd no' believe it now."

Again she tried to turn away. Again he jerked her back. "Confound you, woman, I was looking for Cameron!"

"Maybe you were, but you made a wee detour too. So be it. I gave you leave."

He was ready to pull hairs at this point. "Then why are you raising bloody hell about it?"

"You lied to me! You tried to make me believe it'd be otherwise, and for that I'll no' forgive you!"

She turned away in a huff. His voice stopped her this time, deliberately taunting. "Go ahead, and I'll turn you over my knee."

"You wouldna dare!"

His eyes had narrowed to mere slits. "At the moment, sweetheart, I assure you it would be a pleasure. Now, I'm going to tell you this only once. Whether you believe it or not, I frankly no longer care. The little wench who crawled all over me was just doing her job. She made the offer, I refused it. There was no more to it than that."

With icy control, Roslynn demanded haughtily, "Are you finished?"

After her repeated attempts to do so, it was Anthony who turned and walked away.

Chapter Twenty-six

Roslynn cried herself to sleep that night, the first time she had done so since she was a little girl. That Anthony didn't even try to disturb her in the new room she had moved to was a relief, and yet for some reason she cried the harder. She hated him, never wanted to see him again, but she was stuck with him.

If only she wasn't such a naive little fool. But she had let him convince her that they could have a normal marriage, and now she was paying for her gullibility, with resentment she couldn't seem to help feeling and with a bitterness that was wholly unfamiliar to her. For a few hours that morning she had been in heavenly bliss, which made coming back down to earth so much harder to bear. She wouldn't forgive him for that, for her lost chance at happiness.

Why couldn't he just leave things as they were? Why did he have to give her hope, then turn right around and dash it to bits?

Nettie, not having to be told what happened, since the whole household couldn't help but hear the loud argument, had wisely kept her mouth shut while helping Roslynn change rooms. The next morning, she had cold compresses ready to apply to swollen eyes, again without comment, bless her. And Roslynn's eyes were rather puffy. Chalk up another point against the cur. He was ruining her appearance.

But Nettie's herbal solution erased all evidence of the miserable night her mistress had spent. Too bad she didn't have a magic tonic for what ailed Roslynn inside. Yet when she came downstairs in a sunny yellow dress to counteract her mood, it was virtually impossible to tell that she was still a boiling pot of emotions, none of them good, which was fortunate, since she walked unawares into a parlor full of Malorys, by the looks of them, minus her husband, thank God.

So it had started. Gad, at what a time, when she didn't know if she could bear the sight of Anthony today. And she had no idea what sort of mood he would be in when he came down. He could very well give their troubles away, but she wasn't going to.

She formed a welcoming smile. Just because she wasn't able to get on well with her husband didn't mean she had to be at odds with the rest of the family.

James was the first to notice her entrance and rose immediately to make the introductions. "Good morning, dear girl. As you can see, the elders have arrived to look you over. My brothers Jason and Edward— the blushing bride."

Jason was scowling already, but at James' choice of words. Both men were big, blond, and green-eyed, with Edward the stockier of the two. Jason appeared an older version of James, serious, even to having that aura of ruthlessness about him. Edward was the exact opposite, as she was to learn, good-humored, easygoing, certainly jolly, but staid where business was concerned.

Both men rose, Edward to give Roslynn a hearty hug; Jason, more reserved, bringing her hand to his lips. Jeremy, who didn't need another introduction, simply winked at her. Thank goodness he and James hadn't been home last night to overhear that embarrassing scene in the hall.

"You can't know what a pleasure this is, my dear," Jason was saying, giving her a warm smile as he led her to the sofa to sit next to him. "I had despaired of Tony ever marrying."

"Didn't think the lad had it in him to settle down," Edward added jovially. "Delighted to be proved wrong, though. Simply delighted."

Roslynn didn't know what to say to that, under the circumstances, because Anthony was anything but ready to settle down. But they wanted to believe he was, obviously, so she wouldn't set the record straight on that score. However, she couldn't let them think this was some sort of love match either. It certainly wasn't that by any means.

She began to speak hesitantly. "There were reasons why we married that you should be aware of—"

"Already know, my dear," Edward interrupted. "Reggie's filled us in about your cousin. Doesn't matter, you know. If Tony wasn't ready, he wouldn't have taken the plunge."

"He did it to help me," Roslynn said, only to get three doubting-Thomas smiles, making her insist, "Well, he did."

"Rubbish," Jason replied. "Tony's not the sort to play hero, saving damsels and all that."

"Just the opposite." Edward chuckled.

James added his opinion. "One has only to look at you, dear girl, to know what motivated the lad. Can't say as I blame him in the least."

Jason intercepted the wolfish grin bestowed on Roslynn that had her cheeks blooming. "None of that, now." He scowled at James.

"Oh, give over, Jason. She became safe from me the moment she married."

"Since when did that ever stop you?" Jason demanded brusquely.

"True." James shrugged. "But I draw the line at seducing sisters-in-laws."

Roslynn had no way of knowing this was only bantering. But then she had no way of knowing that these brothers were happiest when they were arguing, even in jest.

"My lords, please," she intervened. "I'm sure James meant no offense."

"There, you see, old man," James said smugly to his brother. "She knew not to take me seriously. What's a look, anyway?"

"Usually an extension of one's true feelings," Jason retorted, still scowling.

"Ah, but never mine. I find it much more amusing not to give myself away so obviously—as you do, brother."

Edward laughed. "He's got you there, Jason. You do look rather fierce at the moment."

"Yes," James agreed, rubbing it in. "You look fierce enough to make the newest member of the family think *you're* serious."

Jason's brow smoothed out as he glanced at Roslynn. "I'm sorry, my dear. What must you think of—"

"That you're a tyrant, and she wouldn't be far off the mark," James couldn't resist saying, even if it did bring Jason's narrowed gaze back to him.

"Not at all," Roslynn intervened again. "I'm an only child myself, so it's . . . interesting, seeing how a large family interacts together. But tell me, who in the family is the referee?"

The question brought hearty laughter, more than she had hoped for. It transformed James, making him even more handsome, if that were possible. It softened the lines on Jason's face too, showing her he was still a devilishly good-looking man at forty-six and not nearly as intimidating as he had seemed. Edward, it just made more lovable. Gad, these Malorys were dangerous to a girl's equilibrium. And, heaven help her, she had married one.

"I told you she was a gem," James said to his brothers. "Has Tony met his match or hasn't he?"

"It would seem so," Edward agreed, wiping the tears of laughter from his eyes. "But I thought you said she was Scottish. I detect no brogue."

A quiet voice from the doorway answered before James could. "It comes with a temper, in moments least expected."

James couldn't let that one pass. "You know from experience, no doubt?"

"No doubt at all," Anthony replied, looking directly at his wife.

Roslynn's fingers clenched into fists, her reaction to seeing him there, oh, so casually leaning a shoulder against the doorframe, arms crossed, one knee bent to cross his feet at his ankles. How dared he? So he wanted to play with words, did he?

She gave Anthony a syrupy sweet smile as she took up the challenge. "Dinna fash yourself, mon. I only hold grudges when they're truly deserved."

James twisted the knife. "Well, then, you've nothing to worry about, Tony, have you?"

"When *does* your ship sail, brother?" was Anthony's retort, gaining a hoot of laughter from James.

The two older brothers and Jeremy came forward then, offering congratulations and good-natured ribbings. Roslynn watched this happy scene, fuming. So he was going to pretend nothing was wrong, was he? Well, she could too, she supposed, as long as his family was here, and as long as he kept his distance from her. But he didn't. He joined her on the sofa, taking Jason's place, and put his arm around her shoulder in a too-husbandly fashion.

"Pleasant night, sweetheart?"

"Go to the devil," she hissed under her breath, but she was smiling as she said it.

Anthony chuckled, managing to keep from wincing when the effort nearly split his head open. He had a royal hangover, thanks to his little wife's stubbornness last night. He would have preferred to simply remain in bed, but couldn't after Willis informed him the elders had arrived. Bloody inconvenient. He couldn't very well have it out with Roslynn with an audience present.

What he should have done was finish it last night. But, fool that he was, he had thought a night's sleep would make her more receptive to reason, and so he had gotten smashed to keep him from breaking her door down. He should have broken the door down. She was nursing her grudge anyway, so it couldn't have made her any angrier. Bloody hell. He'd like to shoot the man who ever said women were malleable creatures.

For the moment, Anthony chose to ignore his wife, but perversely, he kept his arm around her. "So, Eddie, where's the rest of your brood?"

"They'll be along as soon as Charlotte can round them all up. By the by, she wants to give you and Roslynn a party, since we missed the wedding. Nothing too big, mind you. Just family and friends."

"Why not?" Anthony agreed. "Might as well spread some of our happiness around."

He smiled to himself as he heard Roslynn choke.

Chapter Twenty-seven

"I came by yesterday, you know, but you had so many guests—"

"So you just left?" Roslynn stopped buttering her muffin to stare pointedly at Frances. "I wish you hadn't."

"I didn't want to intrude."

"Fran, it was just his family, come by to meet me and wish him well. You would have been welcome, believe me, especially by me. Can you imagine how alone I felt, meeting the whole Malory clan?"

Frances said nothing for a moment. She took a sip of tea, fooled with the napkin on her lap, played with the pastry on her plate that she hadn't touched. Roslynn watched her, holding her breath. She knew what was coming, what hadn't been said yet. She was dreading it, especially now, when she was so regretting her hasty marriage to Anthony. And this was the first she had seen Frances since that marriage. When she had stopped by unexpectedly this morning, just as Roslynn was sitting down to breakfast, she knew she would be eating a dose of censure along with the cook's tempting array of food.

She tried delaying the subject. "I hope you weren't too worried the other night." Hell's teeth, was it only four days ago that she had woken up in Geordie's clutches?

"Too worried?" Frances laughed bitterly. "You were taken from my own house. I was responsible!"

"That you weren't. Geordie was just too tricky for us. But I hope you understand why I had to leave before you got back."

"Yes, that I understand. You couldn't stay with me after he had discovered your whereabouts. But that note you sent me two days ago.

That I'll never understand. How could you do it, Ros? Anthony Malory, of all men?"

Well, there it was, the question she had dreaded, the same one she had been asking herself. The answers just didn't hold up, at least not for her, but she owed them to Frances.

"The night Nettie and I left, I stopped by here to see Anthony."

"You didn't!"

Roslynn flinched. "I know I shouldn't have, but I did. You see, he had offered to help me when we were at Silverley. Regina's husband didn't know my gentlemen that well after all, but Anthony did. He was supposed to clarify certain rumors about them—well, anyway, after that run-in with Geordie, I had run out of time. I came here for a name, nothing else, just a name of the one man out of the five who was most suitable for me to propose to."

"All right. That's reasonable, I suppose, even if highly improper," Frances conceded. "You were frightened, upset. You couldn't have been thinking very clearly that night. So how could it have gone wrong? How did you end up with Sir Anthony instead?"

"He lied to me," Roslynn said simply, her eyes fixed on the uneaten muffin still in her hand. "He convinced me that all five of my gentlemen were so unsuitable, I couldn't possibly marry one of them. Oh, you should have heard some of the horrid stories he invented, the regret he managed in the telling. I never once suspected that he might be lying."

"Then how do you know—"

Roslynn laughed shortly. "He admitted it later, after we were married. Arrogantly confessed the whole thing."

"The cad!"

"Yes, he is that." Roslynn sighed. "But that's not the point. That night I was already desperate when I came here, and then to be told that I was more or less back to the starting point, well, I truly didn't know what to do."

"So you asked him to marry you." Frances drew her own conclusion. "Well, at least I understand now—or think I do. I suppose you felt you had no other choice."

"That's not exactly how it happened," Roslynn admitted, though she decided then and there not to mention her seduction. Frances didn't need to know *everything*. "Even then I didn't consider Anthony as a solution to my problem. Hell's teeth, I was ready to go home to Scotland and marry a crofter. It was Anthony who suggested I marry him instead."

Frances' mouth dropped open. "*He* did?" She collected herself quickly from her surprise. "Well, I naturally thought you would have . . . I mean, you did say before that you wouldn't be afraid to make the proposal, that it would probably be necessary since you had so little time for courting. And here you had run out of time, so I naturally assumed . . . He really did?"

"Yes, and I was just as surprised. In fact, I thought he was joking."

"But he wasn't?"

"No, not at all. I refused, of course."

Frances' mouth dropped open again. "You did?"

"Yes, and went on to Silverley." Frances didn't need to know this had happened the next morning. "But as you can see, I changed my mind. He was offering me a solution, and I decided to treat it as a business arrangement. I still haven't figured out why he did it, but there you have it, the whole story." Less the parts Roslynn couldn't bring herself to mention.

Frances sat back, herself again. "Well, I just hope you don't come to regret it. For your sake, I'll pray for a miracle, that Sir Anthony might somehow turn out to be another Nicholas Eden."

"Good God, bite your tongue, madam," Anthony said as he casually sauntered into the room. "I can barely tolerate the fellow."

Poor Frances turned beet red. Roslynn glared furiously at her husband. "Taken to eavesdropping, my lord?"

"Not at all." He smiled at her, belying the denial. "So the reinforcements have arrived, eh?"

He had Roslynn blushing now as he looked pointedly at Frances with that question. She was remembering that all day yesterday, every time he had tried to talk to her, she had moved off to speak with a member of his family, all of whom had stayed for dinner and much later, giving her excuses to avoid him the whole day. Now they still weren't alone, only this time the visitor was firmly in her camp. His use of the word "reinforcements" was apt, though Frances didn't know what he was referring to.

"You're on your way out?" Roslynn asked hopefully.

"Actually, I'm off to continue the hunt for your dear cousin."

"Oh? And another detour?" She jabbed for blood. "Then I'll see you—when I see you, I suppose."

Anthony braced his hands on the table across from her, leaning forward, his eyes dark with meaning as they locked with hers. "You will *see* me this evening, my dear. You may depend upon it." And then he straightened, his smile tight. "Good day, ladies. You may continue raking me over the coals now."

He turned on his heel and sauntered out as nonchalantly as he had entered, leaving Roslynn bristling and Frances uncomfortably aware that much more had just transpired than was said. But as quietly as he had left the room, he slammed out of the house.

Roslynn grimaced, hearing the noise. Frances raised a questioning brow. "He's displeased about something?"

"You could say that."

"So are you?"

"Frances, I really don't want to talk about it."

"That bad, eh? Well, all I can say is you agreed to this marriage, knowing what he was like. I don't imagine he'll be an easy man to live with, but you must make the best of it. Just don't expect too much."

That was laughable. She hadn't expected a thing, until Anthony had deluded her into thinking he could change. And not twenty-four hours' married and he proved he couldn't. She could have understood a month later, or even a week, but the very next day after he swore he wanted no one but her? The trouble was, she couldn't seem to break through the anger to get back to her original reconcilement to take him as he was.

Anthony's thoughts were simmering along the same lines as he threw himself into the waiting carriage outside. He had every right to be furious and he was, immeasurably so. A business arrangement! He'd like to know what the bloody hell he was to get out of this "business arrangement" as it stood now.

Stubborn, unreasonable, vexing woman. And illogical, for God's sake. If she'd just use some common sense, she'd see how absurd her accusations were. But no, she wouldn't even talk to him about it. Every time he had tried yesterday, she had bestowed her false smile on him and flitted away, using his own family as a barrier against him. And they loved her. And why not? She was charming, intelligent—except in some matters—and beautiful, and they looked on her as his salvation. More likely she was the devil's advocate, sent to drive him mad.

Well, he'd be doubly damned if he'd lose another night's sleep over the contrariness of his wife. She belonged in his bed, not nursing her foolish grudges across the hall. Tonight they'd talk, by God, and without interruption.

Now, how to word a message to James, to suggest he take himself and Jeremy off for the evening, without telling him why?

Chapter Twenty-eight

A while after Frances left, Jeremy came in with a stack of newspapers and a jaunty smile, telling Roslynn the notice would run for two weeks. She found it in each paper, the announcement of her marriage, but she had to admit that Anthony was right in this matter. There was no guarantee that Geordie would see it. So she couldn't help feeling grateful that, even though Anthony was annoyed with her, he was still making an effort to find Geordie to warn him off.

She might be safely married, but if Geordie didn't know it, then how safe was she really? He could at this very moment be working on a new scheme to snatch her and drag her to the altar. He knew where she was—at least he knew that her clothes had come to this address. And if he succeeded in abducting her again, and she had to be the one to tell him he was too late, well, there was no telling what he might do to her in his anger at being thwarted.

Because of that, she elected to stay close to home for a while. Any remodeling she was planning could be done by having the tradesmen come to her, rather than her going to them. And she did plan extensive redecorating of Anthony's house. Nor was she going to bother to tell him about it. And when he saw the damage to his purse, because she had changed her mind about paying for it herself and intended to use only his money, well, he might think twice before getting in her bad graces again with more lies.

A wee voice whispered that she was being wickedly spiteful. Roslynn didn't listen to it. She was going to spend Anthony's money as if he were made of it. She might even insist he build her a new house, a mansion in the country perhaps, but after she had redecorated this one, of course. After all, the town house wasn't that large. It didn't even have a ballroom. How was she expected to entertain?

She could even pauperize the wretched man if she were of a mind to. Yes, there was an idea worth considering. A picture of Anthony humbled and having to come to her for an allowance was delightful indeed, and no more than he deserved for disillusioning her.

But Roslynn didn't devote too much time to vengeful thoughts today, not with Anthony's implied threat hanging over her head that there would be a confrontation between them tonight. She couldn't deny that worried her no small amount. And her nervousness increased during the afternoon, so much so that when James informed her during dinner that he and Jeremy were off to Vauxhall Gardens for the evening, she almost asked to join them. Why tonight of all nights did they both have to go out, never mind that this was the norm rather than the exception? Even though Anthony wasn't home yet, she didn't doubt for a minute that he would show up eventually.

But she didn't ask to intrude on the two Malorys who were still bachelors. She wasn't that much of a coward. At least that was what she told herself before James and Jeremy left. Nevertheless, as soon as the door closed behind the dashing pair, leaving her alone with the servants, Anthony's servants—Nettie didn't count—she found she was a coward after all.

It was a ridiculously early hour to be retiring for the night, but retreat to her bedroom she did, and with all haste. Dobson was told to inform Anthony when he finally came in that she wasn't feeling well and wasn't to be disturbed, for any reason. Whether that would put him off remained to be seen.

In case it didn't, however, she wasn't taking any chances. She donned her most unappealing nightgown, a heavy cotton garment more suitable for a cold Scottish winter in the Highlands, stuck her hair under an ugly nightcap that she borrowed from Nettie, never having liked the use of them herself, and finished her ensemble with a bulky robe that she usually wore only after her bath.

She also considered putting one of Nettie's thick night creams on her face, but that would be doing it up a bit too much. A glance in the mirror showed her that she looked appalling as it was. Anything more would just be obvious arsenal that Anthony might find funny instead of discouraging.

Of course, now that she was so bundled up, she was too warm for bedcovers. But that was just as well. Curled up with a book would be a more natural touch, rather than pretending sleep, which Anthony would likely doubt if he arrived while it was still so early.

No, she had to appear normally indisposed, as if she weren't trying to deliberately avoid him. He would then have to give her the benefit of the doubt and leave her alone. That was, if he didn't heed Dobson's message. That was, if he came home at all.

Hell's teeth, none of this would be necessary if Dobson had been able to find the cursed key to the door yesterday when she had asked for it. But then, might not locking Anthony out be taken as a challenge by someone like him? It would certainly be a clear statement that she didn't want to talk to him, not now, not any time soon. No, this way was better. Let him come, if he must, but she would make him feel guilty as hell for disturbing her when she was feeling, and looking, so poorly.

The book she had on hand was a boring collection of sonnets, gushy in sentimentality, left behind by the previous occupant of the room, whoever that had been. But she was stuck with it. It was too late to risk going down to Anthony's study, where a small library was kept. It would be just her luck that he would walk in and catch her out of bed, ruining the effect she was striving for.

She gave up reading the silly book, however. At any other time she might have been enthralled, for love sonnets, which she surmised most of them were as she flipped through the pages, usually sparked a tender chord in her. But she was in no frame of mind to be romantic tonight. Anything but. She let her mind wander instead, wondering if she ought to allow her malady to last through tomorrow. She could use the time alone to think, to get in control of her emotions again.

Fortunately, Roslynn was still holding the book in front of her and appeared to be reading, because she had no warning that Anthony had returned. The door to her room simply opened and he was there. Unfortunately, he wasn't so easily fooled.

"Very amusing, my dear." His tone was dry, his expression inscrutable. "Did it take all day to think this up, or were you inspired when the Hawke and his pup deserted you?"

Since she had no idea what he was talking about in reference to birds and dogs, she ignored the question altogether. "I asked not to be disturbed."

"I know you did, sweetheart." He shut the door, his smile unnerving. "But a husband is allowed to disturb his wife—anytime, anywhere, any way he wants to."

He was putting another meaning on the word, one that had her cheeks flaming, which he was quick to note. "Ah, it must be a fever," he continued, coming slowly toward the bed. "And no wonder, with that mountain of nightclothes you're wearing. Or is it a cold? No, you haven't bothered to redden your nose with a little pinching. A headache, then, of course. You don't need to produce visible symptoms to claim one, do you?"

His baiting enraged her beyond good sense. "Beast! If I did have one, you wouldn't care, would you?"

"Oh, I don't know." He sat down on the bed, fingering the tie of her robe. His smile was more humorous now that she had given up her ruse. "Do you have one?"

"Yes!"

"Liar."

"I'm learning from a master."

He laughed. "Very good, my dear. I was wondering how I was going to introduce the subject, but you've done it for me."

"What subject?"

"What indeed. Are we going to play dumb now?"

"*We* aren't going to play anything. *You're* going to leave this room."

Of course he didn't. That would have been too much to hope for. He sat back, leaning on one elbow, infuriating her with his quiet scrutiny.

Suddenly he leaned forward and snatched her nightcap away. "That's better." He twirled the cap on his finger as he gazed at the red-gold locks scattered about her shoulders. "You know how I love your hair. I suppose you hid it just to annoy me?"

"You flatter yourself."

"Maybe," he said softly. "And maybe I've known enough women to know how their minds work when they turn vindictive for some supposed wrong. Cold food, cold shoulders, and cold beds. Well, you've served me up all but the food, but I suppose that will come."

She threw the book at him. He dodged it handily.

"If you want to get violent, sweetheart, you've certainly caught me in the right mood for it. In fact, if I had found Cameron today, I think I'd have shot the bastard first and asked questions later. So don't press your luck."

He said it too quietly for her to take him seriously. She was too caught up in her own enraged passions to realize that she'd never seen Anthony like this. He was calm. He was in control. He was furious. She just didn't know it.

"Will you just get out?" she demanded shrilly. "I'm no' ready to talk to you yet, mon!"

"So I see." He threw her nightcap across the room. "But I don't particularly care whether you're ready or not, my dear."

She gasped when he reached for her. Her hands flew up to hold him back. Her action worked only because he allowed it—for the moment.

"Recall the first condition of this marriage, Roslynn. I'm to get you with child, at your own insistence. I agreed to do just that."

"You also agreed to the second condition, and you've done that too. It's the lying that came after that has changed things, mon."

She didn't doubt that he was angry now. It was there in the hard glint of his eyes, the clenched jaw. He was a different man, a frightening man—a fascinating man. He stirred something in her that was primitive, unrecognizable. Shouting she could have dealt with. But this? She didn't know what he would do, what he was capable of, but a part of her wanted to find out.

But Anthony was angry, not crazy. And that spark of desire that flashed in her eyes as she pushed away from him mollified him to a degree. She still wanted him. Even in her fury, she still wanted him. Assured of that, he found he could wait until she got over her pique. It wouldn't be a pleasant wait, but he wasn't about to have her crying rape come morning, putting him right back where he started, only with another grudge for her to hold against him.

"You really should have pinched your nose, my dear. I might have believed that."

Roslynn blinked, doubting her ears. "Oh!"

She shoved against him with all her might. He obliged her by leaving the bed. But his smile was tight as he stared down at her.

"I've been patient, but I give you fair warning. A man's patience is a fickle thing. It shouldn't be tested too often, especially when he's got nothing to apologize for and nothing to feel guilty about—yet."

"Hah!"

Anthony ignored that as he walked to the door. "It might help if you told me how long you intend to punish me."

"I'm not punishing you," she insisted stonily.

"Aren't you, sweetheart?" He turned to chill her with a parting shot. "Well, just remember that two can play this game."

What he might have meant by that bothered Roslynn for the rest of the night.

Chapter Twenty-nine

A jab. Another jab. A left hook, followed by a right cross. The man was down, out cold, and Anthony stood back, swearing because it was over too quickly.

Knighton tossed a towel in his face, swearing too as he jumped into the ring to examine Anthony's partner. "Jesus, Malory! No wonder Billy tried to beg off today after he got one look at you. I always say the ring's a nice place to work out frustrations, but not for you."

"Shut up, Knighton," Anthony snapped as he tore off his gloves.

"The hell I will," the older man shot back angrily. "I'd like to know where I'm going to find another bloke stupid enough to step into the ring with you. But I'll tell you this. I ain't even going to bother looking until you've bedded the wench and got it out of your system. Stay out of my ring until you do."

Anthony had laid men flat for less, but Knighton was a friend. He nearly laid him flat anyway for his bloody insight in calling it too close to the mark. He stood there, the urge overpowering. It was James' voice, breaking into the haze of his rage, that checked him.

"Having trouble finding partners again, Tony?"

"Not if you're still willing to oblige me."

"Do I look like a fool?" James glanced down at his apparel in mock surprise. "And here I thought I was done up quite smartly today."

Anthony laughed, feeling some of his tension drain away. "As if you didn't think you could make short work of me."

"Well, of course I could. No doubt a-tall. Just don't want to."

Anthony snorted, started to remind James of the going-over Montieth had given him, even if James did come out the winner, but changed his mind. No point in putting it to the test when he had no quarrel with his brother.

"I get the impression you're following me, old man. Any particular reason?"

"As a matter of fact, I've a bone to pick—outside of the ring, of course."

Anthony jumped down, reaching for his coat. "Mind if we get out of here first?"

"Come on. I'll buy you a drink."

"Make it more than one and you're on."

The afternoon atmosphere in White's was quiet, soothing, a place to relax, read the dailies, conduct business, discuss politics, gossip, or get drunk, as Anthony contemplated doing, all without the disruptive presence of women, who were not allowed. The lunch crowd was gone, leaving only the regulars, who lived more at the club than at home. The dinner crowd and serious gamblers had yet to arrive, though there were a few games of whist in progress.

"Who kept up my membership all these years?" James asked as they took seats away from the bow window before which the fashionable set would soon be gathering.

"You mean you're still a member? And here I thought you were getting in as my guest."

"Very amusing, dear boy. But I know bloody well Jason and Eddie boy wouldn't have bothered."

Anthony frowned at being cornered. "So I'm a sentimental ass. It's only a few guineas a year, for God's sake. I just didn't want to see your name stricken from the list."

"Or you were certain I'd come back into the fold eventually?"

Anthony shrugged. "There was that, not to mention a bloody long waiting list to get in. Didn't want to see you deserting us for Brook's."

"Malory!" Anthony was hailed and descended upon by a red-cheeked fellow of his acquaintance. "Stopped by your house yesterday, but Dobson said you were out. Wanted to clear up a little wager I have with Hilary. She saw this notice in the paper. You'll never believe it, Malory. It said you'd married. 'Course I knew it couldn't be you. Had to be some other chap, same name. I'm right, aren't I? Tell me it's a bloody coincidence."

Anthony's fingers tightened around his glass, but other than that, there was no inkling that he was bothered by the question. "It's a bloody coincidence," he replied.

"I knew it!" the fellow crowed. "Wait till I tell Hilary. The easiest five pounds I've won from her in a long time."

"Was that wise?" James asked as soon as red-cheeks drifted away. "Imagine the disagreements it's going to cause when he claims to have it from your own lips that you're not married. There'll be fights with those who know better."

"What the hell do I care?" Anthony snarled. "When I feel like I'm married, I'll admit I'm married."

James sat back, a small smile playing about his lips. "So the 'bemoanment' has begun, has it?"

"Oh, shut up." Anthony downed his drink and left to get another. He came back with a bottle. "I thought you had a bone to pick with me. Pick away. It seems to be becoming a habit."

James let the more interesting discovery pass for the moment. "Very well. Jeremy tells me Vauxhall was your idea, not his. If you'd wanted to be rid of us for the evening, why go through the lad?"

"Didn't you enjoy yourselves?"

"That's beside the point. I don't like being manipulated, Tony."

"But that's precisely why I sent the message to the lad." Anthony grinned. "You've admitted how hard it is for you to deny him anything, now that you've become such a doting parent."

"Bloody hell. You could have just asked me. Am I so insensitive that I can't appreciate that you might want to spend an evening alone with your new wife?"

"Come off it, James. You're about as sensitive as a dead tree. If I had asked you to leave last night, you'd have stayed just to see why I wanted you gone."

"Would I?" James' smile came grudgingly. "Yes, I suppose I would. I'd have envisioned you and the little Scot running about the house bare-ass naked, and you'd never have been able to get rid of me. Wouldn't have missed that for the world. So what was it, actually, that you wanted privacy for?"

Anthony poured another drink. "It doesn't matter now. The evening didn't end as I had hoped."

"So there *is* trouble in paradise?"

Anthony slammed the bottle down on the small table next to his chair, exploding. "You wouldn't believe what she's accused me of! Bedding that little twit of a barmaid we met the other night!"

"Careful, lad. I've fond memories of Margie."

"Then you did meet her later?"

"Did you doubt I would, a pretty piece like that? Though the little vixen in breeches would have done . . . never mind." James poured himself another drink, disturbed by the regret he felt at losing that one. "Why didn't you just tell your lady I'd marked the girl for myself? I mean, we've shared women before, but there's something unsavory about sharing in the same day, don't you think?"

"True, but my dear wife wouldn't put any unsavory deed beyond my capabilities. And I resent being put in a position of having to explain that I've done nothing wrong. I shouldn't have to do that. A little trust wouldn't be amiss."

James sighed. "Tony, lad, you've a lot to learn about new brides."

"You've had one, have you, which makes you an expert?" Anthony sneered.

"Of course not," James retorted. "But common sense would tell you it's got to be a very delicate time for a woman. She's feeling her way, adjusting. She's devilish insecure, nervous. Trust? Hah! First impressions are more likely to be the lasting ones. Stands to reason, don't it?"

"It stands to reason you don't know what the deuce you're talking about. When's the last time you even bumped elbows with a lady of quality? Captain Hawke's tastes lean toward a different sort entirely."

"Not *entirely,* lad. Leading a band of brigands does have its drawbacks, mainly in the lower class of establishments one is limited to frequenting. And acquired habits are hard to break. But my tastes, as you put it, are no different from yours. Duchess or whore, as long as she's comely and willing, she'll do. And it hasn't been *that* many years that I can't remember the idiosyncrasies of the duchess. Besides, they're all the same in one respect, dear boy. Jealousy turns them into shrews."

"Jealousy?" Anthony said blankly.

"Well, good God, man, isn't that the problem?"

"I hadn't thought . . . well, now that you mention it, that could be why she's so unreasonable. She's so bloody angry, she won't even talk about it."

"So Knighton was right." James' chuckle turned into an outright laugh. "Where's your finesse gone, dear boy? You've had enough practice in these matters to know how to get around—"

"Look who's talking," Anthony cut in irritably. "The same man who got his shin kicked the other night. Where was the Hawke's finesse—"

"Blister it, Tony," James growled. "If you keep bandying that name about, I'm going to end up with a rope around my neck yet. Hawke's dead. Kindly remember that."

Anthony's mood improved, now that his brother's had taken a turn for the worse. "Relax, old man. These chaps wouldn't know a hawk from a Hawke. But point taken. Since you've gone to the trouble of killing him off, we may as well let him rest in peace. But you never said, you know. What happened to the rest of your brigands?"

"Some went their own way. Some formed an attachment for the *Maiden Anne,* even though she's changed her colors. They're land-locked only till we sail."

"And when, pray tell, will that be?"

"Relax, old man." James tossed the phrase back at him. "I'm having too much fun watching you make a mess of your life to leave just yet."

Chapter Thirty

It was five o'clock in the afternoon when George Amherst assisted the two Malory brothers out of the carriage in front of the brownstone-faced house on Piccadilly, and they did need assistance. George was smiling and had been ever since he came upon the two in White's and smoothed over the disturbance they'd caused. He couldn't help it. He'd never seen Anthony so foxed he didn't know if he was coming or going. And James, well, it was utterly comical to see this intimidating Malory laughing his head off over Anthony's condition when his own was anything but sober.

"She's not going to like this," James was saying as he hooked an arm around Anthony's shoulders, nearly unbalancing them both.

"Who?" Anthony demanded belligerently.

"Your wife."

"Wife?"

George grabbed Anthony as the brothers began to sway and steered them to the door. "Splendid!" He chuckled. "You nearly get yourself kicked out of White's for decking Billings when all he did was offer felicitations on your marriage, and here you can't remember you've got a wife."

George was still getting used to the idea himself. He had been rendered speechless when Anthony had come by his house yesterday morning to tell him personally, before he read about it in the papers.

"One laugh, George . . . one little chuckle . . . and I'll rearrange your nose for you," Anthony had told him with appalling sincerity. "I was out of my mind. That's the only excuse for it. So no congratulations, if you please. Condolences are more in order."

Then he had refused to say another word about it, not who she was or why he'd married her, nor a hint about why he was already regretting it. But George wasn't so sure he was actually regretting it, not when Anthony had dragged him off on a search for this cousin of hers who was some sort of danger to her. The desire to protect her was obvious. The desire not to talk about her was equally as obvious. Most obvious was Anthony's anger, simmering just below the surface all day. George was bloody well relieved they hadn't found the chap Anthony was looking for. He would have hated to see the result if they had.

But a chance remark from James as George was hustling them out of White's put some perspective on the thing. "You've just found a temper to match your own, Tony. Can't say as it's a bad thing in a wife. It'll keep you on your toes, if nothing else." And he had laughed, even when Anthony snarled back, "When you get one of your own, brother, I hope she's as sweet as that little viper who kicked you instead of thanking you for your help the other night."

The door opened just as George was about to pound on it. A wooden-faced Dobson stood there, but the butler's expression relaxed into aggrieved surprise as James abandoned Anthony for a steadier handhold—Dobson.

"Where's Willis, dear fellow? I'm going to need help with my boots, I think."

That wasn't all he would need help with, George thought, grinning, as the skinny Dobson, saying nothing, tried to get the much larger man to the stairs. George was having trouble holding Anthony up as well.

"You'd better call some footmen, Dobson," George suggested.

"I'm afraid," Dobson puffed without looking back, "they're on errands for the mistress, my lord."

"Bloody hell." Anthony perked up, hearing that. "What's she doing dispatching—"

George poked him in the ribs to shut him up. The lady in question had come out of the parlor and stood with hands on hips and an unpleasant gleam in her hazel eyes, which moved over them all. George swallowed hard. *This* was Anthony's wife? Gad, she was breathtaking—and furious.

"Beg pardon, Lady Malory," George offered hesitantly. "I found these two rather deep in their cups. Thought it prudent to get them home to sleep it off."

"And who are you, sir?" Roslynn asked stonily.

George didn't get a chance to answer. Anthony, fixing his gaze on his wife, sneered, "Oh, come now, my dear, you must know old George. He's the very chap responsible for your distrust of the male gender."

George flushed hotly as her eyes narrowed with a distinct golden glow on him. "Blister it, Malory," he hissed, throwing Anthony's arm off his shoulder. "I'll leave you to the tender mercies of your wife. No more than you deserve after that crack." Not that he understood it, but that was no way to introduce one's best friend to one's wife.

To Roslynn, George nodded. "Another time, Lady Malory, hopefully under better circumstances." And he departed angrily, not even bothering to close the door.

Anthony stared after him, bemused and unsuccessfully trying to keep his balance in the middle of the hall. "Was it something I said, George?"

James laughed so hard at that, he and Dobson fell back two steps on the stairs. "You're amazing, Tony. Either you don't remember at all, or you remember more than you should."

Anthony rounded about to stare at James, halfway up the stairs now. His "What the deuce does that mean?" got only another laugh.

When it looked as if Anthony was going to fall flat on his face, Roslynn rushed forward, dragging his arm about her neck, and putting her own around his waist. "I canna believe you've done this, mon," she gritted out, maneuvering him carefully across the hall. "Do you ken what time of day it is, to be coming home like this?"

"Certainly," he replied indignantly. "It's—it's . . . well, whatever time it is, where else would I come home to, except to my own home?"

He tripped on the bottom step, pulling Roslynn down with him to sprawl at the foot of the stairs. "Hell's teeth! I ought to leave you here!"

Anthony misunderstood in his befuddled state. His arm whipped around her, holding her so tight against his chest she couldn't breathe. "You're not leaving me, Roslynn. I won't allow it."

She stared at him incredulously. "You . . . oh, God, save me from drunks and imbeciles," she said in exasperation, pushing away from him. "Come on, you foolish man. Get up."

Somehow, she got him upstairs and into his bedroom. When Dobson appeared at the door a moment later, she waved him away, why, she wasn't sure. She could have used his assistance. But it was a unique situation, having Anthony helpless and unable to do for himself. She was rather enjoying it, now that the first irritation had passed. That she was likely the cause of his condition was satisfying too. Or was she?

"Do you mind telling me why you've come home drunk in the middle of the day?" she asked as she straddled his leg to remove the first boot.

"Drunk? Good God, woman, that's a disgusting word. Gentlemen do not get drunk."

"Oh? Then what do they get?"

He shoved against her backside with his other foot until the boot popped off. "The word is . . . it's . . . what the deuce is it?"

"Drunk," she repeated smugly.

He grunted, and when she came for the second boot, his shove was a bit harder, sending her nearly toppling when the boot came off in her hands. She swung around, eyes narrowed, only to find him grinning innocently at her.

She threw the boot down, coming back to the bed to tackle his coat. "You didn't answer my question, Anthony."

"What question was that?"

"Why are you in this disgusting condition?"

He didn't take offense this time. "Come now, my dear. Why else would a man tip one too many? Either he's lost his wealth, a relative's died, or his bed's empty."

It was her turn to look deliberately innocent. "Did someone die?"

He placed his hands on her hips, pulling her a touch closer between his legs. He was smiling, but there was nothing humorous about it. "Play with fire, sweetheart, and you'll get burned," he warned thickly.

Roslynn yanked hard on his cravat before she pushed him back on the bed. "Sleep it off, *sweetheart*." And she turned on her heel.

"You're a cruel woman, Roslynn Malory," he called after her.

She closed the door with a decisive bang.

Chapter Thirty-one

Anthony woke with a splitting head and a curse on his lips. He sat up to light the lamp by his bed, cursing again. The clock on the mantel said a few minutes after two. It was dark outside his window, so that told him which two o'clock it was. He cursed again, realizing he was wide awake now in the middle of the night, with his head coming off and too damn many hours till dawn.

What the hell had possessed him? Ah, well, he knew what possessed him, but he shouldn't have let it. He vaguely remembered old George bringing them home and something about his having belted Billings—bloody hell. Wished he hadn't done that. Billings was a good sort. He'd have to apologize, probably more than once. Hadn't George left angry? Anthony couldn't quite remember.

Uncomfortable, he glanced down at himself and grimaced. Mean-tempered wife. She could at least have undressed him and tucked him in proper, since it was her fault he'd got foxed to begin with. And hadn't she got snippy there, rubbing it in? He couldn't remember that clearly either.

Anthony leaned forward, gently massaging his temples. Well, he had his options, even at this hour. He could try to get back to sleep, which was doubtful. He'd slept more than his customary hours already. He could change and go back to White's for some whist—that is, if he hadn't behaved too abominably earlier and they'd let him in. Or he could be as mean-tempered as his wife and wake her up to see what might come of it. No, he felt too bloody rotten to want to do anything about it if she did prove amenable suddenly.

He laughed, which made him grimace. Best to just work on getting rid of this hangover before morning. A bath would be nice, but he'd have to wait for a decent hour to rouse the servants. Some food, then.

Slowly, because each step reverberated through his head, Anthony left his room. He stopped just down the hall, seeing the light under his brother's door. He knocked once but entered without waiting for permission, to find James sitting naked on the edge of his bed, holding his head in his hands. Anthony almost laughed but caught himself in time. It hurt too much to indulge.

James didn't glance up to see who had intruded. Softly, ominously, he grated out, "Not above a whisper if you value your life."

"Got a little man hammering in your head too, old man?"

James raised his head slowly. His scowl was murderous. "A dozen at least, and I owe every bloody one to you, you miserable—"

"The devil you do. You're the one who offered to buy me a drink, so if anyone has a right to complain—"

"One drink, not several bottles, you ass!"

They both winced at the raised tone. "Well, I suppose you have me there."

"Good of you to admit it," James snorted as he massaged his temples again.

Anthony's lips began to twitch. It was ludicrous, the punishment they put their bodies through, though James' body didn't look any the worse for wear. Anthony had been surprised for a moment on first entering, not having seen his brother naked since the time he had burst into that countess' bedroom, he couldn't even remember her name now, to warn James that her husband was on his way upstairs. James had changed since that night more than ten years ago. He was broader, more solid. In fact, he fairly bulged with thick muscles running across his chest and arms, down his legs. Must be from climbing all that rigging in ten years of pirating.

"You know, James, you're an incredible brute specimen."

James shook his head at that sudden remark, looking down at himself, then back at Anthony. He finally grinned at his brother's surprise. "The ladies don't seem to mind."

"No, I don't imagine they do." Anthony chuckled. "Care for a few hands at cards? I can't get back to sleep to save my soul."

"As long as you don't break out the brandy."

"God, no! I had coffee in mind, and I seem to recall we missed our dinner."

"Give me a few minutes and I'll meet you in the kitchen."

When Roslynn sat down to breakfast, she was still bleary-eyed, having spent another restless, sleepless night. This time it was her own fault. She felt rather guilty about her treatment of Anthony yesterday afternoon. She could have at least undressed him and made him more comfortable instead of leaving him as she had, not even bothering to see he got under the covers. After all, he was her husband. She was familiar with his body. Nothing to be embarrassed about.

Half a dozen times she had nearly gone up to rectify the matter but changed her mind, afraid he might wake and misconstrue her concern. And after she had gone to bed, well, she wasn't about to enter his bedroom in her nightclothes. *That* would certainly be misconstrued.

It bothered her that she felt guilty at all. She wasn't sympathetic to his plight. If he wanted to get drunk and blame it on her, well, that was his problem. And if he suffered for it this morning with a gruesome hangover, that was also too bad. One had to pay for excesses, didn't one? So why had she lost half a night's sleep thinking about him sprawled helpless on his bed?

"If the food's so bad that you must scowl at it, perhaps I'll eat at my club this morning."

Roslynn glanced up, Anthony's sudden appearance surprising her enough that she replied simply, "There's nothing wrong with the food."

"Splendid!" he said cheerfully. "Then you won't mind if I join you?"

He didn't wait for her to answer, but moved to the sideboard and began piling a mountain of food on his plate. Roslynn stared at his tall frame, immaculately encased in a coat of dark brown superfine, buckskin breeches, and gleaming Hessians. He had no right to look so magnificent, to be so chipper this morning. He should be moaning and groaning and damning his folly.

"You slept late," Roslynn said tersely, stabbing a plump sausage on her plate.

"I've just come back from my morning ride, actually." He took the seat opposite her, his brows raised slightly in inquiry. "Did you only just rise yourself, my dear?"

It was a good thing the sausage hadn't entered her mouth yet, or she would have choked on that seemingly innocent question. How dared he deny her the satisfaction of taking him to task for yesterday's disgraceful behavior? And that was exactly what he was doing, sitting there looking as if he had just had the most wonderful night's sleep of his life.

Anthony didn't expect an answer to his last question, nor did he get one. With an amused glimmer in his cobalt eyes, he watched Roslynn attack her food, determined to ignore him. Perversely, he wouldn't let her.

"I noticed a new rug in the hall."

She didn't spare him a glance, even though it was an insult to call the expensive piece woven to resemble the figured Aubusson tapestry a rug. "Strange you didn't notice it yesterday."

Bravo, sweetheart. He smiled to himself. She was going to get her licks in one way or another.

"And a new Gainsborough too," he went on conversationally, his eyes briefly touching the magnificent painting that now dominated the wall to his left.

"The new rosewood china cabinet and dining table should arrive today."

She still had her eyes fastened on her plate, but Anthony didn't miss the sudden change in her. No longer was she sitting there seething with suppressed anger. Her smug satisfaction was palpable.

Anthony nearly laughed aloud. She was so transparent, his sweet wife. Considering her present antipathy toward him and the subject they were discussing, it wasn't hard to figure out what she was up to. It was an old trick, a wife making her husband pay for her displeasure through his pocketbook. And from various remarks Roslynn had made in the past, he knew she didn't think his pocketbook could bear too much displeasure.

"So you're doing a little redecorating, are you?"

A barely perceptible shrug, but a too-sweet tone. "I knew you wouldn't mind."

"Not at all, my dear. I meant to suggest it myself."

Her head snapped up at those words, but she was quick to reply. "Good, because I've only just begun. And you will be glad to know it isn't going to cost as much as I thought when I first toured the house. Why, I've spent only four thousand pounds so far."

"That's nice."

Roslynn gaped at him, disbelieving her ears. His blatantly bored response was the last thing she had expected. Was it possible he thought she was spending her own money? Well, the wretch would find out differently when the bills started coming in.

She stood up, throwing her napkin down on the table, too chagrined with his reaction, or lack of it, to remain in his company. But she couldn't make the dramatic exit she would have liked. After yesterday, it was imperative that she insist there not be a repeat performance today when she was expecting company.

"Frances is coming for dinner this evening. If you should happen to change your habit of returning late and show up to join us, kindly do so soberly."

It was all Anthony could do to keep his lips from twitching. "Bringing in reinforcements again, my dear?"

"I resent that," she said with icy hauteur before she stalked away, only to whip around at the door, glowering at him. "And for your information, my lord, I don't distrust all men, as you so boorishly pointed out yesterday while introducing me to your friend—only rakes and bounders!"

Chapter Thirty-two

"That be 'im, m'lord."

Geordie Cameron turned to the short, bewhiskered man next to him and could have crowned him. "Which one, ye idiot? There are two of them!"

Wilbert Stow didn't blink an eye at the Scot's abrasive tone. He was used to it by now, used to his impatience, his short temper, his arrogance. If Cameron didn't pay so well, he'd tell him where he could stuff this job. Probably slice his gullet too, just for good measure. But he was paying well, thirty English pounds, a fortune to Wilbert Stow. So he held his tongue as always, letting the insults pass over him.

"The dark one," Wilbert clarified, keeping his tone servile. "'E's the one what owns the 'ouse. Sir Anthony Malory be 'is name."

Geordie trained a spyglass across the street, bringing Malory's features into sharp relief as he turned at the door to say something to the blond chap with him. So this was the Englishman who had been combing the slums for Geordie these past few days, the one who was hiding Roslynn? Oh, Geordie knew she was in there, even if she hadn't shown her face outside the door since he had ordered Wilbert and his brother, Thomas, to keep a constant watch on the house. She had to be in there. This was where her clothes had been sent. And this was where that Grenfell woman had come twice now to visit.

Roslynn thought she was so smart, secreting herself inside that house and not coming out. But it was easier here, keeping watch, what with Green Park just across the street. Plenty of trees for concealment, not like having to sit in a carriage that might draw suspicion, as had been the case on South Audley Street. She couldn't make a move without Wilbert or Thomas knowing it, and they kept an empty coach up the street just waiting to follow her in. It was just a matter of time.

But in the meantime, he would take care of the English fop who was hiding her and who had twice forced Geordie to change location in the last five days because of his infernal snooping. Now that he knew what the dandy looked like, it would be an easy task to settle.

Geordie lowered the spyglass, smiling to himself. *Soon, lass. Soon I'll make ye pay for all this trouble. Ye'll be wishing ye hadna turned against me like yer stupid mother and the auld mon did, may they both be rotting in hell now.*

"Would you care for another sherry, Frances?"

Frances looked at her glass, still nearly full, then back at Roslynn, who was already refilling her glass with the amber liquid. "Will you relax, Ros. If he hasn't shown up by now, it's rather doubtful that he will, don't you think?"

Roslynn glanced over her shoulder at her friend, but she couldn't quite manage the smile she tried for. "I've come to the conclusion that Anthony shows up when least expected, just to keep me nervous."

"*Are* you nervous?"

Roslynn gave a little half laugh, half groan, and took a large swallow of her second sherry before returning to join Frances on the new Adams sofa. "I shouldn't be, should I? After all, he wouldn't do anything outrageous with you here, and I did warn him you were coming."

"But?"

Roslynn finally did smile, though it was more a grimace. "He amazes me, Fran, with his many different moods. I never know which one to expect."

"There's nothing unusual in that, m'dear. We have our moods too, don't we? Now, stop fretting. Tell me what he thought of this new room instead."

Roslynn's deep chuckle was infectious. "He hasn't seen it yet."

Frances' eyes widened. "You mean he didn't approve your choices first? But these pieces are so—so—"

"Delicate and feminine?"

Frances gasped at the twinkle in Roslynn's hazel eyes. "Good God, you did it on purpose! You're hoping he'll hate it, aren't you?"

Roslynn glanced about the once-masculine room that had been drastically transformed with the lovely satinwood furnishings. Now it looked the way a parlor should look, for a parlor was really a woman's domain. Adams might be known for his excessively refined style in delicacy of structure and ornament, but she liked the carved and gilded framework on the two sofas and chairs, and especially the satin brocade upholstery of silver flowers on an olive-green background. The colors weren't really feminine. She had compromised there. But the ornamentation was. Then there was the new wall papering that she hadn't made a decision on yet . . .

"I doubt Anthony will hate it, Frances, and if he does, it's unlikely he would say so. He's like that." Here she shrugged. "But of course, if he does, I'll just get rid of these pieces and buy something else."

Frances frowned. "I think you're too used to spending money without thought to price. You're forgetting your husband isn't quite as rich as you are."

"No, that's the one thing I'm not forgetting."

At that bald statement, Frances sighed. "So that's it. Well, I hope you know what you're doing. Men can have funny reactions where money is concerned, you know. Some can lose twenty thousand pounds and not care. Others would go out and kill themselves for such a loss."

"Don't worry, Frances. Anthony is bound to fall into the not caring category. Now, can I make you another drink before dinner?"

Frances looked at her glass, still half full, then at Roslynn's, empty again. She shook her head, but not in answer to the question. "Go ahead and make light of it, Ros, but you can't tell me you're not anxious over his reaction. Was he very . . . unpleasant when you had this argument you don't want to talk about?"

"It wasn't an argument," Roslynn replied stiffly. "And he's been unpleasant since I married him."

"You weren't exactly gushing over with charm yourself the last time I saw you two together. I would guess that his moods are directly related to yours, m'dear."

Roslynn made a face at this sage observation. "Since he's obviously not going to join us for dinner, and his brother and nephew are out for the evening, it's just the two of us. Surely we can find a more pleasant topic to discuss."

Frances gave in and grinned. "Surely we can if we try hard enough."

Roslynn grinned too, feeling some of her tension drain away. Frances was good for her, even if some of the advice she offered Roslynn didn't want to hear.

She set her glass down and stood up. "Come on. Another drink will spoil the excellent fair cook has prepared, and Dobson has only been waiting for us to adjourn to the dining room to commence serving. And wait until you see the new table that was delivered this afternoon. It is sheer elegance, quite suitable to anyone's taste."

"And no doubt devilish expensive?"

Roslynn chuckled. "That too."

They linked arms and left the parlor to cross over to the small dining room, which had previously been no more than a breakfast room, since Anthony had rarely dined at home before he married and still didn't, for that matter. But Roslynn stopped, noticing Dobson in the process of opening the front door, and then stiffened as Anthony walked in. However, she lost her breath entirely on seeing who was with him. He wouldn't dare! He *had* dared! He had deliberately brought George Amherst home with him, knowing full well that Frances would be here. And from the look of George, who had come to a dead standstill on seeing Frances, he hadn't been warned either.

"Splendid," Anthony said drolly as he handed his hat and gloves to the wooden-faced butler. "I see we're just in time for dinner, George."

Roslynn's fingers curled into fists. Frances' reaction was a bit more dramatic. Ashen-faced, and with a small squeal of horror, she tore away from Roslynn's side and ran back into the parlor.

Anthony clapped his friend on the back, bringing him out of his bemusement. "Well, what are you standing there like an ass for, George? Go after her."

"No!" Roslynn snapped before George could take a step. "Havena you done enough?"

Her contempt sliced into the poor man, but he didn't hesitate another moment in starting toward the parlor. Aghast, Roslynn turned to beat him there, intending to slam the door in his face. But she hadn't counted on Anthony's intervention. Somehow he crossed ten feet of space before she had reached the parlor door, and with a band of steel locking firmly about her waist, he steered her toward the stairs instead.

She was outraged beyond belief by his highhandedness. "Let go of me, you—"

"Now, now, my dear, have a care, if you please," he told her glibly. "I believe we've had quite enough distasteful scenes in that hall for the delectation of the servants. We don't need another."

He was absolutely right, so her voice was lowered, but no less furious. "If you dinna—"

His finger pressed to her lips this time. "Pay attention, sweetheart. She refuses to listen to him. It's time she was forced to, and George can do that here—and without interruption." Then he paused, grinning at her. "Sounds awfully familiar, doesn't it?"

"Not at all," she gritted out beneath her breath. "I listened to you. I just didna believe you!"

"Stubborn chit," he gently chided. "But no matter. You're coming along with me while I change for dinner."

She didn't have any choice but to go along with him, since he practically carried her up the stairs. But once in his room, she jerked away, not even noticing that Willis stood beside the bed.

"That is the most loathsome thing you have ever done!" she exploded.

"Glad to hear it," he replied blithely. "Here I was under the impression that the most loathsome thing I had—"

"Shut up! Just shut up!"

She pushed past him to get to the door. He caught her up about the waist and deposited her in the chaise longue by the mantel. And then with a hand on each side of it, he leaned over, until she had to press back in the chair to keep a distance between them. There was no longer a trace of humor in his expression. He was now deadly serious.

"You're going to stay put, my dear wife, or I will tie you to that chair to see that you do." With just the barest crook of his brow, he added, "Is that perfectly clear?"

"You wouldna do that!"

"You may be absolutely certain that I would."

Her lips set mutinously while their eyes did battle. But when

Anthony wouldn't move away and stayed there hovering over her, she thought it prudent to give in for now.

Her agreement was offered by lowering her eyes and drawing her legs up into the chair to get comfortable. Anthony accepted these signs of surrender and straightened, but his humor did not return. He was aware that in helping George, he had thoroughly damaged his own cause. Whatever progress had been made toward the diminishing of Roslynn's anger by the sheer passage of time was now destroyed. So be it. After all these years, George deserved his chance. What were a few more weeks of Roslynn's renewed bad temper? Torture.

He turned away from the chair, his scowl so black his valet took an involuntary step backward upon seeing it, which finally brought him to Anthony's attention. "Thank you, Willis." His voice was deliberately colorless to sheathe the inner turmoil of his thoughts. "You choice is superb as usual."

Roslynn's head snapped around upon hearing that, her eyes first lighting on Willis, then on the clothes carefully laid out on the bed. "Do you mean to be saying he knew you'd be home for dinner?"

"Of course, my dear," Anthony replied as he shrugged out of his coat. "I always let Willis know when to expect me if I am reasonably certain of my schedule."

She gave Willis an accusatory look that brought hot color to his already ruddy cheeks. "He could have told me," she said to Anthony.

"That is not his responsibility."

"*You* could have told me!"

Anthony glanced over his shoulder at her, wondering if it would do any good to risk turning her anger onto this lesser subject. "Quite true, sweetheart. And if you hadn't flounced off in a pout this morning, I would have."

Her eyes flared. Her feet hit the floor. She came half out of the chair before she remembered his threat and dropped back into it.

But she hadn't lost her voice. "I did no such thing! And how dare you say so?"

"Oh?" Anthony faced her again, his lips slightly curled. "Then what would you call it?"

His shirt dropped into Willis' waiting hand before she could answer. Roslynn turned around so fast, Anthony nearly laughed aloud.

At least the new subject was improving his temper, if not hers. And that she was reluctant to watch him undress was most interesting.

He sat down on the bed so Willis could tackle his boots, but he kept his eyes on his wife. She was wearing her hair differently tonight, more frivolously, with dainty curls dangling from a high-swept coiffure. It had been too long since his hands had been in those glorious red-gold tresses, too long since his lips had tasted the smooth skin along her neck. Her head was turned away, but her body was in profile, the sharp thrust of her breasts particularly drawing his attention.

Anthony was forced to look away before it became an embarrassment to both him and Willis to go any further in his undressing. "You know, my dear, it quite escapes me, the cause of your ill humor this morning."

"You provoked me."

He had to strain to hear her, since she wouldn't face him. "Now how could I have done that when I was so exceedingly well behaved?"

"You called Frances my reinforcements!"

That he heard well enough. "I suppose it will be boorish of me to point this out, sweetheart, but you were in a sulk long before your friend was mentioned."

"You're right," she hissed. "It's boorish of you to be saying so."

He stole another glance at her to see her fingers worrying at the arms of the chair. He had pushed her into a corner. That had not been his intention.

Even-toned, he said, "By the by, Roslynn, until I locate your cousin, I would appreciate it if you wouldn't leave the house without me."

The abrupt change of subject floored her. At any other time she would have retorted that she had already concluded for herself that it was wisest to stay at home for a while. But at the moment she was too grateful that he had given up pressing her about this morning.

"Of course," she agreed simply.

"*Is* there any place you would like to go in the next few days?"

And be forced to endure his company the whole while? "No," she assured him.

"Very well." She sensed his shrug. "But if you change your mind, don't hesitate to tell me."

Did he have to be so bloody reasonable and accommodating? "Aren't you finished yet?"

"As a matter of fact—"

"Malory!" The shout was muffled on the other side of the door, but then George Amherst burst into the room. "Tony! You'll—"

Roslynn shot out of the chair, Amherst's presence canceling Anthony's threat in her mind. She didn't wait to hear what he was so eager to impart to her husband, but rushed past him and out the door, offering up a little prayer that Anthony wouldn't make another scene by trying to stop her.

She didn't look back, either, as she ran down the stairs and straight into the parlor. She came to an abrupt halt on finding Frances still there, standing in front of the white marble fireplace with her back to the room. She turned, and Roslynn felt a lump of misery rise in her throat, seeing the great tears swimming in her friend's eyes.

"Och, Frances, I'm so sorry," Roslynn lamented as she swiftly closed the space between them, catching up Frances in her arms. "I'll never forgive Anthony for interfering. He had no right—"

Frances stepped back to interrupt. "I'm getting married, Ros."

Roslynn just stood there, rendered speechless. Not even the brilliant smile Frances gave her, a smile like one she hadn't seen for years, could make her believe what she had just heard. The tears denied it. The tears . . .

"Then why are you crying?"

Frances laughed shakily. "I can't seem to help it. I've been such a fool, Ros. George says he loves me, that he always has."

"You—you believe him?"

"Yes." And then with more force, "Yes!"

"But, Fran—"

"You're not trying to change her mind, are you, Lady Malory?"

Roslynn started and turned to see the most unfriendly look she had ever received from a man on George Amherst's handsome face as he sauntered forward. And his tone had been rife with menace too, the gray eyes positively frigid.

"No," she said uneasily. "I wouldn't dream—"

"Good!" The transformation was immediate, the smile blinding.

"Because now that I know she still loves me, there isn't anyone I would let come between us."

The implication was there, as plain as the warmth now generating from his eyes, that "anyone" also included Frances. And it was also plain to see that Frances was thrilled by the subtle warning.

She hugged a bemused Roslynn, whispering happily in her ear, "You see now why I don't doubt his sincerity? Isn't he wonderful?"

Wonderful? Roslynn wanted to choke. The man was a rake, a libertine. It was Frances herself who had warned her about trusting such men, and here was her friend, willing to marry the very one who had broken her heart.

"I hope you'll forgive us for running off, m'dear," Frances was saying as she stepped back, a becoming blush staining her cheeks as she finished. "But George and I have so much to talk about."

"I'm sure she understands how we'd like to be alone just now, Franny," George added as he put an arm about Frances' waist, drawing her indecently close. "After all, she's newly married herself."

Roslynn did choke this time, but fortunately, neither of them heard, too involved with gazing into each other's adoring eyes to pay attention to much else. And somehow she must have said the appropriate thing in reply, for less than a minute later she found herself alone in the parlor, staring dazedly at the floor, bombarded with so many conflicting emotions that not one of them could dominate to eliminate her bewilderment.

"I see you've received the good news."

Roslynn turned slowly toward the door, and for a moment every single thought in her head deserted her at the sight of her husband. He had done himself up fancy in a dark emerald coat of satin, with an abundance of snowy lace spilling from his throat. And he had combed his hair back in defiance of the current favored style, but it was so soft it refused discipline, already falling forward over each temple in thick ebony waves. He was stunning, there was no other word for it, so handsome she felt her heart trip over.

But then she noticed the stance, one very familiar to her now, the shoulder braced against the doorjamb, the arms crossed over his chest—and the smugness. Hell's teeth, it fairly dripped from him, the self-satisfied smirk, the laughter in his cobalt eyes, made so much bluer in contrast to the dark green of his coat. He was peacock-proud of himself, the scoundrel, and flaunting it with his usual male arrogance.

"Nothing to say, sweetheart, after you made so much fuss over nothing?"

Now he was taunting her, rubbing it in. Her teeth slammed together, her fingers curling into fists on her hips. Her emotions had found their channel. Fury. But he wasn't finished. He had to go for blood.

"It must be disconcerting to have the very woman who fostered your distrust of men turn traitor and trust one. Rather puts a new light on things, doesn't it?"

"You—" No, she wouldn't do it. She refused to yell like a fishwife again for the servants' amusement. "Actually," she gritted out between clenched teeth, "there's no comparison between my case and hers." And then she hissed, "She'll come to her senses in the morning."

"Knowing old George, I doubt it. The only thing your friend will have on her mind in the morning is how she spent the night. Sound familiar?"

She tried to fight it, to hold it back, but her cheeks bloomed with color despite her effort. "You're disgusting, Anthony. They left here to talk."

"If you say so, sweetheart."

The condescending tone infuriated her. He was right, of course. She knew it. He knew it. It had been so embarrassingly obvious why George and Frances were in such a hurry to leave. But damned if she'd acknowledge it to him!

Tightly, she said, "I believe I've developed a headache. If you'll excuse me . . ." But she had to stop when she reached the door, the space still blocked by his casual pose. "Do you mind?" she asked scathingly.

Anthony straightened up slowly, amused when she gave him her back by twisting to squeeze past him without touching. "Coward," he said softly and grinned when she stopped halfway across the hall, shoulders stiffening. "And I believe I owe you a lesson in a chair, don't I?" He heard her gasp just before she broke into a run for the stairs. His laughter followed her. "Another time, sweetheart."

Chapter Thirty-three

Approaching the wide double-door entrance of Edward Malory's grand ballroom two nights after Frances' defection to the enemy camp, as Roslynn had come to think of her reunion with Amherst, Roslynn was brought up short, dragging her two escorts to a halt as well. The many carriages in front of the Malory mansion should have given some indication, but even so, they wouldn't have accounted for the nearly two hundred people gathered in the large room before her.

"I thought this was only to be a quiet affair of friends and family," Roslynn remarked to Anthony, unable to keep the stiffness from her tone. After all, this party was for them. She should have been given some kind of warning. " 'Nothing too big,' I recall were your brother's very words."

"Actually, this is small for one of Charlotte's entertainments."

"And I suppose these are all *your* friends?"

"I hate to disillusion you, sweetheart, but I'm not that popular." Anthony grinned. "When Eddie boy said friends of the family, I believe he meant friends of each individual member of the family, or so it appears. You're dressed accordingly, my dear."

She wasn't worried about how she was dressed. The moss-green gown of silk crepe, with black lace over satin bandings around the cap sleeves, the deep-scooped neckline, and the high waist and hem, was suitable for any ball, and that was certainly what this had turned out to be. Black evening gloves and satin slippers completed the outfit, but it was the diamonds, dripping from ears, neck, wrists, and several fingers, that made her presentable in her mind, even for a presentation to the Prince Regent.

She said no more. Anthony wasn't exactly paying attention anyway, leisurely scanning the room, which gave her a moment to gaze at him, but only a moment. She forced her eyes away, gritting her teeth.

Arriving with Anthony and James, two of the most handsome men in London, she should have been immeasurably proud, and would have been if she had considered it. But the only thing on Roslynn's mind was how soon she could escape her husband's presence. After the intolerable ride over here, during which she had been forced to sit next to him in the carriage, she was now a mass of screaming nerves.

The ride wouldn't have been so bad, the seats were certainly wide enough, but Anthony had deliberately pulled her close, draping an arm firmly about her shoulders, and she couldn't do anything about that with James sitting across from them, quietly observing them with his misplaced humor. But then that was why Anthony had done it. Because he knew very well she wouldn't make a scene in front of his brother.

But it had been hell, tortured bliss, feeling his thigh burning against hers, his hips, his side pressed so close. And his cursed hand wouldn't be still for a minute, the fingers constantly caressing her bare arm between the short sleeve of her gown and her elbow-length glove. And he knew exactly what it did to her. Even though she was as stiff as a board, she couldn't stop the quickened breath, the hammering of her heart, or the telltale gooseflesh that appeared again and again under his fingers, bringing one shiver after another to tell him how effective was his *innocent* touch.

The ride had seemed to take forever, when it was no more than a few blocks around the corner from Piccadilly to Grosvenor Square, where Edward Malory lived with his wife and five children. And even though they had arrived and Roslynn could breathe normally again by putting a distance between herself and Anthony, she still knew it would be a while yet before she could escape him entirely. With the party in their honor, they would be forced by etiquette to remain together for introductions, and now she saw how long that was going to take, with so many guests to meet. But the very moment she had met the last one . . .

All the Malorys were present. She saw Regina and Nicholas standing with several of Edward's offspring; Jason and his son Derek by the
refreshment table, along with Jeremy, who had come over earlier to
help his aunt Charlotte with the last-minute decorations, which by the
looks of them had entailed raiding Charlotte's garden of every single
flower in bloom. She noticed Frances and George, and several other
people she had met since arriving in London.

And then she realized the hush falling over the room. They had
themselves been noticed, and she groaned inwardly, feeling Anthony's
arm slip around her waist to present a very loving picture. Was there to
be no end to the liberties he was going to take tonight? It seemed not,
for he didn't release her when Edward and Charlotte appeared at their
side with a small group of people in tow, and the introductions began.
The only interruption was when they had to start off the dancing
together as the guests of honor, and that was another excuse for
Anthony to torment her with his closeness.

She soon met *his* friends, the sorriest bunch of lecherous rakes
imaginable. There wasn't one who didn't ogle her shamelessly, flirt
with her, or banter with wicked insinuations. They were amusing. They
were outrageous. And they managed to get her away from Anthony's
side with one dance after another, until when she finally begged for a
moment's respite, Anthony was no longer in sight. At last, Roslynn felt
she could relax and enjoy herself.

"See here, Malory, either you're going to play cards or you're not,"
the Honorable John Willhurst said in exasperation as Anthony rose
from the table for the third time in less than an hour.

The two other players tensed as Anthony placed both hands on the
table and leaned toward Willhurst. "I'm going to stretch my legs, John.
But if you've a problem with that, you know what you can do."

"No—not at all," John Willhurst got out. He was a neighbor of
Jason's and so knew from past experience the explosive tempers of the
Malory brothers, having grown up with them. What *had* he been think-
ing of? "Could use a new drink myself."

Willhurst hurried away from the table himself while Anthony shot
the other players a look to see if there would be any more objections.
There weren't.

Calmly, as if he hadn't just been on the brink of challenging an old family friend, Anthony picked up his drink and left the card room. He stopped at the place he had stopped at previously, the entrance to the ballroom, his eyes scanning the crowd until he found what was repeatedly drawing him back here.

Damnation take her, he couldn't even play a simple game of cards with Roslynn in the same vicinity. Just knowing she was near, but where he couldn't keep his eye on her, destroyed his concentration, so much so that he had already lost nearly a thousand pounds. It was no good. He couldn't stay near her without touching her, but he couldn't stay away from her either.

Across the room, Conrad Sharp nudged James in the ribs. "He's back again."

James glanced in the direction Connie had indicated and chuckled to see Anthony scowling at his wife as she whirled by on the dance floor. "A face worth a thousand words, that. I would say my dear brother is not at all happy."

"You could remedy that by having a little talk with the lady and enlightening her to the truth."

"I suppose I could."

"But you're not going to?"

"And make it easy for Tony? Come now, Connie. It's so much more fun watching him muddle through this on his own. He hasn't the temperament for rejection. He's bound to dig the hole deeper before he finally crawls out."

"If he can crawl out."

"Where's your faith, man? Malorys always win in the end." And here James grinned. "Besides, she's already weakening, if you haven't noticed. Can't keep her eyes from searching the room for him either. If ever there was a woman smitten, it's Lady Roslynn."

"She just doesn't know it, I suppose?"

"Quite so."

"And what are you two grinning about?" Regina asked as she and Nicholas joined them.

James gave her a brief hug. "The foibles of man, sweet. We can be such asses sometimes."

"Speak for yourself, old man," Nicholas retorted.

"I was excluding myself, actually," James replied, a quirk to his lips as his eyes moved over his nephew by marriage. "But then you're a prime example, Montieth."

"Famous." Regina sighed in exasperation, glaring at both before she ignored them to hook her arm through Conrad's. "Connie, would you rescue me with a dance? I'm tired of getting splattered with the blood from their slashes."

"Love to, squirt." Connie grinned.

James snorted as he watched them twirl away. "She puts it rather plain, don't she?"

"You don't know the half of it," Nicholas grumbled, more to himself. "Try sleeping on the sofa when you have a wife annoyed with you."

James couldn't help it. He burst out laughing. "Good God, you too? That's rich, lad. Damn me if it ain't. And what have you done to merit—"

"I haven't forgiven you, that's what." Nicholas scowled at this amusement at his expense. "And well she knows it. Every time you and I have words, she lays into me later. When the devil are you leaving London, anyway?"

"My, but that's becoming a source of keen interest." James continued to chuckle. "If it'll keep you on the sofa, dear boy, I may never leave."

"You're all heart, Malory."

"I like to think so. If it's any consolation, I forgave you a long time ago."

"How magnanimous, when you were at fault to begin with. All I did was best you on the high seas—"

"And land me in gaol," James replied, no longer quite so amused.

"Hah! That was after you landed me in my bed to recover from your thrashing, nearly making me miss my own wedding."

"Which you had to be dragged to," James pointed out sourly.

"That's a bloody lie!"

"Is it? Well, you can't deny my brothers had to do a little arm twisting to get you there. Would that I'd been here at the time—"

"But you were, old man—skulking around alleys trying to way-lay me."

"Skulking? Skulking!" James blustered.

Nicholas groaned. "Now you've done it with your bloody shouting."

James followed the direction of his gaze to see that Regina was no longer dancing. She was standing in the middle of the dance floor watching them and looking none too pleased, with Connie next to her, trying to look as if he hadn't heard their raised voices too.

"I believe I could use another drink," James said abruptly, grinning. "Enjoy your sofa, lad." And he deserted Nicholas for the refreshment table. Passing Anthony on the way, he couldn't resist commenting, "You and Montieth ought to compare notes, dear boy. He suffers from the same complaint as you, don't you know."

"Does he?" Anthony scanned the room until his eyes lit on Nicholas. Dryly, he added, "If he does, he's obviously discovered how to correct it."

James chuckled, seeing Nicholas kissing his wife with flagrant disregard for the audience they were attracting. "Damn me if he hasn't got something there. Regan can't very well rail at him if she can't get her lips free."

But Anthony wasn't there to hear this comment. He had heard once again, and one time too many, Roslynn's throaty laugh at some sally her present partner had made. Weaving his way through the dancers until he came to the pair, he tapped Justin Warton on the shoulder none too gently, bringing them to a sudden halt.

"Is something amiss, Malory?" Lord Warton asked cautiously, sensing the underlying menace in Anthony's stance and expression.

"Not at all." Anthony smiled tightly, but his arm shot out to catch Roslynn as she started to edge away. "Just retrieving what's mine." And with a curt nod, he whirled his wife into the waltz that was still in progress. "Enjoying yourself, sweetheart?"

"I was," Roslynn retorted, keeping her eyes averted from his.

The only indication that the insinuation had struck home was a slight tightening of his fingers on her waist. "Shall we leave, then?"

"No," she said too quickly.

"But if you're having no fun . . ."

"I'm—having—fun," she gritted out.

He smiled down at her, watching her eyes dart about the room, anywhere but up at him. He drew her closer, and saw the pulse beat quicken at her throat, and wondered what she would do if he followed Montieth's strategy.

He asked her. "What would you do, sweetheart, were I to end this dance with a kiss?"

"What?"

He had her eyes locked fast to his now. "That sends you into a panic, does it? Why is that?"

"I'm no' panicked, mon."

"Ah, and there's the brogue, a sure sign—"

"Will you shush!" she hissed, his teasing alarming her so, she missed a step in the dance.

Anthony grinned delightedly and decided to let her off the hook for now. Starting something in a ballroom was not only in bad taste but would get him nowhere.

Noting the fortune in diamonds that sparkled on her with each turn into the light, he said in an impersonal tone, "What does a man give a woman who has everything?"

"Something that canna be bought," Roslynn replied absently, for she was still thinking about what *might* happen when this dance ended.

"His heart, perhaps?"

"Perhaps—no—I mean—" she stammered to a halt, glaring up at him, her tone bitter as she continued. "I'm no' wanting *your* heart, mon, no' anymore."

One hand disturbed the curls along her temple. "But what if it's already yours?" he asked softly.

For a moment, Roslynn lost herself in the vivid blue of his eyes. She actually drifted closer to him, was about to offer him her lips, heedless of the crowded room and what was between them. But she came to her senses with a gasp and drew back, glaring at him again.

Furious at herself, she said, "If your heart's mine, then it's mine to do with as I choose, and I'd be choosing to cut it into wee pieces afore I give it back."

"Heartless wench."

"Not so." She smiled wryly, amusing him though she didn't know it. "My heart's right where it's supposed to be, and that's where it'll be staying."

With that, she jerked loose of his hold and flounced off in the direction of his elder brothers. In their presence was the only place she felt safe from Anthony's bold taunts and the supposedly innocent touches of his caressing hands.

Chapter Thirty-four

George gave the door knocker a few sharp raps, then stood back, whistling a jaunty tune as he waited. It was Dobson who answered.

"You've just missed him, my lord, by five minutes," Dobson informed him before George even started his business.

"The devil, and here I thought I had time to spare," George replied, but he was undaunted. "Right you are, then. He'll be easy enough to find."

George remounted his bay stallion and headed for Hyde Park. He knew the paths Anthony favored, those well away from Rotten Row, where the ladies turned out. He had joined him several times on his morning rides, but then those times had been after a night of carousing, when neither of them had yet to go to bed. Never had he actually gotten up at this ungodly hour to ride or do anything else, for that matter—until recently.

George continued to whistle, his spirits so high he could have been floating along. His habits had changed in the past three days, drastically, but he couldn't have been happier. Early to bed, early to rise, and each day spent with Franny. No, he couldn't be happier, and he owed it all to Anthony. But he had yet to have an opportunity to thank his friend, which was why he had thought to ride with him this morning.

Entering the park, he picked up his pace to catch up with Anthony, but it was a while before he finally spotted him a good distance ahead, and that only because Anthony had stopped at the start of the long run that he usually used for his all-out gallop. George raised his arm, but before he could shout to be heard, a shot was fired.

He heard it, he just didn't believe it. He saw Anthony's horse rear up so far that nearly both rider and horse tumbled over backward, but he still didn't believe it. Anthony did tumble over. The horse found his footing, but he was obviously spooked, shying away, tossing his head, backing into a bush that further spooked him. And a redheaded gent about twenty yards away from Anthony mounted a horse concealed in the brush and took off at an instant gallop.

Anthony had yet to rise, and although it had all happened in the space of only a few seconds, the pieces finally came together in George's mind with heart-stopping clarity. And then Anthony sat up, running a hand through his hair, and the blood rushed back into George's ashen face. He glanced between the fleeing redhead and Anthony pushing himself to his feet, apparently not wounded at all, and made his decision. He turned his horse to follow the redhead.

Anthony had just handed his mount over to the waiting footman to return him to the stable when George cantered up behind him. Bloody hell. He was in no mood for George and his "everything going right" ebullience. Not that Anthony begrudged him his good fortune. He just didn't need to be reminded how opposite was his own state of affairs.

"So you made it home under your own steam," George remarked, grinning at the instant scowl that darkened Anthony's features. "No broken bones, then?"

"I take it you witnessed my unseating? Nice of you to lend a hand in retrieving that bloody nag of mine."

George chuckled at the deliberate sarcasm. "Thought you might rather have this, old man." He tossed a scrap of paper at Anthony.

Anthony's brow rose just a smidgen as he read the address, which meant nothing to him. "Doctor? Or butcher?" he snarled.

George laughed outright, knowing very well he wouldn't consign his favorite mount to the butcher's block. "Neither. You'll find the red-haired chap who used you for target practice there. Strange fellow. He didn't even wait around to see if you were down and out for the count. Probably thinks he's a crack shot."

Anthony's eyes were gleaming now. "So you followed him to this address?"

"After I saw you dragging your bruised bones off the ground, of course."

"Of course." Anthony finally smiled. "My thanks, George. His trail was cold by the time I'd mounted up again."

"He the one you've been looking for?"

"I'd say it's a safe bet."

"You going to pay him a call?"

"You may depend upon it."

George wasn't too sure he liked the cold sparkle in his friend's eyes. "Need some company?"

"Not this time, old man," Anthony replied. "This meeting's long overdue."

Roslynn opened the door to the study but was brought up short to find Anthony seated behind his desk, cleaning a pair of dueling pistols. She hadn't heard him return from his morning ride. She had purposely stayed in her room until she heard him leave, not wanting to face him after having made a fool of herself last night.

Anthony had been so amused when she dragged Jeremy home with them from the ball, against the lad's protests too. He knew exactly why she didn't trust herself alone with him, even for such a short ride. But James had left the ball early with his friend, Conrad Sharp. Jeremy was her only buffer. It had been inconceivable for her to think of being alone with Anthony after the way he had taunted her all evening.

Now here she was alone with him, having come to exchange one book for another from his small library. But he hadn't glanced up when she entered. Perhaps if she left quietly . . .

"Did you want something, my dear?"

He still hadn't glanced up. Roslynn gritted her teeth. "Nothing that can't wait."

Anthony finally gave her his attention, his eyes flitting to the book she was grasping so tightly in her hands. "Ah, the companion of spinsters and widows. There's nothing like a good book to while away an evening when you've nothing else to do, is there?"

She felt like throwing the book at him. Would he always allude to their estrangement every time they encountered each other? Couldn't he back off long enough for her to come to terms with his unfaithfulness? He acted as if *she* were the guilty party.

Her hackles rose with the unfairness of it, and she attacked. "Preparing for a duel, my lord? I've heard it's one of your more favorite pastimes. Which unfortunate husband is it to be this time?"

"Husband?" Anthony smiled tightly. "Not at all, sweetheart. I thought I'd challenge you. Perhaps if I let you draw some of my blood, you might be moved to sympathy, and our little war can end."

Her mouth dropped open for at least five seconds before she snapped it shut. "Be serious!"

He shrugged. "Your dear cousin has decided that if he can get rid of your current husband, he will have another chance at you."

"No!" Roslynn gasped, her eyes flaring wide. "I never considered—"

"Didn't you?" he cut in dryly. "Well, don't let it concern you, sweetheart. I did."

"You mean you married me knowing you were putting your life in danger?"

"Some things are worth putting one's life in jeopardy for—at least I used to think so."

The dig stung, so much so that she couldn't bear to face him another moment and ran from the study, up to her room, where she felt safe to burst into tears. Oh, God, she had thought it would be over once she married. She never dreamed Geordie would try to kill her husband. And her husband was Anthony. She couldn't bear it if anything happened to him because of her.

She had to do something. She had to find Geordie and talk to him herself, give him her fortune, anything. Nothing must happen to Anthony.

Having made up her mind, Roslynn dried her eyes and went back downstairs to tell Anthony what she had decided to do. They would buy Geordie off. All he wanted was the money anyway. But Anthony was gone.

Chapter Thirty-five

Anthony saw now why neither he nor his agents had had any luck in locating Cameron. The Scot had moved away from the docks, letting a flat in a better part of town, which was amazing when such accommodations were at a high premium during the season. The landlord, a congenial chap, admitted that Cameron had been there only a few days, and yes, he was in at present. Whether he was alone, the landlord couldn't say. It made no difference to Anthony.

Campbell was the name Cameron was assuming, and Anthony had little doubt it was assumed. He had found his man. He felt it. His blood pumped with that certainty, the adrenaline flowing through his veins. And once he had settled with Cameron, he would settle with Roslynn. Letting her dictate the rules had gone on long enough.

The room was on the second floor, third door on the left. Anthony knocked softly and had only a few seconds to wait before the door swung open, giving him his first look at Geordie Cameron. The eyes were the giveaway, sky-blue, and bright with recognition.

It took the Scot several moments before his wits returned and panic took over, enough for him to try slamming the door in Anthony's face. A single hand was all it took to prevent the door from closing. A forceful shove and Geordie lost his hold on the handle, cringing as the door slammed into the wall.

Fury and anxiety mixed sickeningly in Geordie's gut. The Englishman hadn't looked this strong from a distance. He hadn't looked this dangerous either. And he was supposed to be dead, or at least seriously wounded, at the very least intimidated by knowing he had a deadly enemy in Geordie Cameron. Roslynn was supposed to have panicked and left the protection of the house on Piccadilly, and Wilbert and Thomas Stow would be there to grab her. The Englishman was *not* supposed to show up at his door, looking disgustingly healthy, lips turned up in an ominous smile that did more to shake Geordie than anything else.

"I'm glad we don't have to waste time introducing ourselves, Cameron," Anthony said as he stepped into the room, forcing Geordie to back up. "I would have been disappointed to have to explain why I'm here. And I'll give you a sporting chance, which is more than you gave me this morning. Are you gentleman enough to accept my challenge?"

The quiet, nonchalant tone gave Geordie back some of his belligerence. "Hah! I'm no' a bloody fool, mon."

"That's debatable, but I didn't think we'd do this in the usual way. So be it, then."

Geordie didn't see the punch coming. It caught him square on the chin and sent him careening into his small dining table, breaking the spindly legs, and knocking over both straight-backed chairs as the table collapsed, Geordie on top of it. He leaped to his feet instantly, to see the Englishman calmly removing his coat, in no hurry. Geordie wiggled his jaw, found it still intact, and eyed his own coat on the foot of his bed across the room. He wondered how much chance he had of reaching the pistol in its pocket.

None at all, he discovered as he turned toward the bed, only to be spun back around. A fist slammed into his midsection; another connected with his cheek. He was on the floor again, not so quick to rise this time. He couldn't breathe either. The bloody bastard had rocks for fists.

Anthony came to stand at his feet. "That was for this morning. Now we'll get down to the real issue."

"I'm no' going tae fight ye, mon," Geordie spat out, tasting blood where his teeth had cut into his cheek.

"But of course you are, dear boy," Anthony replied in the lightest tone. "It's the only choice you have, you see. Whether you defend yourself or not, I'm going to wipe the floor with your blood."

"Ye're crazy!"

"No." Anthony's tone changed, all humor gone. "I'm deadly serious."

He bent over to lift Geordie to his feet. Geordie kicked out to keep him away, but Anthony blocked with his knee, yanking him up anyway. And then he felt those rocks slammed against his jaw again. He only staggered back this time, and had time to raise his own fists before Anthony reached him. Geordie threw a right and struck nothing. He doubled over as two successive punches sank into his stomach. Before he regained his breath this time, his lips were smashed against his teeth.

"En-ough," he tried to get out.

"Not even close, Cameron," Anthony replied, not at all winded from his exertions.

Geordie groaned, and groaned again with the next two punches. He went a little crazy then from the numbing pain. He'd never experienced a beating before in his life. He didn't have the character to take it like a man. He started screaming, throwing wild punches. He laughed when one finally struck, only to find, when he squinted his eyes open, he had hit the wall, breaking three of his own knuckles. Anthony spun him around, and this punch cracked his head back into the wall. His nose was also broken, he realized as he slowly slid to the floor.

He thought that would be the end of it. He was beaten. He knew it. He hurt all over. He was bleeding profusely. It wasn't the end. Anthony pulled him up by his shirtfront, stood him against the wall, and simply pounded away at him. And no matter how Geordie tried warding off the punches, they kept coming, kept landing unerringly.

Finally he didn't feel them anymore. Finally they had stopped. He was slumped on the floor again, siting up only because the wall was supporting his back. Blood was splattered all around him from his mouth, nose, and several cuts on his face. Two ribs were broken. The little finger on his left hand was broken too, from one of his attempted blocks. He could see out of only one eye, and what he saw was Anthony staring down at him in disgust.

"Bloody hell. You give a man no satisfaction at all, Cameron."

That was funny. Geordie tried to smile, but he had no feeling in his lips, couldn't tell if he had managed it or not. But he did manage a single word.

"Bastard."

Anthony grunted and hunkered down in front of him. "You want some more?"

Geordie moaned. "No—no more."

"Then pay attention, Scotsman. Your life may very well depend upon it, because if I have to come looking for you again, I won't use my fists next time. She's mine now, and so's her inheritance. I married her a week ago."

That penetrated Geordie's fuzziness. "Ye're lying! She'd no' have wed ye unless ye signed that stupid contract of hers, and nae mon in his right mind would've done that."

"There you're wrong, dear boy. I did sign it, and in front of witnesses, then promptly burned it after the ceremony."

"Ye couldna. No' wi' witnesses."

"Did I neglect to say the witnesses were related to me?" Anthony taunted.

Geordie tried to sit up farther, but couldn't. "Sae what? She'll still be having it all back when I make her a widow."

"You just don't learn, do you?" Anthony said, grabbing hold of Geordie's shirtfront again.

Geordie quickly grasped his wrists. "I didna mean that, mon, I didna, I swear!"

Anthony let him go this time, deciding to further the lie instead of using more force. "It won't matter to you, Scotsman, whether I die or not. According to my new will, everything I possess, including my wife's inheritance, goes to my family. They'll of course see that my widow doesn't want for anything, but other than that, she gets nothing. She lost it all the day she married me—and so did you."

Geordie's one good eye narrowed furiously. "She mun hate ye fer tricking her!"

"That's my problem, isn't it?" Anthony remarked as he stood up. "Your problem is getting out of London today in your present condition. If you're still here tomorrow, Scotsman, I'll have you arrested for that little stunt you pulled in the park this morning."

"Ye've nae proof, mon."

"No?" Anthony grinned at last. "The Earl of Sherfield witnessed the whole thing and followed you here. How else do you think I finally found you? If my testimony won't put you in prison, his will."

Anthony left him mumbling about how Anthony expected him to leave London when he couldn't even get up off the floor.

Chapter Thirty-six

Fortunately, Roslynn didn't see Anthony when he returned home, and by the time he had bathed and changed, there was no evidence left of the fight. His knuckles might be tender, but thanks to the gloves he had worn, there were no cuts or abrasions from Cameron's teeth. Still, he was disgusted with the whole affair. The man had offered him no challenge at all. It put him in a foul mood, one that wasn't conducive to tackling his next challenge—Roslynn.

He didn't even care to see her at the moment, but, as his luck would have it, she came out of the parlor as he was on his way out again.

"Anthony?"

He frowned at her hesitant tone, so unlike her. "What is it?"

"Did you—challenge Geordie?"

He grunted. "He wouldn't accept."

"Then you saw him?"

"I saw him. And you can relax your guard, my dear. He won't be bothering you again."

"Did you—"

"I did no more than persuade him to leave London. He might have to be carried out, but he'll go. And don't wait dinner on me. I'm going to my club."

Roslynn stared at the closed door after he left, wondering why his terseness upset her so. She should be feeling relief, delight over Geordie's thrashing, for she was sure that was the persuasion Anthony had used; but instead she felt deflated, depressed. It was Anthony's curtness, his cold indifference. He had been in many different moods this past week, but this was a new one she didn't like at all.

She had procrastinated too long, she realized. It was time she reached a decision about her relationship with Anthony, before the decision was no longer hers to make. And it must be done now, today, before he returned.

"Well, Nettie?"

Nettie paused in pulling the brush through Roslynn's fiery hair to stare at her in the mirror. "Is that what ye really mean tae do, lass?"

Roslynn nodded. She had finally told Nettie everything, about Anthony's seduction of her in this very house, about the conditions she had placed on their marrying, even about his lies that he would be faithful, only to have the truth come out the very next day. Nettie had been both furious with and aghast at the two of them. But Roslynn had left nothing out, and had ended by telling Nettie what she had decided to do. She wanted her abigail's opinion, her support.

"I think ye're making a big mistake, lass."

She didn't want *that* opinion. "Why?"

"Ye'll be using him. Ye mark me, he'll no' be liking that one bit."

"I'll be sharing his bed," Roslynn pointed out. "How is that using him?"

"Ye'll be sharing his bed only fer a time."

"He agreed to give me a child!"

"Sae he did. But he didna agree tae leave ye alone once that child is conceived, did he now."

Roslynn's eyes narrowed in a frown. "I'm only protecting myself, Nettie. Constant intimacy with him . . . I don't want to love him."

"Ye already do."

"I dinna!" Roslynn gasped, swinging around to glare at the older woman. "And I willna. I refuse! And I'll be letting him decide. I dinna ken why I told you anyway."

Nettie snorted, not at all perturbed by this outburst.

"Then go and put it tae him. I saw him enter his room afore I came in here."

Roslynn looked away, a cold knot of nervousness tightening in her belly. "Maybe I should wait until tomorrow. He wasn't exactly pleasant when he left today."

"The mon's no' been pleasant since ye moved oout of his room," Nettie reminded her. "But perhaps ye're seeing how silly is yer notion—"

"No," Roslynn replied, determination back in her voice. "And it's not silly. It's self-preservation."

"If ye say sae, hinny." Nettie sighed. "But remember I did warn ye—"

"Good *night*, Nettie."

Roslynn sat there at her new vanity another ten minutes after Nettie left, staring at her reflection in the mirror. She had made the right decision. She wasn't forgiving Anthony. Not in the least. But she had come to the conclusion that she was only thwarting herself with the stand she had taken. Either she could go on hugging her anger to her breast and keeping Anthony at arm's length, or she could get a child. She wanted the child. It was that simple.

But it meant swallowing her pride and going to Anthony. After his coldness today, she had little doubt that she would have to make the first move. But it was only temporary, she reminded herself. He would have to agree to that. She still couldn't convince herself to accept him the way he was, even if she had agreed to when they married. The truth was, she didn't want him as he was anymore. She found she was exceedingly selfish in wanting him all to herself. But since that wasn't to be, she had to remain detached, to keep in mind that she would never be the only woman in his life.

Before she lost her nerve, Roslynn abruptly left her room. Across the hall, she knocked sharply on Anthony's door. The deed done, her presence known, her apprehension returned. Her second knock was so soft only she could have heard it. But the first knock had done it.

Willis opened the door, took one look at her, and silently left the room, leaving the door open for her to enter. She did, hesitantly, closing the door behind her. But she was reluctant to find Anthony in there. She stared at the bed instead, empty but turned down. Her cheeks flushed with color; her palms began to sweat. And then it hit her suddenly what she had come for—to make love to Anthony. Her heart began to pound, and she hadn't even looked at him yet.

He was looking at her. His breath had caught and held at the sight of her in her white silk negligee, the material clinging provocatively to the soft curves of her body, the robe she wore open, of the same thin silk except for the long sleeves, which were transparent, revealing her bare arms beneath. Her hair was loose and flowing in red-gold waves down her back, making his fingers itch to get into it. And she was barefoot.

It was the bare feet that made Anthony consider why she had come to him. Only two reasons came to mind. Either Roslynn was a fool to think she could torture him with her scanty attire and escape back to her room untouched, or she was here to end his torture.

Whatever her reason for seeking him in the privacy of his room and giving him this tantalizing view of what she had been withholding from him all week, he wasn't about to let her leave now. Whether she had set her own trap or was here to end their estrangement, his days of celibacy were over.

"Roslynn?"

There was a question in his voice. He wanted to know why she was here. Hell's teeth, was she going to have to spell it out? Wasn't it obvious? Willis had understood just by her presence, dressed as she was, and that was embarrassing enough. But Anthony was going to make her say it. She should have known this wouldn't be easy.

She finally turned toward the sound of his voice. He was sitting in the overstuffed lounge chair that he had once threatened to tie her down in. She was embarrassed further, remembering that, and remembering that he had forced her to sit there while he had changed clothes that day. Staring at him, watching the way his inscrutable eyes moved over her, she couldn't get any words out.

But her heart continued to pound, harder now that she'd seen him. He was wearing the same silver-blue robe over loose trousers that he'd worn the night they'd first made love, which brought more memories to heat her cheeks and turned that nervous knot in her belly to something entirely different.

"Well, my dear?"

Roslynn cleared her throat, but it did little good. "I—I thought that we might . . ."

She couldn't finish, not with his eyes locked to hers. They were no longer inscrutable, but quite intense, though with what emotion she couldn't tell.

Anthony lost patience, waiting to hear what he wanted to hear.
"Might *what?* There are numerous things you and I might do. What
exactly did you have in mind?"

"You promised me a child!" she blurted out, then sighed with relief
to have it out in the open.

"You're moving back in here?"

Hell's teeth, she'd forgotten about the rest. "No, I . . . when I conceive, there won't be any reason—"

"For you to share my bed?"

The sudden anger in his expression gave her pause, but she had
made her decision. She had to stick with it.

"Exactly."

"I see."

Those two words had such an ominous ring to them, Roslynn actually shivered. Nettie had warned her he wouldn't like it, but she could
see by the tight set of his jaw and the frigid blue of his eyes that he was
quite furious. And yet he didn't move from the chair. His grip might be
a little tighter on the brandy snifter he held in one hand, but his voice
remained soft as he continued—soft and menacing.

"This was not our original agreement."

"Everything has changed since then," she reminded him.

"Nothing has changed, except what you imagine in your suspicious
little mind."

She cringed. "If you won't agree—"

"Stay right where you are, Roslynn," he cut in harshly. "I haven't
finished analyzing this newest condition of yours." He set his glass
down on the table next to him and clasped his hands over his waist, all
the while never taking his eyes off her. And then calmly again, or at
least with self-restraint: "So what you want is the temporary use of my
body for breeding purposes?"

"You needn't be vulgar about it."

"We'll treat the subject as it deserves, my dear. You want a stud,
nothing more. The question is whether I can be detached enough to
give you only what you want. It would be a new experience for me, you
see. I'm not sure I'm capable of performing in a purely perfunctory
manner."

At the moment, he was. He was so angry with her he wanted nothing more than to turn her over his knee and thrash some sense into her. But he would give her exactly what she was requesting and see how long it took her to admit it wasn't what she wanted at all.

Roslynn was already having doubts. He made it sound so—so animalistic. And perfunctory? What the devil did he mean by that? If he was going to be indifferent about it, then how could he make love to her? He himself had said that it couldn't be done unless desire was involved. Of course, that was when he had told her he wanted no other woman but her, and that had all been lies. But even now he said he wasn't sure he could do it. Hell's teeth! He had been after her from the beginning. How could he *not* do it?

He broke into her thoughts with a quiet command. "Come here, Roslynn."

"Anthony, perhaps—"

"You want a child?"

"Yes," she answered in a small voice.

"Then come here."

She approached him, but slowly, and a little fearfully now. She didn't like him this way, so controlled, so cold. And she knew his anger was still simmering just below the surface. Yet her heart was accelerating with each step that brought her closer to him. They were going to make love. How didn't matter. Where didn't matter, though she spared a glance at the empty bed before looking back at the chair. And then suddenly she remembered Anthony's threat the night George and Frances had been here, that he owed her a lesson in a chair. Roslynn stopped cold.

Unfortunately, she stopped too late. She was close enough to Anthony for him to reach out and drag her down onto his lap. She turned to sit sideways, to face him, but he wouldn't let her, maneuvering her the way he wanted, which was sitting straight, with her back to him. The position only made her more nervous because she couldn't see his face behind her. But perhaps that was his intention. She just didn't know what to think at this point.

"You're stiff as a board, my dear. Need I remind you this was your idea?"

"Not in a chair."

"I haven't said we'll do it here . . . but then I haven't said we won't.

What does it matter where? The priority is to first discover if I'm up to this endeavor."

In the position he had placed her, sitting forward on his thighs, she had no way of knowing that he was already up to any endeavor, and had been since she'd walked into the room. She felt him gather her hair in his hands, but again, she didn't know he pressed the silken locks to his lips, to his cheek, couldn't see his eyes close as he savored the feel of her hair against his skin.

"Anthony, I don't think—"

"Shh." He pulled her head back by her hair as he leaned forward to whisper into her ear. "You do entirely too much thinking as it is, my dear. Try a little spontaneity for a change. You might like it."

She held her tongue as he slipped her robe off her shoulders, his hands traveling down her arms, pushing the sleeves down to her wrists and then off, then retracing the path back to her shoulders. He continued touching her, on her shoulders, her neck, but she quickly became aware of the difference between this time and the last time. Even last night in the carriage when he had caressed her bare arm was different from this. Then she had felt his ardor like a hot brand. Now she sensed nothing, only complete indifference, as if touching her were simply a matter of course. Perfunctory—oh, God!

She couldn't bear it, not like this. She started to get up, only to have a hand grip each of her breasts, pulling her back against him.

"You're not going anywhere, my dear. You came here with your damnable conditions, and I agreed to them. It's too late to change your mind—again."

Roslynn's head fell back against his chest. His hands hadn't remained still while he spoke. They had begun kneading, squeezing, drawing a fullness into her breasts. *He* might not be feeling anything, but she certainly was. And she couldn't seem to help it, to stop the warmth from uncoiling in her belly, making her limbs grow languorous one moment, tensed in anticipation the next.

She no longer cared if he was lacking ardor. Her own senses had taken over. It was too late to change her mind. He said it was too late. And it was a means to an end, wasn't it? She had to keep that in mind.

Moments later, she had very little in mind. His hands were roaming the front of her body, stroking gently, roughly, but in no way indifferently now, though she had ceased to notice the difference. Even the silk of her negligee gliding up her legs was a heady caress. And then one hand touched the triangle of hair he had bared and became still.

"Open your legs for me," he commanded, his breath filling her ear with warmth.

Roslynn stiffened for a brief moment, but the words had sent a thrill clear down to her toes. Breathlessly, heart slamming against her chest now, she parted her knees the barest fraction. His hand remained motionless on her titian curls, though the other one slipped up under her negligee, raising it even higher as he sought her breasts, this time without the silk to separate her from his teasing fingers.

His command came again. "Wider, Roslynn."

Her breath caught in her throat, but she obeyed him to the letter this time, moving her knees across his own, until her legs dropped down of their own accord along his outer thighs. That still wasn't enough for him. He parted his own knees, forcing her legs open even wider, and only then did his hand glide lower to insert a single finger inside her.

Roslynn moaned deep in her throat, her back arching away from him, her fingers digging into his jacket behind her head. She wasn't aware of what she was doing, but he was. Each gasp of pleasure she emitted was like a flame licking at his soul. That he was still in control of his own raging passions at this point was beyond his understanding, but he wouldn't be for much longer.

"It doesn't matter, does it?" His question was calculatedly cruel, to keep his anger alive. "Here? On the bed? On the floor?"

She heard the question. All she could do was shake her head no.

"At this moment, I could make you break all your bloody conditions. You know that, don't you, sweetheart?" She was incapable of answering, except with a whimper. "But I won't. I want you to remember this was your choice."

Roslynn didn't care anymore. All that mattered now was the fire he had ignited in her. Anthony didn't care anymore either. She had pushed him past his limits.

Without warning, he moved her forward on his legs to ready himself, then lifted her, positioned himself, and dropped her hard. Her soft cry was ambrosia to his ears. Her hands moved up to grasp his head, the only part of him within her reach. He still had her entire torso at his disposal, and he caressed every inch while she lay back against him, savoring the fullness inside her.

He gave them that brief moment, before recalling that this was not an act of love, but one for a specific purpose only. Damnation take her and her bloody conditions. He wanted to kiss her, to turn her around and take her with all the tenderness and passion he felt for her. But he wouldn't. She had to look back on this with disgust, to admit that she wanted more from him than a child.

With that in mind, he took her hands and placed them on the arms of the chair, leaned forward until she was sitting straight up, then leaned back himself, leaving her astride him, her hair cascading down across his belly. She glanced around, expectant. He knew she was waiting for him to begin, to lead her, that she didn't know the first thing about the many positions available for lovemaking, or that in this one she was in command.

Deliberately, he said, "You wanted the use of my body. You have it. Now ride me." Her eyes widened, but he didn't give her a chance to protest. "Do it!"

She turned back to face forward, her cheeks flaming. But there was that fullness inside her that had to be answered. And if he wouldn't do it . . .

It was easy, once she found her rhythm. It was easy because it felt so wonderful, and she was in control, able to set her own pace. She could rock gently back and forth, or she could lift herself up, to slam down hard if she wanted, or to glide down with exquisite slowness. Her whims, her control—until Anthony took over.

He had no choice. She had caught on too quickly, was doing too good a job on him, and he knew damn well he wouldn't be able to wait for her to climax. He shouldn't wait. He should leave her wanting. After all, it wasn't necessary for her to experience pleasure to get with child. But he couldn't do that to her, whether she deserved it or not.

He sat up, locking an arm around her waist to keep her still while his other hand slid into the soft folds of her lower lips to find the little nub of her pleasure. He brought her to the very pinnacle, then let her go to finish on her own, and she did, riding him so hard and fast that the rolling spasms enveloped them both within mere seconds of one another.

She collapsed back on him in the chair, exhausted, blissful, and he allowed her a few moments, allowed himself the pleasure of wrapping his arms around her—for those few moments. But then he sat up and helped her to her feet.

"Get into bed—my bed. Until you conceive, you will sleep there."

The cold tone broke into her euphoria, shocking her. She turned around to see his expression was bland, his cobalt eyes opaque, making her wonder if her ears had deceived her. Then he looked away, as if he had dismissed her from his mind, while he calmly closed his trousers. And it finally dawned on her that he hadn't removed them. He hadn't even unbelted his robe. For that matter, she was still wearing her negligee.

Tears gathered in her eyes. Anthony looked up to see them, and his face transformed with fury.

"Don't!" he snarled. "Or so help me, I'll blister your backside. You got exactly what you came in here for."

"That's no' true!" she cried.

"Isn't it? Did you expect more when you put desire on a time schedule?"

She turned her back on him so he wouldn't see the tears fall and took refuge in his bed. Much as she wanted to return to her own room at that moment, she didn't dare put it to the test, not in his present mood. But shame washed over her, keeping the tears pouring. He was right. She had come in here thinking he would make love to her as he had before. That she got something entirely different was no more than she deserved. And to her further shame, she had actually experienced pleasure from it.

She had been so sure she had made the right decision. Ah, God, why hadn't she listened to Nettie? Why was she always so self-centered, never considering anyone else's feelings but her own? If Anthony had come to her with the same proposal, that she share his bed only until she conceived, then he wanted nothing more to do with her, she would have been destroyed and thought him the most callous, cruel . . . ah, God, what must he think of her now? *She* wouldn't have agreed to such an outrageous suggestion. She would have been horribly insulted, and yes, furious, just as he was.

At least he didn't love her. She would hate to think what he would be feeling now if he did. But he did feel other things for her, desire, jealousy, possessiveness . . .

Roslynn's eyes rounded with the startling realization that those particular feelings all accompanied love. But he had said he didn't love her! No, he had said it was too soon to speak of love. But he'd never corrected her when she'd mentioned that he didn't love her. He couldn't love her. But what if he did? For that matter, what if he were telling the truth and he hadn't been unfaithful? If that were so, then her actions since they had married would be unforgivable. No—no! She couldn't be wrong about everything!

She sat up to see him still in the chair, his brandy snifter in hand again. "Anthony?"

He didn't glance her way, but his voice was terse, bitter. "Go to sleep, Roslynn. We will breed again at my convenience, not yours."

She flinched, lying back down again. Did he really think she had called him to invite him to "breed" again? No, he was just being nasty, and she couldn't blame him. She would undoubtedly have to put up with a lot more nastiness too, because she couldn't think for the moment how to get out of this latest bargain she had struck with him.

But she didn't sleep. And Anthony didn't come to bed.

Chapter Thirty-seven

It was only half past seven when Roslynn hurried downstairs the next morning. Her cheeks were still blooming with color from the mortifying experience of having come face-to-face with James as she sneaked out of Anthony's room earlier, wearing only her revealing negligee. Still wearing his evening clothes, and still looking impeccable for that matter, he had obviously just come home from a night's carousing and was just opening the door to his room down the corridor when Roslynn saw him and he saw her. And his eyes made sure that he saw *all* of her, moving slowly down her frame, then maddeningly back up, before one infuriating brow crooked in amused inquiry.

Hell's teeth, she had been embarrassed, and, face flaming, she had shot immediately into her own room and soundly closed the door, cringing to hear James' hearty laughter before he entered his own room. She had wanted nothing more than to crawl under the covers on her bed and never come out. It was one thing for James to think that she had made up with Anthony and was sharing his bed again, but quite another for him to see that that wasn't the case, that she was still keeping her own quarters, separate from his. What must James think? She shouldn't care. She had too many other problems on her mind to worry about what Anthony's brother thought of her curious behavior.

One of those problems was finding the bills from all her recent purchases before Anthony did. She realized now how childish was her desire to cause him penury just for spite. It was utterly contemptible for a woman her age to resort to such ploys. And besides, he was too angry with her now for her to risk antagonizing him further if he discovered the enormous amount of money she had spent, all in his name.

She didn't have much time. Though she had left Anthony still sleeping in the chair he had never left last night, he always rose early for his morning ride. She wanted to be out of the house before he came down. Now that it was safe to leave, with Geordie no longer a worry, she could go to the bank and then personally take care of each of those bills. By the time she had to face Anthony again, she would at least have a clear conscience about that. Then she could consider how to get out of the horrible bargain she had made with him without sacrificing her pride or revealing that she still hadn't forgiven him for his lies. As far as she could see, it was going to be impossible to make amends to him without her pride suffering in some way. She had already spent half the night on the problem, with no solution forthcoming.

She carried her reticule and bonnet still in her hands and dropped them into a chair in Anthony's study as she went to search his desk. Her short spencer jacket in brown with a gold weave and the sorrel-brown dress she wore were sedate enough for doing business, and for her mood, which was bordering on depression, and desperation, to see her way out of the hole she was afraid she had dug too deep.

The first drawer contained ledgers and account books, the second personal correspondence she didn't even glance through. In the third drawer she found what she was looking for, more than what she was looking for. It was stuffed full of bills, some opened, some not. Typical of the gentry, and what she had been counting on. Bills tended to be ignored, sometimes for months, sometimes indefinitely, usually at least until they were ready to be paid. Hers hadn't even been opened, as she found to her relief when she recognized the names of the five merchants she had dealt with.

But this time Roslynn couldn't resist glancing through the contents of the drawer. A bill for five hundred pounds from a tailor didn't surprise her; one for two thousand from a jeweler made her brows rise. Another for thirty thousand to a Squire Simmons fairly boggled her eyes, and it didn't even say what it was for! And those were only three creditors of at least twenty bills that she could see piled in the drawer!

Was Anthony already in debt? Hell's teeth, and she had planned to add to it substantially. He would have gone through the roof if he had opened her bills. Thank God he was typical of his class and had just stuffed the things away to be ignored until a later day.

While she was at the bank, she would have to see about having the funds due him from her marriage contract transferred to an account for him and arrange to have the allotted amount added each month. Then she would have to go through the unpleasant task of explaining about the money, for if she didn't tell him, he would never know it was available. And this was *not* the time to talk of money to him. Another cursed problem to worry about.

"Hello, there!"

Roslynn jumped and hastily crumpled the bills in her hand and stuffed them in her skirt pocket, which was, fortunately, below the level of the desk, so Jeremy couldn't see what she was doing. At least it was only he. If it had been Anthony who had caught her behind his desk, she would have had no excuse. With Jeremy, she didn't need one, but was still nervous from the start he had given her.

"You're up early," she pointed out, coming around the desk to get her bonnet and tie it on.

"Derek's picking me up. We're off to a wild party in the country that could last for days."

His excitement fairly bubbled over. God, how she wished she had known Anthony when he was this young and probably looked exactly as Jeremy did now, they were so close in resemblance. But she doubted Anthony had ever been this transparent, even at the tender age of seventeen.

"Does your father know?"

"'Course he does."

This was said too quickly, and Roslynn felt her maternal instincts rise unexpectedly. "Just what do you mean, wild?"

Jeremy winked at her, full of high spirits. "There's to be no ladies, if you get my drift, but lots of women."

"Does your father know about *that?*"

He laughed at her look of censure. "Said he might stop by himself."

Roslynn felt another blush coming on. If it was all right with his father, who was she to say otherwise? The lad was certainly old enough to . . . well, James must think him old enough. But no son of hers would be cavorting with women at seventeen. She would see to that—if she ever had a son.

She sighed, picking up her reticule. "Well, have a—" No, she wouldn't wish him a good time. She just couldn't condone what he was off to do at his age, even if he did look a full-grown man already. "I'll see you when you return, I suppose."

"You're going out?" he asked in sudden concern, her bonnet making that obvious. "Is it safe?"

"Perfectly." She smiled. "Your uncle took care of everything."

"You need a ride, then? Derek will be here shortly."

"No, I have a carriage waiting and one of the footmen is accompanying me, though I'm only going to the bank. Be good, Jeremy," she said in parting, to his chagrin.

It wasn't that short a ride to the bank, but to Roslynn's irritation, she was still too early. She hadn't even thought of the time in her impatience to be out of the house. Rather than just sit there, she had the driver slowly round the block several times, until the bank was finally open.

Her business took just under an hour, longer than she had expected because of opening the account for Anthony. A hundred thousand pounds' lump sum, plus another twenty each month as per her contract, ought to help if he was as deep in debt as she thought. Whether he would appreciate this dowry of hers was another matter. Most men would. She just wasn't sure Anthony was one of them.

Coming out of the bank, Roslynn was distracted, as her driver and the accompanying footman were, by the sight of two men engaged in fisticuffs up the street, something one might expect to see down by the waterfront, not here . . .

She didn't finish the thought. An arm came around her waist from behind, cutting off her breath, and something hard and sharp poked in her side.

"No funny stuff this time, m'lady, or I'll let ye see just 'ow sharp this 'ere sticker be."

She said not a word. She was at first too surprised to, then too afraid when she realized what his "sticker" was. In broad daylight, right in front of a bank—this was incredible. And her carriage was right there, not five feet away. But she was being led behind it while the fight in front of it was still claiming everyone's attention. Had that been planned as a distraction? Hell's teeth, if this was Geordie's doing—but it couldn't be. He had been warned off, violently. He wouldn't dare—would he?

She was shoved into an old coach, one with dark shades over the windows, and the fellow closed the door behind them after following her in. She started to get up off the floor, but a rough hand shoved her back down.

"Give me no trouble, m'lady, an' this'll go real easy fer ye," he said as he stuffed a cloth in her mouth, then quickly tied her hands behind her back. He looked down at his handiwork, noticed her feet, and decided to take no chances, whipping a rope around her ankles. His chuckle was ugly as he plucked her dirk out of her boot. "Ye won't be gettin' another chance to use this on me brother."

Roslynn groaned inwardly, hearing that. So he was one of the men from her last attempted abduction, Geordie's men. Her cousin must be insane to still try and take her. He knew she was married. What the devil did he think he was doing? She stiffened, the answer coming to her. The only thing he could want with her now was revenge for her having eluded his well-planned trap.

The fellow left the coach, left her lying on the floor. A few moments later the old vehicle started to move. Roslynn turned over on her side to try and sit up. The gag in her mouth hadn't been secured, and she frantically worked with her tongue to push it out. She had almost succeeded when the coach slowed down and she heard the driver shout, "That's enough, Tom!"

A second later the door opened and another fellow jumped inside the coach. She recognized this one as the footpad she had taken a chunk out of with her dirk. His lip was bleeding, and he was out of breath. So the distraction *had* been arranged. This was one of the pugilists, who had probably picked a fight with a stranger just so no one would notice when the other fellow led her away. And she had gone along willy-nilly, with a knife pricking her side, not making a single protest.

The fellow, Tom, was grinning at her as he lifted her up and set her on the seat across from him. He tucked her gag back in her mouth too, shaking his head at her in an amused way. At least he wasn't vengeful for the hurt she had caused him the last time, or he didn't seem to be. He was studying her and continued grinning. Finally he laughed.

"God, ye're a bleedin' beauty close up, ye are. Too good fer the likes o' that bastard what's payin' us, I'd say." She tried to speak through the gag, uselessly. "None o' that, now. Thought we'd never get ye, but 'ere ye are. Be good, and there'll be no cause to get rough wi' ye."

Her second warning not to cause trouble. So what would happen if she did? Stupid question, when she was bound up hand and foot and couldn't make a sound louder than a squeak.

Chapter Thirty-eight

They brought her into the building tossed over Tom's shoulder. They had waited first, however, until Wil, as the other, shorter man was called, had said that all was clear. Roslynn's hopes picked up immediately. They were taking her somewhere where someone might stop and question them for treating her in this horrid manner. One good scream, if she got the chance, was all she might need to be rescued.

From her upside-down position, she saw little of the building before they entered it and she was being hurried up some stairs. But across the street were dwellings faced with brownstone, looking as if they belonged in a normal residential area, and one of fair quality. A boarding house, then? Likely, if no one was about at this time of the morning.

So this was where Geordie had moved, to a finer part of town? No wonder Anthony had so much trouble finding him when all he had to go by was that waterfront hovel where she had been taken last time. But little good it had done, his finding Geordie. And she had walked right into the trap, thinking herself safe at last. Hell's teeth, but she despised Geordie for his Scot's stubbornness in refusing to give up.

There was a brief stop while a door was pounded on. Then a few more steps and Roslynn was dumped into a chair. She groaned as she sat back on her bound arms, terribly sore now after the slow, long ride getting here. But she spared only a moment for the discomfort before glancing furiously about the room for a sight of Geordie.

When she saw him standing next to the bed, a folded shirt in hand, his valise open on the bed in the process of being packed, she simply stared, wondering who he was. But the carrot thatch of hair . . .

Roslynn grimaced, unable to help herself. If not for the hair, she wouldn't have recognized him. He looked horrible. He looked as if he belonged in bed, not packing to leave. Good God, what Anthony had done to him! His whole face was discolored and puffed to twice its size, it seemed, one eye black and completely closed, the other bluish-purple and just able to open a mere slit. His nose was swollen and off center. His lips were caked with bloody crusts. There were other ugly scabs on his cheeks and above his eyes where the skin had cracked on bone.

He wasn't looking at her, at least not now. He was staring at the two miscreants responsible for her presence, who were staring at him as if they'd never seen him before. Hadn't they known he'd taken a beating? Hell's teeth, had a mistake been made?

It had been. Geordie threw down his shirt in a rage, then groaned, grabbing his rib cage, the sharp movement ripping him apart with pain. Wilbert and Thomas Stow just stood there, not knowing what to think.

Geordie told them what to think, in a voice choked with rage, the words slurred because of puffed lips. "Ye idiots! Didna the lad I sent tae find ye give ye my note?"

"This?" Tom took out a scrap of paper from his pocket. "We can't read, m'lord," he stated with a shrug, letting the note drop to the floor.

Geordie made an ugly sound in his throat. "'Tis what I get fer hiring English dolts!" He pointed a stiff finger at Roslynn. "I dinna want her now. She married the bloody Englishmon!"

Wilbert and Thomas apparently thought that was funny. They started laughing, and Roslynn watched what wasn't black-and-blue on Geordie's face turn bright red. If what she had gone through to get here wasn't so infuriating, she might have found the situation as it was amusing too.

Geordie didn't. "Get oout, the both of ye!"

The pair stopped laughing. "When ye pay us, m'lord."

Wilbert might have given him the title of respect, but there was no respect in his tone. In fact, the short, thickly bearded fellow looked absolutely menacing as he stared at Geordie. So did the bigger chap beside him. And Geordie had gone quiet, his rage replaced by something else. Roslynn's eyes widened. He was afraid! Didn't he have the money to pay them?

Geordie in fact had only enough money to get back to Scotland. He had counted on Roslynn's money to pay his hirelings off. All that money, gone to the Englishman. It wasn't fair. And now these two would probably kill him. And in his condition, he couldn't even defend himself.

Working her gag while no one was watching, Roslynn finally managed to spit it out. "Untie me, and I'll give you your money—in exchange for my dirk."

"Dinna touch her!" Geordie commanded.

Roslynn turned on him furiously. "Shut up, Geordie! Do you ken what my husband will do to you when he finds out about this? You'd look bonny right now by comparison if he gets his hands on you again."

Wilbert and Thomas didn't miss the significance of that "again," but they were done listening to Geordie anyway. They might have killed a few men in their time, but they had never harmed a woman before. They hadn't liked this job to begin with, and wouldn't have taken it if the Scot hadn't offered what was a bleeding fortune to them.

Wilbert stepped forward and cut Roslynn's bonds with her own dirk. Flipping the blade over in his hand, he handed it to her, but was quick to step back out of her way.

Roslynn was amazed it had been so easy, since she hadn't been at all sure the two ruffians would obey her. But they had, and she felt infinitely better already. And she had obviously guessed right, or Geordie would have gotten them their money before she was cut loose. Instead, he had sat down on the bed, holding his ribs, warily watching all three.

"How much?" she demanded as she stood up.

"Thirty pounds, m'lady."

She spared a contemptuous glance for her cousin. "You're cheap, Geordie. It seems you could have offered a bit more to two such dependable fellows."

"I might have, if they'd have gotten ye afore that bastard married ye!" he spat out.

She clucked her tongue, feeling rather good about having miraculously gotten the upper hand in the confrontation she had so dreaded.

Reaching into the reticule that was still tied to her wrist, she took out a handful of money.

"This will do, I believe, gentlemen." She handed the notes to Wilbert.

Both brothers' eyes gleamed at what amounted to nearly fifty pounds. Wilbert glanced at her reticule. Roslynn intercepted his look, stiffening.

"Don't even think about it," she warned. "And if you don't want to end up looking like him"—she nodded toward Geordie—"you'll never let me see you again."

They both grinned at the little woman threatening *them*. But they had been paid enough. If the Scot hadn't been mashed to a pulp, they would have gotten in a few licks themselves for all his insults. As it was, they were satisfied and, with grinning nods, left.

They stopped grinning, however, at the top of the stairs. Coming up them was the same gent whose house they had been watching for the past ten days, the same gent who was undoubtedly now the lady's husband. He didn't look menacing, didn't even spare them a glance as he slowly mounted the stairs, and yet neither brother could get out of his mind the Scot's condition that this man was responsible for.

Wilbert pulled his knife, just to feel safe, though he palmed it close to his thigh. That would have been the end of it if the nabob wasn't deceptive in his nonchalance. He had in fact noticed the knife and stopped. They both heard him sigh before he spoke.

"Bloody hell. Come along, then, and let's get this over with."

Wilbert glanced once at Thomas before they both charged as one. Their attack didn't turn out as they had expected, however. The nobleman stepped out of the way at the last second, putting his back to the wall, and with one foot extended, Thomas went tumbling down the rest of the stairs. And before Wilbert knew what was happening, he had lost his knife. Seeing it in the noble's hand, he tore down the stairs himself, collected a groaning Thomas up from the floor, and dragged them both out of the building.

Upstairs in the room, Roslynn was pacing furiously before an embittered Geordie. "There are no' enough dirty, loathsome, vile names for what you are, Geordie Cameron. It's shamed I am, you carry that name. You've never brought anything good to it, have you now?"

"And ye have, have ye?"

"Shut up, mon! Because of you I'm married now. Because of you I *had* to get married, when that was no' what I was wanting, at least no' this way!"

"And ye've lost it all, havena ye, ye stupid fool!" he shot back at her. "And I'm glad, do ye hear? If I canna have the Cameron wealth, at least I'm knowing he's tricked ye oout of it as well!"

Roslynn stopped short, glaring at him. "What are you blathering about?"

"He told me he burned yer marriage contract," Geordie replied in what passed for a laugh. "The wily bastard's got it all now, and ye wouldna even be getting it back if he died, 'cause he's leaving it all tae his own kin. Nice husband ye've shackled yerself wi', cousin."

She almost laughed, but if Anthony had gone to the trouble to tell Geordie that lie, she wouldn't take it back. It was brilliant, really, in making Geordie think his chance was forever lost.

"I'd still rather have him than you, *cousin*."

He tried getting up at that slur. He moaned loudly, falling back on the bed. Roslynn goaded him further, not in the least sympathetic.

"You should have left when you had the chance, Geordie. There willna be much left of you if my husband finds out you're still here. He's no' a man to trifle wi', as you've found out. But you deserve it for trying to kill him."

"I was only trying tae scare him into forsaking ye. I didna know then ye'd married the mon. But he only hit me a few times fer shooting at him. The rest was all fer ye. And I'll have ye know, I couldna even get up off the floor where he'd left me until this morning." This was said in what sounded very much like a whine. "But ye can see fer yerself that I was leaving, sae ye've nae tales tae take tae that bloody Spartan."

Spartan? Yes, she supposed Anthony could at times be likened to that austere race known for its strict discipline and military prowess, but only in the lightest sense. His self-control might be absolutely maddening when he chose to use it, but when he didn't, he was as hottempered as any Scot. And look at what he had done to Geordie, without getting even a scratch in the process. Poor Geordie looked like he had been trampled by a horse, not merely beaten by a man's fists.

"I wasn't going to tell Anthony, not if you really are leaving," she conceded.

"Ye're all heart, lass."

It was impossible to mistake the bitter sarcasm, and her outrage shot to the fore again. "If you're expecting me to feel sorry for you, Geordie, I mun disappoint you. I just canna do it, no' after all you've done. You tried to hurt me!"

"I loved ye!"

The words were like a rope around her throat, choking off her breath. Was it possible? He had said that often enough over the years, but she had never believed him. Why did it have a ring of truth to it this time? Or had he deluded himself into thinking it was so?

Quietly, actually afraid of the answer, she demanded, "If that's true, Geordie, then tell me about my mother. Did you put a hole in her boat?"

His head came off the bed, followed more slowly by the rest of his body. "Why did ye no' ask me when it mattered, Ros, when it happened? Why did the auld mon never ask? Nae, I never tampered wi' her boat. I was down by the loch finding worms tae put in cook's stew. That was as close as I ever came tae those boats."

"But your face when you were told? We all saw you were horrified."

"Aye, because I'd wished her dead, fer boxing my ears that morning. I didna mean it, but I thought my wish had been granted. I *felt* I was tae blame."

Roslynn felt sick to her stomach. All these years, they'd blamed him for something he didn't do. And he knew what they thought but never spoke up to defend himself, just harbored his resentment unto himself. It didn't make him a nicer person in her eyes, but it made him innocent of any real crime.

"I'm sorry, Geordie, I really am."

"But ye still wouldna have married me, would ye, knowing the truth?"

"No. And you shouldn't have tried to force me."

"A mon will do anything when he's desperate."

For love or money? She didn't ask. But she wondered if her grandfather's will might have been different if he had known the truth. Somehow, she didn't think so. He had always despised Geordie's weakness, an unforgivable trait for a man of Duncan's strength of character. She wasn't that uncharitable. And she had to salve her conscience for blaming Geordie for her mother's death, which she now realized must have been no more than a freak accident.

She would leave him the money in her reticule that had been intended to pay her bills. Ten thousand pounds wasn't much compared with what she had, but it would be a start for Geordie. And maybe he could do something with it to make his own way, instead of always looking for the easy road that cost him nothing and made him weaker.

Roslynn turned around to remove the money without his seeing. She would leave it where he wouldn't find it until she had gone.

"I'll help you pack, Geordie."

"Dinna do me any favors."

She ignored the bitterness and moved to the bureau, where several articles of clothing still remained in an open drawer. She gathered them up and slipped the money between the clothes before dropping the pile in his valise. It was a mistake to have gotten that close. His hand snaked out, wrapping around her wrist.

"Ros—"

The door opened and she was freed, never to know what Geordie had been about to say. She would like to think it might have been an apology for all he'd put her through. It didn't matter at the moment, not with Anthony's presence filling the room.

"With as quiet as it got, I was afraid you might have killed each other."

She didn't question why he was there, not just then. "Eavesdropping at doors seems to be a habit of yours, my lord."

He didn't deny it. "A useful one, and most times fascinating."

That "most times" referred to his eavesdropping on her and Frances, she knew, and he didn't like what he had overheard then. But there wasn't much he could have overheard this time to annoy him. He might look stern, but by now she knew the difference. He was angry, but not *that* angry. In fact, it could just be a carryover from last night.

"He's leaving, as you can see," she said, walking toward her husband.

"And you came to say good-bye?" Anthony replied dryly. "How thoughtful of you, my dear."

She wasn't going to be baited. "If you've come to take me home, I thank you. I find myself without a ride."

She hoped that that would do it, that he wouldn't direct his attention to Geordie now and start a scene that she would be forced to witness. She didn't particularly want to see Anthony in the mood that could have brought about what he'd already done to Geordie. His level stare made her hold her breath. And then he directed that intense look to Geordie. Roslynn knew her cousin must be trembling in mortal fear.

"I'll be gone wi'in the hour," Geordie volunteered.

Anthony's nerve-racking stare lasted a moment longer. Then he nodded curtly and led Roslynn out the door. His hand on her elbow was impossible to break loose from, so she gave up after one try. Outside, there was no carriage, just his horse being held by a street urchin.

Roslynn decided to attack before he could. "What were you doing back here?"

"Come to see you home, of course."

"Making sure he was gone, you mean, since you couldn't possibly know I'd be here."

"That too."

She gritted her teeth. "*Did* you know?"

"Not until I heard you tearing into the poor man with all the vile, loathsome, and despicable names you never got around to calling him."

So he had been outside the door from the beginning. Had she said anything he shouldn't have heard? No, she didn't think so—not this time. But she was still annoyed.

"You would have been better served to have ferreted out his men, who had still been watching the house—from the park, no doubt. They followed me to the bank and—"

"Yes, Jeremy did mention that was your destination. Imagine my surprise to find you here instead."

He said it as if he didn't believe her. "Hell's teeth, Anthony! I didn't know where he was, so how could I have found him even if I'd wanted to, which I didn't? Those dolts he hired hadn't been told yet that he'd given up."

"Plausible," was all he said as he tossed the youth a coin and mounted his stallion.

She glared at the hand he leaned over to offer her. Sitting next to him all the way home was not very enticing at the moment. She would have preferred to find a hack but saw none on the street.

She took his hand and found herself sitting between his legs, her own draped over his thigh. Color rose swiftly to her cheeks as she was forced to put her arms around him. It was a disconcerting ride, one that brought vividly to mind her main dilemma. Surrounded by his warmth, her nostrils filled with his scent, she could think only about how to get out of the bargain she had struck with him and back into his bed without any stipulations at all.

Chapter Thirty-nine

The ride to Piccadilly seemed to take forever, and yet it wasn't nearly long enough. A hazy kind of euphoria had settled over Roslynn. With no words to distract her, just the steady gait of the horse, the steady beat of Anthony's heart next to her ear, it was easy to forget reality and float in a cocoon of contentment.

So it was quite jarring to be placed on her feet and have her plaguey problems recalled. The suddenness of it left Roslynn disoriented for a moment. In fact, she stared at the crumpled envelope lying at her feet for a good fifteen seconds before she realized what it was and reached for it. Anthony's hand came up the victor.

Roslynn groaned inwardly, having forgotten all about those stupid bills. To have one fall out of her skirt pocket was bad enough. To have Anthony retrieve it was the worst luck. And it was too much to hope he would just hand it back to her. He didn't. He opened it!

"Anthony!"

He shot her a glance with one dark, winged brow arched. "It's addressed to me," was all he said.

She started to walk into the house, as if that would end the matter. His hand on her arm detained her while he still perused the paper in his other hand.

When he spoke, his voice sounded merely curious. "Might I ask what you're doing with this?"

She could see no way out and turned to face him. "It's for some of the furniture I bought."

"I can see what it's for, my dear. I asked what you're doing with it."

"I was going to pay it. That's why . . ."

Her words trailed off as she saw his eyes drift down to her pocket. She followed his gaze and saw another envelope poking out. The bloody ride had worked them loose. And before she could say another word, Anthony's hand was in her pocket and pulling out the rest of the bills.

"You were going to pay these too?"

She nodded, but he wasn't looking at her, so she choked the word out. "Yes."

"Then wouldn't it have been appropriate to have them billed to you instead of me?"

She didn't understand why he was being so calm about this. "I—I meant to, but I forgot."

"No, you didn't," he replied, making her heart sink, only to confuse her by adding, in what was unmistakable amusement, "You're not very good at bargaining, my dear. I could have found these items for half the price you paid for them."

He stuffed the bills into his own pocket, annoying her, because it was just what she would have expected him to do. "Those are *my* purchases," she reminded him.

"They grace *my* house."

"I bought them," she insisted. "I'll bloody well pay for them."

"No, you won't. You had no intention of paying for them to begin with, so let's just leave it as it is, shall we?"

He was smiling at her. Smiling! "Don't be stubborn about this, Anthony. You have enough creditors already. I want to pay for what I—"

"Be quiet, sweetheart," he interrupted, his hands resting on her shoulders. "I suppose I shouldn't have let you go on thinking I was just struggling by, but you were having so much fun trying to put me in debt, I didn't want to spoil it." He chuckled when she lowered her eyes guiltily, and lifted her chin back up. "The truth is, you could have redecorated a hundred households, and I wouldn't have raised a brow."

"But you can't be rich!"

He laughed delightedly. "It pays to have a brother who is a genius where money is concerned. Edward has a golden touch, you might say. And he handles the family's finances with our blessings. If the town house still doesn't suit you after all the trouble you've gone through to redo it, I have several estates in the outlying vicinity, as well as in Kent, Northampton, Norfolk, York, Lincoln, Wiltshire, Devon—"

"Enough!"

"Are you so disappointed I didn't marry you for your money, my dear?"

"You've still got some of it, as per the marriage contract. I put the money into an account for you this morning." There, at least that was out of the way.

So was his amusement. "You'll take yourself back to the bank and put it in a trust for our children. And as long as we're on this subject, I support you, Roslynn. Your clothes, your jewels, anything that adorns your body, I pay for."

"And what am I supposed to do with *my* money?" she demanded sharply.

"Anything you like, as long as it's nothing to do with clothing, food, or shelter, or what is my prerogative to buy you. You might do well to discuss with me first what you decide to spend your money on. We just might avoid future arguments in that way."

Her independent spirit was infuriated. Her woman's heart was delighted. And that word "children" kept buzzing in her head. It implied an eventual end to their difficulties, though she couldn't see that end in sight.

"If this discussion is going to continue, shouldn't we take it inside?"

Anthony grinned at her neutral tone. He had made his point, and his earlier pleasure that she had given up her spite against him returned. For whatever reason, it was a peace offering, and he could make one too. That what he had in mind was more of a necessity after that close ride with her was just plain luck.

"This subject has run its course," Anthony said, leading her inside the house. "But there is another that needs immediate attention."

Roslynn's heart skipped a beat, but she couldn't be sure she had grasped his meaning correctly. So she didn't allow herself to hope until he took her arm and escorted her upstairs to his room. Even then, as he closed the door behind them, she still wasn't certain of his intentions. He crossed the room, removed his coat, and tossed it into that cursed chair they had occupied last night.

She frowned at the chair. Oh, she had learned her lesson in it, as he had promised she would. Resentment bubbled up in her chest, to fight with the powerful arousal she felt just by being in this room again.

"Come here, Roslynn."

He had moved to the bed, was sitting on it, was slowly unbuttoning his white cambric shirt. Her heart picked up double time. He was a temptation beyond imagining, but she didn't think she could bear it if he was going to be "perfunctory" with her once more.

"You—you feel capable of simulating desire, I take it?"

"Simulate?" Both brows shot up. "Oh, I see. You still don't believe in spontaneity, do you, sweetheart? Come here and help me with my boots, will you?"

She did, only because he hadn't answered her question yet, and she didn't feel like running until she knew for sure. The nastiness she could take, but not the lack of passion.

"You're nervous," he noted when she wouldn't turn around after dropping his second boot on the floor. "You needn't be, my dear. You have to take advantage of me when the opportunity presents itself."

He saw her back stiffen and immediately regretted those words. He had made his point last night. She wouldn't forget it. But he couldn't go through that experience again to save his soul.

He reached forward to draw her between his legs, his hands sliding up her ribs to cup her breasts, his cheek pressed against her spencer. Her head fell back. She arched into his hands. Anthony ignited, dropping her down onto the bed, twisting so he leaned over her but kept her legs locked between his.

"Simulation, my dear? I don't believe you and I are capable of such a feat."

His mouth covered hers with a scorching passion that singed all her nerve ends, taking her breath away. It was exquisite. It was what she remembered, this consuming fire between them that defied all reason. Last night was forgotten. He was kissing her now as if he would die if he didn't, hiding nothing from her, and the soul of the woman came alive in his arms.

Chapter Forty

"I'll be leaving in two days, Tony," was the first thing James said as he
entered the dining room.

"Need help packing?"

"Don't be tedious, puppy. You know you've loved having me."

Anthony grunted and resumed eating his breakfast. "When did you
finally decide to be on your way?"

"When I saw how hopeless your situation has become. It's simply
no fun to watch anymore."

Anthony tossed down his fork, glaring at his brother's back as
James walked casually to the sideboard after that remark and heaped
food on a plate. Actually, he thought he'd made a great deal of progress
in the past two weeks. He had only to touch Roslynn now and she
turned into his arms. He failed to see what was hopeless about that.
Soon she would admit that she needed him as much as he needed her.
She would admit her folly and damn her own rules. But until she did, he
would abide by them, to the bloody letter.

"Would you mind explaining that remark?"

James sat down across from him and said maddeningly, "I like this
room now. What'd it cost you?"

"Blister it, James!"

A shrug. "It's obvious, dear boy. Here she is sharing your room, at
all hours of the day, I've noticed, yet when you two aren't ensconced
behind that door, you're bloody strangers. Where's the finesse you're
known for that has women eating out of the palm of your hand? Is she
immune?"

"This is none of your business, you know."

"I know."

Anthony answered him anyway. "She's not immune, but she's not like other women either. She has these infernal notions . . . the point is, I want her to come to me of her own will, not with senses drugged and giving her no choice."

"You mean she won't—come to you, that is?" When Anthony simply scowled at him, James chuckled. "Don't tell me you haven't straightened up that little misunderstanding about sweet Margie?"

"You still remember her name?"

The sneer was obvious, but James chose to ignore his brother's testiness. "Actually, I've been back to see her quite often. She was a delectable piece." But that vixen in breeches hadn't shown up at the tavern again, the real reason he had gone back there. "Did you never think to explain?"

"I did. I won't do it twice."

James sighed at such stubbornness, never mind that his own was just as irksome to friend and foe. "Pride is the advent of fools, dear boy. You've been married nearly a month. If I had known what a bloody mess you were going to make of it, I would have pursued the lady in earnest."

"Over my dead body," Anthony snarled.

"Touchy, aren't we?" James grinned. "But it doesn't matter. You won her. What you've done with the prize, however, is deplorable. A little romancing wouldn't be amiss. She did melt for you in the moonlight, didn't she?"

Anthony just managed to keep his seat when the urge to clobber his brother was overwhelming. "The last thing I need from you is advice, James. I have my own strategy where my wife is concerned, and although it may not appear to be working, it is."

"Strangest bit of strategy I've ever witnessed, enemies by day, lovers by moonlight. I wouldn't have the patience myself. If they don't succumb by the first effort—"

"They're not worth it?"

"Some are. But there are just too many other sweet consolations to be bothered."

"But I've got Roslynn."

James laughed. "Point taken, I suppose. *Is* she worth it?"

Anthony's answer was a slow smile, his first, and James sobered. Yes, he supposed the little Scot was worth a bit a patience. But as for Anthony's strategy, it was obvious to James he was only digging his hole even deeper. James wouldn't be at all surprised if, when he returned to England, Anthony's wife had much in common with Jason's, who used any excuse available to avoid her husband.

Nettie appeared in the doorway. "Excuse me, Sir Anthony, but Lady Roslynn would be liking a word wi' ye."

"Where is she?"

"In her room, my lord. She's no' feeling up tae snuff."

Anthony waved the woman away before growling, "Bloody hell!"

James shook his head in disgust. "There, you see? You hear your wife's ill, and instead of being concerned—"

"Confound you, James, you don't know what the bloody hell's going on, so stay out of it! If she's ill, it's what she's been praying for. I noticed it the other morning when—" Anthony stopped at James' quirked brow. "Damnation. She's going to tell me I'm going to be a father."

"A—but that's splendid!" James said in delight, only to notice Anthony's scowl grow even blacker and add hesitantly, "Isn't it?"

"No, it bloody well isn't!"

"For God's sake, Tony, children usually do follow marriage—"

"I know that, you dolt! I want the child. I just don't want the conditions that come with it."

James started to laugh, misunderstanding. "The price of fatherhood, don't you know. Good God, it's only a few months you'll have to stay out of the lady's bed. You can always find relief elsewhere."

Anthony stood up, his voice calm, but cold enough to freeze. "*If* I wanted relief elsewhere, and *if* it were only for a few months, you might be right, brother. But my celibacy begins the moment my dear wife announces her condition to me."

James was surprised enough to reply, "Whose ridiculous idea was *that?*"

"It bloody well wasn't mine."

"You mean the only reason she came to you was to get a child?"

"None other."

James snorted. "I hate to say it, dear boy, but it sounds like your wife needs her backside treated to a good thrashing."

"No, what she needs is to admit she's wrong, and she will. How soon is the question that's going to drive me crazy."

Chapter Forty-one

Weak tea and dry toast, at Nettie's insistence. Not a very appetizing breakfast, but better than the hot chocolate and pastries that had sent Roslynn flying toward the chamber pot earlier. She had suspected her condition for the past week, after her monthly time was late. She had been sure three days ago, when the most ghastly queasiness had started in the morning, only to vanish come noon. And each day it had gotten a little worse. This morning she had had to stay near the chamber pot for nearly an hour, had heaved her stomach dry. She dreaded what tomorrow would bring, and tomorrow morning was Frances' wedding. She wasn't at all sure she would be able to make it, which was just one more thing to depress her at the moment, when she should have been nothing but overjoyed by her condition.

Her stomach still wasn't settled completely, even with the bland toast she had nibbled on. It was hard for her to remember, considering how she was feeling, that a baby was what she wanted more than anything. Why couldn't she be one of those lucky women who suffered not a day of morning sickness? And to have started so soon! Why, she had made her infamous bargain with Anthony just two weeks ago. And she had suspected she was pregnant one week later, which told her plainly she hadn't needed to make that bargain at all, that she had in all likelihood conceived the very first time they made love.

Roslynn very gently set the teacup back on the table beside the chaise longue on which she was reclining. Undue movement, as she had discovered to her horror the other morning when Anthony made love to her, started her stomach rolling. Extreme concentration had enabled her not to embarrass herself and have to make her confession right then. And she had selfishly gone to him for two more nights without telling him the truth. But she couldn't put it off any longer. This morning she had just barely made it out of his room before he woke up and called her back to bed. And with the nausea getting worse, there was no way she could enjoy morning lovemaking anymore. She had to tell him before he found out for himself and knew she was ignoring their bargain.

Hell's teeth, how she hated that bloody bargain. Anthony had been so wonderfully amorous these past two weeks, at least in his bedroom. He made love to her so often she knew very well he had nothing left to give another woman, that she'd had him all to herself. It was as if each night were her wedding night, with all the passion and tenderness he was capable of, hers for the taking.

But outside his bedroom he was another man entirely, either indifferent or cold and sardonic, but never pleasant. And Roslynn knew this could be blamed on the bargain, his way of letting her know his distaste for her conditions hadn't lessened.

And now it was over. But she didn't want it to be over. Hell's teeth, she had become addicted to Anthony, but by her own idiotic decision, she was going to lose him. Temporary, she had said. Two short weeks was certainly that.

"You wanted to see me?"

He hadn't knocked, but had come right in. He hadn't been in this room since the night she had pretended to be indisposed. There was no pretense now.

Anthony gave the new furnishings a cursory glance before his cobalt eyes settled on her. Roslynn could feel her stomach rioting from her nervousness.

"I'm going to have a baby," she blurted out.

He stood before her, his hands in his pockets. His expression didn't change. That was the worst. He could at least have shown some small pleasure about the child. If not that, then displeasure. She would have welcomed displeasure at the moment. She would have welcomed the fury he had shown the night she had given him her terms.

"How delightful for you," he said in the blandest tone. "So your sojourns to my room are at an end."

"Yes. Unless—"

"Unless?" he cut in deliberately. "Far be it from me to break your rules, sweetheart."

She bit her lip to keep from damning those rules in his presence. She didn't know what she had started to say anyway, before he interrupted. But he obviously hadn't wanted to hear it. And she had been hoping, praying, that *he* would insist she forget their bargain, that he would demand she move back to his room permanently. He wasn't going to. Didn't he care anymore?

She looked away toward the window, her voice toneless when it should have been filled with excitement, considering the subject. "I will need a room for the nursery."

"James is leaving in a few days. You can make over his room."

She had given him the opening. He could have suggested *this* room. It was certainly more convenient, directly across from his.

She continued to stare out the window. "This is your child too, Anthony. Have you any preferences for color—or anything?"

"Whatever pleases you, my dear. By the by, I won't be home for dinner tonight. We're celebrating old George's last night of sanity at the club."

His abrupt change of subject hurt. He obviously had no interest in the baby, nor in her, since he had turned to leave without another word.

Outside the room, Anthony's fist slammed into the wall. Inside, tears were streaming down Roslynn's cheeks. She started from the noise but didn't give it a thought.

She had never felt so miserable in her life, and it was all her own fault. She couldn't even remember the reason for the stupid bargain. Oh, yes. She had been afraid she'd fall in love with Anthony with constant intimacy. Well, it was too bloody late for that, wasn't it? Nettie had been right.

"Was it the news you were expecting?"

Anthony turned to find James standing outside his room. "It was."

"Strategy's not working, then, I take it?"

"Blister it, James. Two days from now isn't soon enough!"

Chapter Forty-two

"Why don't you just tell him, Ros?"

"I can't," Roslynn replied, taking a sip of her second glass of champagne.

They stood away from the others at the party, which was just a small gathering of Frances' friends at her mother's house. The gentlemen weren't the only ones who could celebrate the night before the wedding. But Roslynn didn't feel like celebrating, though she had come to accept that Frances was ecstatic about this marriage, and she was happy for her friend. She just couldn't seem to show it.

Unfortunately, Frances had picked up on her depression and had taken her aside, afraid that Roslynn was still against the marriage. The only way she could convince her friend that she wasn't was to tell her the truth.

"If it were that simple—" Roslynn began, only to have Frances cut in.

"But it is that simple. All you do is say, I love you. Three little words, m'dear, and your problems will be over."

Roslynn shook her head. "The difference, Fran, is that those words are easy for you because you know George returns your love. But Anthony doesn't love me."

"Have you given him anything *to* love?"

Roslynn grimaced. "No. You might say I've been a royal bitch ever since we married."

"Well, you did have your reasons, didn't you? It was really too bad of Sir Anthony, but you did say you're reasonably certain he strayed only that one time. It's up to you, m'dear. You can let him know you've forgiven him his one indiscretion and you want to start over, or you can go on as you are."

Some choice, Roslynn thought, resentment still simmering just below the surface. Why did she have to make all the concessions? Anthony hadn't even apologized, and he wasn't likely to.

"A man like Sir Anthony won't wait forever, you know," Frances continued. "You're going to send him right into the arms of another woman."

"He doesn't need any sending for that," Roslynn replied bitterly.

But Frances had a point. If *she* wasn't sharing Anthony's bed, someone else would eventually. But then she had known that when she made her bargain. She just hadn't wanted to admit at that time that it would matter to her. But it did matter, terribly, because she loved him.

Returning home at eleven, Roslynn had only just removed her evening cloak and gloves when the door opened again and Anthony and George stumbled over the threshold. Dobson took one look at them and sighed. Roslynn felt she had played this scene before, and it had been no more amusing the last time, though this time it appeared Anthony was doing the supporting. George looked half asleep.

"You're home early," Roslynn remarked, keeping her tone neutral.

"The old boy got royally foxed and passed out. Thought I'd better get him to bed."

"So you brought him here instead of taking him home?"

Anthony shrugged. "Habit, my dear. When we used to make a night of it, more times than not old George would end up here. Has his own room, don't you know. Though, actually, come to think of it, you have it now."

They stared at each other a long moment before George broke the contact. "What's that? Who has my room?"

"Don't worry about it, old man. My wife has a few of her things in it that she'll be happy to move for tonight. Won't you, my dear?"

Roslynn's heart turned over. Had he brought George home just so she *would* have to move? And the only place she could move to was his room.

"Don't go to any trouble on my account, Lady Malory."

She understood him perfectly, though his words were terribly slurred and he couldn't seem to locate her, his eyes settling on Dobson instead. "It's no trouble, George," Roslynn assured him. "If you'll just give me a moment—"

"Don't have a moment," Anthony interjected. "He's bloody well heavy, you know. And if I put him down, he'll never get back up. Just proceed us, my dear, and get what you need."

She did, quickly, rushing through the room to gather her things while Anthony dumped George on the bed. George's room? So those were George's sonnets she had found in here. She never would have thought it of such a rakehell, but then you never knew. Frances was luckier than she realized.

She left the room just as quickly, for Anthony hadn't waited to start undressing George. In the corridor, she stared at the door to Anthony's room. This was what he meant for her to do, wasn't it? But then where else could she sleep? Jeremy and James probably weren't home yet, but they would be. And there were only the four rooms upstairs.

She entered the room hesitantly, expecting to find Willis waiting there for Anthony, even though the valet had been scarce these past two weeks, coming only when Anthony summoned him. The room was empty, however. Either Anthony had planned this, or he hadn't yet told Willis to hold himself available again. Then, too, the hour *was* early, by London standards. Willis wouldn't expect Anthony home this soon.

Roslynn sighed, not knowing what to think. But she wasn't going to miss this opportunity. She couldn't have planned it better herself. She wouldn't have to sacrifice her pride and confess what a fool she'd been. She could simply show Anthony that she wasn't adverse to being here, that in fact she wanted to be here.

She began removing her evening apparel. She was down to her chemise when Anthony walked into the room. His gaze rested on her for several heartbeats before he went on into his dressing room. Roslynn hastily got into bed. She wished he had said something. God, how this reminded her of her wedding night. And she was just as nervous now as she had been then.

When he came out, he was wearing only a robe. She at least had thought to slip on a nightgown. She wasn't going to be *that* obvious about what she wanted.

But it was obvious. While he moved about the room to turn down the lamps, desire lit the golden flecks in her eyes as they followed his superb form. She had had too much of him lately. She had found that it wasn't nearly enough. It never would be.

It was dark now, with only a silver stream of moonlight spilling in through the windows. Before her eyes adjusted, her other senses came alive. She could smell him as he drew near. When the bed dipped, she held her breath, waiting. She was experiencing that same giddy feeling she always felt when he was near. He would lean toward her in a moment. His mouth would find hers in the dark, warm, demanding . . .

"Good night, my dear."

Her eyes flew open. Hell's teeth, he hadn't planned the eviction from her room, after all. He was holding to her own rules not to touch her once she had conceived. It wasn't fair. How *could* he, when she was lying right next to him, wanting him more than anything?

"Anthony—"

"Yes?"

His tone was sharp to her ears, killing her courage. "Nothing," she mumbled.

Roslynn lay there, counting her heartbeats, wishing she had drunk more than two glasses of champagne at Frances' party. But she had been thinking of tomorrow morning and the nausea she would have to fight to get to the wedding. She hadn't known sleep was going to be impossible. Just last night she had felt free to turn to Anthony, to rest her head on his chest, to count *his* heartbeats. What a world of difference a single day made. No, not the day. Her cursed bargain.

This just wouldn't do. She was going to have to . . .

She heard the groan just before Anthony's hands reached over and pulled her across his chest. His kiss was wild, full of unleashed passion that set them both aflame. Roslynn didn't question it, she just accepted, so delighted and relieved that she abandoned herself completely, wantonly, to the moment. Pride couldn't equal this. She loved him. She would have to tell him, but now was not the time. Later, when she could think clearly once again.

Chapter Forty-three

It seemed anything and everything was conspiring against Roslynn to keep her from having a private word with Anthony, including herself. She had fallen blissfully asleep after they had made love the other night, and then the next morning Anthony had awakened her simply to tell her that George had left and she could have her room back. Just like that, as if the night had never been. And when she had been about to detain him, her stomach had erupted and she had made it to her room only in the nick of time.

Then there had been the wedding and the luncheon afterward that had taken most of the afternoon. But Anthony hadn't come home with her. He had gone off directly to spend this last evening with his brother, and Roslynn spent a tortuous night wondering what they were up to, because neither of them came home until the small hours of the morning.

And this morning she had been hurried out of bed for the ride to the docks to see the *Maiden Anne* off, with the whole family showing up for the occasion. She stood off to the side now with Jeremy while James' brothers each embraced him and bade him a fair voyage. She had kissed him good-bye herself, a brief peck, what with Anthony's close attention, which James couldn't resist commenting on.

"I suppose you'll miss him terribly, Jeremy?"

The boy grinned at her. "Hell's bells, he won't be gone *that* long. And I doubt I'll have time to miss him. He's laid the law down, don't you know. I'm to bury myself in studies, and get me no bast—ah, that is, I'm to stay out of trouble, mind Uncle Tony, and yourself, of course, and do him proud."

"I'm sure you'll be up to it." Roslynn tried to smile, but the smells of the wharf were doing her in. She had to get to the carriage before she disgraced herself. "I believe it's your turn to tell your father good-bye, laddie."

Jeremy was crushed not only by James but by Conrad as well, and had to listen to another long list of dos and don'ts from the first mate. But he was saved by the tide. It wouldn't wait, and both men were forced to board.

James could blame Anthony for the hangover that nearly made him forget. He called Jeremy up the gangplank and handed him a note. "See your aunt Roslynn gets this, but not when Tony's around."

Jeremy pocketed the note. "It's not a love letter, is it?"

"A love letter?" James snorted. "Get out of here, puppy. And see you—"

"I know, I know." Jeremy threw up his hands, laughing. "I won't do anything you wouldn't."

He ran back down the gangplank before James could take him to task for his impudence. But he was smiling as he turned away, and came face-to-face with Conrad.

"What was that about?"

James shrugged, realizing Connie had seen him pass the note. "I decided to lend a hand after all. At the rate Tony's going, he'd be floundering forever."

"I thought you weren't going to interfere," Connie reminded him.

"Well, he is my brother, isn't he? Though why I bother after the dirty trick he played on me last night, I don't know." At Connie's raised brow, he grinned, despite the slow throb in his head. "Made sure I'd be feeling miserable today to cast off, the bloody sod."

"But you went along with it, naturally?"

"Naturally. Couldn't have the lad drinking me under the table, now, could I? But you'll have to see us off, Connie. I'm afraid I'm done for. Report to me in my cabin after we're under way."

An hour later, Connie poured a measure of rye from the well-stocked cabinet in the captain's cabin and joined James at his desk. "You're not going to worry about the boy, are you?"

"That rascal?" James shook his head, wincing slightly when his headache returned, and took another sip of the tonic Connie had had sent from the galley. "Tony will see he doesn't get into any serious scrapes. If anyone will worry, it's you. You should have had one of your own, Connie."

"I probably do. I just haven't found him yet like you did the lad. You've probably more yourself that you don't know about."

"Good God, one's enough," James replied in mock horror, gaining a chuckle from his friend. "Now what have you to report? How many of the old crew were available?"

"Eighteen. And there was no problem filling the ranks, except for the bos'n, as I told you before."

"So we're sailing without one? That'll put a heavy load on yourself, Connie."

"Aye, if I hadn't found a man yesterday, or rather, if he hadn't volunteered. Wanted to sign on as passengers, him and his brother. When I told him the *Maiden Anne* don't carry passengers, he offered to work his way across. A more persistent Scot I've never seen."

"Another Scot? As if I ain't had enough to do with them lately. I'm bloody well glad your own Scot's ancestors are so far back you don't remember them, Connie. Between hunting down Lady Roslynn's cousin and running into that little vixen and her companion—"

"I thought you'd forgotten about that."

James' answer was a scowl. "How do you know this Scot knows the first thing about rigging?"

"I put him through the paces. I'd say he's had the job before. And he does claim to have sailed before, as quartermaster, ship's carpenter, and bos'n."

"If that's true, he'll come in right handy. Very well. Is there anything else?"

"Johnny got married."

"Johnny? My cabin boy, Johnny?" James' eyes flared. "Good God, he's only fifteen! What the devil does he think he's doing?"

Connie shrugged. "Says he fell in love and can't bear to leave the little woman."

"Little woman?" James sneered. "That cocky little twit needs a mother, not a wife." His head was pounding again, and he swilled down the rest of the tonic.

"I've found you another cabin boy. MacDonell's brother—"

Tonic spewed across James' desk. "Who?" he choked.

"Blister it, James, what's got into you?"

"You said MacDonell? Would his first name be Ian?"

"Aye." Now Connie's eyes flared. "Good God, he's not the Scot from that tavern, is he?"

James waved away the question. "Did you get a good look at the brother?"

"Come to think of it, no. He was a little chap, though, quiet, hiding behind his brother's coattails. I didn't have much choice in signing him on, what with Johnny only letting me know two days ago that he was staying in England. But you can't mean to think—"

"But I do." And suddenly James was laughing. "Oh, God, Connie, this is priceless. I went back to look for that little wench, you know, but she and her Scot had disappeared from the area. Now here she's fallen right into my lap."

Connie grunted. "Well, I can see you're going to have a pleasant crossing."

"You may depend upon it." James' grin was decidedly wolfish. "But we shan't unmask her disguise just yet. I've a mind to play with her first."

"You could be wrong, you know. She might be a boy after all."

"I doubt it," James replied. "But I'll find out when she begins her duties."

And as the *Maiden Anne* left England behind, James contemplated those duties and how he would add to them in the coming weeks. This was indeed going to be a pleasant voyage.

Chapter Forty-four

"You're not going out again, are you?"

Anthony stopped in the process of putting his gloves on. "I was."

Roslynn left the parlor doorway, stepping closer to him. They had been home only a little over an hour. It had taken her this long to get up the courage to approach him, but that courage was fast deserting her now that the opportunity was here. But she had to do it.

"I would like a word with you."

"Very well." He indicated the parlor.

"No, upstairs." At his sharply arched brow, she blushed and quickly added, "In my room." Jeremy was in the house somewhere, but this was one conversation she didn't want interrupted. "We can be private there—for what I have to say."

"Then lead on, my dear."

His tone implied indifference. God, he was not going to make this easy for her. And what if he didn't care? What if she succeeded only in making a fool of herself?

Roslynn hurried upstairs with Anthony slowly following. He was dragging his feet, afraid he wasn't going to like what she had to say. It was too soon for her to say what he wanted to hear. He had figured it would take at least several weeks before she would admit she didn't like sleeping alone. She wouldn't balk then when he put his foot down and demanded she honor her original agreement with him to be a wife in every way.

Roslynn was already seated on the chaise longue when Anthony entered her room. Since that seat was taken and the bed was out of the question, he sat down on the stool at her vanity only a few feet away. He fiddled with the perfume bottles there, waiting for her to begin. The piece of paper was just something else to touch, but when he opened it, James' handwriting caught his immediate attention.

"Anthony, could you at least look at me?" He did, his eyes narrowed now, and she lowered her own. "I don't know how else to say this except . . . I was wrong."

"Wrong?"

"To put limitations on our marriage. I—I would like to start over."

She glanced up then. The last thing she expected to see was anger, but there was no mistaking that he was angry.

"Could this have anything to do with your sudden change of heart?" The paper dangled from his fingers.

"What is it?" she asked warily.

"Don't play games with me, Roslynn! You know exactly what it is," he said tersely.

She matched her tone to his, forgetting for the moment all about reconciliation. "No, I don't! Where did you get it?"

"On your vanity."

"Impossible. I changed clothes when I returned from the docks, and that, whatever it is"—she pointed at the paper—"was *not* on my table."

"There's one way to prove that, isn't there?"

He was furious at James' interference, but mostly at her. How dared she put him through hell, then, because of a simple note, admit she was wrong? He didn't want her bloody contrition. He wanted her to want him without exception. And she would have before long. Then, and only then, would he have convinced her that she had accused him falsely.

He stalked to the door and threw it open, bellowing for Jeremy. Either James had slipped her that note at the docks, which was doubtful since Anthony had been close to her the whole while, or James had given it to Jeremy to give to her. Whichever, he wasn't going to have her lying about it.

When the boy poked his head out of his room down the corridor,

Anthony demanded, "Did your father entrust you with something to give to my wife?"

Jeremy groaned. "Hell's bells, Tony, I thought you'd left. I only just put it . . . you weren't supposed to see it," he finished lamely.

Anthony crumpled the paper in his hand. "That's all right, youngun. No harm done."

He closed the door again, frowning at his own stupid assumption. She hadn't seen the note. That meant . . . bloody hell, and he had just antagonized the hell out of her.

He found her on her feet, her hand outstretched, her eyes glittering with indignation. "I'll be taking that, if you please."

"I don't," he replied, wincing to hear her brogue, a sure sign of her temper. "Look, I'm sorry if I drew the wrong conclusion. The note isn't important. What—"

"I'll determine what's important. If that was on my vanity, then it was meant for me, no' for you."

"Then take it."

He held out his hand, palm up. When she came forward and took the ball of paper, he didn't give her a chance to read it. His fingers closed over hers and he drew her into his arms.

"You can read that later," he said softly. "Tell me first what you meant by being wrong."

She forgot all about the note now crumpled in her fist. "I told you— about the limitations. I should never have—have placed conditions on our marrying."

"True. Is that all?"

He was smiling at her, that melting smile that turned her to honey. "I shouldna have come to you just for the bairn, but I was afraid I'd get so used to having you that nothing else would matter."

"Did you?" His lips brushed her cheek, the side of her mouth.

"What?"

"Get used to having me?"

He didn't let her answer, his lips slanting across hers, warm, beguiling, stealing her breath, her soul. She had to break the contact herself. "Och, mon, if you keep kissing me, I'll never say it all."

He chuckled, still holding her close. "But none of this was necessary, sweetheart. Your problem is, you've taken a bloody lot for granted. You assumed that I would have let this don't-touch-me stand of yours go on indefinitely. Not so. You also seem to think that I would have abided by any rules whatsoever that you set down for this relationship. Wrong again." He softened this news with another deep kiss before continuing. "I hate to disillusion you, sweetheart, but you get away with your outlandish demands for only as long as I allow you to. And I would have allowed you only a few more weeks, no more, to come to your senses."

"Or?"

"Or I would have moved in here."

"Would you, now?" she retorted, but her lips were twitching. "Without my permission, I suppose?"

"We'll never know, will we?" He grinned. "Now, what else did you want to tell me?"

She tried to shrug. It didn't work. Her senses were reeling with his body pressed to hers, his eyes warm, tender, his lips a breath away.

"I love you," she said simply, then squealed when he squeezed her so tight she couldn't breathe.

"Oh, God, Roslynn, I was afraid I'd never hear you say it! Do you really? Despite what an utter ass I've been half the time?"

"Yes." She laughed, giddy from his reaction.

"Then read that note from James."

It was the last thing she expected to hear at the moment. She glanced at him warily as he set her down on her feet and stepped back. But she opened the paper, too curious now not to. The message was brief, addressed to her.

Since Tony's too pigheaded to tell you, I thought you ought to know that the little tavern wench you assumed Tony dallied with was actually mine for the evening. Tony might have been her first choice, as he was yours, but she had no complaints in settling for me. You've been wrong about the lad, dear girl. I do think he loves you.

Roslynn's eyes were moist as they found his and he drew her gently back into his arms. "How can you ever forgive me, Anthony?"

"You forgave me, didn't you?"

"But you weren't guilty!"

"Shh, sweetheart. It doesn't matter now, does it? You're still the only woman I've wanted since I first saw you—bent over peeking in the Crandals' ballroom and presenting me with your sweet little derrière."

"Anthony!"

His laugh was rich and deep as he fastened his arms tighter around her so she couldn't hit him. "Well, it's true, my dear. I was utterly captivated."

"You were a rake!"

"I still am," he assured her. "You wouldn't want me to become morally proper, now, would you? You won't like making love only in the dark, suitably clothed so no skin touches except what is essential— ouch!" She had pinched him. "I'm not teasing you, my dear." He chuckled. "That's how Warton would probably have made love to you. 'Course, he would have died for it . . . now, now, no more pinches."

"Then be serious."

"But I am, my girl, most serious." His fingers slid into her hair, spilling pins this way and that, all the while his eyes remained locked to hers. "You became mine that first night, dashing toward me in the moonlight. You took my breath away. D'you know how much I wanted to make love to you then, right there in the Crandals' garden? What did you feel, sweetheart?"

"I—I was sorry I couldn't have you."

"Were you?" he asked softly, his thumbs caressing her cheeks, his lips just barely touching hers. "Do you want me now?"

"I've always wanted you, Anthony," she whispered, arms wrapping around his neck. "I didn't want it so. I was afraid I could never trust you."

"Do you trust me now?"

"I have to. I love you—even if you don't—"

He put a finger to her lips. "Oh, my beautiful, silly girl. Didn't you read all of my brother's note? My whole family knows I love you to dis- traction without my telling them. Why don't you?"

"You do?" she gasped.

"Would I have let you run rings around me if I didn't?"

"But why didn't you tell me?"

"You didn't want to marry me, sweetheart," he reminded her. "I practically had to twist your arm. And even when you agreed, you did everything possible to keep a distance between us. Would you have believed me then if I had told you I loved you? Roslynn, why else would I marry you?"

"But—" There were no but's. She kissed him, and kissed him again, her heart nearly bursting with joy. "Oh, Anthony, I'm so glad you did. And I'll never, ever be such a fool again, I swear—"

He told her, in between kisses, "You can be a fool . . . whenever you like . . . as long as you don't stop loving me."

"I couldn't, even if I wanted to. Will you?"

"Never, sweetheart. You may depend upon it."

Chapter Forty-five

"I understand congratulations are in order," Nicholas remarked as he joined Anthony for a smoke in the garden. Sunday dinner at Edward's had gathered the whole clan this time, minus James. "You don't think you're a bit old to be starting a family, Malory?"

"When are you going to visit Knighton's Hall, Montieth?" Anthony countered dryly.

Nicholas chuckled, ignoring the gibe. "Regina's been talking about nothing else since Roslynn told her. She wants another of her own now."

"That'll be a bit hard to do, won't it, dear boy? According to James, you're in the doghouse."

"Oh, I never stay there long, old man," Nicholas replied, his grin maddening. "Your niece might have the famous Malory temper, but she's not heartless. Besides, she doesn't like to sleep alone."

Anthony glowered. He still couldn't set it right in his mind that his little Reggie was a woman now—with a lusty rake for a husband. Seemed he ought to punch Montieth out for such a remark. 'Course, the whole family'd be down on his head if he did, Reggie in the lead.

"One of these days, Montieth, I'm going to like you. But don't hold your breath."

Nicholas' laughter followed him back into the house, rubbing him raw. Regina met up with him in the hall, however, to dispel the mood.

"Have you seen Nicholas, Tony?"

"Wish I hadn't, but he's in the garden."

"You didn't have words again, did you?" she asked, frowning.

"What can I say, puss?" He shrugged, then added deliberately, "But you'll notice I left. He goes for blood these days."

"Famous! Oh, when will you two *ever* get along?"

"We're too much alike, my girl, and we know it. But do me a favor and drag him back in the house, will you? I'd like to stroll with the wife, and a little privacy wouldn't be amiss."

Anthony was grinning when he left Regina. Hopefully Montieth would be back in the doghouse tonight, and the poor sod wouldn't even know what he'd done wrong. That thought brought a chuckle. One of these days Reggie was going to realize that he and Nicholas delighted in their verbal sparring. There'd be hell to pay then, but for now, Anthony counted himself the winner of this round.

He found Roslynn had been cornered by Edward, and he just caught her last words as he approached. "But I don't want to double my money. Hell's teeth, what would I do with more of it?"

"I should have warned you, sweetheart, that Eddie boy would be after you. He can't stand to see money just sitting around."

Edward defended himself. "Well, it's preposterous, Tony. No one ever has *too* much money, you know. There are the children to think of, and—"

"And I'm sure Roslynn will let you manage her estate, if she can ever get around to figuring out all it entails."

"That's not fair," Roslynn protested. "I know exactly what I own— I just can't be expected to remember it all." Both men laughed, to her chagrin. "Very well, I'll have my solicitor call on you, Edward. Perhaps this is something I should become interested in."

"Good God, now see what you've done, Eddie," Anthony complained with mock horror. "I don't want her mind filled with figures."

"No, you just want it filled with you." Edward snorted.

"True." Anthony grinned unabashedly. "Now come along, my dear, and let me see if I can find something else for you to be interested in."

Anthony walked her away from the house, until there was only moonlight to light the way. He stopped near the rose bushes, his arms wrapping around her from behind, his chin resting on her shoulder.

"Do you really want to get involved in the empire your grandfather left you?"

"No, but I'm glad you at least asked." She smiled, her arms wrapped over his.

"Whatever makes you happy, Roslynn, since your happiness is mine."

She turned around in his arms, putting her cheek against his chest, loving him so much she could hardly contain it. One finger drew circles on the soft blue velvet of his jacket.

"There is something," she said in a small voice.

"Anything, sweetheart."

There was a long, shy silence before she asked, "Do you think we could try it again in the chair?"

Anthony's delighted laughter filled Grosvenor Square beyond the garden.

GENTLE ROGUE

For my sister-in-law, Lawree,
and her newest joy,
Natasha Kealanoheaakealoha Howard

Chapter One

1818, London

Georgina Anderson held her spoon up backward, placed one of the pared-down radishes from her plate in the bowl of the spoon, pulled the tip back, and shot the radish across the room. She didn't hit the fat cockroach she was aiming for, but she was close enough. The radish splattered on the wall only inches from her target, sending said target scampering for the nearest crack in the wall. Goal accomplished. As long as she couldn't see the little beasts, she could pretend she wasn't sharing accommodations with them.

She turned back to her half-eaten dinner, stared at the boiled food for a moment, then pushed the plate away with a grimace. What she wouldn't give for one of Hannah's rich, seven-course meals right about now. After twelve years as the Andersons' cook, Hannah knew just what pleased each member of the family, and Georgina had been dreaming about her cooking for weeks, not surprising after a month of shipboard fare. She'd gotten only one good meal since she'd arrived in England five days ago, and that was the very night they docked, when Mac had taken her out to a fine restaurant just after they had checked into the Albany Hotel. They'd had to leave the Albany the very next day for much, much cheaper accommodations. But there was nothing else they could do after they returned to the hotel to find all their money missing from their trunks.

Georgie, as she was affectionately known to friends and family, couldn't even in good conscience hold the hotel accountable, not when she and Mac had both been robbed, but from different rooms, even different floors. It was most likely accomplished while the trunks were together on that long ride from the docks on the East End to Piccadilly on the West End, where the prestigious Albany was located, when the trunks were strapped on top of the hack they had rented, with the driver and his helper up top with them, while she and Mac blithely ogled their first sight of London Town.

Talk about your lousy luck, and it hadn't even started there. No, it started when they reached England last week and found out their ship couldn't dock, that it might take anywhere up to three months before it was given quay space to unload its cargo. Passengers were more fortunate in that they could be rowed ashore. But they'd still had to wait several days before this was accomplished.

She shouldn't have been surprised, however. She had known about the congestion problem on the Thames, a very big problem because ships came in seasonally, all being subject to the same unpredictable winds and weather. Her ship had been one of a dozen from America arriving at the same time. There were hundreds of others from all over the world. The appalling congestion problem was one of the reasons her family's merchant line had kept London off its trade routes even before the war. Actually, a Skylark Line ship hadn't been to London since 1807 when England began her blockade of half of Europe in her war with France. The Far Eastern and West Indies trade was just as profitable and far less troublesome for Skylark.

Even after her country had settled its differences with England with the signing of a treaty at the tail end of 1814, the Skylark Line stayed clear of the English trade, because the availability of warehousing was still a serious problem. More times than not, perishable cargoes had to be left on quayside, at the mercy of the elements and the thieves who stole a half million pounds of goods a year. And if the elements didn't ruin perishable goods, then the coal dust that enveloped the whole port would.

It simply wasn't worth the aggravation and loss of profits, not when other trade routes were just as lucrative. Which was why Georgina hadn't come to London on a Skylark ship, and why she wouldn't find free passage home on one, either. Which was going to be an eventual problem, what with Mac and she reduced to a grand total of twenty-five American dollars between them, all that they had been carrying on them at the time of the robbery, and they didn't know how long that would have to last—a good reason why Georgina was presently ensconced in a rented room above a tavern in the Borough of Southwark.

A tavern! If her brothers ever found out . . . but then they were going to kill her when she got home anyway for sailing without their knowing, while each was off in some other part of the world on his own ship, but more to the point, she'd left without their permission. At the least, she could expect to have her allowance suspended for a decade, to be locked in her room for several years, to be whipped by each one of them . . .

Actually, they would probably only do a great deal of shouting at her. But having five angry brothers, all older and much bigger than she, raising their voices in unison and accord, and directing that anger at her when she knew she deserved every bit of it, wasn't at all pleasant to contemplate, and could, in fact, be anticipated with total dread. But, unfortunately, that hadn't stopped Georgina from sailing off to England with only Ian MacDonell as her escort and protector, and he no relation at all to her. Sometimes she had to wonder if the common sense allotted her family hadn't run out by the time she was born.

The knock came at the door just as Georgina pushed away from the little table the room offered for solitary meals. She had to bite back the natural tendency to simply say "Come in," which came from a lifetime of knowing that anyone who knocked on her door would be either servant or family, and welcome. But then, in the whole of her twenty-two years, she had never slept anywhere but in her own bed, in her own room, in her home in Bridgeport, Connecticut; or in a hammock on a Skylark ship, at least until last month. Of course, no one could just come in with the door locked, whether she invited them to or not. And Mac was diligent in reminding her that she had to do such things as keep her door locked at all times, even if the strange, shabby room wasn't a potent enough reminder that she was far away from home and shouldn't be trusting anyone in this inhospitable, crime-infested town.

But her visitor was known to her, the Scottish brogue calling out to her from the other side of the door well recognized as belonging to Ian MacDonell. She let him in, then stepped out of the way as he sauntered through the doorway, his tall frame filling the small room.

"Any luck?"

He snorted before he sat down in the chair she had just vacated. "Depends on how ye look at it, lass."

"Not another detour?"

"Aye, but better than a dead end, I'm thinking."

"I suppose," she replied, but not with much enthusiasm.

She shouldn't really be expecting more, not when they had so little to go on. All Mr. Kimball, one of the sailors on her brother Thomas's ship, the *Portunus*, had been able to tell her was that he was "certain sure" he had seen her long-lost fiancé, Malcolm Cameron, up in the rigging on the British merchantman *Pogrom* when the ships crossed paths during the *Portunus*'s return to Connecticut. Her brother Thomas couldn't even verify it, since Mr. Kimball hadn't bothered to mention it to him until the *Pogrom* was well out of their sights. But the *Pogrom*'s direction had been toward Europe, more than likely to its home port in England, even if it wasn't going directly there.

Regardless, this was the first piece of news she had heard of Malcolm in the six years since he had been impressed with two others right off her brother Warren's ship, the *Nereus*, a month before war had been declared in June of 1812.

Impressment of American sailors by the English navy had been one of the reasons for the war. It was the worst piece of luck that Malcolm had been taken on his very first voyage—and simply because he still had a touch of the Cornishman's accent, having spent the first half of his life in Cornwall, England. But he was an American now, his parents, who were now deceased, having settled in Bridgeport in 1806, with no intention of ever returning to England. But the officer of the HMS *Devastation* wouldn't believe any of that, and Warren had a small scar on his cheek to prove how determined they were to impress every man they could.

And then Georgina had heard that the HMS *Devastation* had been taken out of commission halfway through the war, her crew divided up among a half dozen other warships. But there had been no other news until now. What Malcolm was doing on an English merchantman now that the war was over didn't matter. At least Georgina finally had a means to find him, and she wasn't leaving England until she did.

"So who were you directed to this time?" Georgina asked with a sigh. "Another someone who knows someone, who knows someone, who *might* know where he is?"

Mac chuckled. "Ye make it sound as if we'll be going 'round in circles indefinitely, hinny. We've only been looking these four days. Ye could do wi' a wee bit of Thomas's patience, I'm thinking."

"Don't mention Thomas to me, Mac. I'm that mad at him still for not coming himself to find Malcolm for me."

"He would have—"

"In six months! He wanted me to wait another six months for him to return from his West Indies run, then how many more months for him to come here, find Malcolm, then return with him. Well, that was just too long when I've already waited six years."

"Four years," he corrected. "They wouldna have let ye wed the laddie until ye were eighteen, regardless that he did the asking two years afore that."

"That's beside the point. If any one of my other brothers had been home, you know they would have come here straightaway. But no, it had to be optimistic Thomas, the only one of them who has the patience of a saint, and his *Portunus* the only Skylark ship in port, just my luck. Do you know he laughed when I told him that if I get much older, Malcolm will likely refuse to have me?"

It was all Mac could do to keep from grinning over that sincerely put question. And it was no wonder her brother had laughed if she'd said as much to him. But then the wee lass had never put much store in her looks, not having blossomed into the beauty she was today until she'd been almost nineteen. She'd depended on the ship that was hers when she turned eighteen and her equal interest in the Skylark Line to get her a husband, and Mac was of the opinion that that was just what had motivated young Cameron into asking for her before he left on the Far Eastern route with Warren, a voyage expected to last several years at the least.

Well, a few more years than that had gone by, thanks to British arrogance on the high seas. But the lass wouldn't heed her brothers' advice to forget about Malcolm Cameron. Even when the war had ended and it was reasonable to expect that the lad would find his way home, but didn't, she was still determined to wait for him. That alone should have warned Thomas that she wouldn't be willing to delay while he made his West Indies run, not when he had cargo to deliver to a half dozen different ports, for wasn't she just as adventurous as the rest of the family? It was in their blood. And didn't she lack Thomas's patience, and they all knew it?

Of course, Thomas could be forgiven for thinking that the problem wouldn't be his, since their brother Drew's ship was due in at the end of summer, and Drew always stayed home for several months between his trips anyway. And that fun-loving rogue could never deny his only sister anything. But the lass wouldn't wait for Drew, either. She had looked passage on a ship scheduled to depart just three days after Thomas sailed and had somehow talked Mac into accompanying her, though he still wasn't quite sure how she'd managed to make it seem his idea to do so, instead of hers.

"Well, Georgie lass, we're no' doing sae bad wi' our hunt, considering this here London's got more folks in it than the whole of Connecticut. It could've been much worse was the *Pogrom* no' in port, her crew turned loose. Now the mon I'm tae be meeting tomorrow night is suppose tae know the laddie verra well. The one I spoke wi' today said Malcolm even left the ship wi' this Mr. Willcocks, sae who'd be knowing where he might be found if no' this chum of his."

"That does sound promising," Georgina allowed. "This Mr. Willcocks might even be able to take you to Malcolm directly, so . . . I think I'll go along."

"You willna," Mac snapped, sitting forward to give her a frown. "It's a tavern I'll be meeting him at."

"So?"

"Sae what am I doing here if no' tae see ye dinna do some crazy thing worse than the coming here was?"

"Now, Mac—"

"Dinna 'Now Mac' me, lassie," he told her sternly.

But she was giving him that look that meant she was going to be stubborn about it. He groaned inwardly, well aware that there wasn't much that could move her once she set her mind to something. The proof was her being here, instead of home where her brothers thought her to be.

Chapter Two

Across the river, in the elite West End of town, the coach carrying Sir Anthony Malory stopped before one of the fashionable townhouses on Piccadilly. It had been his bachelor residence, but it no longer was because he was returning now with his new bride, Lady Roslynn.

Inside the townhouse, Anthony's brother, James Malory, who had been residing with Anthony while in London, was drawn into the hall upon hearing the late-hour arrival, just in time to see the bride being carried over the threshold. Since he wasn't aware yet that she *was* a bride, his bland inquiry was perfectly in order.

"I don't suppose I should be witnessing this."

"I was hoping you wouldn't," Anthony said while passing James on the way to the stairs, the female bundle still in his arms. "But since you have, you may as well know I married the girl."

"The devil you say!"

"He really did." The bride laughed in a delightful way. "You don't think I'd allow just anyone to carry me over the threshold, do you?"

Anthony stopped a moment, having caught sight of his brother's incredulous expression. "Good God, James, I've waited a lifetime to see you at a loss for words. But you'll understand if I don't wait around for you to recover, won't you?" And he promptly disappeared up the stairs.

James finally got around to closing his mouth, then opened it again to drain the glass of brandy he was still holding. Astonishing! Anthony leg-shackled! London's most notorious rake—well, most notorious only because James had relinquished that distinction himself when he'd left England ten years ago. But Anthony? Whyever would he do such a ghastly thing?

Of course, the lady was too beautiful for words, but it wasn't as if Anthony couldn't have her any other way. James happened to know that Anthony had already seduced her, in fact, just last night. So what possible reason could he have to marry the girl? She had no family, no one to insist he do so; not that anyone *could* tell him what to do—with the possible exception of their oldest brother, Jason, marquis of Haverston and head of the family. But not even Jason could have insisted Anthony marry. Hadn't Jason been at him to do so for many years with no success?

So no one had held a pistol to Anthony's head, or coerced him in any way to do such a preposterous thing. Besides, Anthony wasn't like Nicholas Eden, the viscount of Montieth, to succumb to pressure from the elders. Nicholas Eden had been forced to marry their niece, Regan, or Reggie, as the rest of the family called her. Anthony had actually pressured Nicholas, with a little help from their brother Edward and Nicholas's own family. By God, James still wished he could have been there to add a few threats of his own, but at the time the family hadn't known he was back in England, and he'd been trying to waylay the same viscount for a sound thrashing he felt he deserved for an entirely different reason. And he'd done just that, almost making the young scamp miss his wedding to Regan, James's favorite niece.

Shaking his head, James returned to the parlor and the decanter of brandy, deciding a few more drinks might bring the answer to him. Love he discounted. If Anthony hadn't succumbed to that emotion in the seventeen years he'd been seducing the fairer sex, then he was as immune to it as James was. And he could also discount the need for an heir, since the number of titles in the family were already secured. Jason, their eldest brother, had his only son Derek, fully grown now and already taking after his younger uncles. Edward, the second oldest Malory, had five children himself, all of marriageable ages except the youngest, Amy. Even James had a son, Jeremy, albeit an illegitimate one whom he'd discovered only six years ago. He hadn't even known about the lad who'd been raised in a tavern by his mother, and had continued working there after she died. But Jeremy was seventeen now and doing his damnedest to take after his father in his rakehell ways—and succeeding admirably. So Anthony, as the fourth son, certainly didn't need to worry about perpetuating the line. The three oldest Malorys had taken care of it.

James stretched out on a couch with the decanter of brandy. Just shy of six feet, his large frame barely fit. He thought about the newly-weds upstairs and what they were doing right about now. Well-shaped, sensual lips curled in a grin. The answer simply wasn't going to come to him about why Anthony had done such a ghastly thing as marry—something James would never make the mistake of doing. But he had to allow that if Anthony were going to take the plunge, it might as well be to a prime article like Roslynn Chadwick—no, she was a Malory now—but still a prime piece.

James had thought of pursuing her himself, despite the fact that Anthony had already staked his claim. But then, when they had both been young rakes about town all those years ago, they had often pursued the same woman for the sport of it, the winner generally tending to be whichever of them the lady happened to clap eyes on first, since Anthony was a handsome devil females found it almost impossible to resist, and James had been called the same himself.

And yet, two brothers couldn't be more dissimilar in looks. Anthony was taller and slimmer, and had the dark looks inherited from their grandmother, with black hair and eyes of cobalt-blue, the same coloring possessed by Regan, Amy, and, annoyingly, James's own son, Jeremy, who, even more annoyingly, looked more like Anthony than like James. James, however, bore the more common Malory looks, blond hair, eyes a medium shade of green, a large-framed body. Big, blond, and handsome, as Regan liked to put it.

James chuckled, thinking of the dear girl. His only sister, Melissa, had died when her daughter was only two, so he and his brothers had raised Regan, equally. She was like a daughter to them all. But she was married to that bounder Eden now, and by choice, so what could James do but tolerate the fellow? But then, Nicholas Eden *was* proving to be an exemplary husband.

Husband again. Anthony had cracked a screw, obviously. At least Eden had an excuse. He adored Regan. But Anthony adored *all* women.

In that, he and James were alike. And James might have just turned thirty-six, but there wasn't a woman alive who could entice him into the matrimonial state. Love them and leave them was the only way to get along with them, a creed that had done well for him all these years, and one he would continue to live by in the years to come.

Chapter Three

Ian MacDonell was a second-generation American, but his Scottish ancestry was proclaimed loudly in his carrot-red hair and the soft burr in his speech. What he didn't have was a typical Scottish temper. His could be considered quite mild, and had been for all of his forty-seven years. And yet what temper he did possess had been tested to the limit last night and half of today by the youngest Anderson sibling.

Being neighbor to the Andersons, Mac had known the family all his life. He'd sailed on their ships for thirty-five years, beginning as old man Anderson's cabin boy when he was only seven, and lastly as first mate on Clinton Anderson's *Neptune*. He'd declined his own captaincy nearly a dozen times. Like Georgina's youngest brother Boyd, he did not want such complete authority to be his—though young Boyd was sure to accept it eventually. But even after Mac had quit the sea five years ago, he hadn't been able to stay away from the ships; it now was his job to see to the fitness of each Skylark vessel when it returned to port.

When the old man had died fifteen years ago, and his wife a few years after, Mac had sort of adopted the surviving children, even though he was only seven years Clinton's senior. But then he'd always been close to the family. He had watched the children grow, had been there to give them advice when the old man wasn't, and had taught the boys—and, the truth be known, Georgina, too—most of what they knew of ships. Unlike their father, who had only stayed at home a month or two between voyages, Mac could let six months to a year go by before the sea called to him again.

As was usually the case when a man was devoted more to the sea than to his family, the Anderson children's births could be marked by their father's voyages. Clinton was the firstborn and forty now, but a four-year absence in the Far East separated his birth from Warren's, who was five years younger. Thomas wasn't born for another four years, and Drew four after that. And Drew's was the only birth the old man had been there to see, since a storm and severe damage to his ship had turned the old man back to port that year, and then one mishap after another had kept him home for nearly a year, long enough to witness Drew's birth and get started on Boyd's, who was born eleven months later.

And then there was the youngest and only girl in the family, with another four-year difference in age between her and Boyd. Unlike the boys, who took to sea as soon as they were old enough, Georgina was always at home to greet each ship when it returned. So it wasn't surprising that Mac was so fond of the lass, having spent more time with her in her growing years than with any one of her brothers. He knew her well, knew all her tricks for getting her way, so it stood to reason that he ought to have been able to stand firm against her latest outlandishness. And yet here she stood next to him at the bar of one of the roughest taverns on the waterfront. It was enough to make a man return to the sea.

If Mac could be grateful for anything, it was that the lass had realized right off that she'd gone a wee bit too far this time with her crazy notions. She was as nervous as a spaniel pup, despite the dirk she had hidden up her sleeve, with a mate tucked in her boot. And yet her confounded stubbornness wouldn't let her leave until Mr. Willcocks put in an appearance. At least they'd managed to conceal her femininity fairly well.

Mac had thought that would be the stumbling block that would keep her from coming with him tonight, but unbeknownst to him, the lass had done some clothesline raiding in the wee hours of the night to be able to show him her disguise this morning when he got around to mentioning that she'd need one, but that they didn't have the money to spare for it.

Her delicate hands were hidden under the grubbiest pair of gloves Mac had ever seen, so big she could barely manage to lift the mug of ale he'd ordered for her, whereas the patched breeches could have used a lot more room in the seat, but at least the sweater covered the tightness in that area—as long as the lass didn't raise her arms, which hiked the sweater up. On her feet were a pair of her own boots mutilated beyond repair, enough to pass for a man's pair that should have been thrown away years ago. Her sable-brown curls were tucked under a woolen cap, pulled down so low it covered her neck, ears, and her dark brown eyes, too, as long as she managed to keep her head lowered, which she did.

She was a sorry-looking thing, to be sure, but in fact, she blended in better with this bunch of wharf rats than Mac did in his own clothes, which weren't fancy, but were certainly of a better quality than anything these rough-looking sailors were sporting—at least until the two upper-class gents came through the door.

Amazing how quickly the out-of-place could quiet a noisy room. In this case, only some heavy breathing could be heard and—perhaps by a few—Georgina's whisper.

"What is it?"

Mac didn't answer, nudging her to be silent, at least until the tense seconds passed while everyone took the newcomers' mettle and decided they'd best be ignored. Then the room's noise gradually rose again, and Mac glanced at his companion to see that she was still working on being unobtrusive by doing nothing more than staring down at her mug of ale.

"It isna our mon, but a couple of lairds, by the bonny look of them. An unusual occurrence, I'm thinking, fer such as them tae be coming here."

Mac heard what sounded like a snort before the quiet whisper, "Haven't I always said they have more arrogance than they know what to do with?"

"Always?" Mac grinned. "Seems tae me ye only started saying such six years back."

"Only because I wasn't aware of it before then," Georgina huffed.

Mac almost burst into laughter at her tone, not to mention such a blatant falsehood. The grudge she bore the English for stealing her Malcolm had not lessened any with the end of the war, and wasn't likely to until she had the lad back. But she bore her aversion so genteelly, or so he'd always thought. Her brothers had been known to rant and rave with some very colorful invectives about the injustices inflicted on Americans by the British, perpetrated by the governing nobility, and this long before the war, when their trade was first affected by Britain's blockade of European ports. If anyone still bore ill will toward the English, the Anderson brothers did.

So for more than ten years, the lass had heard the English referred to as "those arrogant bastards," but she hadn't cared so much then, would just sit back and quietly nod agreement, sympathizing with her brothers' plight but not really relating to it. But once Britain's high-handedness touched her personally with the impressment of her fiancé, it was a different story. Only she still wasn't hot-tempered about it as her brothers could be. Yet no one could doubt her contempt, her total antipathy for all things English. She just expressed it so *politely*.

Georgina sensed Mac's amusement without seeing his grinning face. She felt like kicking him in the shin. Here she was shaking in her boots, afraid even to lift her head in this crowded hellhole, bemoaning her own stubbornness for bringing her here, and he found something to be amused about? She was almost tempted to have a look at those dandy lords, who no doubt must be dressed to the gills in colorful foppery, as their ilk tended to do. She didn't for a moment think that Mac might be amused by what she'd said.

"Willcocks, Mac? Remember him? The reason we're here. If it wouldn't be too much trouble—"

"Now, dinna be getting snippy," he gently chided.

She sighed. "I'm sorry. I just wish the fellow would hurry up and make an appearance if he's going to. Are you positive he isn't already here?"

"There're a few warts on cheeks and noses, as I can see, but none a quarter inch long on the lower lip of a short, pudgy, yellow-haired lad of twenty-five or thereabouts. Wi' such a discription tae go by, it isna likely we'll be missing the mon."

"*If* that description is accurate," Georgina thought she'd better point out.

Mac shrugged. "It's all we got, and better than nothing, I'm thinking. I wouldna like tae be going 'round tae each table here and asking . . . Laird, help us, yer curls are slipping, la—!"

"Shh!" Georgina hissed before he could get that damning "lass" out, but her arm went up immediately to tuck in the falling locks.

Unfortunately, her sweater hiked up in the process, revealing the tightly encased derriere that didn't by a long shot pass for boy's or man's. Just as quickly it was covered again when she put her arms back on the bar, but not before it was noticed by one of the two well-dressed gents who had previously caused such speculation when they'd arrived, and now sat at a table only six feet away.

James Malory was intrigued, though you wouldn't know it to look at him. This was the ninth tavern he and Anthony had visited today, searching for Geordie Cameron, Roslynn's Scottish cousin. He'd just heard the story this morning of how Cameron had been trying to force Roslynn to marry him, had even kidnapped her, though she had managed to escape. *This* was the reason Anthony had married the girl, to protect her from this scurrilous cousin, or so Anthony claimed. And yet Anthony was determined to find the chap, to impress him with a sound thrashing, enlighten him with the news of Roslynn's marriage, and send him back to Scotland with the warning not to trouble her again. All just to protect the new bride, or was his brother just a little more personally involved than that?

Whatever the true motivations that drove him, Anthony was sure he'd found his man when he had seen the red-haired chap at the bar. Which was why they were sitting so close to the bar, hoping they might overhear something, since all they knew of Geordie Cameron was that he was tall, red-haired, blue-eyed, and unmistakably Scottish in his speech. This last was revealed a moment later when the chap's voice rose slightly in what James could have sworn was a scolding for his short friend, but all Anthony noticed was the thick Scottish brogue.

"I've heard enough," Anthony said tersely, swiftly rising to his feet.

James, much more familiar with dockside taverns than Anthony, knew exactly what could happen if a brawl started. In seconds, the original combatants could be joined by the entire room. And Anthony might be a first-rate pugilist, just as James was, but gentlemen's rules didn't apply in places like this. While you were busy fending off the blows of one man, you were likely to get a shiv in the back from another.

Envisioning just such an occurrence, James grabbed his brother's arm, hissing, "You've heard nothing. Be sensible, Tony. There's no telling how many of these chaps in here might be in his pay. We can bloody well wait a little longer for him to leave the premises."

"*You* can wait a little longer. I have a new wife at home I've kept waiting long enough."

Before he took another step, however, James sensibly called out, "Cameron?" hoping no response would end the matter right there, since Anthony wasn't being reasonable. Unfortunately, he got ample response.

Georgina and Mac both swung around at once upon hearing the name Cameron. She was apprehensive about actually facing the entire room, yet did so with the hope of seeing Malcolm. Perhaps it was he who had been hailed. Mac, however, braced himself in an aggressive stance as soon as he saw the tall, dark-haired aristocrat shake off his blond companion's hand, his eyes, clearly hostile, glued to Mac. In seconds, the man had closed the space between them.

Georgina couldn't help it. She gawked at the tall, black-haired man who stepped up to Mac, the most handsome, blue-eyed devil she'd ever seen. In her mind it registered that he had to be one of the "lairds" Mac had tried to tell her about, and that this was not exactly the image she harbored of such creatures. There was nothing foppish about this gentleman. His clothes were obviously of the best quality, but understated; no loud satins or bold velvets here. If not for the excessively fashionable cravat, he was done up as any one of her brothers might be when they chose to turn themselves out elegantly.

All of that registered in her mind, but it didn't stop her nervousness from doubling, for there wasn't anything friendly in the man's demeanor. There was in fact an anger about him that seemed just barely held in check, and it seemed to be directed solely at Mac.

"Cameron?" the man asked Mac in a quiet tone.

"The name's MacDonell, mon, Ian MacDonell."

"You're lying."

Georgina's jaw dropped when she heard that growled accusation, then she gasped as the man jerked Mac forward by his lapels and lifted, until the two men were glowering at each other, their faces only inches apart, Mac's smoky-gray eyes blazing with indignation. She couldn't let them fight, for God's sake. Mac might love a brawl as well as any sailor, but devil take it, that wasn't what they were here for. And they couldn't afford the attention it would draw—at least she couldn't.

Without considering the fact that she didn't know how to wield it, Georgina slipped the knife from her sleeve. She wasn't actually going to *use* the thing, just quietly threaten the elegant gentleman into backing off. But before she could get a good grip on the knife with her oversized gloves, it was knocked out of her hand.

She really panicked then, remembering too late that Mac's accoster wasn't alone. She didn't know why they had chosen her and Mac to pick on when there was a whole room full of tough customers if they were merely looking for some sport. But she had heard of such things, how the arrogant lords liked to throw their weight around, intimidating the lower classes with their rank and the power behind it. But she wasn't going to just stand there and be abused. Oh, no. The fact that she was supposed to remain inconspicuous went right out of her mind at the injustice of this unprovoked attack, like the injustice that had lost her Malcolm.

She turned and attacked, blindly, furiously, with all the bitterness and resentment built up over the last six years toward the English and their aristocrats in particular, kicking and hitting, but, unfortunately, doing nothing more than hurting her fists and toes. The blasted fellow felt like a brick wall. But that only made her so furious she didn't have sense enough to stop.

This might have gone on indefinitely if the brick wall hadn't decided he'd had enough. Georgina was suddenly flipped about and hefted off her feet without the least bit of effort, and horror of horrors, the hand holding her up was clamped to her breast.

If that wasn't bad enough, the dark-haired gent still holding Mac suddenly exclaimed in a loud voice, "Good God, *he's* a woman!"

"I know," the brick wall replied, and Georgina recognized an amused tone when she heard it.

"Now you've done it, you miserable curs!" she snarled at them both, well aware that her disguise had just become useless. "Mac, do something!"

Mac attempted to, but the arm he pulled back and swung at the dark-haired gent was caught by his fist and slammed down on the bar.

"There's no need for that, MacDonell," the dark one said. "I made a mistake. Wrong color eyes. I apologize."

Mac was disconcerted at how easily he had been outmaneuvered. He wasn't that much smaller than the Englishman, yet he couldn't raise his fist off the bar to save his soul. And he had the feeling that even if he could, it wouldn't do him much good.

Prudently, he nodded his acceptance of the apology and gained his release by doing so. But Georgina was still held tight by the other rogue, the blond one Mac had felt instinctively was the more dangerous of the two when he'd first seen them.

"Ye'll be letting go, mon, if ye ken what's good fer ye. I canna let ye monhandle—"

"Be easy, MacDonell," the dark one interjected in a hushed tone. "He means the lass no harm. Perhaps you'll let us accompany you outside?"

"There's nae need—"

"Look around you, dear fellow," the blond one interrupted him. "There appears to be every need, thanks to my brother's loud blunder."

Mac did look and swore under his breath. Just about every eye in the room was gazing with speculation at the lass, who had been transferred to the big gent's hip, one thick arm holding her there like a sack of grain as he carried her toward the door. And, miracle of miracles, she wasn't voicing any complaints at this crude handling, at least not that Mac could notice, for her protest had swiftly died with a tight squeeze about the ribs. So Mac wisely held his tongue, too, and followed, realizing that if it weren't such a menacing-looking fellow who was carrying her, they wouldn't get very far.

Georgina had also come to the realization that she was in deep trouble if she didn't get out of there fast, which was *their* fault, but didn't change the fact. And if the brick wall could get her outside without incident, then she'd let him, even if he was doing it in a way that was absolutely mortifying. This kept her temper simmering impotently.

As it happened, though, they were stopped, but by a pretty barmaid who suddenly appeared and latched possessively onto her toter's free arm. "'Ere now, ye're not leavin', are ye?"

Georgina pulled her cap back enough to see just how lovely the girl really was, and to hear the brick wall reply, "I'll be back later, my dear."

The barmaid brightened, not even bothering to look at Georgina, and she realized with amazement that the girl was actually desirous of this caveman's company. There was just no accounting for some people's taste, she supposed.

"I finish work at two," the barmaid told him.

"Then two it is."

"Two's one too many, I'm thinking." This from a brawny sailor who had stood up and was now blocking their path to the door.

Georgina groaned inwardly. This really was a bruiser, as Boyd, who was an admirer of pugilists, would have called him. And although the brick wall *was* a brick wall, she hadn't really gotten a look at him, didn't know if he might be much smaller than this sailor. But she was forgetting the other lord who had called him brother.

He came up to stand next to them now, and she heard his sigh before he said, "I don't suppose you'd care to put her down and take care of this, James."

"Not particularly."

"I didn't think so."

"Stay out of this, mate," the sailor warned the brother. "He's got no right coming in here and stealing not one but two of our women."

"Two? Is this little ragamuffin yours?" The brother glanced at Georgina, who was looking back with murder in her eyes. Perhaps that was why he hesitated before asking, "Are you his, sweetheart?"

Oh, how she'd like to say yes. If she thought she could escape while the two arrogant lords were being pulverized, she would. But she couldn't take that kind of chance. She might be furious at these two interfering aristocrats, and especially with the one called James who was manhandling her, but she was forced by circumstance to tamp down her anger and give a negative shake of her head.

"I believe that settles it, doesn't it." It was not a question by any means. "Now be a good chap and move out of the way."

Surprisingly, the sailor stood firm. "He's not taking her out of here."

"Oh, bloody hell," the lord said wearily just before his fist flattened on the fellow's jaw.

The sailor landed several feet away from them, out cold. The man he had been sitting with rose from their table with a growl, but not soon enough. A short jab, and he fell back in his chair, his hand flying up to staunch the blood now seeping from his nose.

The lord turned around slowly, one black brow arched questioningly. "Any more comers?"

Mac was grinning behind him, realizing now how fortunate he had been not to take on the Englishman. Not another man in the room made a move to accept the challenge. It had happened too quickly. They recognized a skilled pugilist when they saw one.

"Very nicely done, dear boy," James congratulated his brother. "Now can we quit this place?"

Anthony bowed low, coming up with a grin. "After you, old man."

Outside, James set the girl on her feet in front of him. She got her first good look at him then in the glow of the tavern lamp above the door, enough to make her hesitate a hairbreadth before she kicked him in the shin and bolted down the street. He swore violently and started after her, but stopped after a few feet, seeing that it was useless. She was already out of sight on the darkened street.

He turned back, swearing again when he saw that MacDonell had disappeared as well. "Now where the bloody hell did the Scot go?"

Anthony was too busy laughing to have heard him. "What's that?"

James smiled tightly. "The Scot. He's gone."

Anthony sobered, turning around. "Well, that's gratitude for you. I wanted to ask him why they both turned when they heard the name Cameron."

"To hell with that," James snapped. "How am I going to find her again when I don't know who she is?"

"Find her?" Anthony was chuckling once more. "Gad, you're a glutton for punishment, brother. What do you want with a wench who insists on damaging your person when you have another one counting the minutes until you return?"

The barmaid James had arranged to meet much later when she finished work no longer interested him quite so much. "She intrigued me," James replied simply, then shrugged. "But I suppose you're right. The little barmaid will do just as well even though she spent nearly as much time on your lap as she did on mine." Yet he glanced down the empty street again before they headed toward the waiting carriage.

Chapter Four

Georgina sat shivering at the bottom of a stairway that led down to someone's basement. No light penetrated the deep shadows on the last few steps where she hid. The building, whatever it was, was quiet and dark. Quiet, too, was the street this far away from the tavern.

She wasn't exactly cold. It was summer after all, and the weather here was very like that of her own New England. The shivering must be from shock, delayed reaction—a result of too much anger all at once, too much fear, and one too many surprises. But who would have thought the brick wall would have looked like that?

She could still see his eyes staring down at her from that patrician face, hard eyes, curious, crystal clear, and the color was green, not dark, not pale, but brilliant all the same, and so . . . so . . . Intimidating was the word that came to mind, though she wasn't sure why. They were the kind of eyes that could strike fear in a man, let alone a woman. Direct, fearless, ruthless. She shivered again.

She was letting her imagination run away with her. His eyes had only been curious as he looked at her . . . No, not only that. There had been something else there that she wasn't familiar with, or experienced enough to name, something undeniably disturbing. What?

Oh, what did it matter? What was she doing, anyway, trying to analyze *him?* She'd never see him again and thanked God for that. And as soon as her toes stopped throbbing from that last kick she'd gotten in, she would stop thinking about him, too.

Was James his first name or last? She didn't care. Those shoulders, God, how wide they'd been. Brick wall was apt, a *large* brick wall, but lovely bricks. Lovely? She giggled. All right, handsome bricks, very handsome bricks. No, no, what was she thinking? He was a big ape with interesting features, that was all. He was also an Englishman, too old for her, and one of the hated nobles besides, and probably rich, with the wherewithal to buy whatever he wanted and the temerity to do whatever he wanted. Rules would mean nothing to such a man. Hadn't he abused her outrageously? The rogue, the wretch . . .

"Georgie?"

The whisper floated down to her, not very close. She didn't bother to whisper as she called back, "Down here, Mac!"

A few moments passed while she heard Mac's footsteps approaching, then saw his shadow at the top of the stairs. "Ye can come up now, lass. The street's empty."

"I could hear it was empty," Georgina grumbled as she climbed the stairs. "What took you so long? Did they detain you?"

"Nae, I was waiting aside the tavern tae be sure they'd no' be following ye. I was afeared the yellow-haired one was of a mind tae, but his brother was laughing sae much at his expense, he thought better of it."

"As if he could have caught me, great lumbering ox that he was." Georgina snorted.

"Be glad ye didna have tae be putting it tae the testing," Mac said as he led her off down the street. "And maybe next time ye'll be listening tae me—"

"So help me, Mac, if you say I told you so, I won't speak to you for a week."

"Well, now, I'm thinking that might just be a blessing."

"All right, all right, I was wrong. I admit it. You won't catch me within fifty feet of another tavern other than the one we're forced to lodge in, and there I will only use the back stairs as we agreed. Am I forgiven for almost getting you pulverized?"

"Ye dinna have tae apologize fer what wasna yer fault, lass. It was me those two lairds were mistaking fer someone else, and that had nothing tae do wi' ye."

'But they were looking for a Cameron. What if it's Malcolm?"

"Nae, how could it be? They thought I was Cameron from the look of me. Now I ask ye, do I look at all like the lad?"

Georgina grinned, relieved at least on that score. Malcolm had been a skinny eighteen-year-old when she'd been so thrilled to accept his marriage proposal. Of course he was a man now, had likely filled out some, might even be a little taller. But his coloring would be the same, with black hair and blue eyes very similar to that arrogant Englishman's, and he was still more than twenty years younger than Mac, too.

"Well, whoever their Cameron is, I have nothing but sympathy for the poor man," Georgina remarked.

Mac chuckled. "Frightened ye, did he?"

"He? I recall there were two of them."

"Aye, but I noticed ye only had the one tae deal wi'."

She wasn't going to argue about it. "What was it about him that was so . . . different, Mac? I mean, they were both the same, and yet not the same. Brothers apparently, though you couldn't prove it by looking at them. And yet there was something else that was different about the one called James . . . Oh, never mind. I'm not sure *what* I mean."

"I'm surprised ye sensed it, hinny."

"What?"

"That he was the more dangerous of the two. Ye had only tae look at him tae ken it, tae see the way he looked over that room when they first walked in, staring every mon there right in the eye. He'd have taken on that entire room of cutthroats and laughed while doing it. That one, fer all his fine elegance, felt right at home in that rough crowd."

"All that from the look of him?" She grinned.

"Aye, well, call it instinct, lass, and experience of his kind. Ye felt it, too, sae dinna scoff . . . and be glad ye're a fast runner."

"What's *that* suppose to mean? Don't you think he would have let us go?"

"Me, aye, but yerself, I'm no' sae sure. The mon held ye, lass, like he dinna want tae be losing ye."

Her ribs could attest to that, but Georgina merely clicked her tongue. "If he hadn't held me, I'd have broken his nose."

"Ye tried that, as I recall, wi'out much luck."

"You could humor me a little." Georgina sighed. "I've been through a trying time."

Mac snorted. "Ye've been through worse wi' yer own brothers."

"The sport of children, and years ago, I might point out," she retorted.

"Ye were chasing Boyd through the house just last winter wi' murder in yer eye."

"*He's* still a child, and a terrible prankster."

"He's older than yer Malcolm."

"That's it!" Georgina marched off ahead of him, tossing over her shoulder, "You're as bad as the lot of them, Ian MacDonell."

"Well, if ye'd wanted sympathy, girl, why did ye no' say so?" he called after her before he gave in to the laughter he was holding back.

Chapter Five

Hendon was a rural village, seven miles northwest of London Town. The ride there on the two old nags Mac had rented for the day was a pleasant one, a grand concession for Georgina, who still despised everything English. The wooded countryside they rode through was lovely, with valleys and undulating hills offering splendid views, and many shady lanes with pink and white blossoms on hawthorn hedges, wild roses, honeysuckle, and bluebells by the wayside.

Hendon itself was picturesque, with its cluster of cottages, a comparatively new manor house, even a large red brick almshouse. There was a small inn with too much activity in its yard, so Mac elected to avoid it in favor of the old ivy-covered church with its tall stone tower at the north end of the village, where he hoped they could find out where Malcolm's cottage was.

It had been a surprise to learn Malcolm wasn't actually living in London. It had taken three long weeks to find that out, to finally locate Mr. Willcocks, Malcolm's supposed chum, who turned out not to be a chum of his after all. But he had steered them in another direction, and at last they had some luck, or Mac did, in finding someone who actually knew where Malcolm was.

While Mac spent half of each day working to earn their passage money home and the other half searching for Malcolm, Georgina, by his insistence, had spent the three weeks since the night of the tavern fiasco cooped up in her room, reading and rereading the one book she had brought along for the ocean crossing, until she was so sick of it she'd tossed it out her window, hit one of the tavern's clientele with it as he was leaving, and almost lost her room, the landlord had been so upset. It was the only excitement she'd had, mild as it was, and she'd been about ready to climb the walls, or toss something else out the window to see what would happen, when Mac returned last night with the news that Malcolm was living in Hendon.

She'd be reunited with him today, within a matter of minutes. She was so excited now she could barely stand it. She had spent more time getting ready this morning than it had taken them to get here, more time actually than she ever had before, her appearance usually not a matter of particular importance to her. Her buttercup-yellow gown with its short, matching spencer, was the best of the outfits she had brought with her, and was only slightly mussed from the ride. Her thick brown curls were tucked securely under her silk bonnet, also yellow, the short wisps of hair across her brow and framing her cheeks the more becoming for being windblown. Her cheeks were blooming with color, her lips chewed a bright pink.

She'd been turning heads all morning, perched so prettily on the old nag, intriguing gentlemen in passing carriages and the townsfolk in Hampstead, through which they'd ridden, but only Mac took notice. Georgina was too busy daydreaming, drawing forth her memories of Malcolm, pitifully few actually, but precious for all that.

The day she'd met Malcolm Cameron, she had been dumped over the side of Warren's ship when he'd had enough of her sisterly pestering, and six dockhands had jumped into the harbor to save her. Half of them couldn't swim nearly as well as she could, but Malcolm had been on the wharf with his father and had thought to play the hero, too. As it happened, Georgina pulled herself out of the water, while Malcolm had to be saved. But she had been duly impressed with his intention, and thoroughly infatuated. He was all of fourteen and she twelve, and she decided then and there that he was the handsomest, most wonderful boy in the world.

Those sentiments didn't alter very much in the following years, even though Malcolm had had to be reminded of who she was when next they met, and the time after that, too. Then there had been Mary Ann's party, where Georgina had asked Malcolm to dance, and got her toes stepped on at least a half dozen times. He was sixteen then and

more manly, and though he remembered her, he seemed more interested in her friend Mary Ann, who was closer to his age.

Of course, she hadn't determined to have him for herself yet, nor
had she given him any indication of how certain she was that her infat-
uation with him had turned into love. Another year went by before she
decided to do something about it, and this she did in a wholly logical
manner. Malcolm was still the handsomest boy in town, but his
prospects were not the best. She knew by then that his ambition was to
be captain of his own ship, and that he would have to obtain his goal the
hard way, by working his way up. She also was realistic about herself,
knowing that she had nothing to recommend her in looks, that she sort
of just blended in with the crowd. She had five handsome brothers, but
something had gone wrong when it came to the only female in the family. But what she did have was a handsome dowry—her own Skylark
ship to be hers alone on her eighteenth birthday, just as her brothers had
received theirs. But though she couldn't captain her ship as her brothers
did theirs, her future husband could, and she made sure Malcolm was
aware of this.

It was a calculated plot, to be sure, and she was the tiniest bit
ashamed of it, especially when it worked. Malcolm began courting her
a few months before her sixteenth birthday, and on her birthday, he pro-
posed. Sixteen, in love, and deliriously happy! It was no wonder she
managed to ignore whatever guilt she was feeling in more or less having bought a husband. After all, no one had twisted Malcolm's arm. He
was getting what he wanted just as much as she was. And she was sure
that he felt something for her, and that his feelings would grow to match
hers eventually. So everything would have worked out fine if the English hadn't interfered, blast them.

But they did. Her brothers had tried to interfere, too. She had discovered that they'd only been indulging her when they allowed her to
become engaged at sixteen, assuming she would change her mind at
least a half dozen time before she reached eighteen, when they would
let her marry. She had fooled them though, and since the end of the war,
each time they came home, they would try to talk her into forgetting
about Malcolm and finding another husband. She'd had other offers.
After all, her dowry was still a powerful draw. And she wasn't so scat-

terbrained that she wasn't aware and delighted with the change in her appearance in recent years. But she had remained loyal to her one and only love, even when it got harder and harder to make excuses for why he hadn't returned to marry her in the four years since the war ended. But there would be a good reason, and today she would finally learn what it was. And before she left England, she would be married.

"This be it, lass."

Georgina stared at the lovely little cottage with its whitewashed walls and well-tended rose beds. She rubbed her hands together nervously but made no move to accept Mac's help to dismount. She couldn't even recall stopping at the church and waiting while Mac got directions.

"Maybe he isn't home?"

Mac said nothing, just patiently held up arms to her. They had both seen smoke coming from the single chimney. The cottage was definitely occupied. Georgina chewed her lip a moment longer, then finally squared her shoulders. What was there to be nervous about anyway? She looked her best. She looked far better than Malcolm would remember. He couldn't help but be pleased that she had found him.

She let Mac lift her down, then followed him up the red-bricked walkway to the door. She would have paused another few moments just to get her heartbeat under control, but Mac wasn't taking such things into account. He pounded smartly on the door. And then it opened. And Malcolm Cameron stood there. His face might have become vague in memory, but she recalled it now, for it hadn't really changed at all. There were a few squint lines about the eyes, the mark of a sailor, but otherwise, he seemed not to have aged at all, seemed too young to be twenty-four. But he had grown. He was much, much taller, stood six feet at least, as tall as that James fellow . . . For God's sake, what made her think of him? But Malcolm hadn't widened any to compensate for the gained height. He was slim, almost gangly, but that was all right. Broad chests and thickly muscled arms were on her list of dislikes just now.

Malcolm looked fine, better than fine. He was still so handsome, she barely noticed the toddler he was holding, a pretty little girl of about two, with long blond hair and gray eyes. Georgina had eyes only for Malcolm, who was staring back at her as if, well, frankly, as if he didn't recognize her. But of course he did. She hadn't changed *that* much. He was only surprised, and with reason. She was likely the last person he would expect to turn up on his doorstep.

She should say something, but her mind didn't seem to be working quite properly. And then Malcolm glanced away from her to Mac, and his expression slowly altered, lit up in recognition, and he grinned in welcome, unaware of what this seeming slight did to the girl who had traveled so far to find him.

"Ian MacDonell? Is it really you?"

"Aye, laddie, in the flesh."

"In England?" Malcolm shook his head incredulously, but chuckled. "You've bowled me over, you have. But come in, man, come in. We'll have to have a long visit. Damn me, this is a surprise!"

"Aye, fer all of us, I'm thinking," Mac replied gruffly, but he was looking at Georgina as he said it. "Have ye nothing tae say, lass?"

"Yes." Georgina stepped into what was a small parlor, gave it a cursory glance; then her eyes came back to her fiancé and she asked baldly, "Whose child is that, Malcolm?"

Mac coughed and looked up at the ceiling, as if the open-timbered roof was suddenly of great interest. Malcolm frowned at Georgina as he slowly set the little girl on the floor at his feet.

"Do I know you, miss?"

"You mean you really don't recognize me?" This with a great deal of relief.

Malcolm's frown deepened. "Should I?"

Mac coughed again, or was he choking this time? Georgina spared him a scowl before bestowing one of her brighter smiles on the love of her life.

"You should, yes, but I forgive you that you don't. It's been a long while, after all, and they tell me I've changed more than I think. I suppose now I really must believe it." She gave a nervous laugh. "This is embarrassing, that I must introduce myself to you, of all people. I'm Georgina Anderson, Malcolm, your fiancée."

"Little Georgie?" He started to laugh, but he didn't quite make it, sounded more like he was strangling. "You're not. Georgie?"

"I assure you—"

"But you can't be!" he exclaimed now, looking more horrified than doubtful. "You're beautiful! She wasn't . . . I mean, she didn't look . . . No one can change *that* much."

"Obviously, I must beg to differ," Georgina said with some stiffness. "It didn't happen overnight, you know. Had you been there to see the change come about gradually . . . but you weren't there, were you? Clinton, who was gone for three years, was surprised, but he at least still knew it was me."

"He's your brother!" Malcolm protested.

"And you're my fiancé!" she shot back.

"Oh, Jesus, you can't still be thinking . . . It's been, what, five or six years? I never thought you'd wait, what with the war. It changed everything, don't you see?"

"No, I don't see. You were on an English ship when the war started, but through no fault of your own. You were still an American."

"But that's just it, girl. I never felt right, calling myself an American. It was my folks wanted to settle there, not me."

"What exactly are you saying, Malcolm?"

"I'm an Englishman, always have been. I owned up to it when I was impressed, and young as I was, they believed me that I wasn't a deserter. They let me sign on, which I was glad to do. It made no never mind to me who I sailed with, as long as I sailed. And I'm doing right well, I am. I'm second mate now on the—"

"We know your ship," Georgina cut in sharply. "That's how we found you, though it's taken a month to do so. An American merchantman wouldn't keep such shoddy records, you can be sure. My brothers know where every one of their crewmen can be found when they're in port . . . but that's beside the point, isn't it? You sided with the English! Four of my brothers volunteered their ships as privateers for that war, and you might have come up against any one of them!"

"Easy, lass," Mac intervened. "Ye knew all along that he had tae fight again' us."

"Yes, but not willingly. He's as much as admitted he's a traitor!"

"Nae, he's admitting tae a love fer the country of his birth. Ye canna fault a mon fer that."

No, she couldn't, much as she wanted to. Rot the English. God, how she hated them. They not only stole Malcolm from her, but wooed his sentiments to their cause as well. He *was* an Englishman now, and obviously proud of it. But he was still her fiancé. And the war was over, after all.

Malcolm was red-faced, but whether with embarrassment or chagrin for her condemnation of him, she couldn't tell. She was hot-cheeked herself. This was *not* how she had imagined their reunion would be.

"Mac is right, Malcolm. I'm sorry if I got a little upset over something that . . . well, that no longer matters. Nothing has changed, really. My feelings certainly haven't. My being here is testimony to that."

"And just why is it you've come?"

Georgina stared at him blankly for a moment before her eyes narrowed the tiniest bit. "Why? The answer to that is obvious. The question is, why was it necessary for me to come here, and only you can answer that. Why didn't you return to Bridgeport after the war, Malcolm?"

"There was no reason to."

"No reason?" She gasped. "I beg to differ. There was the little matter of our getting married. Or is that something you chose to forget?"

He couldn't meet her eyes to answer, "I didn't forget. I just didn't think you would still have me, my being an Englishman and all."

"Or you no longer wanted me, my being an American?" she demanded.

"It wasn't like that," he protested. "I honestly didn't think you'd be waiting for me. My ship went down. I figured you would have taken me for dead."

"My family is in shipping, Malcolm. The information we get tends to be accurate. Your ship went down, yes, but no man was lost. We knew that. We just didn't know what became of you after that . . . until recently, when you were seen on the *Pogrom*. But I'll grant you that you might have thought it was pointless to return to a fiancé who only *might* be waiting for you. But the proper thing to do would have been to find out for certain. If you didn't want to make the voyage, then you could have written. Communications had resumed between our countries. An English ship or two has even been seen in our port."

She knew she was being sarcastic, but she couldn't seem to help it. When she thought of how long she might have gone on waiting for this man, how many more years, when he had never intended to return to her! If she hadn't come here herself, she likely would never have seen or heard from him again. She was hurt, she didn't understand his reasoning, and he wouldn't even look at her.

"I did write you a letter."

Georgina knew it for the lie it was, a sop for her pride, the coward's way out for him. Little did he know that her pride had been sacrificed long ago in order for her to have him. It wasn't likely to rear its head now just because he was handing her a passel of excuses that wouldn't hold up under close examination. For God's sake, *she* had come up with better excuses than this for him.

She didn't get angry, though she was very, very disappointed in him. So he wasn't perfect, wasn't considerate or even totally honest. She'd backed him into a corner, and he was trying not to hurt her feelings with the callous truth. In a roundabout way she could count that in his favor, she supposed.

"Obviously, Malcolm, your letter never reached me." She heard Mac snort and could have kicked him. "I assume you wrote that you had survived the war?"

"Aye."

"And likely you mentioned your newly discovered patriotism for a country other than my own?"

"Indeed I did."

"And in consideration of that, did you release me from our engagement?"

"Well, I . . ."

She cut in at his hesitation, "Or did you express the hope that I would still have you?"

"Well, certainly—"

"And then you assumed I wouldn't when you had no answer from me."

"Exactly so."

Georgina sighed. "It's a shame that letter never reached me. So much time wasted."

"What's that?"

"Don't look so surprised, Malcolm. I'll still marry you. It's why I came here, after all. Just don't expect me to live in England. That I won't do even for you. But you can come here as often as you like. As captain of my ship, the *Amphitrite*, you can solicit English trade exclusively if that is your wont."

"I—I . . . Jesus, Georgie . . . I—"

"Malcolm?" A young woman appeared to interrupt him. "Why didn't you tell me we had callers?" and to Georgina with an open smile, "I'm Meg Cameron, ma'am. Are you from the manor, then? Having another party, are they?"

Georgina stared at the woman in the doorway, then at the boy shyly hiding behind her skirt, a boy about five years old, with Malcolm's dark hair, Malcolm's blue eyes, and Malcolm's handsome features. She spared another glance for the boy's father, who looked decidedly ill.

"Your sister, Malcolm?" Georgina asked in the most pleasant of tones.

"No."

"I didn't think so."

Chapter Six

No goodbye. No good wishes. Not even a go-to-hell. Georgina simply turned and walked out of the little white cottage in Hendon, leaving her hopes and girlish dreams behind. She could hear Mac saying something, probably making an excuse to Meg Cameron for Georgina's rudeness. Then he was there at her back and giving her a lift up onto the rented nag.

He didn't say a word to her, at least not until they'd left the village behind. She'd tried to get some speed out of her animal, the urge to be miles away as quickly as possible gnawing at her, but the sorry creature wouldn't oblige. And a fast walk gave Mac plenty of time to study her and see through her calm facade. One thing about Mac, he had an annoying habit of being blunt when you least wanted bluntness.

"Why are ye no' crying, lass?"

She thought about ignoring him. He wouldn't press her if she did. But what was rolling around inside her needed letting out.

"I'm too angry right now. That double-dammed scoundrel must have married that woman on his very first docking, long before the war ended. No wonder he became pro-British. He was converted through marriage!"

"Aye, that's possible. Possible, too, was he saw what he liked and had some, and wasna caught fer it until his second docking."

"What's it matter when or why? All this time I've been sitting at home pining over him, he's been married and making children, having just a swell-dandy time!"

Mac snorted. "Ye've wasted time, all right, but ye were never pining away."

She sniffed at his lack of understanding. "I loved him, Mac."

"Ye loved the idea of having him fer yer own, bonny lad that he was, a child's fancy ye should've outgrown. Were ye less loyal, and less stubborn, ye'd have let go of yer fool's dream long ago."

"That's not—"

"Dinna interrupt me till I've finished. Did ye love him true, ye'd be crying now and angry after, no' the other way around."

"I'm crying inside," she said stiffly. "You just can't see it."

"Well, I thank ye fer sparing me, I surely do. Never could abide a female's tears."

She gave him a fulminating glare. "You men are all alike. You're about as sensitive as a . . . a brick wall!"

"If ye're looking fer sympathy, ye willna get it from me, lass. If ye'll recall, I advised ye tae forget about that mon more'n four years ago. I also recall telling ye that ye'd be regretting coming here, and no' just when yer brothers get ahold of ye. So what has yer stubbornness got ye this time?"

"Disillusionment, humiliation, heartache—"

"Delusion—"

"*Why* are you determined to make me madder than I am?" she snapped hotly.

"Self-preservation, hinny. I told ye, I canna abide tears. And as long as ye're yelling at me, ye willna be weeping on my shoulder . . . Och, now, dinna do that, Georgie lass," he said as her face began to crumble. But the tears started in earnest, and all Mac could do was stop their horses and hold out his arms to her.

Georgina leaped across the short space and curled into his lap. But she wasn't content to just have a good cry on a caring shoulder. There was still a lot of anger inside that came out in a lot of wailing.

"Those beautiful children should have been mine, Mac!"

"Ye'll have yer own bairns, lots of them."

"No I won't. I'm getting too old."

"Aye, all of twenty-two." He nodded sagely, fighting to keep from snorting. "That's mighty auld."

She paused to scowl at him. "You picked a fine time to start agreeing with me."

Both red brows went up in feigned surprise. "Did I now?"

Georgina sniffed, and then wailed again, "Oh, why couldn't that woman have come in a mere minute sooner, before I made such a double-damned fool of myself telling that cur I'd still have him?"

"Sae he's a cur now, is he?"

"The lowest, vilest—"

"I get yer drift, hinny, but it's glad ye should be ye said all ye did tae him, a fine revenge, I'm thinking, if ye wanted revenge."

"Is that some kind of male logic too complicated for the female mind? I didn't get revenge, I got humiliated."

"Nae, ye showed the mon what he lost in forsaking ye, a lass he dinna recognize, she's sae bonny now, and his own ship tae command, which he's long wanted. He's likely kicking his own arse right about now, and it's sure as he did wrong by ye that he'll be regretting what he lost fer many a year."

"The ship maybe, but not me. He's got a job he's proud of, beautiful children, a lovely wife—"

"Lovely, aye, but she's no' Georgina Anderson, owner of the *Amphitrite*, part owner of the Skylark Line, though the puir lass has nae say in the running of that, just an equal share in the profits, *and* they say she's the bonniest lass on the eastern seaboard."

"Is that all?"

"Ye dinna sound verra impressed."

"I'm not. That girl might be a bonny lass now, but she wasn't always, and what good are her fair looks when she's wasted the best years of her life." A rude sound interrupted her, but she chose to ignore it. "And she might have money of her own, a right comfortable amount, but just now she doesn't even have enough to buy her passage home. Her looks and means don't change the fact that she's a fool, and stupid, and gullible, an ill judge of character, and not very smart, and—"

"Ye're repeating yerself. Stupid and not very smart—"

"Don't interrupt."

"I will when all ye're doing is blathering. Now yer tears have stopped. Start looking on the bright side."

"There isn't one."

"Aye, there is. Ye wouldna have been happy wi' such a low, vile . . . cur, was it?"

Her lip trembled a little trying to smile, but not quite making it. "I appreciate what you're doing, Mac, but it's not helping with all that I'm feeling right now. I just want to go home, and hope to God I never meet another Englishman with their oh-so-proper speech, their blasted unshakable composure, their faithless sons."

"I hate tae be the one tae enlighten ye, hinny, but every country has its faithless sons."

"Every country has its brick walls, too, but I wouldn't marry one."

"Marry a . . . Now ye're blathering again, and what's this fixation ye're having wi' brick walls, I'd like tae know?"

"Just take me home, Mac. Find us a ship, any ship. It doesn't have to be an American vessel as long as it's sailing for our part of the world and leaving soon, today preferably. You can use my jade ring to buy the passage."

"Are ye daft, lass? Yer father gave ye that ring, brought it all the way from—"

"I don't care, Mac," she insisted, and she was now wearing the stubborn look he was beginning to really dread seeing. "Unless you're willing to turn thief and steal the money, which I know you're not, it's the only thing we have that will buy us passage. I'm not willing to wait until it's earned, I promise you. And besides, the ring can always be bought back when we get home."

"It's just this quickly ye decided tae come here, lass. Ye're supposed tae learn from yer mistakes, no' jump right in tae making the same ones."

"If you're preaching patience, you can forget it. I've had six years of patience, and *that* was my biggest mistake. I intend to practice impatience from now on."

"Georgie . . ." he began warningly.

"Why are you arguing with me? Until we sail, you're going to have a weeping woman on your hands. I thought you couldn't abide female tears?"

Female stubbornness was far worse, Mac decided, so he gave up gracefully with a sigh. "When ye put it that way . . ."

Chapter Seven

A skyscape of sailless masts didn't guarantee there would be at least one ship, out of so many, sailing for America in the near future. You would think it would. You might even consider it a sure bet. Georgina would have lost the wager if she had thought to make it.

Most of the ships that had come in with theirs last month had long since departed for other ports. Discounting those ships that refused to take on passengers, there were several American vessels still remaining, but none anticipated a return to her home port before next year, too long a voyage for the newly impatient Georgina. And the one ship that *was* scheduled to sail directly for New York, which was close enough to Bridgeport to be ideal, wasn't sailing anytime soon, according to her first mate. Her captain apparently was courting some English miss and had sworn he wouldn't set sail until he was married. Which was just what Georgina needed to hear to make her rip up two dresses and toss the chamber pot out the window.

She wanted to leave England so badly, she was already considering an eight- to ten-month voyage on one of the American ships scheduled to depart within the week, and this after only a few days of trying to find passage. When she told Mac that on the third morning, he came back a few hours later with the names of three English vessels departing the next week. He hadn't mentioned them sooner because he had figured she would discount them out-of-hand simply because they were English and crewed entirely by Englishmen, and escaping all things English was just as important to her right now as getting home was. And discount them is exactly what she did, and quite rudely, too. It was then that Mac hesitantly mentioned an alternative she hadn't considered.

"There be a ship sailing wi' the morning tide. She willna take on passengers, but she's needing a bo's'n . . . and a cabin boy."

Georgina's eyes widened with interest. "You mean work our way home?"

"It was a thought, better'n spending half a year or more at sea wi' a lass *practicing impatience*."

Georgina chuckled at the emphasis he put on that, accompanied with rolling eyes. It was the first thing she'd found amusing since she discovered Malcolm's betrayal.

"Maybe I'll do less practicing once I'm on my way home. Oh, Mac, I think it's a wonderful idea," she said with sudden enthusiasm. "Is it an American ship? Is she big? Where's she bound for?"

"Slow down, lass, she's no' what ye think. She's the *Maiden Anne* out of the West Indies, three-masted and spanking clean. A real beauty. But she has the look of a refitted warship still heavily armed, though she's privately owned."

"A West Indies merchantman would need to be well armed if she frequents those pirate-infested waters. All of our Skylark ships that sail the Caribbean are, and yet they're still occasionally attacked."

"True enough," he agreed. "But the *Maiden Anne* isna a trader, at least no' this voyage. She willna be carrying cargo, just ballast."

"A captain who can sail without making any profit whatsoever?" Georgina teased, knowing how that fact alone would annoy a man who had sailed thirty-five years on merchantmen. "He must be a pirate."

Mac snorted. "He's a mon sails on his whims, going wherever the mood takes him, sae says his crewmon."

"The captain's the owner then, and rich enough to keep a ship just for pleasure?"

"Sae it seems," he said in disgust.

Georgina grinned. "I know how that concept pains you, but it isn't unique by any means. And what's the difference if she's carrying a cargo or not, as long as she gets us home?"

"Aye, well, that's another thing. It's Jamaica she's bound fer, no' America."

"Jamaica?" Some of Georgina's pleasure in finding a ship dimmed, but only for a moment. "But Skylark has offices in Jamaica. And isn't it the third port on Thomas's schedule? We could conceivably arrive there before he departs again, and if not, Skylark has other ships that put in to Jamaica frequently, including Boyd's and Drew's ships, not to mention my own." She was grinning again. "At the most we're talking only a few more weeks' delay in getting home. That's better than half a year, and certainly better than staying here another day."

"I dinna know, lass. The more I think on it, the more I'm thinking I shouldna have mentioned it."

"And the more I think on it, the more I like the idea. Come on, Mac, it's the perfect solution."

"But ye'll have tae work," he reminded her. "Ye'll have tae run the captain's messages, bring his meals, clean his cabin, and whatever else he requires. Ye'll be kept right busy."

"So?" she challenged. "Are you going to tell me you don't think I'm capable of such simple tasks, when I've scrubbed decks, cleaned cannons, scraped hulls, climbed rigging—"

"That were years ago, lass, afore ye started looking like the wee lady ye are now. Yer father and brothers indulged ye, letting ye climb all over their ships when in port, learning things ye had nae business learning. But this be working and living alongside men who dinna know ye, and who canna know ye. The job isna fer a lass, and it isna a lass ye can be if ye take it."

"I didn't miss that point, Mac. So my dresses will have to be left behind. Certain assumptions are automatic when breeches are worn, as we found out. Put a boy in a dress and you see an ugly girl, a girl in breeches and you have a pretty boy. And after all, I did right well that night—"

"Afore ye opened yer mouth or looked anyone in the eye," he cut in to remind her sternly. "Yer disguise dinna last beyond that."

"Because I was trying to pass for a man, which wasn't very smart now that I think of it, not with this face. All right." She stopped him from interrupting again. "So you tried to tell me and I wouldn't listen. Don't belabor the point. This is entirely different, and you know it. A boy can have delicate features. They often do. And with my height and slimness, timbre of voice and"—she looked down at her chest—"some tight binding, I can easily pass for a boy of nine or ten."

She got a disgusted look for that assumption. "Yer intelligence will give ye away."

"All right, so a brilliant twelve-year-old who's slow in maturing." And then quite firmly, "I can do it, Mac. If you didn't think I could, you wouldn't have considered it."

"I mun have been daft, I surely was, but we both ken who be responsible fer *that*."

"Now, now," she chided, grinning. "I'm only one wee lass, soon to be one wee laddie. How difficult can I be?" He made a *very* rude sound. "Well, look at it this way. The sooner I get home, the sooner you can wash your hands of me."

This time a mere grunt. "That's another thing. Ye'd have tae keep up the pretense fer a month or more. That's a long time tae be finding a private spot tae tend nature's calls, when a mon can just stand wi' the wind at his back and—"

"Mac!" She actually blushed, even though with five brothers who sometimes forgot she was around, she'd heard and seen just about everything a girl shouldn't. "I didn't say there wouldn't be *some* difficulties, but I'm resourceful enough to overcome them, whatever they are. Unlike most girls, I know a ship inside out, including the area sailors tend to avoid. I'll manage, even if I have to make use of a rat-infested hold. And besides, if I am found out, what's the worst that can happen? Do you honestly think they'll kick me off the ship in the middle of the ocean? Of course they won't. I'll likely just get locked away somewhere until she docks, and *then* given the boot. And that would be no more than I deserve if I'm careless enough to give myself away."

It took a bit more arguing back and forth before Mac finally sighed. "All right, but I'll be trying first tae get ye on wi'out yer having tae work. They might be agreeable tae that if I decline any pay, and they think ye're my brother who mun come wi' me."

One velvet brow arched, while laughter lit her eyes. "Your brother? Without a Scottish burr?"

"Stepbrother then," he allowed. "Raised separate, which willna be questioned considering the age difference."

"But I thought they *need* a cabin boy? They're more likely to insist if that's the case. I know my brothers wouldn't sail without one."

"I said I'd *try*. They've still the rest of the day tae find another lad fer the job."

"Well, I hope they don't," Georgina replied and meant it. "I'd much rather be working on the crossing than doing nothing, especially since I'll have to be in disguise anyway. And don't think to say I'm your sister instead, because if they won't take me on to have you for bo's'n, then we've lost the opportunity altogether. So let's get going before the job *is* taken."

"Ye'll be needing clothes fit fer a lad."

"We can buy some on the way."

"Ye've yer things tae dispose of."

"The landlord can have them."

"What about yer hair?"

"I'll cut it."

"Ye willna! Yer brothers would kill me, if they dinna anyway!"

She dug the woolen cap she'd used before out of her trunk and waved it under his nose. "There! Now will you quit nitpicking and start moving? Let's go."

"I thought ye were going tae stop practicing impatience," he grumbled.

She laughed as she pushed him out the door. "We haven't sailed yet, Mac. I'll stop tomorrow. I promise."

Chapter Eight

Sir Anthony Malory signaled to the waiter for another bottle of port before he leaned back in his chair to stare at his older brother. "D'you know, James, I think I'm actually going to miss you, damn me if I won't. You should have settled your affairs in the Caribbean before you came home, then you wouldn't have to return there now, just when I've gotten used to having you around again."

"And how was I to know the infamous Hawke's demise could be arranged so easily, so that I could remain here?" James replied. "You forget, the only reason I came home a'tall was to settle the score with Eden. I had no idea that he was about to marry into the family at the time, or that the family would decide to reinstate me now that my pirating days are behind me."

"Presenting the elders with a new nephew in Jeremy helped the matter along, I'd say. They're so bloody sentimental when it comes to family."

"And you're not?"

Anthony chuckled. "So I am. But you will hurry back, won't you? It's been like old times, having you around again."

"We did have some good times in those wild years, didn't we?"

"Chasing the same women." Anthony grinned.

"Getting the same lectures from the elders."

"Our brothers mean well. Jason and Eddie boy just took to this responsibility thing too young, is all. They never had a chance to kick up their own heels, too busy keeping the rest of us in line."

"You don't have to defend them to me, lad," James replied. "You don't think I hold a grudge, d'you? Truth to tell, I'd have disowned me just as swiftly as you three did."

"I never disowned you," Anthony protested.

"Drink up, dear boy," James replied dryly. "It might help to jog your memory."

"My memory is in perfect working order, I tell you. I might have been furious with you for absconding with Reggie that summer eight years ago—three months on a bloody pirate ship, and the dear girl only twelve years old at the time! But I worked that out of my system back then, giving you the thrashing you so richly deserved when you brought her back. And you took that thrashing. I never understood why. Care to tell me now?"

James lifted a tawny brow. "D'you think I could have prevented it, three against one, as it were? You give me more credit than I'm due, dear boy."

"Come off it, brother. You didn't fight back that day. You didn't even try. Jason and Edward might not have noticed, but I'd gone too many rounds with you in the ring not to."

James shrugged. "So I felt I deserved it. I'd thought it a lark at the time, to take her right out from under big brother's nose. I was, shall we say, annoyed enough with Jason to do it, since he'd refused to let me even see Regan after I—"

"Reggie," Anthony corrected automatically.

"Regan," James repeated with more force, beginning the old argument he'd had with each of his brothers over what nickname to call their niece, Regina—an argument that stemmed from a longtime insistence on James's part to be different, go his own way, and follow his own rules. But they both realized at the same moment what they were doing and grinned.

But Anthony went a bit further. He conceded, "All right, Regan for tonight."

James hit one ear with the palm of his hand. "I think there must be something wrong with my hearing."

"Bloody hell," Anthony said with a half growl, half chuckle. "Just get on with your story before I fall asleep. Ah, wait, here's our second bottle."

"You're not thinking of getting me foxed *again*, are you?"

"Wouldn't dream of it," Anthony said as he filled both their glasses to the brim.

"I believe that's what you said the last time we were here at White's, but as I recall, your friend Amherst had to carry us both home . . . in the middle of the afternoon. You never did tell what the little wife had to say about that."

"Quite a bit, thank you, none of it worth repeating," Anthony replied sourly.

James's hearty laugh brought a number of stares to their table. "I honestly don't know what's happened to your finesse, dear boy. You've been in the lady's bad graces ever since the second day of your marriage, simply because you couldn't convince her that that little barmaid who'd squirmed all over your lap for those few minutes wasn't yours for the evening. It was devilish bad luck that the wench left some yellow hair on your lapel for the wife to find, but didn't you tell Roslynn you were only in that tavern on her behalf, searching for her Cameron cousin?"

"Certainly."

"Then you still haven't told her the wench was mine, not yours?"

Anthony shook his head stubbornly. "And I'm not going to, either. It should have been enough that I'd told her nothing happened, that the offer was made and I'd refused it. It's still a matter of trust . . . but I believe we've had this conversation before, and right here, at that. Quit worrying about my love life, brother. My little Scottish bride will come around. I'm working on it in my own way. So let's get back to your grand confession, shall we?"

James reached for his glass first, keeping pace with Anthony. "As I'd said, I was annoyed with Jason for refusing to let me even see Regan."

"Was he supposed to have allowed it? You'd already been pirating for two years."

"I may have been raising hell on the high seas, Tony, but I hadn't changed personally. He knew bloody well I would have left behind anything to do with the Hawke had he allowed me to see her. But he'd disowned me for taking to the seas and disgracing the family as it were, though no one inside England or out knew Captain Hawke and James Malory, viscount of Ryding, were one and the same. Jason had made his stand and wouldn't back down, so what was I to do? Never see her again? Regan's like a daughter to me. We all raised her."

"You *could* have given up pirating," Anthony pointed out reasonably.

James grinned slowly. "Follow Jason's dictates? When did I ever? Besides, I was having a devilish good time playing the pirate. There was the challenge, the danger, but more, I brought discipline back into my life, and for that matter, possibly saved my health. I'd been getting quite dissipated and jaded before I quit London. We'd had our fun, aye, but there was no challenge left save getting in some lady's skirts, and even that no longer mattered when it came right down to it. Hell and fire, no one would even call me out anymore to alleviate the monotony, I'd gotten such a deadly reputation."

Anthony burst out laughing. "You're making my heart bleed, old man."

James tipped the bottle this time. "Drink up, you ass. You've more sympathy when you're drunk."

"I don't get drunk. Tried to tell the wife that, but she wouldn't believe me. So you went to sea and lived the clean, healthy life of a pirate."

"Gentleman pirate," James corrected.

Anthony nodded. "Quite right. Shouldn't miss the distinction. What is the distinction, by the way?"

"I've never sunk a ship, nor taken one without giving her a sporting chance. I've lost a lot of fat prizes that way, letting them elude me, but I never claimed to be a successful pirate, just a persistent one."

"Confound you, James, it was only a game to you, wasn't it? And you deliberately let Jason think you were out there raping and pillaging and feeding men to the sharks!"

"Well, why not? He's not altogether happy unless he's got one of us to condemn. And better me than you, since I don't give a bloody damn, while you, on the other hand, do."

"Now that's a fine attitude to take," Anthony said sarcastically.

"D'you think so?" James smiled and downed his drink. Anthony was quick to refill it. "But then it's the same one I've always had."

"I suppose," Anthony conceded reluctantly. "You were defying and deliberately provoking Jason for as long as I can remember."

James shrugged. "So what is life without its little stimulations, dear boy?"

"I think you just enjoy seeing Jason fly through the roof. Admit it."

"Well, he does it so well, don't you think?"

Anthony grinned and then chuckled. "All right, so the whys and wherefores no longer matter. You've been accepted back into the fold, forgiven all, as it were. But you still haven't answered my question about the thrashing you took."

That golden brow arched again. "Haven't I? Must be because I keep getting interrupted."

"So I'll shut my trap."

"An impossibility."

"James . . ."

"Come now, Tony, just put yourself in my place and you'll have your answer. It's not so very complicated, after all. I wanted my equal time with our darling niece, Regan. I thought she'd enjoy seeing a bit of the world, which she did, by the way. But much as I loved having her with me, I realized the folly of what I'd done before I brought her back. Not that I was an active pirate while I had her. But the sea offers no guarantees. Storms, other pirates, enemies I've made, anything is possible. The risk to her was minimal, but it was still there. And had anything happened to Regan . . ."

"Good God, the unconscionable James Malory plagued by guilt? No wonder I could never figure it out."

"I do have my moments, it would seem," James said dryly, giving Anthony a disgusted look for sitting there laughing.

"What did I say?" Anthony asked innocently. "Never mind. Here, have another drink." And the bottle was tipped again. "You know," he added thoughtfully with a grin. "Between me exposing the dear girl to my jaded friends when I had her to myself each year—all on their best behavior, mind you—and you exposing her to a crew of cutthroats—"

"Who all adored her and were very polite cutthroats while she was on board."

"Yes, well, she certainly had a well-rounded education with our help."

"Hadn't she though? So how is it she ended up married to a bounder like Eden?"

"The puss loves him, more's the pity."

"I figured *that* much out for myself."

"Come now, James, you just don't like him because he's too much like us, and anyone like us isn't good enough for our Reggie."

"Beg to differ, dear boy, but that's why *you* don't like him. *I* took exception to the bloody insults he threw in my face as he sailed away from the encounter I had with him all those years ago at sea, insults that came *after* he'd already disabled my ship."

"But you attacked him," Anthony pointed out, having heard most of the details of that sea battle already, including the fact that James's son was injured in it, which was why James had given up pirating altogether.

"Beside the point," James insisted. "And anyhow, he added insult to injury when he landed me in gaol last year."

"*After* you'd thrashed the daylights out of him. And didn't you say Nicholas had also put up the blunt for your escape before he took off for the West Indies? Because of a guilty conscience, wasn't it?"

"To hear him tell it, it was because he would have missed the hanging."

Anthony hooted. "That sounds like him, the arrogant puppy. But give credit where it's due, brother. If you hadn't been arrested, courtesy of our nephew-by-marriage, you wouldn't have been able to arrange Hawke's supposed demise so neatly, thereby getting the price off your head and burning your bridges behind you. You can now walk the streets of London again without looking over your shoulder."

That deserved the draining of another glassful. "When did you start defending that young cockerel?"

"Good God, is that what I was doing?" Anthony looked utterly horrified. "Beg your pardon, old boy. It won't happen again, you may depend upon it. He's a blighter through and through."

"But Regan makes him pay for it," James said with a gloating smile.

"How's that?"

"He ends up sleeping on the sofa each time he crosses words with one of us and she happens to overhear it."

"The devil you say."

"It's true. Told me himself. You'll really have to visit those two more often while I'm gone."

"I'll drink to that." Anthony laughed. "Eden on the sofa. Gad, that's rich."

"No more amusing than the muddle you're in with your own wife."

"Now don't start in on me again."

"Wouldn't think of it. But I do hope you'll have smoothed the waters before I return in a few months, since I'll be taking Jeremy off your hands then, and *that*, dear boy, will leave you no buffer. Just you and the little Scot . . . alone."

Anthony's smile was quite confident and a little bit wicked. "You will hurry back, won't you?"

Chapter Nine

The whole family had turned out to see James off—Jason and Derek, Edward and his whole brood, Anthony and his little Scot, who was looking quite peaked, but understandably so, since Anthony had recently been told he was to be a father. That scamp, Jeremy, was in high spirits, despite the fact this was the first time he would be separated from James since he'd been found six years ago. He was probably thinking he'd be getting away with murder now, with only his Uncle Tony to keep him in line. He'd find out soon enough that Jason and Eddie boy would be keeping an eye on him, too. He'd be reined in as tight if not tighter than he had been under James and his first mate Conrad's supervision.

The tide put an end to the goodbyes. James's hangover, which he could blame Anthony for, wouldn't take much more back-pounding anyway. But it had also almost made him forget the note he had jotted off for the little Scot, explaining to her about the barmaid she had accused her husband of bedding. He called Jeremy up the gangplank and handed it to him.

"See your Aunt Roslynn gets this, but not when Tony's around."

Jeremy pocketed the note. "It's not a love letter, is it?"

"A love letter?" James snorted. "Get out of here, puppy. And see you—"

"I know, I know." Jeremy threw up his hands, laughing. "I won't do anything you wouldn't."

He ran back down the gangplank before James could take him to task for his impudence. But he was smiling as he turned away, and came face-to-face with Conrad Sharpe, his first mate and best friend.

"What was that about?"

James shrugged, realizing Connie had seen him pass the note. "I decided to lend a hand after all. At the rate Tony's going, he'd be floundering forever."

"I thought you weren't going to interfere," Connie reminded him.

"Well, he is my brother, isn't he? Though why I bother after the dirty trick he played on me last night, I don't know." At Connie's raised brow, he grinned, despite the slow throb in his head. "Made sure I'd be feeling miserable today to cast off, the bloody sod."

"But you went along with it, naturally?"

"Naturally. Couldn't have the lad drinking me under the table, now, could I? But you'll have to see us off, Connie. I'm afraid I'm done for. Report to me in my cabin after we're under way."

An hour later, Connie poured a measure of rye from the well-stocked cabinet in the captain's cabin and joined James at his desk. "You're not going to worry about the boy, are you?"

"That rascal?" James shook his head, wincing slightly when his headache returned, and took another sip of the tonic Connie had had sent from the galley. "Tony will see Jeremy doesn't get into any serious scraps. If anyone will worry, it's you. You should have had one of your own, Connie."

"I probably do. I just haven't found him yet like you did the lad. You've probably more yourself that you don't know about."

"Good God, one's enough," James replied in mock horror, gaining a chuckle from his friend. "Now what have you to report? How many of the old crew were available?"

"Eighteen. And there was no problem filling the ranks, except for the bo's'n, as I told you before."

"So we're sailing without one? That'll put a heavy load on you, Connie."

"Aye, if I hadn't found a man yesterday, or rather, if he hadn't volunteered. Wanted to sign on as passengers, him and his brother. When I told him the *Maiden Anne* don't carry passengers, he offered to work his way across. A more persistent Scot I've never seen."

"Another Scot? As if I ain't had enough to do with them lately. I'm bloody well glad your own Scottish ancestors are so far back you don't remember them, Connie. Between hunting down Lady Roslynn's cousin and running into that little vixen and her companion—"

"I thought you'd forgotten about that."

James's answer was a scowl. "How do you know this Scot knows the first thing about rigging?"

"I put him though the paces. I'd say he's had the job before. And he does claim to have sailed before, as quartermaster, ship's carpenter, and bo's'n."

"If that's true, he'll come in right handy. Very well. Is there anything else?"

"Johnny got married."

"Johnny? My cabin boy, Johnny?" James's eyes flared. "Good God, he's only fifteen! What the devil does he think he's doing?"

Connie shrugged. "Says he fell in love and can't bear to leave the little woman."

"Little woman?" James sneered. "That cocky little twit needs a mother, not a wife." His head was pounding again, and he swilled down the rest of the tonic.

"I've found you another cabin boy. MacDonell's brother—"

Tonic spewed across James's desk. "Who?" he choked.

"Blister it, James, what's got into you?"

"You said MacDonell? Would his first name be Ian?"

"Aye." Now Connie's eyes flared. "Good God, he's not the Scot from the tavern, is he?"

James waved away the question. "Did you get a good look at the brother?"

"Come to think of it, no. He was a little chap, though, quiet, hiding behind his brother's coattails. I didn't have much choice in signing him on, what with Johnny only letting me know two days ago that he was staying in England. But you can't mean to think—"

"But I do." And suddenly James was laughing. "Oh, God, Connie, this is priceless. I went back to look for that little wench, you know, but she and her Scot had disappeared from the area. Now here she's fallen right into my lap."

Connie grunted. "Well, I can see you're going to have a pleasant crossing."

"You may depend upon it." James's grin was decidedly wolfish. "But we shan't unmask her disguise just yet. I've a mind to play with her first."

"You could be wrong, you know. She might be a boy after all."

"I doubt it," James replied. "But I'll find out when she begins her duties."

He slumped back in his comfortably padded chair when Connie left him. He was still grinning, still marveling at the incredible piece of chance that had led the little wench and her Scot to pick his ship out of all those available, especially when it made no sense a'tall.

Connie said they'd tried to buy passage first, so they must have money. Why not just find another ship? James knew of at least two English vessels that would soon be departing for the West Indies, and one of them had ample accommodations for passengers. Why go to the trouble of disguising the girl and taking the risk she'd be discovered? Or was it a disguise? Hell and fire, the last time he'd seen her, she'd been done up the same. It could be her normal way of dress . . . no, he was forgetting her upset when Tony had announced that she was a woman, not a man. She'd been hiding her sex then, was hiding it now—or hoped to do so.

His cabin boy. What nerve she had! James shook his head, chuckling.

It was going to be interesting indeed to see how she planned to get away with it. A poorly lit tavern was one thing, but on a ship, in the bright light of day? And yet she'd obviously fooled Connie. Maybe she could have gotten away with it if James hadn't met her once before. But he had, and he hadn't forgotten the meeting, remembered it quite well, in fact; her cute little backside that had so intrigued him, a tender breast that had fit so nicely in his hand. Her features had been exquisitely delicate: the perfectly molded cheekbones, the pert little nose, the wide, sensual lips. He hadn't seen her brows, nor a bit of her hair, but for those few moments when she'd finally looked up at him outside that tavern, he had become lost in velvety-brown eyes.

He'd gone back not once but half a dozen times trying to find her in the last month. He realized now why he'd had no luck. No one knew anything of the pair because they'd never been in that area before, likely never even been to London before. It would be a safe bet to assume they were from the West Indies and now returning home, rather than the other way around. MacDonell might be a Scot, but the wench wasn't. James hadn't been able to place her distinctive accent, but English it wasn't, of that he was certain.

She was a mystery, all right, and one he meant to solve. But first he was going to amuse himself with her charade by installing her in his cabin and letting her think his cabin boy always slept there. He would have to pretend he didn't recognize her, or let her assume he simply didn't remember their encounter. Of course, there was the possibility that *she* might not remember it, but no matter. Before the voyage was over, she'd share more than his cabin. She'd share his bed.

Chapter Ten

The galley was not exactly the most brilliant place to hide, not with summer still hanging on and the ocean breezes still a far way off. Once they were out to sea it wouldn't be so bad, but now, with the huge brick ovens radiating heat since before the dawn, and steam rolling out of cauldrons on the stove for what promised to be a tasty evening meal, it was hot as the devil's welcome.

The cook and his two helpers had discarded most of their clothes by the time the crew started wandering in for a quick breakfast, a man or two at a time as could be spared, since the hours before castoff were the busiest time aboard. Georgina had watched the activity dockside for a while as the last of the ship's supplies and equipment were delivered and carried to the hold and galley. But it was a familiar sight and so didn't hold her interest very long. And besides, she'd seen enough of England to last her a lifetime.

So she stayed in the galley, out of the way and out of notice, perched on a stool in the opposite corner from where the food supplies were being stacked, barrels and casks and sacks of grain and flour, so much that there was finally no room for any more, and the rest had to be stored in the hold.

If it weren't for the heat, Georgina would really have liked it there, for it was certainly the cleanest galley she'd ever seen. But then the whole ship had a spanking new look to it, and, in fact, she'd been told it had just undergone refurbishing from top to bottom.

Between the ovens and stove was a deep coal bin, full to the brim just now. A long table in the center of the room was barely scarred, with a butcher's cleaving block at the end of it waiting to drip blood from one of the many live animals penned in the hold—a great many animals actually, just about guaranteeing fresh meat for the whole voyage. The room was as cluttered as any galley, with its hung spices and pots, chests and utensils, and everything was carefully secured to the floor, walls, or ceiling.

The lord of all this was a black-haired Irishman by the doubtful name of Shawn O'Shawn, who didn't suspect Georgie MacDonell was other than what he seemed to be. Shawn was a friendly fellow of about twenty-five, with merry green eyes that were constantly surveying his domain. He'd given Georgina permission to stay, though with the warning she might be put to work if she did. She didn't mind that, and every so often she was given a task to do when his helpers were both busy. He was a talkative sort and didn't mind answering questions, but he was a new man himself, and so there wasn't much he could tell her about the ship or her captain.

She hadn't met too many others of the crew yet, even though she and Mac had slept aboard the ship last night, or tried to. What with being wakened repeatedly as the men drifted into the forecastle at all hours from their last night in port, and drunkenly tried to find their hammocks in the dark, sleep wasn't part of the agenda unless you were topsided with drink.

The men were a motley bunch of different nationalities, from what she had seen so far, which wasn't unusual for a ship that traveled far and wide, losing and picking up new men in ports all over the world. Of course, that meant there would be a few Englishmen included in the motley, and there were.

The first mate was one, Conrad Sharpe, known affectionately as Connie, though she'd heard only one man so far dare to call him so. He spoke with a precise accent, almost like a blasted aristocrat, and there was no nonsense about the man. Quite tall and narrow of frame, with red hair shades darker than Mac's and a host of freckles on both arms and hands—suggesting he had them all over. Yet his face was deeply tanned, without a freckle in sight. And his hazel eyes were so direct, there'd been several heart-stopping moments when Georgina had thought she wasn't fooling anyone with her disguise. Yet she was signed on. He had taken her at face value. In fact, there'd been no bargaining with the man, as Mac had found out. Either they worked or they didn't sail with the *Maiden Anne*, which suited Georgina, but Mac had given in only grudgingly.

She could find no fault with Mr. Sharpe—at least not yet. It was on principle alone that she didn't like him. Which wasn't fair by any means, but Georgina didn't care to be fair just now where Englishmen were concerned, placing them all into the category shared with rats and snakes and other detestable creatures. She'd have to keep those feelings to herself, though. It wouldn't do to make an enemy of the man. One tended to watch one's enemies too closely. She'd just avoid him as best she could, him and any other Englishmen aboard.

She hadn't met Captain Malory yet, since he still hadn't arrived before she came down to the galley. She knew she ought to go and find him, introduce herself, discover if there were to be any duties above those she anticipated. All captains were different, after all. Drew demanded a bath be waiting for him in his cabin every day, even if it had to be salt water. Clinton liked warm milk before he retired, and it was his cabin boy's duty to bring it and also tend the cow that produced it. Warren's cabin boy had to do no more than keep his cabin neat, since he liked to fetch his own food and eat with his crew. Mr. Sharpe had named all the normal duties expected of her, but only the captain could tell her what else he would require.

Just now he'd be busy, getting them under way, but that would be to her advantage. Yet she kept dillydallying. He was, after all, the one she had to worry most about fooling, since she would be in his company more than that of any of the other men. And first impressions were the most important, since they tended to stick and affect all other judgments. So if she got through their first meeting without his finding anything amiss, she could pretty much relax.

But she didn't get up to go search him out. There was that very great "if" that kept her in the hot galley long after her clothes began to cling and her hair became a wet mat under the tight-knit stocking and woolen cap that concealed it. *If* the captain saw nothing unusual about her, she'd be fine. But what if he was the one discerning eye aboard that she couldn't fool? And if he unmasked her before they reached the channel, she could well find herself put ashore rather than locked up for the duration of the voyage. A worse possibility, she could be put off ship alone. Mac, after all, was needed a lot more than a cabin boy. And if the captain refused to let Mac go with her, actually detained him until it would be too late for him to follow, there wasn't anything they could do about it.

So Georgina stayed in the galley where she was already accepted as Georgie MacDonell. But she stayed too long, as she realized when Shawn dropped a heavy tray of food on her lap. Seeing all the silver domes and fine cutlery on the tray, she knew it wasn't for her.

"He'd be in his cabin then? Already?"

"Lord love ye, where have ye been, laddie? Word's gone 'round hisself has a head poundin' worse'n the rest of us. It's in his cabin he's been since he came aboard. Mr. Sharpe's cast us off."

"Oh."

Double-damn, why hadn't someone told her? What if she'd been needed, looked for? What if he was angry because no one was there to tend him? That would certainly get them off to a fine start.

"I guess I'd better . . . yes, I'd better—"

"Aye, and quickly. Jesus, careful with that now! Is it too heavy for ye, then? No? Well, never ye mind, boyo. Just remember to duck if it comes back at ye."

The dishes clattered again as Georgina stopped on her way out the door. "Why would it . . . for God's sake, he wouldn't throw it at me, would he?"

Shawn shrugged, grinning widely. "Now how would I be knowin' that? I've yet to clap eyes on the cap'n meself. But when a man's got hisself an achin' head, ye never know what to expect, do ye now? Anticipate, laddie. That's me advice, and good advice it be."

Wonderful. Get the green lad even more nervous than he already was. She hadn't realized Mr. Shawn O'Shawn had such a fine sense of humor, rot him.

It was a long walk to the sterncastle, where the captain's cabin and those of his officers were located, especially long with England still visible off port and starboard. Georgina tried not to look at the riverbanks and how really close they were, tried to look for Mac instead, needing a boost in confidence that a few words with him would give her. But he was nowhere in sight, and the heavy tray was beginning to drag at her arms, so she couldn't delay to look for him. A delay wouldn't be wise anyway. Cold food would not appease a surly, pain-ridden man.

And yet, when she stood outside the captain's door, precariously balancing the tray with one hand so she could knock with the other, she couldn't do it, couldn't make the tiny sound that would gain her entry. She stood rooted, paralyzed except for the trembling in her hands and knees, the tray slowly rocking side to side, all those "what ifs" converging in her mind.

She shouldn't be this nervous. If the worst happened, it wouldn't be the end of the world. She was resourceful enough to find another way home . . . alone . . . eventually.

Devil take it, why hadn't she found out *something* about this captain other than his name? She didn't know if he was young or old, mean or kind, liked or merely respected . . . or hated. She'd known some captains who were real tyrants, the godlike authority they had over their crews going to their heads. She should have asked someone else when Mr. O'Shawn hadn't been able to answer her questions. But it wasn't too late. A few more minutes' delay, a few words with whomever was nearest on deck, and she might learn that Captain Malory was the nicest old softy you could ever hope to sail under. Then her palms would stop sweating and she could forget those "what ifs" . . . but the door opened just as she turned to leave.

Chapter Eleven

———⚭———

Georgina's heart plummeted. The food she was carrying almost did the same as she swung back around to face the captain of the *Maiden Anne*. But it was the first mate who stood there filling the doorway, his hazel eyes moving over her in what seemed close scrutiny, yet it was no more than a brief glance.

"Why, you're just a little squirt, aren't you? Surprised I didn't notice that when I signed you on."

"Perhaps because you were sit—"

The word was choked off when he took her chin between thumb and finger and slowly turned her face this way and that. Georgina blanched, though he didn't seem to notice.

"Not a single whisker," he remarked in what was clearing a disparaging tone.

She started breathing again, and only just managed to tamp down the indignation she felt on Georgie's behalf.

"I'm only twelve, sir," she pointed out reasonably.

"But a small twelve. Damn me, that tray's as big as you are." His fingers wrapped around her upper arm. "Where's your muscle?"

"I'm still growing," Georgina gritted out, getting mad under so much examination. Her nervousness was forgotten for the moment. "In six months you won't recognize me." Which was perfectly true, since she would have cast off her disguise by then.

"Runs in your family, does it?"

Her eyes turned wary. "What?"

"The height, lad. What the devil did you think I meant? Certainly not your looks, since you and your brother don't take after each other a'tall." And then he laughed suddenly, a deeply resounding sound.

"I don't see what you find amusing in that. We merely have different mothers."

"Oh, I gathered something was different, all right. Mothers, is it? And would that explain your lack of a Scottish burr?"

"I didn't realize I had to give my life's history for this job."

"Why so defensive, squirt?"

"Give over, Connie." Another deep voice was heard with very clear warning in it. "We don't want to scare the lad off, now do we?"

"Off to where?" The first mate chuckled.

Georgina's eyes narrowed. Had she thought she didn't like this red-headed Englishman on principle alone?

"This food is getting cold, Mr. Sharpe," she said pointedly, her tone stiffly indignant.

"Then by all means take it in, though I seriously doubt it's food he's in a mood for."

Back came the nervousness, in spades. It had been the *captain's* voice that had interrupted. How had she been able to forget, even for a minute, that he was waiting inside? Worse, he had likely heard everything just said, including her impertinence with his first officer—provoked, but still inexcusable. She was a lowly cabin boy, for God's sake, yet she'd answered Conrad Sharpe as if she were his equal . . . as if she were Georgina Anderson rather than Georgie MacDonell. Any more mistakes like that and she might as well take off her cap and unbind her breasts.

After those last cryptic words, the first mate waved her inside and then left the cabin. It took a concerted effort to get her feet to move, but when they did, she nearly flew through the door to the dining table of Tudor oak in the center of the room, a heavy piece of furniture long enough to accommodate more than a half dozen officers comfortably.

Georgina's eyes fixed on the tray of food and stayed there, even after she set it down. There was a large shape beyond the table, standing in front of the wall of mullioned windows that were beautifully framed in stained glass and filled the room with light. She was just barely aware of the large shape blocking some of the light, but it told her where the captain was.

She had admired the windows yesterday when she had been allowed to familiarize herself with the cabin and make certain it was ready for occupancy. It was that, and fit for a king. She'd never seen anything quite like it, certainly not on any Skylark ship.

The furnishings were all extravagant pieces. At the long dining table sat a single armchair in the newest French Empire style, with bronze mounts on mahogany, and bouquets of colorful flowers embroidered on an ivory background on the thickly cushioned seat, back, and sides. Five more of these chairs were about the cabin, two before the windows, two in front on a desk, one other behind it. The desk was another heavy piece of finery, with large oval pedestals rather than legs, painted in classical scrollwork. The bed, however, was truly a piece of art, an antique of the Italian Renaissance, with tall, deeply carved posts and an even taller headboard in an arched column effect, the mattress covered in white quilted silk.

Instead of a sea chest there was a tall teakwood Chinese cabinet similar to the one her father had given her mother on his first return from the Far East after their marriage, this one decorated with jade, mother-of-pearl, and lapis lazuli. There was also a Queen Anne highboy in burl walnut. Between them and standing just as tall was an ebony and brass clock in the modern style.

Instead of shelves built on the wall, there was an actual mahogany bookcase with gilded and carved decorations and glass doors revealing eight shelves completely filled with books. She recognized the Riesener style in the commode, with marquety, floral decorations, and ormolu moldings. And behind the folding screen, with its painted English countryside on supple leather, that concealed one corner of the room was a porcelain tub that had to be special-made, it was so long and wide, but thankfully not very deep, since she would probably be lugging water to it.

The clutter, what there was of it, consisted of nautical instruments mostly, scattered on or near the desk; a two-foot-tall nude statue in bronze sitting on the floor; and a copper kettle near the washstand behind the screen. Lamps, no two alike, were permanently affixed to the furniture or hung from hooks on the walls and ceilings.

With large and small paintings, thick carpeting from wall to wall, it was a room you might find in a governor's palace, but certainly not on a ship. And it had told her nothing about Captain Malory except that he might be eccentric, or that he liked fine things around him, even if in a hodgepodge order.

Georgina didn't know if the captain was facing her or looking out the windows. She hadn't looked yet, still didn't want to, but the silence was lengthening and stretching her nerves to the breaking point. She wished she could just leave without drawing his attention to her—if his attention wasn't already on her. Why didn't *he* say something? He had to know she was still there, waiting to serve him in whatever capacity he required.

"Your food, Captain . . . sir."

"Why are you whispering?" The voice came to her in a whisper as soft as her own.

"I was told you . . . that is, there was mention that you might be suffering the effects of overindul—" She cleared her throat and raised her pitch to amend briskly, "A headache, sir. My brother Drew always complains about loud noises whenever he . . . has headaches."

"I thought your brother's name was Ian."

"I have other brothers."

"Don't we all, more's the pity," he remarked dryly. "One of mine tried to drink me under the table last night. Thought it would be amusing if I wasn't fit to sail."

Georgina almost smiled. How many times had her brothers done the same thing—not to her, but to each other. And she did get her fair share of pranks, rum in her hot chocolate, bonnet strings tied in knots, her drawers flying from the weather vane, or, worse, strung up the mainmast of another brother's ship, so the guilty one wouldn't get blamed. Obviously, rascally brothers were universal, not confined to Connecticut.

"I sympathize, Captain," she thought to offer. "They can be quite tedious."

"Quite so."

She heard the humor in his tone, as if he found her remark pretentious, and so it was, for a twelve-year-old boy. She really was going to have to weigh her words more carefully before she let them out. She couldn't forget for a single minute that she was supposed to be a boy, and a very young one. But it was extremely hard to remember just at that moment, especially since she had finally noted his accent was decidedly British-sounding. It would be the worst luck imaginable if he was an Englishman, too. She would have been able to avoid the others on the ship, but she couldn't very well avoid the captain.

As she was contemplating swimming for the riverbanks herself, she heard a brisk, "Present yourself, lad, and let's have a look at you."

All right. One thing at a time. The accent could be an affectation. He'd just spent time in England, after all. So she got her feet moving, came around the table, approached the dark shape until a pair of gleaming hessian boots were clearly in her line of vision. Above them were dove-gray breeches molded to a pair of thickly muscled legs. Without raising her bowed head, she stole a quick look higher to see a white lawn shirt with billowing sleeves, cuffed tight at wrists that rested rather arrogantly on narrow hips. But her eyes went no farther than the patch of dark skin visible at mid-chest through the deep V opening of the shirt, and she got that far without abandoning her meek posture only because he was so tall . . . and wide.

"Not in my shadow," he continued to direct her. "To the left, in the light. That's better." And then he remarked the obvious, "You're nervous, are you?"

"This is my first job."

"And understandably you don't want to muck it up. Relax, dear boy. I don't bite off the heads of babes . . . just grown men."

Was that supposed to be an attempt at levity for her benefit? "Glad to hear it." Oh, God, that was too flip sounding by half. *Watch your blasted mouth, Georgie!*

"Is my carpet so fascinating, then?"

"Sir?"

"You can't seem to take your eyes off it. Or have you heard I'm so ugly you'll turn into pea soup if you clap eyes on me?"

She started to grin at what was obviously gentle teasing meant to put her at ease, but thought better of it. It *did* relieve the worst of her anxiety. He was staring at her in full light and she hadn't been denounced. But the interview wasn't over yet. And until it was, it would be better if he still thought her nervous and attributed any more mistakes to that nervousness.

Georgina shook her head in answer to his question, and as a boy of her supposed age might do, she raised her chin very slowly. She was going to execute a quick peak at him, all of him this time, and then duck her head again, a shy, childish action that she hoped might amuse him and fix in his mind her immaturity.

It didn't quite work out that way. She got her sneak peek in, dropped her head again as planned, but that was as far as the planning went. Involuntarily her head snapped back up and her eyes locked on green ones that she remembered as clearly as if they'd been haunting her dreams, and on a few nights they had.

This wasn't possible. The brick wall? Here? The arrogant manhandler she was never supposed to cross paths with again? *Here?* This couldn't be the man she had committed herself to serve. No one could be *that* unlucky.

She watched in fascinated horror as one tawny brow quirked curiously, "Something wrong, lad?"

"No," she squeaked and dropped her eyes to the floor so fast that a pain streaked through her temples.

"You're not going to dissolve into pea soup after all, are you?"

She choked out a negative sound to that droll inquiry.

"Splendid! Don't think my constitution could bear it just now. The mess, you know."

What was he rattling on about? He should be pointing a finger and condemning her with an appalled "You!" Didn't he recognize her? And then it registered. Even after seeing her face clearly, he'd still called her lad. That brought her head back up for closer scrutiny, and in his eyes and expression there was no surprise, no suspicion or doubt. The eyes were still intimidating in their directness, but they merely showed amusement at her nervous behavior. He didn't remember her at all. Not even Mac's name had jarred his memory.

Incredible. Of course, she looked quite different from that night in the tavern when she had been done up in oversized and undersized clothing. Her clothes fit her perfectly now, not too tight or loose, and all new, right down to her shoes. Only her cap was the same. The tight bindings about her breasts and the loose ones around her waist gave her the straight lines of a boy. And then, too, the lighting hadn't been the best that night. Maybe he hadn't gotten as good a look at her as she had of him. Besides, why should he remember the incident? Considering the rough way he had handled her in the tavern, it was possible he had been as drunk as a loon.

James Malory was aware of the exact moment that she relaxed and accepted his pretense of not knowing her. There had been the chance that *she* might bring up their original meeting, and he had held his breath when she first recognized him, afraid she might give up the game then and there with a return of the temper he had been treated to that night at the tavern. But in not suspecting that he was on to her, she had obviously decided to hold her tongue and stick to her disguise, which was exactly what he had hoped she would do.

He could have relaxed himself, except for the sexual tension that had taken hold of him the moment she walked through the door, something he hadn't felt so keenly in the presence of a woman in . . . Good God, it had been so long he couldn't remember the last time. Women had simply become too easily obtainable. Even competing with Anthony for the ladies most fair had lost its challenge long before he had quit England ten years ago. The competition had become the sport, not the prize. The winning of one particular lady simply hadn't mattered when there were so many to choose from.

But here was something altogether different, a true challenge, a conquest that mattered. Why it mattered was disconcerting to a man of his jaded experience. For once, just any woman wouldn't do. He wanted *this* one. It could be because he'd lost her once and been more than a little disappointed over it. Disappointment in itself was unusual for him. It could be simply the mystery she represented. Or it could be no more than that cute little backside he remembered so well.

Whatever the reason, having her was now all-important, yet in no way a foregone conclusion. Which was why his shell of boredom had been cracked, and why he was rife with a tension that wouldn't let him relax with her standing so near. In fact, he was just short of actual arousal, which he found utterly preposterous, considering he hadn't even touched her yet, nor could he, at least not as he would like, if he was going to play this game through. And the game presented too many delightful possibilities to abandon just yet.

So he put some space between himself and temptation, moving to the table to examine the contents under the silver domes. The expected knock at the door came before he finished.

"Georgie, is it?"

"Captain?"

He glanced over his shoulder at her. "Your name?"

"Oh! Yes, it's Georgie."

He nodded. "That will be Artie with my trunks. You can empty them while I pick through this cold fare."

"Would you like me to have it heated, Captain?"

He heard the hopeful note which betrayed her eagerness to leave the room, but he wasn't letting her out of his sight until the *Maiden Anne* left England's shores behind. If she had any degree of intelligence at all, she had to know her risk of discovery was increased by their previous meeting, that even though he didn't appear to remember her now, he could at any time. In light of that, she was likely considering the alternative of abandoning ship before it was too late to do so, even if she had to swim to shore—if she could swim. He wasn't going to give her that option.

"The food will suffice. I haven't much appetite yet, at any rate." And when she continued to just stand where he'd left her, he added, "The door, dear boy. It won't open by itself."

He noted the pursed lips as she marched to the door. She didn't like being prodded. Or was it his dry tone she objected to? He also noted the authoritative way she directed the cantankerous Artie in the placing of the trunks, earning a sour look from the sailor that abruptly changed her manner back to the meekness of a young lad.

James almost laughed aloud, until he realized the wench was going to have a problem with her temper if she forgot who she was supposed to be each time it sparked. The crew wouldn't put up with such haughty airs from a supposed youngun. But short of announcing that the boy was under his personal protection, which would have the new members of his crew snickering behind his back, the old ones looking at the lad more closely, and Connie rolling on the deck in laughter, James would just have to keep a close eye on Georgie MacDonell himself. But that would be no hardship. She really was quite adorable in her lad's togs.

The woolen cap he remembered still hid all her hair from him, though the sable brows indicated her hair would be dark, perhaps the rich brown of her eyes. There were no suspicious lumps under the cap, so either her hair had not been very long to begin with, or she had sheered it off for her disguise, which he sincerely hoped not.

The white tunic was long-sleeved and high-necked, and fell nearly mid-thigh, which effectively hid her cute derriere. He tried to figure out what she'd done with her breasts and, for that matter, the tiny waist he remembered holding. The tunic wasn't bulky but fit narrowly on her frame, giving her straight lines that a wide belt bore testimony to. If there were bumps to be seen, they remained concealed under the short vest worn over the tunic.

Now that was a piece of ingenious clothing ideal for her purposes. Thick with fleece on one side, hard leather on the other, the vest lay on her like a steel cage, so stiff it wouldn't flap open even in a strong wind. Untied, it showed only about three inches of her tunic down the front, three inches of flat chest and flat belly.

The tunic hid the rest until her buff-colored knee breeches began. They ended just below the knee, where thick woolen stockings disguised the slimness of her calves. Being neither too loose nor too tight, they made shapely limbs look like perfectly normal boy's legs instead.

He watched her silently as she meticulously went through each item in his trunks and found a place for it either in the highboy or in the cabinet-converted-wardrobe. Johnny, his previous cabin boy, would have taken armfuls of clothing and just dumped them in the nearest drawer. James had yelled at him enough times for doing just that. But his little Georgie gave herself away with her feminine neatness. He doubted she realized that, doubted she knew any other way to do it. But how long would her disguise last with little blunders like that?

He tried to see her as anyone unaware of her secret would see her. It wasn't easy because he *did* know what was under those clothes. But if he didn't know . . . By God, it wouldn't be *that* easy to guess. It was her size, really, that pulled it off. Connie was right, she really was a tiny thing, no bigger than a ten-year-old, though she had given her age as twelve. Hell and fire, she wasn't *too* young for him, was she? He couldn't very well ask her. No, he couldn't believe that she was, not with what he had felt that night in the tavern, not with that luscious mouth and those soul-sucking eyes. She might be young, but not too young.

She dropped the lid on the second empty trunk and glanced his way. "Should I cart these out, Captain?"

The grin came despite himself. "I doubt you can, dear boy, so don't bother to strain those meager muscles. Artie will return for them later."

"I'm stronger than I look," she insisted stubbornly.

"Are you indeed? That's good to know, since you'll have to be lugging one of those heavy chairs about daily. I usually dine with my first mate in the evenings."

"Only him?" Her eyes darted to the five chairs about the room, not counting the one he was now sitting in. "Not your other officers?"

"This is not a military ship," he pointed out. "And I do like my privacy."

She brightened immediately. "Then I'll leave you—"

"Not so fast, youngun." He stopped her on the way to the door. "Where d'you think you're off to when your duties are only in this cabin?"

"I . . . well . . . assumed, that is . . . you mentioned privacy."

"My tone of voice, was it? Too sharp for you, lad?"

"Sir?"

"You're stuttering."

Her head bowed. "I'm sorry, Captain."

"None of that, now. You'll look me in the eye if you've something to apologize for, which you don't . . . yet. I'm not your father to box your ears or take a strap to you, I'm your captain. So don't cringe every time I raise my voice or if I'm in a bloody rotten mood and I look at you crossly. Do as you're told, without question or argument, and you and I will get along just fine. Is that understood?"

"Clearly."

"Splendid. Then get your arse over here and finish this food for me. Can't have Mr. O'Shawn thinking I don't appreciate his efforts, or there's no telling what I'll find on my plate next time." When she started to protest, he forestalled it with, "You look half starved, damn me if you don't. But we'll put some meat on those bones before we reach Jamaica. You've my word on it."

Georgina had to fight to keep the frown off her face as she grabbed a chair and dragged it to the table, especially when she saw that he'd barely touched his food. Not that she wasn't hungry. She was. But how could she eat with him sitting there staring at her? And she had to find

Mac, not waste precious time here doing nothing more than eating. She had to tell him the startling news of who the captain actually was, before it was too late to do anything about it.

"By the by, youngun, my privacy doesn't apply to you," the captain said as he pushed the tray of cold food across the table to her. "How can it, when your duties require constant attendance on me? And besides, in a few days' time, I won't even notice you underfoot."

That was heartening, but didn't change the fact that he was noticing her right now, and waiting for her to begin eating. Surprisingly, she noted there was no congealing grease on the poached fish, crisply steamed vegetables, and fresh fruits. Cold, it still looked delicious.

All right, the sooner done, the sooner gone. She began shoveling the food down in appalling haste, but after only a few minutes realized her mistake; it was coming right back up. Her eyes widened in horror and flew to the commode, followed by her feet as she ran to get at the chamber pot within, only one thought in her mind—*Please, God, let it be empty*. It was, and she yanked it out just in time, only vaguely hearing the captain's droll "Good God, you're not going to . . . well, I see that you are."

She didn't care what he thought just then as her stomach heaved every bite she had just forced down and then some. Before it was over, she felt a cold, wet cloth on her forehead and a heavy, sympathetic hand on her shoulder.

"I'm sorry, lad. I should have realized you were still too nervous to stomach food. Come on then, let me help you to the bed."

"No, I—"

"Don't argue. You'll probably never be offered the use of it again, and it's a bloody comfortable bed. Take advantage of my remorse and use it."

"But I don't wan—"

"I thought we agreed you'd take your orders as they came? I'm ordering you to lay yourself on that bed and rest awhile. So d'you need carrying, or can you get your arse over there by yourself?"

From gentleness, to briskness, to downright impatience. Georgina didn't answer him; she just ran to the large bed and threw herself on it. He was going to be an autocrat, she could see, one of those who believed that the captain of a ship at sea was God Almighty. But she did feel wretched just now, did need to lie down, only not in *his* blasted bed. And there he was standing over her, now bending over her. She gasped, then prayed he hadn't heard it, for all he did was place the cold cloth back on her forehead.

"You ought to remove that cap and vest; the shoes, too. You'll be more comfortable."

Georgina blanched. Was she going to have to start disobeying him already?

She tried not to sound sarcastic, but put it plainly, "Much as you might think otherwise, Captain, I do know how to take care of myself. I'm fine the way I am."

"Suit yourself," he replied with a shrug and, to her relief, turned away. But a moment later she heard from across the room, "By the by, Georgie, remember to fetch your hammock and belongings from the fo'c'sle later, when you're feeling better. My cabin boy sleeps where he's needed."

Chapter Twelve

"Needed?" Georgina croaked as she sat up in the big bed. Then her eyes narrowed suspiciously on the captain, who was slouching languidly back in the chair she had vacated, so that he was facing her, *and* watching her. "Needed for what in the middle of the night?"

"I'm a light sleeper, don't you know. The sounds of the ship frequently wake me."

"But what has that to do with me?"

"Well, Georgie boy," he said in a tone that implied he was patiently addressing a child. "What if I should need something?" She started to say he could very well get it himself, when he added, "That *is* your duty, after all."

Since her services had yet to be spelled out in their entirety, she couldn't very well deny it. But to have to lose sleep just because he did? And she had actually *wanted* this job? Not anymore. Not when it meant having to serve an autocratic brick wall.

She would allow him his point for now, but wanted clarification. "I suppose you mean duties like fetching you something to eat from the galley?"

"That, certainly," he answered. "But sometimes I merely need to hear a soothing voice to lull me back to sleep. You do read, don't you?"

"Of course," she replied indignantly.

Too late, she realized she could have saved herself one chore at least if she had denied it. That was allowing if she'd still be here, which she was now fervently hoping she would not be. She pictured herself reading to him in the middle of the night, he lying in this bed, she sitting in a chair by it, or even on the edge of it if he complained he couldn't hear her. Only one lamp would be burning for her to read by, and he would be sleepy-eyed and tousled, the dim light softening his features, making him less intimidating, more . . . Devil take it, she had to find Mac, and quick.

She threw her legs over the side of the bed, only to hear a sharp "Lie *down*, Georgie!"

She glanced his way to see he had sat forward in his chair and was frowning at her, giving every indication that if she stood up, so would he, and he happened to be between her and the door. And, blast it all, she didn't have enough nerve just then to put it to the test, not with him looking so formidable.

For God's sake, this is ridiculous, but she lay back down as she thought it. Only she turned on her side to face him, and was just short of glowering back at him.

She did grind her teeth for a moment in frustration before insisting, "This isn't necessary, Captain. I'm feeling much better."

"*I'll* determine when you're better, lad," he said arbitrarily, leaning back in his chair again now that she'd done as she was told. "You're still as pale as that quilt under you, so you'll stay put until I tell you otherwise."

Anger brought color to her cheeks, though she wasn't aware of it. Look at him, sitting there like a pampered lord, and in fact he was, pampered that is, and probably a lord, too. More than likely he had never lifted a finger to do a single thing for himself in his entire life. If she ended up stuck on this ship for the next several weeks because of this unwanted concern he was forcing on her, she'd quickly become worn to a frazzle serving the likes of him, and hating every moment of it. The thought was unbearable. But short of outright defiance, which she wasn't equipped to back up any more than a twelve-year-old boy would be, there was no way to leave the cabin just now.

Accepting that conclusion, Georgina went back to the subject of where he intended her to sleep if she was still on the ship tonight. "I had assumed, Captain, that all available cabins were occupied."

"So they are. What's your point, lad?"

"I'm just wondering where that's going to put me and my hammock, if I'm to be near enough to hear if you summon me in the night."

That got her a laugh. "Where the deuce d'you think it's going to put you?"

His amusement at her expense was as infuriating as his unwanted concern. "In the drafty hall," she retorted. "Which I have to tell you doesn't suit me at—"

"Give over, youngun, before you have me in tears. What bloody nonsense. You'll sleep right here, of course, just as my previous cabin boy did, and every one before him."

She'd been afraid that was what he had in mind. Fortunately, it wasn't unheard of to her, which saved her from making a maidenly display of outrage that would have been quite inappropriate. She knew of several captains who shared their quarters with the youngest members of their crews, simply for the boys' protection. Her brother Clinton was one, ever since a cabin boy of his had been set upon by three crewmen and seriously injured. She had never learned the particulars of what happened, only that Clinton had been furious enough to have the three attackers severely whipped.

This captain, however, knew she had a brother on board who could see to her protection, so his insistence that she move in here with him was for his convenience, not any concern for her welfare. But she wasn't going to argue about it—not that he'd listen to arguments after warning her against making any. It would simply be foolish to protest if this *was* an established policy of his, and apparently it was if his other cabin boys had shared the room with him.

So she had only one question for him. "Right here *where?*"

He tilted his head to indicate the one empty corner in the room, the one to the right of the door. "That will suffice, I'm sure. There's plenty of room for your sea chest and whatever else you've brought along with you. Supports are already in the walls for your hammock."

She saw the hooks he was talking about, spaced just wide enough to accommodate a hammock to cross the space of the corner. Strange, she didn't remember seeing them yesterday when she'd been in the cabin. The corner was at least a long distance from the bed, but that was the best she could say for it, since there wasn't a single piece of furniture between the two areas high enough to give her even a modicum of privacy.

The only thing on that side of the room was the screened-off tub in the other corner near the windows, and the low commode between the corner and the door. The dining table was more in the center of the room, with everything else to the left of the door, the bed behind it, the cabinet and highboy on the far left wall, the bookcase on the same wall, but by the windows again, in the corner where the desk was located in front of the windows to take advantage of the light.

"Will it do, youngun?"

As if he would put her somewhere else if she said no, when she knew very well he wouldn't go to any trouble for the benefit of a mere cabin boy! "I suppose, but would it be all right to make use of the screen?"

"Whatever for?"

For privacy, you dolt! But he was looking so amused by her question, she merely replied, "It was just a thought."

"Then don't think, dear boy. Use common sense instead. That screen's bolted to the floor. Everything is, except for the chairs, and it's your duty to secure them at the first sign of bad weather."

Georgina had no trouble feeling the color flood her cheeks this time. That was something she'd known about all her life. On ship, everything had to be bolted, strapped, or otherwise tacked down, or it ended up someplace other than where it belonged, usually causing a great deal of damage in the process. Where was her mind, to forget such a common piece of knowledge as that?

"I never said I'd sailed before," she replied in defense of that bit of stupidity.

"From England, then, are you?"

"No!" she said, too quickly and too sharply. "I mean, I sailed to get here, yes, but as a passenger." And then peevishly, since she'd only made herself sound even more ignorant, "I just never took note of such things."

"No matter. You'll learn all you need to know, now you're a working member of the crew. Don't be afraid to ask questions, lad."

"Then while you have the time, Captain, would you be so good as to explain my duties to me, other than those you've already men—"

She stopped when one of his golden brows rose in amusement. What the devil had she said this time to have him grinning like a loon?

He didn't keep her in suspense. "Be so good?" He was now laughing. "Good God, lad, I should hope not. I haven't been good since I was your age, but *so* good, never."

"It was merely a figure of speech," she replied in exasperation.

"What it was, was an indication of your upbringing, lad. Manners too fine for a cabin boy."

"Lack of manners were a prerequisite for the job? Someone should have told me."

"Don't get lippy with me, brat, or I'll pin your ears back, that's if they can be found under that bloody cap."

"Oh, they're there, Captain, just pointy and twice the size they should be. Why else would I keep them hidden?"

"You disappoint me, dear boy. I thought surely premature baldness. Only big pointy ears?"

She smiled despite herself. His droll wit was really quite amusing. And who would have thought him capable of being amusing, autocratic brick wall that he was otherwise? If that wasn't surprising enough, where had she gotten the nerve to banter with him? Even more surprising was she hadn't taken him seriously, his calling her brat and threatening to pin her ears back, even though he'd looked quite serious when he'd said it.

"Ah," he said now, taking in her smile and giving one in return. "The boy's got teeth after all. I was beginning to wonder. And pearly-white, too. 'Course, you're young. They'll rot soon enough."

"Yours haven't."

"Meaning I'm so old that I should have lost 'em all by now?"

"I didn't—" She stopped, flustered. "About my duties, Captain?"

"Wasn't Connie specific enough for you when he signed you on?"

"He said I only had to serve you, not the other officers. But no, he wasn't specific, stating only that I would have to do whatever you required of me."

"But that's all there is to it, don't you know."

She gritted her teeth until the exasperation passed, enough to get out, "Captain Malory, I've heard of cabin boys having to milk cows—"

"Good God, they've my complete sympathy!" he said in mock horror, but only a moment passed before his grin came back. "I haven't a fondness for milk myself, lad, so rest easy. That's one task that won't be yours."

"Then what will be mine?" she persisted.

"A catchall of numerous services, you could say. You'll act as footman at table, butler when you're in the cabin, servant in general, and since I've left my valet behind this voyage, that job will also be yours. Nothing too strenuous, you see."

No, just waiting on him hand and foot, exactly what she had figured. It was on the tip of her tongue to ask if she had to scrub his back and wipe his arse, too, but although he'd said she wouldn't get her ears boxed, she didn't care to tempt him to change his mind. It was almost laughable. For God's sake, Drew's cabin boy had to do no more than bring him his meals. Yet out of all the captains to choose from in London harbor, hers had to be a blasted Englishman, and not *just* English, but a useless aristocrat. If he'd ever done a lick of work in his life, she'd eat her cap.

None of which she said to the arrogant man. She was annoyed, not crazy.

James had to bite back his laughter. The wench was making such a valiant effort not to complain of the load he'd just heaped on her. He'd had to make up half of it, particularly the valet part, since he hadn't had one for more than ten years. But the more she had to do to keep her busy in his cabin, the less she would see of his crew; more in point the less they would see of her. He didn't want anyone else discovering her secret until he was ready to discover it himself. Then, too, the more she was in his cabin, the more *he* would have her to himself.

Right now, however, he needed to put more distance than the space of the room between them. Seeing her curled up in his bed this long was giving him ideas that were not for the immediate future.

Self-discipline, old boy, he admonished himself. If you ain't got it, who does?

That was a bloody good joke at the moment. It had been too long since he'd faced an actual temptation, of any kind. Self-control was a simple matter when the emotions were deadened with boredom, something else again when they were hopping-around alert.

Georgina had decided conversation with Captain Malory wasn't worth the aggravation it was turning out to be. Besides, silence might prompt him to seek some other diversion, like maybe captaining the ship. It might get him to leave the cabin, at any rate, and the moment he did, she could, too. She hadn't thought it would bring him to the bed to check on her, but alas, she wasn't having much luck with impromptu plans today.

She opened her eyes and found him looming over her. "Still pale, I see," he said. "And here I thought I'd done a commendable job of putting you at ease to remedy that nervous stomach."

"Oh, you did, Captain," she assured him.

"Not nervous anymore?"

"Not even a little."

"Splendid. Then you shouldn't have to lie abed much longer. But there's no rush, is there? Come to think of it, there's nothing more for you to do until you serve the next meal. A nap might be just the thing, to get the color back in your cheeks."

"But I'm not the least bit—"

"You aren't going to argue with every suggestion I make . . . are you, Georgie?"

Did he have to look like a yes would get her clobbered? He'd lulled her with his affable chitchat into forgetting that he was, after all, a dangerous man.

"Now that you mention it, I didn't get much sleep last night."

Apparently that was the right answer, for his expression altered again. It wasn't quite friendly—well, he'd never really looked all that friendly—but certainly it was less severe, and once again, tinged with amusement. "You're too young to have been doing what the rest of my crew was doing last night, so what kept you awake?"

"Your crew," she answered. "Returning from whatever they'd been doing."

He laughed. "Give it a few years, dear boy, and you'll have more tolerance."

"I'm not ignorant, Captain. I know what sailors usually do on their last night in port."

"Oh? Familiar with that side of life, are you?"

Remember you're a boy, remember you're a boy, and for God's sake, don't blush again!

"Certainly," Georgina answered.

She saw it coming, that devilish crook of brow, laughter gleaming in his so-green eyes. But even being braced for it didn't help when she heard the next question.

"Is that from hearsay . . . or experience?"

Georgina choked on her gasp, and coughed for a good ten seconds, during which time the helpful captain pounded on her back. When she could finally breathe again, she figured she probably had a few broken vertebrae, thanks to the brick wall's bricklike fists.

"I don't believe, Captain Malory, that my experience *or* lack of it, has any bearing whatsoever on this job."

She had a lot more to say about his unorthodox questioning, but his "Quite right" took the wind out of her sails. Which was fortunate, since she wasn't thinking like a twelve-year-old just then. And he had more to say anyway.

"You'll have to forgive me, Georgie. It's my habit to be derogatory, don't you know, and indignation only invites further abuse in my book. So do try not to take it so personally, because to be perfectly honest with you, your displays of chagrin merely amuse me."

She'd never heard anything so . . . so preposterous, and he had said it without a morsel of contrition. Deliberate goading. Deliberate teasing. Deliberate insults. Devil take him, he was a worse scoundrel than she'd first thought.

"Couldn't you just refrain from such provocation . . . sir?" she gritted out.

He gave a short bark of laughter. "And miss little gems of wisdom like that one? No, dear boy, I don't give up my amusements, not for man, woman, or child. I have so few of them, after all."

"Mercy for no one, is that it? Not even sick children get excluded? Or do you finally deem me recovered enough to get up, Captain?"

"You had it right the first go round . . . unless, of course, you're crying pity. I might take that into consideration. Are you?"

"Am I what?"

"Crying pity?"

Rot the man, he was challenging her by bringing pride into it. And boys at the awkward age of twelve had a great deal of pride, which he was undoubtedly counting on. A girl at that age wouldn't only cry pity, she'd be streaming tears along with it. But a boy would rather die than admit he couldn't take a bit of ribbing, even if it was unmerciful ribbing. But devil take it, where did that leave her, a woman who wanted nothing more than to slap his arrogant face, but couldn't because the masquerading *Georgie* wouldn't do something like that?

And look at him, with features gone blank, and a tenseness in those wide shoulders and chest, as if her answer actually held some significance for him. More than likely he had some brilliant piece of sarcasm ready and waiting for her yes that he would be disappointed to waste.

"I have brothers, Captain, all older than myself," she told him in a tight, frosty voice. "So being baited, badgered, and teased is nothing new to me. My brothers delight in it . . . though surely not as much as you do."

"Well said, lad!"

To her chagrin, he looked as pleased as he sounded. Oh, if only she could slap him just once before she deserted the *Maiden Anne*.

But then a whole new set of emotions rose up to choke her as the man bent forward to grasp her chin, just as Mr. Sharpe had done, for a side-to-side examination of her face. Only unlike Mr. Sharpe's, the captain's touch was very gentle, with two fingers spread over her left cheek.

"All that courage, and as Connie said, not a whisker in sight." The fingers trailed down her smooth cheek to her jaw, very, very slowly, or so it seemed to her rioting senses. "You'll do, brat."

Georgina was going to be sick again, if the funny queasiness now stirring in her lower belly was any indication. But her nervous stomach quieted again as soon as the captain took his hand away. And all she could do was stare at his back as he walked out of the cabin.

Chapter Thirteen

The flare-up of Georgina's queasiness might have passed for the moment, but it was still a good five minutes before her tumultuous thoughts quieted down enough for her to realize she was finally alone in the cabin. When she did realize it, her sound of disgust was loud enough to be heard outside the door if anyone happened to be there. No one was, as she discovered a moment later when she yanked the door open.

Mumbling to herself about brick walls and arrogant English lords, she marched to the stairs and was halfway up them before she happened to remember that she'd been more or less ordered to take a nap. She paused, worrying at her lower lip with the "pearly whites" Captain Malory had remarked on. What to do, then? Well, she certainly wasn't going back to bed, regardless of that silly order. Her priorities were straight, and finding Mac and somehow getting off the *Maiden Anne* before it was too late came first.

Yet disobeying a captain's orders was no minor thing, no matter in what terms the order had been couched, or for what reason it was given. So . . . she just had to make sure the captain didn't notice her ignoring his order. Simple.

But what if he hadn't gone far? With her luck today . . . No, she had to think positively. If he was in sight, she could wait a minute or two for him to leave or to become distracted, but no longer than that. She *was* going on deck, whether he was there or not. She could always plead wanting a last look at England if she did get caught by him, though the lie would likely stick in her craw.

As it happened, she was annoyed with herself for wasting precious time worrying about it when she stuck her head cautiously through the open hatch and could find no trace of the captain in the immediate vicinity. Unfortunately, there was no sign of Mac either, not even aloft, where he might be checking the rigging.

Climbing the rest of the companionway, she set off in a hurry toward the bow, not daring to look behind her at the quarterdeck and who might be up there with a clear view of the lower decks. She was just short of running, hoping she wouldn't have to search from stem to stern before finding Mac. But she stopped short amidship in the narrow passage between gunwale and deck housing when her eyes happened to glance starboard. There, as far as the eye could see, was nothing but ocean. Her head snapped around to stern and there was the land she had expected to see passing to port and starboard, not the riverbanks she desperately needed close to hand, but the great bulk of England getting smaller and smaller in the wake of the ship.

Georgina simply stared, watching her chance to abandon ship receding rapidly in the distance. How was it possible? Her eyes shot up to a sky too overcast for her to even hazard a guess at the time of day. Could it have been so late when she had carried that tray of food to the captain? A look at the bowed sails told her the ship was making better than excellent time with storm winds pushing them out to sea, but still, to have left England behind already? They had been navigating the river when she had gone belowdecks to meet the captain.

Anger hit her swift and hard. Double-damn him, if he hadn't been so bent on entertaining himself at her expense with his provoking banter and his unnecessary concern, which she saw now as no more than an opportunity to force his arbitrary will on her, she could have seen the last of him. Now . . . devil take it, she was trapped on his ship, subject to his nasty whims, and likely could expect a great deal more of the aggravation she had experienced at his hands this afternoon. Hadn't he admitted that he *enjoyed* pushing a person to the ends of his temper? As sweet-tempered as she was, and she assured herself that she was, even she couldn't be expected to last long under such deliberate goading. She'd be provoked and provoked until she ended up slapping him or putting up some other such female defense that would give her away.

And then what? With his cruel sense of humor, she couldn't even begin to guess.

Madam Luck had truly deserted her today. So had caution for the moment. When her panicky thoughts were interrupted by a sharp nudge to her shoulder, she came around snapping "What?!" in a voice loaded with haughty exasperation. Such an impudent response naturally enough got her cuffed instantly. The blow to the side of her head slammed her into the gunwale, where her feet slowly slipped forward until her backside hit the deck.

She was surprised more than dazed, though her throbbing ear hurt. And she didn't have to be told what she'd done wrong, though the belligerent sailor standing over her was quick to tell her anyway.

"Sass off to me ag'in, you cheeky little bugger, an' I'll toss you o'er sooner'n you can spit. An' don't let me catch you blockin' the bleedin' way ag'in, neither!"

The area wasn't so narrow that he couldn't have gone around her. He wasn't very big, and was skinny besides. But Georgina didn't point that out. She was too busy getting her sprawled legs out of his way, since he was about to kick them aside rather than step over them to go about his business.

Meanwhile, on the quarterdeck, Conrad Sharpe was having a devil of a time keeping the captain from vaulting over the railing to the deck below, as he had started to do the instant the girl had been cuffed. And to restrain him without appearing to do so was no easy task, either.

"Blister it, Hawke, the worst is over. Interfere now and you—"

"Interfere? I'm going to break the man's bones!"

"Well, there's a brilliant notion," Connie tossed back sarcastically. "How better to show the crew that *Georgie boy* is not to be treated like a cabin boy at all, but as your own personal property? You might as well yank off that silly cap and fetch up a gown. Either way, you'll have the men's interest centered on your little friend until they find out what is so special about him that had you committing murder. And don't raise that brow at me, you bloody fool. Your fists would be lethal on someone that size, and you know it."

"Very well, I'll just have the chap keelhauled."

Hearing the dry tone that signaled James had come to his senses,

Connie grinned and stepped back. "No, you won't. What reason would you give? The wench got lippy. We heard her from here. There isn't a man aboard who wouldn't have done exactly as Tiddles did with such provocation coming from such a little squirt. Besides, looks like the brother's going to take care of it, and no one will wonder about *him* coming to the brat's defense."

They both watched as Ian MacDonell bore down on Tiddles, yanking him around just as he'd been about to kick the girl. Up went the shorter man to dangle from the Scot's fists, each fastened on his checkered shirtfront. And although MacDonell didn't raise his voice, the warning he issued carried across the deck.

"Touch the laddie again, mon, and I'm thinking I'll have tae kill ye."

"He puts it rather well, don't he?" James commented.

"At least no one will remark on it . . . coming from him, that is."

"You made your bloody point, Connie. You don't have to belabor it. Now what the deuce is she saying to the Scot?"

The girl had gotten up and was speaking earnestly but quietly to her brother, who still held Tiddles aloft. "Appears she might be trying to defuse the matter. Smart girl. She knows where the blame belongs. If she hadn't been standing about gawking—"

"I'm partly to blame for that," James cut in.

"Oh? Did I miss something, like seeing you down there nailing her feet to the deck?"

"In high form, aren't we? But notice, old friend, that I'm not amused."

"Pity, since I am." Connie grinned unrepentantly. "But I can see you're perishing to do the noble, so go ahead. Confess why you think you're responsible for the brat's impudence."

"I don't think, I know," James retorted, all but glowering at his friend. "As soon as she recognized me she decided to jump ship."

"She told you that, did she?"

"She didn't have to," James replied. "It was written all over her face."

"I hate to point out little details, old man, but she's still here."

" 'Course she is," James snapped. "But only because I detained her in my cabin until it was too late for her to do anything foolish. She wasn't on the deck gawking. She was watching her only opportunity to escape recede into the distance . . . and prob'ly cursing me to everlasting hell."

"Well, she isn't likely to make the mistake again—of getting in the way, that is. A clout on the ear usually serves as a good lesson."

"But it's set Tiddles against her. Artie, too, was ready to kick her arse a good one, and would have if I hadn't been there. You should have heard the imperious way she was ordering him about."

"You don't suppose the brat's a lady, do you?"

James shrugged. "She's an old hand at directing underlings, whatever she is. Educated, too, or else a great mimicker of her betters."

Connie's humor deserted him. "Damn me, that puts a different light on this, Hawke."

"The devil it does. *I* didn't put her in those breeches. And what the deuce did you think she was? A dockside whore?" Connie's silence was answer enough, and drew a short bark of laughter from James. "Well, you can stow the chivalry, Connie. It don't sit well on your shoulders any more than it does on mine. The cunning little baggage can be a bloody princess for all I care, but for the time being, she's a cabin boy until I say otherwise. It's a role she gave herself to play, and I mean to let her play it out."

"For how long?"

"For as long as I can bear it." And then, watching the Scot release his victim, he added, "Hell and fire, not even a bloody blow! I would've—"

"Broken his bones, I know." Connie sighed. "Appears to me you're taking this a little too personally."

"Not at all. No one can hit a woman while I'm around and hope to get away with it."

"Is that some new sentiment you've adopted since we set sail? Now, Jamie lad," he added placatingly when James turned on him. "Why don't you save those killing looks for the crew, where they might do some . . . All right," he amended with ill grace as James took a step toward him. "I take back every word. So you're a bloody champion of all womankind."

"I wouldn't go *that* far."

Connie's humor returned instantly at the appalled look that came over his friend's face. "Neither would I if you weren't so blasted touchy today."

"Touchy? Me? Just because I want to see that woman beater trounced on?"

"I see I must point out the little details again, such as Tiddles ain't even aware that he hit a woman."

"Irrelevant, but point taken. Child beater then. Can't stomach either one. And before you open up that yapping trap to defend the little twit again, tell me if he would have been so quick to clout Mac-Donell out of his way?"

Connie was forced to concede, "I daresay he would have gone around him."

"Quite so. Now, since you've ruled out all the more preferable forms of reprisal for his bullying tendencies, and the Scot has disappointed me, indeed he has, in merely giving him a warning—"

"I believe the wench saw to that."

"Again irrelevant. Her wishes don't come into this. So the next time I see Mr. Tiddles, it had better be with a prayerbook in his hand."

James wasn't referring to a religious book, but the soft stone used on the hands and knees to renew the deck surfaces that were too small for the larger holystone to get at. After the deck was wetted down, preferably in rainy weather so water didn't have to be hauled up, sand would be sprinkled over the entire surface, then the large holystone with its smooth underside would be dragged fore and aft by means of long ropes attached to the ends. Having to go through the same process on your hands and knees was one of the more unpleasant deck chores.

"You want him sanding decks that are perfectly spotless?" Connie asked for clarification.

"For no less than four watches . . . four consecutive watches."

"Damn me, Hawke, sixteen hours on his knees won't leave much skin on them. He'll be bleeding all over the deck."

Pointing that out did not change James's mind as he'd hoped. "Quite so. But at least his bones will be intact."

"I hope you know this will only make him resent your *lad* the more."

"Not at all. I'm sure you can find *something* about the chap to warrant such a mild punishment. Even the cut of his clothes or their condition will do. His shirtfront ought to be nicely wrinkled from

MacDonell's fists, don't you think? But whatever you find fault with, you're the dear fellow who'll be resented, not Georgie."

"Thanks much," Connie sneered. "You *could* just let it go, you know. They have."

James watched as the two MacDonells headed toward the forecastle. Georgie had her hand pressed to the ear that had been clouted.

"I doubt they have, but under no circumstances will I. So don't quibble any more about my means of retribution, Connie. It's either that or the cat-o'-nine-tails. And if you want to talk about blood getting all over the deck . . ."

Chapter Fourteen

"Blathering about brick walls again, are ye? Did that mon hit ye sae hard then? Ye should've let me do some damage tae—"

"I meant the captain," Georgina hissed as she hurried Mac along in search of a private spot where they could talk. "He's the same two-ton ox who carted me out of the tavern that night I had hoped to forget."

Mac stopped in his tracks. "Ye canna mean that yellow-haired laird? *He's* yer brick wall?"

"*He's* our captain."

"Och, now, that isna good news."

She blinked at that calm reply. "Didn't you hear me? Captain Malory is the same man—"

"Aye, I heard ye aright. But ye're no' locked up in the hold, or hasna he seen ye yet?"

"He didn't recognize me."

Mac's brows shot up, not because he was surprised at that answer, but because Georgina sounded piqued that it was so. "Are ye sure he got a good look at ye?"

"From top to bottom," she insisted. "He simply doesn't remember me."

"Aye, well, dinna take it personally, Georgie. They had other things on their minds that night, the both of them. They'd been drinking as well, and some men can ferget their own names after a bad night."

"I thought of that. And I'm not taking it personally." She sniffed indignantly at the very thought. "I was nothing but relieved . . . after I got over my shock of seeing him here. But that's not to say something might stir his memory yet, like seeing you."

"Ye've a point there," Mac said thoughtfully. He glanced over his shoulder to where England was no more than a speck on the horizon.

"It's too late for that," she said, reading his mind correctly.

"So it is," he agreed, then, "come. There's tae many ears here."

He led her not to the forecastle, but belowdecks to the boatswain's domain, now his, a room where the extra rigging was stored. Georgina plopped down on a fat coil of rope while Mac went through the motions of thinking: a bit of pacing, a bit of sighing, and tongue clicking.

Georgina practiced patience as long as she could, all of five minutes, before demanding, "Well? What are we going to do now?"

"I can avoid the mon as long as possible."

"And when it's no longer possible?"

"I hope I'll have grown some hair on my face by then," he said, offering her a grin. "A red bush tae cover this old leather will be as good a disguise as yer own, I'm thinking."

"It will, won't it?" she said, brightening, but only for a moment. "But that only solves one problem."

"I thought we only had the one."

She shook her head before slouching back against the bulkhead. "We also have to figure out a way for me to avoid the man."

"Ye know that isna possible, lass . . . unless ye take sick." He beamed, thinking he'd just solved the matter. "Ye wouldna be feeling poorly, would ye?"

"That won't work, Mac."

"It will."

She shook her head again. "It would if I was to sleep in the fo'c'sle as we assumed, but I've already been informed otherwise." And then she sneered, "The captain's magnanimously offered to share his own cabin with me."

"What!?"

"My sentiments exactly, but the blasted man insisted. He wants me close to hand in case he needs something in the middle of the night, the lazy cur. But what can you expect of a pampered English lord?"

"Then he'll have tae be told."

It was her turn to gasp as she shot to her feet, "What!? You can't be serious!"

"Ye better believe I am, lass." Mac nodded resolutely. "Ye'll no' be sharing a cabin wi' a mon who's nae friend or kin tae ye."

"But he thinks I'm a boy."

"That doesna matter. Yer brothers—"

"Will never know," she cut in angrily. "For God's sake, if you tell Malory, I could end up sharing his cabin anyway, but in a manner even less to my liking. Did you think of that?"

"He wouldna dare!" Mac growled.

"Oh, wouldn't he?" she demanded. "Are you forgetting so soon who's captain around here? He can do anything he blasted well pleases, and protesting on your part will only get you clapped in irons."

"Only the blackest scoundrel would be taking such advantage."

"True. But what makes you think he isn't just that? Are you willing to risk my virtue on the thin likelihood that the man has a scrap of honor? I'm not."

"But, lassie—"

"I mean it, Mac," she insisted stubbornly. "Not a word to him. If I'm found out some other way it will be soon enough to learn if the Englishman has any decency, but I tell you true, I doubt it. And sleeping in his cabin is the least of my worries. It's being around him otherwise that will be a test of my fortitude. You would not believe how despicable he is, how he takes pleasure in being downright nasty. He actually admitted to me it's one of the few enjoyments he has."

"What is?"

"Putting people on the defensive, making them squirm. He treats them like butterflies, his barbs the pins that nail them to the spot."

"Are ye no' exaggerating a wee bit, lass, disliking the mon as ye do?"

She was, but she didn't care to admit it to him. If she really was the boy the captain thought her to be, she wouldn't have taken offense at what was merely an older man ribbing a younger one about his lack of experience, something males invariably tended to do. And the topic of sex was a natural one between men when women weren't around. Hadn't she overheard enough conversations among her brothers, when they weren't aware that she was about, to know that?

Fortunately, the door opening just then kept her from having to answer Mac. A young sailor rushed in and showed relief at finding the boatswain there.

"The topsail halyard is fraying under these winds, sir. Mr. Sharpe sent me for a new one when he couldn't find you."

"I'll see tae it, mon," Mac said curtly, already turning to locate the proper rope.

The inexperienced sailor left gratefully. Georgina sighed, aware that Mac had no more time for her right now. But she didn't want to leave their conversation on such a bad note, or have him worrying about her.

The only way to do that was to give in and admit, "You were right, Mac. I have been letting my dislike of the man persuade me he's worse than he is. He said himself that he probably won't even notice me underfoot in a few days, which means he's tested my mettle and now won't bother himself with me anymore."

"And ye'll do yer best tae stay unnoticed?"

"I won't even spit in his soup before I serve it up to the great ox."

She grinned to show she was only teasing. He looked horrified to show he knew it. They both laughed before Mac headed toward the door.

"Are ye coming then?"

"No," she said, rubbing her ear under her cap. "I've decided the deck is more hazardous than I remember it being."

"Aye, this wasna a good idea, lass," he said regretfully, referring to their working their way home. It had been his idea, even if he had tried to talk her out of it afterward. If anything happened . . .

She smiled, not blaming him in the least for the way it had turned out. It was no more than bad luck that had made an Englishman, and that particular one, owner and captain of this ship.

"Now, none of that. We're on our way home, and that's all that matters. There's nothing else to do but grin and bear it for a month. I can do it, Mac, I promise. I'm practicing patience, remember?"

"Aye, ye just remember tae practice around him," he replied gruffly.

"Him most of all. Now go on before someone else comes down for that halyard. I think I'll just stay in here for the time being, until duty calls again."

He nodded and left her. Georgina wedged herself between two fat bundles of rope and rested her head back against the bulkhead. She sighed, thinking the day couldn't get any worse. Malory. No, he had a first name. James Malory. She decided she didn't like the name any more than she did the man. *Be honest, Georgina, you can't stand the sight of him. For God's sake, his touch even made you sick.* All right, so she disliked him a lot, a whole lot, and not even just because he was English. There still wasn't anything to be done about it. In fact, she'd have to pretend otherwise, or at least pretend indifference.

She yawned and rubbed at the binding cutting into the skin around her breasts. She wished she could take the thing off for a few hours, but she knew she didn't dare. Getting discovered now would be worse than she had counted on because *he* would be the one to decide her fate. But as she started to nod off, her lips tilted up into a smug little smile. The man was as stupid as he was obnoxious. He'd been so easy to fool, seeing only what she wanted him to see, and that was worth gloating over.

Chapter Fifteen

"Georgie!"

Her head had rolled forward in sleep, but now it slammed back against the bulkhead as she was startled awake. Fortunately the bulk of her hair and the cap cushioned the blow, but she still glared up at Mac, who continued to shake her shoulder. She opened her mouth to snap at him, but he got his say in first.

"What the devil are ye still doing down here? He's got men searching the whole ship fer ye!"

"What? Who?" And then it came rushing at her, where she was and who else was on this ship. "Oh, him." She snorted. "Well, he can . . ." No, wrong attitude. "What time is it? Am I late serving his dinner?"

"More'n an hour late, I'd say."

She swore under her breath as she scrambled to her feet and headed directly for the door. "Should I go straight to him, do you think, or get his dinner first?" she asked him over her shoulder.

"Food first. If he's hungry, it might help."

She swung around to face him. "Help what? He's not angry, is he?"

"I havena seen him, but use yer head, lass," Mac admonished. "This is yer first day serving under him, and already ye've neglected—"

"I can't help it if I fell asleep," she cut in, her tone a bit too defensive. "Besides, he as much as ordered me to take a nap."

"Well, then, I wouldna worry about it. Just get yerself going afore any more time's wasted."

She did, but she worried, too. The captain might have told her to sleep, but in his cabin, where he could have awakened her when it was time to fetch his food. Wasn't that why he wanted her near, so she'd be there for whatever he needed doing? And here he'd had to send people looking for her. Damn, double-damn. And she had thought she was through with anxious moments for this day at least.

She rushed into the galley so quickly, the three men there stopped what they were doing to gawk at her. "The captain's tray, is it ready, Mr. O'Shawn?"

He pointed a flour-coated finger. "Been ready—"

"But is it hot?"

He drew himself up to his medium height in an affronted manner. "Sure and why wouldn't it be, when I've just now filled it for the third time. I was going to send Hogan . . . here . . ."

His words trailed off as she left as quickly as she'd entered, the heavy tray, much larger than the one she'd delivered earlier, weighing down her arms but not slowing her down. Three men called to her on the way that the captain was looking for her. She didn't stop to answer. She just got more anxious.

He said he won't box your ears. He said he won't. But she had to keep reminding herself of that all the way to his door, once again before she knocked and heard the curt command to enter, and still one more time before she did.

And the first thing she heard as she stepped inside was the first mate's voice saying, "Ought to box his ears."

Oh, she did hate that man, she truly did. But instead of revealing to him the flash of heat in her eyes, she bowed her head, waiting to hear James Malory's opinion, which was the one that counted.

She heard only silence, however, tortuous silence, since it told her nothing of the captain's mood. And she refused to look at him, imagining his expression to be at its most intimidating, which would only increase her trepidation.

She jumped when he finally asked, "Well, what have you to say, youngun?"

Reasonable. He was going to be reasonable and listen to whatever excuse she had to offer. She hadn't expected that, but it brought her head up to meet those bright green eyes. He was sitting at his table, his *empty* table, with Conrad Sharpe, and she realized suddenly that because of her tardiness, both men had had to wait for their dinner. And yet she was feeling relief because the captain wasn't looking like thunder held over. He was still intimidating, but then he always would be, big ox that he was. But there was no hint of anger about him. Of course, she had to remind herself, she didn't know how this man would look when he got angry. He might look just as he did now.

"Maybe a flogging, too," Conrad suggested into the continuing silence. "To teach the brat to answer when he's asked a question."

Georgina didn't hesitate to blast him this time with a fulminating glare, but all it got her was a chuckle from the tall redhead. A glance back at the captain showed he was still waiting, his expression still inscrutable.

"I'm sorry, sir," she said at last, putting as much contrition into her tone as she could manage. "I was sleeping . . . as you told me to do."

One golden brow crooked in what she decided was a very irritating affectation. "Imagine that, Connie," the captain said, though his eyes never left her. "He was only doing what I told him to do. Of course, as I recall, I told him to sleep here, in that bed yonder."

Georgina winced. "I know, and I tried, really I did. I was just too uncomfortable in . . . What I mean is . . . Devil take it, your bed was too soft." There, better that lie than admitting the only reason she couldn't sleep there was because it was *his* bed.

"So you don't like my bed?"

The first mate was laughing, though she couldn't imagine why. And the captain's irritating brow actually rose up a bit higher. And was that amusement in his eyes now? She should be relieved. Instead she felt she was the butt of some joke that had no punchline, and she was really getting tired of being a source of entertainment without knowing why.

Patience, Georgina. Indifference. You're the only Anderson besides Thomas who doesn't have a temper. Everyone says so.

"I'm sure your bed is nice, sir, the best there is, if you like things soft and cushiony to sleep on. I prefer firmer stuff myself, so—"

She broke off, frowning, as the first mate burst into another round of hearty laughter. James Malory had apparently choked on something, for he was bent over in his chair, coughing. She almost demanded to know what Sharpe found so funny this time, but the tray was getting heavier to hold up. And since they were thoughtlessly forcing her to stand there with it while she explained her late arrival, she would rather get it over with.

"So," she continued, throwing the word out sharply to regain their attention, "I thought to collect my hammock, as you also told me to do. But on the way to the fo'c'sle, I . . . well, I saw my brother, who wanted a word with me. So I followed him below for just a minute, but then . . . well, my stomach acted up again suddenly. I was only going to lie down for a second or two, until it passed. But the next thing I knew, Mac was waking me up and giving me a blistering scolding for falling asleep and neglecting my duties."

"A blistering scolding, eh? Is that all?"

What did he want, blood? "Actually, I got my ears boxed. They're likely twice as big now."

"Are they? Saves me the trouble, then, don't it?" But then he added in a softer tone. "Did it hurt, Georgie?"

"Well, of course it hurt," she retorted. "Do you want to see the damage?"

"You'd show me your pointy ears, lad? I'm flattered, indeed I am."

She was glowering by now. "Well, don't be, because I won't. You'll just have to take my word for it. And I know you think this is highly amusing, Captain, but you wouldn't if you'd ever had your own ears boxed."

"Oh, but I have, innumerable times . . . until I began boxing back. I'd be pleased to show you how."

"How what?"

"To defend yourself, dear boy."

"Defend . . . against my own brother?" Her tone implied she wouldn't even consider it.

"Your brother, or anyone else who bothers you."

Her eyes narrowed then, suspiciously. "You saw what happened, didn't you?"

"I haven't the faintest notion what you seem to be accusing me of. Now, d'you want lessons at fisticuffs or not?"

She almost laughed at the absurdity of it. She almost said yes, for it might be a useful thing to know, at least while she was on this ship. But lessons from him would only mean more time spent with him.

"No, thank you, sir. I'll manage on my own."

He shrugged. "Suit yourself. But, Georgie, the next time I tell you to do something, see that you do it as I tell you, not as you might prefer.

And if I ever find myself put to the inconvenience of worrying again that you might have fallen overboard, I'll bloody well confine you to this cabin."

She blinked at him. He said it without the slightest raised inflection, but that was a dire warning if she'd ever heard one, and she didn't doubt for a moment that he meant it. But it was ridiculous. It was on the tip of her tongue to tell him she likely knew her way around a ship better than half his crew, that the chances of her falling overboard were nil. But she couldn't say that when she'd pretended ignorance of ships previously. Of course, his having worried over her she didn't believe at all. Inconvenience said it all, no worry but an empty belly, which he meant to see never happened again. He was a blasted autocrat, was all, but she'd already known that.

Into the silence came Mr. Sharpe's dry inquiry, "If we're not going to have the cat-o'-nine sent for, James, d'you mind terribly if we have our dinner instead?"

"You always were ruled by your gut, Connie," the captain retorted dryly.

"So some of us are easy to please. Well, what are you waiting for, brat?"

Georgina thought how nice the tray of food would look dumped in the first mate's lap. She wondered if she dared pretend to trip. No, better not, or he'd fetch that cat-o'-nine-tails himself.

"We'll serve ourselves, Georgie, since you're running late tonight in your duties," the captain said as she shoved the tray on the table between them.

She looked at him in mild inquiry. She wasn't about to feel guilty about forgetting to do something she hadn't been told about. But he got a rise out of her anyway when he wasn't forthcoming with an explanation, wasn't even paying attention to her now as he examined the meal that was quickly being revealed by his loathsome friend.

"*What* duty have I overlooked, Captain?"

"What? Oh, my bath, of course. I like it directly after dinner."

"With fresh water or sea?"

"Fresh, always. There's more than enough. Hot, but not scalding. It usually requires about eight buckets full."

"Eight!" She dropped her head quickly, hoping he hadn't noticed her dismay. "Yes, sir, eight. And will that be once a week or every other?"

"Very amusing, dear boy," he said with a chuckle. "That's every day, of course."

She groaned. She couldn't help it. And she didn't care if he heard her or not. The big ox *would* have to be fastidious. She would love a bath every day, too, but not when it meant lugging heavy buckets all the way from the galley.

She turned to leave, but was arrested by the first mate's comment. "There's a bucket rail housed on the poopdeck, squirt. You can try it, but I doubt you've the muscle to tote four buckets at a crack. So use the water cask at the top of the stairs for the cold fill. It'll save you a bit of time, and I'll see it's replenished for you each evening."

She nodded her thanks, the best she could do at the moment. So what if he was actually being nice, in making the suggestion. She still didn't like him or his *clean* captain.

Once the door closed behind her, Connie wanted to know, "Since when d'you bathe every evening when you're aboard ship, Hawke?"

"Since I acquired that darling girl to assist me."

"I should have known." Connie snorted. "But she won't thank you for it when she counts all the blisters on her hands."

"You don't think I mean to have her tote all those buckets, d'you? Heaven forbid she should develop muscle where she doesn't need it. No, I've already arranged for Henry to show what a kindhearted chap he is."

"Henry?" Connie grinned. "Kindhearted?" And then, "You didn't tell him—?"

"'Course I didn't."

"And he didn't ask you why?"

James chuckled. "Connie, old man, you're so accustomed to questioning every bloody thing I do that you forget no one else dares."

Chapter Sixteen

Georgina's hands were trembling a bit as she piled the dishes back onto the tray and cleaned up the captain's table, and not because they'd been put to heavy use. No, she'd had to do no more than carry all those buckets from the door to the tub, thanks to a blustery Frenchman who'd gotten all upset when she sloshed water on the deck. His name was Henry, and he wouldn't listen to her protests when he ordered two crewmen, not much older than Georgie was supposed to be, to carry the buckets for her. Of course, the boys were a lot bigger than she was, and certainly stronger, and she had only protested because she felt she ought to, and because she figured they would grumble at having to do her job for her.

But they didn't protest, and Henry's last testy word on the subject was that she should grow a little before she attempted to do a man's job. She almost took offense at that, but wisely held her tongue. The man was helping her, after all, even if he didn't see it that way.

She'd still had to do some carrying, since her helpers dropped their load outside the door, refusing to enter the captain's cabin. She didn't blame them at all. She wouldn't enter his domain, either, if she didn't have to. But the little bit of carrying she did wasn't responsible for her trembling hands. No, they trembled because James Malory was behind the bath screen taking his clothes off, and just knowing that was making her more nervous than she had been at any other time today.

Fortunately, she didn't have to stay in the cabin. She had the dishes to return to the galley, and she still had her hammock to collect from the crew's quarters in the forecastle. But she wasn't out of the room yet. And she was still there when she heard the water splash.

She tried to force it away, but an image came to her mind of that big body easing into the hot water, steam coming up to surround him and wilt that thick mass of golden hair. Beads of moisture would form across his massive chest until his skin reflected the light of the lantern hanging over him. He would lean back and close his eyes for a moment as his body relaxed in the soothing heat . . . and there the image ended. Georgina simply couldn't picture that man relaxed.

Her eyes flared wide when she realized what she'd been doing. Was she crazy? No, it was the stress and strain of a perfectly horrid day, and the day wasn't even over yet. Angrily, she tossed the last dish on the tray and swiped it up, heading for the door. But she didn't quite reach it before the captain's deep voice floated out to her.

"I need my robe, Georgie."

His robe? Where had she put it? Oh, yes, she'd hung it in the cabinet, a thin piece of emerald silk that likely wouldn't fall past his knees. It certainly wouldn't offer any warmth. She'd wondered when she'd seen it earlier what it was even used for. But when she couldn't find any nightshirts in the captain's belongings, she decided he must sleep in it.

She returned the tray to the table, quickly grabbed the robe out of the cabinet, and nearly ran across the room to toss it over the screen. But she'd no sooner pivoted back toward the table when she heard from him again.

"Come around here, lad."

Oh, no. No and no again. She didn't *want* to see him relaxed. She didn't want to see the glistening skin she had just pictured in her mind.

"I have to fetch my hammock, sir."

"It can wait."

"But I don't want to disturb you setting it up."

"You won't."

"But—"

"Come *here,* Georgie." She heard the impatience in his voice. "This will only take a minute."

She glanced wistfully at the door, her only escape. Even a knock just then would save her from having to go behind that screen, but there was no knock, no escape. He'd made it an order.

She gave herself a mental shake and stiffened her spine. What was she afraid of, anyway? She'd seen her brothers at their baths, and at all ages, too. She'd fetched towels for them, washed their hair for them, even washed Boyd entirely that time he burned both hands. Of course, he'd only been ten and she six, but it wasn't as if she'd never seen a man unclothed. With five brothers under her roof, it was a wonder she hadn't had more than just one or two embarrassing glimpses in all these years.

"Georgie . . ."

"I'm coming, for God's . . . I mean—" She came around the screen. "What can I do . . . for . . . you?"

Oh, God, it just wasn't the same. He wasn't her brother. He was a big, handsome man who was no relation to her at all. And his skin was glistening wet bronze, and stretched so tautly over those bricklike muscles, bulging muscles. His hair hadn't wilted, either. It was too thick to wilt, except for a few strands that curled damply over his forehead. She might think of him as an ox, but only because he was so big and broad. He was indeed broad, but solid. She doubted there was a soft part on his whole body . . . except maybe one. She flamed at the thought, and prayed fervently he didn't notice.

"What the devil is wrong with you, youngun?"

She'd annoyed him, obviously, in not coming immediately. She lowered her eyes to the floor, a safe place at the moment, and hoped she looked suitably contrite.

"I'm sorry, sir. I'll learn to move quicker."

"See that you do. Here."

The washrag with the soap inside it hit her square in the chest. The soap dropped to the floor. She caught the rag. Her eyes were now huge circles of dread.

"You want a new one?" she asked hopefully.

She heard a snort. "That one will do just fine. Come and wash my back with it."

She'd been afraid he was going to say something like that. She couldn't do it. Get close to that naked skin? Touch it? How could she? *But you're a boy, Georgie, and he's a man. He sees nothing wrong in asking you to wash his back, and there wouldn't be, if you were a boy.*

"Getting your ears boxed affected your hearing, did it?"

"Yes . . . I mean, no." She sighed. "It's been a long day, Captain."

"And nervous tension can wear a boy out. I understand perfectly, lad. You can turn in early, since I've nothing more for you to do tonight . . . after you do my back."

She stiffened. She'd thought for a second there that she was getting a reprieve, but she should have known better. All right, she'd wash his blasted back. What choice did she have? And maybe she could take some skin off while doing it.

She swiped up the soap and came around the end of the tub. He leaned forward as she did, so when she got there, his entire back was presented to her, so long, so wide, so . . . masculine. The water, as much as she'd poured in, still only rose up a few inches above his hips, the tub was so big. And it wasn't murky. The man had nice buttocks.

She caught herself staring, just staring, and wondered for how long. Not long, or he would have said something, impatient devil that he was.

Annoyed with herself, furious with him for making her do this, she slammed the washrag into the water, then mutilated the soap with it until she had enough suds to wash ten bodies. This she slapped against his back, then began to rub with all her might. He didn't say a word. And she began to feel guilty after a moment, seeing the red marks she was leaving behind.

She eased the pressure, and her anger eased with it. She was staring again, fascinated at the gooseflesh that appeared if she touched a sensitive spot, watching the dark bronze skin disappear under bubbles, then reappear as they popped. The cloth was so thin, it was almost as if it weren't there, as if there was nothing between her hand and his slick skin. Her movements became slower. She was washing areas she'd already washed.

And then it happened. The food she'd gulped down while waiting for the bathwater to boil in the galley was starting to churn in her stomach. It was the weirdest feeling, but she didn't doubt for a moment that it was going to be full-fledged nausea. And she'd be mortified if she threw up again in his presence. *Can I help it if it makes me sick to get near you, Captain?* That would really go over well, wouldn't it?

"I'm finished, sir." She handed the washrag over his shoulder.

He didn't take it. "Not quite, lad. My lower back."

Her eyes dropped to that area, streaked with suds that had dribbled down. But she couldn't actually remember if she'd washed there or not. She attacked it swiftly, relieved that enough suds floated in the water now that she could no longer see through it. She even plunged the cloth the few inches below the water to the very base of his spine, giving him no excuse to say she hadn't done a thorough job. But she had to bend way down to reach it, bringing her closer to him, so close she could smell his hair. She could smell his clean body, too. And she had no trouble hearing his groan.

She jerked back so fast, she hit the wall behind her. He jerked around just as fast to stare up at her. The heat in his eyes impaled her where she was.

"I'm sorry," she gasped. "I didn't mean to hurt you, I swear I didn't."

"Be easy, Georgie." He turned back around, dropping his head onto his raised knees. "It's just a minor . . . stiffness. Nothing you could have known about. Go on, I can finish easily enough now."

She bit her lip. The man sounded as if he were in pain. She ought to be glad, but for some reason she wasn't. For some reason she had an urge to . . . to what? Soothe his hurt? Had she gone absolutely mad? She got out of there as fast as she could.

Chapter Seventeen

James was on his second glass of brandy by the time Georgie returned to the cabin. He had himself in hand again but was still smarting over how easily the girl's innocent touch had aroused him. Talk about well-laid plans gone down the bloody drain. He'd meant to have her rinse him, to hand him his towel, to help him into his robe. He meant to see those pretty cheeks blush with color. Instead, he would have been the one with the hot cheeks if he'd stood up at that point. He'd never in his life suffered an embarrassment over an honest reaction of his body, and he wouldn't have this time, except that to her mind, his reaction would have been caused by a boy.

Damnation, what a coil, when the game was to have been so simple. The advantage was to be his, while she was between wind and water as they say, which was a vulnerable position. He'd envisioned seducing her with his manly form, until she would be so overcome with lust that she would toss off her cap and implore him to take her. A splendid fantasy, where he would play the innocent, unsuspecting male attacked by his wanton cabin boy. He would protest. She would beg sweetly for his body. He would then do the gentlemanly thing and give in.

But how was any of that to come about if the old John Henry raised his head every time she got near? And if she happened to notice, the darling chit would think he had a fondness for boys, and *that* wouldn't inspire anything in her but disgust. Bloody hell, he'd have her confessing who she was just so he *wouldn't* get any ideas.

His eyes followed her as she crossed over to the corner he'd assigned her. She carried a canvas bag tucked under her arm, a hammock slung over her shoulder. The bag was fat enough to contain more than a few articles of boy's attire. There was likely a dress or two inside, and maybe something that would shed some light on the mystery surrounding her.

He'd picked up a few more pieces of the puzzle tonight. Connie had pointed out the very natural way she'd said "fo'c'sle" instead of "forecastle." Only someone familiar with ships would use the abbreviated term, yet she'd claimed an ignorance of all things nautical.

And she called her brother Mac. Now there was a telling little tidbit, leading him to believe the Scot was no relation to her at all. Friends and acquaintances might call MacDonell Mac, but family would use his given name or some other nickname, not one that each family member could equally claim for himself, all being MacDonells. Yet she did have a brother or two. She'd mentioned them without having to think about it. So who was the Scot to her? Friend, lover . . . husband? By God, she'd better not have a lover. She could have all the bloody husbands she liked, dozens for all he cared, but a lover was serious business, what he intended to be himself.

Georgina could feel his eyes on her as she hooked her hammock to the wall. She'd located him sitting behind his desk when she came in, but as he hadn't said anything to her, she didn't speak either; nor had she looked his way again. But that one glance . . .

He was wearing that emerald robe. She'd never realized what a splendid color emerald could be on the right person. On him it darkened the green of his eyes, highlighted the fairness of his blond locks, mellowed the deep bronze of his skin. And so much skin was visible. The closing V of the robe was so wide and deep, it barely covered his chest. A mat of golden hair sheened in the lamplight, from nipple to nipple, from above his chest to . . . below.

Georgina pulled the high neckline of her shirt away from her skin. This blasted cabin seemed awfully hot this evening. Her clothes felt more weighty, her bindings more uncomfortable. But the most she dared remove for sleeping was her boots. She did that now, sitting on the floor to pull them off and set them neatly up against the wall.

And she could still feel James Malory's eyes, watching her every movement.

Of course, she had to be imagining it. What reason would he have to watch her, unless . . . She glanced at her hammock and grinned. The captain was probably waiting to see her climb into her swinging bed and fall flat on her arse. He probably even had some droll comment ready to toss at her about clumsiness or inexperience, something really nasty and guaranteed to embarrass her. Well, not this time. She'd been in and out of hammocks since she could walk, had played in them as a child, napped in them when she was older and spent whole days on whatever Skylark ship was in port. There was less likelihood of her falling out of one than out of a normal bed. The captain would just have to swallow his ridicule this time, and she hoped he'd choke doing it.

She settled into her swinging bunk with the ease of an old salt, then glanced quickly toward the desk in the opposite corner of the room, hoping to catch the captain's surprise. He *was* looking her way, but to her chagrin, his expression gave nothing away.

"You're not actually going to sleep in those clothes, are you, youngun?"

"Actually, Captain, I am."

She must have scored with that, for he was frowning now. "I didn't mean to give the impression you'd be in and out of bed all night long, you know. Did you assume so?"

"I didn't." She did, but everything he knew about her was a lie anyway, so what was one more? "I always sleep with my clothes on. I can't remember why I started doing so, it's been so long, but it's a habit now." And for good measure, just in case he had the audacity to suggest she change her habits, she added, "I doubt I could get to sleep without being fully clothed."

"Suit yourself. I have my sleeping habits, too, though I daresay they're quite the opposite of yours."

What was that supposed to mean? Georgina wondered, but didn't have long to find out. The man stood up, came around his desk heading for his bed, and stripped out of his robe on the way.

Oh, God, oh, God, this isn't happening to me. He's not strutting across the room naked and giving me a full frontal view of him doing it.

But he was, and her female sensibilities were outraged. Yet she didn't squeeze her eyes shut, not immediately anyway. After all, this was not something she saw every day, not something she would likely have ever seen, for he was truly a splendid specimen of manhood right down to his toes. She couldn't deny it, no matter how much she wished he had some fleshy sides, or a pot belly, or a tiny . . .

Don't blush, you ninny. No one heard you think it but yourself, and you didn't even complete the thought. So he's extra fine-looking in every *respect. It's nothing to you.*

Her eyes closed tight finally, but she'd already seen more than was good for her. His naked image was not something she was likely to forget anytime soon. Devil take him, the man simply had no shame. No, that wasn't fair. She was supposed to be a boy. What was a little nakedness between males? An eye-popping experience for her, that's what.

"Would you put out the lamps, Georgie?"

She groaned and was afraid he'd heard her when he sighed and added, "Never mind. You're already abed, and we wouldn't want to test the fates that put you there on your first try."

Her teeth gnashed together. So he'd gotten the blasted gibe in anyway. The man was a devil clear to the core. She almost said she'd see to the lanterns anyway. She'd show him that the fates had nothing to do with her and her hammock. But she'd have to open her eyes to do it, and he wasn't in bed yet and covered up. And coming face-to-face with him undressed . . . Well, she'd be smart not to.

But her eyes cracked open anyway. The temptation was just too great to resist. And besides, if the man was going to put on a show, she reasoned, he ought to have an audience to appreciate it. Not that she did. Certainly not. It was just curious fascination, not to mention self-preservation. She'd keep her eye on a snake if it was this close to her, wouldn't she?

But as interesting as she found this unusual experience, she wished he'd hurry up. She was starting to feel nauseous again, and this time he wasn't even close to her. Lord, but he had nice buttocks. Was the room getting hotter? And such long legs, such firm flanks. His masculinity was overwhelming, blatant, intimidating.

Oh, God, was he coming toward her? He was! Why? Oh, the lantern over the tub. Double-damn him for frightening her like that. When he doused it, her end of the room darkened. Only one light remained by the bed. She closed her eyes and kept them closed. She would *not* watch him getting into that heavenly soft bed. What if he didn't use a cover? The moon had already risen, had lit the deck above quite brightly, and was bound to light the cabin through that wall of windows. She wouldn't open her eyes again to save her soul. Well, that was a bit extreme. Maybe just to save her soul.

Where was he now? She hadn't heard his feet padding back toward his bed.

"By the by, lad, is Georgie your given name, or just a pet name your family has burdened you with?"

He's not standing right next to me, stark naked. He's not! I'm imagining it, imagining the whole thing. He never dropped his robe. We're both sleeping already.

"What's that? I didn't hear you, lad?"

Didn't hear what? She hadn't said a word. She wasn't going to, either. Let him think she was asleep. But what if he touched her to wake her, just for her answer to his stupid question? As tense as she was right now, she'd probably scream her head off, and that just wouldn't do. *Answer him, you ninny, and he'll go away!*

"It's my given name . . . sir."

"I was afraid you'd say that. It really won't do, you know. Why, I've known females to call themselves that, short for Georgette or Georgiana, or some other godawful long name. And you wouldn't care to be likened to a female, would you?"

"I never gave it much thought one way or the other," she replied in a fluctuating tone, half growl, half squeak.

"Well, don't worry about it, lad. It might be the name you're stuck with, but I've decided to call you George. Much more manly, don't you think?"

He didn't give a fig what she thought, and she cared even less what he thought. But she wasn't going to argue with a naked man standing only inches away from her.

"Whatever pleases you, Captain."

"Whatever pleases me? I like your attitude, George, indeed I do."

She sighed as he walked away. She didn't even wonder why he was chuckling to himself. And despite her firm resolve, after a moment her eyes cracked open again. But she'd waited too long this time. He was in bed and decently covered. But moonlight did indeed flood the room, so she had a clear view of him stretched out on his bed, his arms crossed behind his head, and smiling. Smiling? It had to be a trick of the light. And what difference did it make anyway?

Disgusted with herself, she turned over to face the corner so she wouldn't be tempted to look at him anymore. And she sighed again, unaware that this time it was a purely deflated sound.

Chapter Eighteen

Georgina had had the worst time getting to sleep that night, but the next thing she knew, the captain's voice was calling, "Show a leg, George," the age-old sailors' adage that meant shed the covers quick and get moving. She blinked, and sure enough, daylight filled the cabin, bright enough for her to suppose she'd overslept.

She located the reason behind her lack of sleep and found him dressed, thank God, or at least partially so. Breeches and stockings were better than nothing. And even as she watched, he slipped into a black silk shirt similar in style to the white one he'd worn yesterday, though he didn't lace up the front closing. The breeches were black, too. Give him an earring, and the cursed man would look like a pirate in that billowing shirt and tight pants, she thought uncharitably, and then sucked in her breath as she noticed he *was* wearing an earring today, a small golden one just barely visible under the blond locks still disarrayed from sleep and not combed back yet.

"You're wearing an earring!"

That brought those bright green eyes to her, and the affectation she considered his most arrogant *and* irritating habit, the raising of just one golden brow. "Noticed, did you? And what d'you think of it?"

She wasn't awake enough yet to think of being flattering instead of truthful. Baldly, she said, "It makes you look piratical."

His grin was positively wicked. "D'you think so? I would have said rakish myself."

She caught herself about to snort. She managed to just sound curious instead, "Why would you want to wear an earring?"

"Why not?"

Well, he was a fount of information this morning, wasn't he? And what did she care if he wanted to look like a pirate, as long as he wasn't one in actuality?

"Well, come along, George," he said briskly now. "The morning's half gone."

She gritted her teeth as she sat up, swung with the hammock a few times, then dropped to the floor. He called her George with a good deal of relish, it seemed, as if he knew how it would irritate her. More manly sounding indeed. She knew of a number of Georges called Georgie, but not another female other than herself with that shortened name.

"Not used to sleeping in a hammock, are you?"

She glared at him, really fed up with his inaccurate assumptions. "Actually—"

"I could hear you tossing about all night long. All that squeaking rope woke me a number of times, I don't mind telling you. I trust that's not going to be a nightly occurrence, George. I suppose I'd have to offer to share my bed with you just so I won't be disturbed."

She blanched, even though he sounded as if he'd hate doing it. She had little doubt he'd do it anyway, *and* insist, no matter her protests. Over her dead body.

"It won't happen again, Captain."

"See that it don't. Now, I hope you've a steady hand."

"Why?"

"Because you'll be scraping the whiskers from my cheeks."

She would? No, how could she? She might get sick again, and she could just see herself puking in his lap. She'd have to tell him about this propensity she had for getting nauseous when she got too close to him.

She groaned inwardly. How could she tell him something like that? He'd be so insulted, there was no telling what he'd do to her. He could, after all, make her life utterly miserable, much worse than it already was.

"I've never shaved anyone, Captain. I'd likely nick you to pieces."

"I sincerely hope not, dear boy, since this is one of your duties. And as a valet, you'll have to improve. Notice I've had to dress myself this morning."

She was going to cry. There was just no way she would be able to avoid getting close to him. And he'd eventually notice that she had a serious aversion to him. How could he not if she ran for the chamber pot several times a day?

But maybe it wasn't him. Maybe she was seasick. When she'd sailed the eastern coast with her brothers on short runs and never suffered it? When she'd crossed the ocean to England without the tiniest upset? It was him. But she could tell him she was seasick, couldn't she?

She felt much better suddenly and even smiled as she promised, "I'll do better tomorrow, Captain."

Why he just stared at her for a long moment before answering curtly, she didn't know. "Very well. I have to confer with Connie, so you've about ten minutes to fetch some warm water and dig out my razors. Don't keep me waiting, George."

Well, he was certainly put out that he'd had to dress himself, wasn't he? she thought as he slammed the door behind him. He hadn't even bothered to put on boots. She hoped he got splinters in his feet. No, he'd probably make her pick them out.

She sighed, then realized she had the cabin to herself for a few minutes. She didn't hesitate to head straight for the commode. If it weren't for Malory's blasted time schedule, she wouldn't chance it. But she'd never make it down to the hold to the chamber pot she'd hidden away there, not in the ten minutes allotted her to fetch the water for his shaving. Nor could she wait until she was finished shaving him. But after this, she was going to have to work on getting up *before* he did so she had more time.

James slammed back into the cabin the same way he'd left, with a lot of noise, the door hitting the wall this time. He expected to startle Georgie and meant to, her with her unexpected smile that he'd felt clear to his gut. Well, he'd startled her all right. If the color of her cheeks was any indication, she was going up in flames of mortification, too. But he was still the more startled. What a bloody dense ass he was, not to have considered how a female pretending not to be a female would manage such things as bathing and nature's calls, even changing her clothes, on a ship full of men. By moving her into his cabin, he'd given her more privacy than she would have had otherwise, but that was for his sake, not hers, part of his game. There was still no lock on the door, no place where she could be *assured* of a little privacy.

With his mind centered on getting her pants off, he really should have considered these things. She must have, before she decided on this pretense. And it would be a safe bet that his cabin was not the place she had determined would offer the least risk of discovery. He'd more or less forced her to take this chance by rousing her from sleep and ordering her immediately to her duties. It was his fault she was now hiding her face against her pretty bare knees. And there wasn't a bloody thing he could do about her embarrassment, and still keep up the pretense. If she really were a George, he wouldn't back out of the room making apologies, would he? He'd treat the matter as nothing out of the ordinary, and it wouldn't be, if she were a George.

But she wasn't, and by God, there was nothing ordinary about this situation. The darling girl did have her pants down, and his senses had been relishing that fact since he'd stormed into the room.

James rolled his eyes ceilingward and stomped around the bed to find his boots. This is too much, he thought. She smiles at me and I get aroused. She sits on a bloody chamber pot and I get aroused.

"Don't mind me, George," he snapped out more sharply than he meant to. "I forgot my boots."

"Captain, please!"

"Now don't get missish. D'you think the rest of us never have to use that thing?"

Her groan told him plain enough he wasn't helping, so he simply got out of there, slamming the door once again, and carrying his boots out with him. He was afraid the incident was going to be a setback for him. Some women could be peculiar about such things, like never wanting to set eyes again on a man who'd witnessed their embarrassment, or caused it. And a man didn't have a prayer if he happened to do both.

Bloody everlasting hell. He had no idea how this girl would react, whether she'd laugh it off, blush for a few days, or dive under the nearest bed and refuse to come out. He hoped she was made of sterner stuff. Her masquerade suggested she had courage and a good deal of audacity. But he just didn't know. And his mood took a swing for the worse that he was having any kind of setback at all, especially after the progress he had made last night.

Georgina wasn't thinking about hiding under any beds. Her options were quite clear. She could jump ship, keep company with the rats in the hold for the rest of the voyage, or murder James Malory. And the last had the most appeal no matter how she looked at it. But when she got up on deck she heard that the captain was passing out punishments left and right, and for no good reasons, or, as one sailor put it, because he had a barnacle up his arse. And that, translated simply, meant he was displeased about something and taking it out on anyone foolish enough to cross his path this morning.

Some of the color that had still been riding her cheeks receded immediately. By the time she got back to the cabin with the warm water for his lordship's shaving, she decided that he just might be more embarrassed than she was . . . well, not more. No one in the entire world could ever have been more mortified than she. But if he had felt even a tiny bit of that, then she could live with it, she supposed, especially if it had so upset him as to put him in a black mood.

Of course, that reasoning gave him a sensitivity she wouldn't have thought him capable of. His reaction was directly related to hers. If she hadn't behaved like such a ninny, missish he'd called her, then he would have thought nothing of it. But he knew he'd embarrassed her worse than any of his taunts could ever do, and so he was ashamed to have done it.

The door opened hesitantly a few minutes later, and Georgina almost laughed when the captain of the *Maiden Anne* actually stuck his head around the door to see if it was safe to come in this time. "Well, are you ready to cut my throat with my own razors, youngun?"

"I hope I'm not that unskilled."

"I sincerely share that hope."

He shed his uncertainty, which had been comical, it was so unsuited to the man, and sauntered toward the table where she had set the basin of water. His razors were spread out on a towel, next to which more towels were stacked, and she had already whipped up a lather in the cup she found for that use. He had been gone much longer than ten minutes, so she had also set the room to rights, making his bed, stowing her own, picking up his discarded clothes to wash later. The only thing she hadn't done was fetch his breakfast, but Shawn O'Shawn was cooking that now.

Looking over the setup, he remarked, "So you have done this before?"

"No, I've watched my brothers do it."

"Better than total ignorance, I suppose. Well, have at it then."

He peeled his shirt off and tossed it farther down the table, then turned his chair sideways and sat down facing her. Georgina just stared. She hadn't expected to work on him while he was half dressed. It wasn't necessary. She had extra towels, big ones, to wrap around his shoulders to protect his shirt. Devil take him, she'd use them anyway.

But when she tried to, he pushed them away. "If I want you to smother me, George, I'll let you know."

The idea of cutting his throat appealed to her more and more. If it wouldn't be so messy, and if she wouldn't have to clean up the blood, she'd give in to the impulse. With all that skin to distract her, it just might happen anyway—accidentally, of course.

She could shave him. She had to do it. And best do it quickly, before that wretched nausea flared up to make it an even more difficult task. *Just don't look down, Georgie, or up, or anywhere but at his very ordinary whiskers. How disturbing can whiskers be?*

At arm's length, she spread the lather on thickly, but she had to get closer to do the actual scraping. She was looking at his cheeks, concentrating on her task, or trying to. He was staring up at her eyes. When her gaze happened to collide with his, her pulse picked up its beat. And he didn't look away. She did, but she could still feel his eyes on her, and the sudden heat they were causing.

"Stop those blushes, now," he chided. "What's a little bare arse between men?"

She hadn't even been thinking of *that,* curse and rot him. But now her face was twice as hot, and got hotter, for he wasn't going to let the subject pass.

"I don't know why I should, since it's my cabin," he said testily, "but I'm going to apologize, George, for what happened earlier. You'd think I walked in on a bloody girl, the way you carried on."

"I'm sorry, sir."

"Never mind that. Just put a damned sign on the door next time if your privacy means so much to you. I'll honor the bloody thing, and no one else comes in here without permission."

A lock on the door would be even better, but she didn't suggest it. She hadn't expected this much, was amazed that the man could be so considerate, generous even, when he didn't have to be. She might even be able to take a real bath now, instead of a quick sponge-off down in the hold.

"Blister it, George, I'm rather fond of this face. Leave me some skin on it, will you?"

He startled her so, she thoughtlessly snapped, "Then do it yourself!" and threw the razor down on the table.

She was stalking away from him when his dry tone hit her in the back. "Oh, my. The brat has a temper, does he?"

She stopped, her eyes widening with the realization of what she'd just done. Her groan was quite loud, and when she turned about, she looked as apprehensive as she felt.

"I'm sorry, Captain. I don't know what came over me. A bit of everything, maybe, but honestly, I don't have a temper. You can ask Mac."

"But I asked you. Now, you aren't afraid to be truthful with me, are you, George?"

That was worth another groan, though she kept this one to herself. "Not at all. Should I be?"

"I don't see why. Your size gives you an advantage, you know. You're too small to cuff or flog, and I wouldn't inconvenience myself by assigning you extra duty as punishment, now would I? So you *can* feel free to speak your mind to me, George. Ours is a close relationship, after all."

"And if I should cross the line into being disrespectful?" she couldn't resist asking.

"Why, I'd blister your backside, of course. That is about the only recourse I have for a lad your age. But that isn't going to be necessary, is it, George?"

"No, sir, it most certainly isn't," she gritted out, horrified and enraged at once.

"Then come along and finish my shave. And do try and be a little more careful this time."

"If you would . . . not talk, I might be able to concentrate better."
She couched it as a suggestion. Her tone was utterly respectful. But his
despised brow still shot upward. "Well, you said I could speak my
mind," she mumbled angrily as she stepped forward and picked up the
razor again. "And as long as I'm at it, I hate it when you do that."

The other brow rose to join the first, but now in surprise. "Do
what?"

She waved the hand that held the razor toward his face. "That
supercilious lifting of the eyebrows."

"Good God, brat, you bowl me over with your diction, indeed
you do."

"So now you think it's funny?"

"What I think, dear boy, is that you took me much too literally.
When I said you could speak your mind, it was not with the thought that
you would be foolish enough to criticize your captain. In that you cross
the line, as I believe you well know."

She did know it, and had only been combing the waters, so to
speak, to see just how far she would sink before drowning. Not far at
all, obviously.

"I'm sorry, Captain."

"I thought we agreed yesterday that you'd look me in the eye if you
were going to apologize. That's better. So you hate it, d'you?"

Devil take it, now he was amused. And she hated that even more
than his brow raising, especially since he never bothered to share the
joke with her.

"I feel it's in my best interests not to answer that, Captain."

He burst into laughter at that. "Well said, George! You're learning,
indeed you are."

His pleasure with her included a clap on the shoulder. Unfortunately, this sent her careening into his open thigh, which precipitated
his having to grab her to keep her from tumbling over his leg. She'd
grabbed him, too, to stop the fall herself. When they both realized they
were holding on to each other, the ship could have sunk and they
wouldn't have noticed. But the electrifying moment was come and
gone in a matter of seconds, for he released her as fast as she did him.

As if fire hadn't leaped between them in that brief span of time, the
captain said, albeit unsteadily, "My whiskers have likely grown an inch

since you got started, George. I do hope you'll get the hang of this before we reach Jamaica."

Georgina was too flustered to answer, so she just brought the razor up to his face and began working on the side she'd yet to scrape. Her heart was fluttering wildly, but why shouldn't it? She'd thought she was going over his leg headfirst. It had nothing to do with touching him.

But when she turned his face to finish up the other side, she saw the dots of blood where she'd nicked him. Without thinking about it, her fingers gently wiped the spots.

"I didn't mean to hurt you."

If her voice had been soft in saying it, his was much, much softer in his reply. "I know."

Oh, God, here comes the nausea, she thought.

Chapter Nineteen

"Are ye ailing, Georgie lad?"

"Just Georgie will do, Mac."

"Nae, it willna." He glanced around the poopdeck to make sure they were alone before adding, "I've caught myself nearly calling ye lass when I shouldna. I need the reminding."

"Suit yourself."

Georgina reached listlessly into the basket sitting between them for another rope to splice to the one in her lap, which she'd already joined to three others by interweaving the rope ends together. She'd offered to help Mac with the mundane chore just to pass the time, but wasn't paying much attention to what she was doing. Already he'd had to open one of her splices with a marlinespike and have her start over. She hadn't said a word or noticed the mistake herself.

Mac, watching her, shook his head. "Och, ye are ailing. Ye're being much too agreeable."

That got a rise out of her, but only just barely. "I'm always agreeable."

"No' since ye got it into yer wee head tae sail off tae England, ye havena been. Ye've been a prime pain in the arse since that notion took ye."

He had her full attention now. "Well, I like that," she huffed. "You didn't have to come along, you know. I could have reached England perfectly well without you."

"Ye knew verra well I'd never let ye sail alone. Short of locking ye up, I had nae choice. But I'm thinking I should've locked ye up."

"Maybe you should have."

He heard her sigh and snorted. "There ye go agreeing wi' me again. And ye've been acting passing strange all week. Is the mon working ye tae hard?"

Hard? She couldn't say that he was. In fact, half the things the captain had told her she'd have to do, she'd never gotten around to doing.

He was usually up and partially dressed before her in the morning. The one time she beat him out of bed, he behaved as if she'd done something wrong rather than right. She was learning to distinguish his moods, from his customary drollery to his really nasty taunts when he was annoyed about something, and that morning he'd been seriously annoyed. He'd made it seem like a punishment, her having to dress him that day. His comments, his manner, everything made it seem so, and had her swearing she'd be a slugabed the rest of the voyage.

She hoped she'd never have to experience anything so nerve-racking again. Having to get close to him was bad enough, but to do it when she knew him to be angry . . . Well, so far it hadn't happened again. Nor had he ever asked her to help him undress for his bath in the evening.

Even that hadn't turned out to be an everyday occurrence as he had implied it would. He still wanted his back scrubbed when he did bathe, but two nights out of the last seven he'd told her not to bother with the bath at all, had even offered her the use of his tub instead. She declined, of course. She hadn't been ready to risk a total strip-down yet, even if he had been honoring the sign she set outside his door several times each day.

Then there was the shaving of him. That first time, she didn't know why she hadn't been sick. It had felt like all hell had broken loose in her belly. If she had had to stand there much longer, the morning would likely have had a different ending. Instead, she'd finished his chin with a few strokes, tossed a towel at him, and run out of the cabin before he could stop her, yelling that she'd be back in a trice with his breakfast.

He'd only asked her to shave him once more, and that time she'd nicked him in so many places, he'd told her sarcastically that he'd be wise to grow a beard. But he didn't. Most of the crew did, including the first mate, but the captain continued to shave each day, either in the morning or in the late afternoon. He just did it himself now.

Not once had she had to play footman for him. He either ate right from the tray she brought in or waved her away when she tried to place the dishes before him. And not once had he disturbed her sleep to ask for something in the middle of the night, as he'd assured her he would.

All in all, she had very little to do and a lot of free time on her hands. This she spent in the cabin when it was vacant, or on deck with Mac when it wasn't, trying to limit her times with the captain to only what was necessary. But if she was acting strange, enough for Mac to notice, it was entirely James Malory's fault.

The scant week she had been on his ship seemed more like forever. She was constantly tense, had lost her appetite, was losing sleep, too. And she still got nauseous if he came too close to her, when he looked at her in a certain way, sometimes even when she stared at him too long, and *every* time she was treated to the flagrant flaunting of his naked body, which was every blasted night. It was no wonder she wasn't sleeping well, no wonder she was a bundle of nerves. And it was no wonder Mac noticed.

She would have preferred not to discuss it at all, she was so confused over what she was feeling. But Mac was sitting there staring at her, awaiting some kind of answer. Maybe some common-sense advice from him was just what she needed to put a new perspective on what was bothering her.

"The work isn't hard physically," Georgina allowed, staring down at the rope in her lap. "What's hard is having to serve an Englishman. If he were anyone else . . ."

"Aye, I ken yer meaning. Here ye were in a snit tae leave—"

Her head snapped up. "A snit? A snit!"

"Practicing impatience then, but the point is ye were in a hurry tae leave England and all things English behind, and it was that verra impatience that has ye stuck now wi' just what ye were trying tae get away from. Him being a laird only makes it worse."

"He acts like one, I agree," she said disdainfully. "But I doubt he actually is. Don't they have some cardinal rule about aristocrats and trade not mixing?"

"Something of the like, but they dinna all follow it. Besides, there's nae cargo, if ye'll recall, sae he isna in trade, at least no' this voyage. But he is a laird, a viscount as I heard it."

"How splendid for him," she sneered, then sighed heavily. "You were right. That actually does make it worse. A blasted aristocrat. I don't know why I doubted it."

"Look on this experience as atoning fer yer impulsiveness and hope yer brothers take that into account afore they drop the roof on yer head."

She grinned slightly. "I knew I could count on you to cheer me up."

He snorted and went back to splicing. She did, too, but she was soon brooding again over what was really bothering her. She finally decided to broach it.

"Have you ever heard of a person getting sick when they get too close to something, Mac?"

His light gray eyes pinned her with a curious frown. "Sick how?"

"Sick. You know, nauseous."

His brow cleared instantly. "Oh, aye, lots of foods will do that, when a mon's already feeling poorly from drink, or a woman's going tae have a bairn."

"No, not when something is already wrong with you. I meant when you're feeling perfectly fine, until you get close to a certain thing."

He was frowning again. "A certain thing, is it? And will ye be telling me what this thing is that's making ye sick?"

"I didn't say it was me."

"Georgie . . ."

"Oh, all right," she snapped. "So it's the captain. Half the time I get near him, my stomach reacts horribly."

"Only half?"

"Yes. It doesn't happen every time."

"And ye've actually been sick? Actually vomited?"

"Once, yes, but . . . well, that was the first day, when I'd just found out who he was. He forced me to eat, and I was just too nervous and upset to hold anything down. Since then, it's just been the nausea, sometimes worse than other times, but I haven't vomited again—yet."

Mac pulled at the red whiskers now covering his chin, mulling over what she'd said. What he suspected, he discounted, and so didn't even mention it to her. She disliked the captain too much to be attracted to him, much less to be experiencing any sort of sexual desire that she might be mistaking for nausea.

Finally, he said, "Could it be the scent he wears, lass, or the soap he uses? Or maybe even something he puts on his hair?"

Her eyes widened just before she laughed. "Now why didn't I think of that?" She jumped up, dropping her pile of rope into his lap.

"And where are ye off tae?"

"It's not his soap. I use it myself to sponge off. And he doesn't use anything on his hair, just lets it fly any which way. But he's got a bottle of something he uses after he shaves. I'm going to go smell it now, and if that's it, you can guess where it's going."

He was pleased to see her smiling again, but reminded her, "He'll miss it if ye just toss it over the side."

She almost said she'd worry about that later, but there was no point in courting trouble with that attitude. "So I'll tell him the truth. He's an arrogant beast, but . . . well, he's not so insensitive that he'd continue to use something if he knew it made me ill. I'll see you later, Mac, or tomorrow at any rate," she amended, noting the sun was on its downward swing.

"Ye promise ye willna do anything tae get yerself punished?"

If he knew what punishment she'd been warned of, he wouldn't have to ask that. "I promise."

And she meant it. If it was the captain's cologne that had been causing her such distress, there was no reason not to tell him about it. She should have mentioned it sooner, she was thinking, just before she ran right into him on the lower deck.

Her stomach flipped over, which brought a grimace to her face that she wasn't quick enough to hide.

"Ah," James Malory remarked, seeing it. "You must have read my mind, George."

"Captain?"

"Your expression. You've divined that I have a bone to pick with you about your bathing habits, or should I say, your lack thereof?"

Her face turned pink, then almost purple with indignation. "How dare—"

"Oh, come now, George. D'you think I don't know lads your age look on bathing as some kind of heinous torture? I was a lad once myself, you know. But you're sharing my cabin—"

"Not by choice," she got in.

"Regardless, I have certain standards I adhere to, cleanliness among them, or at the very least, the smell of cleanliness."

He twitched his nose just for good measure, she was sure. And if she weren't so furiously affronted, she might have burst into laughter, considering what she and Mac had just been discussing. *He* found *her* smell offensive? God, how ironic, and what poetic justice if it also made him ill.

He was continuing, "And since you haven't made the slightest effort to rise to my standards—"

"I'll have you know—"

"Do *not* interrupt me again, George," he cut in in his most autocratic tone. "The matter has already been decided. Henceforth, you will make use of my tub for a thorough scrubbing no less than once a week, more often if you like, and you will begin today. And that, dear boy, is an order. So I suggest you get busy if you're still missish in desiring privacy for such things. You will have until the dinner hour."

She opened her mouth to protest this new high-handedness of his, but the raising of that detestable golden brow reminded her that she didn't dare, not when he'd made it a blasted order.

"Yes, *sir*," she said, infusing the "sir" with as much contempt as she could manage without getting cuffed for it.

James frowned as he watched her stomp away, wondering if he hadn't just made a colossal mistake. He had thought he'd be doing her a favor by ordering her to take a bath, at the same time assuring her she'd have the privacy to do it. As closely as he kept tabs on her, he knew she hadn't had a decent one since she'd come aboard. But he also knew that most women, ladies in particular, cherished their baths. He was sure that Georgie was simply still too fearful of discovery to chance it; ergo, he would take the matter into his hands and force her to do what she would be most grateful for. What he had not expected was that she would get indignant about it, though if he had been thinking clearly, which he couldn't quite seem to manage lately, he would have.

You do not tell a lady she stinks, you bloody ass.

Chapter Twenty

Georgina's anger dissolved in the warm water the very moment she lay back in the long tub. It was heavenly, almost as good as her own tub at home. Hers conformed more to her size, but having the extra room was nice, really nice. The only thing she lacked were her scented oils and her maid to help rinse her long hair—and the confidence that she wouldn't be disturbed.

But the tub was long enough to submerge completely, hair and all. The chafed and deeply grooved skin around her breasts burned when the water first covered it, but even that was minor compared to the joy of being totally clean, totally unbound. If only the captain hadn't insisted . . .

Oh, devil take it, she was glad he had. It would have taken her at least another week to get up the nerve to do it on her own. And she'd been feeling very sticky lately from the salt air, the heat in the galley, not to mention how hot this cabin got every time the captain took off his clothes. A hurried sponge bath just wasn't enough.

But as much as she wanted to, she still couldn't linger in the tub. She had to be back in disguise before the dinner hour, hair dried and stuffed away, breasts flattened again. And there was always the possibility that the captain might actually need something from the cabin, and in that case, he wasn't likely to honor her privacy sign. The screen was there to hide her, but still, just the thought of being completely naked with him in the same room was enough to make her blush.

But he was true to his word and didn't come below until much later. By then she'd had her dinner, had his waiting for him, enough for two, though Conrad Sharpe didn't join him that evening. It wasn't until she left to fetch the water for his bath that she remembered that bottle of sweetwater he used. She decided she'd have a sniff of it the moment he stepped behind the screen, but as it happened, he sent her off for extra water tonight to wash and rinse his hair with, and by the time she got back with it, he was ready to have his back scrubbed.

Annoyed now, mostly with herself for having missed the opportunity to get to that bottle when he wasn't around, she made short work of washing his back. She would still have the few moments while he dried himself, and thinking of that rather than what she was doing helped to keep the nausea down, though she didn't even notice its absence this once.

Since she always kept his towels near enough for him to reach, she left him as soon as she sluiced the last bucket of water over his back, and headed straight for his highboy. But as her luck had been running lately, it wasn't surprising that he came around the screen while she was still standing there with the bottle in her hand. And the only reason she was caught was that she'd been so disappointed after taking a whiff of the cologne, she didn't put it away immediately. The scent was spicy, a little musky, but it didn't bring on her nausea as she'd been so sure it would. No, it *was* the captain who made her sick, not the smell of him.

"I hope you haven't disobeyed a direct order, George," his voice came at her sharply.

"Sir?"

"What d'you think you're doing with that bottle?"

She realized then what he was implying and quickly corked the bottle and put it back. "It's not what you think, Captain. I wasn't going to use it, even if there was a need to, which there isn't. I *did* bathe; I promise you I did. I'm not so foolish as to think I could mask an offensive smell with a little sweet scent from a bottle. I know some people do, but I'd rather be . . . that is, I wouldn't.'"

"Glad to know it, but that does not answer my question, lad."

"Oh, your question. I just wanted to—" *Sniff it, when he wears it all the time? He'll never buy that, Georgie. And what's wrong with the truth? After all, he wasn't a bit hesitant in telling you that he found your scent offensive.* "Actually, Captain—"

"Present yourself, George. I'll see for myself if you're telling the truth."

She gritted her teeth in exasperation. The blasted man wanted to *smell* her, and it wouldn't do a bit of good to protest. He'd just make it an order, and get annoyed himself because he had to. But he was only wearing that indecently thin robe. She was beginning to feel the heat already.

She came around the bed slowly. She was wringing her hands by the time she stood before him. And he made no pretense about it. He bent, stuck his nose by her neck, and sniffed. She might have gotten through it without incident if his cheek hadn't rubbed against hers.

"What the deuce are *you* groaning about?"

He said it as if he should be the one groaning. And he sounded quite put out. But she couldn't help it. She felt as if everything inside her was clamoring to get out. She stepped back quickly, far back, so she could breathe again. She couldn't meet his eyes.

"I'm sorry, Captain, but . . . there's no delicate way to put this. You make me ill."

She wouldn't have been surprised if he came forward and clobbered her, but he didn't move an inch. He simply said in the most indignant tone she'd ever heard from him, "I beg your pardon."

She would have preferred to be clouted than try to explain this. What had made her think she could tell him the truth, when the truth was so horribly embarrassing, for her, not him? Obviously, this was her problem. There was something wrong with her, since no one else got sick around him. And he might not even believe her, might think she was merely trying to get back at him for implying that she smelled bad, when she knew very well she didn't. In fact, he was more than likely going to think just that, and get mad. The devil take it, why hadn't she just kept her mouth shut?

But it was too late now, and quickly, before he decided to stomp all over her, she explained, "I'm not trying to insult you, Captain, I swear I'm not. I don't know what the problem is. I asked Mac, and he thought maybe your scent was doing it. That's what I was doing with your bottle, smelling it . . . but it's not that. I wish it was, but it's not. It could be only coincidence." She brightened with that thought, which just might save her neck, and even dared to glance up at him to expound on it. "Yes, I'm sure it's just a coincidence."

"What is?"

Thank God, he sounded calm, looked it, too. She'd been afraid he would be mottled with rage by now.

"That I only get sick when you're around, mostly when I get too near you." Best not to mention the times when just looking at him did it, or his looking at her. In fact, she'd be smart to end this subject and fast. "But it's my problem, sir. And I won't let it interfere with my duties. Please, just forget I mentioned it."

"Forget . . . ?"

He sounded as if he were choking. She squirmed, wishing she could drop through the floor. He wasn't calm as she'd thought. Maybe he was in shock over her audacity, or so angry that words failed him.

"What . . . kind . . . of sick?"

Worse and worse. He wanted details. Did he believe her, or was he hoping to prove she was just being spiteful so he could feel justified in clobbering her? And if she tried to pass it off as nothing now, he really would think she'd only been trying to get back at him, but was now regretting it.

She was indeed regretting opening her big mouth, but as long as she'd gone this far, she'd better stick with the truth.

But she braced herself before saying, "I'm sorry, Captain, but the closest comparison I can think of is nausea."

"Have you actually—?"

"No! It's just this real funny queasiness I feel, and shortness of breath, and I get so warm, well . . . actually hot, but I'm almost positive it's not fever. And this weakness comes over me, like my strength is just draining away."

James just stared, unable to believe what he was hearing. Didn't the wench know what she was describing? She couldn't be that innocent. And then it hit him, where it hurt the most, and he felt every one of her symptoms himself. *She wanted him.* His unorthodox seduction had worked and he hadn't even known it. And he hadn't known it because *she* didn't know it. Bloody hell. Ignorance was supposedly bliss, but in this case hers had caused him pure hell.

He had to rethink his strategy. If she didn't know what she was feeling, then she wouldn't be attacking him and begging him to take her, would she? So much for that splendid fantasy. But he still wanted her confession first. It would give him the upper hand in dealing with her if she didn't know he'd seen through her disguise.

"These symptoms, are they terribly unpleasant?" he asked carefully.

Georgina frowned. Unpleasant? They were frightening because she'd never experienced anything like it before, but unpleasant?

"Not terribly," she admitted.

"Well, I wouldn't worry about it any longer, George. I've heard of this problem before."

She blinked in surprise. "You have?"

"Most definitely. I also know the cure."

"You do?"

"Absolutely. So you may go on to bed, dear boy, and leave the matter to me. I'll take care of it . . . personally. You may depend upon it."

His grin was so wicked, she had the feeling he was funning with her. Maybe he hadn't believed her after all.

Chapter Twenty-one

"Are you asleep yet, George?"

She ought to be. She'd turned in more than an hour ago. But she was still wide awake. And she didn't have the captain's nakedness to blame for it tonight, for she'd kept her eyes firmly closed this time from the moment she climbed into her hammock. No, tonight it was just plain old curiosity keeping her awake, wondering if the captain really did know what was ailing her and if there really was a cure for it. If there was a cure, what could it possibly be? It was probably some vile concoction that would taste horrible. If it didn't, he would probably make sure it did.

"George?"

She considered feigning sleep, but why bother. A trip to the galley to fetch him something might tire her out, if that was what he wanted.

"Yes?"

"I can't sleep."

She rolled her eyes, already having figured that out. "Can I get you something?"

"No, I need something to soothe me. Perhaps if you read to me for a while. Yes, that ought to do it. Light a lamp, will you?"

As if she had any choice, she thought as she rolled out of her hammock. He'd warned her she might be called upon to do this. But she hadn't been sleeping, either, so it made no difference tonight. She knew why she wasn't sleeping, but she wondered what was keeping him awake.

She lit the lantern hanging by her bed and took it with her to the bookcase. "Is there anything in particular you'd like to hear, Captain?"

"There's a thin volume, bottom shelf, far right. That should do the trick. And pull up a chair. It's a quiet, soothing voice I need, not shouting across the room."

She paused, but only for a second. She really hated the idea of getting near his bed while he was in it. But she reminded herself that he was decently covered, nor did she have to look at him. He only wanted her to read, and maybe the book would be boring enough to put her to sleep, too.

She did as he'd instructed, dragging a chair over near the foot of his bed and setting the lantern on the dining table behind her.

"I believe there's a page marked," he said as she settled in the chair. "You may begin there."

She found the page, cleared her throat, and began to read. " 'There was nary a doubt that I had ever seen such big ones, round and ripe. My teeth ached to bite them.' " *God, what tripe. This would have them both asleep in minutes.* " 'I pinched one and heard her gasp of delight. The other beckoned my mouth, which was panting to oblige. Oh, heaven! Oh, sweet bliss, the taste of those succulent . . . breasts . . . ' "

Georgina slammed the book closed with a horrified gasp. "This . . . this—"

"Yes, I know. It's called erotica, dear boy. Don't tell me you've never read such garbage before? All boys your age do, those that can read, that is."

She knew she ought to be one of all those boys, but she was too embarrassed to care. "Well, I haven't."

"Are we being missish again, George? Well, read on, anyway. You'll find it educational, if nothing else."

It was times like this that she hated the pretense of her disguise the most. Georgina wanted to blister his ears about corrupting the morals of young boys, but Georgie would likely welcome the corruption.

"Do you actually like this—garbage, I believe you called it?"

"Good God, no. If I liked it, it wouldn't put me to sleep, now would it?"

That he sounded so appalled lessened some of her embarrassment.

But not even the threat of torture could get her to open that disgusting book again—at least not while he was around.

"If you don't mind, Captain, I'd rather find some other book to bore you with, something less . . . less . . ."

"Priggish as well as missish, are you?" A long sigh came from the bed. "I can see I'm not going to make a man of you in just a few weeks. Well, never mind, George. It's a bloody headache that's keeping me awake, anyway, but your fingers can take care of it just as well. Come and massage my temples, and I'll be asleep before you know it."

Massage, as in touching *and* getting closer? She didn't budge from her chair.

"I wouldn't know how—"

"'Course you wouldn't, not until I show you. So give us your hands."

She groaned inwardly. "Captain—"

"Damnation, George!" he cut in sharply. "Don't argue with a man who's in pain. Or do you mean for me to suffer all night?" When she still didn't move, he lowered his voice, though its tone was still brusque. "If it's that ailment you're worried about, lad, putting it from your mind will help. But whether it takes you or not, my malady takes precedence over yours just now."

He was right, of course. The captain was all-important, while she was just his lowly cabin boy. To try and put herself before him would come across as the actions of a spoiled, thoughtless child.

She changed positions slowly, sitting down very gingerly beside him on the bed.

Put it from your mind as he said, and whatever you do, don't look at him.

She kept her eyes trained on the arched columns in the headboard behind him, so she started when his fingers closed over hers and drew them to his face.

Pretend he's Mac. You'd do this willingly for Mac or any one of your brothers.

Her fingertips were pressed to his temples, then moved in very small circles.

"Relax, George. This isn't going to kill you."

That was going to be her own next thought, but Georgina wouldn't have put it quite as dryly as he did. What must he be thinking? *That you're afraid of him.* Well, she was, though she couldn't say exactly why anymore. Living so closely with him this week, she honestly didn't think he would hurt her, but . . . then what?

"You're on your own now, George. Just keep up the same motion."

The warmth of his hands holding hers was gone, but it made her notice the warmth of his skin beneath her fingertips. She was actually touching him. It wasn't so bad . . . until he moved slightly and his hair fell over the backs of her fingers. How soft his hair was, and cool. Such contrast. But there was more heat. She could feel it coming off his body near her hip. It made her realize he didn't have the thick, quilted cover drawn up, only the silk sheet, *the thin silk sheet* that would do no more than cling to him.

There was no reason for her to look, no reason at all. But what if he fell asleep? Was she supposed to just go on massaging when it was no longer necessary? But he'd snore once he was asleep. That would let her know. But she had yet to hear the man snore a single time. Maybe he never did. And maybe he was asleep already.

Look! Just do it and get it over with!

She did, and her instincts had been right . . . she shouldn't have. The man looked positively blissful, eyes closed, lips curved in a sensual smile, and so handsome it was sinful. He wasn't asleep. He was just enjoying her touch . . . Oh God! It came on her in waves, the heat, the weakness, a tempest set loose inside her. Her hands fell away from him. He caught them so quickly she gasped. And slowly he returned them, not to his temples, but to his cheeks.

She was cupping his cheeks, and staring into his eyes, piercing eyes, hot green, mesmerizing green. And then it happened, lips to lips, his to hers, covering, opening, flaming hot. She was sucked into the vortex, sinking, a whirlpool of sensation taking her deeper and deeper.

How much time passed she'd never know, but gradually Georgina became aware of what was happening. James Malory was kissing her with all the passion a man could put into a kiss, and she was kissing him back as if her very life depended on it. It felt as if it did, but it felt right.

Her nausea had returned worse than ever before, but it felt wonderful now, and right, too. Right? No, something wasn't right. He was kissing her . . . No, he was kissing Georgie!

She went hot, then cold with shock. She pushed away from him frantically, but he held her fast. She only managed to break the kiss, but that was enough.

"Captain! Stop! Are you mad? Let me—"

"Shut up, you darling girl. I can't play this game anymore."

"What game? You *are* mad! No, wait . . . !"

She was drawn over him, then under him, his weight pinning her down in the soft bed. For a moment she couldn't think again. The familiar nausea, not so familiar now, much too pleasant now, was spreading. And then it clicked. *You darling girl?*

"You know!" she gasped, shoving his shoulders back so she could see his face and accuse him properly. "You've known all along, haven't you?"

James was in the throes of the most powerful lust he had ever experienced in his life. But he still wasn't so far gone that he was going to make the mistake of 'fessing up to that one, not when it looked as if what promised to be a prime temper was gathering steam.

"I wish to bloody hell I had known," he growled low as he shoved the vest off her shoulders. "And I'll have an accounting from you later, you may depend upon it."

"Then how . . . ? Oh!"

She clung to him as his mouth seared her neck to her ear. When his tongue swirled about her earlobe, she shivered deliciously.

"They're not pointy at all, you little liar."

She heard his deep chuckle and felt an urge to smile in answer, and that surprised her. She should be apprehensive over her unmasking, but with his mouth on her, she wasn't. She should be stopping what he was doing, but with his mouth on her, she couldn't. She hadn't an ounce of strength or will to even try.

She did hold her breath when a single tug took away her cap and stocking both, spilling the dark mass of her hair out on the pillow and unmasking her in truth. The apprehension she felt now, however, was wholly female in nature, in hoping he wouldn't be disappointed with what he saw. And he was most thorough in his examination, and very still as he looked her over. When his green eyes finally met hers, they were blazing with intensity again.

"I ought to thrash you for hiding all this from me."

The words didn't frighten her. The way he was looking at her belied any serious intent toward thrashing. On the contrary. The meaning behind the words sent a pleasant thrill right down to her toes. The voracious kiss that followed sent the thrill rushing everywhere else.

It was quite some time before she could breathe again. Who needed to breathe? She didn't. And she still wasn't doing it right, was gasping really as those experienced lips moved around her face and neck. When her shirt was removed with such subtle finesse, she barely noticed. But she did notice the teeth at her breast bindings that started a tear his hands quickly ripped apart.

She hadn't been expecting that, but then everything that was happening was so far out of her experience, there was no hope of anticipating anything. Somewhere in the muddle of her mind was the thought that disrobing her was a consequence of her deceit, that he was doing it only to make absolutely sure there would be no more surprises for him. Then why all the kisses? But she couldn't hold on to that thought, not when he was staring at her breasts.

"Now this was a crime, love, what you did to these poor beauties."

The man could make her blush with a look, but his words . . . It was a wonder her skin tone wasn't permanently pink. It was a wonder, too, that she had any thoughts left, for no sooner had he made the remark than his tongue was tracing the red lines and grooves left from the bindings. And his hands, they had each covered a breast and were gently massaging, soothing, as if he were merely trying to offer commiseration for their long imprisonment. She would have done the same thing had she removed the tight bindings herself, so she didn't even think to suggest he not do that. And then his hand plumped up one breast to offer to his mouth, and she had no more thoughts for a while, just feelings.

Unlike Georgina's, all of James's faculties were working perfectly. They just weren't very manageable. But then it wasn't necessary to concentrate as he would with any other seduction, not with the darling girl cooperating so enthusiastically. In fact, he had to wonder who was seducing whom. Not that it made the least bit of difference at this point.

By God, she was exquisite, much more than he had supposed. The delicate features he had come to know were incredibly enhanced by the wealth of dark hair now framing her small face. And even in all his imaginings, he hadn't guessed how luscious her little body would be. There had been no indication that her breasts would be so bountiful, her waist so narrow. But he'd known all along that the cute little derriere that had so intrigued him in that tavern would be perfect in shape and resiliency, and he wasn't disappointed. He kissed each cheek as he bared it, and promised himself he'd devote more time to that adorable area later, but right now . . .

Georgina wasn't ignorant of lovemaking. She'd overheard her brothers too many times discussing such things in plain and sometimes crude terms not to have gathered a general idea about how it was done. But she hadn't associated that with what was happening to her—until now, when she felt his body with all of hers, skin to skin, heat feeding heat.

She didn't even wonder how or when he'd finished her disrobing. She realized she was now as naked as he, but she was feeling too many other things to be embarrassed. He was on top of her, pressing her down, surrounding her in a purely dominant way. Vaguely she thought she ought to be crushed, brick wall that he was, but she wasn't, not at all. His large hands were holding her face while he kissed her and kissed her, slowly, tenderly, then with scorching intensity. His tongue delved, tasted her, let her know the taste of him.

She didn't want any of this to stop, what he was doing, what she was feeling, and yet . . . shouldn't she stop it, at least make an effort to? To succumb knowingly, and she was reasonably certain now where this was leading, was to agree and accept. But did she? Really and truly?

How could she know for sure when she could barely put two thoughts together? Set her ten feet away from him, no, make that twenty, and she'd know. But right now, she liked the fact that there wasn't even an inch separating them. Oh, God, she must have succumbed already. She just didn't know it. No! She had to make an effort to be sure, for the sake of the conscience that was going to ask "What happened?" tomorrow.

"Captain?" she got out between kisses.

"Hmmm?"

"You're making love to me?"

"Oh, yes, my darling girl."

"Do you really think you should?"

"Absolutely. It's the cure, after all, for what's been ailing you."

"You can't be serious."

"But I am. Your nausea, dear girl, was nothing more than a healthy desire . . . for me."

She wanted him? But she didn't even like him. Yet that would explain perfectly why she was enjoying this so much. Obviously, one didn't have to like the object of one's passion. And she had her answer. Talking, concentrating, getting her mind off what she was feeling, if only for a minute, hadn't made any of it go away. It was all still there and wildly exciting. Yes, she wanted him, at least this one time.

You have my permission to proceed, Captain.

She didn't say it aloud, for he would only be amused, and she didn't want to amuse him just now. The thought had been for her conscience anyway. She communicated the same thing, however, subtly, by wrapping her arms around him. And he took the hint, quite swiftly, in fact.

Exciting? Not nearly explicit enough. He settled between her legs, and everything inside her seemed to roll over to make room for him. His lips returned to hers, then moved down her neck, down to her breasts. He raised himself. She regretted that. She liked his weight. But there was compensation, more pressure below, and, God, the heat there. And she could feel him, thick and hard, pressing into the heat, so tight, filling her, thrilling her. She knew his body, knew just what was entering hers. She wasn't afraid . . . but then, no one had ever told her it would be painful.

She gasped, mostly in surprise, but there was no denying it. That had hurt.

"Captain, did I mention that I've never done this before?"

His weight had returned to her, had more or less collapsed on her. His face was turned toward her neck, his lips hot on her skin there.

"I believe I've just discovered that on my own," she just barely heard him say. "And I think it would be permissible for you to call me James now."

"I'll consider it, but would you mind terribly if I asked you to stop now?"

"Yes."

Was he laughing? His body was certainly shaking.

"Was I too polite?" she wanted to know.

There was no doubt that he was laughing now, loudly and clearly. "I'm sorry, love, I swear I am, but . . . Good God, the shock. You weren't supposed to be . . . that is, you were too passionate . . . Oh, bloody hell."

"Stuttering, Captain?"

"So it seems." He raised up to lightly brush his lips across hers before he grinned down at her. "My dear, there's no need to stop now, even if I could. But the damage is done, and your virgin's pain is over." He moved in her to prove it, and her eyes flared, for the movement was nothing but sensually pleasant. "So do you still want me to stop?"

This is for you, conscience. "No."

"Thank God!"

His obvious relief made her smile. The kiss he treated her to then made her groan. Accompanied by the slow movement of his hips, the sensations built again gradually, but escalated and surpassed anything she'd felt before, until the crowning glory was upon her, exploding in tiny shocks that left her dazed. She'd cried out, but the sound had gone from her mouth to his, and as his own climax was reached, was given right back to her.

Still dazed, Georgina was having difficulty believing she'd felt what she did, that anything could feel like that. But she held fast to the man who had shown her what her body was capable of. Feelings of gratitude and tenderness mixed with something else that made her want to thank him, kiss him, tell him how magnificent he'd been, how euphoric she felt now. She didn't, of course. She just continued to hold him, occasionally she caressed him, finally she kissed his shoulder so softly, he couldn't possibly have noticed.

But he did notice. James Malory, connoisseur of women, jaded aristocrat, was in such a state of heightened awareness, he felt each and every little movement the girl made, and was touched by her tenderness more than he cared to admit. He'd never felt anything like it, and it was bloody well frightening.

Chapter Twenty-two

"I understand now why people do this sort of thing."

James sighed in relief. That was just what he needed to hear, some silly bit of nonsense to put things in their proper perspective. She was just a wench, albeit a prime piece. But she was no different from any other woman he'd set out to seduce. With the challenge gone, there was nothing left to hold his interest. So why didn't he get off her and send her back to her own bed? Because he bloody well didn't want to yet.

He rose up to his elbows to gaze down at her. Her skin was still flushed, her lips appeared well-ravaged. With his finger he gently tried to sooth them. And there was a soft look in her velvety-brown eyes that for some reason delighted him. It certainly wasn't a look he was accustomed to from her. Usually her eyes expressed her nervousness, or frustration, or outright irritation, so amusing in her lad's disguise . . . By God, he'd forgotten about that, her masquerade, her reasons for it. There was still the mystery of her to hold his interest, wasn't there?

"This sort of thing, George?"

The fact that his brow went up told her more plainly than words that she'd amused him. Well, so what? The mannerism wasn't quite so annoying just now, either. "That wasn't very romantic sounding, was it?" she inquired softly, feeling incredibly shy all of a sudden.

"Not very loverlike, either, but I didn't miss the point, dear girl. You enjoyed yourself, did you?"

She couldn't quite manage to say the word, so she nodded, then felt a delicious thrill at the smile he bestowed on her. "Did you?" *Georgie! Are you mad to ask him that?* "I mean—"

He threw back his head in laughter, rolled to the side, but brought her with him. She was now looking down at him, a bit more in control in this new position, until he opened his legs and she slid between them.

"What am I going to do with you, George?"

He was still laughing, and hugging her to him. She didn't really mind his amusement, except, as usual, she'd missed the joke.

"You could stop calling me George, to begin with."

As soon as she said it, she wished she hadn't. She went very still, hoping she hadn't brought her deception to mind with that remark. But he became just as still. The smile was still there, but the change in him was almost palpable. The sardonic autocrat was back.

"And what, pray tell, should I call you? By your true name perhaps?"

"Georgie is my true name."

"Try again, sweet, and this time make me believe you." No answer. In fact, her expression became quite mulish. "Ah, so I'm going to have to drag it out of you, am I? Shall I bring on the instruments of the Inquisition, whips and racks and all that?"

"That isn't funny," she retorted.

"I daresay you wouldn't think so, but I might find it entertaining . . . No, don't squirm, love. It feels delightful, but I'm in the mood for explanations just now. And why don't we begin with the reason for your charade."

She sighed and laid her head on his chest. "I had to leave England."

"Were you in trouble?"

"No, I just couldn't stand it there another day."

"Then why didn't you leave in the customary fashion, by purchasing passage?"

"Because the only ships crossing the Atlantic were English."

"I imagine that's supposed to make sense. Give me a moment and I might figure it out . . . then again, I might not. What the deuce is wrong with English ships?"

She leaned up to frown at him. "*You* wouldn't find anything wrong with them, but *I* happen to despise all things English."

"Do you indeed? And am I included in that package?"

When his brow went up this time, she had the greatest urge to yank it back down. "You were. I haven't made up my mind whether you still are."

He grinned, then chuckled. "I'm beginning to see the light,

George. You wouldn't happen to be one of those hotheaded Americans, would you? That would certainly account for the accent I haven't been able to place."

"And what if I am?" she demanded defensively.

"Why, I'd consider locking you up, of course. Safest place for people who like to start wars so much."

"*We* didn't start—"

He kissed her silent. Then, holding her head in both hands, he kissed her thoroughly, until she was breathless enough for him to announce, "I'm not going to argue dead issues with you, dear girl. So you're an American. I can forgive you for that."

"Why you—"

What works is worth repeating, James had always found, so he silenced her with another kiss, and kept this one up until she was quite dazed. By then he was aroused himself, and sorry he'd teased her.

"I don't give a bloody damn what nationality you are," he said against her lips. "I wasn't involved in that ridiculous war, didn't support it or the policies that led to it. I was, in fact, living in the West Indies at the time."

"You're still English," she said, but with very little heat now.

"Quite true. But we're not going to let that matter, are we, love?"

Because he asked while he was nibbling on her lips, she couldn't think of a single reason that it should matter. She gave him a whispered no, and began some nibbling of her own. She'd felt the change in his body when it occurred, and had an idea now what it meant. And in the back of her mind came the thought that the questioning might end if they made love again. Of course, the fact that those marvelous feelings were stirring inside her again had nothing to do with it.

But a while later, after the bedsheets were a bit more rumpled and she was once again rolled on top of him, though only partially this time, he said, "Now, shall we discuss how I felt upon discovering that you're a wench rather than the lad I took under my wing? My mortification in recalling the times you'd assisted me at my bath, the times that I . . . disrobed in your presence?"

With it put that way, Georgina felt absolutely terrible. Her deception alone was bad enough, but much worse was allowing the captain to put himself unknowingly into positions that he now found embarrassing. She should have confessed the truth that very first day when he called her into the area of his bath. Instead, she had foolishly thought she could make it through the whole voyage without being found out.

He had every right to be furious with her, and so it was with a good deal of hesitancy that she asked, "Are you very angry?"

"Not very, not anymore. I'd say I've been adequately compensated for all embarrassments. In fact, you've just paid for your passage and anything else you'd like."

Georgina drew in her breath sharply in disbelief. How could he say something like that after the intimacy they'd just shared? *Easily, you ninny. He's an Englishman, isn't he; an arrogant, blasted lord? And what did he call you? A wench, which says plain enough how lowly he thinks you.*

She sat up slowly. By the time she looked down at him, her features set in lines of fury, there wasn't a single doubt in James's mind that she felt insulted.

"You could have waited until morning before you got nasty again, you son of a bitch."

"I beg your pardon?"

"As well you should!"

James reached for her, but she bounded off the bed. He tried to explain, "I didn't mean that the way it sounded, George."

She whirled around to glare down at him. "Don't call me that!"

He was beginning to see the absurdity in what was happening, which kept his voice calm as he pointed out. "Well, you haven't given me your name yet, you know."

"It's Georgina."

"Good Lord, you've my utter sympathy. I'll stick with George, thank you."

Was that supposed to coax a smile from her? With the expression of feigned horror that accompanied it, it almost did. But not quite. That crack about having paid for her passage hurt.

"I'm going to bed, Captain. *My* bed," she said with stiff hauteur, and she pulled it off superbly, even standing there naked. "I would appreciate it if you would arrange other quarters for me in the morning."

"So we're seeing the true George at last, are we, complete with a formidable temper?"

"Go to the devil," she mumbled as she came around the bed, swiping up her clothes as she went.

"All this huffiness, and all I did was pay you a compliment . . . in my fashion."

"Well, your *fashion* stinks," she said, then added as an afterthought that was laced with contempt, "sir."

James sighed, but after a moment, as he watched her march across the room, her dark brown hair swishing about that cute little backside of hers, he was grinning, almost laughing. What a delightful surprise she was turning out to be.

"However did you manage a full week of meekness, George?"

"By biting holes in my tongue, how else!" she called back at him.

He did laugh this time, but softly, so she wouldn't hear. He turned on his side to watch her antics as she threw her clothes down in her corner in a demonstration of feminine pique. But almost immediately she realized what she'd done and retrieved her shirt to put on. That done, she started to get into her hammock, but hesitated, and after a moment, retrieved her breeches and yanked them on, too. Apparently satisfied that she was properly covered for the moment, she rolled into her hammock. Her ease with which she did so, however, recalled to James's mind that she'd never really had any difficulty with that precarious bed.

"You've sailed before, haven't you, George, in addition to your jaunt to England?"

"I think I have proven, quite adequately, as you put it, that I'm not a George."

"So humor me, dear girl. I rather like you as a George. And you have sailed—"

"Certainly," she cut in, then turned over to face the wall, hoping he'd take the hint. But she couldn't resist adding, "I own my own ship, after all."

"Of course you do, dear girl," he humored her.

"I really do, Captain."

"Oh, I believe you, indeed I do. So what took you to England, hating it as you do?"

She was still gritting her teeth over being humored. "*That* is none of your business."

"I'll get it out of you eventually, George, so you might as well tell me now."

"Good *night,* Captain. On second thought, I hope your headache returns . . . if you even had one, which I'm beginning to doubt."

She heard his laughter this time. He simply couldn't prevent it when it occurred to him that her display of temper tonight would be as nothing in comparison to how she would feel if she ever learned that he'd known she was a female from the start. The next time he got bored, he might just tell her, merely to see what would happen.

Chapter Twenty-three

James stood next to the hammock a long while the next morning, watching the girl sleep. The moment he had awakened, he had regretted not bringing her back to his bed last night. A man of strong drives, he very frequently woke in an amorous mood, and any female found snuggling at his side was treated to more of what she experienced in the night.

It was for that reason, several days ago, that he'd been so sharp with Georgina for being up and about before him, for he then had no excuse not to have her dress him, as was her supposed duty. He'd had one hell of a difficult time getting his body under control at first, but somehow he'd managed.

He smiled at the thought that that problem would no longer be a problem. He no longer had to hide the fact that he found the wench extremely desirable. Yes, he most definitely regretted his decision last night to give up sleeping beside that soft little body, to allow her her one night of pique. There'd be no more of that. Tonight she'd share his bed again, and stay there.

"Show a leg, George." He kneed her hammock, setting it aswing. "I've decided not to announce to our little world at sea that you're other than you've been appearing to be. So get those lovely breasts tucked away again, and go fetch my breakfast."

She merely stared at him, eyes only partly open. She yawned, blinked up at him, then came fully awake with a widening of those velvety-brown eyes.

"I'm still to act as your cabin boy?" she asked him incredulously.

"Excellent conclusion, George," James replied in his most obnoxious dry voice.

"But . . ."

She paused as the idea of going on as she had been really set in. She wouldn't have to tell Mac, then, that she'd been discovered. She wouldn't have to explain what had happened—as if she could. Even she wasn't sure what had happened, but she was positively sure she didn't want anyone else to know about it.

"Very well, Captain, but I want my own quarters."

"Out of the question." He held up his hand when she started to argue. "You've been sleeping in here for a week, dear girl. To move now will give rise to entirely too much speculation. Besides, there are no other quarters, as you well know. And don't think to mention the fo'c'sle, because I'd put you under lock and key before I'd allow you to return there."

She frowned at him. "But what difference can it make, if I'm still thought to be a boy?"

"I deduced the truth easily enough."

"Because of that silly confession of mine that was so embarrassingly naive," she said with half-disgust.

The smile he gave her then was one of the tenderest she'd ever seen. It made her catch her breath, it was so heartwarming.

"I thought that confession of yours was rather sweet, my darling girl." The back of his fingers brushed her cheek. "You wouldn't happen to be feeling, ah . . . nauseous now, would you?"

His touch had a powerful effect on her. Well, that smile had really done it. But she wasn't going to make another mistake like the one she'd made last night, to leave herself wide open for his derision again. Besides, what had happened last night couldn't happen again. This man was not for her, even if he did make her pulses race and her insides quiver. He was an Englishman, for God's sake, and worse, a despised aristocrat. Hadn't his country just put hers through four years of hell? And even before the war, her brothers had been railing against England's high-handedness. That couldn't be ignored, no matter how much she might wish it could be. Why, her brothers wouldn't even let the man in the house! No, James Malory, lord of the realm, was definitely not for her. She had to keep that in mind at all times from now on, and make sure he knew it, even if she had to lie through her teeth.

"No, Captain, I'm not feeling a bit *nauseous*. You promised a cure and it apparently worked, for which I thank you. I won't need any more doses."

That he was still smiling told her he wasn't buying her attempt to put him off even a little. "A pity," was all he said, but that was enough to make her blush.

"About those quarters . . . ?" she prompted as she crawled out of the hammock and put a little distance between them.

"No longer under discussion, George. You'll stay here and that's the end of it."

Her mouth opened to argue again, but she closed it just as quickly. She could give ground on that, as long as he understood she wasn't his to command in *every* way. Actually, if she couldn't have a room to herself, then his cabin was preferable to any other quarters. At least here she would be able to remove her bindings and sleep more comfortably for the duration of the voyage.

"Very well, as long as the sleeping arrangements remain the same." That was putting it plainly enough. "And I don't think I should be scrubbing your back anymore . . . sir."

James almost laughed. How prim the little wench was sounding this morning, and entirely too demanding. He wondered again what kind of life she led when she wasn't sporting breeches. He supposed he had to rule out dockside doxy after last night.

"Need I remind you, George, that you're the only cabin boy I've got. You put yourself in that position, so you'll stay in it until I tell you otherwise. Or have you also forgotten that I'm captain around here?"

"And you intend to be difficult, I see."

"Not at all. I'm merely pointing out that you yourself give me no choice but to insist. But you aren't by any chance thinking I mean to take advantage of you just because you were so accommodating last night?"

She eyed him narrowly, but his expression gave away nothing. Finally she sighed. Until he gave some indication that he might force his attentions on her, she really had no choice but to be fair and assume the man wouldn't bother her unless invited to do so.

"Very well, we'll go on as we did before . . . before last night, that is." With the concession, she even offered him a tentative smile. "And now I'll dress more thoroughly, as you suggested, sir, then fetch your breakfast."

He watched her scoop up the rest of her clothing from the floor and head for the concealment of the leather screen. He had to bite his tongue to keep from making some comment about her modesty after she'd marched gloriously naked across the room last night.

He remarked instead, "You don't have to keep sirring me, you know."

She paused to glance back at him. "Sorry. It just seems appropriate. After all, you're old enough to be my father, and I've always given my elders a measure of respect."

He looked for the twitch of her lips, the triumph in her eyes, anything to show that she was deliberately trying to insult him. And it was a direct hit. Not only did he feel indignant, but his pride and vanity were also seriously wounded. But there was nothing in her expression. If anything, she looked as if the comment had been entirely casual, even automatic, without any forethought at all.

James gritted his teeth. For once, his golden brows didn't move even a miniscule amount. "Your father? I'll have you know, dear girl, that that is an impossibility. I may have a seventeen-year-old son, but—"

"You have a son?" She turned about fully. "Have you a wife, too?"

He hesitated in answering, only because she surprised him with her crestfallen look. Could it be disappointment? But she recovered during his hesitation.

"*Seventeen?*" she practically shouted, sounding totally incredulous, then added quite triumphantly, "I rest my case," and marched on toward the screen.

James, for once at a loss for a proper rejoinder, turned and left the cabin before he gave in to the urge to throttle the saucy chit. *Rest my case, indeed*. He was bloody well in his prime. How dare the wench call him old?

In the cabin, behind the screen, Georgina was smiling—for all of five minutes. And then her conscience began to prick her.

You shouldn't have attacked his self-esteem, Georgie. Now he's mad.

What do you care? You don't like him any more than I do. Besides, he deserved it. He was entirely too smug.

With reason. Before he reverted to form last night, you thought he was the greatest thing God had ever put breath in.

I knew it! You just couldn't wait to gloat because you think I made a colossal mistake. So what if I did? It's my life to make mistakes with, and I'm not denying it. I gave him my permission.

He didn't need it. He'd have taken you with or without it.

If that's the case, what could I have actually done about it one way or the other?

You were too complaisant.

I didn't hear you complaining very much last night . . . Oh, God, I'm talking to myself.

Chapter Twenty-four

"Brandy, George?"

Georgina started. He'd been so quiet, sitting there at his desk, that she'd almost forgotten James was in the room. Almost, but not quite. He was not, in any way, shape, or form, a man who could be easily ignored.

"No, thank you, Captain." She cast him a saucy smile. "Never touch the stuff."

"Too young to drink, are you?"

She stiffened. It wasn't the first time he'd made a remark that implied she was a child, or childish in her thoughts, or too young to know better, and this after he knew very well she was a woman full-grown. And she knew very well he was only doing it to get back at her for implying he was too old for her. But she hadn't let him rile her, not yet anyway. He had been, after all, quite courteous to her otherwise, coldly courteous actually, telling her plainly just how offended he really was by her remarks about his age.

Three days had gone by since that fateful night of her discovery, and although he had said that they would go on exactly as before, he hadn't asked for her assistance at his bath, didn't flaunt his nakedness before her anymore, and even wore his pants under his robe before he retired, as he was doing now. Nor had he touched her again since that morning he tenderly brushed her cheek with his fingers. Deep down, where she was honest with herself to a fault, she admitted a certain regret that he wasn't even going to try to make love to her again. Not that she would let him, but he could at least have made an effort.

She'd finished her chores early tonight. She'd been lying in her hammock, gently rocking, and biting her nails short so they more resembled a boy's. She was prepared to sleep, with everything removed except her breeches and shirt, but she wasn't the least bit tired.

Now she glanced sideways toward the desk and the man behind it. She wouldn't half mind an argument to clear the air, an opportunity for him to get his resentment off his chest. On the other hand, she wasn't sure she wanted the other James back, the one that could melt her with a look. Better to let him nurse his chagrin for the remainder of the voyage.

"Actually, Captain," she said in answer to his caustic remark, "it's a matter of preference. I never acquired a taste for brandy. Port, on the other hand—"

"Just how old are you, brat?"

So he'd finally asked, and quite irritably at that. She'd wondered how long he would resist. "Twenty-two."

He snorted. "I would have thought anyone as lippy as you to be at least twenty-six."

Oh, my, so *he* was looking for an argument, was he? She grinned suddenly, mischievously deciding not to oblige him.

"Do you think so, James?" she asked sweetly. "I'll take that as a compliment. I've always despaired that I look too young for my age."

"As I said, too bloody lippy."

"My, but you're grouchy this evening." She was just short of laughing. "I wonder why."

"Not at all," he demurred cooly as he opened a drawer on his desk. "And as luck would have it, I just happen to have your preference here, so pull up a chair and join me."

She hadn't anticipated that. She sat up slowly, wondering how she could refuse gracefully, even as she watched him tip the bottle of port to half fill an extra glass, which had also been concealed in the drawer. But then she shrugged, deciding a half glass wouldn't hurt and might even relax her enough to let her get to sleep. She confiscated his chair from the dining table and dragged the heavy thing over to his desk. She accepted the glass from him before she sat down, careful not to get trapped by those brooding green eyes or touch his fingers as she did.

Casually, still grinning, she lifted her glass to him before she took a sip. "This is very sociable of you, James, I must say." The use of his name now, when she hadn't used it before, was annoying him as she had figured it would. "Especially," she continued, "since I've had the impression that you're angry with me for some reason."

"Angry? With such a charming brat? Whyever would you think so?"

She almost choked on the sweet red wine, hearing that. "The fire in your eyes?" she offered cheekily.

"Passion, dear girl. Pure . . . unadulterated . . . passion."

Her heart did a double pound as she went very still. Against her better judgment, her eyes rose to his, and there it was, the very passion he just bespoke, hot, mesmerizing, and so sensual it went right to the core of her. Was she a puddle on the floor yet? Good Lord, if not, she ought to be.

She downed the remainder of her port and this time choked on it for real, which was fortunate, since doing so broke the spell for a moment, long enough for her to say sensibly, "I was right. Passionate enragement if I ever saw it."

His lips turned up the slightest bit. "You're in top form, brat. No—no, don't run away," he added quite firmly when she put her glass down and started to rise. "We haven't ascertained yet the cause of my . . . passionate enragement. I like that, indeed I do. I must remember to use it on Jason the next time he flies through the roof."

"Jason?" Anything to make him let go of this pulse-disturbing subject.

"A brother." He shrugged. "One of many. But let's not digress here, sweet."

"No, let's do. I'm really very tired," she said, frowning as she watched him tip the bottle to her glass again.

"Coward."

He said it with amusement tinging his tone, but she still stiffened at such an outright challenge. "Very well." She swiped up the refilled glass, nearly spilling it since it was more than half full this time, and sat back in her chair to take a fortifying gulp. "What would you like to discuss?"

"My passionate enragement, of course. Now, why, I wonder, would you think of rage when I mention passion?"

"Because . . . because . . . oh, devil take it, Malory, you know very well you've been annoyed with me."

"I don't know anything of the kind." He was really smiling now, like a cat moving in for the kill. "Perhaps you'll tell me why I should be annoyed with you?"

Admitting she had struck at his pride would be admitting she had done it deliberately. "I haven't the faintest notion," she insisted, eyes as innocently wide as she could make them.

"Haven't you?" The golden brow arched, and she realized she'd missed that affectation of his these last few days. "Come here, George."

Her eyes widened. "Oh, no," she said, shaking her head emphatically.

"I'm merely going to prove that I'm not the least bit enraged with you."

"I will accept your word on it, I assure you."

"George—"

"No!"

"Then I'll come to you."

She leaped up and ludicrously held out her glass as if it might ward him off. "Captain, I must protest."

"So must I," he said on his way around the desk, while she started around the other side to keep it between them. "Don't you trust me, George?"

This was no time to be diplomatic. "No."

His chuckle kept her from elaborating. "Smart girl. They do tell me, after all, that I'm a most reprehensible rake, but I prefer Regan's more discerning 'connoisseur of women.' It has a much nicer ring to it, don't you think?"

"I think you're drunk."

"My brother would take exception to that word."

"Blast your brother and you, too!" she snapped. "This is absurd, Captain."

She stopped moving around the desk only when he did. She'd kept her glass in hand and somehow managed not to spill a drop. She set it down now and glared at him. He looked back with a grin.

"I quite agree, George. You're not really going to make me chase you around this thing, are you? This is the sport of doddering old fools and parlormaids."

"If the shoe fits," she retorted automatically, then gasped, realizing her mistake.

All traces of humor left him. "I'll make you eat the bloody shoe this time," he growled low just before he leaped over the desk.

Georgina was too stunned to flee, but she wouldn't have gotten far in the mere seconds it took James to land in front of her. The next thing she knew, those big, muscular arms were wrapping around her, gathering her in to press close, closer, until she could feel every inch of his hard frame along hers. She should have been stiff, outraged, at least flattened. Instead her body seemed to sigh into his, yielding where it shouldn't, fitting so perfectly it felt like home.

Her mind, working under delayed reaction, began gathering wits to protest, but too late. She fell victim to a leisurely kiss so enticingly sweet and sensual, it wrapped her in a spell of wonder impossible to break. It went on and on, working on her in degrees, until she couldn't say exactly when contentment turned to burgeoning desire.

He was nibbling gently at her lips when she knew for certain she didn't want to be let go. Her hands twisting in his thick mane of hair told him. Her body pressing for closer contact told him. Finally she told him in the soft whisper of his name, which got her that heartwarming smile of his that could turn her to mush.

"Has prim little George actually retired for the night?" he inquired huskily.

"He's fast asleep."

"And here I thought I was losing my touch . . . in my old age."

"Ouch." She winced, to give him his due.

"Sorry, love," he said, but he was grinning unrepentently just the same.

"That's quite all right. I'm used to men who simply can't resist a little gloating."

"In that case, does it taste good?"

"What?"

"The shoe."

The man was a veritable devil, to be able to make her laugh when all she wanted to do was crawl into him. "Not especially. But you do."

"What?"

Her tongue came out to lick sensually at his lower lip. "Taste good."

Georgina's breath choked off, he squeezed her so tightly. "Remarks like that will get you an apology and anything else you want."

"And if all I want is you?"

"My darling girl, that goes without question," he assured her as he swept her into his arms to carry her to his bed.

Georgina held on tight, despite feeling weightless in his strong arms. She simply wanted the closer contact and was reluctant to let go even long enough to allow him to remove their clothes. Had she really thought she could ignore the things this man had made her feel before, the same things she was feeling now? She'd tried to these last days, she really had. His anger had made it easier to do so. But he wasn't angry anymore, and she was tired of trying to resist something as powerful as this. God, the feelings . . .

She gasped at the heat that seared her skin as his mouth settled over one of her breasts. And she was squirming before he finished with the other. She wanted him right now, but he was taking his time with her, turning her over, driving her crazy in his devotion to every inch of her, in particular the firm globes of her derriere, which he kneaded, kissed, and nipped until she thought she was going up in flames. When he finally rolled her back over, it was the finger that moved into her that was her undoing. She cried out, and his mouth came back to hers to accept this accolade to his skill. And when he entered her moments later, and treated her to a further demonstration of his experience, each thrust different, somehow more pleasurable than the one before, each with the power to draw forth another gasp if he weren't still kissing her. Connoisseur of women? Thank God.

A short while later, Georgina found herself stretched out on one side of the bed, with James on the other side, and a sturdy chessboard between them. Whatever had possessed her to answer yes when he asked if she played the game? But now that it was started, the challenge had her wide awake, and the promise that she could spend the morning in bed kept the play at an unhurried pace. Also, the prospect of beating James Malory had been too tempting to resist and still was, particularly since she suspected he was trying to destroy her concentration by keeping a conversation going while they played. He'd find that wouldn't work, since she'd been taught the game with her whole family present, and her family was never quiet when they were in the same room together.

"Very good, George," James said as she captured a pawn, opening a path to his bishop and leaving him nothing of hers to take, and his own bishop to protect.

"Well, you didn't think this would be easy, did you?"

"I'd hoped not. So good of you not to disappoint me." He moved his queen over a space to protect his bishop, a wasted move, and they both knew it. "Now, who did you say MacDonell is to you?"

She almost laughed at the way he'd slipped that in, probably hoping she'd answer without thinking about it. She had to give him points for cleverness, but it wasn't necessary. There was no longer a need to pretend Mac was her brother.

"I didn't say. Are you asking?"

"Well, we have established he's not your brother."

"Oh? When did we establish that?"

"Damnation, George, he's not, is he?"

She made him wait while she made her next move, which put his queen in jeopardy. "No, he's not. Mac is just a very good friend of the family, sort of like a beloved uncle, actually. He's always been around, and he sort of thinks of me as the daughter he never had. Your move, James."

"Quite so."

Instead of blocking her last move to protect his queen, he captured one of her pawns with his knight, a move that put her own queen in danger. And since neither of them was ready to lose a queen yet, Georgina retreated for the moment, giving James the advantage of attack. He wasn't expecting that, and so had to take a moment to study the board.

She decided two could use his strategy of distraction. "Why the interest in Mac all of a sudden? Have you spoken with him?"

" 'Course I have, love. He is my bo's'n, after all."

Georgina went very still. It might not matter that he knew Mac wasn't her brother, but she still didn't want him recognizing Mac and remembering their first meeting in a tavern. That would lead to a whole set of questions that she didn't care to answer—in particular, what she was doing there. And besides, James might get angry at what he could very well see as a double deceit, not just her disguise, but the fact that she'd met him before.

"And?" she asked carefully.

"And what, George?"

"Devil take it, James, did you rec— Ah, that is, did you say anything to him about us?"

"Us?"

"You know *exactly* what I mean, James Malory, and if you don't answer me this minute, I'll—I'll bash you with this chessboard!"

He burst into laughter. "Gad, I adore this temper of yours, sweet, indeed I do. Such spit and fire in such a little package." He reached across the board to tweak her hair. "'Course I didn't mention us to your friend. We spoke of the ship, nothing personal."

And he would have said something if he'd recognized Mac, wouldn't he? Mac would have, too. Georgina relaxed with that conclusion.

"You should have let me bash you with the board," she said now, her humor returned. "You're losing, after all."

"The devil I am." He snorted. "I'll have your king in three more moves.

Four moves later, James found himself on the defensive, so he tried distraction again and tried to appease his curiosity at the same time. "Why are you going to Jamaica?"

Georgina grinned cheekily. "Because you are."

Up went the single brow, just as she expected it would for such an answer. "Dare I be flattered?"

"No. Yours was just the first ship heading to this side of the world, one that wasn't English, that is, and I was too impatient to wait for another. Had I known *you* were English—"

"We're not going to start *that* again, are we?"

"No." She laughed. "And what about you? Are you returning to Jamaica, or just visiting?"

"Both. It was my home for a long time, but I've decided to return to England for good, so I need to settle my affairs in Jamaica."

"Oh," she said, aware of the disappointment his answer brought her, but she hoped he didn't detect it.

She shouldn't have assumed he'd be staying in Jamaica just because Mac had said the vessel was out of the West Indies. Jamaica, at least, had been an acceptable place she could come back to. England she never wanted to see again. Of course, this voyage wasn't over, and yet— Georgina shook herself mentally. What was she thinking? That there might be a future for her with this man? She knew how impossible that was, that her family would never accept him. And she wasn't even sure what *she* felt for him, other than passion.

"So you won't be in the islands long?" she concluded.

"Not long a'tall. The chap on a neighboring plantation there has been after me to sell him mine for some time. I likely could have handled the matter through correspondence."

Then they'd never have met a second time, she thought. "I'm glad you decided to see to it personally."

"So am I, dear girl. And your own destination?"

"Home, of course. New England."

"Not immediately, I hope."

She shrugged, leaving him to draw his own conclusion. It depended on him, but she wasn't brazen enough to say so. Actually, it also depended on how soon a Skylark vessel would be in port, but there was no reason to tell him that. That was something she didn't want to think about yet. And to get his own mind off it, she put him in checkmate.

"Bloody hell," he said, looking at what she'd just done. "Very clever, George, to distract me into losing."

"Me!? With you asking all the questions? I like that," she huffed. "Just like a man to find excuses for getting beat by a woman."

He chuckled and lifted her across to his side of the bed. "I said nothing about questions, you darling girl. It's this luscious body of yours that's been the distraction, for which I don't mind losing a'tall."

"I'm wearing my shirt," she protested.

"But nothing else."

"You should talk, with this skimpy robe," she said, fingering the silky material.

"Was it distracting?"

"I refuse to answer that."

He feigned amazement. "By God, don't tell me you're finally at a loss for words. I was beginning to think I was losing my touch."

"To render people speechless with your drollery?"

"Quite so. And as long as I've got you speechless, love . . ."

She meant to tell him that he wasn't as merciless with his wit as he liked to think, at least not all the time, but she got distracted again.

Chapter Twenty-five

It was difficult to keep up the pretense of being Georgie MacDonell, cabin boy, when Georgina was with James outside of his cabin. And more and more as the days passed and they neared the West Indies, he wanted her with him on deck, by his side, or just nearby where he could keep an eye on her. What was most difficult, she'd found, was keeping what she was feeling out of her expression, and especially out of her eyes, which would fill either with tenderness or passion whenever she looked at James.

Yes, it was difficult, but she was managing, at least she thought she was managing. She had to wonder sometimes, though, if some of his crew didn't know or suspect, when they'd smile or nod at her in passing, or give her a good-day greeting, these men who had previously barely noticed her. Even the cantankerous Artie, and the grouchy Frenchman, Henry, were more courteous to her now. Of course, time breeds familiarity, and she'd been on the ship almost a month now. That the crew should have gotten used to her in that amount of time was to be expected, she supposed. And the only reason she was hoping that her pretense was still working was for Mac's sake . . . well, actually for her own sake, since she knew exactly what kind of reaction she'd get from him if he knew she'd accepted James Malory as her lover. He'd fly through the roof, as James would say, and with reason. She still sometimes doubted that it was true herself.

But it was true. James was her lover now, in every sense of the word except one—he didn't actually love her. But he did want her. There was no doubt of that. And she did want him. She hadn't even tried to deny it again after that second time she'd succumbed to his gentle persuasion. She'd told herself in plain terms that a man like this only happened once in a girl's lifetime, if even that. So why, for God's sake, couldn't she enjoy him while she had this chance to? They'd be parting soon enough, at journey's end, he to settle his affairs in the islands, and she to return home on the first Skylark ship to put in to Jamaica. But she'd be going home to what? Just existing again, as she'd been doing for the last six years, just living day by day, without excitement, without a man in her life, just memories of one. At least this time, of this man, her memories would be the stuff of dreams and fantasies.

So she told herself, but in truth, she tried not to think of their parting, which was inevitable. That would only ruin the here-and-now, and she didn't want to do that. She wanted instead to savor every minute that she spent with her "reprehensible rake."

She savored him right now, leaning back against the rail on the quarterdeck with nothing to do but watch him. He bent over charts, discussing their course with Connie, for the moment ignoring her. She was supposed to be there to carry messages for him, though he rarely sent her off to do so, merely relaying such messages to Connie, who would in turn boom them across the deck to whomever they were intended for.

She didn't mind being ignored right then. It gave her a chance to calm down from James's last glance her way, which had been so heated and full of promises of what he would do to her as soon as they returned to his cabin, that anyone else who looked at her would have thought she'd had too much sun that morning, she flushed so with pleasure. Morning, noon, night; their lovemaking followed no schedule. When he wanted her, he let her know in no uncertain terms, and no matter the time of day, she was most willing to comply.

Georgina Anderson, you have become a shameless hussy.

She merely grinned to her conscience. I know, and I'm enjoying every minute of it, thank you.

She was, oh, how she was, and how she loved to just watch him like this, and experience her "nausea" to the fullest, knowing that he'd soon cure it in his special way. He'd discarded his jacket. The wind was brisk but warm as they neared Caribbean waters, and it played with his pirate's shirt, as she'd come to think of those full-sleeved, laced-up-the-front tunics he liked to sport, and made him look so wickedly handsome in combination with his single gold earring, tight breeches, and knee-high boots. The wind loved him, caressed those powerful limbs of his, as she wanted to do . . . Was she supposed to be calming down?

In self-defense, just so she wouldn't be tempted to drag *him* off to their cabin as he'd done so many times to her in recent days, Georgina turned seaward and saw the ship in the distance at the precise moment that the warning came down from the crow's-nest. Well, there was nothing unusual in that. They'd passed several other vessels at sea. They'd also had another trailing them as this one was, though they'd lost sight of that ship after a brief storm. But this one was different, according to the next information shouted down by the lookout. Pirates.

Georgina stood very still, gripping the rail, hoping the lad above would call down that he'd made a mistake. Her brothers had all had encounters with pirates in one way or another over the many years they'd been sailing the seas. But she did not want to make it a unanimous family custom. And dear Lord, James carried no cargo, just ballast. Nothing could get blood-thirsty pirates angrier than to discover their prize had an empty hold.

"Obliging, ain't they, to give us a little diversion?" she heard Connie remark behind her to James. "Do you want to play with them first, or come about and wait?"

"Waiting would only confuse them, don't you think?" James replied.

"Confusion has its advantages."

"Quite so."

Georgina turned around slowly. It wasn't just the words that shocked her, but the calm nonchalance in their tones. They both had spyglasses trained on the approaching vessel, but to listen to them, neither seemed the least bit concerned. That was taking English imperturbability a bit too blasted far. Didn't they realize the danger?

James happened to lower his spyglass then and glance at her, and in that second before he schooled his features upon noticing her upset, she saw that he wasn't nonchalant at all. The man had looked eager, *delighted* even, that a pirate ship was bearing down on them. And she realized that it had to be the challenge that inspired him, an opportunity to pit his seamanship skills against an adversary, regardless that that adversary might be out to murder him if he lost, rather than wish him better luck next time.

"Actually, Connie," he said, without taking his eyes from Georgina. "I think we'll just take a leaf from young Eden's book and thumb our noses at them as we sail away."

"Sail away? Without firing a single shot?"

The first mate sounded incredulous. Georgina didn't glance his way to see if he looked it, too. Her eyes were caught by bright green ones that wouldn't let go.

"And need I remind you," Connie added, "that you almost killed that young pup Eden for thumbing his nose at you?"

James merely shrugged, still with his eyes holding Georgina's, and his words going right to her center. "Nonetheless, I'm not in a mood to play . . . with them."

Connie finally followed his gaze, then snorted. "You could think of the rest of us. We don't have our own personal diversions aboard, you know."

He sounded so disgruntled that James laughed, but it didn't stop him from grabbing Georgina's hand and heading for the stairs. "Just lose them, Connie, and try to do it without me, will you?"

James didn't wait for an answer. He was off the quarterdeck and moving briskly down the next set of stairs before Georgina could draw breath to question his intentions. But she should have known what they were. He pulled her inside his cabin and was kissing her even as the door slammed shut behind them. He'd found an outlet for the blood-rushing excitement that had briefly flared when he'd contemplated battle. And he found this outlet just as pleasurable, and went after it just as ruthlessly, as he would have waged the battle.

The battle? For God's sake, there were pirates in their wake! How could he possibly think of making love *now?*

"James!"

She pulled her lips away from him, but he didn't stop kissing her. He just changed locations. Her neck. And then lower.

"You would have challenged pirates!" she said accusingly, even as her heavy vest dropped to the floor behind her. "Do you know how fool-hardy that is? No, wait, not my shirt!"

Her shirt was gone. So were her bindings. So swiftly! She'd never seen him this . . . this impassioned, impatient.

"James, this is serious!"

"I beg to differ, love," he said as he lifted her so his mouth had direct access to her breasts while he bore her backward to the bed. "That is a nuisance. *This* is serious."

His mouth closed over one breast to leave her in no doubt as to what *this* was, nor did his mouth leave her as he stripped off the rest of her clothes, and his own. He had a wonderful mouth; God, did he have a wonderful mouth. No one could say James Malory wasn't a magnificent lover who knew exactly what he was about. Well, not everyone could know that, but she was in a position to know at the moment, a very nice position to know.

"But, James," she tried one more time, weakly though, to remind him about the pirates.

His tongue was dipping into her navel when he said, between laves, "Not another bloody word, George, unless they're love words."

"What kind of love words?"

" 'I like what you're doing, James. More, James. Lower . . . James.' " She gasped as he did move lower, and he added, "That will do, too. Ah, love, you're already hot and wet for me, aren't you?"

"Are . . . those your . . . love words?" She could barely speak, the pleasure was so intense.

"Do they make you want me inside you?"

"Yes!"

"Then they'll do." He caught his breath as he entered her, swiftly, deeply, his hands cupping her derriere, bringing her up to take all of him. "For now."

Fortunately, the pirates were left far behind, but Georgina couldn't have cared less anymore.

Chapter Twenty-six

"Your carriage just arrived, James," Connie announced from the open doorway.

"There's no hurry. With that congestion out there, I'd just as soon wait until the wagons loading that American vessel in the next berth clear off the quay. Come join me for a drink, old man."

They'd docked several hours ago. Georgina had packed James's trunks that morning, but he hadn't told her yet that she would be staying at his plantation. He wanted to surprise her with the grandeur of his island home, and then tonight, over a candlelit dinner of Jamaican delicacies, he was going to ask her to be his mistress.

Connie crossed the room to stand next to the desk, looking out windows that showed a clear view of the American ship and the activity going on as it prepared to set sail. "She looks familiar, don't she?"

"Perhaps one of the Hawke's prizes?"

Connie grinned. "I wouldn't be surprised."

"Then it's just as well she's about to leave."

"Why?" Connie asked. "The *Maiden Anne* never sailed under her own name. And since when wouldn't you welcome a little diversion, such as being accused of piracy when there's no proof to back it up? You passed up the opportunity for a little sport at sea—"

"With reason," James reminded him. He wasn't about to put his little Georgie at risk for a mere few hours of stimulating adventure. "And actually, I'd rather not be bothered just now, either."

Connie turned as he accepted his drink. "You *are* looking rather complacent. Any reason in particular?"

"You're looking at a man about to commit himself, Connie. I've decided to keep George around for a while. And don't look so bloody surprised."

"Well, I bloody well am surprised, and with reason. The last woman you sailed with . . . What was her name?"

James frowned at the question. "Estelle or Stella. What difference does it make?"

"You decided to keep her around for a while, too. You even allowed her to decorate this cabin with these atrociously mismatched pieces—"

"I rather like this furniture now that I've grown accustomed to it."

"You're deliberately missing the point. You were well pleased with the wench, generous with her to a fault, but less than a week at sea with her, you turned the ship around to dump her back where you'd found her. Such close confinement with her had driven you crazy. I'd say I was safe in assuming that after all these weeks of being cooped up with the brat, you couldn't wait to get away from her now that we've docked."

"So George is a much more charming companion."

"Charming? That saucy-mouthed—"

"Watch it, Connie. This is my soon-to-be-mistress we are discussing."

Conrad's brows shot up. "You're going to go *that* far in committing yourself? Whatever for?"

"Now that's a stupid question," James replied irritably. "What the devil do you think for? I've grown fond of the little Yank. She might not show her sweet self to you, but George has been decidedly agreeable to me ever since we did away with pretenses."

"Correct me if I'm wrong, but aren't you the man who swore off keeping mistresses? Something about their always getting marriage-minded, despite their protests to the contrary? You have faithfully stayed clear of commitments for a good number of years, Hawke, and I might add, without ever once lacking for female companionship when you wanted it. Damned less expensive, too."

James waved that reasoning aside. "So I'm due for a change. Besides, George isn't the least bit interested in marriage. I set her straight on the subject, and she hasn't said another word about it."

"*All* women are interested in marriage. You've said so yourself."

"Damnation, Connie, if you're trying to talk me out of keeping her, you bloody well can't. I've given it a good deal of thought this last week, and I'm simply not ready to see the last of her yet."

"And what does she think about it?"

"She'll be delighted, of course. The wench is quite fond of me as well."

"Glad to hear it," Connie replied dryly. "So what's she doing over on yonder ship?"

James turned around so fast, he nearly tipped his chair over. It took him a few seconds to scan the deck of the American ship before he saw what Conrad had seen. Georgina, with the Scot standing behind her. She appeared to be talking to one of the ship's officers, possibly even her captain. James had the feeling she was acquainted with the chap, especially when the man gripped her arms and began to shake her, then, in the next moment, pulled her close to embrace her. James shot to his feet, seeing that. His chair did tip over this time.

He was heading for the door, swearing under his breath, when Connie remarked, "If you intend to fetch her back—"

"I intend to break that chap's face, *then* I'll collect George."

James hadn't stopped to reply, was already out the door, so Connie had to shout after him, "You'll find it a bit difficult doing either, old man! The ship's already cast off!"

"The devil she has!" was heard from out in the hall, and then as James appeared back in the doorway to stare out the windows at the slowly departing vessel, "Bloody hell!"

"Look on the bright side, Hawke," Connie said without the least bit of sympathy. "You would only have had a few weeks more with her, until we returned to England. Even if you had considered taking her back with you, from what you've told me of her aversion to the motherland, she'd never have agreed—"

"Blister it, Connie, the wench has deserted me, and without a by-your-leave. Don't talk to me about problems I might have faced, when this one's knocked me on my arse."

He ignored Conrad's derisive short. He stared at the now-empty berth next to the *Maiden Anne* and still couldn't believe Georgie was gone. Just that morning she'd awakened him with her sweet lips on his, her little hands holding his face, and what he thought of as her take-me smile, the one she bestowed on him only when they were abed, the one that never failed to stir primitive urges he'd never even known he possessed. Gone?

"No, by God," he said aloud, then pinned Conrad with a resolute look that made the redhead groan. "How many of the crew have gone ashore?"

"For God's sake, James, you can't mean to—"

"I bloody well do mean to," James cut in, the anger that was starting to rise reflected clearly in his tone. "Get them back while I find out what I can about that ship. I mean to be on her tail within the hour."

Georgina defied her brother Drew's order to get herself to his cabin as soon as his back was turned. He'd already promised her a walloping that would have her standing the whole voyage home. Whether that was just his anger talking, or he really meant to take his belt to her, she found she didn't much care at the moment.

Oh, he was indeed mad, furiously so. She'd merely surprised Drew at first when he turned around and found her standing there grinning at him. And then he'd been alarmed, assuming only some grave catastrophe could have brought her to Jamaica looking for him. When she'd assured him no one had died, his relief turned to irritation. He'd shaken her then for scaring him, but just as quickly hugged her because he really was relieved not to be hearing bad news, and, of course, the fact that she was his only sister and well loved had a little to do with it. It was when she'd casually dropped the news that she'd just returned from England that the shouting began. And this was one of her more mellow brothers, the most even-tempered next to Thomas.

Unlike Warren, who had an explosive temper that no one cared to get on the wrong side of, or Boyd and Clinton, who were too serious by half sometimes, Drew was the devil-may-care rogue in the family who had women chasing after him by the hordes. So he out of all of them should have understood why she had thought it necessary to chase after Malcolm. Instead, he'd been so angry, she'd almost seen some color in his black eyes. If she got a walloping from him, she could just imagine what she'd get from Clinton or Warren, her oldest brothers, when they found out. But she didn't much care at the moment.

She hadn't realized when she'd become so excited upon seeing Drew's ship and had rushed right over to her, that the *Triton* was making ready to depart, had in fact cast off her lines while Drew was still ranting and raving. She stood at the rail now, the sparkling Caribbean waters separating her from the *Maiden Anne* more and more, frantically searching the deck of the other ship for a last sight of James.

When she did finally see him appear on deck, his golden hair whipping about in the breeze, those wide, wide shoulders that couldn't be mistaken for any other man's, she could barely breathe for the lump that rose in her throat. She prayed he would look her way. She was too far away already to shout and hope to have him hear her, but she could at least wave. But he didn't look out to sea. She watched him leave his ship, move off briskly down the wharf, and then disappear into the crowd.

Oh, God, he didn't even know she was gone. He probably assumed she was somewhere on the *Maiden Anne,* assumed she'd be there when he returned. After all, her belongings were still there, and among them the cherished ring her father had given her. She hadn't known there would be no time to collect them, not that she cared about them at the moment. What was tearing her up inside was that she'd had no opportunity to say goodbye to James, to tell him . . . what? That she'd fallen in love with him.

She almost laughed. It was funny, it really was. Love thine enemy—but not literally. A hated Englishman, a despised, arrogant aristocrat, and he still got under her skin, still worked his way right into her heart. So stupid to let that happen, but so much worse if she'd actually told him. She'd asked him one night while his arms were around her and his heart beat steadily under her ear, if he were married.

"Good God, no!" he'd exclaimed in horror. "You won't see me ever making that fool's mistake."

"And why not?" she'd wanted to know.

"Because all women become faithless jades as soon as they get that ring on their finger. No offense, love, but it's bloody well true."

His comment had reminded her so much of her brother Warren's attitude about women that she mistakenly drew her own conclusion. "I'm sorry. I should have realized there had to have been a woman you loved at some point in your life who betrayed you. But you shouldn't blame all women for the unfaithfulness of just one. My brother Warren does exactly that, but it's wrong."

"I hate to disappoint you, George, but there was never a great love in my life. I was speaking of the many women whose unfaithfulness I know of from firsthand experience since I happen to be the one they were unfaithful with. Marriage is for idiots who don't know any better."

But she'd already had a feeling his answer would be something in that vein to begin with. In that he was still so much like her brother Warren it was uncanny. But at least Warren had an excuse for swearing he'd never marry, for the abominable way he now treated women, using them without ever letting them get close to him. He'd been hurt really badly once by a woman he'd intended to marry. But James had no such excuse. He'd said so himself. He was simply what he'd told her he was, a reprehensible rake. He wasn't even ashamed of it.

"Come now, lass, the lad's nae really going tae beat ye," Mac said, having come up beside her. "Ye've nae reason tae be crying. But best ye get yerself below like he said. Give Drew a chance tae calm down afore he sees ye again and has tae hear the worst of it."

She glanced sideways as she swiped at her cheeks. "Worst of it?"

"That we had tae work fer our passage."

"Oh, that," she sniffed, thankful to have something else to think about, and that Mac assumed she was merely upset over Drew's anger. She added with a sigh, "No, I don't suppose his knowing that will go over very well just now. Is there any reason we have to tell him?"

"Ye'd lie tae yer own brother?"

"He's threatened to beat me, Mac," she reminded him with a measure of disgust. "And this is Drew, *Drew,* for God's sake. I'd just as soon not find out his reaction if he learns I've slept in the same cabin with an Englishman for the last month."

"Aye, I see what ye mean. Sae maybe a little lie wouldna hurt, or just the omission that we were robbed of our money. Ye've still the others tae be facing yet, after all, and their reactions will be even worse, I'm thinking."

"Thanks, Mac. You've been the dearest—"

"Georgina!" Drew's voice cut in with clear warning. "I'm taking off my belt."

She swung around to see that he wasn't doing any such thing, but her handsome brother looked as if he would if she didn't disappear, and quick. Instead she closed the distance between them and glared up at the six-foot-four-inch tall captain of the *Triton*.

"You're being an insensitive brute, Drew. Malcolm married another women, and all you can do is yell at me." And she promptly burst into heartrending tears.

Mac snorted in disgust. He'd never seen a man so quickly disarmed of his anger as Drew Anderson just was.

Chapter Twenty-seven

Georgina had been feeling somewhat better, certainly much more optimistic about the rest of her brothers' reactions after Drew proved to be so sympathetic to her heartache. Of course, Drew thought all her tears were over Malcolm. She saw no reason to tell him that she never even thought of Malcolm anymore, except when his name was mentioned. No, her thoughts and emotions were centered on another man, one whose name had never been spoken other than to explain he was the captain of the ship that brought her to Jamaica.

She felt bad about deceiving Drew. More than once she had thought about telling him the truth. But she didn't want him to be angry with her again. His anger had really surprised her. This was her fun-loving brother, the one who teased her most, the one who could always be counted on to cheer her up. He'd managed to do that. He just didn't know what was truly depressing her.

He would know eventually. They all would. But the worst news could wait awhile more, until the hurt had a chance to heal a little bit, until she found out how badly the rest of them were going to react to what she saw now as a minor thing, at least in comparison to what she would have to tell them in a month or two when they demanded to know whose baby was stretching her waistline. What was it James had said about his brother Jason? He frequently flew through the roof? Well, she'd have five brothers doing it.

She wasn't sure yet how she felt about the consequence of her brief fall from grace. Scared, certainly. A little bewildered, a little— glad. She couldn't deny it. It was going to cause all kinds of difficulty, not to mention scandal, but nevertheless, her feelings could be summed up in two words. James's baby. What else could matter next to that? It was crazy. She should be devastated to think of bearing a child and raising it without a husband, but she wasn't. She couldn't have James, and no other man would do after him, but she could have his child, *and* keep it, and that was exactly what she would do. She loved James too much not to.

The baby, and Georgina's certainty that it was real and not just a possibility, accounted for her improved mood by the time the *Triton* sailed into Long Island Sound on the last leg of their journey home, three weeks after leaving Jamaica. And by the time Bridgeport was sighted and they'd turned into the Pequonnock River, which helped form a deep harbor for oceangoing vessels, she was excited to be home, especially at this time of year, her favorite, when the weather wasn't too cold yet, and the sunset colors of autumn still lingered everywhere. At least she was excited until she saw just how many Skylark ships were in port, three in particular that she wished were anywhere else but here.

The ride to the red brick mansion that she called home on the outskirts of town was a quiet one. Drew sat next to her in the carriage, holding her hand, squeezing it occasionally for encouragement. He was firmly on her side now, but a lot of good that would do her when she faced the older brothers. Drew had never been able to hold his own against them anymore than she could, especially when they were united.

Her cabin boy's clothes were gone. That outfit had been partly to blame for Drew's towering anger, so at least that was one thing less the others could complain about. She'd scrounged clothes from Drew's crew for the voyage, but right now she was wearing the lovely gown Drew had been bringing home to his Bridgeport sweetheart as a present. Likely he'd buy another here to take to his sweetheart in the next port.

"Smile, Georgie girl. It's not the end of the world, you know."

She glanced sideways at Drew. He was beginning to see some humor in her situation, which she didn't appreciate the least bit. But a comment like that was so typical of him. He was so different from her other brothers. He was the only one in the family with eyes so dark they couldn't be called anything but black. He was also the only one who could be knocked down and come up laughing, which had happened numerous times when he'd rubbed Warren or Boyd the wrong way. And yet he looked so much like Warren it was uncanny.

They both had the same golden-brown hair, which was more often than not a mop of unruly curls. They both had the same towering height, the same features that were entirely too handsome. But where Drew's eyes were black as pitch, Warren's were a light limegreen like Thomas's. And where the ladies adored Drew for his winsome charm and boyish manner, they were wary of Warren with his brooding cynicism and explosive temper—but not wary enough, obviously.

Warren was, without a doubt, a cad where women were concerned. Georgina pitied any woman who succumbed to his cold seduction. Yet so many did. There was just something about him that they found irresistible. She couldn't see it herself. His temper, on the other hand, she saw all the time, since that was something he'd always possessed, and had nothing to do with women.

Reminded of Warren's temper, she replied to Drew's remark with, "That's easy for you to say. D'you think they will listen to an explanation before they kill me? I rather doubt it."

"Well, Clinton won't listen for very long if he detects that ghastly English accent you've picked up. Maybe you ought to let me do the talking."

"That's sweet of you, Drew, but if Warren is around—"

"I know what you mean." He grinned boyishly, remembering the last time Warren had chewed off a piece of his hide. "So let's hope he's spent the night at Duck's Inn and won't get his two cents in until after Clinton's laid down his verdict. It's lucky for you Clinton's home."

"Lucky? Lucky!"

"Shh!" he hissed. "We've arrived. No need to give them warning."

"Someone will have told them by now that the *Triton* has docked."

"Aye, but not that you were on her. The element of surprise, Georgie, just might let you have your say."

It might have, too, if Boyd weren't in the study with both Clinton and Warren when Georgina entered, with Drew right behind her. Her youngest brother saw her first and bounded out of his chair. By the time he got through hugging, shaking, and throwing questions at her so fast she had no chance to answer any of them, the two older men had recovered from any surprise she might have given them and were approaching her with looks that said the shaking had only just begun. They also looked as if they just might come to blows to see who could get his hands on her first.

What little confidence Georgina had that her brothers wouldn't *really* hurt her, not seriously anyway, departed upon seeing them bearing down on her. She swiftly extricated herself from Boyd's hold, dragged him back with her so he stood shoulder-to-shoulder with Drew, and wisely placed herself behind them.

Peeking over Boyd's shoulder, no easy matter since Boyd, like Thomas, stood nearly six feet tall—but was still half a head shorter than Drew—Georgina shouted at Clinton first, "I can explain!" then to Warren she added, "I really can!"

And when they didn't stop, but came one around each side of her barricade, she squeezed between Boyd and Drew to run straight for Clinton's desk and around it, though she remembered belatedly how a desk hadn't stopped someone *else* from getting at her. And it appeared that she'd only made Clinton and Warren angrier by running from them. But her own temper was sparked when she saw Drew grab Warren's shoulder to keep him from following her, and just barely manage to duck a blow for his effort.

"Blast you both, you're being unfair—"

"Shut up, Georgie!" Warren growled.

"I won't. I'm not answerable to you, Warren Anderson, not as long as Clinton is here. So you can just stop right there or I'll—" She picked up the nearest thing within reach on the desk. "I'll clobber you."

He did stop, but whether in surprise that she was standing up to him when she never had before, or because he thought she was serious about braining him, she didn't know. But Clinton stopped, too. In fact, they both looked kind of alarmed.

"Put the vase down, Georgie," Clinton said very softly. "It's too valuable to waste on Warren's head."

"*He* wouldn't think so," she replied in disgust.

"Actually," Warren choked out just as softly, "I would."

"Jesus, Georgie," Boyd was heard from next. "You don't know what you've got there. Listen to Clinton, will you?"

Drew glanced at his younger brother's blanched expression, then the two stiff backs in front of him, then his little sister beyond them, still holding up the vase under discussion as if it were a club. He suddenly burst out laughing.

"You've done it, Georgie girl, damned if you haven't," he crowed in delight.

She just barely spared him a glance. "I'm in no mood for your humor just now, Drew," but then, "What have I done?"

"Got them over a barrel, that's what. They'll listen to you now, see if they don't."

Her eyes moved curiously back to her oldest brother. "Is that true, Clinton?"

He'd been debating what approach to take with her, stern insistence or gentle coaxing, but Drew's unwelcome interference settled it. "I'm willing to listen, yes, if you'll—"

"No ifs," she cut in. "Yes or—"

"Blast it, Georgina!" Warren finally exploded. "Give me that—"

"Shut up, Warren," Clinton hissed. "before you frighten her into dropping it." And then to his sister, "Now, look, Georgie, you don't understand what you've got there."

She was looking, but at the vase she still held aloft. It elicited a small gasp from her, because she'd never seen anything quite so lovely. So thin it was actually translucent, and painted in pure gold on white with an Oriental scene in exquisite detail. She understood now, perfectly, and her first instinct was to put the beautiful piece of ancient porcelain down before she accidentally dropped it.

She almost did just that, put it down very carefully, afraid a mere breath could shatter something this delicate. But the collective sighs she heard made her change her mind at the last moment.

With a raised brow that was a perfect imitation of what she had once found so irritating in a certain English captain, she inquired of Clinton, "Valuable, did you say?"

Boyd groaned. Warren turned about so she wouldn't hear him swearing, which she could hear perfectly fine since he was shouting every word. Drew just chuckled, while Clinton looked extremely angry again.

"That's blackmail, Georgina," Clinton muttered between clinched teeth.

"Not at all. Self-preservation is more like it. Besides, I haven't finished admiring this—"

"You've made your point, girl. Perhaps we should all sit down, so you can rest the vase in your lap."

"I'm all for that."

When he made the suggestion, Clinton hadn't expected her to take his seat behind the desk. He flushed a bit when she did just that, his angry look getting worse. Georgina knew she was pushing her luck, but it was a heady feeling to have her brothers in such a unique position. Of course, she just might have to keep the vase they were all so worried about with her indefinitely now.

"Would you mind telling me why you're all so angry with me? All I did was go to—"

"England!" Boyd exclaimed. "Of all places, Georgie! That's the devil's birthing ground and you know it."

"It wasn't *that* bad—"

"And alone!" Clinton pointed out. "You went alone, for God's sake! Where was your sense?"

"Mac was with me."

"He's not your brother."

"Oh, come now, Clinton, you know he's like a father to us all."

"But he's too soft where you're concerned. He lets you walk all over him."

She couldn't very well deny it, and they all knew it, which was why her cheeks bloomed with color, especially when she realized she'd never have lost her innocence, or her heart, to an English rogue like James Malory if one of her brothers had been with her instead of Mac. She'd never even have met James, or discovered such bliss. Or such hell. And there wouldn't be a babe resting under her heart that was going to cause a scandal the likes of which Bridgeport had never seen before. But it was so pointless to bring up should-have-dones. And she couldn't honestly say that she wished she'd done anything different.

"Maybe I was a bit impulsive—"

"A bit!" Warren again, and not even a little calmed down yet.

"All right, so maybe a lot. But doesn't it matter *why* I felt I had to go?"

"Absolutely not!"

And Clinton added to that with, "There's no explanation that can make up for the worry you put us through. That was inexcusable, selfish—"

"But you weren't supposed to worry!" she cried defensively. "You weren't supposed to even know about my going until after I got back. I should have been home before any of you, and what *are* you doing home, anyway?"

"That's a long story, wrapped up in that vase you're holding, but don't change the subject, girl. You know you had no business going off to England, but you did it anyway. You knew we would object, knew exactly what our sentiments are toward that particular country, and still you went there."

Drew had heard enough. Seeing Georgina's shoulders drop under that load of guilt, his protective instincts came to the fore, making him snap, "You've made your point, Clinton, but Georgie's suffered enough. She doesn't need all this added grief from you three."

"What she needs is a good spanking!" Warren insisted. "And if Clinton doesn't get around to it, you can damned well believe I will!"

"She's a bit old for that, don't you think?" Drew demanded, overlooking the fact that he'd been of the same opinion when he'd found her in Jamaica.

"Women are never too old to be spanked."

The imaginings that disgruntled reply engendered had Drew grinning, Boyd chuckling, and Clinton rolling his eyes. They'd all, for the moment, forgotten that Georgina was even in the room. But sitting there listening to this outlandishness, she was no longer cowed, was instead bristling, and was quite ready to throw the precious vase at Warren's head.

And Drew didn't exactly redeem himself when he said, "Women in general, aye, but sisters fall into a different category. And what's got you so hot under the collar, anyway?"

When Warren refused to answer, Boyd did. "He only docked yesterday, but as soon as we told him what she'd done, he had his ship refitted, and was in fact leaving this afternoon—for England."

Georgina started, thoroughly bemused. "Were you actually coming after me, Warren?"

The small scar on his left cheek ticked. Obviously, he didn't like it known that he'd worried about her as much as, if not more than, the rest of them. And he wasn't going to answer her anymore than he had Drew.

But she didn't need an answer. "Why, Warren Anderson, that has to be the nicest thing you've ever considered doing for me."

"Oh, hell," he groaned.

"Now don't be embarrassed." She grinned. "No one is here except family to witness that you're not as cold and callous as you like people to think."

"Black and blue, Georgie, I promise you."

She didn't take his warning to heart, maybe because there was no longer any heat behind it. She just gave him a tender smile that said she loved him, too.

But into the silence, Boyd demanded of Drew, albeit belatedly, "What the devil did you mean, she's suffered enough?"

"She found her Malcolm, more's the pity."

"And?"

"And you don't see him here, do you?"

"You mean he wouldn't have her?" Boyd asked incredulously.

"Worse than that." Drew snorted. "He married someone else, about five years ago."

"Why that—"

"—good for nothing—"

"—son of a bitch!"

Georgina blinked at their renewed anger, this time on her behalf. She hadn't expected that, but she should have, knowing how protective they were of her. She could just imagine what they'd say about James when it came time for the big confession. She couldn't bear to think of it.

They were still commiserating in their own way, with colorful invectives, when the middle brother walked into the room. "I still don't believe it," he said, drawing everyone's startled attention. "All five of us home at the same time. Hell, it must be ten years at least since we've managed that."

"Thomas!" Clinton exclaimed.

"Well, hell, Tom, you must have come in on my waves," Drew said.

"Just about." He chuckled. "I spotted you off the Virginia coast, but then lost you again." And then he gave his attention to Georgina, only because he was surprised to see her sitting behind Clinton's desk. "No greeting, sweetheart? You aren't still angry with me, are you, for delaying your trip to England?"

Angry? She was suddenly furious. It was just like Thomas to put little stock in her feelings, to assume that everything would be swell-dandy-fine now that he was home.

"*My* trip?" She came around the desk, toting the vase under her arm, so angry she forgot she was even holding it. "I didn't want to go to England, Thomas. I asked you to go for me. I begged you to go for me. But you wouldn't, would you? My little concerns weren't important enough to interfere with your blasted schedule."

"Now, Georgie," he said in his calm way. "I'm willing to go now, and you're welcome to come along or not."

"She's already been," Drew informed him dryly.

"Been what?"

"Been to England and back."

"The devil she has." Thomas's lime-green eyes came back to Georgina, flared with upset. "Georgie, you couldn't be that foolish—"

"Couldn't I?" she cut in sharply, but then unexpectedly her eyes filled with unwanted tears. "It's your fault that I'm—I'm . . . oh, here!"

She tossed the vase at him as she ran out of the room, ashamed to be crying again over a heartless Englishman by the name of Malory. But she left pandemonium behind, and not because anyone had noticed her tears.

Thomas caught the vase she'd thrown to him, but not before four grown men fell at his feet in their efforts to catch it if he didn't.

Chapter Twenty-eight

James stood impatiently at the rail, waiting for the small skiff that had finally been sighted on its way back to the ship. Three days he'd waited in this little bay on the Connecticut coast. If he'd known it was going to take this long for Artie and Henry to return with the information he wanted, he would have gone ashore himself.

He almost had, yesterday. But Connie had calmly pointed out that his present mood was a deterrent, that if the Americans didn't clam up simply because he reeked of British nobility, authority, and condescension, his mood would make anyone distrustful, possibly even hostile. James had objected to the condescension part. Connie had merely laughed. And two out of three had still made his point.

James was totally unfamiliar with these American waters, but he'd decided not to follow the vessel he'd been trailing into port, since he didn't want to give Georgie any prior warning that he was here. He'd merely assured himself that her ship had actually docked at the coastal town, rather than sailing up the river she had entered. He'd then anchored the *Maiden Anne* just around the point of land that jutted out at the mouth of the river and sent Artie and Henry into the town to find out what they could. But it shouldn't have taken three days. He'd only wanted to know where he could find the wench, not details of the whole town.

But they were back now, and the moment they climbed aboard, he demanded, "Well?" only to change his mind and snap, "In my cabin."

Neither man was overly concerned with his abruptness. They had an earful to report, and besides, the captain's manner was no different than it had been since leaving Jamaica.

They followed him below, as did Connie. But James didn't even wait to settle behind his desk before he again asked for an accounting.

Artie was the first to speak up. "Ye won't like it none, Cap'n . . . or maybe ye will. That ship we was after followin', she's one o' the Sky-lark Line."

James frowned thoughtfully as he slowly eased into his chair. "Now why does that name have a familiar ring to it?"

Connie's memory had no trouble supplying the answer. "Maybe because as the Hawke, you had encounters with two Skylark ships. One we captured, the other got away, but not before we did considerable damage to her."

"And this Bridgeport 'ere is 'ome port o' the line," Artie added. "There's more'n a 'alf dozen o' their ships docked right now."

James accepted the significance of that with a grin. "It appears my decision to avoid that harbor was a fortuitous one, don't it, Connie?"

"Indeed. The *Maiden Anne* might not be recognizable, but you certainly are. And I guess that settles the matter of your going ashore."

"Does it?"

Connie stiffened. "Blister it, James, the wench isn't worth getting hanged for!"

"Do try not to exaggerate so," came the dry reply. "I might have been easily visible whenever we bore down on a prize, but I also sported a beard in those days, which you'll notice I no longer do. I'm no more recognizable than my ship is, and furthermore, the Hawke retired more than five years ago. Time dims all memories."

"In your case, it must also have eroded good sense," Connie grumbled. "There's no reason you have to take any risk a'tall, when we can just as easily bring the brat to you."

"And if she doesn't want to come?"

"I'll see that she does."

"Are we considering abduction, Connie? Strike me if I'm wrong, but isn't that a crime?"

Red-faced with frustration, Connie demanded, "You just aren't going to take this seriously, are you?"

James's lips twitched the slightest bit. "I'm just remembering that the last time we tried abduction of a fair damsel, we ended up pulling my sweet niece out of the bag. And the time before that, when Regan was quite willing to be abducted, I ended up being disowned and soundly thrashed by my dear brothers. But that's neither here nor there. I didn't come all this way to let your worry over what is no more than a slim possibility at most change my plans."

"Just what are your plans?"

That particular question brought back James's irritation, and then some. "I haven't any yet, but that's beside the bloody point," and then, "Artie, where the hell is the wench? You two laggards *did* discover her whereabouts, didn't you?"

"Aye, Cap'n. She lives in a big 'ouse just outside o' Bridgeport."

"Outside? Then I can find her without actually going through the town?"

"Easily, but—"

James didn't let him finish. "There, you see, Connie? You were worried over nothing."

"Cap'n—?"

"I won't have to go anywhere near the harbor."

"*Merde!*" Henry was finally heard from as he glowered at his friend. "When will you tell him, *mon ami?* After he has entered the tiger's house?"

"That's lion's 'ouse, 'Enry, and what do ye think I've been tryin' to do, eh?"

They had James's full attention again after that. "It's lion's den, gentlemen, and if I am to enter one, I suppose I must assume I'm missing something pertinent. What would that be?"

"Just that it's the girl's family what owns them Skylark ships, 'er brothers that sail 'em."

"Bloody hell," Connie mumbled, while James started laughing.

"By God, that's irony for you. She said she owned a ship, but I'll be damned if I believed her. Thought she was just being lippy again."

"Appears she was being modest instead," Connie said. "And there's nothing funny about it, James. You can't very well—"

"'Course I can. I'll just have to choose a time when she's likely to be alone."

"That won't be today, Cap'n. They're givin' a sorry tonight."

"A soiree?"

"Aye, one o' them. 'Alf the town's been invited."

"To celebrate the whole family is home," Henry added. "Such an occurrence apparently does not happen often."

"I can see now what took you so bloody long," James said in disgust. "I send you to locate the wench, and you come back with her family history. All right, what else will I find of interest? I don't suppose you discovered what she was doing in England, by any chance?"

"Lookin' for 'er intended."

"Her intended what?"

"Her fiancé," Henry clarified.

James sat forward slowly. All three of his companions recognized the signs. If he'd been in a simmering rage since they'd left Jamaica, it was nothing compared to what that single word just did to him.

"She . . . has . . . a . . . *fiancé?*"

"No longer," Henry quickly explained.

"She found 'im wed to an English wench, and after she'd waited six years for—Ouch! Jesus, 'Enry, that's my bleedin' foot ye're steppin' on!"

"It should be your mouth, *mon ami!*"

"She . . . waited . . . *six* . . . years?"

Artie flinched. "Well, 'e got 'imself impressed, Cap'n, and then the war . . . They didn't know what became o' the lad until earlier this year. It ain't common knowledge, at least that she went searchin' for 'im. 'Enry 'ad to sweet talk one o' the 'ousemaids—"

"Six years," James said again, but this time to himself. In a louder voice he added, "Sounds like George was very much in love, don't it, Connie?"

"Damn me, James, I can't believe you're letting that bother you. I've heard you say a number of times that a woman on the rebound makes for a splendid tumble. And you didn't *want* the brat falling in love with you, did you? It always annoys the hell out of you when they do."

"Quite so."

"Then what the devil are you still glowering about?"

Chapter Twenty-nine

"Where the hell have you been, Clinton?" Drew demanded belligerently as soon as his brother entered the large study, which was the general gathering place for the men in the house.

Clinton glanced at Warren and Thomas lounging on a maroon sofa for an explanation of Drew's unusual greeting, but since Drew hadn't bothered to tell either of them why he'd been so impatient for Clinton's return, they both merely shrugged.

He continued on to his desk before he replied. "I believe it's my habit to attend to business when I'm home. I spent the morning at the Skylark offices. Had you bothered to ask Hannah, she would have told you that."

Drew recognized a subtle reprimand when he heard it. He flushed slightly, but only because he hadn't thought to question their housekeeper-cook.

"Hannah was too busy preparing for the party to be bothered."

Clinton had to tamp down the urge to smile at that mumbled reply. Drew's displays of temper were very rare and so surprising when they occurred. There was no point in aggravating the one he was demonstrating just now. Warren felt no such qualms.

"You could have asked me, blockhead." Warren chuckled. "I could have told you—"

Drew was on his way to the sofa before Warren finished, so Warren didn't bother to finish. He just stood up to meet his younger brother head on.

"Drew!"

The warning had to be repeated in an even louder tone before Drew turned back to glare at Clinton. The last time those two had a difference of opinion in his study, he had to have his desk repaired and two lamps and a table replaced.

"You might both remember that we're entertaining this evening," Clinton admonished sternly. "With the whole blasted town likely to show up, this room as well as every other in the house is certain to be used. I'd appreciate it if it didn't have to be rearranged beforehand."

Warren unclenched his fists and sat back down. Thomas shook his head at the lot of them.

"What's troubling you, Drew, that you couldn't discuss it with Warren or myself?" he asked, his tone meant to be soothing. "You didn't have to wait for—"

"Neither of you was home last night, but Clinton was," Drew snapped, but said no more, as if that had explained it all.

Thomas's renowned patience was clearly in evidence as he said, "You went out yourself, didn't you? So what's this in reference to?"

"I want to know what the hell happened while I was gone, that's what!" Drew then rounded on his oldest brother again. "So help me, Clinton, if you spanked Georgie after you said you wouldn't—"

"I did no such thing!" Clinton returned indignantly.

"But he should have," Warren put in his opinion.

"A good walloping would have lifted the guilt from her shoulders."

"What guilt?"

"For worrying us. It's had her moping around the house—"

"If you've seen her moping, it's because she hasn't gotten over Cameron yet. She loved—"

"What nonsense," Warren scoffed. "She never loved that little bastard. She just wanted him because he was the best-looking boy the town had to offer, though why she thought so I'll never understand."

"If that's so, brother, then what had her crying every blasted day for a full week after we left Jamaica? It broke my heart to see her eyes all red and puffy. And it was all I could do to cheer her up before we got home. But I managed it. So I want to know what set her off again. Did you say something to her, Clinton?"

"I barely spoke two words to her. She spent most of the evening in her room."

"Are you saying she was crying again, Drew?" Thomas asked carefully. "Is that what you're so upset about?"

Drew shoved his hands in his pockets as he nodded curtly. "I can't stand it, I really can't."

"Get used to it, blockhead," Warren inserted. "They've all got their store of tears ready to discharge at a moment's notice."

"No one would expect an asinine cynic to know the difference between real tears and fake ones," Drew retorted.

Clinton was about to jump in when he saw that Warren was ready to take serious exception to that last remark. But he didn't have to bother. Thomas defused Warren's temper merely by placing his hand on his arm and giving him a slight shake of his head.

Clinton's lips turned down in chagrin, seeing that. The whole family admired Thomas's ability to remain calm under any circumstances—ironically, Warren most of all. Warren also tended to take Thomas's censure to heart, whereas he usually ignored Clinton's, a fact that annoyed Clinton no end, especially since Thomas was four years Warren's junior, and also a half foot shorter.

"You're forgetting that you were of the same opinion as the rest of us, Drew, when we agreed to allow that ridiculous engagement," Clinton pointed out. "None of us thought that Georgina's affections were seriously involved. For God's sake, she was just a child of sixteen—"

"The reasons we agreed don't matter when she's gone and proved us all wrong," Drew insisted.

"All that has been proven is that Georgie is incredibly loyal . . . and unbelievably stubborn," Clinton replied. "And I'm inclined to agree with Warren. I still don't think she actually loved Cameron."

"Then why would she wait six—?"

"Don't be a total ass, Drew," Warren cut in. "The situation around here hasn't changed in all these years. There still aren't a great number of unmarried men in this town for her to choose from. So why shouldn't she wait for Cameron to come back? She didn't find anyone else in the meantime that she would prefer to him. If she had, you can bet she would have forgotten that Cornishman in the blink of an eye."

"Then why did she run off to find him?" Drew asked hotly. "Answer me that?"

"Obviously, she felt she'd waited long enough. Clinton and I had already come to the same conclusion. He was going to take her with him when he went to New Haven to visit his children this trip home. His mother-in-law is still active in the social whirl there."

"What social whirl?" Drew snorted. "New Haven is not much bigger than Bridgeport."

"If that didn't work, then I was going to take her to New York."

"*You* were?"

Warren's scowl became positively threatening. "You think I don't know how to escort a woman about?"

"A woman, aye, but not a sister. What man would approach her with you near at hand . . . the perpetual brooder."

That brought Warren to his feet again with eyes flashing. "I don't brood—"

"If you two would stop trying to provoke each other," Thomas managed to interrupt without raising his voice. "You might realize that you've gotten away from the point. What was intended is irrelevant at the moment. The fact remains that Georgie is obviously more unhappy than the rest of us thought. If she's been crying . . . Did you ask her why, Drew?"

"Why?" Drew exclaimed. "Why else? She's heartbroken, I tell you!"

"But did she tell you that?"

"She didn't have to. The day she found me in Jamaica she said that Malcolm had married another woman and then she immediately burst into tears."

"She hasn't seemed the least bit heartbroken," Clinton remarked. "She's been damned bossy, if you ask me, after getting away with what she did the other day when she arrived. This blasted party tonight was her idea, too, and she's thrown herself into preparing for it."

"Well, you don't see her down here this morning, do you? She's probably hiding in her room because her eyes are all puffy again."

Thomas actually frowned. "It's time someone had a talk with her. Clinton?"

"What the hell do I know about these things?"

"Warren?" But before Warren could answer, Thomas chuckled. "No, better not you."

"I'll do it," Drew offered reluctantly.

"When all you can do is make assumptions, and you turn to mush at the first sign of a few tears?" Warren sneered.

Before they could begin another argument, Thomas rose and started for the door, saying, "With Boyd likely still asleep after being out half the night, I suppose that leaves me."

"Lots of luck," Drew called after him, "Or have you forgotten she's still mad at you?"

Thomas paused to glance back at Drew. "Did it occur to you to wonder why?"

"There's nothing to wonder about. She didn't *want* to go to England. She wanted you to go."

"Exactly," Thomas replied. "Which means she didn't really care if she saw Cameron again or not. She just wanted the matter settled."

"Well, hell," Drew said after he'd gone. "Was that supposed to be significant?"

Warren couldn't let that one pass. "It's a wonder you aren't still a virgin, Drew, with as little as you know about women."

"Me?" Drew choked out. "Well, at least I leave them smiling. It's a wonder that *your* women don't freeze to death in your bed!"

They were too near to each other for that kind of exchange. All Clinton could do was yell, "Watch the blasted furniture!"

Chapter Thirty

"Thomas!" Georgina exclaimed when she lifted the corner of the damp cloth covering her eyes to find her brother walking toward her bed, rather than her maid. "Since when do you just walk into my room without knocking?"

"Since my welcome became doubtful. What's wrong with your eyes?"

She tossed the cloth on the table next to her bed and threw her legs over the side to sit up. "Nothing," she mumbled indistinctly.

"What's wrong with *you* then, that you're still in bed? Do you know what hour it is?"

That managed to get a glare out of her. "I've been up. Does this look like my nightclothes?" she asked, indicating the bright yellow morning gown she was wearing.

"So you've just become lazy, is that it, with so much inactivity on your recent voyages?"

Her mouth dropped open before it pulled into a tight line of irritation. "What *do* you want?"

"To find out when you're going to start talking to me again."

He smiled as he said it, and sat down at the foot of the bed where he could lean back against the bed-post to face her. She wasn't fooled. He wanted something else. And whenever Thomas didn't come right to the point, the point was almost invariably delicate or distasteful, neither of which she cared to face just now.

As for talking to him again, she'd already decided that she had to assure him he was forgiven and blameless *before* her condition became known, so he wouldn't feel guilty or feel he was partly responsible. He wasn't. She could have kept James Malory from making love to her if she'd really wanted to, but she hadn't wanted to. Her conscience could attest to that.

She might as well get it over with while he was here. "I'm sorry, Thomas, if I led you to believe that I'm angry with you. I'm not, you know."

"I wasn't the only one who had that impression. Drew assures me—"

"Drew is just being overprotective," she insisted with a good deal of exasperation. "Honestly, it's not like him to get so involved in our affairs. I can't imagine why he—"

"Can't you?" he interrupted gently. "It's not like you to behave impetuously, but you have. He's reacting to your reactions. So is Warren, for that matter. He's being deliberately provoking—"

"He's *always* provoking."

Thomas chuckled. "So he is, but usually he's a bit more subtle about it. Let me put it another way. He's actively looking for a brawl just now, and I don't think he cares who obliges him."

"But why?"

"It's one way of getting rid of emotions that he has trouble containing."

She made a moue of distaste. "Well, I wish he'd find another outlet. I wish he'd fall in love again. *That* would give him a different direction for his passions. Then maybe he'd stop—"

"Did I hear you correctly, Georgina Anderson?"

She flushed hotly at his censuring tone, having forgotten for a moment that she was talking to a brother. "For God's sake, Thomas," she said defensively. "Do you think I know absolutely nothing about life?"

"No more than you should know, which is very little about *that* side of life."

She groaned inwardly, but staunchly maintained, "You have got to be joking. After all the conversations I've overheard in this house? Granted, I shouldn't have listened, but when the subject is soooo fascinating . . ." She grinned when he leaned his head back against the post, closing his eyes. "Have I made my point, Thomas?"

One eye popped open. "You've changed, Georgie. Clinton calls it bossiness, but I'd call it—"

"Assertiveness, and it's about time I showed some, don't you think?"

"Willfulness is more like it."

"Well, I'm due some of that, too." She grinned.

"And downright lippy."

"So I've been told recently."

"Well?"

"Well, what?"

"What's responsible for this new sister I've come home to find?"

She shrugged. "I guess I've just figured out that I can make my own decisions about my life, *and* accept the consequences for them."

"Such as going off to England?" he asked carefully.

"For one."

"There's more?"

"I'm not getting married, Thomas," she said so softly he assumed she referred to Malcolm.

"We know that, sweetheart, but—"

"Ever."

Fireworks going off inside the room couldn't have had more impact than that one word, especially when every instinct told him she wasn't just being melodramatic, was in fact absolutely in earnest.

"Isn't that . . . a bit drastic?"

"No," she said simply.

"I see . . . no, actually I don't. In fact, it looks like I'm as bad as Drew is at making assumptions. By the way, he's terribly upset."

She stood up, sensing by his tone that the conversation was going to take a turn now that she'd rather avoid for the time being. "Thomas—"

"He heard you crying last night."

"Thomas, I don't—"

"He insists your heart is broken. Is it, Georgie?"

He sounded so sympathetic, she felt the tears coming on again. She quickly gave him her back until she could get her emotions under control. Thomas, of course, had the patience to wait.

Finally she said in a forlorn little voice, "It feels like it."

It wouldn't have occurred to Thomas to ask his next question a few hours ago, but he was done with making assumptions. "Because of Malcolm?"

She swung around in surprise. She'd so hoped she wouldn't have to say any more. But Thomas was being entirely too perceptive, not to mention persistent. She wondered why she was even trying to be misleading. What did it matter now? Because she didn't want to talk about James. Talking about him would have her crying again, and she didn't want to cry any more. Damn, but she'd thought last night's bout would hold her for a while.

She dropped back on the bed with a sigh. "I really wish all I felt now was what I felt when I discovered Malcolm's betrayal. That was so easy to deal with . . . and get over. I was merely furious."

"So it *is* something else that has you so melancholy?"

"Melancholy?" She laughed shortly. "How little that really says." And then she asked a question of her own. "Why haven't you married yet, Thomas?"

"Georgie . . ."

"Demonstrate your patience, brother. Why haven't you?"

"I haven't found what I'm looking for yet."

"But you are looking?"

"Yes."

"Clinton isn't, and look how many years it's been since his wife died. He says he just doesn't want to go through that again. Warren isn't, but of course he's still nursing his bitterness and will likely change his mind eventually, as fond as he is of children. Boyd isn't. He claims he's much too young to settle down. Drew, now, says he's not ready to give up the fun of looking—"

"He *told* you that?" Thomas came very close to raising his voice.

"No." She grinned. "That was just one of the things I overheard."

He gave her a purely disgruntled look. "What's your point, Georgina? That you've decided you're not going to look anymore?"

"No, I've just met someone with still another view on marriage. And I can safely say he thinks hell would be preferable."

"My God!" Thomas gasped as all the pieces came together. "No wonder it didn't make sense. Who is he?"

"An Englishman."

She cringed, waiting for the explosion. But this was Thomas. He merely asked, "What's his name?" But Georgina had already said more than she'd intended to.

"His name doesn't matter. You won't be meeting him, and I'll never see him again."

"Did he know how you felt about him?"

"No . . . maybe. Oh, I don't know."

"How did he feel about you?"

"He liked me well enough."

"But not enough to marry you?"

"I told you, Thomas, he thinks marriage is a fool's mistake. And those were his exact words, no doubt said to keep me from hoping."

"I'm sorry, sweetheart, I truly am. But you know, this is no reason to set yourself against marriage. There will be other men, maybe not here, but Clinton means to take you to New Haven with him when he visits our two nieces. And if no one appeals to you there, Warren intends to take you to New York."

She had to smile at that. Her brothers, all of them, meant well. And she'd enjoy seeing her nieces again. She had wanted to raise them herself when Clinton's wife died, but she'd been only twelve at the time and was being raised more or less by servants herself, or whichever brother was home at the time. So it had been decided that they'd live with their grandparents in New Haven, since Clinton was so rarely home himself. Fortunately, New Haven wasn't so very far away.

But if she was going to visit anywhere, she'd have to do it soon, before she started showing and all hell broke loose. Maybe most of her brothers would be back to sea by then. She could hope.

Right now, she'd agree to anything to end this discussion, before Thomas thought to get even more personal in his questioning.

"I'll consider going, Thomas . . . if you'll do me a favor. Don't tell the others about . . . well, what I've told you. They wouldn't understand how I could fall in love with an Englishman. I don't understand it myself. You know, I really couldn't stand him at first, his arrogance, his . . . Well, you know how those blasted lords can be."

"A lord, too?" He rolled his eyes. "No, I can't see any good reason to mention that to my dear brothers. They'd likely want to start up the war again."

Chapter Thirty-one

"Blast it, Georgie! Don't you know better than to do that to a man?"

Georgina blinked at Drew's sharp tone, before his words sunk in. "Do what?" she asked innocently, already realizing by the way he was clutching the vase he was holding that he'd nearly dropped it when he'd glanced at her. Why she'd surprised him, though, she wasn't sure, since she'd spoken to him when she entered the study.

"Come into a room looking like that," he explained testily, glaring at the low cut of her evening gown.

She blinked again. "Well, for God's sake, Drew, how am I supposed to look for a party? Should I have worn one of my old work dresses? Maybe my gardening one, replete with grass stains?"

"You know what I meant." He glowered. "That one is much too—too—"

"There is nothing wrong with this gown. Mrs. Mullins, my seamstress, assured me it's in very good taste."

"Then Mrs. Mullins doesn't have any."

"Any what?"

"Good taste herself." When that brought a gasp and then a narrowing of her chocolate eyes, Drew decided he'd better back off. "Now, Georgie, it's not so much the dress, but what it doesn't cover, if you get my meaning."

"I got your meaning right off, Drew Anderson," she said indignantly. "Am I supposed to dress out of fashion just because my brother objects to the cut of my bodice? I'll wager you've never complained about this particular style on other women, have you?"

Since he hadn't, he decided it might be prudent to shut his mouth on the subject. But still—Damn, but she'd given him a turn. He'd known she'd blossomed into a little beauty, but this was broadcasting it from the mainmast.

Georgina took pity on his flushed discomfort. After all, she hadn't had occasion to dress up the last few times Drew was home, so it had been several years since he had seen her in anything other than her modest day dresses—and more recently, her boy's attire. She'd had this gown made up last Christmas for the Willards' annual ball, but a severe cold had kept her from wearing it then. But the Grecian style was still in the height of fashion, as was the thinness of the material, in this case a sheer rose batiste over white silk. And her mother's ruby necklace was the perfect touch to fill in the bare expanse below her neck, which Drew was objecting to.

But his objection really was a bit ridiculous. It wasn't as if she were in danger of exposing herself. There was a good inch and a half of ribbon-threaded material above her nipples, a considerable amount compared to some gowns she had seen on other women. So a little cleft was showing. A little cleft was supposed to show.

"It's all right, Drew." She grinned now. "I promise not to drop anything. And if I do, I'll let someone else pick it up for me."

He accepted that out gracefully. "See that you do," but couldn't resist adding, "you'll be lucky if Warren doesn't put a sack over your head."

She rolled her eyes. This was just what she needed to make the evening go smoothly, brothers all over the room glaring at any man who got near her, or surrounding her themselves so no man could get near.

"What were you doing with that?" she asked, indicating the vase to change the subject.

"Just having a closer look at what's cost us our China trade."

Georgina had heard the story the night of her homecoming. The vase wasn't just an antique, but a priceless piece of art from the Tang dynasty, some nine hundred years old, and Warren had won it in a game of chance. If that wasn't incredible enough, he'd wagered his ship against it! If she hadn't also heard that Warren was quite drunk at the time, she wouldn't have believed it, since the *Nereus* was the most important thing in his life.

But Clinton had confirmed it. He'd been there at the time and hadn't even tried to talk Warren out of the game, not that he could have. Apparently, he'd wanted the vase just as badly to take the risk of losing one of the Skylark ships. Of course, one ship was nothing in comparison to the value of that vase.

What neither of them had realized at the time was that the Chinese warlord who had wagered his vase against Warren's ship had no intention of honoring the bet if he lost, which he did. A group of his followers had attacked them on the way back to their ships, and if their crews hadn't come to the rescue, neither of them would have survived that night. As it was, they just barely escaped Canton without having their ships fired upon. And having to leave so suddenly was the reason they were home much sooner than expected.

As she watched Drew carefully lock the vase back in Clinton's desk, she remarked. "I'm surprised Clinton has taken it so well, that it will be a very long time before a Skylark ship dares venture into Chinese waters again."

"Oh, I don't know. As lucrative as the Canton trade was, I think he was getting tired himself of the long voyages. I know Warren was. And they did make several European stops on the way back, to establish new markets."

She hadn't heard that before. "Is England being forgiven then and considered for one of those markets?"

He looked at her and chuckled. "You must be joking. With as much money as they cost us with their arbitrary blockade before the war? Not to mention how many of their blasted warships stopped ours to impress their so-called deserters. It'll be a cold day in hell before Clinton deals with an Englishman again, even if we were desperate for their trade, which we're certainly not."

Her grimace was inward. If there had been a secret hope that she might someday return to England to see James again, she might as well bury it. If only that trip to Jamaica hadn't been his last, she could have gone back there easily enough. But he'd confessed that he had only gone there to dispose of his holdings, that he was returning to England for good.

"I didn't think so," she said now in a small voice.

"What's the frown for, Georgie? Have *you* forgiven England, after those bastards stole your Malcolm and caused you such grief?"

She almost laughed. England, no, but one particular Englishman she'd forgive anything, if only he . . . what? Had loved her a little instead of just desiring her? That was asking for the moon.

But Drew was waiting for an answer, and she gave him the one he most likely expected. "Certainly not," she snapped, and turned to leave, only to find Warren on his way into the room. His eyes went straight to her decolletage, and his expression immediately started gathering storm clouds, and she snapped again, "Not one word, Warren, or I'll rip it off and come down to the party naked, see if I don't!"

"I wouldn't," Drew cautioned when Warren started to follow her out of the room.

"Did you see the bosoms on that girl?" Warren's tone was half outrage, half amazement.

"Couldn't miss 'em." Drew smiled wryly. "I mentioned it myself, and received a quelling set-down. The girl grew up, Warren, when we weren't looking."

"She'll still have to change into something more—"

"She won't, and if you try and insist, she's likely to do exactly as she said."

"Don't be an ass, Drew. She wouldn't—"

"Are you so sure?" Drew interrupted again. "Our little Georgie has changed, and I don't just mean into a raving beauty. That was more gradual. This is so sudden, it's like she's a new woman."

"What is?"

"Her willfulness. The temper she'd been demonstrating. And don't ask me where she might have picked it up, but she's developed a droll wit that is really quite amusing at times. And snippy. Hell, it's hard to even tease her anymore, she sasses back so quickly."

"None of which has anything to do with that blasted gown she's wearing."

"Now who's being an ass?" Drew snorted, and borrowed from Georgina's own retaliation. "You wouldn't mind seeing it on any other woman, now would you? Those low-cut bits of nothing are, after all, highly fashionable," and he added with a grin, "thank God."

And that just got him a glower that Warren was still wearing when he stood in the receiving line a while later to greet their guests and intimidate any of the male gender who happened to stare at Georgina too long. No one else, of course, thought anything the least bit wrong with her lovely gown. It was, if anything, modest next to a few others worn by some of their female neighbors.

As was usually the case in a seafaring town, there were many more women present than men. But for an impromptu party, there was a fine turnout. The main gathering was in the drawing room, but with so many people showing up, and still more trickling in as the evening progressed, every room on the first floor had a small crowd of people in it.

Georgina was enjoying herself, despite the fact that Warren was never more than a few feet away. At least he'd stopped scowling. Boyd, too, after his first sight of her, was right there at her side every time a man approached her, no matter what age the man happened to be, and even if he was accompanied by a wife. Drew remained close by just to watch the other two playing big brothers, which was amusing him no end.

"Clinton informed us that you'll be sailing to New Haven soon."

"So it seems," Georgina replied to the stout lady who'd just joined her small group.

Mrs. Wiggins had married a farmer, but she came from townfolk herself and had never quite made the adjustment. She flicked open an ornate fan and began stirring the air around them. The crowded room *was* getting a bit warm.

"But you've just returned from England," the older lady pointed out, as if Georgina could forget. "By the way, dear, how did you find it?"

"Dreadful," she said in all sincerity. "Crowded. Rife with thieves and beggars." She didn't bother to mention the beautiful countryside, or the quaint villages that had, oddly enough, reminded her of Bridgeport.

"You see, Amos?" Mrs. Wiggins told her husband. "It's just as we imagined. A den of iniquity."

Georgina wouldn't have gone that far in her description. There were, after all, two sides to London—the poor and the rich—maybe she would go that far. The rich might not be thieves, but she'd met one of their lords and he was as wicked as they come.

"It's fortunate that you weren't there very long," Mrs. Wiggins continued.

"Yes," Georgina agreed. "I was able to conclude my business quite swiftly."

It was obvious the lady was dying to ask what that business was, but she wasn't quite audacious enough to do it. And Georgina wasn't about to volunteer the information that she'd been betrayed, jilted, forsaken. It still bridled that she'd been such a fool, clinging to a childhood fancy for so long. And she'd already come to the conclusion that she didn't even have love as an excuse. What she had felt for Malcolm was nothing next to what she felt for James Malory.

She blamed his name being in her thoughts for the tingling shiver of premonition that crawled down her spine a moment later when she saw Mrs. Wiggins staring in clear amazement at the doorway behind her. Of course it was absurd, wishful thinking. She had only to glance around and her pulse would slow down again. But she couldn't do it. The hope was there, regardless how unfounded, and she wanted to savor it, cling to it, before it was dashed to nothing.

"Who is he, I wonder?" Mrs. Wiggins crashed into Georgina's thoughts. "One of your brother's men, Georgina?"

Probably. Surely. They were always picking up new crewmen in other ports, and new faces always engendered curiosity here in Bridgeport. She still wouldn't look.

"He doesn't have the look of a sailor," Mr. Wiggins had concluded and said so.

"No, he doesn't." This surprisingly from Boyd, whom Georgina had forgotten was even beside her.

"But he does look familiar. I've met him before, or seen him somewhere . . . I just can't place where."

So much for raised hopes, Georgina thought in disgust. Her pulse slowed. She started breathing again. And she turned around to see who the devil they were so curious about . . . and had the floor drop out from under her.

He stood not ten feet away, big, blond, elegant, and so handsome it was painful. But the green eyes that pinned her to the spot and took her breath away were the coldest, most menacing eyes she'd ever seen in her life. Her love, her Englishman, and—the realization was fast dawning and rising up to choke her—her downfall.

Chapter Thirty-two

"What is it, Georgie?" Boyd asked in alarm. "You don't look well at all."

She couldn't answer her brother. She felt the pressure of his hand on her arm but couldn't look his way. She couldn't take her eyes off James, or believe, despite the silly game of hope she had just played with herself, that he was truly here.

He'd cut his hair. That was the first thought she was able to fix in her mind with any coherency. He'd been tying it back as they had neared Jamaica, it had grown so long, and with that golden earring flashing, he'd looked more like a pirate than ever to her adoring eyes. But he looked nothing like a pirate now. His tawny mane of hair was as flyaway as ever, as if he'd just come in out of a violent storm, but as it was a style other men spent hours trying to achieve, it looked perfectly in order. The locks that fell over his ears concealed whether he still sported the golden earring.

He could have been walking into a ball given for royalty, he was so finely turned out in velvet and silk. Had she thought he looked stunning in emerald? He looked positively devastating in dark burgundy, the nap of the velvet so fine, the many lights in the rooms cast it in jewel tones. His silk stockings were as snowy-white as the stylish cravat at his throat. A fat diamond winked there, so big it was surely drawing notice if the man himself wasn't.

Georgina had noticed all this when her eyes first swept him, before they locked with his riveting gaze, a gaze that was sending off warning signals that should have had her running for her life. She'd seen James

Malory in many different moods over the weeks she'd spent with him, several of those moods quite dark, but she'd never actually seen him truly angry, enough to lose his temper—if he even had one. But what she saw now in his eyes could have frozen a hot coal. He was angry all right, so angry, she couldn't begin to guess what he might do. For a moment, all he was doing was letting her know.

"Do *you* know him, too?"

Too? Oh, that was right. Boyd thought he looked somehow familiar. He was obviously wrong. But before she could comment at all, if she could manage to get a word past the tightness in her throat, James started to walk toward her in a deceivingly lazy stride.

"George in a dress? How unique." His dry voice carried across the space to her and everyone around her. "It becomes you, though, indeed it does. But I must say I prefer your breeches. Much more revealing of certain delectable—"

"Who are you, mister?" Boyd demanded aggressively, stepping in front of James to cut off his derogatory flow of words as well as his path.

For a moment it looked as if James would just brush him aside, and Georgina didn't doubt that he could. They might be of a height, but where Boyd was lean and hard like the rest of his brothers, James was a brick wall, broad, solid, and massively muscled. And Boyd might be a man to reckon with at twenty-six years of age, but next to James, he looked a mere boy fresh out of the schoolroom.

"Bless me, you're not actually thinking of interfering, are you, lad?"

"I asked who you are," Boyd repeated, flushing under the amused condescension he detected, but he added, with a measure of his own derision, "Aside from being an Englishman."

All signs of amusement instantly dropped. "Aside from being an Englishman, I'm James Malory. Now be a good chap and step aside."

"Not so fast." Warren moved next to Boyd to block James's path even more. "A name doesn't tell us who you are or what you're doing here."

"Another one? Shall we do this the hard way, George?"

He asked it even though he could no longer see her with Warren's towering shoulders as an obstruction. But she didn't have the least little doubt of James's meaning, whether her brothers did or not. And she found she could move after all, and quite quickly, to come around their protective wall.

"They're my brothers, James. Please don't—"

"Brothers?" he cut in sneeringly, and those frigid green eyes were back on her. "And here I thought something entirely different, with the way they were hovering over you."

There was enough insinuation in his tone for no one to mistake his meaning. Georgina gasped. Boyd flushed beet-red. Warren just threw his first punch. That it was deflected with ease disconcerted him for a moment. In that moment, Drew arrived to prevent Warren from swinging again.

"Have you lost your senses?" he hissed in an embarrassed whisper. "We've got a room full of people here, Warren. Guests, remember? Hell, I thought you'd gotten it out of your system this afternoon when you laid into me."

"You didn't hear what that son of a—"

"Actually, I did, but unlike you, I happen to know that he's the captain of the ship that brought Georgie to Jamaica. Instead of beating him to a pulp, why don't we find out what he's doing here, and why he's being so . . . provoking?"

"Obviously drunk," Boyd offered.

James didn't deign to answer that charge. He was still staring down at Georgina, his expression keeping her from showing any joy that he was here.

"You were absolutely right, George. Yours are quite tedious."

He was referring to her brothers, of course, and the remark she had made about them that first day on his ship, when she admitted she had other brothers—besides Mac. Fortunately, her three siblings didn't realize that.

Georgina didn't know what to do. She was afraid to ask James why he was here, or why he was so obviously furious with her. She wanted to get him away from her brothers before all hell broke loose, but she wasn't sure she wanted to be left alone with him. But she'd have to.

She put her hand on Warren's arm and could feel how tense he was. "I'd like a private word with the captain."

"No," was all he said.

From Warren's expression, she knew there'd be no getting around him, so she appealed for help from a different quarter. "Drew?"

Drew was more diplomatic. He merely ignored her, keeping his eyes on James. "Why exactly *are* you here, Captain Malory?" he asked in a most reasonable tone.

"If you must know, I've come to return George's belongings, which she thoughtlessly left behind in our cabin."

Georgina groaned inwardly after a quick glance at her brothers. That "our" had stood out like a flashing beacon on a moonless night, and not one of them had missed the implication. She'd been right in her first assumption. Her downfall was imminent, especially since James at his nastiest was embarrassing in the extreme, but he was obviously going for blood. She might as well dig a hole and bury herself.

"I can explain—" she began to tell her brothers, but didn't think she'd get far, and she was right.

"I'd rather hear Malory explain." Warren's tone was barely under control, much less his anger.

"But—"

"So would I," Drew was next to interrupt, his tone no longer reasonable, either.

Georgina, quite understandably, lost her temper at that point. "Blast you both! Can't you see he's deliberately looking for a fight? You ought to recognize the signs, Warren. You do the same thing all the time."

"Would someone mind telling me what is going on here?" Clinton demanded.

Georgina was almost glad to see him arrive, and with Thomas beside him. Maybe, just maybe, James might feel it would be prudent now to desist in his assassination of her reputation. She had little doubt that was his intention. She just didn't know why.

"Are you all right, sweetheart?" Thomas asked her, putting his arm protectively around her shoulders.

She just had time to nod before James said mockingly, "Sweetheart?"

"Don't even think of going that route again, James Malory," she warned in a furious undertone. "This is my brother Thomas."

"And the mountain?"

"My brother Clinton," she gritted out.

James merely shrugged. "The mistake was natural, considering there's no family resemblance. Which was it, different mothers, or fathers?"

"You're a fine one to talk about resemblance, when your brother is as dark as sin."

"Anthony will appreciate the simile, indeed he will. And I'm delighted to know you remember meeting him, George. He wouldn't have forgotten you either . . . no more than I would have."

She could be forgiven for missing the implication of that statement, as upset as she was. And Clinton was still waiting for an explanation, if the sharp clearing of his throat was any indication. Boyd beat her to it.

"He's the captain of the ship Georgie left England on, and English to boot."

"I'd already detected that much. Is *that* why you're putting on this little show for our guests?"

The condemnation in Clinton's tone left Boyd shamefaced and silent, but Drew took up where he left off. "We didn't start this, Clint. The bastard was insulting Georgie the moment he walked into the room."

James's lips curled disdainfully. "By remarking that I prefer the darling girl in breeches? That's a matter of opinion, dear boy, hardly an insult."

"That wasn't exactly how you put it, Malory, and you know it," Warren told him in a furious hiss. "And that's not the only rubbish he's been spouting, Clinton. He's also made the ridiculous claim that Georgina's belongings were kept in *his* cabin, implying—"

"Well, of course they were," James interrupted quite mildly. "Where else would her belongings be? She was, after all, my cabin boy."

He could have said lover, Georgina reminded herself as she lost every bit of color in her face. That would have been worse, but not by much.

While each of her brothers was looking at her to deny it, all she could do was stare at James. There was no triumph in his eyes, still as frigid as before. She was afraid that last thrust wasn't the final one yet.

"Georgina?"

Her thoughts clattered desperately this way and that, but could find no way to get out of the dilemma James had put her in, short of lying, which was out of the question with him standing there.

"It's a long story, Clinton. Can't it wait until lat—"

"Now!"

Wonderful. Now Clinton was furious. Even Thomas was frowning. Burying herself in a hole in the ground was likely to end up her only option.

"Very well," she said stiffly. "But in the study, if you don't mind."

"By all means."

She headed in that direction, without waiting to see who was following, but that James was the first one through the door behind her gave her a start. "*You* weren't invited."

"Ah, but I was, love. Those young pups weren't budging without me."

In answer she glowered at him, while her brothers filed through the door. Only one couple was in the room, and Drew quickly ousted them from the sofa with little fuss. Georgina tapped her toes, waiting. She might as well make a clean breast of everything and let her brothers kill James. Who the devil did he think he was dealing with here, anyway—calm, reasonable men? Ha! He was in for a rude awakening, and if his rotten plan backfired in his face, that was no more than he deserved just now.

"Well, Georgina?"

"You don't have to take that head-of-the-family tone with me, Clinton. I haven't done a single thing I'm sorry for. Circumstances forced Mac and me to work our way home, but I was disguised as a boy."

"And where did this boy-in-disguise sleep?"

"So the captain kindly offered to share his cabin with me. You've done the same for your cabin boy, as a means of protection. And it wasn't as if he knew I . . . was . . . a—" Her eyes flew to James, flaring wide and then filling with murderous lights as his previous words finally clicked. "You son of a bitch! What do you mean, you wouldn't have forgotten me? Are you saying you knew I was a girl all along, that you only *pretended* to see through my disguise later?"

With supreme nonchalance, James replied, "Quite so."

There was nothing tepid about Georgina's reaction. With a low cry of rage, she leaped across the space between them. Thomas jerked her back just short of her target and held on to her, since Warren had already claimed James's attention, swinging him about to face him.

"You compromised her, didn't you?" Warren demanded without preamble.

"Your sister behaved like a dockside doxy. She signed on as my cabin boy. She helped to dress me, even to bathe me, with nary a single protest of maidenly airs. She was compromised before I ever laid hands on her."

"My God!" Warren said. "You're actually admitting that you . . . that . . ."

Warren didn't wait for an answer, or even to finish. For the second time that evening, his emotions carried him along and he swung his fist. And for the second time, the punch was easily deflected. Only James followed it with a short jab to Warren's chin that snapped his head back, but otherwise left him standing in the same place, just slightly dazed. While he blinked away his surprise, Clinton swung James around to face him.

"Why don't you try that with me, Malory?"

Georgina couldn't believe her ears. Clinton, about to engage in fisticuffs? Staid, no-nonsense Clinton?

"Thomas, do something," she said.

"If I didn't think you'd interfere if I let you go, I'd hold that bastard myself while Clinton rearranges his face."

"Thomas!" she gasped, incredulous.

Had all of her brothers lost their senses? She could expect such remarks from the more hot-tempered three, but for God's sake, Thomas never lost his temper. And Clinton never engaged in fights. But look at him, standing there bristling, the only man in the room older than James, and perhaps the only one a match for him. And James, that devil rogue, couldn't have cared less that he had managed to fire all of this heated emotion.

"You're welcome to have a go at me, Yank," he said with a mocking slant to his mouth. "But I should warn you that I'm rather good at this sort of thing."

Taunting? Daring? The man was suicidal. Did he honestly think he'd only have Clinton to deal with? Of course, he didn't know her brothers. They might pick on each other mercilessly, but against a common enemy they united.

The two older men faced off, but after a few minutes it was readily apparent that James hadn't been bragging. Clinton had gotten in one blow, but James had landed a half dozen, each one taking its toll with those bricklike fists.

When Clinton staggered back from one particularly grueling punch, Boyd stepped in. Unfortunately, Georgina's youngest brother didn't stand a chance and likely knew it, only he was too furious to care. An uppercut and then a hard right landed him on the floor in short order . . . and then it was Warren's turn again.

He was more prepared this time. He wasn't unskilled as a fighter by any means. In fact, Warren rarely lost a fight. And his greater height and longer reach should have given him the advantage here. He'd just never come up against anyone who'd trained in the ring before. But he did acquit himself better than Clinton. His right connected solidly again and again. His blows just didn't seem to be doing any damage. It was like hitting . . . a brick wall.

He went down after about ten minutes, taking a table with him. Georgina glanced at Drew, wondering if he was going to be foolish enough to get into this, and sure enough he was grinning as he removed his coat.

"I have to hand it to you, Captain Malory. Your 'rather good' was putting it mildly. Maybe I should call for pistols instead."

"By all means. But again I should warn you—"

"Don't tell me. You're rather good at that, too?"

James actually laughed at Drew's dry tone. "Better than good, dear boy. And in all fairness, I was merely going to arm you with the same knowledge that the young cockerels at home are aware of, that I have fourteen wins to my credit, no losses. In fact, the only battles I've ever lost have been at sea."

"That's all right then. I'll take the advantage that you must be tiring."

"Oh, hell, I don't believe it!" Boyd suddenly exclaimed, to Drew's annoyance.

"Stay out of this, baby brother," Drew told him. "You had your turn."

"No, you dolt, I've just remembered where I've seen him before. Don't you recognize him, Thomas? Imagine him with a beard—"

"My God," Thomas said incredulously. "He's that damned pirate, Hawke, who had me limping into port."

"Aye, and he walked off with my entire cargo, and on my first voyage on the *Oceanus* as sole owner, too."

"Are you certain?" Clinton demanded.

"Oh, for God's sake, Clinton," Georgina scoffed at this point. "You can't take them seriously. A pirate? He's a damned English lord, a viscount something-or-other—"

"Of Ryding," James supplied.

"Thank you," she replied automatically, but went right on as if there'd been no interruption. "To accuse him of being a blasted pirate is so ludicrous, it—"

"That's gentleman pirate, love, if you don't mind," James interrupted her once again in his drollest tone of voice. "And retired, not that it matters."

She didn't thank him this time. The man was positively insane. There was no other excuse for what he'd just admitted. And that admission was all her brothers had needed to converge on him in force.

She watched for a moment, until they all crashed onto the floor, a small mountain of sprawled legs and swinging arms. She finally turned to Thomas, who still had his arm firmly about her shoulder, as if he thought her stupid enough to get in the middle of *that*.

"You have to stop them, Thomas!"

She didn't know how urgent she sounded. And Thomas wasn't dense. Unlike his brothers, he'd been watching the two principals involved in this distasteful affair rather closely. The Englishman's baleful stares lasted only as long as Georgina was looking at him. When she wasn't, there was something else entirely in his eyes. And Georgina's emotions were even more revealing.

"He's the one you've been crying over, isn't he, Georgie?" he asked her very gently. "The one you—"

"He was, but he's not anymore," she replied emphatically.

"Then why should I try to interfere?"

"Because they're going to *hurt* him!"

"I see. And here I thought that was the idea."

"Thomas! They're just using that piracy nonsense as an excuse to stop being fair about this, because they weren't getting anywhere fighting him individually."

"That's possible, but this piracy business isn't nonsense, Georgie. He *is* a pirate."

"Was," she staunchly maintained. "You heard him say he's retired."

"Sweetheart, that doesn't alter the fact that during his unsavory career, the man crippled two of our ships and stole a valuable cargo."

"He can make reparations."

The argument lost its point just then as the combatants began rising from the floor. All but James Malory. Brick walls weren't invincible after all.

Chapter Thirty-three

James managed to keep the groan from escaping his swollen lips as he regained consciousness. He took a quick mental inventory, but didn't think his ribs were more than badly bruised. His jaw he wasn't so sure about.

Well, he'd bloody well asked for it, hadn't he? He couldn't just keep his mouth shut and play ignorant when those two younger brothers had remembered him and brought his past into it. Even George had defended him in her moment of disbelief. But no, he had to let the skeletons out of the closet for a clean breast of it.

It wouldn't have been so bad if there weren't so many of them. Hell and fire, *five* of the bloody Yanks! Where were Artie and Henry's wits to have failed to mention that? Where were his, for that matter, in abandoning his original plan to confront George alone? Connie had warned him, indeed he had. And Connie was going to gloat to England and back over this, might even mention it to Anthony just to rub it in further, and then James would never hear the end of it.

And what the devil had he thought to accomplish in coming to their bloody party anyway, aside from embarrassing the darling girl as she deserved? It was the party, or the idea of it, and George flitting around enjoying herself with a dozen beaus surrounding her, that made James lose his wits. And damned if he hadn't found her so well protected by those idiots she was related to that no one could get near her, not even him.

Their voices were buzzing around him, coming from different directions, some far away, some close, just above him in fact. He imagined one of them was watching for signs of his coming awake, and he thought briefly of changing places with the chap. He'd gone easy on them for Georgie's sake, and look what it had gotten him, when he could just as easily have taken each of them out within a matter of seconds while they were still being fair-minded about it. On second thought, perhaps he wasn't quite up to making the effort just now, after they'd tried pounding him through the bloody floor. He'd do better to concentrate on what they were saying, but that effort was almost as difficult through the haze of pain clamoring for attention.

"I'm not believing it, Thomas, until I hear it from Georgie."

"She tried to clobber him herself, you know."

"I was here, Boyd." The only voice that was easy to listen to, and it was so soothing. "I was the one who stopped her. But it makes no difference. I tell you she—"

"But she was still pining over Malcolm!"

"Drew, you ass, how many times do you have to be told, that was pure stubbornness on her part."

"Why the hell don't you stay out of this entirely, Warren! The only thing that comes out of your mouth these days is rubbish anyway."

A brief scuffle, and then, "For God's sake, you two, haven't you garnered enough bruises for one day?"

"Well, I've had enough of his damned bitterness dropping in my corner, Clinton, I really have. The Englishman could take lessons from him."

"I'd say that was the other way around, but that's neither here nor there. Kindly shut up, Warren, if you can't contribute anything constructive. And stop being so blasted touchy, Drew. You're not helping matters any."

"Well, I don't believe it anymore than Boyd does." James was beginning to distinguish voices, and this one from the hot-tempered Warren grated along points already throbbing. "The blockhead doubts it, too, so—"

More scuffling ended that revelation. James sincerely hoped they killed each other—after he found out what they were so doubting of. He was about to sit up and ask when they crashed into his feet, jarring his whole body. His groan was telling enough.

"How are you feeling, Malory?" he was asked by a surprisingly amused voice. "Fit enough for a wedding?"

James cracked his eyelids open to see the baby-faced Boyd grinning down at him. With all the contempt he was capable of, he said, "My own brothers have done a better job on me than you puling pups."

"Then maybe we should give it another go-round," said the one whose name ought to be cut in half. War suited him so much better.

"Sit *down,* Warren!"

The order came from Thomas, surprising them all, except James, who had no idea this Anderson brother rarely raised his voice. And he really couldn't have cared less just then. Determinedly, he concentrated everything he had on sitting up without flinching.

And then it hit him, "What the bloody hell d'you mean, wedding?"

"Yours, Englishman, and Georgie's. You compromised her, you'll marry her, or we'll very cheerfully kill you."

"Then smile away, dear boy, and pull the trigger. I won't be forced—"

"Isn't that what you came here for, Malory?" Thomas asked enigmatically.

James glowered at him, while the brothers all reacted in different degrees of amazement.

"Have you gone crazy, Thomas?"

"Well, that explains everything, doesn't it?" This, sarcastically.

"Where are you getting these ridiculous notions from, first about Georgie, now this?"

"Would you like to explain that, Tom?"

"It doesn't matter," Thomas replied, watching James. "The English mind is too complicated by half."

James wasn't going to comment on that. Talking to these imbeciles was a headache in itself. Slowly, with extreme care, he got to his feet. As he did, so did Warren and Clinton, who had been sitting down. James almost laughed. Did they really think he had anything left in him that they need worry about just now? Bloody giants. Little George couldn't have a *normal* family, could she?

"By the by, where is George?" he wanted to know.

The young one, who'd been pacing the floorboards in agitation, stopped in front of him to glower hotly. "That's not her name, Malory."

"Good God, indignation over a name, now." And with a lack of the indifference James was known for, "I'll call her any bloody thing I like, puppy. Now where have you put her?"

"We haven't *put* her anywhere," Drew's voice came from behind him. "She's right here."

James swung around, winced at what the sharp movement did to him, saw Drew first, standing between him and the sofa. And on the sofa, stretched out and looking as pale as death, and quite unconscious, Georgina.

"What the bloody hell!"

Drew, the only one to actually see the murderous expression that crossed James's face as he started toward the sofa, tried to stop him, but wished he hadn't as he landed with slamming force against the wall. The impact tilted every picture on the wall, and a crash was heard out in the hall, where one of the servants was so startled by the sudden loud noise that she dropped her tray of glasses.

"Let it go, Warren," Thomas cautioned. "He's not going to hurt her." And to James, "She merely fainted, man, when she got a good look at you."

"She never faints," Boyd insisted. "I tell you she's playing possum so she won't have to listen to Clinton yell at her."

"You should have beat her when you had the chance, Clint," This bit of disgruntlement came from Warren, which got him exasperated looks from each of his brothers, but something altogether unexpected from the only non-family member in the room.

"You lay a bloody hand on her and you're dead."

James didn't even turn around to snarl that warning. He was on his knees beside the sofa, gently patting Georgina's ashen cheek, trying to bring her around.

Into the pregnant silence that followed, Thomas looked at Clinton and said calmly, "I told you."

"So you did. All the more reason we don't drag our feet about this."

"If you'd just let me turn him over to Governor Wolcott for hanging, there'd be no problem."

"He's still compromised her, Warren," Clinton reminded him.

"There will be a wedding to amend that before we discuss anything else."

Their voices droned on behind him, but James was only vaguely listening. He didn't like Georgina's color. Her breathing was too shallow, too. Of course, he'd never dealt with a fainting woman himself before. Someone else was always around to do that and stick smelling salts under her nose. Her brothers must not have any salts, or they'd have used it. Weren't burnt feathers supposed to do the trick, too? He eyed the sofa, wondering what it was stuffed with.

"You might try tickling her feet," Drew suggested, coming up to stand behind James. "They're very sensitive."

"I know that." James replied, remembering the time his hand had merely brushed against her bare instep and she'd practically kicked him out of his bed in reflex.

"You know? How the devil do you know?"

James sighed, hearing the belligerence back in Drew's tone. "By accident, dear boy. You don't think I'd participate in such childish antics as tickling, do you?"

"I wonder just what antics you *have* participated in with my sister?"

"No more than you've already assumed."

Drew inhaled sharply before replying, "I'll say this for you, Englishman. You know how to dig a hole very deep for yourself."

James glanced over his shoulder. He would have smiled if it wouldn't have hurt to do so. "Not at all. Would you have me lie about it?"

"Yes, by God, I wish you had!"

"Sorry, lad, but I haven't the conscience you seem burdened with. As I told your sister, I'm quite reprehensible when it comes to certain aspects of my life."

"Meaning women?"

"Well, aren't you the discerning fellow."

Drew flushed with ire, fists clenching. "You *are* worse than Warren, by God! If you want some more—"

"Back off, puppy. Your heart's in the right place, I'm sure, but you're not capable of taking me on and you know it. So why don't you make yourself useful instead and fetch something to revive your sister? She really ought to join this particular party."

Drew stomped off angrily to follow his suggestion, but was back in a moment with a glass half full of water. James eyed it skeptically. "What, pray tell, am I supposed to do with that?" For answer Drew splashed the contents in Georgina's face. "Well, I'm bloody well glad you did it rather than me," James told Drew as Georgina sat up sputtering, shrieking, and looking around for the culprit.

"You fainted, Georgie," Drew told her quickly by way of explanation.

"There must be a dozen women in the other room with smelling salts," she said furiously as she sat up and began rubbing water off her cheeks and upper chest with stiff fingers. "Couldn't you have asked one?"

"Didn't think of that."

"Well, you could have at least brought a towel with the water," and then, aghast, "Blast you, Drew, look what you've done to my gown!"

"A gown you never should have been wearing in the first place," he retorted. "*Now* maybe you'll go change it."

"I'll wear it till it rots off if you did this just so I'd—"

"Children, if you don't mind . . ." James cut in pointedly, bringing Georgina's eyes to him.

"Oh, James, look at your face!"

"That's rather difficult to do, brat. But I wouldn't talk, with yours still dripping."

"With water, you ass, not blood!" she snapped, then turned to Drew. "Well, haven't you at least got a handkerchief?"

He dug in his pocket and handed over a white square, expecting her to wipe her face with it. Instead he watched in bemusement as she leaned forward and carefully dabbed at the blood encrusted around the Englishman's mouth. And the man let her, just knelt there on his knees and let her attend him as if he hadn't been looking daggers at her earlier, and he hadn't embarrassed her in front of family and friends, and they hadn't *just* been snapping at each other.

He glanced around to see if his brothers had noticed this irrational behavior, too. Clinton and Warren hadn't. They were too busy still arguing. But Boyd met his glance and rolled his eyes. Drew quite agreed with him. And Thomas was shaking his head, though obviously amused. Drew couldn't find *anything* about any of this amusing. He was damned if he wanted a pirate for a brother-in-law, retired or not.

Worse, an English pirate. Even worse, a lord of the old realm. And he damned well couldn't believe that his sister had actually fallen in love with the fellow. It simply defied reason.

So what was Georgina doing fussing over him right now? And why had she fainted just because they'd messed up his face a little?

Drew admitted the Englishman was a fine figure of a man. An unmatched pugilist, too, that Drew might admire, but Georgie wouldn't. And he supposed he might even say the fellow could be called handsome, at least he had been before they'd puffed up his face. But would Georgina let such minor things sway her when he had so many black marks against him? Oh, hell, nothing had made sense to him since he'd found her in Jamaica.

"You're quite handy with your fists, aren't you?"

Drew's attention snapped back upon hearing that testy question out of his sister. He eyed Malory for his reaction, but it was hard to distinguish any expression at all under so much damage.

"You could say I've trained a bit in the ring."

"Wherever did you find the time," Georgina came back with sarcasm, "between running a plantation in the islands *and* pirating?"

"You've told me yourself how *old* I am, brat. Stands to reason I've had time for a great many pursuits in my lifetime, don't it?"

Drew almost choked, hearing that. The noise he did make drew Georgina's attention back to him. "You're still just standing about, when you could be helpful? His eye needs something cold for the swelling . . . Yours does, too, for that matter."

"Oh, no, Georgie girl. Horses couldn't drag me out of here just now, so save your breath. But if you want me to step back so you can have a word alone with this scoundrel, why don't you just ask?"

"I want nothing of the sort," she insisted indignantly. "I have absolutely nothing to say to him"—her eyes came back to James to clarify—"to you. Nothing . . . except that your behavior tonight has gone beyond your usual unpleasantness to the despicable. I should have realized you were capable of such meanness. All the signs were there. But no, I foolishly deemed your particular brand of ridicule as harmless, a habit as you say, without serious malice. I believed that! But you proved me wrong, didn't you? That double-damned tongue of yours has shown itself to be viciously lethal. Well, are you happy with what you've wrought? Has it quite amused you? Has it? And what the devil are you doing on your knees? They should have put you to bed."

She worked herself up to a fine rage, and then to end with a note of concern for him! James sat back on his heels and laughed. It hurt like bloody hell, but he couldn't seem to help himself.

"So good of you to spare me, George, and say nothing," he finally said.

She glared at him a moment, then asked quite seriously, "What are you doing here, James?"

With that one question, his humor was shattered. In the blink of an eye, his hostility was back.

"You neglected to say goodbye, love. I thought I'd give you an opportunity to correct that oversight."

So there was motive to his madness? He'd felt slighted? And for that petty, vengeful little reason, he'd destroyed her reputation *and* what she felt for him? Well, she could be grateful for the latter. To think she'd actually been eating herself up with grief because she thought she would never see him again. Now she *wished* she'd never see him again.

"Oh, well, how thoughtless of me," she said in a purringly brittle tone as she pushed to her feet, "and soooo easy to rectify. *Goodbye,* Captain Malory."

Georgina brushed passed him, ready to make the most splendid exit of her life, and came face-to-face with her brothers, all looking at her, and all having heard every word of her heated exchange with James. How *could* she have forgotten they were in the room?

Chapter Thirty-four

"Well now, it's plain to see that you two are *well* acquainted."

Georgina frowned at Warren's snide remark, her defenses rising along with her embarrassment and underlying anger. "And what's that supposed to insinuate, Warren? I spent five weeks on his ship in the capacity of a cabin boy, as he so *thoughtfully* informed you."

"And in his bed?"

"Oh, are we finally getting around to asking me?" A single brow rose in a perfect imitation of James's affectation, and she wasn't even aware that the royal vernacular "we" she had just used was also his habit, not hers. Sarcasm was not her forte, after all, and in attempting it, it was only natural to draw from a master. "And here I thought you didn't need any further confirmation beyond an admitted pirate's word. That *is* why you four pounced on the man and tried to kill him, isn't it? Because you *believed* his every word? It didn't even once occur to you that he might be lying?"

Clinton and Boyd were feeling enough guilt over that to give themselves away with red faces. She couldn't see Drew's reaction behind her, but Warren was obviously feeling justified.

"No man in his right mind would claim lawless activities if it weren't true."

"No? If you knew him, Warren, you'd know it's just like him to admit to something like that whether it was true or not, just for effect and reaction. He thrives on dissension, you see. And besides, who says he's in his right mind?"

"Now I object to that, George, indeed I do," James protested mildly from the sofa, where he had moved his sore body. "Furthermore, your dear brothers recognized me, or have you forgotten that?"

"Rot you, James!" she threw over her shoulder at him. "Can't you keep quiet for a few blasted minutes? You've made more than enough contributions to this discussion—"

"This is not a discussion, Georgina," Clinton interrupted, his voice sternly disapproving. "You were asked a question. You might as well answer it now and save yourself all this procrastinating."

Georgina groaned inwardly. There *was* no getting around it. And she shouldn't feel so—so ashamed, but these were her brothers, for God's sake. You just didn't tell overly protective brothers that you'd been intimate with a man who wasn't your husband. Such things weren't discussed without a great deal of embarrassment even if you *were* married.

For about half a second she considered lying. But there was the proof that would start showing itself soon in the form of her baby. And there was James, who wasn't likely to let her get away with denying it after he'd taken such pains to make their intimacy known, just to appease the blasted vanity she'd wounded.

Frustrated and backed into a corner, she opted for bravado. "How would you like to hear it? Should I spell it out, or will it suffice to say that in this case, Captain Malory was telling the truth?"

"Ah, hell, Georgie, a blasted pirate?"

"Did I *know* that, Boyd?"

"An Englishman!" from Drew.

"Now there's a fact I couldn't miss," she said dryly. "It comes out of his mouth with every word he speaks."

"Don't get snippy, Georgie," Clinton warned her. "Your choice in men is deplorable."

"At least she's consistent," Warren interjected. "From bad to worse."

"I don't think they like me, George," James put his two cents in.

It was the last straw, as far as she was concerned. "You can all just stop it. So I made a mistake. I'm sure I'm not the first woman to do so, and I won't be the last. But at least I'm not foolishly blinded anymore. I know now that he set out to seduce me from the start, something the lot of you practice on a regular basis, so you'd be hypocrites to blame him for that. He was very subtle about it, so subtle I didn't know what he was doing. But then I was under the misconception that he thought I was a boy, which I now know to be false. *I* have reason to be furious, but you don't, since I can picture at least half of you doing exactly as James did if presented with similar circumstances. But regardless of the ways and means, I was a willing participant. I knew exactly what I was doing. My conscience can attest to that."

"Your *what?*"

"Well said, George," James remarked behind her, rather amazed at how she'd blamed and defended in the same breath. "But I'm sure they'd much rather have heard that you were raped, or in some other dastardly way taken advantage of."

She swung about, eyes narrowed on the cause of her woes. "You *don't* think I was taken advantage of?"

"Hardly, dear girl. I wasn't the one who confessed to being nauseous."

She flamed red, noticeably red, at that reminder. Oh, God, he wasn't going to tell them about *that*, was he?

"What's this?" Drew wanted to know, the only one to see her heightened color.

"Nothing . . . a private joke," she choked out, while her eyes beseeched James to keep his mouth shut for once.

Of course he wouldn't. "A joke, George? Is that what you call—"

"I'm going to kill you, James Malory, I swear I am!"

"Not before you marry him, you're not."

"*What?*" she shrieked, and turned to stare incredulously at the brother who'd uttered those ridiculous words. "Clinton, you can't be serious! You don't *want* him in the family, do you?"

"That's beside the point. You chose him—"

"I did no such thing! And he won't marry me—" She paused to glance back at James, a long pause, full of sudden hesitancy. "Will you?"

"Certainly not," he replied testily, only to look a bit hesitant himself before asking, "Do you *want* me to?"

"Certainly not." Her pride forced the words out, well aware of his feelings on the subject. She turned back to her brothers. "I believe that settles it."

"It was already settled, Georgie, while both you and the captain were unconscious," Thomas told her. "You'll be married tonight."

"*You* instigated this, didn't you?" she said accusingly, their conversation of this morning suddenly bright in her mind.

"We're only doing what's right for you."

"But this isn't right for me, Thomas. I won't marry a man who doesn't want me."

"There was never any question about wanting you, brat," James said, a distinct irritation in his tone now. "You'd make a fine mistress."

Georgina just gasped. Her brothers were more vocal.

"You bastard!"

"You'll marry her or—"

"Yes, I know," James cut in before they got carried away again. "You'll shoot me."

"We'll do better than that, man," Warren growled. "We'll fire your ship!"

James sat up at that, only to hear from Clinton, "Someone has already been dispatched to discover her location, since it's obvious you didn't sail her into port or we would have heard about it."

James stood up at that, only to hear from Warren again, "They will also arrange for the detainment of your crew. Then the lot of you can be turned over to the governor for hanging."

Into the charged silence following that announcement, Boyd asked reasonably, "Do you think we ought to hang him if he's Georgie's husband? It doesn't seem right, hanging a brother-in-law."

"Hanging!" Georgina exclaimed, having been unconscious during the previous mention of this option. "Have you all gone mad?"

"He confessed to piracy, Georgie, and I'm sure Skylark hasn't been his only victim. In good conscience, that can't be overlooked."

"The devil it can't. He'll make restitution. Tell them you'll make restitution, James." But when she glanced at him for confirmation that might get him out of this, he was looking like hell warmed over, and four-fifths was pride, which kept his mouth firmly closed. "Thomas!" she wailed then, feeling very close to panic. "This is getting out of hand! We're talking about crimes committed . . . years ago!"

"Seven or eight," he replied with a careless shrug. "My memory seems to be quite faulty, though Captain Malory's hostility does seem to jog it remarkably well."

James laughed at that point, but it wasn't a pleasant sound by any means. "Blackmail now, to go along with coercion? Threats of violence and mayhem? And you bloody colonials call me the pirate?"

"We only mean to turn you over for trial, but as Boyd and myself are the only witnesses against you . . ."

The rest was left unsaid, but even Georgina grasped what Thomas was implying. If James would cooperate, nothing would come of his so-called trial, for lack of positive testimony. She even started to relax, until another brother was heard from.

"*Your* memory might get mucked up with sentiment, Thomas," Warren said. "But I very clearly heard the man's confession. And I'll damned well bear witness to it."

"Your strategy boggles the mind, Yanks. Which is it to be? Vindictiveness or vindication? Or are you under the misconception that the one complements the other?"

James's mordant humor threw sparks on Warren's frothing enmity. "There won't be any vindication if I have anything to say about it, and there's no need to dangle that carrot before you, *Hawke*." The name was said with such contempt, it had the distinct sound of an epithet. "There's still your ship and your crew. And if you don't care about the one, what you decide right now will determine whether your crew should be brought up on charges alongside you."

It took a considerable lot to overset the smooth urbanity of James's personality these days. He'd long ago mastered the dangerous temper of his youth, and although he still got angry occasionally, it took someone who'd known him for years to even notice. But you didn't threaten his family and hope to come away unscathed, and half of his crew was like family to him.

He started toward Warren slowly. Georgina, watching him, had a suspicion that her brother had prodded him too far, but not that the dangerous capabilities she and Mac had both sensed in the man at their first meeting had just been unleashed.

Even his voice was deceiving in its soft abrasion as he warned, "You go beyond your rights as pertains to this business in bringing my ship and crew into it."

Warren snorted with disdain. "If she's a British vessel lurking in our waters? Furthermore, a ship suspected of piracy? We are clearly within our rights."

"Then so am I."

It happened so fast, everyone in the room was held momentarily in shock, in particular Warren, who felt the incredibly strong hands tightening inexorably around his throat. He was no weakling himself, but his fingers couldn't break the hold. Clinton and Drew, each jumping forward to grab one of James's arms, couldn't manage to pull him off, either. And James's fingers were slowly, relentlessly squeezing.

Warren's face was purpling vividly before Thomas found something heavy enough to knock James unconscious with. But he didn't have to use it. Georgina, with her heart in her throat, had leaped on James's back and was screaming in his ear, "James, please, he's my brother!" and the man simply let go.

Clinton and Drew did likewise, to catch Warren as he started sinking to the floor. They helped him to the nearest chair, examined his neck, and decided nothing was crushed. He was coughing now as he labored to fill his starved lungs.

Georgina slid off James's back, still shaken by what he'd almost done. Her anger hadn't set in yet, but as he turned to face her, she saw that his was still in full bloom.

"I could have snapped his bloody neck in two seconds! Do you know that?"

She cringed under the blast of his rage. "Yes, I—I think we do."

For a moment he just glared at her. She had the feeling that he hadn't released nearly enough of his anger on Warren, that he had a good store of it in reserve for her. It blazed from his eyes, showed in the tension in his big body.

But after the intense moment passed, he surprised her and everyone else in the room by growling, "Then bring on your parson before I'm tempted again."

It took less than five minutes to locate the good Reverend Teal, who was a guest at the party still going on in the rest of the house. So in short order, Georgina was married to James Malory, viscount of Ryding, retired pirate and God only knew what else. It was not exactly how she had imagined her wedding would be, all those years she had thought about it as she waited patiently for Malcolm to return to her. Patiently? No, she realized now it had been merely indifference. But there was nothing of indifference in any of the occupants gathered in the study.

James had given in, but with complete ill grace. Resentment and ire were just a few of the inappropriate emotions he was displaying at his wedding. And Georgina's brothers were no better, absolutely determined to see her married, but hating every minute of it, and showing every bit of it. For herself, she'd realized she couldn't play stubborn and let her pride prevent this farce as she wanted, not with a baby to think about who would benefit from its father's name.

She'd wondered briefly if anyone's attitude would change if they knew about the baby, but she doubted it. James was being forced to marry either way, and there was no getting around that humiliating fact. Maybe afterward it might make a difference to him, lighten the blow, as it were. She'd have to tell him sometime, she supposed . . . or maybe she wouldn't, if Warren had his way.

And he had his way the moment the good reverend pronounced them man and wife. "Lock him up. He's already had all the wedding nights he's going to get."

Chapter Thirty-five

"You don't really think that will work again, do you, Georgie?"

Georgina poked her head over Clinton's desk where she'd been trying to break into the locked drawer. Drew was standing there, shaking his dark golden head at her. Boyd stood next to him, looking baffled over Drew's question.

Georgina stood up slowly, furious that she'd been caught. Double-damn, she'd been so sure they'd all gone to bed. And Drew was too discerning by half, having guessed what she was up to. She brazened it out anyway.

"I don't know what you mean."

"Aye, you do, sweetheart." Drew grinned at her. "Even if you got your hands on it, that vase becomes insignificant next to what that Englishman did to you. Warren would sacrifice the vase rather than let Captain Hawke go."

"I wish you wouldn't call him that," she said, wearily dropping into the chair behind the desk.

"Am I hearing this right?" Boyd demanded. "You want to let that blackguard go free, Georgie?"

Her chin rose a notch. "What if I do? All of you have overlooked the fact that James came here because of me. If he hadn't, he wouldn't have been recognized by you and Thomas, wouldn't be locked in the cellar right now. Do you think my conscience could bear it if he goes to trial and gets sentenced to hang?"

"He could also be cleared in a trial if Thomas has anything to do about it," Boyd pointed out.

"I'm not taking that chance."

Drew's brows narrowed speculatively. "Do you love him, Georgie?"

"What nonsense," she scoffed.

"Thank God." His sigh was quite loud. "I'd truly thought you'd lost your senses."

"Well, if I did," she retorted stiffly, "I've thankfully regained them. But I'm still not going to let Warren and Clinton have their way."

"Clinton couldn't care less that he's the infamous Hawke," Drew said. "He just wants him never to darken our door again. He's still smarting that he couldn't get the better of him."

"Neither could you two, but I haven't heard you calling for the rope."

Boyd chuckled. "You've got to be kidding, Georgie. Weren't you watching the man? We were so outclassed, it was a joke even trying to take him on. There's no shame in losing to someone that skilled with his fists."

Drew just smiled. "Boyd's right. There's a lot to admire in the man, if he weren't so—so—"

"Antagonizing? Insulting? Disparaging in his every remark?" Georgina almost laughed. "I hate to be the one to tell you, but that happens to be the way he is *all* the time, even to his close friends."

"But that would drive me crazy," Boyd exclaimed. "Didn't it you?"

Georgina shrugged. "Once you get used to it, it's kind of amusing. But as habits go, it's a dangerous one, since he simply doesn't care if he rubs someone the wrong way . . . like tonight. But regardless of his habits, or his past crimes, or anything else, I don't think he's been dealt with fairly by us."

"Fair enough," Boyd insisted, "considering what he did to you."

"Let's not bring me into this. You don't hang a man for seducing a woman, or you'd both be in trouble yourselves, wouldn't you?" Boyd had the grace to blush, but Drew just grinned maddeningly. "I'll put it another way," Georgina continued, giving Drew a disgusted look. "I don't care if he was a pirate, I don't want him to hang. And his crew should never have been brought into it, either. He was right about that."

"Maybe so, but I don't see what you can do about it," Boyd replied. "What you've said isn't going to make the least bit of difference to Warren."

"He's right," Drew added. "You might as well go to bed and hope for the best."

"I can't do that," she said simply and slumped back in her chair.

She was starting to feel that insidious panic again that had brought her in here to try desperate measures. She forced it back. Panic didn't help. She had to think. And then it came to her as she watched her two youngest brothers head toward the liquor cabinet, likely what had brought them both here. She wasn't surprised they needed a little help sleeping tonight, as bruised as they both were. She tried not to think of how much worse James had been injured.

She began by stating the facts. "James is your brother-in-law now. You all saw to that. Will you two help?"

"You want us to wrestle the key away from Warren?" Drew grinned. "I'm all for that."

Boyd, in the process of taking a sip of brandy, choked. "Don't even think about it!"

"That's not what I had in mind," Georgina clarified. "There's no reason for either of you to get in Warren's bad graces, no reason for him to know that any of us did anything, for that matter."

"I suppose we could break that old lock on the cellar door easy enough," Drew allowed.

"No, that won't do, either," Georgina said. "James won't leave without his crew or his ship, but he's in no condition to free either one. He may *think* he is, but—"

"So you want us to help him with that, too?"

"That's just it. As angry as he is just now, I honestly don't think he'd accept your help. He'd try to do it all himself and end up caught again. But if we free his ship and crew first, then it will be an easy matter for them to break James out and help him back to his ship. Then they'll be gone by morning, and Warren will have to assume that his men missed one or two of them, who were able to help the rest escape."

"And what about the guard Warren has left on the *Maiden Anne* who will tell him exactly who came aboard?"

"Those men can't tell him if they don't recognize anyone," Georgina said confidently. "I'll explain on our way there. Just give me a few minutes to change my clothes."

As she came around the desk, though, Drew grabbed her arm to ask softly, "Will you go with him?"

There was no hesitation or emotion in her reply, "No, he doesn't want me."

"Seems I heard something different."

She stiffened at the reminder that they'd all heard James say she'd make a fine mistress. "Then let me rephrase that. He doesn't want a wife."

"Well, there's no arguing with that. And neither Clinton nor Warren would let you go, anyway. They might have married you to him, but I can tell you true, it wasn't with the intention of letting you live with him."

And she couldn't argue with that, nor did she want to live with James. She'd meant it earlier when she said she didn't love him. She didn't anymore, she really didn't, and if she kept saying it often enough, it was going to be absolutely true.

Chapter Thirty-six

Forty minutes later, the three youngest Andersons found the small bay where the *Maiden Anne* was still anchored. Warren's crew had captured her with the pretense of an official boarding by the harbor master, and there'd been little Conrad Sharpe could do since he didn't know whether Bridgeport had jurisdiction over this area of the coast or not. Fortunately, no one had been hurt. The deceit had worked perfectly in getting enough of Warren's crew transferred over from the *Nereus* to the *Maiden Anne* for them to then take control of the unsuspecting ship. And since Warren hadn't given his men orders to bring either the ship or crew into Bridgeport, his men had simply locked the *Maiden Anne*'s crew in their own hold and left a small contingent of men to guard them and the ship. The *Nereus* hadn't even remained behind, but had returned to Bridgeport with most of her crew.

With the whole thing having been accomplished from ship to ship, Georgina was hoping there would be a skiff somewhere along the shore that James had used to land, and they could use to get out to the ship. But after ten minutes of searching, it appeared that James had merely been dropped off.

"I hope you know I hadn't figured on a midnight swim being part of this crazy scheme. It's the middle of October, if you hadn't noticed. We're going to freeze our . . . you-know-whats . . . George."

Georgina flinched at the new name both her brothers had been ribbing her with since she surprised them by coming downstairs dressed in her old boy's togs, which James had so thoughtfully returned to her. Drew had gone one further to really embarrass her in remarking, "I

766

really don't like you in those breeches, now that your Englishman has pointed out what parts of you can be so easily admired in them."

"I don't know what you're complaining about, Boyd," she said testily now. "Imagine how much more difficult this would have been had they brought her into the harbor where we'd have the watch on every nearby ship to contend with, not just Warren's men."

"Had they done that, little sister, you'd never have gotten me to agree to this business in the first place."

"Well, you did agree," she said testily. "So get your shoes off and let's get it over with. These men do need *some* sort of head start, just in case Warren gets *really* ridiculous and decides to go after them."

"Warren might be feeling justified where your captain is concerned," Drew pointed out, "but he's not suicidal. Those aren't toy cannon poking out of those gunports on yonder ship, sweetheart. And the Hawke says he's retired?"

"Old habits die hard, I imagine," she said in James's defense, which was becoming a habit she ought to break. "Besides, he was sailing in the West Indies, where pirates do still roam."

That piece of logic brought chuckles from both brothers, with Drew remarking, "That's rich, an expirate worried about attack from his old buddies."

With memories reminding her how true that statement was, Georgina only said, "If you two don't show a leg, you can stay with the horses. I'll go on without you."

"Clinton was right, by God," Drew told Boyd as he hopped on one foot to get the boot off his other. "Bossy, that's what she's become, plain and . . . Now hold on, Georgie, you aren't going up that anchor cable first!"

But she was already in the water, and they both had to scramble to catch up with her. As they were strong swimmers, it didn't take long, and soon the three of them were gliding smoothly across the bay. Ten minutes later, they neared the ship and swam around to the anchor cable, which they would now have to use to climb aboard.

The original plan had included the use of James's skiff, to just brazenly approach the ship in it and claim they'd found another of the *Maiden Anne*'s crewmen in town and had brought him out for safekeeping with the others. Georgina would have done the talking and stayed in front, since she was the least likely of the three of them to be recognized. Drew would have kept behind them, and Boyd was to be the "prisoner" in the middle. Then as soon as she got close enough to one of the guards, she was to duck and let Boyd bash him. Very simple. But since they weren't likely to swim out to the ship with a prisoner in tow, those plans had to be abandoned, at least until the deck was secured. And neither Drew nor Boyd was about to let Georgina participate in that, which left her twiddling her thumbs in the water while they both disappeared over the side of the ship.

She waited, but none too patiently, as the minutes passed and she had no way of knowing what was happening above. The lack of any noise was heartening, but what might she really hear with the water lapping in her ears, and her ears covered by the woolen cap which completed her disguise? And with nothing to distract her, it wasn't long before her position in the water began to work on her imagination.

Were there sharks in the area? Hadn't one of her neighbors caught a shark just last year when he'd gone fishing up the coast? In the shadow of the ship, she couldn't see anything on the surface of the water, much less anything swimming around under her.

Once the question arose, it was less than a minute before Georgina was out of that water and climbing the anchor cable. Not to go all the way up, though. She'd been told to wait with an added "or else," and had no intention of getting Boyd and Drew angry with her after they'd been so obliging to help her. But intentions didn't take into account that her hands weren't made for dangling from a thick cable. In fact, she only just barely made it to the top rail before her hold gave out. And considering that she would have gone splashing back into what she was now absolutely positive was shark-infested water, she was pretty relieved to pull herself over the side—until she saw the dozen men standing there ready to greet her.

Chapter Thirty-seven

Standing in the puddle of water pooling at her feet, shivering in the frigid night wind whipping across the deck, Georgina heard the dry, disparaging voice say, "Well, if it isn't old George. Come to pay us a visit, have you?"

"Connie?" Georgina said on a gasp as the tall red-head stepped toward her to drop a heavy coat around her shoulders. "But . . . what are you doing free?"

"So you know what's happened here?"

"Of course I . . . but I don't understand. Did you escape on your own?"

"As soon as the hatch opened. These countrymen of yours aren't too smart, are they, squirt? It was no trouble a'tall changing places with them."

"Oh, God, you didn't hurt them, did you?"

He frowned at that. "No more than was necessary to dump them where they'd dumped us. Why?"

"They were letting you out! Didn't you give them a chance to explain?"

"Not bloody likely," he replied emphatically. "Am I to assume then that they were friends of yours?"

"Just my brothers, that's all."

He chuckled at her disgruntled tone. "Well, no harm done. Henry, go fetch us the two lads, and be nice to them this time." And then, "Now, George, perhaps you'd be so good as to tell us where James is?"

"Ah, that's kind of a long story, and since time happens to be a problem, you might want to let me explain on our way back to shore."

It was her sudden unease rather than her words that Connie reacted to. "He *is* all right, isn't he?"

"Certainly . . . just a little bruised . . . and in need of your assistance in getting out of a locked cellar."

"Locked in, eh?" Connie started laughing, to Georgina's chagrin.

"It's not funny, Mr. Sharpe. They mean to see he stands trial for piracy," she told him bluntly, which took care of his amusement quite quickly.

"Bloody hell, I warned him!"

"Well, maybe you should have sat on him instead, because it's every bit of it his own fault, him and his grand confessions."

She prodded the first mate into hurrying then, but didn't get away with not explaining the rest of it on the way. Her brothers were left temporarily behind, much to their loud irritation, so Connie could make use of their horses to bring several of his own men along. Georgina got the honor of riding double with the first mate, but as she'd feared, so he could get every last detail out of her, which he did, interrupting only occasionally with "He didn't!" or "The devil he did!" and finally with an angry "You were doing fine up to that point, George, but you'll never get me to believe James Malory has got himself leg-shackled," to which she replied, "You don't have to believe me. I'm only the other half who got shackled."

And since she didn't even try to convince him beyond that, by the time they reached her home, he was still unconvinced. Much she cared. By that time she was annoyed enough that she wouldn't even have showed them the way to the cellar if she didn't think they'd wake one of the servants stumbling around in the dark to find it on their own.

But she really wished she hadn't waited around for the door to be pried open. With the one candle she'd garnered from the kitchen, James had no difficulty in seeing who his rescuers were, aside from her, since she stood well back of the door. But she didn't think he'd have said anything different had he known she was there.

"You shouldn't have bother, old man. I bloody well deserve to hang for what I allowed to happen here."

Georgina placed no significance on the word "allowed." All she heard was James's disgust over his married state. And Connie must have heard the same.

"So it's true? You actually married the brat?"

"And how did you find that out?"

"Why, the little bride told me, of course." Connie started laughing before he got the last word out. "Should I . . . offer . . . congrat—"

"You do, and I'll bloody well see to it you have difficulty ever saying another word," James snarled, and then, "If you've seen her, where'd you leave the faithless little jade?"

Connie glanced around. "She *was* right here."

"George!"

Georgina stopped at the top of the stairs, cringing at what sounded like a cannon blast. And she'd thought her brothers had loud, carrying voices. Gritting her teeth, clenching her fists, she stomped back down the stairs to do some blasting of her own.

"You doubled-damned idiot! Are you just trying to wake the whole house, or my neighbors, too? Or did you like the cellar so—"

She'd unfortunately reached him by that point and was summarily silenced by a wide hand clamping over her mouth. That it was James's hand gave her pause for a moment, but he was nothing if not swift, and before she even thought to struggle, his hand was replaced by his cravat, which turned out to be quite an effective gag after it was wrapped around her head several times.

Connie, watching the whole process, said not a word, particularly when he noted that Georgina just stood perfectly still the whole while. And Jame's behavior was even more interesting. He could have asked for assistance, but didn't. But neither would he let go of the hold he had about the girl's waist even long enough to tie the gag off, which made it necessary for him to use his teeth to pull one side of it tight, and that had to have hurt, as cut and swollen as James's mouth was. Finished, he tucked the girl firmly under his arm, and only then did he notice Connie watching him.

"Well, it's plain to see she can't be left behind," James said irritably.

" 'Course she can't." Connie nodded.

"She'd clearly give the alarm."

" 'Course she would."

"You don't *have* to agree with me, you know."

" 'Course I do. My teeth, don't you know. I'm rather fond of them."

Chapter Thirty-eight

Georgina sat slumped in the chair she'd pulled up in front of the wall of windows, pensively watching the choppy surface of the cold Atlantic surrounding the *Maiden Anne*. She heard the door open behind her, then footsteps crossing the room, but she wasn't interested in who had disturbed her solitude. Not that she didn't know. James was the only one who entered the cabin without knocking.

But she wasn't speaking to James Malory, and hadn't said more than two words to him since that night a week ago when he had carted her aboard his ship in the exact same manner he had once carted her out of an English tavern. And this undignified treatment wasn't even the worst of it that night. No, the very moment he saw her brothers on the deck of his ship, he ordered them tossed over the side. And the man had had the unmitigated gall to tell them, just before they went over, that she had decided to sail with them, as if they couldn't see the gag about her mouth, or the way he was holding her like a blasted piece of baggage.

Of course, no one had bothered to tell him what Drew and Boyd were doing on his ship in the first place. Any one of his men could have volunteered the information that if it weren't for her brothers, they'd still be in the hold and the *Nereus*'s men would still be walking the decks, rather than trussed up and deposited on the shore. But apparently they didn't have the nerve to interrupt their crazy captain to enlighten him to that fact. Connie in particular should have said something, but one glance at him showed he was being much too entertained by the whole affair to see it ended by anything so mundane as an explanation.

It was possible that James knew by now that he'd behaved like an ungrateful wretch that night. But if he didn't, he wasn't going to hear it from her, since she was never talking to him again. And the blasted man didn't even care. "Sulking, are we?" he'd remarked when he noticed. "Splendid! If a man must be burdened with a wife, thank God for small favors."

That had really hurt, especially since she didn't doubt for a moment that he sincerely meant it. And he must have meant it, since he hadn't once tried to coax her into talking to him, railing at him, or anything else.

They shared the same cabin, she in her hammock, he in his great bed, and did everything possible to ignore each other. He succeeded admirably, but she had found, much to her chagrin, that when he was there, he was *there*. At least her senses knew it, going a little crazy every time he was near; sight, smell, hearing all attuned, heightened by remembered touch, remembered taste.

Even now, despite the desire not to, Georgina found herself watching James from the corner of her eyes as he sat down behind his desk. He appeared as relaxed as if he were alone, while she was now stiff with her awareness of him. He didn't glance her way any more than she would turn her head to face him. She might as well not be there. In fact, she couldn't for the life of her figure out why she was there, when it would have been much more in line with his behavior that night, if James had dumped her into the bay with her brothers.

She hadn't asked why she was sailing with him. She'd have to talk to him to ask, and she'd cut her tongue out before she would give up her silent sulk, as he termed it. And if she was appearing childish with the attitude she'd adopted, well, so what? Was that any worse than his being a boorish madman with piratical tendencies toward kidnapping and plank walking or pushing, as the case were?

"Do you mind, George? That constant staring is getting on my bloody nerves."

Georgina's eyes snapped back to the boring view outside the window. Double-damn him, how did he know she'd been covertly watching him?

"It's becoming quite tedious, you know," he went on to remark.

She said nothing.

"Your sulking."

She said nothing.

"'Course, what can one expect of a wench raised among barbarians."

That did it. "If you mean my brothers—"

"I *mean* your whole bloody country."

"Well you're a fine one to talk, coming from a country of snobs."

"Better snobs than ill-mannered hotheads."

"Ill-mannered?!" she shrieked, coming out of her chair in a burst of long-suppressed fury that took her across the room, right up to the side of his desk. "When you couldn't even say thank-you for getting your life saved?"

He'd stood up before she got there, but it was not intimidation that had her backing up as he approached, merely an unconscious desire not to get walked over. "And just who was I to thank? Those benighted Philistines you call kin? The very ones who dumped me in a cellar to await transport to a hanging?"

"A circumstance you courted with every word out of your mouth!" she shouted up at him. "But despite what you deserved or didn't, that was Warren's doing. Not Boyd's and Drew's. They went against their own brother to help you, knowing full well that he'd beat the daylights out of them if he found out."

"I'm not lacking in intelligence, brat. No one needed to tell me what they'd done. Why do you think I refrained from breaking their bloody necks?"

"Oh, that's nice. And to think I wondered what I was doing here. I should have realized it was no more than another blow against my brothers, since you couldn't stay in the area to do any worse damage. That's it, isn't it? Taking me along was your idea of the perfect revenge, because you knew it would drive my brothers crazy with worry."

"Absolutely!"

She didn't notice the color that had flooded his neck and face, proof positive that her deduction had more than doubled his anger and was responsible for his answer. All she heard was the answer, a death knell to her last hope, which she'd never have admitted clinging to.

So it was pain that made her lash out with retaliating scorn, "No more than I could expect of an English *lord*, a Caribbean *pirate!*"

"I hate to point this out, you little witch, but those aren't epithets."

"They are as far as I'm concerned! My God, and to think I'm going to have your baby."

"The devil you are! I'm not touching you again!"

She was stomping away from him when he heard, "You won't have to, you stupid man!" and James felt as if he'd been poleaxed, or kicked in the arse by a berserk mule, which was no more than he figured he deserved at that moment.

But Georgina wasn't the least bit interested in his reaction. High dudgeon carried her out the door, slammed it for her, and kept her from hearing what began as chuckles, but soon turned into delighted laughter.

He found her a half hour later in the galley, taking her wrath out on Shawn O'Shawn and his helpers in a tirade against men in general, and James Malory in particular. And considering that the word had gone out that their Georgie, back in breeches again, though borrowed this time, was now the captain's wife, they weren't inclined to disagree with anything she had to say.

James listened to her for a moment before he interrupted, hearing himself likened to a member of the mule family, a brainless ox, and a brick wall, all in the same breath. Brick wall? Well, there was no accounting for American similes, he supposed.

"I'd like a word with you, George, if you don't mind."

"I do mind."

She didn't glance at him to say it. In fact, all he'd noted was a slight stiffening of her back when he'd spoken. Politeness was obviously the wrong tack to take.

Georgina would have called James's smile devilish had she seen it, but as she wasn't facing him, only the others in the room noted it as he came up behind her and lifted her off the barrel she'd been perched on. "If you'll excuse us, gentlemen, George has been neglecting her duties of late," James said as he turned and carried her from the room in a position she was quite familiar with.

"You ought to curb these barbaric tendencies, Captain," she said in a furious undertone, knowing from experience that there was nothing she could do to get him to put her down until he was ready to do so. "But then breeding speaks for itself, doesn't it?"

"We'll get there quicker if you'll shut up, George."

She was stunned almost speechless by the humor she detected in his tone. What, for God's sake, did he find amusing in their present situation, where they both now despised each other? And less than an hour ago he'd been a fire-breathing dragon. But he was an Englishman, so what other explanation was needed?

"Get where quicker?" she demanded. "And what duties have I neglected? Need I remind you that I'm no longer your cabin boy?"

"I'm well aware of what you are now, dear girl. And although I've nothing good to say about marriage, it does have one small benefit that even I can't complain about."

It took her about five seconds to mull that over before the fireworks went off. "Are you crazy or just senile? I heard you plain and clear when you told me *and* the whole ship that you weren't touching me again! I've surely got witnesses!"

"The whole ship?"

"You said it loud enough."

"So I lied."

"Just like that? You lied? Well, I've got news for you—"

"How you do go on, George. This propensity you have for airing our dirty laundry—"

"I'll do more than that, you addled ox!" But she was finally aware of the snickers and chuckles following in their wake, and her voice dropped to a whispered hiss, "You just try and . . . Well, you just try it and see what happens."

"Good of you to make it more interesting, sweet, but totally unnecessary, I assure you."

She didn't mistake his meaning. It suffused her with heat in all the wrong places, wrong just now, since she wanted nothing to do with him. *Why* was he doing this? They'd been at sea a whole week and all she'd gotten was dark, brooding looks from him, if he bothered to look her way at all. But he'd started that fight in the cabin, provoked her into giving up her sulk, and now this. If he was trying to drive her crazy with confusion, he was well on the road to success.

He shifted her before he started down the stairs to his cabin, swinging her legs around and up so she ended up cradled in his arms, a position no easier to get out of than the other. She was really starting to resent his strength, and his ability to put his anger aside, while hers just seemed to increase.

"Why, James?" she asked in a tight, resentful little voice. "Just tell me that, if you dare."

She could look at him now in her new position, and was, but when he briefly glanced down at her, she saw it all in those green eyes. She didn't have to hear it. He told her anyway.

"Don't look for hidden meanings, love. My motives are simple and basic. All that passionate anger we were spewing at each other got me a bit . . . nauseous."

"Good," she bit out, closing her eyes in pure self-defense against that potent look of his. "I hope you puke."

His laughter shook her. "You know that's not what I meant. And I'll wager all that heated passion worked on you as well."

It had, but he'd never know it. Yet he was determined to know it.

His voice turned seductively husky, "Are you feeling nauseous?"

"Not the least little—"

"You do know how to reduce self-confidence to a low ebb, dearest girl."

She slid down the front of him when her legs were released, but her feet never quite touched the floor with his one arm still about her back. She hadn't noticed entering the cabin they shared, but she heard the door close with a resounding click. Her heartbeat sounded louder.

"And I'll be the first to admit that I seem to have totally lost my finesse when it comes to dealing with you," he continued as his other arm came around her, both shifting now, one moving lower until his hand cupped her buttocks, pressing her into his hips, while the other moved up, the fingers gliding under her hair, along her scalp, until her head was firmly in his grip. She saw his sensual smile, the heat in his eyes, felt his breath on her lips when he added, "Allow me to see if I can find it again."

"James, no . . ."

But his mouth was already slanting across hers, and he'd already ensured there'd be no escape from it. Leisurely, with infinite care, he bestowed on her the finesse of a lifetime, kisses meant to entice, to mesmerize, to tap every sensual impulse she possessed. Her arms were already encircling his neck when his tongue seduced her lips to part, entered, and took her swiftly to that realm of not-caring-what-he-did. Beneath the tender onslaught, she felt the urgency. Hers or his? She didn't know. She was in the center of an erotic storm that consumed awareness of everything except the man and what he was doing to her.

God, the taste of him, the feel of him, the hard heat surrounding her, flaying her senses with exquisite pleasure. She'd forgotten . . . No, she'd just doubted the reality, that anything could so overwhelm her with feeling that she would lose herself completely to it . . . to him.

"My God, woman, you make me tremble."

She heard the wonder in his voice, felt the vibration in his body . . . or was it her own limbs shaking, about to shatter?

She was holding on to him now for dear life, so it was an easy matter for him to lift her legs and wrap them around his hips. The intimate contact, the friction as he walked her to his bed, released a heat wave in her loins that had her groaning into his mouth as he continued to ravage her with his tongue.

They fell on the bed together, a bit clumsily, but Georgina didn't notice that James's finesse had once again deserted him beneath a need that far surpassed hers, and hers had escalated beyond anything she'd previously experienced with this man. In short order they were ripping each other's clothes off, literally, and not even aware that they'd reverted to primitive instinct.

And then he was inside her, deeply buried, and her whole body seemed to sigh in relieved welcome. This lasted all of a moment before there was a stab of alarm when his arms hooked under her knees, something he'd never done before, raising them so high, she was given a feeling of total defenselessness. But the alarm was so brief it was instantly forgotten, for the position embedded him so deeply inside her, she felt touched to her very core. And the starburst of fire exploded in that moment, sending out waves of tingling awareness from her center to every extremity, but surrounding him, throbbing against him, every shuddering spasm of pleasure felt by him.

She'd screamed, but didn't know it. She'd left bleeding half moons on his shoulders, but didn't know it. She'd just given him her soul once again. Neither of them knew it.

When Georgina reached a point of knowing anything, it was that she was weighted with sweet languor . . . and her lips were being softly nibbled on, which led her to believe James hadn't shared that magnificent experience with her.

"Didn't you—?"

" 'Course I did."

"Oh."

But in her mind she said another "Oh," with much more surprise. So soon? Did she want to lose herself like that again? Dare she? But the urge was almost overpowering to do some nibbling of her own, and that gave her the only answer she wanted at the moment.

Chapter Thirty-nine

"Marriage used to be for gain, don't you know, or to unite great families . . . which would never have applied to us in any case, would it, love? But these days it's back to primitive basics, society's sanction of lust. In that, we're quite compatible, I'd say."

Those words kept coming back to Georgina in the two weeks that followed her fateful surrender to James Malory's finesse, reminding her that she shouldn't have tried to read more into the return of his desire for her. All she'd asked him was what he intended to do about their marriage, if he meant to honor it or get out of it. She wouldn't call his answer an answer. And she hadn't needed to be told that all they shared was mutual lust as far as he was concerned.

And yet, there was so much tenderness in that lust; so often when she lay in his arms she felt cherished . . . almost loved. And that more than anything else kept her tongue still each time she thought to ask again about the future. Of course, getting straight answers out of James was next to impossible anymore. If his replies weren't derogatory, which annoyed her into shutting up, then they were evasive. And she had learned very quickly that if she tried to bring up what had happened in Connecticut, or even came close to mentioning her brothers, she'd get singed by the fire-breathing dragon again.

So they existed much as they had before, as lovers and companions, with one exception. Touchy subjects were forbidden. It was almost like having an unspoken truce; at least Georgina looked at it that way. And if she wanted to savor and enjoy this time with James, and she did want that at least, then she had to bury her pride and anxieties for a while. When they arrived at their destination it would be soon enough to find out where she stood, if James meant to keep her or send her home.

And it was such a short while. Without having to fight the westerly winds, the *Maiden Anne* made such good time, she was sailing up the Thames almost three weeks to the day after she'd left the American coast behind.

Georgina had known right from that first night that she was going to be visiting England again, since James had discussed their course with Connie while she was still tucked to his hip. She didn't even have to wonder long why he wasn't returning to Jamaica to finish his business there. That was one of the forbidden subjects, so she didn't bother to ask him, but Connie could be questioned on impersonal matters, and he'd informed her that James had fortunately found an agent to dispose of his property in the islands while he was waiting for his crew to be rounded up. At least she didn't have that to be held against her, too, though she had to wonder if she'd ever know what had really brought James Malory to Connecticut in such a vengeful state of mind.

Once again Georgina had packed James's trunks for him in preparation for departure, this time including her few articles of borrowed clothing. But this time when she came on deck, she found Artie and Henry stationed on either side of the gangplank, both men making no pretense about keeping an eye on her.

She found that amusing. Had she been able to speak of it, she could have told James that he'd never find a Skylark vessel in London harbor. So, he could have been assured that she had nowhere to run off to, if he didn't care to lose her just yet. But he knew that she had no money with her, so setting watchdogs on her was really absurd. She did have her jade ring back, given to her for a wedding ring since James happened to be wearing it on a chain around his neck at the time, but she wasn't going to consider parting with it again.

The ring on her finger was now a reminder of what was so easily forgotten, that she was a married woman. Easily forgotten, too, was her pregnancy, since she was suffering not the least bit of discomfort or sickness with it, nor had she even begun to expand, except for a very slight enlargement in her breasts. Yet she was now two and a half months along. But she'd never mentioned it again to James, nor had he ever spoken of it even once. She wasn't even sure he'd heard her that day she'd blurted it out in her anger as she slammed out of his cabin.

Just now, Georgina pulled James's heavy Garrick coat closer about her to ward off the chill. The harbor was a bleak-looking place in the middle of November. Cold, overcast, the day was as gloomy as her thoughts were becoming as she waited for James to join her.

What, if anything, awaited her here?

Georgina remembered Piccadilly. She almost mentioned it to James, that she and Mac had stayed in the Albany Hotel, which the rented carriage had just passed. But one look at her husband's expression changed her mind. He'd been like that since they left the ship, actually since they'd first sighted England.

She didn't bother to ask what had turned his mood so dark. He'd just give her some careless remark that would tell her absolutely nothing, and that would only irritate her. And she was trying her best not to aggravate the situation by giving her own gloomy mood free rein. But she would have thought James would be glad to be home. She knew he had family here, even a son . . . Good Lord, how could she have forgotten that? He had a seventeen-year-old son, a boy only five years her junior. Was James worried about having to explain why he was coming home with a wife? Would he even bother to explain? Was he even bringing her home?

For God's sake, this was utterly ridiculous, when a little communication would put her mind at ease . . . or not, as the case might be. "James—?"

"We're here."

The carriage stopped just as he said it, and he was out the door before she'd even gotten a look out the window. "Here, where?"

His hands reached back in to lift her down to the curb. "My brother's townhouse."

"Which brother?"

"Anthony. You'll remember him. Dark as sin, I believe you called him once."

Her brows drew together with a sudden suspicion that released all her pent-up anxiety in a burst of anger. "You're dumping me here, aren't you? You haven't the guts to take me home with you, so you're leaving me with your rakehell brother. Which is it you don't want to explain to your son, that I'm an American or that I'm your wife?"

"I despise that word. Call yourself anything else you like, but kindly strike that word from your vocabulary."

That he said it calmly only infuriated her more. "All right. Will whore do?"

"Preferably."

"You bastard!"

"My dear girl, you really must curb this propensity you have for swearing. And as usual, you've managed to air our dirty laundry for the delectation of the masses."

The "masses" happened to be Dobson, Anthony's butler, who had diligently opened the door before it was required of him, having heard the carriage arriving. Georgina blushed profusely to have been caught shouting profanities. But to look at the stoic-faced Englishman, you'd have thought he hadn't heard a word.

"Welcome home, Lord Malory," he said as he thrust the door open wider.

At that point, Georgina almost had to be dragged inside. Despite her boy's clothes, which couldn't be helped, she had *so* wanted to make a good impression today of all days, what with the possibility of meeting James's family. But then he hadn't denied he was going to drop her off here with Anthony, and everything she'd ever heard him say about this brother, and what she'd seen for herself, had led her to believe he was as disreputable a fellow as James was, so what was the difference? She had no care to impress *him*. Still, servants gossiped, and this one likely knew the servants of the rest of the family. Devil take it, she could kick James for making her finally lose her temper.

And James could have kicked himself for making things worse with her, but he couldn't seem to break the habit of a lifetime. But she was so bloody thin-skinned. She ought to know by now he didn't mean it. But he *was* damned annoyed with her.

She'd had more than enough time to give him some clue about how she felt about him now, but not one bloody word had passed her lips on the subject. And he'd never felt more insecure in his entire life. The only thing he was sure about was that she desired him as much as he did her. But he'd known too many women not to know that that meant absolutely nothing where their true feelings were concerned.

The truth was, she hadn't wanted to marry him. She'd told her brothers so. She'd told him so. She was going to have his baby, but still she'd flatly refused to marry him. She'd had to be forced right along with him, and everything she'd done since had led him to believe she was just biding her time, waiting for an opportunity to run from him again. And now she'd have all the opportunity she could want, which put him in a devil of a bad temper. But he hadn't meant to take it out on her. He ought to apologize . . . damned if he would.

"I don't suppose my brother is at home this time of day?" James inquired of Dobson.

"Sir Anthony is at Knighton's Hall, I believe, for his customary exercise in the pugilist ring."

"I could do with a bit of that myself just now. And Lady Roslynn?"

"Visiting the countess of Sherfield."

"Countess? Ah, that's right, Amherst wed Roslynn's friend not too long ago." His eyes locked with Georgina's before he added, "Poor man," and he was satisfied to note that her expression of embarrassment switched to one of anger. "And is my son at school, Dobson?"

"He got sent home for the week, my lord, but Sir Anthony has already filed a complaint with the headmaster, and his lordship the marquis is also looking into the matter."

"And the lad was likely totally to blame for whatever it was they say he did. Damned scamp. I leave him alone for a few months—"

"Father!"

Georgina turned to see a young man practically flying down the stairs and then slamming into the brick wall that was her husband, and apparently his father, though it was not a foregone conclusion by any means. The boy didn't look all of seventeen as she'd been told, but much closer to her own age. Was it just the height? He was as tall as James, though not nearly as broad of frame. He was more on the slim side, yet his shoulders promised to get wider. He was being crushed right now in a bear hug, and laughing, and she realized with a start that he bore no resemblance to James at all, though no one could deny he was just as handsome.

"But what's happened, then?" Jeremy was asking. "You're back so soon. Did you decide to keep the plantation?"

"No," James said. "I just found an agent to dispose of it, is all."

"So you could hurry back? Missed me, did you?"

"Get that grin off your face, puppy. I thought I'd warned you to stay out of trouble."

The boy gave Dobson a look of reproach for spilling the news so soon, but he was grinning unrepentently again when he looked back at his father. "Well, she was a prime piece. What was I to do?"

"What *did* you do?"

"Just had a bloody good time, is all. But they weren't very understanding about finding the wench in my room, so I told 'em she followed me back, that she refused to leave without making a fuss."

"And they believed that clanker?"

"The headmaster didn't." Jeremy grinned roguishly. "But Uncle Tony did."

James laughed here. "Tony doesn't *know* you well enough yet." But he tamped down his humor when he noticed Georgina's look of disgust. "But you'll attend to your entertainments outside of the school grounds from now on, scamp, that's if they even allow you back, and you bloody well better hope they do, or I'll be kicking your arse around the block."

Jeremy's grin didn't waver the least little bit, as if he'd heard such dire warnings a hundred times before and had never once taken them seriously. But he had followed his father's glance to Georgina, and he was now looking her over himself. Still wrapped up in James's Garrick coat, and with her hair tucked under her cap, which she'd worn to limit her embarrassment in being dressed as she was, she found it understandable that the boy showed only the mildest interest in her.

But Georgina was still simmering over her latest heated exchange with James, which was aggravated by what she'd just heard. The man was no more than amused that his son was following in his footsteps . . . another reprehensible rake to be set loose on womankind.

That, coupled with her embarrassment over her shabby appearance, prompted her cutting remark. "He doesn't look anything like you, James. In fact, he looks more like your brother." She paused to raise a brow tauntingly. "Are you sure he's yours?"

"I know you feel justified, love, but don't take it out on the youngun."

He said it in a way that guaranteed she'd feel ashamed of herself for behaving pettishly, and she did, extremely so. But instead of cowing her, it only made her angrier. And James, unfortunately, didn't notice.

"Jeremy," he continued. "Meet George—"

"His *wife*," she cut in scathingly, taking a good deal of satisfaction in saying it, since she was sure James wouldn't have said it. And then she added innocently, "But I forgot. I'm supposed to delete that word from my vocabulary. And that would make me—"

"George!"

She merely gave James an owl-eyed look, not at all impressed by his bellow. But Jeremy's interest was now piqued and he stepped closer to her, though it was his father he addressed his questions to.

"Wife? She's a girl, then?"

"Oh, she's female all right," James said testily.

Jeremy yanked off Georgina's cap before she could stop him. "Oh, I say," came out with a good deal of male appreciation as her long dark hair tumbled down her shoulders. "Do I get to kiss the bride?"

"Not in the way you'd like to, scamp." James was scowling now.

But all Georgina wanted to know, was, "Why isn't he surprised?"

"Because he doesn't believe a word of it," James retorted.

She'd anticipated a lot of reactions, but flat disbelief wasn't one of them. The boy thought they were ribbing him. At the moment, she wished they were.

"Well, that's just swell-dandy-fine," she said indignantly. "I'm damned if I care what your family thinks, James Malory, but you can certainly be sure that as long as they *don't* think I'm your wife, I'll be sleeping alone." And she turned to glare at the butler. "You may show me to a room that is far removed from *his*."

"As you wish, my lady," the butler replied without the slightest crack in his bland expression.

But Georgina, in high dudgeon, explained haughtily, "I'm not *your lady*, my good man. I'm American."

That didn't get a reaction out of him, either, not that she was trying for one. But as she followed the man up the stairs, her exasperation did increase when she heard Jeremy's remark.

"Hell's bells, you can't mean to install your mistress here! Aunt Roslynn won't stand for it."

"Your aunt will bloody well be delighted, lad. You may depend upon it. George *is* a Malory, after all."

"Sure, and I'm legitimate."

Chapter Forty

"Show a leg, George. Your new in-laws will be returning home soon."

Georgina cracked an eyelid to find James sitting on the side of the bed. Doing so had made her roll toward him in her sleep, so that her hips were pressed up against his thigh. But that didn't alarm her nearly as much as his hand resting on her buttocks.

"How'd you get in here?" she demanded, wide awake.

"Walked in, of course. It was wise of Dobson to put you in my room."

"*Your* room? I told him—"

"Yes, and he took you literally. After all, he didn't hear me deny your status, and only Jeremy is doubting of it, not the whole family."

"You mean he *still* is? You didn't bother to try and convince him?"

"Didn't see much point in it."

Georgina sat up and turned away from him so he couldn't see how that answer affected her. So now she knew. She wasn't going to be here long enough for it to matter whether his son believed he'd married or not. James probably planned to put her on the first ship he could find sailing for America. Well and good, the sooner the better. She didn't want to live in England anyway. And she certainly didn't want to live with a man who merely shared a mutual attraction with her. That was fine for temporary, but not for permanent. For permanent she needed much, much more. And she wouldn't cry, not this time. She'd done enough crying over this man. If he didn't care, she wouldn't either, and that's all he was going to know . . . if it killed her.

James had no idea what conclusion she'd drawn from his remark, but then he was overlooking the fact that Georgina didn't know his son. In his doubt, Jeremy was merely being loyal to James, since he was well aware of James's sentiments towards marriage, and also that he had sworn never to marry. And James wasn't ready to explain why he'd changed those sentiments, since that was also going to be doubted. So what was the point in letting his hardheaded son frustrate him over the matter, when time would tell?

"You're absolutely right, James," Georgina said, coming off the bed.

"I am?" His brow rose sharply. "Dare I ask what you're agreeing with me about?"

"That there's no point in convincing anyone about our . . . connection."

He frowned as he watched her cross to the chair where he'd dumped a pile of clothes for her. "I was referring only to Jeremy," he explained. "It won't be necessary to convince anyone else."

"But if it is, why bother? And I don't see much point in my meeting the rest of your family, either."

"You've let the lad give you cold feet, have you?"

"Certainly not," she retorted, turning to glare at him for drawing that conclusion.

"Then what are you worried about? Unlike *your* family, mine will adore you. And you'll get along famously with Roslynn. She's only a few years older than you are, I believe."

"Your sister-in-law Roslynn? The one who's going to object to my staying here? And which brother does she happen to be married to?"

"Anthony, of course. This is his house."

"You mean he's married?"

"He put the shackle on just the day before I met you, as a matter of fact, and that's about as long as his wedded bliss lasted. He was still at odds with his little Scottish bride when I left here. It'll be interesting to see how the lad's getting on with her now, though Jeremy assures me Tony's no longer in the doghouse."

"Sounds like a good place for you to be, though," she said pointedly. "You could have told me all of this *before* we got here, James."

He shrugged carelessly. "Didn't think you'd be interested in my family. I'm certainly not interested in yours. Now what's this?" he asked when he saw her chin go up just before she gave him her back again. "It's no insult to you, love, that I can't tolerate those barbarians you call brothers."

"My brothers wouldn't have behaved like barbarians if you hadn't deliberately provoked them. I wonder how your family would react if I did the same thing."

"I guarantee they won't trounce you or cart you off to Tyburn Hill for hanging."

"Probably not, but they wouldn't like me. And they'd wonder if you hadn't lost your mind, bringing me here."

He chuckled as he came up behind her. "On the contrary, you darling girl. Do or say anything you like. You'll find it won't make the least bit of difference to your welcome."

"Why?"

"Because you've become a Malory through me."

"Is that supposed to be significant?"

"I'm sure you'll hear all about it soon enough, but you won't if you don't get dressed. Shall I help you?"

She slapped away the hand that reached around for the hem of her shirt. "I think I can manage myself, thank you. Whose clothes are these, anyway? Roslynn's?"

"That would have been more convenient, but no. She's a mite bigger than you just now, or so her maid assured me. So I sent round to Regan's, who happens to be just your size."

Georgina turned in his arms and shoved him back. "Regan? Ah, yes, the one who prefers to call you a 'connoisseur of women' rather than a reprehensible rake."

"D'you never forget anything?" he said on a sigh, which she totally ignored.

"And here I thought at the time that Regan was a male friend of yours." And then she surprised him by jabbing a finger in his chest and demanding with a good deal of heat, "So who is she? A mistress you left behind? If you've borrowed clothes from a mistress for me, James Malory, so help me I'll—

His laughter cut her off. "I hate to interrupt such a splendid display of jealousy, George, but Regan's my beloved niece."

There was but a moment's blank expression before she cringed. "Your niece?"

"She'll be amused to hear you thought otherwise."

"Well, for God's sake, don't tell her!" she said, aghast. "It was a perfectly natural mistake, considering you're a confessed reprobate."

"Now I resent that, indeed I do," he replied in one of his drier tones. "There's a world of difference between a rake and a reprobate, dear girl. And your perfectly natural mistake wasn't so natural, since I haven't kept a mistress for years."

"What did you call Jeremy's lie? A clanker?"

"Very amusing, George, but it happens to be true. I've always preferred variety. And mistresses can be quite tedious in their demands. I'd have made an exception for you, however."

"Should I be flattered? I'm not."

"You were my lover on the *Maiden Anne*. Where's the bloody difference?"

"And now I'm your wife, if you'll pardon that ghastly word. Where's the difference?"

She'd hoped to annoy him with the comparison, but instead he grinned at her. "You're getting very good at this, George."

"At what?" Suspiciously.

"Disagreeing with me. There aren't many who dare, you know."

She gave an unladylike snort. "If that's supposed to be more flattery, your score is zero."

"Well, if we're keeping score, how will this one rate? I want you."

He drew her up against him as he said it, so she could feel with her body that he wasn't speaking in a general sense, but about the present moment. He was aroused, and whenever James was aroused, his whole body seduced, hips grinding against loins, chest tantalizing nipples to hard points, touch seeking only the sensitive, and mouth stealing any protest. What protest? Georgina was lost the moment she felt his need.

In her surrender, she could tease, albeit a bit breathlessly. "What about the in-laws I'm supposed to meet?"

"Devil them," James said, his own breathing already labored. "This is more important."

His thigh thrust between hers, and his hands clasped her buttocks to drag her up the surface of it. She moaned at the friction, her arms wrapping about his neck, her legs about his waist, her head thrown back so his mouth could sear her throat. There was no more thought for teasing or anything beyond the moment and their burgeoning passion.

And into this heated scene walked Anthony Malory. "Thought the youngun was only bamming me, but I see he wasn't."

James's head came up, and his growl was indicative of a very frustrated annoyance. "Blister it, Tony, your timing is bloody rotten!"

Georgina slid slowly back to the floor, though her footing was none too steady. It took her about that long to realize they'd been intruded upon by one of the in-laws. Fortunately, James's arms were still about her for support, but they couldn't prevent the mortified flush that was fast staining her cheeks.

She remembered Anthony from that night in the tavern when he'd mistaken Mac for someone else, remembered thinking he was the most handsome blue-eyed devil she'd ever seen—until she noticed James. But Anthony was still incredibly good-looking. And she hadn't been being only spiteful earlier when she'd told James that his son looked more like Anthony. Jeremy was in fact a younger image of Anthony, even to the cobalt-blue eyes and coal-black hair. She had to wonder if James really *was* sure that Jeremy was his. And she had to wonder what Anthony must think of her in the brief glance he gave her.

Put a patch over her eye and she'd look like a pirate just now in James's flowing white shirt, which he'd managed to unlace exceedingly low, his wide belt, cut down to her size, which she was wearing over the shirt because it was so blasted big, and her own tight breeches. And she was barefooted and bare-calved. She'd done no more than take off her shoes and stockings before she'd dropped onto the bed earlier to seethe and had fallen asleep instead.

Oh, she was mortified all right to be found looking like this, and in such an intimate position, but at least this time it wasn't her fault. She had been behind closed doors, doing what she had every right to do. Anthony should be the one embarrassed for just walking in without warning, but he didn't look the least bit embarrassed. He looked merely annoyed.

"It's good to see you, too, brother," he said in reply to James's heated statement. "But not your little wench there. You've got about two minutes to dispose of the chit before the wife comes up to welcome you home."

"George isn't going anywhere, but you can take yourself out of here."

"You're foxed, is that it? Can't remember that this ain't a bachelor residence anymore?"

"There's nothing wrong with my memory, old boy, and there's no need to hide George. She's—"

"Now we're done for," Anthony interrupted in vexation as they heard someone coming down the hall. "Stick her under the bed or something . . . Well, don't just stand there!" and he reached for Georgina himself.

"Touch her, lad," James warned softly, "and you'll end up stretched out on the floor yourself."

"Well, I like that," Anthony replied huffily, but he backed off. "Fine. Then you talk your way out of this. But if I end up having a row with Roslynn over it, I'll bloody well take it out of your hide, see if I don't."

"Anthony," James said simply. "Shut up."

He did just that. Leaning back against the wall, crossing his arms over his chest, he waited for the fireworks to start. He'd barely spared Georgina more than a cursory glance. Now he watched the open doorway, waiting for his wife to appear.

By this time, Georgina was expecting a veritable dragon to enter the room. Anyone who could cause that tall, physically perfect man to worry that she might be upset with him had to be very formidable indeed. But Roslynn Malory didn't look intimidating when she came through the door, offering James a blinding smile, which she passed on to Georgina. She was a stunningly beautiful woman, not much taller than Georgina, not much older, and, by the looks of it, not much more pregnant than Georgina was.

"Jeremy just stopped me on the stairs to tell me you've gotten married, James. Is this true?"

"Married?" Anthony's interest perked up.

"I thought you said you hadn't convinced Jeremy," Georgina said to James.

"I didn't. The dear boy is being tediously loyal where he thinks it will count. Notice he didn't tell Tony the same thing. Because he still doesn't believe it himself."

"Married?" Anthony said again, and got no more notice than before. Roslynn asked. "What doesn't Jeremy believe?"

"That George here is my viscountess."

"Clever of you to find another name for it, James," Georgina said. "But that one *I* object to, so find another. You won't be sticking any English titles on me."

"Too late, love. The title came with the name."

"Married?" Anthony shouted this time, and finally got James's attention. "That's doing it up a bit much, isn't it, just to get out of a scolding?"

And before James could comment one way or the other, Roslynn asked her husband, "Who in their right mind would try to scold *him?*"

"You would, sweetheart."

Roslynn chuckled, a deep, husky sound that had Georgina blinking in surprise to hear it. "I seriously doubt that, Anthony, but why don't you tell me why you think I would."

Anthony waved a hand in Georgina's general direction, not even deigning to look at her. "Because he's come home with . . . with his latest . . . well, with *her.*"

And that was just a little bit too much for Georgina to tolerate without her temper rising. "I'm not a 'her,' you pompous ass," she said quietly, but with a good deal of bristling animosity in her expression. "I'm an American, and, for the moment, a Malory."

"Well, bully for you, sweetheart," Anthony came back sneeringly. "But then you'd say anything he told you to say, wouldn't you?"

At that, Georgina turned on James and poked him in the ribs. "It won't be necessary to convince anyone else? Isn't that what you said?"

"Now, George," James said placatingly. "This is nothing to lose your temper over."

"I don't have a temper!" she yelled at him. "And I don't have a marriage either, as far as your family's concerned. So I guess that means you'll be finding yourself another room, won't you?"

It was the wrong thing to threaten him with, when his body had yet to completely cool down from what they'd been doing before they were so rudely interrupted. "Like bloody hell I will. You want him convinced? I'll show you just how easy my baby brother is to convince." And he started toward Anthony with fists clenched.

Alarmed at this sudden turn, Roslynn quickly stepped in front of James, who looked as if he might just tear her husband limb from limb if he reached him. "Och now, there'll be no fighting in my home. Why have you let him rile you, man? You ken how he is."

And Anthony said, a bit more diplomatically, "You *are* pulling our collective leg here aren't you, old man?"

"If you'd use your head instead of your arse to think with, you'd know this is one subject I would never joke about," came James's scathing reply.

Anthony straightened slowly, coming away from the wall. Georgina, watching him, could have said to the very second when he finally believed James, his expression turned so comical in his amazement. It still took about five more seconds before he burst out, "Good God, you actually did it, didn't you?" and he promptly started laughing, so hard he had to hold on to the wall for support.

"Bloody hell," James swore under his breath.

Roslynn sent Georgina an apologetic smile, but to James, who was staring at Anthony in disgust, she said, "You should have expected this. I've heard you ribbed him unmercifully when he married me."

"Not because he married you, my dear, but because he couldn't find his way over the wall you set down in the center of the marriage bed."

Roslynn pinkened with the reminder of how long it had taken for her to forgive Anthony for his supposed infidelity. Anthony started to sober, for that was a subject he didn't find amusing now, any more than he had then. But into the pause following James's vexing remark, Georgina let them all know she was none too amused herself. In fact, she'd briefly contemplated putting on one of her shoes just so she could kick both Malory men.

Instead, she said, "Now, there's a problem you just might be facing yourself, James Malory."

And that sent Anthony off with a new peal of laughter, and turned James's scowl on his wife. "Blister it, George, you can see he's convinced."

"What he is, is convulsed with hilarity, and I'd like to know just *what* is so funny about your having married me?"

"Damnation, it's nothing to do with you! It's that I've married at all!"

"Then why don't you tell him it wasn't your idea, that my brothers—"

"George—!"

"—forced you?"

Having failed in his effort to stop her, James closed his eyes in anticipation of what that little gem was going to produce by way of reactions. It was too much to hope Anthony might not have heard her.

"Forced?" Anthony said incredulously, pausing only long enough to wipe moisture from his eyes. "Well, now, that makes more sense, indeed it does. Should have said so right off, old boy." But he'd held back too long to say that much. "Forced?" he choked out once more before bursting into laughter again, even harder than before.

Very quietly, James told Roslynn, "Either drag him out of here or he's not going to be much use to you for several months . . . possibly a whole bloody year."

"Now, James," she tried to placate him and keep the grin off her own lips while doing it. "You have to admit it's rather farfetched that you could be forced . . ." His darker glower turned her attention to her husband instead. "Anthony, do stop. It's not *that* funny."

"Devil . . . it . . . ain't," he gasped out. "How many, James? Three? Four?" When James just scowled at him, he looked to Georgina for the answer.

She was also scowling at him, but said, "If you're asking how many brothers I have, there were five at last count."

"Thank God!" Anthony gave a mock sigh between chuckles. "Thought you were slipping there for a moment, brother. Now you've got my complete sympathy."

"Like hell I do," James snarled, and started toward Anthony again.

But Roslynn intervened once more, this time grabbing her husband's arm. "You just don't know when to quit, do you?" she admonished, pulling him toward the door.

"I've hardly begun," he protested, but a glance back at James made him amend, "You're right, sweetheart, indeed you are. And didn't you tell Jason we'd pay him a visit while he's in town? By God, I don't think I've ever looked forward so to seeing the elders, or had such interesting news to tell 'em."

Anthony was barely out the door before it was slammed behind him, but that only started his laughter again, particularly when he heard the muffled string of oaths from the other side.

Roslynn gave him an exasperated look. "You really shouldn't have done that."

"I know." Anthony grinned.

"He might not forgive you."

"I know." His grin widened measurably.

She clicked her tongue. "You're not the least bit repentant, are you?"

"Not one bloody bit." He chuckled. "But damn me, I forgot to congratulate him."

She jerked him back sharply. "Don't you dare! I happen to like your head on your shoulders."

In an abrupt change of interest, he cornered her up against the wall there in the hallway. "Do you?"

"Anthony, stop!" She laughed, trying only halfheartedly to avoid his lips. "You're incorrigible."

"I'm in love," he countered huskily. "And men in love usually are incorrigible."

She gasped as he nipped her ear. "Well, when you put it that way . . . our room *is* just down the hall."

Chapter Forty-one

〰️

"Good God!" Anthony said when James and Georgina entered the dining room the next morning. "How the devil did I fail to notice you've got yourself a prime article there, James?"

"Because you were too busy ribbing me," James replied. "And don't start again, lad. Be grateful my night was more pleasant *after* your departure."

Georgina blushed, wanting to kick him for saying something like that. Anthony was saved from the same wish, simply because she had no idea the prime article he referred to was herself. And since the night had been very pleasant for her as well, and she was now looking her best in a deep plum-colored gown of plush velvet that fit her perfectly, She was feeling mellow enough not to make a comment to either of them.

But Anthony couldn't seem to take his eyes off her, and his wife finally did some kicking of her own—under the table. He flinched but was not the least bit put off, even when James started frowning at him.

Finally he said, with some exasperation, "Where the deuce have I seen you before, George? You look damned familiar, damn me if you don't."

"My name isn't George," she told him as she took her seat. "It's Georgina, or Georgie to my friends and family. Only James can't seem to remember that."

"Are we hinting that I'm senile again?" James asked, one brow crooking.

She grinned sweetly at him. "If the shoe fits."

"If memory serves, I made you eat that shoe the last time you tried forcing it on my foot."

"And if memory serves," she countered, "I believe it was delicious."

Anthony had watched this byplay with interest while he patiently waited to repeat his question. But the question was quite forgotten when he noted that James's eyes were suddenly smoldering with an inner heat that had nothing to do with anger. Passion flaring over a shoe? And she'd eaten the thing?

"Is this a private joke?" he asked mildly, "or do we get to hear the punch line?"

"You get to hear how we met, Sir Anthony."

"Ah ha!" he said triumphantly. "I knew it. I'm deuced good at this sort of thing, don't you know. So where was it? Vauxhall? Drury Lane?"

"A smoky tavern, actually."

And Anthony's eyes went from her to James, one brow slanting, an affectation that must run in the family, Georgina decided. "I should have known. After all, you had developed a taste for barmaids."

But James wasn't in a mood to be riled just now. Grinning, he said, "You're thinking with your arse again, dear boy. She didn't work there. Come to think of it, I never did find out what she was doing there."

"The same thing you were, James," Georgina told him. "Looking for someone."

"And who were you looking for?" Anthony asked his brother.

"Not me, you. This was the day you dragged me over half of London searching for your wife's cousin."

A day Anthony would *never* forget, so he was quick to point out, "But your Margie was a blond."

"And my George is a brunette, with a fondness for male togs."

And Anthony's eyes came back to Georgina with perfect recall. "Good God, the vixen who leaves bruises on shins! I thought you'd had no luck finding her, James."

"I didn't. She found me. Dropped right into my arms, so to speak. She signed—"

"James!" Georgina cut in, appalled that he was going to confess all again. "It isn't necessary to get into particulars, is it?"

"This is family, love," he told her with unconcern. "Don't matter if they know."

"Is that so?" she replied stiffly, her brows snapping together. "And is that the attitude you had when you told *my* family all about it?"

James frowned, clearly displeased that she'd brought the subject around to something *he* didn't want discussed. And he didn't bother to answer. He moved to the sideboard where the breakfast fare was laid out, giving the table his back.

Roslynn, aware that the atmosphere had drastically changed, said diplomatically. "May I fix you a plate, Georgie? We serve ourselves in the morning."

"Thank you—"

But James cut in, his tone clearly grumbling, "I can bloody well do it."

Georgina's lips pursed in annoyance. She supposed she shouldn't have introduced the one topic guaranteed to sour his mood, but devil take it, was she supposed to let him scandalize his own family, and thoroughly embarrass her in the process? He might not care what he told to whom, or what waves it created, but she did.

But her pique didn't last beyond getting the plate of food from her husband, which he dropped loudly in front of her. It was a small mountain of eggs, kippers, meat pies, and sausage, rounded with biscuits and great scoops of jellies, more food than four people could eat. Georgina stared at it wide-eyed, turned to see that James's plate was piled even higher. Both were so obviously prepared with a total absence of thought that her humor was pricked.

"Why, thank you, James," she said, resisting the smile that was tugging at her lips. "I *am* famished, actually, though I can't image why. It's not as if I've been very . . . energetic this morning."

The outright lie was designed to cajole him back to a more agreeable mood, since they had both exhibited an abundance of energy this morning before they even left their bed. But she should have known better than to attempt word games with James Malory.

"You should always be so lazy, George," he replied with one of his more devilish smiles, and there was absolutely nothing that could have stopped her cheeks from going up in flames.

"I don't know why she's blushing," Anthony said into the ensuing silence. "It's not as if we *should* understand the implications there. Not that we don't, but we shouldn't. Had a hard time getting out of bed myself this morn—"

Roslynn's napkin hitting him in the mouth ended that round of teasing. "Leave the poor girl alone, you rogue. Hell's teeth, being married to a Malory is—"

"Bliss?" Anthony prompted.

"Who says so?" she snorted.

"You do, sweetheart, most frequently."

"Moments of madness surely." She sighed, gaining a chuckle from her husband.

By this time Georgina's cheeks had cooled down, but she was still grateful to Roslynn, who managed to steer the conversation into subjects nonpersonal after that, or at least nonembarrassing. She learned that a seamstress would be visiting her that very afternoon to provide a complete new wardrobe, that there were several upcoming balls over the winter season that she *must* attend—both Malory men groaned at that point—as well as routs and soirees by the dozen, where she could be introduced properly to the *ton*. Taking into account that these things implied she had a future here, which wasn't an established fact by any means, she'd looked at James with an is-all-this-necessary? look, and had gotten back total inscrutability.

Georgina also found out that there was to be a family gathering tonight, which was when Anthony admitted, "By the by, I didn't visit the elders last night after all. Got detained." Here he wiggled his brows and kissed the air toward his wife, while she looked for another napkin to throw at him. Chuckling, he added to James, "Besides, old boy, I realized they simply wouldn't believe the news unless they hear it from you, and you have such a unique way of telling it, without actually saying it, that I didn't want to deprive you of the opportunity to blunder through it again."

To that, James replied, "If you're visiting Knighton's Hall today, I'll be delighted to join you."

"Well, if I'm damned anyway, I might as well ask it," Anthony said, and asked it. "What the devil did you tell her family that you can't tell your own?"

"Ask George." James grunted. "She's the one who doesn't want it repeated."

But when those cobalt-blue eyes turned on her in inquiry, Georgina's lips closed stubbornly, prompting Anthony to say with a blinding smile, "Come on, sweetheart, you might as well 'fess up. I'll only bring up the matter at every opportunity, in whatever company, until you do."

"You wouldn't!"

"He bloody well would," James put in sourly.

Thoroughly vexed, Georgina demanded of her husband, "Well, can't you do something about it?"

"Oh, I intend to," James said with distinct menace. "You may depend upon it. But that ain't going to stop him."

"'Course it wouldn't." Anthony grinned. "No more than it would you, old man."

Georgina sat back in a huff and said, "I'm beginning to have the same sentiments toward your family as you have toward mine, James Malory."

"I'd be surprised if you didn't, George."

With no help for it, she gave Anthony a fulminating glare and snapped out, "I was his cabin boy. That was what he told my brothers; that and the fact that I'd shared his cabin. Now are you quite satisfied, you odious man?"

"I don't suppose he knew they were your brothers?" Anthony inquired mildly.

"He knew," she grouched.

"Perhaps he didn't know there were so many of them?"

"He knew that, too."

Anthony then turned a very knowing and maddening look on James. "Sort of like pulling the trigger yourself, ain't it, old boy?"

"Oh, shut up, you ass," James snarled.

To which Anthony threw his head back and laughed uproariously. When he slowed to chuckles, he said, "Didn't think you'd go so far to fulfill my hopes, old man."

"What hopes?"

"You don't recall my remark that when you get one of your own, she be as sweet as the little viper who kicked you instead of thanking you for your help? Didn't mean for you to get *the* very one."

James did recall the remark then, and the fact that it had been given when Anthony was in a black mood because he'd had no luck the previous night in wooing his angry wife back to his bed. "Now that you mention it, I do recall your saying something to that effect . . . and why you said it, and that you were drowning your miseries in drink that day. Foxed by five o'clock, and the wife wouldn't even put you to bed, would she?"

"Bloody hell." Anthony's expression was now quite sour, while James was now smiling. "You were foxed yourself that day. How the devil d'you remember all that?"

"You have to ask, when you were being so bloody entertaining? Wouldn't have missed a moment of it, dear boy."

"I do believe they're about to go at it again," Roslynn told Georgina. "Why don't we leave them to it. They might kill each other if we're not around to watch," and with a pointed look at her husband, she added, "which will save *us* the trouble."

"If you leave, he won't be nearly so annoyed by my digs," Anthony protested as both women left the table.

"That's the point, darling." Roslynn smiled at him, then said to his brother, "By the by, James, I sent off word to Silverley last evening, about your return. So you might want to keep yourself available today, since Reggie isn't likely to wait until this evening to show up. And you know how devastated she'll be if she misses you."

Georgina paused upon hearing that to demand, "And just *who* is Reggie?"

"Regan," James told her, grinning with the memory of her jealousy, and what looked to be a return of it.

But Anthony added, with a baleful look passed on to James, "It's a longstanding point of disagreement, what we call her, but she's our favorite niece. The four of us raised her, you know, after our sister died."

Georgina could not, by any means, picture that. But as long as this Regan-Reggie was merely related to James, she lost interest in her. Still, even if Georgina wasn't going to be around long, she really ought to make a point of learning a bit more about this large family of his, if just to keep her dander from rising each time she heard a female name in connection with his. It would have been nice if he had bothered to sort it all out for her before they got here, but he had been very closed-mouthed about his family—possibly to make sure she was closed-mouthed about hers. Fair was fair, after all.

Chapter Forty-two

"Men *do* get married, you know," Georgina said reasonably, if a bit sarcastically. "They even do it on a regular basis, same as women do. So would someone mind telling me why the first and so far unanimous reaction to James's getting married is shock, followed closely by disbelief? For God's sake, he's not a monk."

"You're absolutely right. No one could *ever* accuse him of being that." And the speaker went into a round of giggles.

Reggie, or Regan, as the case were, turned out to actually be Regina Eden, viscountess of Montieth. But she was a very young viscountess, only twenty years old, and no bigger than Georgina. And no one could deny that she was a member of the Malory clan, at least Anthony and Jeremy's side of it, for she had the same black hair and cobalt-blue eyes that they'd been born with. But Georgina was to learn that they were the exceptions, along with Amy, one of Edward's daughters. All of the other Malorys resembled James, being blond and mostly green-eyed.

Georgina also found, to her relief, that Regina Eden was immensely likable. In quick order she found her to be lively, charming, open, teasing, and quite, quite outspoken. She'd been bubbling with good humor ever since she'd arrived earlier that afternoon, but especially after she'd asked James, "And which mistress did you lend my clothes to?" since she hadn't been home for the borrowing of them. And while James was mulling over the easiest way to break the news, Anthony simply couldn't resist answering, "The one he married, puss." Fortunately, the girl had been sitting down at the time. But Georgina had heard at least nine times, "I don't believe it"—she was counting—and there'd been a good ten times, "Oh, this is famous!" and that in the space of only a few hours.

Georgina was upstairs now having her hair artfully arranged by Roslynn's maid, Nettie MacDonald, a feisty Scot of middle years whose soft brogue and softer green eyes had Georgina thinking how Mac would really like this woman. Roslynn and Regina were also present, supposedly to make sure she was turned out just right to meet the elders, James's older brothers, but actually they were making sure she didn't get nervous by regaling her with amusing anecdotes about the family and answering all her questions.

"I suppose it does seem a bit strange to someone who isn't familiar with Uncle James's history." Regina had quieted down enough to answer Georgina's question. "This is a man who swore he would never marry, and no one doubted he was absolutely serious. But to understand why, you have to realize he was a . . . well, he . . ."

"Was a connoisseur of women?" Georgina supplied helpfully.

"Why, that's a splendid way to put it! I've said the same myself."

Georgina only smiled. Roslynn rolled her eyes. She'd heard her Anthony described the same way by this minx, but she preferred to call a rake a rake.

"But Uncle James wasn't just a connoisseur," Regina went on to explain. "And if I may be blunt . . . ?"

"By all means," Georgina replied.

But Roslynn warned first, "Now don't try to make her jealous, Reggie."

"Of past peccadilloes?" The girl snorted. "I for one, am eternally grateful for every one of my Nicholas's past mistresses. Without the experience—"

"I think we get your drift, m'dear," Roslynn cut in, and couldn't help grinning. "And we might even agree," she added, seeing that Georgina was smiling, too.

"Well, as I was saying, Uncle James was a bit more than just a connoisseur of women. For a while after he first embarked on what was to be a very jaded career, you might have called him a glutton. Morning, noon, and night, and never with the same woman."

"Oh, bosh," Roslynn scoffed. "Morning, noon, *and* night?"

And Georgina nearly choked, holding her breath, waiting to hear that ridiculous "never with the same woman," questioned, too, but apparently that part wasn't in doubt.

"It's perfectly true," Regina insisted. "Ask Tony if you don't believe me, or Uncle Jason, whose misfortune it was to try and curb James's wildness while he was still living at home—unsuccessfully, I might add. Of course, half of what Uncle James ever did was just to rile Jason. But James *was* wild. From the youngest age, he always went his own way, always had to be different from his brothers. It's no wonder he had his first duel before he was even twenty. 'Course he won that one. He's won them all, don't you know. Jason was a superb marksman, after all, and he taught all his brothers. Anthony and James, though, developed a fondness for fisticuffs, too, and many of their challenges were seen to in the ring rather than the dueling field."

"At least that's not so lethal."

"Oh, he never actually killed anyone on the field of honor, at least not that I recall hearing about. It's the angry challenger who usually tries to kill his opponent."

"Anthony used to ask his opponents where they would like to receive their wounds," Roslynn put in. "A question like that really undermines a chap's confidence."

Regina giggled. "But who do you think he picked that habit up from?"

"James?"

"The very one."

Georgina was beginning to wish she hadn't started this. "But you still haven't really answered my question."

"It's all part and parcel, m'dear. By the time Uncle James moved to London, he was already a disreputable rakehell. But he no longer chased everything in skirts, because he didn't have to. By then, they were chasing him. And most of the women throwing themselves at him were married women."

"I think I'm beginning to understand," Georgina said.

"I thought you would. Most every challenge issued to him was quite legitimate, all from husbands. The irony is, James might have taken what was offered, but he never kissed and told. Those batty women were so impressed with him—well, he *was* a devilish handsome man when he was younger, too—that *they* did the bragging if he so much as looked at them. So it stands to reason that he wouldn't have much respect for the married state, seeing firsthand nothing but constant infidelities."

"Which he contributed to," Georgina said a bit testily.

"No one can deny that." Regina grinned. "He was, after all, the most notorious rake in London. He even put Tony to shame, and Tony was quite scandalous himself in his day."

"I'll thank you to leave Anthony out of this," Roslynn said. "He's a totally reformed rake."

"Well, so is my Nicholas, I'll have you know. But as for Uncle James, after so many years of seeing only the worst side of marriage, it was no wonder he despised the hypocrisy of it, and unfaithful wives in particular, with which the *ton* abounds. He swore he'd never have one of his own, and we all thought he meant it."

"I'm sure he did mean it. He didn't ask to marry me, after all."

Regina didn't question that. She'd already been told that James had been forced to marry, and by James himself—before Anthony could. But she did question the "forced" part.

"I have to wonder about that, Georgie," she said thoughtfully. "You just don't know my Uncle James—"

"But that's what you're doing, telling me about him. It's rare that I get anything of a personal nature out of him, after all. Is there anything else you think I ought to know?"

"Well, the fact that the family disowned him for a while might come up tonight. He was gone from England for about ten years during that time. 'Course, he's reinstated now. I don't suppose he told you about any of that?"

"No."

"Well, that's one subject that you'll have to ask him about, since it's not my place to say—"

"That he was the infamous Captain Hawke?"

Regina's eyes flared. "So he *did* tell you?"

"No, he admitted it to my brothers, after they'd recognized him. I suppose you could say it was the worst luck that two of them happened to meet up with James on the high seas before he retired from pirating."

Regina gasped, "You mean your brothers all knew? Good Lord, it's lucky they didn't hang him!"

"Oh, they wanted to, at least Warren did," Georgina said in disgust. "But James was so full of confessions that night, he deserved hanging."

"And how is it . . . he didn't hang?" Regina asked carefully.

"He escaped."

"With your help?"

"Well I couldn't let Warren have his way, just because he was furious at James because of me. He's a womanizer himself, that hypocrite."

"Well, all's well that ends well, as the saying goes," Roslynn said, and got a snort out of Regina.

"It doesn't sound like all's well to me, not when Uncle James has her whole family against him."

"Come now, Reggie, you don't really think he's going to let a little thing like that bother him, do you? Particularly when he's here and they're a whole ocean away. When he's ready, I'm sure he'll make it up with them, for Georgie's sake."

"James?"

Roslynn's rich chuckle filled the room at Regina's exaggerated incredulity. "Perhaps you're right. He's a man who doesn't go out of his way to forgive or forget. Your poor husband has learned that firsthand, hasn't he?"

"Don't remind me. And I'm sure Nicholas is going to quite enjoy getting in a few digs tonight, especially if he hears that James married under the same circumstances as Nicholas married me." At Georgina's questioning look, she added, "Your husband was not the only one who got shoved up to the altar. In Nicholas's case, it took a little blackmail, a little bribery, and of course Tony praying he'd refuse so he could cut Nicholas into little pieces."

"And James?"

"Oh, he wasn't part of that. We didn't even know he was back in England yet. But as it happens, my husband also clashed with Captain Hawke on the high seas at one time. So if they appear to be mortal enemies tonight, think nothing of it."

At that Georgina burst into laughter.

Chapter Forty-three

Despite the fact that this was to be no more than a family gathering, Georgina discovered that such events were still quite formal affairs here when Regina produced a sparkling evening gown for her to wear. The rich brown material shimmered so, it looked like polished bronze, and with the bodice overlaid with sequined tulle, Georgina really did sparkle in the lovely creation. At any rate, she was delighted with it. Having been condemned to pastels for so long, she was eager for the darker, matronly colors it was now acceptable for her to wear. In fact, she had chosen nothing but bold, vibrant colors for the wardrobe she had ordered earlier.

Coming downstairs later, they met the men of the household in the parlor, finding they had done themselves up just as grandly. Anthony was unfashionably all in black, except for the pristine whiteness of his carelessly tied cravat. James was sporting a satin coat for the occasion, but in an emerald-green so dark it could not in any way be called dandyish. And what that color did for his eyes! They appeared like jewels with fire captured at their center, lighting them to a more vivid, brilliant green that fairly glowed. And Jeremy, that scamp, was a dandy personified in a glaringly cardinal-red coat, with godawful chartreuse knee-breeches, a combination that, Regina told Georgina in a side whisper, was being worn just to annoy his father.

Conrad Sharpe was also present, not surprising since James and Jeremy both considered him family. Georgina had never seen him done up formally before, though, even to the point of having shaved off his sea beard. But likewise, this was the first time he was seeing her in anything other than her boy's togs, and it was too much to hope that he might overlook that fact.

"Well, Good God, George, you haven't misplaced your breeches, have you?"

"Very funny," she mumbled.

While Connie and Anthony chuckled, and James just stared at her deeply scooped decolletage, Regina remarked, "For shame, Connie. That's not the way you compliment a lady."

"So you've already championed her, little squirt?" he said, drawing her close for a hug. "Well, sheathe your claws. George here don't need flattery any more than you do, or protection, for that matter. Besides, it ain't safe to compliment her when her husband's around."

James ignored that bit of foolery to tell his niece, "Since I know that must be one of your ensembles, sweet, I have to say you're wearing your bodices too low these days."

"Nicholas doesn't mind." The girl grinned.

"That wastrel wouldn't."

"Oh, famous. He's not even here yet, and you're already starting on him," and she moved off in a huff to greet Jeremy.

But when James's eyes came back to Georgina, particularly to her bodice, she was so reminded of a similar scene that she said, "If my brothers were here they would make some ridiculous remark right about now, like I ought to change into something less revealing. You wouldn't by any chance be thinking the same thing?"

"And agree with them? God forbid!"

With a teasing grin, Connie said to Anthony, "D'you get the feeling he don't like her brothers?"

"I can't imagine why," Anthony replied, straight-faced. "After what you told me about 'em, they sound like such enterprising chaps."

"Tony . . ." James warned, but Anthony had held his laughter in too long.

"Locked in a cellar!" he hooted. "By God, I wish I could've seen it, indeed I do."

If James hadn't heard enough, Georgina had. "My brothers, the lot of them, happen to be as big or bigger than yourself, Sir Anthony. You wouldn't have fared any better against them, I assure you," she said and then marched off to join Regina across the room.

Anthony, if not put in his place, was at least surprised. "Well, damn me, I do believe the chit just defended you, James."

James merely smiled, but Roslynn, who'd listened to her husband with growing exasperation, said, "If you don't stop ribbing him in front of her, she's liable to do more than that. And if she doesn't, I might," and the last lady deserted them.

Connie chuckled at Anthony's changed expression, which was cha-grined now. He nudged James to have a look. "If he's not careful, he might be sleeping with the dogs again."

"You may be right, old man," James replied. "So let's not discour-age him."

Connie shrugged. "If you can bear it, it's no skin off my back."

"I can bloody well put up with anything for the desired results."

"I suppose you can, even getting locked in cellars."

"I heard that!" Anthony interjected. "So I had the right of it. There *was* motive to your madness—"

"Oh, shut up, Tony."

It wasn't much longer before the elders arrived, as James and Anthony liked to refer to their older brothers. Jason Malory, the third marquis of Haverston and head of the family, was a surprise to Georgina. She'd been told he was forty-six, and indeed, he merely looked a slightly older version of James. But right there the similarities ended. While James had his droll charm, his abnormal sense of humor, and his devilishly sensual smiles, Jason was sobriety itself. And she had thought her brother Clinton was too serious-minded. Jason put him to shame, and worse, she'd been told all that grimness came with a hot temper that was more often than not directed at his younger brothers. Of course, she'd also been told, and had no reason to doubt it if James and Anthony were any indication, that the Malory brothers were happi-est when they were arguing among themselves.

Edward Malory, now, was unlike any of the other three. A year younger than Jason, he was stockier than Jason and James, though he had the same blond hair and green eyes. Nothing seemed to be able to mar his joviality. He could banter with the rest of them, but good-humoredly. In fact, like her brother Thomas, he seemed totally lacking in temper.

And when James dropped the news on them? Well, at least their disbelief didn't last nearly as long as Anthony's.

"I had doubts that Tony would ever settle down, but James? Good God, he was a lost cause," Jason commented.

"I'm amazed, James," Edward said, "but of course delighted, absolutely delighted."

Georgina couldn't doubt her welcome into the family. Both older brothers looked at her as if she were a miracle worker. Of course, they hadn't been told yet the rest of the circumstances of her marriage, and Anthony, for once, kept his mouth shut. But she couldn't help wondering why James was letting them all think that everything was swell-dandy-fine.

It would be rather awkward for him to explain if he sent her home now, but she knew that wouldn't stop him if he was going to. So was he going to? If the question weren't so damned important, she'd put herself out of misery and ask it again, and pray that this time she'd get a straight answer. But if he didn't have plans to live with her permanently, she really didn't want to know it now, when she was starting to have hope again.

Edward had arrived with his wife, Charlotte, and Amy, the youngest of his five children. The others all had had previous commitments, but had promised to drop by during the week. Derek, Jason's only son, was supposedly out of town, likely committing deviltry—word was he was fast following in his younger uncles' footsteps—at least no one had been able to locate him. And Jason's wife, Frances, never came to London, so her absence was not unexpected. Regina had, in fact, confided that Frances had only endured marriage to provide Derek and Regina with a mother figure, and now that they were grown, she preferred to live separately from her austere husband.

"Don't worry, you'll figure out who's who in no time," Roslynn had assured her. "It's when dear Charlotte regales you with the *ton*'s latest scandals that you'll get confused. So *many*, you know, and yet you're likely to meet everyone involved eventually."

Meet the cream of England's aristocracy? She could do without that, thank you. And yet she nearly choked with wry humor when she realized that aside from Connie and Jeremy, every single person in the room *was* a titled aristocrat, herself now included. And irony of ironies, she didn't find them the least bit contemptible, snobbish, or unlikable . . . well, with the possible exception of her youngest brother-in-law. Anthony, with his provoking taunts and innuendos, was not endearing himself to her at all. Quite the opposite.

It wasn't much later, however, that Georgina had her first opportunity to see how Malorys banded together. No sooner did Nicholas Eden, viscount of Montieth, walk into the room, than Anthony and James stopped going for each other's throats and went for his instead.

"You're late, Eden," Anthony greeted him with cool curtness. "And here I was hoping you'd forgotten where I live."

"I've tried, old man, but the wife keeps reminding me," Nicholas replied, his tight smile anything but congenial. "You don't think I *like* coming here, d'you?"

"Well, you'd best pretend otherwise, puppy. Your wife has noticed that you've arrived, and you know how annoyed she gets when she sees you provoking her dear uncles."

"*Me* provoking?" The poor man nearly choked in strangled outrage.

But when he glanced over to where Regina was embroiled in conversation with Amy and Charlotte, his whole countenance changed. She signaled she'd join him in a minute. He winked and smiled at her with unbelievable tenderness. Georgina was trying to be neutral, even though she'd heard the stories about why these three men were so at odds with one another and thought it ridiculous that it had gone on for more than a year. But after just watching that tender exchange, she favored Nicholas Eden's side . . . until he turned back to the three of them and his eyes lit on James.

"Back so soon? And here I'd so been hoping you'd sink at sea or something."

James actually chuckled. "Sorry to disappoint you, lad, but I had precious cargo this trip, so was extra careful. And how have you been? Sleeping on the couch lately?"

Nicholas scowled. "Not since you've been gone, you bloody sod, but I suppose that will change now," he grumbled.

"Depend upon it, dear boy." James grinned devilishly. "We do love to assist in a good cause, after all."

"You're all heart, Malory." And then those amber eyes dropped to Georgina, standing between the brothers, but with James's arm draped over her shoulders. "And who is this, as if I need to ask?"

The insinuation was clear, and Georgina bristled at being demoted back to mistress. But before she could think of a scathing enough reply, and before James could retaliate even more harshly, Anthony came to her defense, shocking not only her, but Nicholas, too.

"Get that sneer out of your tone, Eden," he said, his anger all the more telling for its quietness. "That's my sister-in-law you're dragging through the gutter of your thoughts."

"I beg your pardon," Nicholas said to Georgina, thoroughly embarrassed and contrite to have made such a horrid mistake. And yet his confusion quickly took over. To Anthony, he said, with a good deal of suspicion that he might have just had his leg pulled, "I thought your wife was an only child."

"She is."

"Then how can she be . . . ?" Those beautiful amber eyes jumped back to James, widened incredulously now. "Oh, Good God, you can't mean *you've* taken a wife! You must have had to sail to the ends of the earth to find a woman who wouldn't be scared off by your sordid reputation." He looked to Georgina again to add, "Did you *know* you were getting a bloody pirate for a husband?"

"That *was* mentioned before the wedding, I believe," she answered wryly.

"And did you know that he carries grudges to the ends of time?"

"I'm beginning to see why," she countered, causing both Anthony and James to burst into laughter.

Nicholas grudgingly smiled. "Very good, m'dear, but did you also know he is a philandering rogue, so jaded—?"

James interrupted at that point with a soft growl, "Keep it up, lad, and you'll force me to—"

"Force you?" Regina said as she came up beside her husband to slip her arm through his. "You *told* him, Uncle James? Famous! I could have sworn that was one little tidbit you wouldn't have wanted Nicholas, of all people, to know about. After all, you do so hate to have anything in common with him, and that you were both forced to wed is having a *lot* in common, isn't it?"

Nicholas said nothing to that. He stared at his wife, probably trying to ascertain if she were serious or not. But he was going to laugh. Georgina could see it in his eyes. He held back only until he saw James's chagrined look.

Surprisingly, Anthony didn't join Nicholas in his laughter. He'd either gotten it all out of his system the previous night, or, more likely, he just didn't want to share anything with the young viscount, even something they both found vastly amusing.

"Reggie, puss," he said with marked displeasure. "I don't know whether to strangle you or send you to your room."

"I don't have a room here anymore, Tony."

"Then strangle her," James said, looking as if he actually meant it, until his eyes dropped to his niece with a mixture of fondness and exasperation. "You did that on purpose, didn't you, sweet?"

She didn't even try to deny it. "Well, you two always stand solidly against him, which is hardly fair, now is it, two to one? But don't be mad at me. I've just realized that *I'm* going to have to listen to his crowing about it a lot more than you will. I live with him, after all."

That did not, by any means, make it better, when Nicholas Eden was standing there grinning from ear to ear. "Perhaps I ought to come live with you myself, Regan," James said. "At least until the townhouse Eddie boy found for me is refurbished."

At that, Nicholas was brought up short. "Over my dead body."

"That, dear boy, can be arranged."

And at that moment, Edward joined them. "By the by, James, in all the excitement of your wonderful news, I forgot to mention that a chap stopped by the house this evening looking for you. Would have told him where you could be found except, well, dash it all, he was rather hostile in his inquiry. Figured if he were a friend, he'd have better manners."

"Did he leave a name?"

"None a'tall. He was a big chap though, very tall, and an American by the sound of him."

James turned slowly toward Georgina, his brows drawn together, storm clouds gathering in his eyes. "Those barbarous louts you're related to wouldn't have followed us here, would they, m'dear?"

Her chin rose a little in defiance of his reaction, but she still couldn't conceal the amusement that touched her eyes. "My brothers happen to care about me, James, so perhaps if you'll recall Drew's and Boyd's last sight of me on your ship, you'll have your answer."

His frame of mind that memorable night of their wedding might have been a little off center with volatile emotions, but he did recall that he'd brought her aboard his ship gagged, and that he'd kept her close to hand, under his arm, actually.

Now he said quietly, but with feeling, "Bloody everlasting hell."

Chapter Forty-four

"Devil take it, you can't be serious!" Georgina said furiously. "I have to at least see them. They've come all this way—"

"I don't give a bloody damn how far they've come!" James shot back just as furiously.

She hadn't had a chance to broach the subject of her brothers last night, since she had gone up to her room soon after the elders left, and though she'd waited and waited for James to join her, she'd fallen asleep before he did. Now, this morning, he'd flatly refused to take her to the harbor, flatly refused to arrange a carriage for her when she asked for that instead, and finally told her in words she couldn't possibly misunderstand, that she wouldn't be seeing her brothers at all, and that was that.

She drew herself up now and tried to inject some rationality into the discussion by asking calmly, "Would you mind telling me why you're taking this attitude? You must know they've only come here to assure themselves that I'm all right."

"Like bloody hell!" he snarled, unwilling or unable to be rational, reasonable, or anything moderate just now. "They've come to take you back."

It was a question she could no longer put off. "And isn't that what you intended all along, to send me back?"

She held her breath while he continued to scowl at her for several long moments. And then he snorted, as if she'd asked something utterly ridiculous.

"Where the deuce did you get that notion from? Have I ever said as much?"

"You didn't have to. I was at our wedding, remember? You were not an eager groom by any means."

"What I remember, George, is that you ran off from me without a by-your-leave!"

She blinked in surprise at hearing that brought up at this late date, and not at all in connection with what she'd asked. "Ran off? What I did was go home, James. That *is* what I was doing on your ship in the first place—going home."

"Without telling me!"

"Now that wasn't my fault. I would have told you, but the *Triton* had already sailed by the time Drew was done yelling at me for showing up in Jamaica, when he'd assumed I was at home. Was I supposed to jump overboard just to tell you goodbye?"

"You weren't supposed to leave at all!"

"Now that's ridiculous. We had no understanding, no spoken agreement that might have led me to believe you wanted to continue our relationship on a permanent basis—or any basis, for that matter. Was I supposed to read your mind? *Did* you have something permanent in mind?"

"I was going to ask you to be my . . ." He hesitated over the word when he saw the narrowing of her eyes. "Well, you don't have to look insulted," he ended huffily.

"I'm not," she said tightly, which told him plainly that she was. "My answer, by the way, would have been no!"

"Then I'm bloody well glad I didn't ask!" and he headed toward the door.

"Don't you dare leave yet!" she shouted after him. "You haven't answered my question."

"Haven't I?" He turned with raised brow, which warned her immediately that he was done with showing her his temper, and was now going to be merely difficult, which was far worse as far as she was concerned. "Suffice it to say that you're my wife, and as such, you aren't going anywhere."

And that infuriated her no end. "Oh, are we admitting it now, that

I'm your wife? Just because my brothers have come? Is this more revenge on your part, James Malory?"

"Think what you like, but your damned brothers can rot in the harbor for all I care. They won't know where to find you, and you bloody well aren't going to them. End of discussion, love," and he slammed out of the bedroom.

And by the time Georgina had slammed the door three more times for good measure, none of which brought her exasperating husband back to finish the argument properly, she'd decided he was still a blasted brick wall. But brick walls could be climbed if they couldn't be toppled.

"Have you told her you love her yet?"

James slowly put his cards down on the table and picked up his drink instead. The question, unrelated to anything said previously, had his brow raising. He looked first at George Amherst to his left, who was studying his cards as if he'd never seen them before, then at Connie across from him, who was trying to keep a straight face, and finally at Anthony, who'd tossed out that loaded question.

"You weren't by any chance speaking to me, were you, old boy?"

"None other." Anthony grinned.

"You've been sitting there all evening wondering about it, have you? No wonder you've been losing steadily."

Anthony picked up his own drink and lazily swirled the amber liquid around in the glass, watching it rather than his brother. "Actually, I wondered about it this morning when I heard all that noise going on upstairs. Then again this afternoon when you caught the dear girl surreptitiously sneaking out the front door and ordered her to her room. That was a bit much, don't you think?"

"She stayed put, didn't she?"

"Indeed, so much so she wouldn't come down for dinner, which got *my* wife annoyed enough to go off visiting."

"So the little darling sulks," James said, shrugging with little concern. "It's a rather amusing habit of hers that can be got around quite easily. I'm just not ready to get around it yet."

"Oh, ho." Anthony chuckled. "That's confidence a bit misplaced I'd say, particularly if you haven't told her you love her."

James's brow shot up a bit higher. "You're not proposing to give me advice, are you, Tony?"

"As your wife puts it, if the shoe fits."

"But yours don't fit a'tall. Aren't you the lad who was so mired in the muck of misery that he—"

"We aren't discussing me," Anthony said laconically, a frown settling between his brows.

"Very well," James allowed, only to add, "But you'd still be floundering if I hadn't left Roslynn that note that exonerated you."

"I hate to break it to you, old man," Anthony gritted out. "But I'd already mended that fence before she ever clapped eyes on your note."

"Gentlemen, the game is whist," George Amherst said pointedly, "and I'm two hundred pounds down, if you don't mind."

And Connie finally burst out laughing. "Give it up, puppy," he said to Anthony. "He's going to remain mired in his own muck until it suits him to crawl out of the hole, and not a moment sooner. Besides, I do believe he's enjoying his muck . . . the challenge, you know. If she don't know how he feels, then it stands to reason she ain't going to tell him how she feels. Keeps him on his toes, don't it?"

Anthony turned to James for confirmation of this interesting idea, but all he got was a scoffing snort and a scowl.

As the Malory brothers were picking up their cards to continue the game, Georgina was slipping out the backdoor to stumble her way across backyards and alleys to Park Lane, where after an anxious fifteen-minute wait, she was able to hail a passing hack to take her to the London docks. Unfortunately, she'd already been let off and the hack gone before she belatedly recalled something she'd learned on her first trip to England. London, reputedly the largest commercial and shipping center in the world, didn't have just one dock. There was the London Dock at Wapping, the East India at Blackwall, Hermitage Dock, Shadwell Dock—and those were just a few of them that spread for miles along the Thames, and on both the south bank of the river and the north.

How the devil was she supposed to find a ship or two—and it was doubtful that her brothers would have brought more than that to England, knowing the berthing difficulties—this late at night, when most of the docks were locked up behind their high, protective walls? The best she could hope to do was some questioning, and that would have to be done on the wharves where incoming sailors would be found. More specifically, in the waterfront taverns along the quay.

She had to be crazy to even consider it. No, just exceedingly angry. What other choice did she have when James was being so ridiculously unreasonable? He wouldn't even let her out of the blasted house! And although she would rather try and locate her brothers during the day, when the area she was now in could be considered safer, she knew she'd never make it out of the townhouse undetected in the day, when there were so many servants and family about. And she was *not* going to let her brothers go home thinking she'd been done away with by the dastardly ex-pirate they'd married her to, simply because they'd been unable to find her.

But as she neared the area of the wharves where people were having rousing good times in whatever entertainments could be found late at night, her anger lessened in proportion to her rising nervousness. She really shouldn't be here. She wasn't dressed appropriately for what she was considering, wearing one of Regina's lovely dresses with matching spencer, which did not keep out the cold at all. And she wasn't adept at questioning people. What she wouldn't give to have Mac with her just now. But he was an ocean away, and when she watched two drunks leave one tavern and get no more than ten feet away before starting a fight with each other, she concluded that she *was* crazy to have come down here.

She would just have to work on James some more to get him to change his mind. She had wiles, didn't she? All women were supposed to have them, and what good were they if she didn't use them?

Georgina turned to go back the way she'd come, which at the moment seemed the safer avenue, or at least the more quiet, when she spotted what looked like another hack at the other end of the street. But she'd have to pass two taverns competing in noise to get to it, one on either side of the street so that she'd actually have to pass in front of one or the other to reach the hack, and the doors of both happened to be open to allow the escape of smoke and to let cold air in to cool the customers. She hesitated, weighing the long walk down deserted streets just to get to an area where she *might* be able to find transportation back to the West End, against this dimly lit street—except directly in front of the taverns where light blazed out—that was actually empty except for the two men now rolling on the ground in the middle of the street as they continued to pound on each other. A minute at a hurried pace and she'd be out of there, with nothing left to worry about except how she was going to get back into the house on Piccadilly undetected.

That settled it as far as she was concerned, and she set off at a brisk walk that picked up to a near run as she started to cross the front of the tavern on her right, since that one seemed to be a little less noisy. Keeping her head averted toward the street, she slammed right into a solid chest and would have sent both her and the owner of that solid chest falling except for someone else quickly steadying them.

"I beg your pardon," she began quickly, only to feel arms come around her instead of setting her back as they should have done.

"Not at all, love," she heard a husky voice say with a good deal of enthusiasm. "You can run me down any time, indeed you can."

She didn't know whether to be grateful or not that those tones were cultured, but she was going to assume that this was a gentleman, even if he hadn't let go of her yet. And a glance up at a well-dressed chest confirmed it. But when her eyes reached the top of him, she was given pause. Big, blond, and handsome, the young man reminded her uncannily of her husband, except for the eyes, which were more hazel than green.

"Perhaps she'd like to join us," came another voice, slightly slurred.

Georgina glanced over to see the fellow who'd kept them from falling, doing a bit of swaying on his feet himself. A young gentlemen, too, and she guessed uncomfortably that they were rakehells out slumming.

"A splendid idea, Percy, damn me if it ain't," the blond one holding her agreed, and to her, "Would you, love? Like to join us, that is?"

"No," she said flatly and distinctly as she tried to push away from him. The chap wasn't letting go, though.

"Now don't be hasty in deciding," he cajoled her, and then, "Gad, you're a pretty thing. Whoever's keeping you, sweetheart, I'll top his price and then some, and make sure you never have to walk these streets again."

Georgina was too stunned by the proposition to reply immediately, giving someone else an opportunity to say behind her, "Good God, cousin, you're talking to a lady. Take a gander at them togs she's wearing if you doubt me."

Three of them, Georgina realized, not just two. She was getting really uneasy now, particularly since the big one she was pushing against still wouldn't release her.

"Don't be an ass, dear boy," he said dryly to their third companion. "Here? And alone?" Then to her, with a smile that would probably have worked magic on any other woman, because the fellow really was exceedingly handsome, "You're not a lady, are you, love? Please say you aren't?"

She almost laughed at that point. He was honest-to-God hoping she wasn't, and she was no longer the innocent to be left wondering why.

"Much as I hate to admit it, I do have a 'lady' tacked on in front of my name now, thanks to my recent marriage. But regardless, mister, I believe you've detained me long enough. Kindly *let go*."

She'd said it firmly enough, but all he did was grin down at her in a maddening way. She was thinking about kicking him and then making a run for it when she heard a sharp intake of breath right behind her, and an incredulous voice.

"Hell's bells, Derek, I know that voice, damn me if I don't. If I'm not mistaken, that's your newest aunt you're trying to seduce."

"Very funny, Jeremy," Derek snorted.

"Jeremy?" Georgina twisted around, and sure enough, James's son was the one standing behind her.

"And my stepmother," the lad added, just before he started to laugh. "You're bloody well lucky you didn't try snatching a kiss from her like you did the last wench that caught your eye, cousin. My father would prob'ly kill you, if your father didn't beat him to it."

Georgina was released so fast, she stumbled. Three sets of hands immediately came up to steady her but dropped away just as quickly. For God's sake, if she was going to run in to family down here on the docks, why couldn't it have been hers instead of James's?

Derek Malory, Jason's only son and heir, was scowling blackly now, and Jeremy had stopped laughing as he looked around for his father, didn't see him, and concluded correctly that she was there without him.

"Does this mean the chit ain't going to be joining us?" Percy wanted to know.

"Watch your mouth," Derek warned his friend in a growl. "The lady is James Malory's wife."

"You mean the chap who nearly killed my friend Nick? Gad, you *are* done for, ain't you, Malory, trespassing with his—"

"Shut up, Percy, you ass. The lad *told* you she's my aunt."

"Beg to differ," Percy replied indignantly. "He told you. He did not tell me."

"Well, you *know* James is my uncle. He's not going to— Oh, devil it, never mind." And then his scowl came back to Georgina. More and more, he was reminding her of James ten years younger, which was probably about how old Derek was. "I suppose I should apologize, Aunt . . . George, ain't it?"

"Georgie," she corrected, unable to fathom why he appeared so annoyed with her now, but his next words brought a little understanding.

"Can't say as I'm thrilled just now to welcome you to the family."

She blinked. "You're not?"

"No, I'm not, not when I'd much prefer we weren't related." And then he said to Jeremy, "Bloody, hell, where *do* my uncles find 'em?"

"Well, my father found this one in a tavern." Jeremy was frowning at her now, too, but she quickly realized his anger was merely on his father's behalf. "So I suppose it's not so strange, after all, seeing her down here."

"For God's sake, it's not what it looks like, Jeremy," she protested with a bit of her own annoyance surfacing. "Your father was being totally unreasonable in not allowing me to see my brothers."

"So you set out to find them for yourself?"

"Well . . . yes."

"Do you even know where to look for them?"

"Well . . . no."

To that he gave a disgusted snort. "Then I think we'd better take you home, don't you?"

She sighed. "I suppose, but I *was* on my way home, you know. I meant to hire that hack—"

"Which would've left you walking, since that's Derek's carriage, and his driver would've just ignored you . . . unless of course you'd have given him your name, which you likely wouldn't've thought to do. Hell's bells, you're bloody lucky we found you . . . George."

Like father like son, she thought, gritting her teeth, and realizing, at that point, that there wouldn't be much hope now of getting back into the townhouse without James finding out about her little adventure, unless . . .

"I don't suppose you could refrain from mentioning this to your father?"

"No," he said simply.

Her teeth were really gnashing now. "You're a rotten stepson, Jeremy Malory."

And that amused the young scamp enough to bring back his laughter.

Chapter Forty-five

By the time Derek's carriage stopped in front of the townhouse on Piccadilly, Georgina wasn't just annoyed anymore with her escort, she was quite angry. Jeremy's humor had gotten thoroughly on her nerves, and his dire predictions of what she could expect from an enraged husband didn't help. Derek was still chagrined that he'd tried to seduce his own aunt, albeit unknowingly, and so his continued scowls weren't helping, either. And Percy, that half-wit, was simply too much to put up with at *any* time.

But she wasn't kidding herself. She knew very well that her anger now was more defensive than anything else, because despite the fact that James's stubbornness had driven her to that impulsive trip to the river, she knew she shouldn't have gone, and he really did have every right to be furious with her. And James angry, really angry, was nothing pleasant to deal with. Hadn't he nearly killed Warren with his bare hands? But to hear Jeremy tell it, that was nothing compared to what *she* could expect. It was understandable then that she might be feeling a good deal of trepidation, and understandable that she might hide it under her own anger.

At any rate, she fully intended to march into that house and keep right on going, right up to her room. Her rotten stepson could tattle on her to his heart's content, but she was going to be behind a barricaded door before her husband exploded with his reaction.

So she thought, but Jeremy had other ideas, and letting him lift her down from the carriage was her mistake. When she tried to brush past him to enter the house first, he caught her hand and wouldn't let go.

And she might be older than he was, but there was no doubt that he was bigger, and stronger, and determined to lay her *and* her misdeeds right before James so she'd get her just desserts.

But they weren't in the house yet, though the door *was* already being opened by the ever-efficient Dobson. "Let go of me, Jeremy, before I clobber you," she whispered furiously at him while giving the butler a smile.

"Now is that any way for a mother to talk to her—"

"You wretched boy, you're enjoying this, aren't you?"

That question only got her a grin and a tug which brought her into the hall. It was empty, of course, except for Dobson, so there was still a chance. The stairs were right there. But Jeremy didn't waste a blasted second before calling for his father, quite cheerfully at the top of his lungs. And so Georgina didn't waste another second before she kicked him. Unfortunately, that only made him yell louder, not let her go, and, much worse, the parlor door was thrown open while she was in the process of kicking him again.

It was really too much, after a day fraught with so many disturbing emotions. James just had to be there, didn't he? He couldn't have discovered her missing and gone off to search for her, could he? No, he had to be there, right there, watching her trying to abuse his son. And were those brows of his drawing together in suspicion, as if he knew exactly why? And even with his father's presence, had Jeremy released her yet? No, he had not!

It *was* too much, and just enough for Georgina's oft-denied temper to explode for real. "Tell this wretched child of yours to let go of me, James Malory, or I'm going to kick him where it will really hurt!"

"Oh, I say, does she mean what I think she means?"

"Shut up, Percy," someone said, Derek probably.

Georgina barely heard. She marched over to James, dragging Jeremy with her, because the scamp *still* hadn't let go, and glared up at her husband, totally ignoring Anthony, Connie, and George Amherst, who crowded around him.

"I don't give a fig what you say about it, so there!" she told him.

"Dare I ask, about what?"

"About where I went. If you hadn't been an unnatural husband—"

"Unnatural?"

"Yes, unnatural! Denying me my own family. What is that if not unnatural?"

"Prudence."

"Oh! Very well, maintain your ridiculous stand. But if you hadn't been *prudent*, then I wouldn't have resorted to desperate measures, so before you get all hot under the collar, consider who's actually at fault here."

All James did was turn to Jeremy and ask, "Where did you find her?"

Georgina could have screamed at that point. She'd been trying to shake off Jeremy's hand while she'd had her say but still couldn't, and heaping guilt on James's shoulders didn't appear to have worked, either. And now the scamp would have his say, and she wouldn't be surprised if James throttled her right there in front of brother, nephew, son, and assorted friends, all of whom were on *his* side and not likely to lift a finger to her aid.

But then she gasped, finding herself jerked behind Jeremy's broad back and hearing him say to his father, "It's not as bad as you might be thinking. She was on the waterfront, aye, but she was well protected. She'd hired her own carriage and had these two huge, monstrously huge, drivers who weren't letting anyone get near—"

"What a clanker," Percy interrupted, chuckling to himself. "How'd she run smack into Derek's arms, then, to almost get herself kissed?"

Derek, flushing from hot pink to hot red, reached over and grabbed Percy's cravat, twisting it around his hand until the poor man was almost choking. "Are you calling my cousin a liar?" he snarled, his eyes a true green now, foretelling just how upset he was.

"Gad, no! Wouldn't dream of it," Percy quickly assured him, yet his confusion was evident, and he was heard to protest, "But I was *there* Derek. Ought to know what I seen." The cravat twisted tighter. "Then again, what do I know?"

"Gentlemen, if you please," Anthony's dry tones entered the dispute. "My wife deplores bloodshed in her hall."

Georgina, well shielded by Jeremy's tall form, was sorry for all the bad thoughts she'd had of the lad. She'd already realized he'd kept hold of her to protect her from his father's wrath, rather than to assure that she couldn't escape it as she'd thought. He'd even lied for her, which had just endeared him to her for all time, but thanks to that double-damned Percy, it was all for naught.

She was afraid now to peek around his shoulder to see how James was taking all of this. He'd frowned when he first saw her, but other than that, he'd displayed his usual imperturbability, had just stood there and listened to her tell him what was what without showing the least bit of emotion.

From where she stood, or cowered, as the case were, she could see Anthony to one side of James, Connie on the other. Connie was grinning at her, plainly enjoying the situation. Anthony appeared to be bored with it all, a reaction that was usually James's, but she didn't think James would be showing the same just now. And when she felt Jeremy tense in front of her, she guessed she was right. And when Jeremy turned around and whispered to her, "I think you better run now," she knew it for certain.

James didn't move as he watched her race up the stairs, merely noting that she'd hiked her skirt up to accomplish her flight, leaving not only her ankles but her calves on display for everyone to see, and a glance about the hall told him everyone was indeed seeing, and admiring, which brought more fire to his eyes than had already been there. Not until the door slammed upstairs did his eyes return to Jeremy, the only one who hadn't watched Georgina's exit, who'd been warily watching his father instead.

"Switched loyalties, have you, lad?" James said very quietly.

It was the softness of his tone that had Jeremy squirming and blurting out, "Well, I didn't want to see you going through what Uncle Tony did, just because you might get a little angry with the wench, and she might get a lot angry back at you. She's got a bloody temper if you ain't noticed."

"You thought I'd have to find a new bed, is that it?"

"Something like that."

Hearing his past difficulties aired so nonchalantly, Anthony let his assumed boredom drop clean away with a choking sound and then a growl, "If your father don't blister your hide, youngun, I'm bloody well thinking of doing it!"

But Jeremy wasn't concerned with his uncle's chagrin just now, real or not. "What are you going to do?" he asked his father.

As if it were a foregone conclusion, James replied, "I'm going to go up and beat my wife, of course."

No matter how mildly he'd said it, six voices rose in immediate protest. James almost laughed, it was so absurd. They knew him better than that, or ought to, yet even Anthony was suggesting he think about it first. He hadn't said another word, or made a move to do as he'd said, but they were still arguing their points when Dobson opened the front door again and Warren Anderson pushed past him.

Anthony was the first to see this mountain of male fury heading straight for his brother and, with a nudge to James's ribs, asked, "Friend of yours?"

James followed his gaze and swore, "Bloody hell, enemy is more like it."

"One of your brothers-in-law by any chance?" Anthony guessed as he wisely got out of the way.

James was given no opportunity to answer since Warren had reached him by that time and immediately took a swing at him. James blocked the first punch easily, but Warren ducked his return swing and came up with a solid blow to James's middle.

With the breath momentarily knocked out of him, he heard Warren sneer, "I learn from my mistakes, Malory."

One swift jab to daze him, and one hard right landed Warren on the floor at James's feet for James to reply, "Not well enough, apparently."

As Warren was shaking his head to clear it, Anthony asked James, "Is this the one that wanted to hang you?"

"One and the same."

Anthony offered Warren a hand up, but held on when Warren was standing and tried to get his hand back. And there was pure menace in his voice as he asked Warren, "How does it feel, having the tables turned, Yank?"

Warren merely glared at Anthony. "What's that supposed to mean?"

"Look around you. It's not your family that surrounds you this time, but his. I'd bloody well keep my fists in my pockets were I you."

"Go to hell," Warren said as he snatched his hand back.

Anthony could well have taken exception to that, but instead he laughed and cast James a look that said clearly, Well, I tried. It's your turn again. But James didn't want another turn. He just wanted Warren Anderson out of there, out of England, out of his life. If the man weren't so belligerent, obnoxious, and plainly hostile, he might try explaining things rationally to him. But Warren Anderson was not a rational man. Besides, James simply didn't like the fellow, understandable since this was the chap who'd wanted to see his neck stretched by a rope.

Coldly, ominously, James warned him, "We can do this the hard way and I can beat you to a bloody pulp—and don't doubt it, dear boy, I won't need any help to do so—or you can just leave."

"I'm not leaving without my sister," Warren maintained staunchly.

"Now there you're wrong, Yank. You gave her to me, and I'm keeping her, and I'm especially keeping her away from you and your bloody propensity toward violence."

"You didn't want her!"

"Like hell I didn't!" James growled. "I wanted her enough to let you nearly hang me!"

"You don't make sense, man," Warren said, frowning now.

"'Course he does," Anthony interjected at this point, laughing. "Perfect sense."

James ignored his brother to assure his brother-in-law, "Even if I didn't want her, Anderson, you still wouldn't get her back now."

"Why the hell not?"

"Because she's having my baby, and I haven't forgotten that you're the man who thinks beating her will solve everything."

"But didn't Malory say he was going to—"

"Shut *up*, Percy!" came from three different directions.

Warren was too shaken up now to notice. "My God, Malory, I wouldn't hurt her even if she weren't . . . Hell, she's my sister!"

"She's *my* wife, which gives me all rights in the matter, one of which is my right to deny you access to her. You want to see her, you'll have to make your peace with me first."

Warren's response to that wasn't surprising, considering James looked anything but peaceable at the moment. "Like hell I will, and your rights be damned. If you think we'll leave her in the hands of a pirate, think again!"

They were impotent last words, but Warren knew he'd have no luck getting Georgina out of that house right then, since he had come alone, while Malory was surrounded by family and friends. It enraged him beyond measure that he'd have to leave without her, but for the moment he had no choice. He left furious, and the only reason the door didn't slam behind him as he stormed out was that Dobson had snatched it open before he reached it.

Anthony rocked back on his heels and gave a hoot of laughter. "Don't know whether to congratulate you about the baby, old man, or because you got rid of its uncle."

"I need a bloody drink," was James's only response, and he headed back into the parlor to find one.

Much as he would have liked it otherwise, the whole lot of them followed. By the time the rest of the congratulations had died down, James was on his way to being quite foxed.

"Little George wasn't too far off the mark when she described her brothers, was she?" Anthony remarked, still quite amused over the whole affair. "Are they all as big as that one?"

"Just about," James mumbled.

"He'll be back, you know," Anthony speculated. "And likely with reinforcements."

James disagreed. "The others happen to be a bit more levelheaded. Not by much, mind you, but a bit. They'll go home now. What can they do, after all? She's my wife. They saw to it."

Anthony chuckled, not believing a word of it. "That ghastly word's coming easier to you, is it?"

"What word?"

"Wife."

"Go to the devil."

Chapter Forty-six

Georgina couldn't believe it. He'd locked her in. And no matter how much she'd pounded on the door all through the night, finally giving up in exhaustion, no one had come to let her out. And they were still ignoring her this morning. How *could* Warren do this to her? And after she'd defied her husband's dictates just to relieve his mind about her welfare.

She wished now that she'd never heard his voice last night, raised so loud as he shouted at her husband in the hall below. But she did, and of course it had drawn her out of her room with every intention of rushing right down to him.

But before she'd reached the stairs, she'd heard James refuse to let Warren see her, and she knew she'd only get him angrier at her than he already was if she just went down to join them. So she thought she'd been real clever in deciding to sneak out the back way once again so she could come around to wait for Warren to leave. And she didn't doubt that he'd be leaving. James's refusal had been more than adamant.

So she'd waited out front and surprised Warren when he stormed out of the house. She'd wanted to assure him she was all right. She'd wanted to tell him not to worry about her anymore. She hadn't expected him to thrust her into his carriage and drive off with her. Devil take it, why couldn't James have thought to lock her in instead, then she wouldn't be here, on Warren's ship, panicking because he had every intention of taking her home, not to James, but to Connecticut. And he wouldn't listen to the fact that she didn't want to go. He hadn't listened to anything she'd had to say. She was afraid, too, that he wasn't even going to tell the rest of her brothers that he had her!

In that she was wrong, as she found when the door opened and Thomas stepped into the cabin. "Thank God" were her first words, because it was her one brother who didn't let temper affect his judgments.

"My sentiments exactly, sweetheart," he said as he held out his arms to her and she quickly entered them. "We'd about given up hope of finding you."

"No, I didn't mean . . ." She leaned back to demand, "Did you know Warren had locked me in?"

"He did mention it last night when he returned to the hotel and told us what had happened."

She pushed away from him. "You mean you left me here all night!"

"Calm down, sweetheart. There was no point in letting you out sooner, when you aren't going anywhere."

"The devil I'm not!" she said furiously on her way to the door. "I'm going home!"

"I don't think so, Georgie." This from Drew, who appeared in the doorway right then to effectively cut off her exit. To Thomas, he said, "Well, she looks fit enough, doesn't she? No bruises. Spitting mad."

Georgina felt like spitting, or screaming. Instead she took a deep breath, took another, then asked in a perfectly calm voice, "Warren didn't tell you, did he, that I wasn't in need of rescuing? Right? He forgot to mention that I'm in love with my husband? Is that why neither of you bothered to let me out of here sooner?"

"He didn't mention the love part, no," Thomas admitted. "I seriously doubt he believes it. But he did say you'd demanded to be taken back to your husband. He thinks you're suffering under misplaced loyalty because you're going to have the man's baby. How are you feeling, by the way?"

"I'm . . . How did you know?"

"Malory told Warren, of course. He used that as one of the reasons he's keeping you."

One of the reasons? It was probably the only reason, and why hadn't she thought of that before? Because she'd begun to think James really hadn't heard her when she'd told him about the baby, since he'd never once mentioned it to her.

She moved over to the bed and sat down, trying to fight the depression that was sneaking up on her. She couldn't let the reasons matter, she just couldn't. She loved James Malory enough for the both of them. And as long as he wanted to keep her, then she wanted to stay with him. There, that settled that. So why didn't she feel any better?

Thomas startled her when he sat down next to her. "What did I say to upset you, Georgie?"

"Nothing . . . everything." She was grateful to have something to take her mind off the fact that James didn't love her. Them! Her brothers were being too high-handed by half. "Would you two mind telling me what I'm doing here?"

"It's all part of the plan, Georgie."

"What plan? To drive me crazy?"

"No." Thomas chuckled. "To get your husband to be reasonable."

"I don't understand."

"Would he let Warren see you?" Drew asked her.

"Well, no."

"Would he have changed his mind about it, do you think?" Thomas asked.

"Well, no, but—"

"He's got to be made to see that he can't keep you from us, Georgie."

Her eyes flared. "You intend to take me all the way home just to teach him a lesson?" she cried.

Thomas grinned at her chagrin. "I doubt it will be necessary to go that far."

"But if he thinks we will . . ." Drew didn't feel it necessary to elaborate, and it wasn't.

Georgina sighed. "You don't know my husband. All this is going to do is get him mad."

"Maybe. But I guarantee it will also work."

She doubted it, but wasn't going to argue about it. "So why couldn't Warren have told me all this last night?"

Drew snorted before answering, "Because our dear Warren never agreed to the plan. He has every intention of taking you home with us."

"What!"

"Now don't worry about Warren, sweetheart," Thomas told her.

"We won't be leaving for at least a week, and your husband is sure to show up long before then to settle this thing."

"A week? You came all this way, won't you stay longer than that?"

"We'll be back." Thomas chuckled. "And quite regularly, it seems, since Clinton has decided that as long as we're here anyway, we might as well make this rescue profitable. He's off right now arranging for future cargoes."

Georgina might have laughed at that if she weren't so upset by all of this. "I'm delighted to hear it, but I didn't need rescuing."

"We didn't know that, sweetheart. We've been worried sick about you, especially since, according to Boyd and Drew, you didn't go willingly with Malory."

"But you know now that I did so why won't Warren give it up?"

"Warren is hard to understand at the best of times, but in this case . . . Georgie, don't you know that you're the only woman that he has any kind of feelings at all for?"

"Are you trying to tell me he's given up women?" She snorted.

"I don't mean *those* kind of feelings, but the tender kind. I think it actually upsets him that he has any feelings at all. He wants to be completely hard-hearted, but there you are, making him care."

"He's right, Georgie," Drew added. "Boyd said that he'd never in his life seen Warren so upset as when he came home and found you gone off to England."

"And then Malory arrived, and he saw it as his inability to protect you."

"But that's absurd," she protested.

"Actually, it's not. Warren takes your welfare very personally, perhaps more personally than any of the rest of us do, because you *are* the only woman he cares about. If you take that into consideration, then it's not so surprising, this hostility he feels for your husband, particularly after everything the man said and did when he showed up in Bridgeport."

"Why *did* he set out to ruin your reputation that night, Georgie?" Drew asked her curiously.

She made a face of disgust. "He felt slighted because I sailed off with you without saying goodbye to him."

"You must be joking," Thomas said. "He didn't strike me as a man who would go to such extremes for petty revenge."

"I'm just telling you what he told me."

"Then why don't you ask him again. You'll probably hear a completely different reason."

"I'd rather not. You don't know how infuriated that night still makes him. After all, you men throttled him, married him off, confiscated his ship, *and* locked him in a cellar to await hanging. I don't dare mention your names to him." Saying all that made her realize how hopeless their plan really was. "Devil take it, he's *not* going to change his mind, you know. What he'll probably do is bring *his* whole family down here and tear this ship apart."

"Well, let's hope it doesn't come to that. We are reasonable men, after all."

"Warren isn't." Drew grinned.

"James isn't, either." Georgina frowned.

"But I'd like to think the rest of us are," Thomas said. "We *will* settle this thing, Georgie, I promise you, even if your James has to be reminded that he provoked our hostilities in the first place."

"Well, that's sure to make him amiable."

"Is she being sarcastic?" Drew asked Thomas.

"She's being difficult," Thomas replied.

"I'm allowed," Georgina retorted, scowling darkly at them both. "It's not every day that I get abducted by my own brothers."

Chapter Forty-seven

Thomas and Drew had managed to convince Georgina, somehow, to remain in the cabin so they wouldn't have to lock her in again. But an hour had passed since they'd left her, and she was beginning to wonder why she was going along with their crazy scheme when she knew very well it wasn't going to work on someone of James's unpredictable temperament. You just didn't force him to do something against his will and expect him to blithely go along with it. He was more likely to dig in his heels and *never* change his mind about allowing her to see her family . . . that was assuming he got her back, which wasn't a guaranteed outcome just now. After all, her brothers could be stubborn, too.

Why was she just sitting here, waiting for circumstances to determine her future, when all she had to do was sneak off the *Nereus* and make her own way home to James? After all, it would be easy to find a hack on the dock, and she was still wearing the same clothes she'd made her escape in yesterday, so her pockets were still lined with the money that both Regina and Roslynn had forced on her when they'd learned that James was deliberately keeping her without funds. And for all she knew, James might have already had a change of heart after she'd proven to him yesterday how serious she was about seeing her family again. She'd never gotten a chance to argue that out with him last night. Warren's high-handed abduction of her just might have ruined whatever headway her risk taking had gained her.

Annoyed now that she'd backslided into letting her brothers make her decisions for her again, she was on her way to the door when it opened, and Drew announced grimly, "You'd better come up. He's arrived."

"James?"

"The one and only. And Warren's furious that Malory actually managed to get on board when he had his crew watching for him just so he could prevent it." Drew grinned then, despite the seriousness of the situation. "I think our brother expected James to bring an army with him, and that's what everyone was watching for. But your Englishman is either fearless or foolhardy, because he's come alone."

"Where's Thomas?"

"Sorry, sweetheart, but our mediator left to meet Clinton."

She didn't waste any more time after hearing that. God, they'd probably killed each other already, without Thomas there to help control Warren's temper. But when she rushed on deck, it was merely to hear Warren ordering James to get off his ship. But that didn't mean violence wouldn't follow. Warren was up on the quarterdeck, gripping the rail, his body stiff with malice. James had gotten no more than a few feet on deck before a solid line of sailors had appeared to block him from going any farther.

Georgina started straight for James, but Drew yanked her back and pushed her toward the quarterdeck instead. "Give the plan a chance, Georgie. What harm can it do? Besides, they won't let you get to him, anymore than they're going to let him through. They've got their orders, which only Warren can rescind, so if you want to talk to your husband, you know whose permission you'll have to get first . . . unless of course, you're up to shouting back and forth at him."

Drew was grinning after that. *He* was finding this amusing, the rogue. She wasn't, and neither was anyone else, in particular James. Finally able to see him clearly from the quarterdeck, she thought he looked like hell warmed over.

He felt like it, too, though she didn't know that. Waking up with a head-pounding hangover, discovering he'd passed out in the parlor along with all six of last night's drinking companions, then girding himself for the confrontation with his wife only to find her gone again—this had *not* put him in a very good mood. The only thing that he could look on with favor this morning was that he'd already discovered where the three Skylark ships were berthed, and the first one he'd boarded happened to be the one his wife was hiding on. And that she was hiding wasn't the worst of his conclusions. He had little doubt that she'd decided to leave him to go home with her brothers. Why else would she be here?

Georgina had no idea what conclusions James had drawn, but actually, it wouldn't have mattered if she did. She still had to defuse this situation before it got out of hand, no matter who he was furious with.

"Warren, please—" she began as she came up beside him, but he didn't even glance down at her.

"Stay out of this, Georgie," was all he said.

"I can't. He's my husband."

"That can and will be rectified."

She gritted her teeth over such hard-nosed stubbornness. "Didn't you hear a single thing I said to you last night?"

But by then James had noticed her appearance, and was heard to bellow, "George, you are *not* leaving!"

Oh, God, did he have to sound so arbitrary? How could she reason with Warren when James was standing down there making belligerent demands? And Drew was right. She would have to shout to him if she wanted to talk to him, and how could she say anything personal that way? And if Thomas was to be believed—and looking at Warren she didn't doubt it—even if she could get James to concede, Warren still wouldn't let her go back to him. Without the rest of her brothers there to back her up, nothing could be settled one way or the other. Drew might be there, but he'd never been able to sway Warren to anything, so he'd be no help.

She'd waited too long to answer James. He'd begun taking matters into his own hands, or fists, rather.

He'd already flattened two of Warren's crew when Warren shouted, "Throw him o—"

Georgina's elbow meeting her brother's ribs cut him off temporarily. The glowing fury that had leaped into her eyes kept him quiet a bit longer. And she was furious now, not just with him, but James, too.

Double-damned idiots! How dare they totally ignore her wishes, as if it weren't *her* future that was at issue here?

"James Malory, stop it right now!" she shouted down to the deck just as another sailor went flying.

"Then get down here, George!"

"I can't," she said, and meant to add "not yet," but he didn't give her a chance to finish.

"What you can't do is leave me!"

He was thrown back. There were still six crewmen standing against him. That wasn't deterring him in the least, however, which only infuriated her the more. The fool man was going to get tossed in the river yet.

She might do it herself. She was, after all, fed up with being told what she could or couldn't do. "And why can't I leave you?"

"Because I love you!"

He hadn't even paused in throwing another punch to shout that. Georgina, however, went very still, and breathless, and nearly sat down on the deck, her knees had gone so weak with the incredible emotion that welled up inside her.

"Did you hear that?" she whispered to Warren.

"The whole blasted harbor heard it," he grouched. "But it doesn't make the least bit of difference."

Her eyes rounded in disbelief. "You must be joking! It makes all the difference in the world, because I love him, too."

"You wanted Cameron, too. You don't know what you want."

"I'm not *her*, Warren." He looked away at the mention of the woman who had played him so false, the one who was responsible for the cold way he treated women now, but Georgina caught his face between her hands, forcing him to look into her eyes.

"I love you. I know you're trying to do right by me, but you have to trust me on this, Warren. Malcolm was a child's fancy. James is my life. He's all that I want, all that I'll ever want. Don't try and keep me from him any longer, please."

"Are we supposed to just stand back and let him keep you from us? That's what he means to do, you know. We'll never see you again if he has his way!"

She smiled now, knowing she'd swayed him, that he was merely objecting now to what she knew they all feared. "Warren, he loves me. You heard him. I'll see it set right, but let *me* do it. You only manage to bring out the worst in him."

With total ill grace: "Oh, for God's sake, go on then!"

She gave a glad cry and hugged him, but wasted not another second in swinging around . . . and slamming right into a brick wall.

"So you love me, do you?"

She didn't wonder how he'd gotten up there. A few loud groans from the lower deck told that story. She didn't care, either, that he'd obviously heard what she'd told her brother. She just took advantage of the fact that she was already pressed tightly to him, and slipped her arms around him to keep it that way.

"You're not going to yell at me in front of my brothers, are you?"

"I wouldn't dream of it, brat."

But he wasn't smiling, and he wasn't staying there. She gasped as he swung her up into his arms and turned to leave.

"It would go over much better if it didn't look like you were *taking* me away," she told him.

"I *am* taking you away, dear girl."

Well, all right. She hadn't really thought the rest was going to be easy.

"At least invite them to dinner."

"Like hell I will."

"James!"

There was a low growl deep in his chest, but he stopped and turned back. Only it was Drew he looked at, not Warren. "You're bloody well invited to dinner!"

"For God's sake," she said as he continued on his way. "That was the most graceless, ill—"

"Shut up, George. You haven't seen it *set right* yet."

She winced, wishing he hadn't heard that bit of confidence on her part. Yet she was confident. He'd already made the first concession, with ill grace, true, but it was a definite start.

"James?"

"Umm?"

"You're going to enjoy my efforts to make you give in."

One golden brow crooked as he glanced down at her. "I am, am I?"
She ran a finger slowly over his lower lip. "You are."

He stopped right there on the dock, a long way yet from his
carriage, and started kissing her. Georgina wasn't sure how they got
home.

Chapter Forty-eight

"James, shouldn't we go down? The carriages have been arriving for the last hour."

"That's my family showing up for this momentous occasion. With luck, yours won't find the house."

She twisted a lock of his golden hair about her finger and gently tugged. "You aren't still going to be difficult, are you?"

"I'm never difficult, love. You just haven't convinced me yet to forgive your brothers."

Her eyes flared, then flared some more when he rolled over on the bed, putting her beneath him again. Her temper wanted to flare, too, but when James rested between her thighs, anger was the farthest thing from her mind.

Still, she reminded him, "You invited them here."

"I invited them, but it's Tony's house. He can bloody well kick them out."

"James!"

"So convince me."

The horrid man was grinning at her, and she couldn't help grinning back. "You're impossible. I never should have said that you'd enjoy this."

"But you did . . . and I am."

She giggled as his lips trailed along her neck, then down to capture the peak of one already pebbled nipple. But then she gasped as her desire ignited fully, pulled from her with the suction of his mouth. Her hands moved down over his back, loving the feel of him, all of him, everywhere.

"James . . . James, tell me again."

"I love you, my darling girl."

"When?"

"When what?"

"When did you know?"

His mouth came back to hers for a long, deeply stirring kiss before he replied, "I've always known m'dear. Why do you think I married you?"

Carefully, hating to mention it at a moment like this, she reminded him, "You were forced to marry me."

One kiss, one grin, and he said, "I forced your family to force me, George. There is a difference."

"You did *what?*"

"Now, love—"

"James Malory—"

"Well, what the bloody hell else could I do?" he asked indignantly. "I'd sworn I'd never get leg-shackled. The whole bloody world knew it. So I couldn't forswear myself and actually ask you, now could I? But I remembered how that bounder my darling niece calls husband got himself wed, and I figured what's good enough for him would do me as well."

"I don't believe I'm hearing this. All deliberate? They beat you senseless! Had you counted on that?"

"The price one pays to get what he wants."

Hearing that, the heat went right out of her, the angry heat, that is. The other kind was coming back.

But she shook her head at him. "You amaze me. I always suspected you were a madman."

"Just a determined man, love. But I was bloody well amazed myself. I don't know how you did it, but you crawled into my heart and wouldn't get out. I'm learning to accept your presence there, however."

"Oh, you are, are you? It's not too crowded?"

"There's room for a few offspring to join you there." He grinned at her.

And that got him a kiss, until she recalled, "So why did you have to confess to being the Hawke? They were already determined that you would marry me."

"Are you forgetting they'd recognized me?"

"I could have convinced them they were mistaken if you'd kept your mouth shut," she huffed.

He shrugged. "It seemed only reasonable to get it out of the way, George, rather than let it cause unpleasantness later, after we'd settled into married bliss."

"Is that what you call this," she asked softly. "Married bliss?"

"Well, I'm bloody well feeling blissful at the moment." She gasped when he suddenly entered her. There was a deep chuckle before he added, "What about you?"

"You may . . . depend upon it."

When they entered the parlor a while later, it was to find Malorys squared off against Andersons, each on opposite sides of the room, and her poor brothers were most definitely outnumbered, for the entire Malory clan had shown up this time. And it wasn't hard to guess that James's family was united in their loyalty to him. There wouldn't be any overtures made until he let them know the feud was ended, and all he'd told Anthony earlier, when he'd carried her up to their room was to expect unpleasant company for dinner, which of course that rogue understood perfectly to mean her brothers were coming.

But her husband's frowning countenance as he stared at the five Anderson men didn't bode well for getting this group together. Georgina was having none of that.

She used the same trick that had worked on Warren that morning to get him to listen to her and jabbed her elbow into her husband's ribs. "Love me, love my family," she warned him, sweetly, of course.

He smiled down at her as he tucked her arm more firmly under his so she couldn't do any more jabbing. "Beg to differ, George. Love you, *tolerate* your family." But then he sighed. "Oh, bloody hell," and began making introductions.

"They're *all* eligible, you say?" Regina asked her shortly thereafter. "We'll have to do something about that."

Georgina grinned, deciding she wouldn't warn her brothers that there was a matchmaker in the room, but she did point out, "They're not going to be here that long, Regan."

"Bloody hell, would you listen to that?" Anthony remarked in passing to Jason. "She's picked up his bad habits."

"What bad habits?" Georgina demanded of James's brothers, ready to defend her husband.

But they hadn't stopped, and Regina, with a giggle, told her. "My name. They'll never agree on what to call me. But it's not nearly so bad anymore. They used to almost come to blows over it."

Georgina rolled her eyes and caught James's long-suffering expression across the room where Thomas and Boyd were speaking to him. She smiled. Not one derogatory word had he said to four of her brothers. Warren, however, he wasn't getting anywhere near.

Nor was Warren being very sociable with anyone. The others had surprised her though, particularly Clinton, by how well they were getting along with the hated English. And Mac would be stopping by later, she'd been told. She'd have to remember to introduce him to Nettie MacDonald. Regina wasn't the only one who could play matchmaker.

Still later, Anthony and James stood alone, each watching their respective wives as they spoke. "Shall we betroth them?"

James choked on the sip of brandy he'd just taken, since the subject they'd been discussing was their upcoming fatherhood. "They're not even born yet, you ass."

"So?"

"So they could end up the same gender."

A degree of visible disappointment accompanied a sigh from Anthony. "I suppose."

"Besides, they'd be first cousins."

"So?" again.

"That's not at all the thing these days."

"Well, how the bloody hell should I know?"

"I agree," Nicholas said, coming up behind them. "You don't know much." And to James, "Nice family you've acquired there."

"You *would* think so."

Nicholas smiled. "That chap Warren don't like you very much. He's been looking daggers at you all evening."

James said to Anthony, "Would you like the honors, or do I get the pleasure?"

Nicholas sobered, understanding perfectly that they were talking about trouncing him. "You wouldn't dare. You'd have both your brothers on your heads, not to mention my wife."

"I do believe, dear boy, it would be worth it," James told him, then smiled as Nicholas wisely took himself off again.

Anthony was chuckling. "The lad does like to press his luck, don't he?"

"I'm learning to tolerate him," James conceded, then, "Bloody hell, I'm learning to tolerate a lot."

Anthony laughed at that, following James's glance to Warren Anderson. "Old Nick was right. That chap really don't like you a'tall."

"The feeling is entirely mutual, I do assure you."

"Think you'll have trouble with him?"

"Not at all. We'll have a whole bloody ocean between us very shortly, thank God."

"The fellow was just protecting his sister, old boy," Anthony pointed out. "Same as you or I would have done for Melissa."

"Are you trying to deny me the pleasure of hating him, when he's so very hatable?"

"Wouldn't dream of it," Anthony said, then waited until James took another sip of his drink before adding, "By the by, James, did I ever tell you I love you?"

Brandy spewed across the carpet. "God, a few drinks and you get maudlin!"

"Well, did I?"

"Don't believe so."

"Then consider it said."

After a long pause, he grumbled, "Then consider it returned."

Anthony grinned. "Love the elders, too, but I don't dare tell 'em . . . the shock, you know."

James quirked a brow. "But it's all right for me to keel over?"

"'Course it is, old man."

"What is?" Georgina asked, joining them.

"Nothing, love. My dear brother is just being a pain in the arse . . . as usual."

"No more than mine is, I imagine."

James stiffened upon hearing that. "Has he said anything to you?"

"Of course not," she assured him. "It's that he's not saying any-thing to *anyone.*" And then she sighed. "It might help, James, if you made the first—"

"Bite your tongue, George," he said in mock horror, which wasn't all that feigned. "I'm in the same room with him. That's more than enough."

"James—" she started cajolingly.

"George," he said warningly.

"Please."

Anthony started laughing. He knew a doomed man when he saw one. His amusement earned him one of James's darker looks, even as James was allowing his wife to drag him across the room to her most obnoxious brother.

It still took another jab in the ribs to get him to open his mouth, and then it was only a curt "Anderson."

"Malory" came back at him just as curtly.

At that point James started to laugh, confounding both Anderson siblings. "I suppose I'll have to give over," James said, still chuckling. "Since you obviously haven't learned how to dislike a fellow in a civi-lized fashion."

"What's that supposed to mean?" Warren demanded.

"You're supposed to *enjoy* the discord, dear boy."

"I'd rather—"

"Warren!" Georgina snapped. "Oh, for God's sake."

He glowered at her a moment. Then with a look of disgust he stuck out his hand to James, who accepted that begrudged peace offering, still grinning.

"I know how that pained you, old chap, but be assured you're leaving your sister in the hands of a man who loves the breath out of her."

"The breath?" Georgina frowned.

James's golden brow crooked at her, an affectation she now found more endearing than she could say. "Well, weren't you gasping for breath in our bed just a little while ago?" he asked in all innocence.

"James!" She gasped now, her cheeks flaming that he'd say that in front of Warren, of all people.

But Warren said, his lips finally lifting just the slightest bit, "All right, Malory, you've made your point. Just see that you continue to make her happy, and I won't have to come back over here to kill you."

"Much, much better, dear boy," James replied, chuckling. And to his wife, "He's learning, George, damned if he ain't."